Pay Dirt

ALSO BY SARA PARETSKY

Pay Dirt

A V.I. Warshawski Novel

Sara Paretsky

HARPER LARGE PRINT

An Imprint of HarperCollinsPublishers

PAY DIRT. Copyright © 2024 by Sara Paretsky. All rights reserved. Printed in the United States of America. No part of this book may be used or reproduced in any manner whatsoever without written permission except in the case of brief quotations embodied in critical articles and reviews. For information, address HarperCollins Publishers, 195 Broadway, New York, NY 10007.

HarperCollins books may be purchased for educational, business, or sales promotional use. For information, please e-mail the Special Markets Department at SPsales@harpercollins.com.

FIRST HARPER LARGE PRINT EDITION

ISBN: 978-0-06-335982-6

Library of Congress Cataloging-in-Publication Data is available upon request.

24 25 26 27 28 LBC 5 4 3 2 1

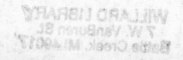

for Eve, part of my beating heart

Pay Dirt

1
Nightmare

Gunshot. When you hear it, you know it's not a backfire, not an M-80. Sprint up the stairs. Peter shoves past me into the room. I grab his arm. "You can't go in there blind. You don't know who's shooting, who they're shooting at."

He shoves me aside and plunges into the room.

A second shot, a third. Screams. I follow him in.

Blood, brain, bone. I slip in them. The air, acrid, thick with smoke. I can't see who's alive, who's injured, who has weapons. Stumble on Peter lying across Taylor's body, bellowing, "No! No!"

The cry woke me. I was weeping. I reached for the lamp switch, hand finding empty air. I was in a strange place, alone. Panic hit me. Taylor's mother had kidnapped me, I'd been jumped in a Chicago alley, I was in a KGB prison. I tried leaping out of bed, but the sheets were knotted around me like a mummy's tapes and I landed on the floor.

And finally remembered I was in Kansas. Lawrence. Not in a dump in Chicago's Uptown where Taylor Constanza had been murdered by their father. Taylor had died five months ago, but the nightmares wouldn't release their grip on me.

It was my own thrashing that had knotted up the sheets. I extricated myself, remade the bed. My sleep shirt was soaked through with sweat. I took it off, washed myself off in the B and B's small bathroom, put on a T-shirt. It was only three in the morning. I tried to go back to sleep.

I'd driven down to Lawrence to see Angela Creedy join an elite group of basketball players who'd broken the three-thousand-point lifetime scoring marker. She was a star on Northwestern University's team, a star attracting international attention. She was also a housemate of Bernardine Fouchard, Bernie to me, who was a hockey player and my sort of goddaughter.

Angela and her Northwestern Wildcats had beaten the hometown Jayhawks in last night's game, but it had been close, exciting to watch. Dozens of girls in Kansas regalia had crowded around Angela when she left the visitors' dressing room, thrusting their programs at her.

She'd squatted with easy grace to their head-level and signed their programs, chatting in a way that left the girls starstruck. When the crowd thinned, she joined me and Bernie in the hall, along with their other roommates. Angela and Bernie were close, so I'd grown close to her as well. The three other women I knew only in passing.

Angela embraced me. "Vic, I know it wasn't easy for you to come, but thank you! It means so much to have you here, especially since my mom couldn't make it. We're going downtown to celebrate. Come along, won't you, please?"

Angela's mother was a nurse in Shreveport. Her rare days off were spent caring for her own aging mother, and soaking her swollen feet in a eucalyptus bath.

"Yes, Vic, you should come," Bernie said. "We are going to a place called the Lion's Heart. Everyone on the team will be there."

"Thanks, babe, but the night belongs to Angela and your friends. I'll find some tamer form of entertainment."

Bernie Fouchard grabbed my arm as I moved away from the group. "Vic, you cannot go back to your room alone. When you are alone, you—" She flung her hands up, trying to think in English, but gave it up. "*Broies du noir*! You must be with other people."

I could guess the meaning. My smile tightened. "Bernie, don't pretend to know what I need or not. I'll be happier alone than in a noisy bar with drunk students."

She put both hands on my arm. "Vic, I only want you to be well, not to insult you!"

I pulled away, roughly. "You persuaded me to join you in Kansas. I'm glad I came, glad I got to see Angela in triumph, but that's my limit. Join your friends, have a good time, but not so riotous you can't be safe on the road tomorrow. Text me when you get back to Evanston."

She looked at me for a long moment, her expression disconsolate, but she finally joined the group around Angela. I had an impulse to cross over to her to apologize, but they left before I acted.

I'd driven to Lawrence by myself, needing privacy from the high-octane energy of five NCAA athletes, needing privacy most of all from Bernie's insistent hammering at me: when you fall, when you're injured, you get back on the ice *immédiatement!* She'd pressured me into coming down to watch Angela, which was probably a good thing, but she couldn't stop at one good thing. She relied on me as an example of women's strength; she needed me to be who I was last September, not who I'd become since Peter's and my Incident.

Peter Sanson was an archaeologist and director of a

famed institute at the University of Chicago. He was my lover, and I was in love with him, which had not happened to me in many years. This made the Incident harder to overcome.

Taylor Constanza had been one of his second-year students. Taylor disappeared the week the fall term began. The parents were frantic, threatening to sue the university for dereliction of fiduciary responsibility and threatening Peter in more ominous language. Taylor was a trans femme who'd been on a month-long dig with Peter and five other students in August. The parents were claiming Peter had coerced their son into a sex change to fulfill his sexual fantasies.

It was a sickening scenario. When the police came up empty, I agreed to look. Sadly enough, Taylor had been easy to find. They were sheltering with other runaways in an Uptown firetrap. Taylor pleaded with me to keep the location secret; they were frightened of their parents, who'd reacted violently when they came out after the August dig.

I'd promised, but Peter felt he needed to let the school and the parents know that Taylor was safe but needed time away from both. The parents were furious with me and with the university, which in turn pressured both Peter and me to reveal the address. When we wouldn't, the parents hired another detective who easily followed the same trail as me. This second investigator ignored Taylor's plea for safety.

The next day I got a terrified text from the student. Their father had shown up, with a gun. By the time an ambulance arrived, father and child were both dead.

Afterward, Peter suffered in every way. One of the bullets had winged him. He needed multiple surgeries to recover from damage to his shoulder, and the pain was unrelenting.

He was also awash in guilt. Even though I'd told him the student was afraid of their parents, he'd felt he had to let Mrs. Constanza know I'd found her child. Peter had a high sense of responsibility to his students; he felt he'd let Taylor down badly. The university didn't make his life easier. Their lawyers deposed him along with everyone else on the August dig, hoping to prove Peter had never touched Taylor.

Peter knew he shouldn't blame me, but he did. If I hadn't been a detective, skilled at finding the hidden, he would have left matters to the university. He could have kept himself three removes from the carnage.

I knew I needed to cut him slack, but I'd been the one who stayed to comfort the other runaways in the apartment. I was the one who answered hours of cop questions at Area 2, while I still had bits of bone and brain on my clothes. I was also the one who spent hours on the phone with the dead student's mother. My own nerves were sheared to the root. I'd hung up on her, and ignored the university's demands that I make myself endlessly available to lawyers, both Mrs. Constanza's and the university's.

Peter and I wore each other out. We fought, made up, fought again. Peter had always been a steady person, not prone to furies. If we argued, he could almost maddeningly see my side as well as his own. Now it horrified him to see how easily he gave way to anger.

Finally, exhausted by his demons, he decamped to Malaga, Spain, where he was helping excavate a three-thousand-year-old Phoenician settlement on the shores of the Mediterranean. It was a relief for both of us when I dropped him off at O'Hare shortly before Christmas.

It was after he left that the nightmares began. Sometimes, like tonight, I'd re-enact the moment of Taylor's murder. Other times I'd have dreams about my mother. Gabriella had died of ovarian cancer when I was in my teens. I was an only child, born after numerous miscarriages. She was fierce in her love for me, but she pushed me also to be independent, to stand up for myself, not to settle for second best. Her loss left a hole that no other love ever completely filled.

Gabriella had been an immigrant in a neighborhood

with many immigrants, but she'd also been a Jew in a neighborhood without them. The physical battles I'd fought on South Chicago's playgrounds, to defend her from the insults the local kids liked to chant, distressed both her and my father. Now, in my current nightmares, she was under attack and I was helpless to protect her.

After Taylor's murder, I started second-guessing my work decisions, forgot important meetings, left invoices unsent. I began retreating from my friends, taking long runs up the lakefront with the dogs, even avoiding my elderly downstairs neighbor. He was 1,000 percent in my court, but his constant fulminations against Peter wore on me. (*I thought he was better than those losers you usually bring around, but he's just as bad as that Murray Ryerson, only thinking of hisself.*)

It was Bernie Fouchard who forced open a crack in my shell, or rather, Bernie's mother, Arlette. Bernie herself had driven me to fury, with her badgering me on "getting back on the ice after a bad fall."

"People depend on you. Everyone is hurting in their lives, not only you, but only you can help people who are in trouble."

"I'm not a superhero and I'm not a robot. Trauma shatters me the way it does everyone. So take your platitudes and your naïveté back to the hockey arena."

She looked shocked and hurt, but she mercifully shut up and disappeared. In January, though, her mother flew to Chicago with the Canadiens. Her husband had been my cousin Boom-Boom's closest friend when the two of them played for the Blackhawks. Boom-Boom was Bernie's godfather, and when he died, he more or less bequeathed the godparenting to me.

Arlette Fouchard pushed past me into my apartment. "Bernardine has been telling me your troubles."

"Bernie thinks I'm made of titanium, not flesh and bone. She wants me to be something nonhuman. She and everyone else." Clients, friends, strangers who contacted me online, either wanting to know how to protect their trans children, or vilifying me for brainwashing a boy into thinking he was a girl, using language whose ferocity and obscenities were terrifying.

"Bernardine is not subtle or tactful," Arlette said, "but she understands you better than you are able to believe."

She moved into my kitchen and began washing the dishes I'd let stack up on the table and in the sink. I watched in irritation, but finally dug a clean towel from a drawer and dried the plates and put them away.

"Victoria, it's true that people depend on you, and that is a burden for you right now," she said when the last pot was scrubbed shiny. "I'm not here to persuade you otherwise. You witnessed something beyond bearing, a man murdering his own child. It is—is—*accablant*—something that can make the strongest person deranged.

"I'm here to speak to *you*. Not for your clients or your friends, but concerning what you need for your own nurture. If you don't have money, you need to work, *n'est-ce pas*? But if detecting work no longer nourishes you, then find new work. You need to stay in motion, though, unless you wish to become an opera heroine, some Juliette or Aida, locked in a tomb and dying out of martyrdom."

With the dishes done, she made tea, which I normally drink only when I'm sick. But I was sick, sick of myself, of the vileness and violence that surrounded me.

We took tea into my living room and sat on the couch, not speaking much. At length, she said, "Victoria, I only ask this of you: to be less harsh. With yourself, *bien sûr*, but with others as well. Most of us have been spared the horrors you saw, but these times are hard for everyone. The insults against you on social media, they are dreadful, but most people mean well, including my daughter. If she is *maladroite*, it is not out of malice. We all have seen too much of death, too much of anger from the strain of this Covid, from the strain of war and other violences, from the hastening of the death we all must face. Try not to be so severe."

She waited a moment for my response, but I couldn't give her one. She went into the kitchen again and put together an omelet, which she brought out to me in the living room. She left when I started eating. I took the dirty dishes back to the kitchen. It seemed wrong to put them in the scrubbed and shining sink, so I washed them.

The next day I began picking up the pieces of my practice. I still felt fragile, as if I were an uncooked egg whose shell might shatter at any moment, but Arlette was right: staying in motion created a rhythm that was in and of itself healing. I put to one side the question of whether I wished to continue to be an investigator and returned to work.

In February, when Bernie urged me to witness Angela's moment of glory, I was still feeling rocky, but I'd regained enough balance that I'd felt able to join her in Kansas.

2
Changing the Climate

The February evening had turned cold during the game and the wind had picked up. When I left the field house, a gust pushed air back into my lungs. I bent down, choking, and was almost knocked over by a group of excited girls coming out behind me.

"She signed my program, too. *Love, Angela,*" one was saying.

"It's not like she's in love with you, Rina—that's what she put on all our programs," another said scornfully.

"I think she was trying to say she loved all you girls for wanting to be your best in the world," an adult suggested.

I moved out of their way, smiling a little over the exchange, when a man running full tilt toward the field house barreled into me.

"Whoa," I cried. "Plenty of room here for everyone."

He ignored me but pelted on to where the girls were standing. He grabbed one by the arm and yanked her from the group.

"You're not to come near my daughter. Not ever!" He bellowed at the adult so loudly I could hear him above the wind and the sound of the cars exiting the lot.

I turned, dumbfounded. The girl he'd grabbed was the one who'd sighed so happily over Angela's signature. She started to cry now, silently, the wind crystallizing the tears on her lashes. I couldn't hear the response from the adult with the group. I trotted back into earshot.

"You've been suspended without pay, Perec." The man was still shouting. "That means you don't come near any children in my school district."

"You don't own the county, Santich, even if you did get your school board to suspend me. Ruthie's mom asked me to bring the girls, since she tested positive."

"Cady Perec?" I blurted, astonished by the interchange. "It's V.I. Warshawski." We'd met when I came down to Lawrence on a case a few years earlier.

"I don't care if you're Wyatt Earp's ghost," the man bellowed at me. "I'm talking to Perec, so mind your own business."

"You almost knocked me down, you were so eager to make your daughter cry, so you are my business," I said.

Santich surprised me by looking down at his daughter. When he saw her tears, he put an arm around her and said in a soft voice, "I'm sorry, honey, sorry to get you upset. I'm just trying to protect you."

Just as quickly, he resumed his attack on Cady. "As for Lela Abernathy, if she thought you could be trusted with her daughter, I'll have a few words with her and Keith. I'll give the rest of you girls a ride home."

The girls pressed closer to Cady, who said, "Their parents are coming for them, Santich, just like you came for Rina, so don't get your undies in a bundle."

Several people had stopped to watch. Santich glared at Cady, me, at the onlookers, while his daughter turned her back on the other girls, perhaps embarrassed by her father. At that moment, one of the mothers arrived. A ripple of relief flowed through the group as she thanked Cady for chaperoning the outing.

"Was it wonderful?" she added to the girls. "I heard on the radio that the player from Chicago broke a record."

"She was awesome, Mom," her daughter said, but

without enthusiasm: Santich had drained the excitement from the group.

In another few minutes the rest of the parents arrived, leaving only one girl with Cady. Santich told her he'd drive her home.

She looked at him stonily. "My mom wants Ms. Perec to take me home."

He put out a hand for her, but dropped it when he saw me and the other bystanders watching. He scowled, but shepherded his own daughter away.

"What was that about?" I asked. I didn't know Cady well, but molestation seemed out of character. Besides, if she'd been accused of molesting a student, what parent would trust their daughter with her?

"He and I had a policy disagreement," she said tightly. "I need to get Ruthie home."

She and Ruthie were headed into the parking lot when we heard another bellow from Santich. He was next to a Kia SUV with its doors open, but he'd seized someone by the shoulders and was roaring at him. The second man shook himself free.

Not your business, I reminded myself, but I walked over to them anyway. Two of the bystanders who'd been watching Santich with Cady tagged after me.

"Damn you, Garrity! Defacing my property and right out in public!"

"I wasn't defacing it, asshole. I was improving it. You should thank me."

Garrity was a thin man with a halo of wild hair. He was wearing an old army parka, unzipped to show a faded sweatshirt with the ubiquitous Jayhawk on the front.

"I'm calling the cops," Santich snarled. "You're going to be in front of a judge first thing tomorrow."

A squad car pulled up, but not from the city police; it had the university's seal on the door. The driver got out.

"What's going on here, folks?" he said. His south-western twang was so thick I could barely make out the words, but that's the time-honored response of a cop to a family dispute.

"I want him ticketed," Santich said. "Vandalizing property."

"What'd you do this time, Trig?" the patrolman asked.

"Like I said to his royal heinie here, I was improving the look of his gas guzzler. Or at least, I was helping him let the world know he's aware of what he's doing."

Santich pointed to the back of the car. I followed the patrolman around and saw that Garrity had put a bumper sticker on, one of the ones urban guerillas used to tag SUVs twenty years ago: I'M CHANGING THE CLIMATE: ASK ME HOW.

"Just the fact you think I'm desecrating your guzzler tells me you know you're destroying the planet," Garrity said. "Case closed."

Santich demanded that the patrolman arrest Garrity or at least ticket him for defacing property.

"Daddy, please," Rina cried from the back of the SUV. "Can't we go home? I'm freezing, and Mom texted, she wants to know where we are."

"Yes, why don't you take your little girl home, Mr. Santich?" the campus cop said. "Tomorrow if you still want to press charges, we'll write him up, but let's all sleep on it. You, too, Trig. And get out of this parking lot before I ticket you for vagrancy."

"Where were you when Lord Santich here was harassing Cady Perec?" Garrity demanded. "It's okay for him to attack her in front of a bunch of kids, but it's against the law for me to confront him? That is justice in America, plain and simple, before you wrap it up in a pretty package of Constitutional rights that only the rich get to have. No wonder you got Perec fired, Santich: you're afraid she'll teach your kid to think."

Santich lunged at him, trying to punch him, but the patrolman grabbed his arm. "Not saying Trig doesn't deserve it, but you get on home. You don't want your kid to see me writing you up for assault."

"What?" Trig cried. "He owns the county, so I

deserve to get hit by his platinum arm, but you make sure he goes home safe and sound?"

The patrolman's lips tightened. "Trig, you get off the university's property in five or you'll be in a holding cell for the night."

Trig hunched down into the parka, scowling as fiercely as Santich, but he shambled off in the direction of the campus. Santich climbed into his Kia and roared out of the lot with a great squealing of rubber.

"That seems like a long-standing feud," I said to the campus cop. "What was the business about Cady Perec?"

"If you don't know, it's not my job to tell you." The patrolman got back in his car. He shut the door but didn't move until Trig was off the premises. The remaining onlookers took off, leaving me alone in the parking lot with my Mustang.

3

On Your Mark

The place I'd found to stay in was built into the side of a hill, so that the back was underground. The front, which had its own entrance, was glassed in.

When I got back, I sat by the picture window facing down to the town and searched online for news about Cady Perec. A local paper, the *Douglas County Herald*, had covered her troubles. When I'd been here before, Cady had taught social studies in one of the Lawrence schools, but she'd moved to a new consolidated school in Yancy, northwest of town.

Cady had come under fire for her segment on Douglas County in the 1850s and '60s. She'd put together a curriculum where kids acted out arguments over slavery, built a replica of the kind of shanties where Free

State homesteaders lived, even tried to survive for a week on the meager rations the Free Staters scrounged.

Yancy parents had gotten riled up over a part of the curriculum dealing with the Delaware Nation, who had helped the Free Staters during the Civil War. It was hard to tell what had gone amiss from the *Herald*'s sketchy reports, but I read an account of a fiery school board meeting, where the board had voted to suspend Cady pending a full inquiry into her teaching methods.

The next week, a woman named Clarina Coffin had started picketing the school and writing rambling letters to the *Herald* about Indigenous rights. Trig Garrity had picketed with her. For the first few days, university students joined them, demanding that the full history of Indigenous people and of Black settlers in Kansas be told. And then parents showed up, shouting that they didn't want their kids indoctrinated with critical race theory.

Oh, and the chair of the school board was Brett Santich. Bad blood all the way round.

This was old news, or oldish, since it had happened last fall, shortly after the start of the school year. I didn't see any more recent news about Cady, but Trig's name popped up quite a few times, shouting at county or commission meetings on a variety of issues, or picketing construction sites. He seemed to have moved on from Cady Perec's woes, but a later story, really just a paragraph, announced that Yancy had suspended her without pay for the remainder of the year, with her contract terminated effective the following June.

I got ready for bed but didn't draw the curtains. I lay watching the lights twinkling around the town, every now and then punctuated by police strobes. Maybe it was Bernie and her friends, lighting up the town, hammering home the visitors' victory. Or maybe it was Trig Garrity. He was furious with Santich, the man with the platinum arm, and was breaking windows in downtown Lawrence to let off steam.

I slipped into sleep, thinking of the happy girls whose mood Santich had broken. Maybe that was why my demon dream woke me at three. It was a long time before I fell asleep again, but it wasn't really sleep, just that gritty state one step below wakefulness.

My phone jolted me fully awake at six. I was hoping for Peter, but the screen told me it was Bernie Fouchard. I let it go to voicemail, but as I was drifting off again, she called a second time, and then a third.

"Okay, Bernie, you woke me. Where's the fire?"

"It is not a fire, Vic, but Sabrina. We can't find Sabrina."

My brain was muzzy from sleeplessness. "Sabrina?" I echoed.

"Vic, please! Sabrina! You know her, my housemate, she plays soccer, you saw her only last night, you must remember her!"

I did remember, now that Bernie had goaded me. Sabrina was a soccer forward, apparently a leading scorer in the Big Ten conference. At the restaurant where I'd met Bernie and her friends for supper before the game, Sabrina had looked thin, almost to the point of anorexia, with a waxy pallor. I'd had trouble imagining her breaking through an opposing line to score.

"Sabrina isn't here. Did she say she was coming to see me?"

"She has said nothing because no one has seen her since last night." Bernie was shouting, her voice pitched high from fear. "Hear what I am saying! We don't know where she is."

"Wasn't she staying with you at that motel?"

"She was supposed to, but Amber says she never came to bed. We must leave for Chicago now. We must be back by five—Angela and I have practice, we all are past due with essays."

"Send Sabrina a text and tell her you have to leave without her."

"Of course we have done this! That is not the point."

I put my phone down and lay flat. I knew what the point was. I didn't want to hear it. Bernie continued for a minute, so loud I could make out her demand that I search for Sabrina. Finally the phone went silent.

I longed for sleep, that clean cool rest that knits the ravelled sleave of care, not the febrile state I'd been in before the phone rang. I lay still, trying to breathe, but I couldn't let go of fear, the fear that if I got involved, Sabrina would end up dead. I would be covered in blood and bone. All my friends would turn against me, but not as harshly as I would turn against myself.

I watched the eastern sky turn light, watched a sickly sun rise over the Kansas River Valley. I was going to drive back to Chicago later today myself. I had planned a run and a cortado at the Decadent Hippo before setting out, but when I tried to put on my sweats, my legs felt too heavy to lift. I tried to do some warmups, but I kept stopping mid leg lift or arm lift, unable to coordinate my movements.

I shuffled into a shower that my landlady had built in an old closet. I could pick up coffee and something to eat on my way out of town. When I came back into the room, wrapped only in a towel, my landlady was there. Norma Something. I'd corresponded with her about the room but couldn't remember her surname.

She apologized brusquely for showing up unannounced. "I'm on my way to work. A young woman is upstairs. She says she's your niece and she needs to see you. I didn't want to let her in without checking first—"

"Vic!" Bernie burst in behind her. "Vic, please! You have to help us."

"Of course I do," I said brittlely. "No consideration about my own obligations, let alone my state of my mind or state of dress, should come ahead of what you need."

"Oh, Vic, don't. Don't talk in that mean way. I can't stay on down here, and anyway, I don't have any idea how to start looking for Sabrina, but you would." Bernie wasn't a person who cried often, and when she realized she was crying, she brushed the tears away with an angry hand.

"Who is missing?" Norma asked.

I was still clutching the towel around my breasts. I put my T-shirt back on while Bernie explained Sabrina to my landlady. "She is a soccer player, for Northwestern University—we are all athletes in different sports. Sabrina rode with us from Chicago to watch our friend Angela Creedy play basketball. Now she is not in her room, she is not answering her phone. We have to drive back today, now, *enfin*, and where is she?"

"You don't think she hooked up with someone?" Norma asked drily.

The obvious explanation. I was so unraveled by the death of Peter's student I couldn't think simply anymore.

"Maybe," Bernie said doubtfully. "Of course, it is possible. In fact, Angela says she saw Sabrina at the bar with three boys. No one in our group saw her leave, but if she went with them—!"

She turned back to me, wringing her hands in anguish. "Oh, Vic, please! Can't you wait until afternoon to leave? At least can you call the police to see if someone found her? Perhaps these boys—Rohypnol or something even worse—she is so—so *faible*—"

"I'll check with the hospital, just in case," my landlady said. "I'm on the nursing staff there. What's your friend's name? Her date of birth?

"Sabrina Granev. I don't know her birthday."

Bernie watched anxiously, moving from foot to foot, while my landlady phoned. "Norma Rolfson here. I'm running a few minutes late but I need to check whether there was an overnight admission."

She spelled out Sabrina's last name, but shook her head at Bernie when she finished. "I have to run, but Ms. Warshawski, if you need to stay on, I don't have any other bookings for a few days. Let me know."

She left the way she'd come, through the door that

led to her basement and her garage. Bernie was looking at me pleadingly.

"Bernie, do you know what you're asking of me? To try to find a missing student?" My throat felt as though something large, a basketball perhaps, was lodged in it. I could barely get the words out.

She blinked back more tears. "I'm sorry, Vic. *Maman* told me not to ask it of you, but I'm so used to you being calm, figuring out what to do when there is a problem, and if you don't know what to do, how can I know?"

I sat down heavily, hands over my eyes.

Bernie came over to me, shoulders drooping. "I am sorry, Vic. I see—*Maman* is right. You are a wounded eagle, she said, and that is the truth. We must leave now, but I will report Sabrina missing to the soccer coach when we get home."

A car had been honking in front of Norma's house for several minutes. "Amber and Chantel are waiting for me. It is necessary that I go."

I made myself look at her. Her face was pinched and pale with distress.

I wrapped the towel around my waist and got up to put an arm across her shoulders. "Okay, babe. I'll see if she was picked up on a disorderly, but police don't consider a person who's been gone only overnight as missing. Do you know Sabrina's parents' names? Where they live?"

"Sabrina, she is not truly part of our group. She only came to live in our house in October when we were looking for a fifth person to help with the rent, so I don't know her well. Also, soon after that, she broke her ankle. Her mother came, *bien sûr*, but Mme. Granev stayed in a hotel, so really, we spoke only to say, hello, yes, we can bring you coffee. She was always on her phone, her computer, except when she was pushing Sabrina to work on her rehab.

"Everyone in our house, we are all serious athletes, and Sabrina was, too. She toured with a national youth team, she is already scouted by different clubs, and so at first she was working hard, but something went wrong with the joint. The harder she worked the worse the bone got. That was when she started acting so differently.

"We hoped the mother would notice at Christmas, but after the winter vacation, it was even worse. Sabrina stayed in her room all the time. We tried to talk to her and she became angry. Angrier. So why she decided to come to Kansas with us—I don't know."

The car honking became more insistent, and then someone rang the upstairs bell. Bernie blinked at me nervously.

"I must run, I am sorry. As to where the parents are, that I'm not sure. The West, I know that. Colorado? Maybe New Mexico?"

"Ask the others if anyone knows where her parents live. I'll try to reach them. And I'll call Angela, see if she can describe the boys at the bar."

"I—thank you, Vic. I will ask the others. Angela, she's on the team bus, but Chantel or Amber, they may know where to find the parents." She hugged me convulsively and darted through the outside door to the street.

4

Get Set

After she left, I collapsed onto the bed. My body felt as though someone had laid an iron weight on me, pushing my belly button into my spine. I lay without moving, not sleeping, not thinking. Maybe this was how a caterpillar felt inside a cocoon. No ticking clock, no responsibilities, floating to music only nature could hear.

After a time, something in me shifted and my mind went reluctantly to the missing student. Missing, not dead, not shot. Arlette Fouchard had told her daughter I was a wounded eagle. That was grandiose. I was just wounded, along with most of the planet these days.

The papers are full of reports of people walking away from work, but most people keep going to their jobs. Something keeps them going, even if the job feels like drudgery. Before Covid, maybe it was workplace camaraderie, or family responsibilities. Now, with disease, political upheaval, economic uncertainty, it was hard to keep going.

Personally, I was tired of responsibility. I hadn't become a private eye to take on the weight of other people's worries but for the excitement of uncovering what lay behind a given crime. Even more, I got pleasure from those times I could make justice happen.

My dad had been a cop. After law school I'd been with the public defender for three years, handling street crime, so I didn't have dewy-eyed notions of law and order. While I was defending inarticulate street youth, trying to get them not to plead their lives away, it made me crazy that the big offenders, the ones who damaged hundreds or thousands of lives, walked off whistling a happy tune and pocketing a few billion more dollars. I chose detective work to try to take some of the air out of those whistles.

The challenges were greater today than when I started because the deck had been stacked ever more heavily on the whistlers' side. That meant I either should quit completely, or become smarter and wilier than when I started.

Smarter and wilier. That required at a minimum

that I get out of bed, get my head back in the game. I rummaged in my overnight bag for a pair of clean jeans and a long-sleeved knit top. As I dressed, I could still feel the weight on my chest, but it receded to a small point under my heart. I could almost ignore it, and focus instead on what I knew of Sabrina Granev.

Bernie had said Sabrina was something of an outsider to the group of women who shared the Evanston house. They were all athletes, all attending university on athletic scholarships, but in different sports. While they often cheered each other's home games, they didn't have the time to go to away games. Last night had been an exception: they all wanted to see Angela's big moment in the spotlight.

At dinner with the women before last night's game, I hadn't tried to join the conversation, which was in a kind of code, young people speaking in fragments, punctuating their comments with bursts of laughter or cries of "No way!"

The dinner party had strained my endurance. The young women's exuberance made me feel invisible, made me want to walk away. Only my affection for Bernie kept me at the table. I'd noticed Sabrina Granev because, like me, she seemed listless, forcing herself to take part in jokes, but toying with her meal.

Depression over her ankle, I'd thought last night. It

would be natural enough for her to envy her healthy housemates while she remained on the bench.

She'd been restless, twitching, during the meal. Drugs. I hadn't thought it consciously, but of course that was Bernie's worry—not that Sabrina had hooked up for sex but that she'd been desperate for drugs. Bernie and the other roommates were protecting Sabrina, but they knew she was using.

I texted my landlady to say I would be staying an extra night. I texted my dog walking service in Chicago, asking them to put in another day with Mitch and Peppy. I called Mr. Contreras, my downstairs neighbor in Chicago. He keeps close tabs on my comings and goings—closer, since last fall's debacle—but he's in his nineties and not able to take the dogs for long walks these days.

He loves me, but he dotes on Bernie; he was vehement in his applause that I was going to help her.

"I don't want to help her," I growled. "I want to take the dogs and sit on a warm beach where the only thing I have to find is a dry towel when I get out of the ocean."

"Don't go talking like that, doll. You wouldn't be happy with yourself if you left little Bernie in the lurch, you know that."

I hung up before I started a longer whine about how

it was my turn to get looked after. "No one is going to shoot Sabrina," I told my face in the mirror. "She will not bleed out in your arms. You will find her because you are a clever detective."

I tried to figure out where to start my search. In Chicago, I have friends in the police who could tell me if someone had been brought in overnight. I was a stranger here, not someone with contacts who might tell me where a young woman seeking—what? oxy? fentanyl?—might have gone. Still, the police department was the logical place to start.

I drove down to the Decadent Hippo for my coffee, which they make the way I like. I drove the two miles to the cop shop. They'd moved since the last time I was here, to a shiny new building on the town's expanding west side. At the information counter, I produced some ID, including my PI license, and asked if Sabrina Granev was in their system.

The woman behind the counter checked her database. Sabrina hadn't been booked, at least not under her own name.

"Do you have any Jane Does?"

The woman looked at her screen and gave a little snort of laughter. "Just one, who can't be your missing gal. Aside from the fact that everyone in town knows who he is."

"Trig Garrity?" I suggested.

She put both hands on the countertop. "What game are you playing, Ms. Chicago Detective?"

"Sorry. Not a game, a wild guess. He went after someone in the field house parking lot last night. University security broke it up, but I wondered if he'd been angry enough to attack the other guy later."

She gave me the old cop look: *I've been spun a lot of lines, and I know when I'm hearing one.* I looked back steadily: *I am an honest loyal citizen who speaks nothing but the truth.*

"If you're here for Garrity, his bail hearing will be at eleven in Judge Bhagavatula's courtroom. If you're really here about a missing student, what does she look like?"

"About five-eight, thin enough to see through, white with dull skin, lots of brown hair pulled into a ponytail, or at least it was the last time I saw her."

The woman didn't write any of this down. Maybe she'd been trying to trip me up—if I couldn't manufacture a description quickly I wasn't here on legitimate business. Instead, she repeated my landlady's suggestion, that Sabrina had hooked up with someone and wasn't answering her phone.

"I don't know this young woman well," I said. "I'm the godmother to one of the friends she rode down with, but I was wondering more about whether she'd hooked up with drugs rather than sex. If an outsider is looking to buy here, where would they go?"

The woman picked up a file folder and slapped the counter with it. "Is that what you were really hoping to find? A place to score? If that's what you need, you're on your own, Chicago."

I knew a sergeant in the Lawrence force, a man named Deke Everard whom I'd met when I was here before. He wasn't in, the woman said. I didn't believe her, but I didn't have a way of challenging her.

Back in my car, I stayed in the police lot while I called Angela. The team bus was noisy, but earbuds let us carry on a conversation.

"Bernie told me she'd talked you into looking for Sabrina. I'm sorry, Vic—sorry she pressured you when you're so—well, vulnerable. I love her, but sometimes she's such a giant mosquito the only appropriate answer is to swat her."

Laughing at the image made me feel a bit better. "She told me you saw Sabrina at the bar with three white guys. What did they look like?"

"They were strutting. The kind of boys we stayed as far from as possible when I was in high school. They like to get you in trouble and then laugh at you while you try to dig your way out. And just because a woman is white, like Sabrina, isn't any protection from guys like that. I called over to Sabrina to come back to our table, and one of the boys said, 'You her nanny?'"

I sucked in a breath, involuntary.

"Yes." Angela's voice was as dry as the dust on my windshield. "Sabrina said, 'She's our star. I'm just one of her planets.' So I walked away. I didn't look back at them. Maybe Sabrina left with them. Probably she left with them, but I didn't want to know. She has a way of making me not want to be my sister's keeper."

"I hear that," I said. "I couldn't help thinking drugs when I saw her twitching at our pregame supper last night. Your strutting boys may have offered her oxy or fent."

"Could be," Angela agreed.

"Can you describe any of them more than that they were cocky?"

"You mean, like, did one have a Proud Boy tattoo on his neck? The bar was full, I wanted to recapture my mood. I didn't try to memorize their faces. One had a lot of curly dark hair, that's the only detail I remember. And they were wearing Tom Brady's sportswear line— that's why I figured they were rich."

I thanked her. "Forget the boys, forget Sabrina, go back to your well-deserved high. See you soon in the Big Garlic."

"Big Garlic?" she echoed.

"You know, New York is the Big Apple. In fifth grade we were taught that Chicago was named for some kind of wild garlic. Why not?"

That made her laugh in turn. "Got it, Vic. Thank you for—well, everything."

Back in the old downtown, I parked in a free city lot. What an incredible luxury—free parking in the central business district. Did these people have any idea how lucky they were?

I figured there were some things I could look up in the library. On my way there, I walked past too many rough sleepers in shop doorways, still wrapped in blankets or sleeping bags as the town came to life.

My route took me past the Meadowlark, a bakery cum sandwich shop. Since the Incident, I never seemed to be hungry, but I hadn't had breakfast. A sourdough roll with espresso would do. The espresso was thin and bitter, but I made myself eat the whole roll.

I signed up for one of the computers on the library's lower level and went into the law enforcement databases to read incident reports for both the town and the county. I covered the most recent six months, looking for drug busts. I found several. I opened a map app in another window and looked up the locations. There'd been one in a newer part of town to the southeast, but most were in the parts of the county with the sparsest population. I noted the coordinates, although if the cops had busted a place, they'd have shut it down.

I also came on suicide reports. The numbers seemed high for a county this size. Like the drug busts, most had happened in the remote parts of the county, but some were on the college campus. That conjured a fresh worry about Sabrina Granev. Far from healing, her ankle had deteriorated. A young woman who'd been an international star six months ago, using opioids (perhaps), she could be seriously at risk.

Bernie hadn't gotten back to me with information about Sabrina's family, but I found them in one of my subscription databases. Her parents lived in a suburb of Albuquerque. Both had been athletes—her father a budding footballer in Zagreb when the Serbian civil war prompted his own parents to emigrate to the States. Her mother had also been a soccer star. The pair met at the University of New Mexico. Sabrina was their only child.

I found photographs of Sabrina easily enough—Instagram, TikTok, Facebook—all showing a bright-faced athletic young person, not the gray, drained woman at last night's dinner table.

I went outside to call the parents. Both phones sent me to voicemail. The message I left—who I was, where I was, Sabrina's phone wasn't answering—sounded thin.

I walked back to the lot where I'd left my car, shoulders hunched, mood somber. This wasn't the first time Bernie Fouchard had talked me into doing something that wore me out.

5

(Dis)order in the Court

The local cops hadn't been helpful, but the university had its own force, as I'd learned last night. I phoned instead of trying to go in person. I was a worried aunt who'd come down from Chicago for last night's game. The officer on duty checked their incident reports for the past twenty-four hours. They'd picked up three drunks and one assault victim, but they could identify her. She wasn't Sabrina.

I hung up, unsure what to do next. It was eleven o'clock. The woman at the police information counter had said that was when Trig Garrity was having his bond hearing. It was a long shot, but there would be cops in court. Depending on why Trig had been arrested, Deke Everard himself might be present. If not, maybe an officer on active patrol would be willing to smuggle a message to the sergeant.

The county courts were in an old stone building a short walk from the Hippo. By the time I'd gone through security and found Judge Bhagavatula's courtroom, it was a quarter past the hour, but the judge was hearing enough cases that Garrity was still in the courtroom. Even though I'd only seen him under a streetlight, his wild hair and dirty parka stood out.

Three uniformed officers were sitting in the front row, all male. I couldn't tell from behind if any of them was the sergeant. A small number of spectators was sprinkled among the benches.

Two people were called ahead of Trig, one for attacking a man with a broken beer bottle, the other for attacking a grain silo with a backhoe. The backhoe earned a higher bond than the beer bottle. One drunk more or less was negligible, but this was farm country, and the backhoer was destroying the livelihood of many farmers.

A woman in the front row had a cell phone trained on the bench. Illinois doesn't allow journalists to record court proceedings, but Kansas apparently did.

The backhoer's attorney tried to plead some mitigating circumstances, namely the plaintiff had stolen his client's backhoe and the client had come to take it back. The judge deplored that argument and sent him away with a fifty-thousand-dollar bond. The woman with the cell phonee scribbled a note.

"Irwin Garrity," the clerk read. "Charged with violating a peace bond by willfully invading the property at"—he rattled off a set of coordinates—"with the intent to damage said property. How do you plead?"

The woman with the cell phone trained her device on Garrity, who stayed seated. The lawyer who'd been arguing for the backhoer scurried to his side and began a whispered argument with him.

"Irwin Garrity, if you don't come forward, I'm going to hold you in contempt and give you a fine as big as your head of hair," the judge said.

"I do not answer to the name Irwin."

"That's what's on your driver's license," the district attorney said.

"I told the low-paid flunkey who arrested me to use 'Trig,' which is the name I've used for thirty years."

"Then you should change it legally," the DA said.

The judge rubbed his forehead, eyes shut. "Mr. Garrity, will you approach the bench and tell us how you plead?"

Garrity got to his feet and stepped forward with a world-weary sigh. "Not guilty. No matter what the billionaire's flunkeys say."

"No editorials, Mr. Garrity," Bhagavatula said.

The DA explained that Garrity had been on a piece of private land. Someone had seen him nailing a sign to a tree inside the property, and had called the sheriff.

The deputy who'd made the arrest wasn't in the courtroom. The judge asked what was on the sign.

The DA looked at his tablet. "'Murderer! Destroying life for profit.'"

"No direct threats were made against the person or property of the owners, is that correct?"

"No, Your Honor, but the defendant was on private land that he's been bonded to stay away from."

"Why can't you come out and call it Brett Santich's land? Is his name too sacred to say out loud in court?"

"Mr. Santich's name isn't on the complaint," the judge said. "Sheriff's deputy Hanover wrote the ticket in response to a call from the night watchman at Kirmek Construction."

"Typical bullshit," Trig said. "All those layers between Santich and the public he's working to poison."

"You're not helping your case by flinging around slanderous comments," the judge said.

Trig started to argue that truth was a defense against slander, but the judge silenced him. "Mr. Garrity, you were here five months ago for disrupting a planning commission meeting. You were in front of me three months ago for harassing administrators at the Yancy Consolidated School. Six weeks ago you allegedly violated NO TRESPASS signs at the Wakarusa coal plant. What else do you do with your time besides create a public nuisance?"

"I'm a watchdog. This county and this town require a great deal of watching, because every time I blink, some rich, powerful person is taking steps to destroy free speech, or the air we breathe, or the river where we get our drinking water."

Bhagavatula thumbed through some papers that his clerk handed to him, along with a whispered comment. The judge looked back at Trig. "If you were serious about watchdogging, Mr. Garrity, you would start with basic research. Brett Santich doesn't own that land."

"Because he sold it to some equally brazen billionaire."

"Because he sold it to a brazen billionaire, *Your Honor*," Bhagavatula said. "This land had three mortgages on it. The owner sold it six years ago to a trust administered by the Pioneer State Bank and Trust."

Garrity looked goggle-eyed at the judge.

"Since the arresting officer isn't here, I'm dismissing the charges. However, although you call yourself a watchdog, you do not get to decide what the law is in Douglas County or the State of Kansas. The next time you're in front of me I'm going to lock you up for sixty days for the good of the community."

Garrity made a sweeping bow, a parody of a costume drama courtier. "The king's justice is an avatar for the king's person."

He walked backward down the central aisle.

"Lucas, if you can't control your client, I'm going to fine you, too," Bhagavatula growled.

The defense lawyer grabbed Garrity's shoulder. He turned him around and frog-marched him to the exit. The woman with the cell phone followed.

"I will not defend you the next time they pick you up," the lawyer hissed as he opened the door. "You deliberately break the law. Then you turn the courtroom into a circus. I won't support a defendant whose only goal is to mock the law."

"Pity Martin Luther King didn't have you for a lawyer," Garrity said. "Or John Lewis. All that law-breaking over a piddling thing like the vote. Or in my case, a piddling thing like destruction of the planet."

The lawyer looked murderous but didn't try to prolong the battle. When the door shut again, the judge called a ten-minute recess.

We all rose. I left as the defense attorney said to the DA, "I wish Bhagavatula would lock him up. I'm tired of trying to defend assholes who don't want a defense."

I remembered that feeling well from my days with the Cook County public defender, but I still felt some sympathy for Trig.

The three cops went into the hallway. I followed, hoping to interest them either in Sabrina's disappearance, or getting a message from me to Deke Everard. They weren't rude, but they weren't willing to help, either.

Farther down the hallway, the journalist with the cell phone was interviewing Garrity. I went to a quiet corner at the opposite end to check my messages. Sabrina's parents hadn't gotten back to me. I tried them again, as well as Sabrina, but all three still went to voicemail. I did have a text from Bernie—she'd come up with the name of a friend of Sabrina's.

I reached Bernie while her group was taking a lunch break in Des Moines. "We texted this friend, Darla Browder her name is. She plays for Iowa, but she and Sabrina have been besties since their first soccer camp," Bernie reported, "Darla hasn't heard from Sabrina since before we left Evanston."

I took the friend's name and number and sent her a text, explaining who I was, before phoning. Darla took my call. She was worried about Sabrina, but she couldn't tell me much.

"Angela Creedy said Sabrina was talking to three guys at a bar," I said.

"Probably they were hitting on her," Darla said. "She's beautiful, with a lot of charisma. At least, before her injury she was always the center of attention. Not showing off, just a vibe she radiates. Used to radiate. She's not into guys, but they always glom on to her. Now she's pretty depressed. It's been hard for her to be on the bench with her ankle, so she's acting different in a lot of ways."

"Different how? Would she be medicating herself?"

"Medicating? Oh . . . You mean, is she taking drugs, besides Tylenol or something? She's an athlete, she knows better, she knows that's how you ruin yourself."

Phone interrogations are frustrating. You can't see the person's face or what they're doing with their hands, and the transmission flattens a lot of the emotion out of the conversation. I couldn't tell if Sabrina was doing drugs and Darla didn't know about it, or if she knew and was protecting her friend.

I pushed, but gently. I couldn't alienate her if I needed her help down the road. Instead I asked her to text me some photos.

"I want to start showing her picture to people, and all I have is her team photo, and some murky selfies her roommates took last night."

I gave her my number and tried to figure out what else I could or should do. Lunch, maybe, and return to the library to work on projects for my own clients. I was walking slowly along Massachusetts Street, hunched down in my coat, when the young woman from the courtroom appeared next to me.

"Hi. I'm Zoë Cruickshank with the *Douglas County Herald*. I saw you at Trig's hearing just now." She was very young, probably not thirty, and pulsing with energy.

I introduced myself. "That was a very theatrical event. I used to be a public defender in Chicago, and our most dramatic moments usually came from the bench."

She laughed, revealing crooked lower teeth. "That bow Trig gave on his way out? I figure he must have practiced for a month to make sure he didn't fall over. Fortunately, I got it on video so I can post it to the *Herald*'s web page. Is that why you were in court? To compare Kansas justice to Chicago?"

She had her phone out, ready to record me.

"Why do you want to talk to me?" I said.

"I'm the entire news desk for the *Herald* and I'm trying to turn Trig's court appearance into a story. It's hard to make news about him anymore, since he's always protesting something, and he's often in court for stuff like violating a peace bond. If you're an old friend, it would give me another angle."

"What was the 'murderer' placard about? Is Santich operating an abortion clinic?"

"Good grief, no. Santich's family owned all this land going back about a hundred years. He sold it, like the judge said. I haven't been able to burrow behind the Pioneer State's trust to get the actual owner's name, but they're building a giant resort on top of Yancy Hill. They've cut down a lot of old-growth trees, and Trig is trying to rouse opposition, but he fights so many wars no one listens to him anymore. He can't even get the Students for Environmental Justice to work with him. If you don't know Trig, why did you come to court?"

"People do, you know. Cold February day, it's free entertainment."

"What, you really were comparing Kansas and Illinois courts?"

I relented. "Deke Everard is an acquaintance of mine. Do you know him? Sergeant with the LKPD. They wouldn't let me try to reach him at the station, but I'm hoping he might help me in a search for a missing Chicago-area athlete, a young woman who came down to watch last night's game. I saw Trig mixing it up with Brett Santich in the field house parking lot after the game. When I learned Trig was going to be in court today, I was hoping Everard might be present, or at least that one of the officers there could get a message to him. The LKPD isn't interested, but Everard might help me for old times' sake."

"Missing student?" Zoë's dark eyes gleamed. A real story. "What's her name?"

The more information I could spread around, the better my chance of finding Sabrina. I gave Zoë what I knew, including the pictures Darla Browder had texted. Most were selfies of the two of them—under an umbrella on a beach, playing volleyball in the sand, hugging after a soccer match.

In the photos, Sabrina did radiate a vitality more attractive than conventional beauty. They were a pointed and poignant contrast to the sallow young woman I'd seen last night. I AirDropped them to Zoë so that she could put them on the *Herald*'s web page.

Zoë still wanted to interview me. I assured her I didn't have a story to tell, but I went with her to the *Herald* office. They were in one of the old buildings along the river, where rents were cheap because the owners didn't put any money into maintenance.

The lock was loose, and she had to work the key around for a bit until the tumblers engaged. She led me down an unlit hall to her office.

"This whole building used to belong to us." She sighed. "We had printing presses in the basement, and a big editorial and reporting staff. Now it's just me, a guy who covers sports, and an editor who doubles as an ad manager. Most days, they don't even come in, but I like to work here. I like to feel I'm part of a real newspaper, even if we don't set type for it."

It felt colder inside her office than on the street, even when she turned on an arthritic space heater. She questioned me about Trig's confrontation with Santich last night, and then she wanted a detailed rundown on Sabrina.

I told her the little I knew, omitting my suspicion about opioids. Before I left, I asked her about Cady Perec.

"I met her along with Sergeant Everard when I was here two years ago. Cady was at the game last night. Right before Trig had his blowup with Brett Santich, Santich attacked Cady. I read—I guess it must have been your piece, right?—in the local paper, but it didn't seem to justify Santich's rage."

Zoë preened a little over my finding her work, but said, "That was Trig, too. He and this woman who sometimes protests with him, they started picketing the Yancy school after Cady was suspended. See, Cady was reprimanded for pushing critical race theory on to unsuspecting students, but the hearing was to decide whether she should be punished in some bigger way.

Of course, I wrote it up—it was news—which was how Trig heard about it."

I told her I'd read the story in the *Herald*'s online version.

Zoë grinned again. "The online version is all there is anymore. I loved covering Cady's troubles—so much action. They even picked up my story on Kansas City's TV stations. Trig and Clarina Coffin, they carried signs comparing Santich to Stalin: toe the party line or be sent to the gulag. And Trig has a bullhorn, so he was bellowing through that. It was during the day, school was in session, and Santich went nuts.

"Cady's been a respected teacher for seven or eight years, first at a junior high here in Lawrence, and then out in Yancy, plus her grandmother knows everyone in town, including the people on all the different school boards, even the one out in Yancy. The board probably wouldn't have fired Cady, would have stopped at a reprimand, if Trig hadn't gotten them so angry. One of the families who fought with Cady when she was a social studies teacher here in the town came to the meeting and said some ugly stuff. That added to everyone's hysteria."

"I guess that explains why no one wants to join Trig in his fights. That, and the little bombshell the judge dropped. Did you talk to Trig about that in your post-court interview?"

Zoë made a wry face. "He felt a little bit ashamed. It never occurred to him to ask about who owned the land, and really, Brett sold it to a hedge fund, something anonymous, years ago.

"See, until they actually started bulldozing the top of Yancy Hill, Brett kept farming the land. The top, it was woodland, with natural springs, which made the next level down the hill ideal for crops. If anyone even thought about it, they must have assumed Brett had gotten the land back. Now it turns out he was leasing the farmland from the Trust owners until they started building, which was only a few months ago. Brett still owns a little patch at the bottom of the hill, with a few buildings on it."

I got to my feet. "You seem to know everything in this county. If I wanted something like fentanyl, where would I go?"

"Fentanyl? You don't want anything like that. Leave it alone. It's super-bad stuff."

I didn't say anything.

"You do look thin," Zoë said. "Get yourself into rehab, but don't go looking for drugs like that here."

"What—Douglas County is so pure you don't have dealers?"

"We have way too many dealers. They are a creepy bunch."

I nodded: dealers are always creepy, whether they're in the city or the country. It seemed like a good time to leave, before she connected the drugs to my questions about Sabrina.

6
Blood on the Pizza

I walked along the river, kicking at rocks on the path. The water was slate colored, reflecting the dirty gray clouds overhead. An eagle was perched on a dead tree on a sandbank. I stopped and watched until it swooped down and pulled up a fish.

Maybe that's what I needed—not a live fish, but lunch, something to augment the sourdough roll I'd eaten at nine. Massachusetts, the town's main street, was packed with eateries, offering almost any kind of food you might want, from pizza to Asian or South American or Greek. Nothing sounded appealing.

I caught sight of myself in the store window. My jeans were hanging loose around my hips, and my cheekbones were pronounced. Not as extreme as

Sabrina's gray pallor and downy anorectic face, but thin enough to make Zoë Cruickshank think I had a habit to feed. If Peter saw me now, would he be repelled, or moved by pity?

Queen Margherita's Pizza Palace stood across the street, next to a diner advertising Vietnamese, Thai, and Chinese food. Pizza seemed a safer bet. I bought two slices and took them outside to one of the benches the city placed on its main street.

When I opened the box, the tomato sauce looked like congealing blood. My stomach heaved, and I started to my feet, looking for a trash can, then saw myself again in the storefront. I could not continue like this.

In my years as an investigator, I've seen the bodies of other brutally murdered people. It's never easy, but with Taylor's slaying I felt as if my skin had become a sausage casing, holding not my own inner self, but all the bone and blood and brain I've witnessed over the decades.

It was the times, the times of pandemic, the times of fake news, endless wars, assaults on our government, assaults on thought. The times they aren't so much a-changin' as grinding us into sand.

I looked at the pizza for a long moment, then made myself eat a slice. One bite at a time, slowly, chewing, eyes shut so I didn't see the red sauce. I'd bought a bottle of water and I drank half to wash down the pizza.

"This tastes like tomato and olives, it does not taste like blood. The water tastes clean."

I said it out loud and a man in a nearby doorway looked up. He had a scraggly beard and matted brownish hair that stuck out from under a moth-eaten ski cap.

"Blood? You got a mouth full of blood? Like this here?" He poked the roof of his mouth open with one grimy finger so that I could see all the holes where he used to have teeth.

His face was as crusted as his finger. For a moment I thought I wouldn't be able to keep the pizza down. I forced myself to study him clinically. The teeth that remained were black, and the gums were full of lesions. Meth, maybe, or heroin.

"Something like that," I agreed. "I've been covered in too much blood lately. You?"

He rolled up his pant leg, and I could see the blood trails where he'd been injecting himself sloppily. "You got these?"

"Not for public consumption," I said primly.

"Public consumption. That's a good one. But there you are, consuming pizza in public while starving people are bleeding into the sidewalk all around you."

I squatted on the sidewalk near him and handed him

the box. He took the second slice, inspected it for a second, then folded it in half and ate it in one long noisy mouthful.

"Yep. These here are definitely tomatoes, not blood." He eyed me hopefully. "You got any more food you're scared of? Can of Pepsi?"

"Right now I'm mostly scared I won't be able to find me any oxy before the end of the day. Or trams, I'd settle for a tab if I had to."

"Don't look at me." He backed away, anger and fear chasing each other across his face. "Just because I'm on the street doesn't mean I'm an addict or nothing."

"Of course not! But I bet you see and hear a lot out here on the street. Someone told me I could find a connection at the Lion's Heart, but I don't know who to ask for."

"You a cop?"

"I am not a cop. I came down here for the basketball game and I can't get back to Chicago until tomorrow. I have to get something to tide me over. Soon!"

"Oh. You're an athlete. I get it."

"So who do I ask for at the Liony place? Or is there somewhere else better?"

"You give me fifty bucks. That'll buy me food for a week."

Or drugs for a day, but I kept that unhappy thought to myself. "How about twenty."

"How about you do your own research?"

When we compromised on twenty-five, he laughed, showing his rotting gums. "You want drugs, you got to be connected to a network. You got to know what bars the dealers go to, what bars the cops go to, see? Last night maybe they was at the Lion, tonight, maybe at the Boat Yard or Peewee's Palace. You're from out of town, so you don't have connections."

"You're right," I said, voice humble. "I don't have connections, which is why I'm talking to you. One of my team scored oxy at the Liony place last night. She said she was talking to three white boys, who looked like frat boys, but she knows I want to get in line ahead of her, so maybe she was lying. Maybe she really found a heavy from Kansas City."

My friend sucked on his toothless gums. "Don't know. Rumor is some frat boys deal for fun, or maybe to pay for their rides. I see 'em cruising sometimes in one of those fancy Jeeps. One might have a Porsche. Three white boys having a good time, could be from the Omicron fraternity."

I got to my feet, forgetting to move like a desperate addict. My friend said, "You are a cop!"

I pulled up my hoodie and the sweatshirt under it. "No wire," I said. "I'm not a cop."

"You better not be. I find you ratted me, I'll come

up to Chicago and break your face in so you can get all the blood in your food you want."

"That's scary," I agreed.

I went back to my car and tried Sabrina and her parents again, but still had no answer. I tried the LKPD again, but Deke Everard also wasn't available.

I went over to the Lion's Heart. This was a student bar, decorated with plastic Jayhawks, ceramic Jayhawks, Jayhawk jerseys, and this year's men's basketball schedule. It was an ill-lit space in a half-basement, with a story above it that was connected by an interior staircase. It might be a perfect place for a dealer to hand out wares, but in midafternoon, the only customers were older, nursing a beer or a shot. I sat at the far end of the bar, next to the cash register, where the stink of stale beer was strong enough to make me feel drunk.

The bartender was wiping glasses in the time-honored fashion of bartenders everywhere. The cloth looked surprisingly clean.

"What'll it be?"

Close up, I saw he was wearing a blue sweatshirt with the ubiquitous Jayhawk on the front.

"Help, I hope." I laid my phone on the bar, with a twenty underneath and showed him Sabrina.

"She's disappeared. The last time anyone saw her

was late last night when three frat boys were talking to her here at the bar. Were you on duty?"

"Duty? I was working. Didn't know that included being on duty for coeds who drink too much and get themselves into trouble."

"People tell me the frat boys are dealing here in the bar."

"People will tell you anything." He pushed the twenty toward me. "If you're looking to score, go someplace else. Lion's Heart is clean."

A thickset man came over from a table in the back of the room. "Trouble here, Joey?"

"No trouble," I said. "I'm just trying to find the boys who went off with my niece last night. She was here celebrating with friends from Chicago, and the last they saw of her, she was at your bar with three white guys."

"There were probably three dozen white guys here last night and maybe another ten or twelve Black. If your niece hooked up with someone, that was something she did on her own, not something my bar would arrange or condone. Anything else?"

"They came in a Porsche," I said, wondering how reliable my rough sleeper's narrative was.

"They could have come in a helicopter, but they wouldn't have driven it inside the bar, so that doesn't

ID them for me. You talk to the cops, file a missing person, don't come bothering me."

From the way he was looking at me, I suspected that he knew more, but I couldn't think of a way to get him to reveal it. I left the bar, panicking at my inability to come up with a coherent way to look for Sabrina.

My rough sleeper's story was thin, but it was the only story I had. Would a college fraternity really be able to run a drug operation without the campus cops and all their friends and neighbors noticing? It was hard to believe, even harder when I drove up the hill to the university campus.

The sun was starting to set, and gold light glinted on the limestone buildings. A warm and friendly place, where you'd be glad to send your child. They would be safe here. No one would be peddling tabs or powders.

The Omicron Delta Beta house was on the northwest edge of the campus. It was a well-maintained brick building with mullioned windows and fake Tudor beams across the front, set in carefully planted and groomed grounds. I wandered around the perimeter until I found the parking garage.

I'd thought my homeless friend had thrown in Porsches to make his story more colorful. There actually were two Porsches, an older Carrera with Kansas plates, and a new silver Boxster 718 from Virginia. An assortment of muscle cars, including a newer version of my own Mustang, and a good half dozen Jeeps.

I photographed the plates on the Jeeps and the Porsches.

"What the fuck do you think you're doing?" It was a young man in chinos and a yellow cashmere sweater. Sockless loafers despite the February wind.

"Admiring the wheels," I said. I hadn't heard him approach. Not good.

"Admire them somewhere else. This is private property, off limits without an invitation."

"I'd love an invitation," I said. "I hear some boys were cruising around the Lion's Heart last night, offering people something more special than craft beer. Friends of yours?"

A ghost of a smirk twisted the left corner of his mouth. "Lion's Heart is where nickel girls can move up to dime. You look like about two cents. Maybe just one."

"And where's the bank where you move those nickels around?" I asked.

"You could be funny," he said, "but you're trying too hard."

I walked around the Carrera. Mud was caked in the hubcaps and had splattered the fenders.

"Your bank must be in the country. This car isn't happy crawling around the mud."

The smirk became more pronounced. "Could be. Now get out of the garage. Unless you'd like to leave on a stretcher."

I studied him up and down, pretty sure I could take him, even as out of shape as I was. Wondering what I would gain if I did so.

I gave a mock salute. "Got it, frat boy. See you at Salamis."

"Is that where old worn-out ho's drink?" He drawled his words to make sure I knew how offensive they were.

I clicked my tongue on my teeth. "Oh, little boy, you'd better start spending some of your mommy's money on your classes. Salamis, where the Greeks wiped out a Persian force more than twice their size. You should try to pick up a little knowledge to tide you over when the drug money runs out."

"You're not just old and ugly, you're crazy," the boy said.

"Crazy is unpredictable, more dangerous than sane. Better go to your psych classes as well, to be on the safe side." I sauntered out of the garage, not looking at him but bracing myself in case he jumped me. In a way I was sad he didn't—I would have enjoyed showing him what an older woman could do to a punk.

Back in my own muscle car, I couldn't say the visit was wasted. The punk's smirk suggested that he could be one of the boys Sabrina had been talking to at the Lion's Heart last night.

Trouble was, I still had no idea where she might be. The countryside around the town was vast. If that mud-spattered Carrera had ferried Sabrina to an abandoned house out in the country, I'd need a Persian-size army of my own to hunt for her.

I looked up the other two bars my rough sleeper had mentioned. The Boat Yard was on the north side of the river, Peewee's Palace on the south, where the university and most of the town were located. I tried the Palace first.

As at the Lion's Heart, the Palace held a handful of older drinkers, male and female, at a grimy bar. They stared ahead, as if the foggy mirror behind the bottles could show them something happier than their own thoughts.

The bartender, who was as apathetic as his clientele, was unmoved by my missing niece who'd last been seen with three college boys. Even when I showed him the picture of her glowing with health on a beach, he hunched a heavy shoulder and said coeds were always getting in over their heads, not his problem. Anyway, rich boys with expensive cars went to Kansas City or St. Louis to drink.

The Boat Yard was a different story. They were

doing a lively business, mostly early supper for families with small children, along with long-haul truckers coming off the nearby interstate exit. It didn't seem like a probable drug haven, but you never know.

Two waitresses, both brisk, middle-aged, exuding a kind of maternal cheer with their customers, were racing from kitchen to tables. I had to wait ten minutes before I could speak to anyone.

The bartender turned out to be the Boat Yard's owner. He was sure no one ever came around selling drugs, or seducing young women. Certainly no one in a Porsche. Lawrence wasn't that kind of town.

He turned back to a couple at the end of the bar, old friends, apparently, who were laughing at some long story he was telling.

I left, feeling helpless and useless. Night was closing in, but the highway lights and all the little bars and shops north of the river made the stars invisible.

I had my hand on the Mustang door when someone behind me called out, "Miss! Miss? Don't go just yet."

I turned to see one of the waitresses in her pink-striped dress, not even a sweater against the night chill. She had her hands rolled up in her apron.

"Greg doesn't want to admit anything could go wrong in this place, but I've seen those boys you're talking about. They don't cruise here often, we're more family and truckers, but—" She looked over her shoulder, to see if anyone was listening.

I moved up next to her, close enough to read the name HOLLY on the plastic tag pinned to her dress.

"It's my sister," Holly breathed. "We fight about this all the time, but she cleans a house out west of town, on Yancy. She knows as well as me that they're holding drug parties there, but she says she never sees anyone using. She gets a message to have everything set up— glasses, napkins, fresh towels in the toilets. They leave a hundred dollars for her on the kitchen table and she does the whole downstairs, comes back the next day to clean it all up. Sometimes there's all this puke, they should pay her double, but really, she shouldn't work there at all."

"I'm a stranger here," I said. "Yancy?"

"It's a hill just outside town, farms, woods. Right now they're doing construction on top. Anyways, there's an old brick house on East 1450 Road. I don't know whose land it's on, but it's been abandoned a long time. Sometimes I drive past, wondering what mess Ivy's got herself into, and I see a fancy sports car there. Couldn't tell you the make."

I thanked her effusively. She waved off the twenty the Lion's Heart bartender had rejected and trotted back into the restaurant.

7

Three Crows Means a Summons

Yancy. The name kept cropping up, first in Bhaga-vatula's courtroom, then at the school whose board fired Cady Perec for corrupting the children of Doug-las County. Finally, it was the site of a house where a woman named Ivy cleaned up after drug parties. Three crows means a summons. That must mean I was des-tined to go to Yancy.

It had been cold in Chicago when I left, so I'd worn my heavy winter jacket. I needed clothes that allowed for quick movement over country terrain. In an outlet mall behind the Boat Yard, I bought a thick hoodie, navy with the inevitable Jayhawk over the heart, and fleece leggings. Socks, since the pair I was traveling in was dirty enough to make my toes itch. A cheap pair of trail shoes. A flashlight so I wouldn't drain my phone battery.

Bernie had texted while I was shopping. Back in my car, I called her, hoping Sabrina had surfaced on her own.

"No, Vic, it is not so. We are now home with no word from her, and her phone is still turned off."

I told her I hadn't had any luck, either. "I have one slim lead. If it doesn't pan out, I'll be coming home tomorrow."

I'd been afraid she might start hectoring me, but she agreed in an unusually sober, un-Bernie-like way. She was sharing her worry over Sabrina's possible opioid use when my phone told me I had an incoming call from Valerie Granev. I switched to her immediately.

"Ms. Granev! This is V.I. Warshawski. Have you heard from your daughter? I haven't—"

"Ms. Warshawski? Have you found her? What happened to her? I should never have let her go to Kansas with her friends. But she sounded better—"

She was frantic, almost incoherent. I was finally able to interject a few words.

"Sabrina went with her friends to a bar here in Lawrence. The last they saw of her she was talking to some boys there. Did she text you, let you know what she was planning?"

"I knew those other girls wouldn't take care of her," Valerie cried. "I've been in a high-security meeting all day, we couldn't access our phones, this is my first chance to call you. I'm on my way to the airport. I'll be getting to Lawrence about one in the morning. Tell me where to meet you, or can you meet my plane? What do you know?"

"Very little, I'm afraid. I may have found at least one of the boys Sabrina was talking to, but I don't have any leverage here."

"She wouldn't go off with strange boys, not without a good reason. But if she was abducted—"

"Abducted?" The horror stories of young women held captive flashed across my mind.

"My work," Valerie was saying. "Someone—the Russians and Chinese want this technology—someone could work for them, hold Sabrina for ransom. You have to stop looking. A hundred thousand things could go wrong if you find her and they feel cornered."

"Has someone approached you, Ms. Granev? Someone demanding ransom? Have you talked to the FBI?"

She didn't answer, just wailed, "I wish I knew what—who to trust—anyway, I'm on a plane, I'll be there as soon as I can, but don't do anything until you see me."

The connection went. What kind of investigator are

you, V.I., that you didn't dig deep enough to learn what kind of powerhouse job Valerie Granev held?

I started my car, turned on the heater. My eyelids felt heavy, my brain full of cotton.

I couldn't let the lassitude of the last few months encase me again. I turned on the overhead light and looked up Valerie Granev. She headed the electronic engineering unit for the aeronautics division of Tulloh Industries. Access to her research on avionics was blocked. Access to her research reports was blocked. Even if I could access her work, I wouldn't understand it; I wouldn't know if a foreign power would want it badly enough to kidnap her daughter.

Maybe the FBI should be involved. I thought Sabrina had been looking for drugs. In fact, if she was addicted, it would be easy for someone to abduct her—she would go with anyone promising her access. Trouble was, I couldn't see the Bureau listening to me. Missing student whom I barely knew? They'd be all over Bernie and her friends as well as me, and would be unlikely to start a serious search for Sabrina.

I took a look at Valerie's husband to see if he was also some kind of engineering wizard. Ramir Granev had apparently embraced the great Southwest with gusto. He worked for a sports equipment store but when I called the store, the manager told me Ramir was on a weeklong trek in the Sangre de Cristo mountains with a group of teen skiers. No cell phone coverage there.

"He takes kids wilderness camping all year round," the manager said.

"There's a family crisis," I said. "Has his wife been in touch?"

"What kind of crisis?" the manager tried to sound concerned but came across as eager.

"Ms. Granev was pretty rattled," I said. "She seems to think their daughter is at risk. She didn't give me details but I thought her husband should know."

Ramir was reachable only by sat phone, but the manager assured me Valerie would know that. "She probably got him some souped-up phone that can make calls to Venus in an emergency. Even if she called him, it would take Ram eight or more hours to hike out to where they left the vehicles. But Ram would be the first to say, let Valerie take care of a crisis, unless it's like a rescue mission in the mountains, where he definitely knows what to do."

I blinked at the flow of information, although it did offer an insight into the Granevs' relationship. I asked how I could call into Ramir Granev's sat phone. I couldn't, as it turned out, unless I had a device that would transform my cell phone into a satellite phone.

By the time the store manager finished telling me

everything he knew about phones, which was a lot, the February night had shut down completely. Despite running the heater, the damp cold was seeping through the windows.

Stay here and freeze, feeling sorry for myself, so Lotty and Mr. Contreras could erect a tombstone with SHE DROWNED IN SELF-PITY on it. Or get moving.

I found the card Zoë Cruickshank had given me and called her cell phone. "I have some news for you. Have your sources already told you that my missing college student has a high-powered mom? No? Valerie Granev, she's a significant electronics person for Tulloh Industries. She's afraid Sabrina was kidnapped to force her mom to reveal national secrets."

"How do you know? Is the FBI involved? Where can I find the mom?"

"She's flying in from Albuquerque. She begged me to stop looking for her daughter because she worries my search could get Sabrina killed. The hell of it is I don't know if Valerie has reason to suspect kidnapping, or it's her way of denying her daughter might be in other kinds of trouble."

Of course Zoë had a thousand questions, including what secrets Valerie had access to.

"All her work is blocked off by security fences. Even if I had the skill to climb over them, I wouldn't

understand her work. I barely understand what 'avionics' means. She could be sitting on an entire Ve-
suvius of inventions for the air force. If you do run
across any Bureau types, write your story up and
publish before they slap an injunction on you. They
can suppress the story if you run it, but once it's on
the Web it won't disappear completely."

"Do you think Sabrina was kidnapped?"

"I don't know," I said. "She could be anywhere in
the world right now. Even if she's still here in Douglas County, it would take an army to go through every
possible hiding place. I don't know," I repeated.

Valerie's and Bernie's calls had sidetracked me
before I'd written down the address that the waitress
had given me. I shut my eyes, slow breaths, going into
track, my old physics professor used to call it. As if
Professor Wright were whispering in my ear, the address came to me: E. 1450 Road.

My map app showed a single road on the hilly out-
cropping that was Yancy. The satellite view showed
cultivated land on the hill's lower reaches, pockmarked
by sections of woodland. East 1450 Road was easy to
spot. There was only one building on it that could be
the house the waitress had mentioned.

I needed to rest. I'd been on the go since early this

morning, with another stint looming. Back in my room, I set the timer on my phone for ninety minutes and fell heavily into sleep. Before the timer rang, my landlady came in and shook me awake. She turned on the bedside lamp, and I blinked up at her.

"You told me I could stay another night. Didn't you get the message that I'd be here?"

"I'm sorry, Ms. Warshawski, it's not about that, but someone is here from the FBI."

"FBI?" I repeated.

A man came in behind my landlady. He flashed a credential that glinted gold in the lamplight. "Cornell Stamoran, FBI."

I sat up. I was naked except for a T-shirt, which seemed to be my dress code for greeting visitors. "Have you found Sabrina?"

Stamoran looked away from my crotch. Good. I had some privacy.

"I need you to answer some questions about her," he said.

I went into the bathroom and soaked a facecloth in hot water, rubbed my face and eyes. Cornell Stamoran stayed in the doorway, perhaps to make sure I didn't have Sabrina hidden in the shower. I ostentatiously wrapped my torso in a towel, took my time combing my hair. Stamoran followed me back into the sleeping room and watched as I put on my new fleece leggings, clean socks, sweatshirt, hoodie.

"Tell me about Sabrina," I said.

He shook his head. "We need answers to some questions before we decide what action to take."

I waited.

"How much research did you do into the Granev family before you started looking for Sabrina?"

This was the entrance to a hall of mirrors, where they tried to prove I had done something with Sabrina Granev in order to get a reward or a ransom or something from her parents.

"I didn't have a chance to study your credentials," I said. "Let me make sure you're really with the Bureau."

Nurse Norma the landlady had stayed in the room, standing behind Cornell near the exit to the street. She nodded approvingly.

The agent's mouth tightened, but he pulled out his badge again. I took it from him and studied it. He was from the Bureau. Or it was a good AI forgery.

"How much did you know about the Granev family when you started your search for Sabrina?" he prodded.

I took my phone out and turned on the recording app. "This is V.I. Warshawski, making a statement to

Cornell Stamoran from the FBI about Sabrina Granev."
I gave the date and time.

"Sabrina Granev drove to Kansas with three of her
housemates to watch a fifth friend play basketball on
Sunday evening. Sabrina's housemates came to me
Monday morning, concerned because she had not
returned to their motel Sunday night. They asked me
to delay my return to Chicago to look for her. I found
her parents' phone numbers online and kept phoning
them, as well as Sabrina, until I connected with Valerie
Granev, who told me she was afraid her daughter had
been kidnapped. She was frantic, as any parent would
be, and it was painful to tell her I'd made no progress in
finding her daughter. Beyond those bare facts, I know
nothing about Ms. Granev. I know nothing about her
family."

Stamoran ignored my speech. "You have a reputation for impulsive, even violent action, to achieve your
goals."

I said nothing.

"You made a major mistake looking for a student in
Chicago last October."

I studied my fingernails to keep from damaging
Agent Stamoran in a violent impulsive act.

"It's been suggested that you hid Sabrina yourself,

hoping you could find her and erase the mistake you made in the winter."

I pressed the play button on my phone, and my statement repeated itself in the small room.

"You say you knew nothing about the Granev family. How much do you know about Valerie Granev's work?"

"I know nothing about her work."

"You know she works for Tulloh Industries."

"I learned from Ms. Valerie Granev that she worked for Tulloh. I did not know that before we spoke."

"You deny that you abducted Sabrina Granev in order to collect a large ransom from Tulloh Industries?"

"I don't understand the question," I said.

He repeated it, raising his voice. I repeated my answer. He tried shouting the question. I stopped trying to answer.

Stamoran finally gave up and asked something more sensible. "You said you made no progress in looking for her. What steps did you take?"

"I checked with the Lawrence police, to see if she'd been picked up overnight. I tried to file a missing persons report, but the police told me Sabrina had not been missing long enough to qualify. I gave her picture to the local newspaper and asked them to run it online so that anyone who'd seen her could get in touch with me. My landlady checked with the hospital in case she'd been in an accident."

Norma said, "That's right. I'm a nurse at the Lawrence hospital. I was leaving for work when the young women came over to consult Ms. Warshawski because they were worried about their friend. The young woman hadn't been admitted, either to the main hospital or the university's."

"I think you know where the girl is," Stamoran said, "but just in case you're telling the truth, back off from your search. You could jeopardize her life. Got it?"

"Got it," I said, wondering what he thought I was agreeing to.

Stamoran finally left, without him arresting me or me slugging him.

When Norma had seen him out of her house, she came back and studied my face, looking troubled. "You didn't abduct her, did you?"

I gave a tired smile. "I did not abduct her. Her mother apparently does something high-powered with aviation electronics, and thinks someone could kidnap Sabrina and ask for her mom's secret research as ransom. I guess that's why the Bureau got involved, but if they really thought Russia or China had snatched Sabrina, they would have sent a sharper guy than this Stamoran to investigate."

Norma smiled. "When you put it like that, I can't disagree. Can you tell me what happened to the student the agent was talking about? The one where things went wrong?"

I gave her an outline of the Incident.

Norma nodded thoughtfully. "What went wrong wasn't because you did anything, but because the parents were unbalanced. Is that affecting your judgment? Are you afraid if you tell the parents where Sabrina is they might, well, react in the same way?"

"You're right. It's why I didn't want to start looking in the first place. But now that I'm looking, I have one lead on a place where I might find Sabrina. I think she might have a serious opioid problem, and I've learned about a house out in the country that hosts drug parties. I want to drive out there. This FBI agent might be watching your house to see what I'm doing. Would you be willing to drive my car into the next street and let me leave through your upstairs door?"

Norma's eyes widened. She studied my face for a long minute, then held out her hand for the keys.

8

This Old House

The road to Yancy was a two-lane job with ditches on either side and no shoulder. When I left the town limits, I drove by a cluster of new houses at the base of the hill. A sign pointed to the turnoff for the Yancy Consolidated School. After I passed that subdevelopment, I was shrouded in dark. The county had installed streetlamps at the crossroads, but these were a quarter mile apart. I stuck to the middle of the road to avoid the ditches.

My headlights picked up patches of mist rising from the land. An occasional fox or raccoon sauntered across the road. If the Omicron frat boys were selling product, I couldn't believe they'd chosen this isolated terrain.

When my GPS told me I'd reached my destination, I

couldn't see anything but trees and bracken. I thought at first my aerial map must be out-of-date, but after a moment I spotted a rutted muddy drive leading into the overgrowth. My headlights glinted on windowpanes at the end of the drive.

I backed away, reluctant to park there. You couldn't see the house from the road, and I didn't want to risk parking in the muddy cul-de-sac.

Beyond the house, the road curved past a plowed field. I found a farm track about a quarter mile away and bounced the Mustang along it until I came to the shelter of a tree.

If I'd had a chance to scout the terrain in daylight, I might have risked walking cross-country so I could come at the house from the back, but I had to stick to the road. I pulled the hoodie well forward over my head.

The walk along the dark road was more unnerving than a Chicago alleyway at night. I used the flashlight to keep out of the ditches, but this made me visible and vulnerable. Bushes grew wild on the far side of the ditches. Anyone could have been lurking there.

A car passed me, the first I'd seen since turning onto 1450 Road. The driver turned on their brights, blinding me. I hugged the edge of the tarmac until they'd passed.

When I reached the turnoff to the house, I saw

that the drive had been covered in gravel, although the damp ground meant that the cars that used it had gouged tracks into it. There had been a lot of traffic, and a lot of it was recent. Perhaps this was where the Porsche hubcaps had become caked in mud.

I worked my way to the house without the flash, tripping over potholes and tufts of grass, but managing to stay on my feet. The drive ended in a small turning circle near the house's back door. Risking the flash again, I could see more signs of recent traffic. Very recent, judging by the freshness of the mud under the gravel. Had an Omicron party been in progress? Had the frat boys sent everyone home so they could lie in wait for me?

The house was brick, the soft rose-colored clay that's stood up to the weather for a long time. It needed remortaring, but there weren't any broken windows.

Hugging the side of the house, in case anyone was watching from the windows, I made a circuit, stumbling on bottles and machine pieces that had been dumped in the tall grasses in the back. No lights seeped around the window blinds. No vehicles stood between the house and the encroaching woodland behind.

I returned to the side entrance. The door was heavy, with a new lock. When I tried the handle, it opened silently. A new door with well-oiled hinges. In a movie that's the sign that the heroine is about to be violently attacked if she goes inside.

I opened the door just wide enough to slip through. Pointed my flash at the checkerboard linoleum on the floor. An enameled table in the middle of the room was covered with half-empty boxes of carryout food. There were bottles of designer vodka and gin on a sideboard, beer, melting ice in a large chest, stacks of plastic glasses. There'd definitely been a party underway, one that had been abandoned in a hurry.

The kitchen was cold, but I could feel a bit of warmth in the radiator. The pipes wouldn't freeze and burst.

I moved resolutely toward the interior of the house, through three small rooms that held cushions and balance balls along with a few old-fashioned chairs and a settee. Beer bottles and half-drunk glasses were scattered around the floor. Ivy would earn her hundred dollars when she next came to clean.

The third room must have been the house's formal room when it was built; it had a fireplace, and an archway that opened on a small hallway, with a front door that special visitors would use, and a stairway to an upper floor.

I shone my flash on the front door. And saw a bundle wedged against it.

A cold sweat drenched me. I dropped the flashlight

and couldn't see where it landed. Pulled my phone from my hip pocket, but I was shivering with cold and had trouble swiping it open.

I pulled the hoodie sleeve down over my hand, rubbed some circulation into my fingers, turned on the flashlight app.

I knelt and prodded the bundle, gingerly at first, but when I couldn't feel flesh or bone I pushed my hand down onto it. I sat back on my heels. An empty tartan blanket, not a dead soccer player. My heart settled down, and I found my flashlight in the corner by the door.

I was getting to my feet when I heard a whimper. I stood still. Heard the sound again. Not my own wheezing breath or a night creature. Someone was in the house, on the upper floor.

The staircase was steep, the risers so narrow that the heels of my trail shoes hung over the edges. The stairs ended at a small circular landing. Three doors opened onto it, two open, one shut. The two open rooms both held a couple of bare mattresses. You could come up here to sleep off your drugs, I guess, or have sex.

I paused at the door of the third room. Heard the whimper. Flung the door open, burst into the room.

My flashlight picked out a figure wrapped around

itself so tightly that it looked like a ball. Brown hair visible between the knees.

"Sabrina Granev? Your mother is worried and the FBI is looking for you. Let's get you out of here."

She didn't hear me, but kept whimpering, rocking herself. I knelt beside her, trying to talk her into responding, but she kept herself tucked into a tight ball. I tried to pull her hands away from her shoulders so that I could lift her. She was clenching her muscles so hard that I was panting in earnest by the time I had prized her arms and legs apart. I put my hands under her armpits and dragged her, lifeguard fashion, to the stairs.

She screamed in terror, words that I couldn't make out, and began kicking and thrashing, jerking me around in a circle. I dropped her arms, and she scuttled back to the room.

I called her name in the low, firm voice that lifeguards are supposed to use with frenzied victims. She screamed louder.

I did a two-finger whistle, loud, I was the coach. She stopped screaming. I whistled again.

"You cannot stay in this house, Granev. I am here to take you away. Get to your feet. Now!" I used the sternest voice I had, coach unhappy with a lackluster team effort, ten laps around the track.

"I am Coach Warshawski. You need to do exactly what I tell you. Do you understand? Say, 'yes, Coach!'"

After a moment, she said, "Yes, Coach," in a trembling voice.

"Come to me and take my hand." I turned on the flashlight on my phone and shone it on my face and hand, then pointed it at her. She stumbled forward, grabbed my hand.

I led her down the steep staircase, moving step to step on my butt in case she started thrashing again.

When we reached the bottom, Sabrina was shaking so violently I could barely hold her. She clung to me but didn't fight me. I marched her through the rooms to the kitchen door. She was icy after her long hours in the underheated house, but she apparently still had enough remnants of an athlete's physique to keep going.

When we were outside, I took off my heavy hoodie and wrapped it around her. Athlete's physique or not, she was too depleted to walk back to my car. I was trying to figure out the warmest, safest place to park her when strobe lights split the night. A trio of squad cars turned up the drive. They squealed to a halt with a great spraying of what was left of the gravel.

The lead car turned on its spotlight. A voice bellowed through a bullhorn. "Let the girl go and no one will get hurt."

9
Academic Exercises

I spent a long night with Lawrence's finest, along with deputies from the sheriff's office. FBI Agent Stamoran had apparently been monitoring the police frequency, because he showed up with a subordinate. There was the usual jurisdictional squabble you get anytime the feds step in, but everyone had the same basic question: What had I been doing in the abandoned house?

We were meeting in the LKPD's big conference room, but the number of LEOs meant that Agent Stamoran was forced to stand. He and I were the only two wearing masks, which did not turn us into BFFs.

"Just be glad we knew to go to that house," Stamoran said to me. "Otherwise you could be facing a murder charge if the Granev girl had died."

"Since I had nothing to do with the young *woman* being in that house, there is no possible way a murder or any other charge of grievous harm could be made. How did you know to drive out there?"

"A neighbor reported suspicious activity," Stamoran said.

"Oh, my," I said. "That's the kind of session we're going to have? Where you disrespect me so blatantly that you don't pretend to make up a credible lie?"

"What is that supposed to mean?" Stamoran asked.

"There are no neighbors closer than a quarter mile away. Unless someone was flying drones over the place, I don't know what activity they could have seen."

"We all know you've been struggling since that student you were looking for killed himself," Stamoran said. "We know you have a tendency for violence. We figure you could have drugged Sabrina Granev and hidden her so you could find her and look like a hero."

I felt a wave of vertigo, dug my nails into my palms to steady myself. And felt something viscous in my right palm. Blood. Not now, don't do this, not when you need your wits, don't go seeing blood. My left hand was clean. I shut my eyes, looked again. Real blood, someone else's. Sabrina's?

"Well?" Stamoran bawled. "Nothing to say? I guess we can all agree that's how it went down."

The whole room was staring at me, not my hand, which they couldn't see. Jackals, wanting to bite and be done with it.

"How it went down?" I made myself smile at him, my evil smile. "That's a TV cop cliché, a fallback for the times when you don't know how to think. You're referring to a tragedy, about which you know so little that I know you didn't get your information from the Bureau or the Chicago Police Department. Maybe someone gave you a Classic Comics version to save you reading the big words."

My eyes swept the room. A few people were hiding smiles at my insult: the agent hadn't made himself popular. "Agent Stamoran is talking about a tragedy in Chicago last fall. A student was murdered. The horrible details are a matter of record: the student, a young trans woman, was murdered by their father and the death is considered infanticide: a child murdered by its parent."

The junior LEOs shifted uncomfortably in their seats. One of the county deputies cleared his throat and asked why I'd gone out to the house on Yancy Hill tonight—the Dundee place, he called it.

"Sabrina Granev's friends were worried that she had an opioid problem after her injury. I talked to street people who told me college kids were dealing in the area bars. I made a tour of downtown bars. Someone told me about the house—they didn't tell me it was called the Dundee place. I didn't know Sabrina would be there. It was the only lead I had, so I followed it."

"You should have reported that to us!" a town cop said.

"I ordered you to stop looking," Stamoran said to me, and then turned a dull mahogany as he realized how stupid that made him look.

"I tried talking to the Lawrence department this morning—I guess by now that was yesterday morning—and your team dismissed me, treating me like an addict looking for a score."

More uncomfortable shifting among the troops. I eyed them sardonically, before continuing my report.

"I'd tried reaching Sabrina's parents all day yesterday, and finally connected with her mother. As you can imagine, Valerie Granev was frantic. She didn't want to believe her daughter would be using drugs—no parent wants to face that. She said what Stamoran here repeated, that she feared her daughter had been kidnapped. Ms. Granev apparently works on sensitive projects for the DOD. She worried that someone could use her daughter as leverage to pry out national secrets.

"If she was right, I didn't want to get in the FBI's way, but I didn't think looking at a possible drug house would cross national security lines. And, in fact, there was plenty of evidence of drug use at the Dundee house. And Sabrina Granev was, in fact, there, in the grip of a pretty horrifying drug overdose."

That caused a general outcry and a new volley of questions: the identity of the dealers, the identity of whoever told me about the Dundee place, and, from Stamoran, an accusation about my role in getting Sabrina out to the house.

"You're recording this session," I said. "Play my remarks back. They explain everything I did and why."

As I spoke, Zoë Cruickshank, the young reporter with the *Douglas County Herald,* burst into the room. When she saw me, she forced her way through the mob of LEOs to my side.

"Oh, no! I got here after you finished your statement. Did you record it? Can I copy it from your phone? I heard on my scanner that someone found a body in the old Dundee place. Was it that student you were looking for?"

"Who let her in?" a Lawrence cop groaned.

"You know me, Deke, I can track you to the ends of the county if you're part of a story. Chicago—how'd you know the old Dundee place was a drug house? Pretty smart work for a stranger in town."

Deke Everard. The sergeant I'd tried to reach yesterday. In the chaos, both in the room and in my head, I hadn't recognized him.

Everyone seemed to know Cruickshank, all but the two feds. Deke and his team treated her like an annoying kid sister, someone whose questions made them laugh but not take seriously. In the middle of their chaffing, a young cop raised a timid hand.

"Uh, Deke, uh, Sarge—I put out a request to Uber and Lyft to see if someone drove Sabrina Granev out there Sunday night. I just got a message from the Uber driver who took her to Yancy. He says he picked her up outside the Lion's Heart just before midnight. She was alone."

"Did she die out in the drug house?" Zoë demanded.

"No," I said. "She was alive when I found her. I think they took her to your local hospital. Was she wounded? Bleeding?"

Sergeant Everard shook his head. "Not that I know. We don't have all the details yet, but the EMTs said she was suffering from hypothermia and an OD."

At that, Agent Stamoran seemed to think his expertise was needed elsewhere. He packed up his subordinate and left, without even looking at me.

"He was so sure the Granev girl had been kidnapped, he'd already taken over the chief's conference room as a federal incident room," Deke explained to the rest of us. "Meanwhile, Warshawski, let's have the name of the bartender who sent you to the Dundee place. It's okay if you use big words with me—I move my lips when I read them to make sure I get them right."

His team laughed—with him, with me. Stamoran had rubbed them all the wrong way. I decided not to remind him that Sabrina was a woman, not a girl—they were on my side, at least for the moment. Don't spoil it.

"People kept telling me that a group of frat boys from the Omicron Delta Beta house were dealing. Then someone in the parking lot at the Boat Yard told me she thought there were wild parties out at the Dundee place. That didn't seem like a big enough tip to bother you with, but, as I said, it was the only lead I had."

I hoped by positioning Holly in the parking lot, she would sound like a customer. I didn't want to put her and her sister in police sights. Even though I knew they both should be questioned, I was feeling protective, as if they were friends or clients.

Deke started handing out assignments, who was to follow up at the Boat Yard, who was to go around to other bars to see if the dealers could be identified, who was to go to the Omicron house to see what they could find.

Zoë turned to me. "I want an exclusive, Chicago. Tell me what happened tonight."

"It's not very interesting: I went into what I now

know is the Dundee house, heard Sabrina crying on the floor above me, and walked up and found her."

"Details." She held her phone under my nose.

"Not at three in the morning," I said.

"And not when she needs to talk to the LKPD." Deke moved between Zoë's phone and me.

He beckoned to a young officer to accompany us into the cubicle that served as his office. He asked for more details about anything I'd noticed at the Dundee house, and anything I'd seen in the Omicron garage.

We went through a few more routine questions and then Deke asked about the blood on my hand. He'd been watching me more closely than I'd realized, which was a discomforting thought.

"It's why I wondered if Sabrina had been wounded. Getting her out of that room and down the stairs was a—it was an intense physical experience. There's blood on my leggings, too."

He got up and looked at my hand and legs. "You know, Warshawski, you should get an HIV test. Drug house, blood, and that stuff hadn't congealed when you landed in it. I'll pass the word on to the county that they'd better have a hazmat team when they go through the place." He made a note.

I got up to leave but asked if Valerie Granev had made it into town.

"Yes. She was actually at the station with the chief when the call came in that you'd found her daughter. She was hot to get out to the Dundee place, but the chief persuaded her to meet the ambulance crew at the hospital. She's probably still there. I don't know why the fed was throwing his muscle around. It was like he'd hoped the girl had been kidnapped so he could strut his stuff. You made him look bad by finding she was a druggie.

"That kid you found in Chicago—the one whose father murdered them in front of you—most cops never have to witness that kind of horror show. Sorry Stamoran rubbed your face in it."

"It keeps haunting me, way more than any other violent crime I've witnessed. I keep seeing blood everywhere."

"Maybe because we're so awash in blood these days," Deke said drily. "When are you heading back?"

"Tomorrow. When I wake up. Do you have someone who could drive me to my B and B? I was hustled into town in a squad car and my Mustang is out on 1450 Road somewhere."

Zoë Cruickshank had been hovering outside his door. When she offered to drive me, the sergeant said, "Give the lady a chance to sleep, Cruickshank. I'll take her home."

Interlude I
Gertrude and Cady

Gertrude Perec was at the computer in the alcove she used as an office when Cady came down to the kitchen. Gertrude was sitting with shoulders that would do a marine proud, but she managed to stiffen them farther at her granddaughter's footsteps.

"Nine A.M., missy. You planning to spend the rest of your life sulking over losing that job?"

"I'm not allowed to be depressed? To mourn my career?" Cady spoke to the steel spine.

"I expect better from you than feel-good jargon. Depressed. Mourning your career. Even when I lost your mother, and the grief felt like a saw cutting my body in half, I didn't lie in bed feeling sorry for myself."

Cady shut her eyes. She thought she might scream

if her grandmother bragged once again about her stoic commitment to duty.

"Open your eyes when I'm speaking to you, missy."

Cady's face must be reflected in the computer screen. Or Gertrude was a seer. That was entirely possible.

"If you want to fight the firing, go to your union representative, or get your own lawyer. If you want to turn a page and move forward in your life, start figuring out what your next step is. But don't droop like a willow tree—it's hard on the people around you and does you no good in the bargain."

Cady took half a grapefruit from the refrigerator and moved to the breakfast nook without speaking. When five minutes passed in silence, Gertrude said, "Pat Everard was at breakfast this morning."

Cady grunted. The breakfast was a midweek ritual among the most enthusiastic members of Riverside Congregational's women's group. Pat Everard ran the group with Gram, so it wasn't news that she was at the breakfast.

"That Chicago detective is back in town."

"I know," Cady said. She was texting, but she looked up from her phone. "I saw her after the game Sunday."

"You didn't mention that. I never liked that woman."

"I know, Gram. It's why I didn't tell you." Cady looked at her screen and ate another section of grapefruit.

"Cold, I thought. Arrogant, even if she knows her business. As she did in this case—she found that missing student—in time to save her life, Deke told Pat."

"That's good." Cady paused. "Brett Santich was in the parking lot when I was leaving the game. He as good as called me a pedophile."

"Sticks and stones, Miss Cady," Gertrude said sharply. "And you know it's rude to text while I'm talking to you."

"The tongue has no bones, but it's strong enough to break them," Cady said. "Trig Garrity got into a fight, practically a physical one, with Brett over the land on Yancy. Everyone who was still in the parking lot stopped to watch—that's when I saw the detective."

"Trig would fight a dead rabbit if he thought it looked at him sideways. I don't like the deal Brett did over the land, either. Once he sold it, he lost control over it, but that was years ago, not yesterday. There's no point to screaming about it now, the way Trig does. The land means something to me, something personal, which it never did to him. Apparently not to Brett, either."

Gram's family had owned the land when the town was being built in the 1860s, but they'd had to sell during the Great Depression of the 1930s. It hadn't been in her family for close to a century, but she still acted as though she had a stake in it.

"I guess Brett got overextended when he built that little subdivision on Yancy," Gertrude added. "He mortgaged just about everything, from what Pat and I could make out, when he applied for planning permission. And then he did a deal with that Topeka bank."

For Gertrude, doing business with an out-of-town bank was like doing a deal with the devil, even if the out-of-town was only twenty-five miles away.

Gertrude gave a snort of bitter laughter and added, "If Trig Garrity didn't make me see red, white, and blue, I'd have joined in his protest. Anyway, it was out there on Yancy land where that missing student turned up. The Dundee place, that old brick house on the south side of the hill."

"Is that who owned the land at the bottom of the hill? Dundees? Were they cousins or something I never heard of?"

"When my mother was a girl, when the family still owned the land, they leased it to a tenant farmer. Schapen, I think, but definitely not Dundee or even Santich. Santiches rented it out during the 1960s, the hippie craze, you know, when all the long-haired kids wanted to lie around in the country pretending to raise their own food but smoking pot. Whoever Dundee was predated all that history."

"Gee, Gram, if you don't know, the Dundees probably never existed."

Gertrude narrowed her eyes—was it a joke or a criticism? Cady liked to accuse her of getting overinvolved in local people's lives.

She sidestepped the issue. "Pat Everard said the place was being used as a drug house, but no one knew, either in the sheriff's office or the city."

"Oh, please, Gram! If V.I. Warshawski discovered it after being in town twenty-four hours, the cops must have known about it. Not to mention Brett himself. He's just trying to avoid legal liability. The students' parents could sue him for operating a dangerous business, so he's trying to pretend he doesn't know. Ditto for the police, even if Aunt Pat's your oldest friend and Deke is the best-looking single guy in town."

Cady put her grapefruit skin in the compost bin and the spoon and bowl in the sink. She was leaving the room, but turned back to kiss Gertrude on the head.

"I'm okay, Gram. I just need to sort out where I go from here. I am tired of parents screaming at me because their baby got an F for not doing any work, or because I want their kids to think in bigger ways about the big world around them. Maybe I'll join Trig on the barricades, screaming at Santich until he admits he's a jerk."

10
Rope Bridge

I showered when I got back to my room, Lady Mac-beth scrubbing blood from my hands. I hoped the hot water would relax me, but when I slid beneath the comforter, I couldn't sleep. Every time I turned over I seemed to feel Sabrina's bones, sharp, too close to her skin, poking into my breasts.

Bernie phoned at seven, just as I'd managed to drop off. I had texted her when I got to my room, to let her know Sabrina was safe, but I'd forgotten to silence my phone. Bernie wanted to know where I'd found Sabrina and how.

My first impulse—hang up—I put aside. Talk to her now, get it done.

"The guys Angela saw her talking to in the bar

must have given her the address of the house where I found her."

"Ah, Vic, I knew you would make it happen, almost like magic."

"It wasn't magic, Bernie, it was luck, luck plus following the only trail I could turn up."

"Even so, I am grateful, Angela is also. Thank you for doing what was painful. Now maybe the Granevs will take Sabrina out of school and send her to a clinic. Living with her has made us all *stressées*. She is depressed, not eating, us guessing she is using while the parents and coaches act as if she had flu, an illness she will recover from swiftly."

"You and Angela had a difficult fall trying to support her," I said. "Did you talk to your own coaches about her behavior?"

"We were afraid maybe we would be responsible for her losing her scholarship," Bernie said. "Anyway, now can you see that you are wrong to let doubts devour you? You are still the brilliant problem solver."

My stomach twisted. "You know those rope bridges you see in movies? The ones that connect two inaccessible mountain peaks? In the movies the ropes are fraying. The hero makes it across seconds before the last strand breaks. That's me, Bernie. The last strand is fraying."

"But, Vic, I don't see this at all. In one day you discover a drug house, you recover a person close to death. You should feel as high as angels. You proved you are still a great detective. This is what you needed."

I hung up before my anger overcame me and I began shouting at Bernie: *I don't need this, more blood, used needles, I need to sit by a stream on a sunny day with a cool drink, listening to birds and not thinking of anything.*

I lay back down, trying to take those deep breaths that fitness mavens say are key to relaxation, but I couldn't relax back into sleep. I finally gave up on it. Got up, tried to move my tired muscles into some stretches, bathed my gritty eyes in hot water. Sergeant Everard had asked me to stay in town another day in case there were follow-up questions, but I planned to leave as soon as possible.

The cleanest clothes I had right now were the ones I'd worn when I drove down on Sunday. They were clean only relative to the soiled hoodie and trail shoes I'd bought yesterday. I took those and the bloodstained leggings out to Nurse Norma's garbage can. Maybe the dirt could be cleaned off, but not the memory of Sabrina Granev gibbering on the floor.

When I was packed, and had put my used linens in Nurse Norma's washing machine, I phoned Sabrina's mother. The call went to voicemail. I left a message, saying I was glad I'd found Sabrina in time but would like an update on her condition. I sent a text to Nurse Norma, thanking her for helping me evade possible surveillance last night. You may have seen the news that I found the missing student in a drug house northwest of town.

Zoë Cruickshank phoned as I was starting to summon an Uber to take me to my car. "Chicago! I need my exclusive."

Her energy was as nerve-jarring as Bernie's. "I can't tell you anything more than you can learn from the police," I said.

"You're wrong, Chicago: they won't talk to me, not even Deke. Please—this is my big chance!"

"Addiction up close and personal is your big chance?" My voice was harsh.

"I didn't mean it like that," she muttered. "You have an important career, you're a success, but I'm getting by on part-time jobs because the paper can only pay me twelve thousand a year. If I can cover an important story then I could get more freelance work."

Put like that—twenty-five years old or so, ambitious but with bleak prospects—she didn't need me stomping on her dreams. I said if she'd drive me out to my car, I'd tell her what I could.

She was at the curb in ten minutes. One big attraction to Lawrence: you could get anywhere fast. On the way out to 1450 Road, Zoë had her phone on the dash, recording our conversation. I repeated what I'd told the cops last night.

"I was surprised that no one was there when I arrived," I said. "The tire tracks and empties made it look as though they'd had a big crowd, but it wasn't even midnight when I showed up. The amount of debris in the house, and the number of tire tracks stirring up the driveway, there must have been a good-size crowd."

By the time I finished answering Zoë's questions, we'd reached the bend in the road where the Dundee house stood. Zoë stopped at the mouth of the driveway. "That's Trig Garrity's car up there."

She turned in and pulled up behind a battered van. It was hard to tell what the original color might have been. The rear bumper was plastered with stickers advocating to save the earth, whales, and democracy, and to overturn *Citizens United* and *Hobby Lobby*.

Zoë got out and dashed up to the house. Trig, still in his faded army parka, was at the kitchen door. He seemed about to knock out a pane of glass with a rock when we arrived.

"I know it's a fucking crime scene, Cruickshank. It's a crime that the whole county puts up with this house and what goes on in it. I pointed that out to Prince Santich, but he said it wasn't his problem."

"At the police station, they called it the Dundee house," I said. "Does it actually belong to Santich?"

Trig glared at me. "Who are you? Some hotshot lawyer?"

"She's a hotshot detective from Chicago," Zoë said. "She found Sabrina Granev in this house last night when the police and even the FBI didn't know where to look."

"Local pigs couldn't find a cornfield if they drove into it." Trig spat. "They're all in bed with Santich. Yes, your moneyness, no, your moneyness, tell me how low to stoop, your moneyness."

"That's so not fair!" Zoë cried. "Deke Everard is a good cop and so is—"

"Everard's arrested me five times on Brett Santsnitch's say-so. And then Brett started after Cady, because she was speaking truth to power. And now he's going after Clarina Coffin for the crime of supporting my work."

I didn't want to hear Trig rant about his work as the county watchdog, so I repeated my question about whether the Dundee house belonged to Santich.

"The Dundees aren't around to defend it so Santich probably stole it from them," Trig said.

He swung his arm back to smash the glass door pane, but I grabbed his wrist and pulled his hand down.

"Why do you want to go to prison?" I asked.

"What—you come all the way from Chicago to arrest me?"

"I'm a private investigator. No arrest powers."

"Private, public, pigs both."

I let go of his wrist. "Go ahead. I can see why your PD is tired of trying to defend you."

"Trig, don't be an asshole," Zoë said. "You know if the sheriff or Chief McDowell find out the house has been broken into, they'll want to talk to you. Vic is smart; you should pay attention to her."

"Tell me something, then, Ms. Smart-from-Chicago."

"Can't tell you anything," I said. "You know it all already. However, if I were investigating, I'd wonder what use you were making of this house. Did you store stuff here, figuring the dealers and users wouldn't bother about it? Posters and bullhorns, or something bigger, more worrying if a sheriff's deputy found it?"

He gave a bark of something like a laugh. "You are so far off base you're not even playing the right game."

He stomped over to his van and took off. The doors rattled and the tires were balding, but the engine ran quietly, and he didn't leave an exhaust trail.

I looked after him. "In court Monday, the judge said Santich didn't own the land, that some corporation did."

"I went over to the recorder's office," Zoë said. "The little bit of the property Brett hung on to includes this house. He still owns and farms that field"—she pointed toward where I'd parked my car—"but he lives over in that subdivision around Yancy School. He raised the money to build it, but then he got slammed in the downturn and had to sell the houses to some hedge fund. Back in the 1930s the Santiches were super rich. Gertrude Perec's family couldn't hang on to the farmland they owned here on Yancy, so they sold to Santiches, I think to Brett's grandfather. Anyway, it must be unlucky land because whoever owns it can't afford to keep it."

She laughed. "Maybe I'll do a little paragraph on how it's unlucky to own land on Yancy—can the new resort going up break the curse?"

"If Brett is bankrupt, why is Trig so hot against him?"

Zoë shrugged. "Maybe it's like Judge Bhagavatula said, Trig didn't do his homework. Anyway, Brett's family are like so many farmers around here, they can't compete with the big corporate farms in the west of the state, and so they scramble to hang on to their land. Only Brett lost most of his with some unlucky investments. It's a shame, really, that Trig doesn't understand the odds farm families are fighting. They could use some support."

"What about the Dundees? Are they another local family?"

Zoë shook her head. "I never heard of them. Not that that means anything—I didn't grow up here and so all these family connections, they're something I have to learn as I go along. I've been working for the *Herald* for two years now and I'm hoping it will lead to better things—which this drug story could make happen."

Her face brightened, and she put a hand on my arm. "Why don't you stay and find out what's been going on in this house, and who the Dundees are. I could report the investigation as it unfolds, like a docudrama!"

"And your twelve thousand a year would cover paying for my time and expertise? I charge by the hour, plus expenses, which in this case would include moving my household to Kansas. Why don't you investigate and do a daily podcast on your progress? That would get you a big audience and a new career direction."

"It would be better with two people," she wheedled.

My face must have looked ominous—she hastily moved away to take pictures of the outside of the house. While I was waiting on her, I got a call from someone named Jenna Ettenberg who said she was the Granev family's attorney.

"Valerie Granev wants to talk to you. She's staying with her daughter at the local hospital; if you could meet her there it would be a help. Text her when you get to the lobby."

11
Take Me to the Limit

Valerie Granev's face belonged in a funhouse mirror. She'd started the day yesterday with makeup, but her foundation had caked and cracked. She had mascara smears under her eyes, accentuating her look of unbearable grief.

"How is Sabrina doing?" I asked.

"Not too well." She swallowed, looked away. "When we got to the hospital, she was screaming, having frightening hallucinations. She said monsters were waiting outside the window, she begged me to make them go away.

"I—I was useless, I thought if we went to the window she would see—but the nurses explained it was hallucinations from cold and dehydration and"—

she flinched—"whatever drugs she'd taken. At least when they put in the IVs she calmed down. They let me sleep with her and at seven she woke up and screamed 'they're still there, they're still there, make them go away.' I told her that Daddy had gotten rid of them and she went back to sleep, but right before you got here she started seeing them again."

She squeezed her eyes shut. "I've been so—negligent. I saw at Christmas that she wasn't well. Ram—my husband—we're an athletic family. For New Year's, we always go to a place in Utah to ski. Sabrina couldn't ski—this year—her broken ankle wasn't healing—she was in a lot of pain. She was already too thin, not eating, not working at her rehab."

Granev kneaded her fingers. "I pushed her to take her rehab seriously. She—she was ranked among the top twenty young U.S. soccer players before the ankle break. Twenty Under Twenty. She's competitive and ambitious."

A sob caught up with her.

"She was. That's my nature, and she has it, too. But at Christmas she was apathetic, didn't seem to care, and all I did was scold her.

"I flew to Chicago at Thanksgiving and saw she wasn't making an effort with her rehab. I lectured her but didn't really pay attention—I was under a deadline, as if killing more Russians was more worth my time than my own daughter."

Her mouth twisted in a spasm of self-loathing. "Instead, I tried getting her housemates to push her to do her rehab, but of course they couldn't. It wasn't fair to them. I—I didn't want to see the problem."

I nodded, not speaking.

"The young Black woman Sabrina lives with—the basketball star—she tried to tell me when I came back with Sabrina after the winter break, and all I did was tell Sabrina to follow—what's her name? Angela? Angela's training schedule and she'd be back on her feet. How cold was that? The truth is, I was annoyed with Sabrina for not taking her career as seriously as Angela takes hers. I didn't want to know she was struggling with these damned drugs.

"And now—we don't know how much damage she has. Brain, body—will she walk properly, let alone play, or have a family—" The enormity of her daughter's losses crashed in on her, and she began to weep in earnest.

A hospital staffer stopped near us, looking down in concern. *Water?* I mouthed. She nodded and came back in a moment with a bottle and a cup.

"Were you able to reach your husband?" I asked. "I gather he's up in the mountains away from normal phone service."

"Yes, wilderness camping is his great love and he longs to run year-round programs, and get the resources for less-able children. We used to go camping in the Uinta Mountains when Sabrina was little, but then my career got more demanding, and when Sabrina was a teen she wanted to spend spring break at soccer camps or with her friends. I—I used to argue with Ram that he didn't care about her future, and he said I cared enough for two, so he turned his attention to the youth programs he works with."

She rubbed her eyes, further smearing the mascara.

"Ram is hiking down from the camp, but with the kids and equipment it will take hours and then—anyway, as soon as it's safe to move Sabrina, we're getting her to a rehab clinic that works with—with addicts, so there's no point him coming here. Although maybe if Ram shows up he can persuade her that Daddy got rid of her monsters."

She went over her failures like an accountant with a spreadsheet, her coldness, her imperceptiveness, her absorption in her avionics career. "I loved being one of the 'Forty Under Forty STEM Women to Look Out For.'" Her voice cracked. "And when Sabrina was one of Twenty Under Twenty, I was so proud, like these numbers mean something more than paying attention to your own child."

She was crying in earnest. I let her cry, found more water and a box of tissues.

She finally wound down and looked at me. "I know I owe her life to you, the police told me that, but how— how did you know where to find her?"

"I didn't," I said. "I'm a stranger in this town. When I asked questions of likely people, the house where I found her was the only thing close to a lead I turned up. I wasn't expecting to find your daughter, but I thought if there was a party going on, I'd get leads on other places to look for someone trying to score—trying to find meds. The FBI agent ordered me to stop looking, in case she'd been kidnapped, but I thought finding leads to dealers wouldn't interfere with a kidnapping investigation."

"Agent Stamoran thinks you got her to go out there. He said you need to look like a hero after making a big mistake with a different college student last fall."

"Yes, he made that slanderous and outrageous statement in the police station last night. I don't know why he felt he needed to discredit me, but he is, in fact, wrong."

"He says you can't prove you didn't take Sabrina out there." She didn't sound accusatory, more anguished and uncertain.

"You can't prove a negative, Ms. Granev." Big lies,

small lies, all circulating on the net, destroying life after life. The sheer tawdriness of life today made the whole world appear gray.

I summoned what I hoped was a reassuring tone. "Even though we disagree on my role in what happened to Sabrina, your FBI agent should be able to track down the dealers who sold drugs to her. The Bureau has the resources for that kind of work."

She gave a little headshake. "He's not my agent. I don't know who called the Bureau about Sabrina's disappearance. It wasn't me, but anyone who heard me on the phone with you or with Ram—I was so distraught I wasn't careful where I spoke."

She pressed the heel of her hand against her forehead. "I can't finish a coherent thought today. Agent Stamoran—maybe old Mr. Tulloh called the Bureau. If he heard about Sabrina—everyone jostles for space close to the head man—anyone could have told him. When you're a billionaire, you know everyone wants to do you favors, even the FBI, so maybe that's why they sent Stamoran over from the Topeka office."

She produced a smile to keep from crying again. "I saw Stamoran this morning. He says since Sabrina wasn't kidnapped, the Bureau doesn't have jurisdiction to track down dealers, that it's the business of the local police. I know I should care more, get on some soapbox and demand they protect other people's children, but that doesn't matter to me."

"Don't add that to the list of other things you're beating yourself up over," I said. "You have one job right now, looking after your daughter. The local cops are good; they'll follow up."

"There's one thing I wanted to ask you." She looked up at me again. Her mascara had turned into black stalactites, reaching from her eyes to her jaw.

"I know Sabrina is hallucinating when she's screaming about the monsters coming to the window, but what if she really saw something last night? If it's someone who could come after her—I—she doesn't seem to remember anything else. I'm asking you—you did what no one else could, finding Sabrina. I want you to find out what she really saw when she was in that house."

"No!" My response was involuntary. She winced, and I tried to soften my answer—my home was in Chicago, my clients as well as my elderly neighbor needed me, I was here without clothes or even my computer.

"Today and tomorrow," she said. "I can pay whatever your fee is, send it by Zelle to your bank. The FBI and the police, they won't pay attention. You could go out to that place and see—I don't know what a detective can see."

I started to say "no" more forcefully, and then I

thought of the blanket by the front door, with blood on it still fresh last night at midnight. A party had been interrupted, everyone but Sabrina had fled. She'd been screaming when she saw me, nonsense syllables I'd thought at the time, but maybe she'd thought I was one of her monsters.

It hadn't occurred to me last night, but I'd gone into a house where a party had been at full swing not too much earlier, and yet I hadn't seen any cars leaving as I walked to the house from the farm track where I'd parked. The blood on the blanket was just starting to congeal. That meant someone had been dripping blood less than fifteen minutes before my arrival.

I pulled up one of my contracts on the app I'd created for my business. Valerie filled it out and signed it, including her private cell phone number, and sent me four thousand dollars without blinking.

12
Monsters

I parked in the same place I'd used before and walked
down the road to the Dundee house. The day was
dull, with snow threatening. The wind had risen, stirring dust devils in the plowed field on the south side of
the road.

Despite the cold air, I moved slowly up the drive,
trying to see if anyone had driven here after Zoë and
I left this morning. I was hoping to find signs of the
Omicron boys' Porsche. The county hadn't sent a
crime scene unit in yet; the fraternity crew might have
come to collect leftover product, but I didn't see any
signs of them.

The kitchen door was unlocked. Trig apparently
hadn't tried the handle but had gone straight for a rock.

He wanted to go inside, but when I suggested he was hiding something in the house he'd been scornful: I was so far off base I wasn't even playing the right game.

What was the right game? Drugs? The protests he was running with the woman named Clarina? Or had Cady Perec's firing felt personal to him?

I waited for a moment inside the kitchen door, ready to run if anyone tried to jump me, but the house felt empty.

The kitchen looked worse in daylight. When I turned on a light, roaches skittered away from the cartons of food. I could see more drug detritus—not needles, but the foil wraps and test-tube bottles that tabs and powders come in. Ivy hadn't shown for her cleanup gig. Or she'd come, not seen her pay, and left again.

I stood still, listening for a creaking floorboard, stifled cough, but didn't hear anything except the wind rattling the windows. I moved past the downstairs rooms into the front hall.

The blanket was gone. Someone had returned for it. Someone could be in here now, silent as a grave, waiting for me.

"Don't go there, V.I." I said out loud. "Keep your head."

I climbed the stairs to the upper floor, stomping loudly on the narrow risers. At the top, I hugged the wall, making myself as small a target as possible, but no one appeared, no one shot at me.

I checked the three small bedrooms, found a bathroom tucked into what had been a closet, saw nothing.

The window in the room where I'd found Sabrina overlooked the woods behind the house. If she'd seen monsters, they would have come across the fields or through the woods. Maybe deer or some other animal that her drug-riddled brain had turned into something from a horror film.

Back in the kitchen, I saw another door that I'd overlooked before. The cellar. I found a string attached to a naked bulb that swung above my head like a noose.

Another steep narrow staircase. No handrail. In movies, you yell at the heroine not to go down those stairs. I wasn't a heroine, though, but something less dazzling, an exhausted detective far from home.

I almost missed the woman. She was propped against the wall under the stairs. Her head had flopped to one side, but her eyes were open, irises cloudy. She was wearing a down coat that someone had stuffed her into, unskillfully, one arm in, one showing where her clothes had been ripped away from her body.

I didn't touch her, but bent over her. Bra unhooked, pants pulled away from her hips. Her feet were bare.

The blood on last night's blanket had come from the

back of her head. Someone had smashed it, hard, probably more than once. Blood and bone chips had fallen onto the coat's collar.

"*Poverina*," I whispered, blinking back tears. "Who hated you this much?"

13
Whose Woods These Are

You have serious explaining to do." Deke Everard's voice was raw with fatigue. He probably hadn't been to bed at all since dropping me at Norma's place in the predawn.

"What would you like me to explain?"

"What you really know about the Dundee house. You conveniently uncovered two crimes there in"—he looked at his wrist—"just about twelve hours. Don't bat your eyes and tell me you never heard of the place before."

"I'm not an eye batter, Sergeant, but I never heard of the place before last night."

He smacked the tabletop. "Don't give me that crap. The DA is looking into what we can charge you with.

Obstruction, concealing a crime for starters. Just so you know, that fed has shown up again, making more noises about kidnapping."

We were in an interrogation room at the LKPD headquarters. The building was new, so new that the interrogation rooms didn't yet smell of blood, sweat, and tears.

"Who was the woman whose body I found?" I asked.

"Clarina Coffin. Tell me what you know about her."

"Nothing," I said. Zoë had told me about Clarina Coffin's role in getting Cady Perec fired, but you don't do yourself any favors by rambling on to the cops.

Deke demanded that I tell him what I was doing at the Dundee place this morning.

"You know I didn't put Ms. Coffin's body in that basement," I said. "Nor did I hit her over the head hard enough to kill her."

"You had blood on you last night," he said. "Where did it come from?"

"A blanket by the front door. I was terrified Sabrina Granev's body might be inside, but when I unrolled it, nothing was there."

"And you didn't think to report it?"

"I mentioned the blood to you, but in the stress of finding Sabrina, I forgot about the blanket." I kept my voice steady. Don't push on a cop who's already close to the edge. "There'd been a party going on, which apparently broke up abruptly. You surely noticed all the booze and foil wraps and so on, right? No cars when I got to the house last night. But if I'd thought about the bloody blanket at all, I'd have guessed a fight among the partygoers. You find out who set up the party? Was it the Omicron boys?"

All the time I was talking, I knew I should keep my mouth shut. I could hear how a DA would spin this in court: *The defendant had a bloody blanket in her possession. The defendant was at the crime scene off and on during twelve hours when a woman was murdered and a second woman close to death from an overdose.* I had always told my clients, *Don't talk if you don't have a lawyer with you and even then, don't talk.* Yet here I was, saying way more than I should.

"You disappeared after the emergency crew showed," Deke said. "Where did you go?"

"I gave a statement to the first responders. And then I went to my car. I was badly shaken. The woman's dead body was hard enough, but the way her clothes had been ripped—the violence—the violation—"

I'd sat in the Mustang's passenger seat, my knees pulled to my chin in a little Sabrina-like ball. I probably would have screamed like Sabrina if someone had tried to pry me out of my car.

In the months after the Incident in Chicago, I'd consulted a trauma specialist. She'd suggested a technique—arms crossed over the chest, tapping side to side in a heart-like rhythm, chanting something. This morning I tried "You are safe/You will survive." After a time I was able to uncoil myself, drink some water. I dozed for almost an hour.

By the time I woke and drove back to the Dundee house, the emergency responders had left. I tried calling Valerie, to let her know that her daughter's monsters had brought a woman's body into the house. The call went to voicemail.

I stood irresolutely in the drive, the dust and sleet stinging my face. I tried to work out a timeline for the monsters. How had they avoided the party and me both last night?

The blood had been fresh when I went to the house last night, but since there'd been no cars, I thought it likely that the body had been carried through the woods. I went into the undergrowth north of the house. Not directly in the line of sight from Sabrina's window, but parallel to it.

The bushes and trees immediately behind the house hadn't been tended to for years. It was easy to see breaks in the branches, but the ground was still hard in mid-February, not holding footprints. About ten yards beyond the thickest undergrowth, I found a trail, overgrown but a definite path up the hill. I followed it, my running shoes slipping in the rotting leaves.

A little farther along, I came upon the remains of a chimney, the kind they used to build up the sides of houses when the fireplace was the main heat source. When I squatted to study the area, I could see a dimple in the ground where the foundation had been laid.

The trail, or what was left of it, continued upward through woods that hadn't been pruned for so long that dead trees blocked the trail in places. I found ruins from three other buildings, including an old well with a rusted cover bolted over it. Some kind of little community had tried to make a go of it here, but only the Dundee house had survived.

I finally came to a fence, with a worn sign proclaiming PRIVATE PRO . . . TRESPASSERS WILL . . . It was as if Piglet from Winnie-the-Pooh had set up house nearby. I looked around and was unnerved to see an actual owl, a big tawny creature who watched me with amused contempt: *You're no match for the countryside, detective. Go back to Chicago where you belong.*

The TRESPASSERS WILL sign had pulled the wire away from the fence post. I stepped on it, pushing it to the ground, and walked on. The land was flattening out, and the area had been clear-cut. I came to a more formidable fence, a new Cyclone number that also was signposted, this time spelling out the prosecution that awaited trespassers (the full extent of the law! Be afraid!).

It was cold on the hilltop. A steady wind was blowing from Chicago. I put up my arms, begging the wind to pull me aloft, fly me home. Nothing happened.

Zoë had said that someone was building a resort up here, maybe some apartment buildings as well. The hilltop had been leveled. In the middle of it was a slab of concrete, perhaps a hundred yards square, with the pipe sticking up from the edges, showing where electrics and plumbing fittings would go.

Industrial lampposts dotted the perimeter, providing cones of light that gave a sense of the size of the project. A road led into the site on the side of the plowed field farthest from me. Trucks were beetling up and down, stirring up clouds of dust.

The south side, where I was standing, held the trailers that served as offices. One was labeled KIRMEK CONSTRUCTION, PROJECT MANAGER. The other was for the project architect and engineer.

When I'd watched Trig's court appearance last week, the judge had said it was a night manager at Kirmek who had filed the trespassing complaint against Trig. This was where he'd been protesting the destruction of old-growth trees.

I wandered over to the western edge of the open field, where outsize machinery was standing near some equipment sheds. These were what you'd need for building something big—bulldozer, giant steam shovel, drilling rig, blazoned with the letter K in a circle. They'd installed the tower for a pylon, but hadn't yet built the cage, nor laid any cable as far as I could tell.

On the north side of the giant concrete slab, stack of poles, like outsize Lincoln Logs, lay on the ground next to a piling hammer. I guessed a second pylon would go up there. It would be more challenging to build pylons on the slope, but the essential equipment seemed to be in place.

I didn't see anything that looked like the foundations for hotels or shops. There was one small structure built from cement blocks that looked more permanent than the trailers.

I headed toward that, eyes on the ground, hoping to find something, a fragment of cloth, something that would show the dead woman had been carried over the fence last night. I didn't see anything, but as I reached the cement blocks I heard shouting.

On the far side of the building, two men were in an angry confrontation. The wind was too strong to carry their words, but they were poking each other with index fingers when they weren't balling their hands into fists. One had a hard hat on; the other, bareheaded, looked like the man Trig Garrity had been baiting in the field house parking lot the other night.

"Mr. Santich!"

The pair had been so wrapped in their fight they hadn't seen me approach.

"Who the fuck are you and how did you get here?" the hard hat roared.

"I'm a detective. I'm detecting how a dead woman's body ended up in the Dundee house."

"You can be an astronaut looking for the moon, but you don't do it on this land. It's posted. Clearly. Private Property."

The hard hat hadn't registered my words, but Santich had.

"What are you talking about? A dead woman? What—that Chicago girl who went missing?"

"You're not keeping up, Mr. Santich. The Chicago *woman* isn't dead, she's in the hospital recovering from a drug overdose. Haven't the police talked to you about drug parties happening in your house?"

I paused, but he didn't say anything.

"No, what I found was the body of an older woman, recently dead, in your basement."

"I live on the other side of the hill," he muttered.

"The Dundee house doesn't belong to you? I thought that bit of land it sits on was still yours."

"Yes, it's my land, but the house—no one's lived there for years."

"Someone rents it from you? To use for entertainment?" I prodded.

"I don't have time to look after the house. It's historic, it can't be torn down, but if someone's been in it, no one's told me. You seen activity down there?" he asked the hard hat.

"I don't have time to go crawling around all those trees down below. My responsibility stops at the fence, which *you* have trespassed." On the last phrase, he turned to lean over me, making sure I saw the handle of a large-caliber something in a shoulder holster underneath his bomber jacket.

I didn't move, although he was close enough that I could have counted his nose hairs if I'd wanted to.

He stepped back. "Let's see your badge."

"No badge," I said. "I'm private, not public."

"What, are you part of that asshole Urine's harassment brigade?"

"Asshole Urine?" I repeated.

"Don't play dumb with me, bitch. I didn't just fall off a turnip truck."

"No, indeed," I agreed. "You damaged your brain years ago."

He reddened and reflexively put a hand on his gun grips.

"Off the land, now," he roared.

I saluted and turned around. My shoulders itched, worrying about a bullet, but I refused to look back or to move fast.

I wished I knew what he and Santich had been arguing about. Santich hadn't known about the dead woman, I was pretty sure of that, but maybe the hard hat did. And who was the asshole Urine with a harassment brigade? Or was he saying, the asshole's urine?

Asshole Urine. Of course. In court yesterday, Judge Bhagavatula had called him Irwin, and Trig had reacted. It was the kind of ugly nickname bullies would have slapped on him in third grade. No wonder he wanted to be called Trig.

But who was on Trig's harassment brigade? The dead woman? She'd meet him at the Dundee house during the day—there was no risk of any drug parties at noon—and they'd map out strategy? Had he been there this morning because he had a meeting scheduled with Clarina Coffin?

The woodland near the fence had held the usual dreary litter of modern life—Styrofoam, chip bags, bottles—but between the hilltop and the clearing around the Dundee house, the woods were clean. I hoped Santich could hang on to the land so there'd be a little refuge from trash. Was that what made Trig so angry with Santich? He knew the guy was planning a secret deal for these woods?

Close to the wellhead by the remaining chimney stack, I saw a scrap of paper. Litter after all. I picked it up, hoping for some revelation, but it was just a few lines torn from a larger document. Someone had been disappointed or angry and torn it up.

through the grapevine that
eries about Kansas his
like to be first in line to
dy to reveal your work to
lunch in our offices in Westbro

I was going to drop it back on the trail, but I stuck it in my pocket. It might be a clue, although to what it was impossible to say.

14

Insecurity Blanket

When I finally made it back into town, I tried again to reach Valerie. I left a second message, saying it was possible Sabrina's monsters had been real people carrying a dying woman through the woods into the house.

Clarina had been wrapped in a blanket. I pictured Sabrina at the top of the steep stairs, watching the men maneuver Clarina through the house to the basement. It's not easy to carry a dead person. The blanket flipped open, Sabrina saw the face. She hadn't cried out—if she had she would have been killed herself. The sight cut the last strand tethering Sabrina to the world around her. I couldn't prove it, but it was a workable scenario.

When I called Norma to extend my stay yet again,

she said, "You can have one more night, but I have a couple arriving tomorrow evening who've booked the suite for a week. I hope you can go home tomorrow so that you're not left hanging."

I hoped so, too.

I had two messages from Deke Everard, three from Zoë. *Chicago, I told you we needed to team up. Did you know Clarina was dead when we were at the house this morning? Call me!*

Deke wanted me at the LKPD headquarters on the double. I bought yet another pair of clean jeans, went back to Norma's to wash the woods out of my hair, and got to the cop shop only ninety minutes after Deke's second text.

I told him what I'd been doing, although I left out the part where I was huddling in my car on the brink of a meltdown. I suggested they look at Santich's finances to see if he was making money from drugs at the Dundee house. I asked if he knew what the relationship was between Santich and the construction on top of Yancy.

"You're sounding like Trig, wanting to blame Santich for all the problems in the world. Santich grew up here, everyone knows him. He sells insurance to support his family. He's well-respected in the town, even if he went a bit overboard with Cady."

"Sergeant," I said, "the house is on land that he still owns. It isn't blaming him for the evils of the world to ask why he's letting someone hold drug parties there. He claims he doesn't know about them, but that is hard to believe."

"Santich lives on the other side of Yancy," Deke objected. "The Omicron Delts, or some group like them, probably took advantage of an empty house where the owner wouldn't see their activity."

"I went up the hill a little bit ago to see if I could find any trace of Sabrina's monsters," I said. "I came on Santich arguing, quite fiercely, with someone on the construction site."

"That isn't proof that Santich murdered the Coffin woman, or hid her in the Dundee house."

"Convenient," I said. "It's always the Dundee house, never the Santich house."

"It's how things are in this county," Deke said. "People called Larkin have lived in my family's old home for fifty years, but folks still call it the Everard place. You find something that proved Santich murdered the Coffin woman?"

His jeering tone made me reluctant to share, but I showed him the scrap of paper I'd found in the woods.

"This could be anything from anyone," he said,

impatient. "It doesn't have any connection to the Coffin woman's death, or to activities at the Dundee place."

"One thing you can see is that the paper is fresh," I said sharply. "It hasn't been lying about in the woods long enough for the paper to start disintegrating."

"Yeah, maybe." He made a sour face but put it in an evidence bag. "I still think it's irrelevant. I'm not spending time and resources on maybes. Stamoran and the DA, Frank Karas, are breathing down my neck, wanting proof that you were responsible for bringing both Sabrina whosis and Clarina to the Dundee house. Don't make it hard for me to stand up for you!"

"Not that I'm not grateful for your support, but all I'm guilty of is stumbling on a dead woman and a nearly dead young woman. I was here two years ago. You saw me working, you know who I am and how I do what I do. Why would you think I'd suddenly become a deranged drug dealer and killer?"

Deke ran his hands through his hair. "Two years ago you hadn't witnessed a man killing his son."

"Daughter," I snapped. "Taylor was denied their rightful identity in life; don't take it away from them in this interrogation room. Their murder makes me weep, even now, but it did not change my own rightful identity. I've said everything you're going to hear from me, and I've said way too much. From now on, you'll speak to my lawyer."

I got up and swept from the room. And ran into Zoë in the lobby.

"Chicago!" Zoë cried. "Didn't you get my messages? How did you find Clarina?"

"Old-fashioned legwork," I said. "The sergeant can tell you everything you want to know—he has my story plus all the forensic evidence they've gathered so far. And you know who Clarina is, or at least what she was doing in Lawrence, which I don't."

"Before you turn the LKPD into your private conference room, how did you get back here, Cruickshank?" Deke said.

"Us reporters have to cultivate contacts." She grinned saucily at him.

"I don't have anything for you. The chief will make a statement to the press later today. Now, off you go." He spoke in the indulgent tones of a big brother with a sister whom he liked to tease.

"People are saying that Clarina was assaulted," Zoë said.

"She was murdered," Deke said more seriously. "We don't have forensic evidence back yet, so I can't tell you more than that. Was she sexually assaulted? I don't know. Her body was taken to the Kansas City lab for a postmortem. We'll release results when we know them.

"The only hopeful thing I can tell you, not for publication until we have an official report." He paused to make sure Zoë understood that. "Her clothes had been torn from her body, but she was dead, or close to death, when that happened, our own CSI says—something about how blood pooled around the garments."

He pushed Zoë toward the exit. While she flung more questions at him, I made good my escape. I did not want to dwell on the dead woman's abused body.

Zoë caught up with me in the parking lot, where she repeated the question from her text: Had I known Clarina was in the Dundee house when we'd been there this morning?

I assured her I did not, and got into my car to call my lawyer. Freeman Carter had already read about my finding Sabrina: anytime one of his clients appears in the news he gets an alert. I told him about my potential legal troubles, both with the FBI agent and with the Lawrence cops. He promised to find a good criminal defense lawyer in the area.

"Don't insert yourself into an investigation that belongs to the Kansas crews," he said.

"I'm not inserting myself; I'm being shoved into it. They want to make me an interested party, if not a guilty one, because I was lucky enough to find a student who was overdosing, and then unlucky enough to find a dead body."

I talked Freeman through what was going on, gave him the local DA's name, as well as Deke Everard's.

Murray Ryerson had called, indignant that a tiny local publication knew what I was doing before he did. Mr. Contreras wanted to know if I was safe. Lotty sent love. Three of my clients wanted to know if I was hotdogging in Kansas at their expense. Valerie Granev was still not answering her phone.

Zoë was still waiting expectantly next to my car. I rolled down my window. "Zoë, I need to go to the hospital. I'll catch up with you after that."

At the ICU entrance, I explained to the charge nurse that I had important information for Valerie that might help her deal with her daughter's fears.

"I am an investigator," I explained when the nurse hesitated. "Ms. Granev hired me this morning hoping I could find out what Sabrina might have witnessed in the drug house where I found her late Monday night."

The charge nurse pointed me toward a waiting area and said she would check with Ms. Granev. Two families were also in the waiting area, the children sprawled on the floor playing with crayons or tablets, but everyone spoke in a soft murmur.

The chairs were cushioned and deep, covered in soft colors, purples and greens, and the walls were hung with photos of prairie grasses and rivers. A circulating waterfall created enough background noise to make private conversations possible. I leaned back in one of the chairs.

Valerie woke me about twenty minutes later. She'd had a chance to shower and change. With fresh makeup, a severe white shirt and blazer, she looked like an important corporate player, not a terrified mother.

"Ms. Warshawski, I was beside myself when I talked to you earlier. I sent you off on a wild goose chase without thinking, or taking time to consult my husband. I have to apologize. We have good news about Sabrina."

"That's great." I was dopey from my brief sleep, but Valerie's manner meant I needed to be alert. "You're able to get some answers from her? How she came to be at that house, and what she saw there?"

Valerie's poise faltered briefly, but she produced a tight smile. "Not that great. She's far from out of the woods. But there's a rehab facility in Florida that's considered one of the best in the nation for people with, well, with damage like my daughter's. We—Ram and I—we learned about an hour ago that they have space for Sabrina. She'll be medevacked out there today. I'm taking care of all the paperwork now.

"As I said, I owe you an apology for sending you off looking for—for—"

"Monsters," I supplied, before she could come up with a euphemism. "When I went back to the house, I found the dead body of a woman. I wondered if Sabrina had seen her killers. She might have watched them from a window, or seen them at the bottom of the stairs. The killers had wrapped—"

"Enough!" Valerie put up her hands, shielding herself from unpleasant information. "I just explained to you that I hired you without thinking it through or talking it over with my team. We can't subject Sabrina to any kind of interrogation. I must ask you to stop. Send me an itemized account of your expenses; if they exceed the retainer I paid you, we'll take care of it. If there's an overpayment, consider it a goodwill offering for your time."

She turned on her heel—a highly polished boot—and retreated.

"The helicopter will be here in about forty-five minutes, and there is a lot of paperwork to complete," the nurse said. "Families in crisis are often abrupt with other people. Try not to take it personally."

"I'm taking it professionally," I said, "which means I'm baffled by what she's afraid I'll tell her. The people who treat Sabrina should know that there's a reality to her monster fears. You heard what I just said to Sabrina's mother? Can you make a note on Sabrina's chart?

"There was a dead woman in the basement of the house where I found Sabrina. It's possible she saw the woman being carried to the house. That's a lot for a sober person to process, but the nightmares will haunt Sabrina more if no one knows they're grounded in reality."

The nurse backed away from me. Perhaps I sounded overwrought, talking about bodies in basements. I invoked Nurse Norma's name, which got this woman to add my name and phone number to Sabrina's chart—but with no explanation of who I was or what my connection to her was.

While I'd been talking to Valerie, my car had sent a message to my phone. Someone had opened the door, someone had opened the trunk.

Zoë was waiting for me in the lobby, but I ran past her to the parking lot. The trunk was shut, but the driver's door was unlocked. I used my remote to pop the trunk, standing well back in case of explosives. When no fire erupted, I went to look inside. A dirty tartan blanket had been dumped there, on top of my own overnight bag.

Interlude II
Gertrude and Cady

Clarina's Death

I suppose someone told you Clarina Coffin is dead," Gertrude said over supper.

"Yes," Cady agreed. "Zoë Cruickshank called. She wanted a comment. I suppose she wanted me to shout, *She had it coming,* or some crap like that."

"That young woman is a menace, prying into everyone's lives. But that doesn't mean I want to hear you use that kind of language at the dinner table. Or anywhere else, for that matter."

"Zoë works hard in a dying field. I don't have a problem with that." Cady cut the beans on her plate in half, and then halved them again. Gertrude tried not to watch as she sliced them into smaller pieces without eating them.

"Anyway, I didn't wish Clarina ill, at least not in that way. I wished her to mind her own business, instead of trying to design my lesson plans for me, but I didn't wish any of the school board, not even Brett Santich, to die for the way they treated me."

Gertrude put down her knife and fork. "I thought, from what Pat said, she was found dead of an overdose."

"Zoë says Deke told her she was hit over the head. Probably she was left to die in the basement out there. Zoë says—rats—"

She took her plate of uneaten food and scraped it into the compost bin.

Gertrude's voice didn't soften, but she pleaded with Cady to eat something. "Even ice cream."

Cady went to her grandmother and kissed her forehead. "You are worried, aren't you, Gram, if you're offering me dessert when I haven't eaten my dinner."

She brought a carton of butter pecan and two bowls to the table. Gertrude hadn't eaten much of her meal, either, but she put her plate to one side and filled both bowls.

"Did Zoë have other information?" Gertrude asked after a moment.

"You mean, something else Deke wouldn't have told Aunt Pat?"

"I wondered if the police talked to the Chicago detective. After all, she was in that house looking for the missing student."

"V.I. Warshawski is the person who found the body, and according to Zoë, Deke's been questioning her hard. She found the student with the overdose, she found Clarina, and then she found a blanket in her car that maybe was used by Clarina's killers. Zoë apparently was bird-dogging her all day."

Cady grimaced. "Zoë's like a terrier, you know. She sees our little crime wave as her ticket to the big time. If she hears that Clarina annoyed the Riverside women's group, she'll come around questioning you."

"Clarina annoyed us because she acted as though she knew more about Lawrence history than people who've lived here their whole lives, and their grandparents before them," Gertrude said. "She pretended she knew our deepest secrets, as if a bunch of middle-aged women running a food bank and a homeless shelter have deep secrets."

She paused. "When you get old, your sleep is light. Footsteps, doors shutting, they wake you."

Cady was loading the dishwasher, but she stood up

to face her grandmother. "Do they, now? And can you tell if the noisy walker was in the house, watching the garage, or coming from the outside?"

The two women stared at each other. Before either spoke again, the front doorbell rang. Cady switched on the porch light and looked through the glass.

"It's Deke Everard with another man," she called to her grandmother. "What on earth do they want this time of night?"

15

Mr. Watson, Come Here!

Lawrence cops had impounded my Mustang. They hadn't arrested me, but they were moving closer. They'd told me I couldn't leave town until they'd done a complete inspection of my car. When I asked how long it would take, Deke Everard said, "As long as it takes."

Since Zoë had been present when I found the blanket, she followed me back to the cop shop, where they kept me until well past dark. By the time we finished, Zoë had left: an overturned semi had sent chickens all over the road. I was grateful to the chickens. The last thing I needed was Zoë peppering me on top of the LKPD interrogation.

Lawrence had a free bus service, I learned from the officer on desk duty. She handed me a printed schedule and instructed me on how to find the closest stop. Waiting at the bus stop, anonymous in the dark, I asked myself the same questions the cops had pounded me with.

Why had someone chosen my car to plant the blanket—assuming this was the blanket I'd stumbled on in the Dundee house Monday night? Deke kept asking me that, and of course I didn't know.

"Maybe because they figure you're putting me in the frame," I said. "You won't look further if you have a suspect." I stopped on the brink of adding: "time-honored cop behavior."

My car had been alone in a field near the Dundee house; it was distinctive, a red Mustang with Illinois plates. Anyone who'd spotted it there would have recognized it in the hospital parking lot.

"Maybe the Omicron boys are behind this. They'd feel it was payback for touring their garage to ask about their drug business Monday afternoon."

"Are you accusing a fraternity of murdering Clarina Coffin?" Deke asked.

"I'm not accusing anyone of anything. I'm trying to understand why my car was picked as an evidence-dumping ground."

We went around the same questions so many times I felt I'd been on a whirligig by the time they gave me a statement to sign, along with an admonition not to leave the area.

Waiting for the bus, I kept asking myself the questions the cops had dwelt on. I had explained to Deke and the LKPD major who joined him for the interrogation about Granev hiring and then firing me in rapid order. I gave them her private phone number so they could verify it with her, but they didn't seem to think Valerie Granev was relevant to the story. The question still remained, though: Why had she pushed me away after begging me to find the source of Sabrina's monsters?

The bus was almost empty when I got on, but it picked up students along the way. I kept an eye on the street signs to make sure I didn't miss my stop, but it wasn't until we were a few blocks east of Westbrooke Circle that the name struck me.

"Lunch in our offices in Westbro"—the scrap of paper I'd found in the woods had read. I got off at the next stop and walked back up the street to explore the circle.

The circle was small; the one significant building on the land belonged to the University of Kansas press.

Someone had been invited to lunch at the press and had torn up the invitation. A piece had landed in the woods behind the Dundee House.

Zoë said Clarina Coffin had thought of herself as an expert on Kansas history, and that she'd upended Cady Perec's teaching career over Cady's approach to teaching Kansas history. Maybe Coffin had been a serious historian; perhaps the university press wanted to publish her work.

While I waited for another bus, I thought about texting the suggestion to Deke, but cops look with heightened suspicion at anyone who tries to help them find clues, even a trained investigator. Maybe especially a trained investigator. Keep it to yourself, Warshawski. Solve this murder, make them look like hamburger past its shelf date.

The bus decanted me a few blocks from Nurse Norma's home on the hillside near the university. My long day had worn me out. I took off my shoes, thinking I'd lie down for ten minutes, and woke up an hour later.

I got up feeling stiff and dirty and stood under Norma's shower for ten minutes, washing cop grime and Dundee house dirt out of my mind. I couldn't answer any questions about Valerie Granev's behavior, but I could search for information on Clarina Coffin.

After burrowing through my subscription databases, which harvest far too many personal secrets, I began to think Clarina was a myth, some kind of 3D figure created by artificial intelligence. There wasn't a single record about her before she showed up in Lawrence some two years ago, and even here I could find only wisps of information.

If she had a phone, it wasn't registered in her name. Whether she was renting or owning, she was either paying cash or paying under a different name. I found a Kansas suffragist named Clarina Nicholls, but I didn't discover any descendants named Coffin.

I couldn't even find photos of her on the *Douglas County Herald* website, beyond the blurry shots Zoë had taken of her picketing the Yancy school. Trig was with her, recognizable with his halo of graying curls, but there were other people, carrying signs proclaiming, BLACK LIVES MATTER, NO CRT IN OUR SCHOOLS, OUR HISTORY IS YOUR HISTORY, NATIVE NATIONS WERE HERE BEFORE THE *MAYFLOWER*, and no one's face showed up clearly.

I sent what I had to Murray—he has access to sources that I don't—and added "I'll call tomorrow. Cops have me talked out tonight."

I walked into the town to find some supper. I felt lonely, desolate, and over a meal in a quiet café I sent a long message to Peter.

Everyone thinks I'm unstable because of Taylor's death. I suppose I am in some ways. I find myself crying or forgetting to eat. But I am not kidnapping college students, or bringing them to the point of death to salvage my honor.

I hope you're having an easier time in Malaga. I miss you. xxxVI

When I walked back up the street to Norma's place, Cady Perec got out of a car in front of the house.

"Vic. I'm sorry to show up unannounced. I need to talk to someone, someone besides Gram and Zoë, I mean, and you know how the police work. Deke Everard—I've been knowing him since I was born, but he came around and interviewed me like he thought I'd killed Clarina."

"Did you?" I asked.

"Vic! Please, I need help."

I gritted my teeth but let her in. She produced a bottle of white wine. I found some glasses in the kitchenette.

"Did he say why he was talking to you?" I asked.

"I guess because her wild talking got me fired. He wonders if I'm bearing a grudge so intense I'd kill to get my job back."

"Tell me about the firing, or about her. Clarina isn't

in any of my databases. Did she ever talk about where she came from?"

Cady shook her head. "She wasn't the kind of person I wanted to know. She came to the women's group at Riverside Congregational—the church Gram and I belong to—a few times, but I'm not active in the group. She rubbed a lot of the women the wrong way, Gram says, because she pretended she wanted to pick their brains on local history, but really what she wanted was to show how much more she knew than everyone else. Gram's words."

I'd met Gertrude Perec when I was here two years ago. She had not hidden her displeasure with me for involving myself in her and Cady's affairs. I tried to imagine her hitting Clarina over the head for the crime of showing off. People have killed for many strange reasons, but it was hard to picture.

"What about when Clarina picketed your school? Did she get in touch then?"

Cady's lips were tight with anger. "She certainly did. I'd been asked to take a few days' leave while the board looked at my curriculum. Of course that pissed me off, the board second-guessing a teacher with my experience, but I thought we could sort it out. Then Zoë called wanting my comment on Clarina and Trig picketing. I drove over to the school, and there they were, with kids from the university campus. I begged Trig and Clarina to stop.

"That was what did me in: someone photographed me talking to Clarina, and parents claimed I was joining in the picket. I tried to explain, but you can't prove a negative. When Zoë talked to Clarina during the picket, Clarina claimed I was privately happy to have her there but couldn't say so publicly. I wanted to—" She cut herself short.

"Slug her?" I suggested.

She turned crimson. "Something like that."

"Did you try to talk to her again?"

"No. My union rep advised me not to, and so did Gram—it was clear Clarina would twist anything I said the wrong way."

"What about before the suspension and picketing and so on, when she wanted to get involved with your syllabus?" I asked.

"I don't know how she learned about my lesson plan, but she started wanting to be part of it. She thought she knew a ton about Kansas history, Civil War stuff, what happened to the Kansa and Delaware nations after the war, all kinds of stuff. She'd say she could prove what she was talking about, but when I asked her to show me, she wouldn't or couldn't."

The lesson plan had been called "We All Have a

Kansas History." Students were going to write essays on their own family's history in the state—where they came from, why and when they landed here. Cady had also planned segments on the state's geological and ecological history, with help not just from the school's science teachers, but also from graduate students at the University of Kansas, whose main campus was in Lawrence. She also had someone from Haskell, the local Indian Nations University, lined up to speak.

"Clarina called my class 'woke lite,'" Cady said with a brittle smile. "I was certainly going to cover the way both the national government and local European settlers forced Native Americans first to come here from farther north and east, and then after the Civil War, pushed them into Oklahoma, but that was just a piece of the lesson plan.

"Clarina lectured me about my reading list. Did I know what the first governor did to the Delaware nation after the war? Did I know about recent murders of Native Americans in the county? Did I know this, did I know that. She told me I should start the syllabus with an acknowledgment that we in Lawrence were occupying lands that had been the historic home of the Delaware and the Kansa nations, and that our own ancestors had forcibly removed these original inhabitants from their land."

Cady gulped down her wine and poured herself a second glass. "I wouldn't talk to her after that first phone call, but she wrote a letter to the *Herald*, saying my class was a perfect chance for students at Yancy to learn the true history of the land they lived on. 'The land their families stole' was how she put it, and that my lesson plan should be required throughout the state. So then some of the parents got angry, because I was woke, and teaching critical race theory, if they even knew what that is. I was called in front of the board. Clarina and Trig declared themselves my champions, and then I got fired. Suspended without pay, technically."

"I can't find a phone number for Clarina. How did she call you?"

Cady looked blank. "On the phone. What do you mean?"

"Sorry—if she had cell or land service in her name, it should show up somewhere. When she called, did her name appear on your screen, or 'unknown caller'?"

Cady squinted, trying to look into the past. "'Unknown caller,' I guess, but she did leave a number for me to call back. Only I didn't keep it because I didn't want to talk to her."

I returned to the controversy that had landed Cady in trouble. I hadn't seen Clarina's letter when I looked for her in the *Herald* archives, but Cady pulled it up for me. It was long, the kind of essay-cum-harangue that everyone grinding an ax writes these days.

Clarina included a lot of history, including dates and atrocities, and ended her letter by declaiming that "everyone here does have a Kansas history. We all have some of that blood on our hands, and it's time our children learned to see it."

"Had she written a book about all this?" I asked.

"A book?" Cady echoed. "I never thought her ideas were organized or coherent enough for a book. Why?"

"Grasping at straws," I said, "or scraps of paper. I found a fragment near the Dundee house suggesting a meeting at the university press. It's such a small fragment, it doesn't include any names. I just wondered if it could have been sent to Clarina."

Cady's mouth twisted in bitterness. "I couldn't stand it if she turned out really to be an expert on Kansas history! I know she's dead, but honestly! All that stuff she put in her letters, it got the parents riled up against me. The police seem to think it's a motive for me killing her, and if there's a book—it will look like I tried to shut her up before she could make all her ideas public."

She picked at her cuticles. Blood pooled around her forefinger.

"Deke came with a Major Somebody in the department. Because Gram used to be his Sunday school teacher, he couldn't question either of us himself, he just babysat while the major interrogated us separately. When he was talking to me, the major said no one could seriously think Gram killed anyone, but he says, if she did, it was to support me. He *encouraged* me to say what reason she'd have to protect me."

She saw the blood and wiped her finger on her jeans. "Vic, could I hire you? To investigate Clarina's death?"

I was startled. "The cops suspect me, Cady. They've impounded my car."

She ignored that. "They say Gram went out to the Dundee house, like at three in the morning, after you found Sabrina and all the emergency responders were back in town. First she got on her high horse, denied it, but someone sent in an anonymous photo.

"So then Gram said, she got a message, phone message, saying one of her friends was having car trouble out there. And when she got to the Dundee house, there was no sign of Lela Abernathy, but Trig was there; he'd gotten a message about something different, something about Brett Santich, or at least he claims that was what it was.

"Gram and Trig waited for an hour and then they left. She says." She squeezed her bloody finger, so hard I thought she might break it.

"Vic, the two of us living together all these years—

since I was born—we hide our secrets. It's how we can live together and have some privacy. We know not to poke each other's secret spots. But—we both heard each other in the night, coming and going."

"And you came and went?" I asked.

"I have trouble sleeping these days. Since I got fired. I went for a walk, down to the river. When I got home, the garage door was open. Gram's car wasn't there. I wondered if someone had stolen it, but when I went to her room to tell her, she wasn't in bed. I waited for her to come home, listened to her on the stairs, then went up myself. We heard each other, but we didn't talk about it."

"You told the cops?"

Cady shook her head, face unhappy. "I guess the reason they didn't arrest Gram is they can't prove she was inside the Dundee house."

"Also, they suspect me. And probably Trig," I said drily.

"But they took all our coats," Cady said. "They want to test them to see if there's any trace of Clarina's blood on them. Please say you'll help. I can't pay what you probably usually ask, but Zoë told me you need a place to stay after tonight. We have an apartment over our garage. You could use it rent-free instead of a fee."

"If they don't have any evidence linking you or your

grandmother to the murder, the two of you should be able to ride it out," I added.

"Please!" Cady cried. "Maybe in a big city you can 'ride out' an accusation like that, but a town the size of Lawrence, where everyone who counts has known you since your first day of preschool? And then, people are saying if Gram killed Clarina it was to punish her for destroying my career. I'll never get a teaching job while that kind of accusation is floating around. Maybe not even after we prove we're innocent—nothing disappears from the internet, after all."

I knew all too well how unforgiving internet stories were, even for someone who lives in a large city.

"Your grandmother can't stand me," I reminded Cady. "How are you going to persuade her to let me live over the garage?"

"She's worried. I told her I was going to invite you and she said, 'Sip with the devil, make sure you have a long spoon.'"

"So I'm the devil now? Lines up with a lot of my trolls' posts, except their language is earthier."

"Sorry, Vic," she said in a small voice. "But if you have to stay here anyway, I could really use your help."

I felt a sinking in my middle. Was this how Alexander Graham Bell's assistant felt when he got the world's first phone call? *Mr. Watson, come here, I want you, no matter what is going on in your own life?*

I wanted to be the prima donna for once, the person who got to say, I need you, and my minions dropped whatever they were doing to race to my side. Instead, I pulled up my app, got Cady to sign a contract and pay me a hundred dollars as a token fee. We also agreed on a modest rent. I explained that if I found evidence condemning her or Gertrude, living rent-free would make it hard to share anything I found with the police.

"There's nothing for you to find," she insisted.

"Including proof of your middle-of-the-night walk along the river in the freezing air?" I said.

"You don't have the right to ask—"

"Cady, that's going to be the problem. The only way to get answers is to ask questions. If my questions touch you on the raw that much, then I'm giving back your retainer and erasing the contract."

She bit her lip, fortunately not hard enough to draw blood. "I didn't kill Clarina. Neither did Gram. I'll try to answer your questions, but when they are offensive, I—well, I'm offended."

She walked out of the room, leaving the bottle of wine behind.

16
New Life in Old Metal

The next morning, the thin February sun was just warm enough that I could sit outside the Decadent Hippo, nursing a cortado. Zoë Cruickshank bounced up the street.

"This is going to be great, Chicago, you working with me to solve Douglas County's crime wave. And you're staying with another prime suspect, so I can cover the whole story with one interview."

"How did you know I'm going to be at the Perecs'?" I asked.

She grinned. "Gertrude Perec told me."

"*Gertrude* Perec?"

"Yep, her and me, we're BFF's." Zoë laughed. "Actually, she looks at me like I'm a piece of fish a cat dug out of a dumpster, but I talked to her because I needed to know how her interview with the police went. I went to a meeting of Bring Lawrence Home—it's an organization trying to find housing for Lawrence's homeless population.

"Of course, Gertrude is on the board—she runs just about every important civic organization in the county. Her and Pat Everard. Anyway, she couldn't throw me out of the meeting, since they want the coverage. I made sure to walk inside at the same time as her, even though I had to lurk in the lobby for ten minutes. She was pissed that I'd caught her in public where she couldn't hang up on me. She wouldn't tell me anything about the police interview, but she did say if I wanted to know anything about the investigation I should talk to you, since Cady was letting you snoop around the house."

"Those her exact words?"

"Not exactly," Zoë admitted. "She said since I was Lawrence's self-appointed busybody, I'd find out sooner or later that Cady had invited you to move in. She called you that 'interfering know-it-all from Chicago,' and said you and I would make the perfect couple."

Zoë's teeth flashed white in her dark face. "Of course, I took that as a great compliment. Gertrude said she couldn't have both you and me nosing into her personal business, but I thought, that is exactly what we need. You go over for dinner tonight and tell me what she says and how she says it."

"That sounds like tons of fun for everyone," I said. "Me at the Perec dinner table isn't likely to happen—especially since the last time I was in Kansas, she sprayed Lysol on me whenever I passed her house."

Zoë laughed again. "But you must know why the police interviewed her. I mean, if Cady invited you to stay with them, she must be scared about what they're finding out about Gertrude."

"I don't think those Perec women frighten easily. Tell me more about Clarina. I haven't turned up the faintest whiff on where she came from. How about you?"

Zoë shook her head. "No one I've talked to even knows when she arrived in town. All I can say is, she definitely is not from here, or people would know about her.

"About two years ago, not long after I graduated and joined the *Herald,* she started showing up at local history meetings, correcting mistakes she thought people made in their presentations. She did research in the university archives, and people say they saw her over in Topeka at the Kansas Origins Museum, but after one meeting, where she was correcting this history professor!—can you believe that?—I asked her what she'd published.

"She got all huffy: she wasn't giving away her hard work for free to a small-town paper. But, you know, to me that was saying she'd never really written anything."

"Where did she live? She must have given some kind of personal information to a Realtor if she was renting or buying."

Zoë shook her head. "You'd think, but she sublet a trailer in a mobile home park south of town, and the manager of the park doesn't know anything about her, except that she was a good tenant. She didn't have to give a credit history because she's subletting. The manager says Clarina pays—paid—the rent on time, didn't keep pets or smoke or play loud music or fire her gun at cockroaches."

"She has—had—a gun?"

Zoë hunched a shoulder. "That was on the list of things bad tenants do, according to the manager. Not guns, we're four-square for unregulated weapons here in Kansas, but shooting cockroaches. It sounds made up, but the woman said it happened. 'Not that we want roaches in our park, but there are easier ways to deal with them than shooting out the doors and windows.'"

"Clarina paid the manager herself? Cash?"

"Gosh, I didn't ask. Is it important?"

"A check or credit card would give you an entrée into her financial records, and maybe a way to find her personal history."

"See—we're already better as a team. I wouldn't have thought of that, but it would have been harder for you to find where she sublet."

Her phone beeped. "Fire over in North Lawrence. I should go look at it."

She got to her feet but was reluctant to leave, asking me more questions about what I planned to do, and whether I thought Gertrude or Cady were guilty.

"Of course not. Cady is my client, and my clients are never guilty."

Zoë finally left, trying to make me promise to see her tonight to tell her what I'd uncovered. I agreed to a phone chat, since that was the only way I could get her to give me the name of the trailer park where Clarina had lived: Prairie View.

Clarina had been an ardent amateur historian who never published anything. That scrap of paper I'd found with the address (probably) of the University Press could have been addressed to Clarina, or to someone who knew Clarina. Of course, as Deke had said, it most likely had nothing at all to do with her murder.

I needed a car if I was going to be here any length of time. And if I had to stay here for days, or even weeks, I needed to get back to Chicago to move my office down here. I called Deke for an update on my car. They'd get to it when they got to it, was the essence of his response.

I looked up car leasing. The $4,100 my Kansas clients had paid me so far would not cover a long-term car rental as well as living expenses.

I walked across the bridge to the north side of town. I'd thought about Uber, but I didn't want a computer trail of my moves.

I spotted the billboard, newly painted, as soon as I crossed the train tracks on the far side of the bridge. LOU & ED: BREATHING NEW LIFE INTO OLD METAL. I breathed a sigh of relief: they'd survived the pandemic.

When I reached the scrapyard, I saw they'd put up a high fence since I was last here, but otherwise, the place looked the same—rusted car fenders and plowshares, rebar, and a lot of machinery I couldn't identify.

I had to press a button for admittance, but when I said my name over the intercom, the gates swung open. One of the men was on the concrete apron in front of the shop building, working with a welding torch. He didn't stop, but his partner came out of the building. Lou Arata, I saw when he walked over.

"We heard you were in town. Wondered if you'd remember us," he said.

"I'll never forget you and Ed or what I owe you," I said.

"Saw all the ruckus on TV about you and that student, volleyball player, was she?"

"Soccer."

"Thought for sure you'd stop by."

"I'm sorry," I said. "I wasn't expecting to stay in town. I wasn't expecting to end up under a police microscope. It has me rattled, more than it should, maybe."

Lou looked at me more closely. "You are rattled. You lost weight. You haven't taken up dieting, have you?"

"Never. I—it's been a stressful winter. I'm getting better, but having the FBI blame me for finding a student who could have died hasn't helped get my balance back. There was another student in Chicago—" I broke off.

"Read about that," Lou said. "Not your fault, but you got caught in the middle, didn't you. This gal, this soccer player, local cops don't really buy that *federale*'s line, do they?"

"I hope not, but yesterday, I found a dead woman in the drug house basement."

Lou grunted. "You are definitely a whiz as a magician, but maybe you need to tone down your act—say, rabbits and hats instead of bodies and basements."

"It's hard to attract an audience these days unless you have shock value," I said.

"Give you credit, you've got that and more where it came from. Law think you put the woman down there?"

"I'm in the top four people of interest, maybe top two now: someone planted a blanket in my trunk that may be tied to the dead woman. I know they're looking at Cady Perec and her grandmother—Cady's a schoolteacher who might have lost her job because of the murder victim's interference."

"Yes, read about Cady's troubles for trying to teach some indigestible version of Kansas history," Lou said. "Can't believe Five-O would go after the grandmother. She's in charge of the town, or big chunks of it. Anyone arresting her would find themselves out of a job."

"That's why I'm leading the pack of suspects," I said. "The shortest distance to the nearest powerless person makes the problem go away."

"You want us to hide you here at the yard?" Lou asked.

His words were bantering, but his tone was serious. He knew I'd come for a favor, and he was bracing himself for the ask.

"They've impounded my car. I was hoping you had a working wreck here I might rent."

Lou led us over to Ed, who nodded, finished the join he was working on, and turned off the fire. "Bad penny turned up, Ed. She needs help."

The men looked at each other, stepped back a few paces and began talking in low voices. After half an hour, and a couple of phone calls, the men came back to me.

"Got a Toyota you can use. We're looking after it for the owner while he's laid up. He says you can borrow it. You pay the insurance plus a hundred twenty a week."

"Just so you know, I'm not supposed to leave the jurisdiction," I said. "I have to drive back to Chicago, to collect clothes and computer files and all those things. If I get stopped, I guess the cops could seize that car, too. Your guy okay with that?"

Ed curled a lip. "What with drones and all that surveillance, seems like a jurisdiction covers a lot of ground these days. Keep to the speed limit. Don't run any red lights. Don't drink and drive."

"And bring the princess back with you. You need the company," Lou added. He meant Peppy.

"He thinks he's going to persuade you to trade her highness for a tractor," Ed said.

The Toyota was at their home, some ten miles farther out in the country. Ed went back to his welding while Lou drove me out to pick up the car.

When I first met them, I thought they were brothers, they looked so much alike, same height, same square jaws, same gray-green eyes in their coffee-colored faces. It was later that I realized they were a couple. No rings, but each with a tattoo: TIL DEATH on Ed's right forearm; US DO PART on Lou's left.

They'd changed their names, too: Ed Lyndes became Ed Arata Lyndes and Lou became Lou Lyndes Arata.

If Peter ever got back to me, if we ever got back together, how would he feel about becoming Peter Warshawski Sanson?

Lou pulled up in front of the house and turned off the engine. "The dead woman, Coffin, she came to talk to us a year or so back."

"What did she want?"

"She was looking for old diaries or letters, any kind of family papers we had. She said she was talking to all the 'people of color,' she called us, in the county, hoping to do a proper history of Black folks in Kansas."

"She say anything about what she was writing? I mean, a book, or some articles, or a podcast?"

Lou shook his head. "I didn't pay that much attention. Something about her seemed a little off-kilter, if you know what I mean. Ed and I, we talked it over with some of the neighbors. One Black woman over at the university, she thought it was an opportunity to get more complete Black history out in the world, but the prof ain't from here, so she didn't have the kind of documents the Clarina woman was looking for."

"Was Clarina Black?" I asked. "I haven't seen a clear photo of her."

"Ed and I thought she was a wannabe, thought maybe she wanted to produce a history to prove she was."

He got out of the truck. I followed him behind the barn, where they'd parked the Toyota. It was exactly the car I needed—beige, a couple of dings on the fenders, but in good working order. Lou handed me the Toyota keys. I gave him seven twenties—a week's rental plus the insurance.

"You get in over your head, and you don't call me and Ed, that will be the crime we won't forgive or forget, you hear? And fuck's sake, Warshawski, start eating. That skinny white-girl look is never attractive, least of all on you."

"Got it," I said, a lump in my throat. I'd been needing a true ally down here.

17

New Life in Old Detectives

The route back into town led past the Boat Yard. I pulled into their lot. Ten A.M., business was light. Greg, the bartending owner, was talking with a couple of truckers standing at the counter drinking coffee.

Holly was setting up tables for lunch. She looked up when I came in and frowned, worried.

"Am I too late for breakfast?" I asked. "A short stack?"

She nodded and went to the kitchen window to put in the order, bringing a thermos of coffee on her way back to me. She poured without asking if I wanted it.

"I saw where you found your missing girl out in that house on Yancy."

"I did," I agreed. "I didn't feed you to the police, if

you're worried about that. Or your sister, but I wondered if she showed up yesterday morning to clean the place."

She shook her head. "I was scared about that when I saw the news, but she said someone told her to stay away."

"Who?" I asked.

She hunched a shoulder.

"I'd like to talk to her," I said, "see what she can tell me about who's running those parties."

"Please don't," Holly begged. "She needs the money."

"No one's going to be doing anything in that house for quite some time," I said. "It's a major crime scene, and anyway, now that the sheriff knows someone's selling drugs there, they'll shut it down."

"But she could be arrested as an accessory or something, if the police learn she knew drugs were being used there and didn't report it."

A ding from the kitchen window called her to pick up my order. She set the plate in front of me, said, "Anything else?" and left the tab on the table. She stayed well away from me—when I got up to pay, she went into the kitchen, leaving me to settle the bill with Greg.

"You weren't harassing Holly, were you"—he held my credit card close to his face—"V.I. Warshki?"

I shook my head. "I was looking for someone I thought she might know, that's all."

He eyed me narrowly. "Not that I don't appreciate your business, but if it means upsetting my team, maybe you should eat somewhere else."

I smiled, signed the slip, average tip so I didn't look guilty. "Your team is lucky to have you in their corner."

The truckers followed me out, watched me get into the Camry before climbing back into their rigs. Holly was lucky to have a protective boss. Greg was lucky to have loyal customers. I was lucky for some reason. I just couldn't put my finger on it at the moment.

The strip mall where I'd bought my change of clothes yesterday was right behind the Boat Yard, but I thought it prudent to leave the parking lot. My overnight bag had been in the Mustang's trunk. The police hadn't let me take it with me, which meant I had to buy yet more jeans, socks, toothbrush, change of underwear.

Murray called while I was clothes shopping to say he'd also come up blank on Clarina. "Maybe the Coffin woman was a Chinese or Iranian spy, with such a deeply buried backstory she didn't know herself who she was."

I gave him a full interview while sitting in the Camry, including all the details of finding Clarina, and finding the blanket in my trunk.

Before he hung up, Murray said casually, "Sabrina's plight seems to have had some positive fallout. Some anonymous angel gave her father a hundred grand to build a youth camp in the mountains."

"Any hints on the ID?" I asked.

"No one's using their trumpet yet."

I hadn't bothered looking at the Granevs or the Perecs on my different news feeds. I squinted now at the screen, the gray day making it hard to read.

It was an Albuquerque story picked up on the national wires because my rescue of Sabrina had made the national news. "If this happened before one week ago, I am dancing up the mountain, so happy to have money for my youth camp," Ramir Granev said. "Now? Now I am grateful, very grateful, but my own child, my own heart, lies between life and death. My heart is sliced in two: joy, sorrow."

"You still there?" Murray demanded.

"Just catching up on the story. Ramir seems like a good guy," I said. "His wife is more puzzling. I was looking to see if she's mentioned anywhere. After unraveling on me and persuading me to go look for monsters at the drug house where I found her child, she told me we were done. They'd gotten a spot for Sabrina at some exclusive Florida facility. She was medevacked out yesterday afternoon."

Murray whistled. "Private clinic? Could run over fifty K for a month. Maybe Ram will have to leverage his gift for youth camping or whatever it is."

"Valerie is a higher-up in Tulloh Industries' aeronautics division. The Granevs probably have gold-plated insurance and cash in the bank, too. The part that bothers me is that at the moment I found a likely source of her daughter's terrified screams, Valerie axed me. I'm wondering if it was under pressure from the FBI."

"Why? Jurisdictional jealousy?"

"Yesterday morning, when she was sharing her fears and so on, Valerie said it was Tulloh who got the Bureau involved. She seemed uncomfortable with the agent, guy named Stamoran. Stamoran acts as though he wants to print and book me but doesn't have enough evidence. The LKPD is also gunning for me, so I'm supposed to stay here and wait for the DA to decide whether to charge me with being an outsider in Lawrence's power structure. It didn't move the local sergeant to know I'm here without a computer or clothes or toothpaste, so I'm driving up tomorrow to collect what I need for a week or two down here."

"Oh, boy. Warshawski, the fugitive from justice. This is going to be my story when they pick you up, not that Kansas newbie's."

"The Kansas newbie gets twelve thousand a year to do real journalism. She's making an amazing job of it, so don't try to push her to the margins. Anyway, can you let Sal know I'm coming? I'll call Lotty and Mr. Contreras. We can have a good old-fashioned get-together at the Glow before I head south again."

When we finished, I saw I had a message from my lawyer, Freeman Carter. He'd found a criminal lawyer in Kansas City for me, a woman named Faye Mitchell who'd been in law school with one of Freeman's associates. She'd be expecting a call from me. I didn't tell Freeman I was planning a quick trip north, or that I wouldn't call Mitchell until I was back in Lawrence. I wasn't really fleeing the jurisdiction, but better to ask forgiveness, and so on.

I called my Chicago clients to assure them their affairs were uppermost in my mind. Yes, I knew I'd been in the news over a murder and a drug house; I'd be in Kansas for a week sorting things out but I would be taking care of everything they needed from me, not to worry.

I looked at myself in the rearview mirror. Dark circles under the eyes, cheekbones still too gaunt. I am a chronic overachiever, I chanted. I can free myself of suspicion, find Coffin's murder, solve the drug-use problem of Douglas County, and run my business. *Come on, V.I.,* I adjured myself. *Breathe new life into old detectives.*

My final call was to Mr. Contreras. He was ecstatic that I was coming home, even for a day. He didn't want me taking Peppy, but he understood, doll, he understood she'd look after me. After forty-five minutes, I gently disengaged myself so that I could move into the Perec garage.

I apologized to Cady for being late—I'd said I would be there an hour earlier.

She shrugged. "I wasn't doing much. Gram is on me to stop moping around feeling sorry for myself, so I'm tutoring in the library's after-school program, but I still need to pull my socks up and get marching, Gram says. Apply for jobs, rethink my career goals, all the stuff that self-help books tell you marks the difference between success and failure."

"I always wonder about those books," I said. "They seem to me to be a form of fantasy fiction. 'In my dream world I was an Olympic diver who became the person who brokered peace in Sudan. In my real life I'm a checkout clerk in a grocery store.' Maybe with artificial intelligence coming to dominate us, we won't be able to tell the difference, but for now, keep doing what you're doing."

She laughed and showed me where to park. She escorted me up the stairs, which ran outside the garage, mercifully on the far side from the house so that Gertrude couldn't monitor my comings and goings.

It was a small space, but one with plenty of light. The furniture seemed to be leftovers from generations of Gertrude's family: a bureau with a marble top and an old streaked mirror, a rocking chair, a narrow couch with crocodiles carved into the arms and legs. A bookcase next to the narrow bed held a selection of mysteries and Kansas history books.

Cady had clearly scrubbed it down in my honor, and had even put a bunch of flowers in the middle of the table.

"Gram built this place when my mom was pregnant with me, hoping she would stay here, only of course she died when I was a few months old." Cady offered this in a matter-of-fact voice, repeating a story she'd been told many times.

She watched while I put away my few belongings. "Have you learned anything about Clarina?"

"So far, only that no one knows anything about her, except for her obsession with Kansas history. I have to stay here until I clear my name, but I'm going to drive up to Chicago tomorrow to get my computer and clothes and so on. I'll be bringing my dog back with me, so let me know if I need to look for a different place."

She assured me the dog would be fine as long as she was housebroken. She seemed eager for a longer tête-a-tête, but I told her I had to start investigating or I'd be in Gertrude's garage until Memorial Day.

As I drove off, I saw her in the rearview mirror, shoulders slumped when she thought I was no longer watching her.

I made my way around the town on side streets that turned into county roads, checking for company. Lawrence was well supplied with traffic cams; I expect Deke could track me online if he knew about the Camry, but at least for now no one was following me.

The Prairie View Mobile Home Park where Clarina had lived was between Yancy Hill and the town. If Clarina had been an energetic walker, she could have gotten to the Dundee house and the Yancy school on foot.

Some prairie remained for park residents to view, but the north side of the development faced a fertilizer plant, while the east backed onto a busy county road. The entrance, on the west side, listed the amenities: Wi-Fi, running water and electricity, a community room with a gym, and a park. The manager's home/office immediately inside the entrance was clearly marked.

I pulled into a parking space next to the office trailer. A pair of cement blocks served as a step up to a muddy stoop, but the doorframe was freshly painted. The manager's name was also freshly painted on a white plaque with a border of bright flowers: MIGNON TRAVERS.

She buzzed me in and called out, "To your right."

To my right was her home office, filled with green plants along with a television, a recliner, and a desk. Travers was in the recliner, playing a computer game on a tablet with fierce attention. She was a heavy woman, her dark hair scraped back into a bun that accentuated her round cheeks.

She didn't glance up from her screen. "You looking to rent or buy?"

"Neither. I'm a detective, I want to look at Clarina Coffin's place."

"Sheriff and city cops both have been through here already. Which one you with?" She looked up for a moment, eyes shrewd behind her dark heavy frames.

"I'm private. Coffin was a historian. I've been hired to look for her papers, to see if she has anything in shape to be published." I took my PI license from my wallet, but Mignon wasn't interested.

"Somebody already went through that place. God knows what they were looking for. Cops was plenty mad about it when they saw the damage, like I'm supposed to be a security guard or something. All I do is make sure trash on the *outside* of the homes is picked up, rent collected on time, nobody shooting guns inside the homes, even if they're the owners, 'cause we all live close together and between you, me, and that geranium over there, the walls are not that sturdy."

"Is it true someone was shooting at roaches?" I asked.

"*They* said, not me." Her thumbs were moving furiously.

"Even if someone went through Coffin's place already, I'd still like to see for myself."

"Got to earn your fee, I suppose." She flicked her eyes at the wall by the door. "Keys are hanging there. 1732 Squash Blossom Lane."

Duplicate keys for all the homes were hanging on a pegboard, addresses written on white disks in a neat hand. I found 1732 easily enough. Anyone could have found it if Travers ever left her recliner long enough for someone to pop in.

"I understand she sublet. Who was the owner?"

"You ever going to finish talking? I'm concentrating here. I have to answer back to the cops, but not to a private."

"I'll be gone so fast you won't know I was ever here," I said. "Just tell me who she rented from."

"A fund, like a bush. Not local, but who knows where they're located. They own about twenty of the units, and we only have but forty-eight."

"A hedge fund," I said, but she didn't answer. Hedge funds, Squash Blossoms, Mignon herself, a kind of plant. It was an effort to turn a spartan space into a garden. The hedge fund was probably not much help.

The homes themselves were trailers, some single wide, some double, set on a grid of streets around a rectangle of grass with playground equipment—I guess that was the park part of the community. I drove there and inspected the layout on my map app. Squash Blossom Lane was four streets down. I parked and walked over.

The homes were close together, close enough that if neighbors weren't mindful about their TV volume everyone on both sides could hear it. Even though it was the middle of the day, plenty of people were inside, devices loudly competing among country, rap, and soaps.

The February freeze and thaw had left the ground raw, but some dormant grasses were still there, along with a few spindly bushes. The streets were cleaner than in my neighborhood at home; Mignon did a good job of making sure people picked up their trash, or maybe Kansans were naturally tidier than Chicagoans.

1732 Squash Blossom was a single wide, which meant a single bedroom at one end, with a bathroom tucked in between that, and a kitchen-dining-living room at the end where the door was.

I studied the lock before I stuck the key in. It hadn't been jimmied, and the hinges were all straight. Whoever came in before me either was skilled with a picklock or, more likely, picked up a key while Mignon wasn't looking.

My predecessors in the search hadn't been interested in hiding their presence. Every possession Clarina Coffin had owned had been pulled from cupboards and drawers and dumped where the intruders had stood when they examined it. I could hear them cursing, getting angrier as they moved through the narrow space, because the destruction in the bedroom was worse than in the main room. The couch had been upended and the cushions unzipped, but in the bedroom, they'd slit open the mattress and the pillows.

Mignon, or the hedge fund, had turned the power off to the trailer. It was dark and cold and my phone flash didn't give enough light for a thorough inspection, but I wore down the battery poking through the debris. I didn't find any personal papers, or even scholarly papers. Of course, I was third in line. I was assuming her killers had been the first—they'd killed her looking for something, and had been furious when they couldn't find it. They or the cops would have impounded any digital devices.

The only personal items I found, if you could call them personal, were three pictures. One was a black-and-white photo of a white woman in the kind of dress I associated with Mary Todd Lincoln—a tight bodice and full skirt. She was sitting with her hands folded in her lap. The print was old and faded; the black of her dress had turned a kind of sienna.

I would have thought the woman was wearing mourning, except she seemed to have a wreath of flowers looped around the wings of hair that covered her ears. She had a large brooch pinned to where the collar met at her throat, and she was staring at the camera with seeming defiance.

The vandals had broken the frame around the photo. A piece of glass was embedded in the woman's skirt. I removed it, carefully, trying not to tear the paper itself.

The other two pictures had had the grainy, blurry quality that comes from printing from microform or digitized files. One showed a fight in progress, white against Black, apparently at a train station. Pieces of broken furniture were scattered around, along with a few chickens and a calf.

The third picture showed the smoking remains of a building that had burned to the foundation. There were no people in the picture, and no label to tell me whether it had been a house or a business.

The flashlight had worn out my phone battery. I wrapped the pictures carefully inside a dish towel and went back into the cold day.

18
Rebel with Too Many Causes

Trig Garrity was the one person I could identify who'd spent time with Clarina. I was sure the cops had already been on him, but that might make him more willing to speak to an independent investigator.

Trig lived in the old part of town, in a tired house on Vermont Street, with cracked siding and gaps in the foundation that would make the place an easy mark for rodents. Dead plants sat stiffly in pots along the porch railing. A child's tricycle, missing a wheel, was upside down below them. Four mailboxes hung next to the front door.

I buzzed 2-E, Trig's apartment, several times, but didn't get an answer. A woman came out as I was heading back to my car. She wore a backpack and had her face stuck on her device while she scrolled through her screen.

"Excuse me," I repeated loudly when she didn't stop scrolling.

"Sorry," she said, drawing out the second syllable in annoyance.

"I'm sorry to interrupt you," I said. "But I'm looking for Trig."

"You one of the protesters? He's at work, but you can sign up at Kansans4Freedom."

"Where does he work?"

"Prairie State Recycling over in Eudora, last I heard, unless he was fired." She looked back at her screen, swore under her breath, and started down the street at a jog, the backpack thumping into her.

"You late somewhere? I'll give you a lift."

She thanked me effusively; she was a student, heading up the hill to class, which started in nine minutes. "I wasn't watching the time. Thank you, thank you. I've been late the last three classes and Prof. Rand is threatening to lower my grade."

"How long have you been living in the same building as Trig?" I asked as she shut the passenger door.

"Just this year. He's been in that house forever; he has the best apartment, the one with the sunroom overlooking the garden. Well, yard. It's mostly weeds and dirt, but, still, when the trees are in leaf it's pretty. Are you a protester?"

"Just an ordinary person with some questions about a murdered woman. She used to take part in some of his events."

"Oh! That woman someone found walled up in a basement!"

"Not walled up. But dead in a basement out in the country. Her name was Clarina Coffin. I'm trying to find out who she was and what brought her to Lawrence. Did you ever meet her?"

"She came around a few times when Trig was protesting at some school."

I started up the steep hill to the campus, the Toyota slow but not complaining.

"Do the police suspect Trig?" She was suddenly alert, a hostile undertone in her voice.

"I'm not with the police, so I don't know what they're thinking. Did she ever say anything about where she came from? People say she was exploring Lawrence history, but no one seems to know what her background was."

The young woman shook her head. "She never really talked to me, except to see if I'd come out to that school with her and Trig. He gets a bad rap—he's such a good-hearted person, caring about the planet, and all kinds of injustices, it's hard for him to understand why some of us don't have his time or energy for protests. When I first moved into the building I helped him paint some signs, but it all got to be too much. The stuff he protests, he's right about all these issues, so if the police or whoever are trying to stop him, it's because they're not paying attention."

We'd reached the campus security checkpoint. I couldn't drive past it without a permit, but my passenger gave me another brilliant smile, she was only four minutes away if she ran, and for sure I'd saved her life.

I pulled over on a side street and consulted my GPS for directions to Prairie State Recycling. Eudora was a town to the east, about eight miles in a direct line from where I was parked. I started down the hill. I was turning onto Fifteenth Street when I remembered Lou's admonition about skinny white girls.

I hadn't eaten much of the pancakes at the Boat Yard. I drove back into town, where I made myself eat a large bowl of chicken-noodle soup. It rested uneasily in my stomach, but I reminded myself of the Warshawski coat of arms: a dinner plate, with knife and fork rampant, and the motto *Never Skip a Meal, Always Clean Your Plate.*

Prairie State Recycling was easy to find. Signs told me where to park, in a lot around the side, away from heavy machinery and debris. Signs told me where to deposit my material. Another sign begged me to do a simple sort before I dropped off anything. IT SAVES WEAR AND TEAR ON OUR NERVES AND ON OUR MACHINES, AND LOWERS THE COST TO YOU!

The center itself was in a large, simply built shed, whose outer doors were raised so that conveyor belts could feed material into shipping containers outside.

A couple of people were emptying bags onto a belt. The light inside the shed was dim, but Trig's halo of wiry curls was easy to spot. He was facing the belt and moving items onto smaller belts, hand-sorting glass from different metals, tossing nonrecyclables into a bin at his feet. Prairie State Recycling's customers apparently ignored the signs and didn't do a simple sort themselves.

The din from the machinery and the clanging of bottles and metal on the belts was intense. Even if I'd wanted to interrupt Trig midtask, no one could have heard me over the racket.

A woman who'd been emptying bags onto the belt came over to me, lifting her earmuffs from her head.

"Can I help you?" she bellowed. "Are you a member?"

"I want to talk to Trig," I shouted back. "How long before he finishes?"

She looked at a giant clock on the wall. "You one of his marchers? He'll take a break in about ten minutes."

I went back to the Toyota, where I could block out the worst of the noise. GATES INTO THE YARD ARE SHUT PROMPTLY AT FOUR, a sign read. If I were a member, I could enter my code on the pad and leave my recyclables in the yard.

I was studying the sign when the woman came over to me and said Trig was taking a break. "No one can work the belts for more than thirty minutes at a stretch."

I agreed that the work looked both tedious and dangerous.

"It baffles me how people completely disregard our instructions and jumble everything together, but no one ever said life was supposed to be easy."

When I got back to the shed, the noise was down because the belts weren't running. Trig was leaning against the wall, scrolling through his phone. He'd put on the army parka I'd seen him wearing in the courthouse.

"Tina said you wanted to volunteer," he said when I introduced myself. "But she didn't say what you wanted to do. It's best if you go to the website."

"I'm sorry—all I told her was that I wanted to talk to you. I'm an investigator, trying to learn more about Clarina Coffin."

His expression soured. "Oh, yes. The private pig hanging around with Zoë. Every step I take, one of you jerks is writing me a ticket for moving my feet the wrong way."

"Mr. Garrity, I don't have ticket-writing powers. I'm interested in you only insofar as you can tell me anything about Clarina Coffin. Do you know her home was trashed? Someone was trying to find something there. If you have a whiff of an idea about what it could be, I'd love to hear about it."

He scowled. "Why do you care about Clarina?"

In time-honored pig fashion, I sidestepped the question. "Do you know her background, where she lived before she came to Lawrence? She talked to people like Cady Perec about her interest in history. I just searched the trailer she was renting. Whoever trashed her apartment took anything she might have written, including any computers she might have written on. Do you know what she wrote?"

He hunched a shoulder and muttered she'd never shown him her work.

"In the woods behind the Dundee house I found a fragment of a letter suggesting a lunch date at the University of Kansas press building. I wonder if it's a letter she received?"

"You really are a snooper, aren't you? Busy in her trailer, busy in the woods?"

Bhagavatula had a ton more patience than me—I would have locked him up months ago. I tried to keep my irritation from showing. "Did she mention a possible meeting with anyone at the press?"

"Not to me," he said after a pause, perhaps reluctant to admit she hadn't confided in him.

"Trig!" Tina called from the shed. "We're going to start up the line again."

He turned back toward the shed.

I put a hand on his arm. "Can we meet for coffee or a drink when you get off work so we can finish this conversation? I'll wait for you at the Decadent Hippo."

"What, so you can try to frame me? I know how the police work. If you can't pin Clarina's murder on me, you'll round up some Black or Native person to arrest, case closed, next!" He mimed a judge banging a gavel.

"On top of having no ticket-writing powers, I have no power to arrest anyone. You're in the top tier of people they're interested in because you keep showing up at the Dundee house."

"So do you, and for that matter, so does Queen

Gertrude. I guess I should thank you—if the two of you hadn't gone out there, I'd be in a cell, for sure."

"Very likely," I agreed. "Judge Bhagavatula can't be the only person on the bench who you've pissed off. However, the sooner I can find out who actually killed her, the sooner I can return to Chicago and a vestige of normal life."

Tina called his name again, and he stomped off toward the shed.

"And stop it with the pig-naming," I called after him. "It's a worn-out cliché. You're clever enough to think of something new."

19

Dreams of Glory

O ne of the junior editors, Kayla Huang, at the University Press remembered Clarina, not with enthusiasm. "Her murder is shocking, and I'm sorry for it, but she came around several times, maybe eighteen months or two years ago. I was the newbie, so they sent her to me. She thought she had a great memoir to tell, about her life in the context of her family's involvement in the abolitionist movement, but she didn't have anything in writing to show me. She had this whole file of clippings from the *New York Times* on memoirs that had been written by ghost writers, where the books had surprised their publishers by generating huge sales."

Huang took me into her office, a cubbyhole filled with books and manuscripts, some on the floor, some stacked on chairs. She let me read the correspondence between the press and Clarina, a series of increasingly angry letters from Clarina, accusing everyone in Lawrence of bigotry and a refusal to acknowledge true Kansas history.

When I showed Huang the photo I'd taken of the letter fragment, she frowned over it. "I can't tell if it came from our offices or not. There's no sign it was written on letterhead. I supposed if it was an invitation to meet in Westbrooke Circle, it would have meant to come here, but there's no way of telling. And you can't see who it was written to, either."

Huang took me back to the reception area. A red-headed woman in a blue cleaner's smock was emptying the trash by the counter into a blue cart labeled RECY-CLABLE PAPER AND CARDBOARD ONLY.

Huang asked the young man at the counter if Clarina had been in anytime in the last few weeks. "She might have thought someone had a lunch date with her."

He looked at the visitors log, but Clarina's name wasn't in it. "Bruce had a lunch here with Tracy Clark, and Nandar had one over at the faculty club with Lori Rader-Day. That's all for the past month, but I can get you a list for the rest of the year if you want."

"The paper was fresh," I said, "not stained by snow or dirt, so I don't think it would go back very far."

The woman taking care of the trash stood holding the empty container, waiting for us to get out of her way.

"I'll send out an email blast to everyone on staff asking if they saw or corresponded with Clarina in the last month," Huang said. "I'd be surprised—she might have refused to work with me, since I hadn't gotten her the contract she wanted, but they would have sent her to me first if she came around recently."

When I thanked her and left, I saw the woman with the trash still standing in the hall, staring after me.

I drove back to what the map app called "Old Lawrence," the part of town close to the river where the nineteenth-century pioneers had settled. Gertrude Perec lived in the tony section, big houses, big lots, trim and siding painted, streets and sidewalks well maintained. It was only a short walk east from her place to small houses that seemed to stay upright due to some anti-gravity device. The sidewalks there were brick, and buckling.

Everything in Old Lawrence, including the homes, the shops and the courts, was in a walkable area about a mile square. I parked the Toyota in front of a tumbledown house and walked back to the Perec garage. I couldn't hide from the cops indefinitely, but the longer it took them to connect me to the Camry, the easier it would be for me to slide out of town tomorrow.

When I'd dropped off my supplies, and eaten some cheese, I walked back into town. It was a transition hour at the Hippo, from coffee to cocktails. In the mornings only three or four people would sit at the big wood tables inside, but it was nearly five when I got there; the place was filling up.

The Hippo's signature cocktail was the River Bottom, a mix of bourbon, Aperol, and orange pulp. I don't usually drink this early in the day, and rarely cocktails, but I ordered a River Bottom and wedged myself into a spot behind the door. It was too cold to wait outside, but I wanted air on me, even if people claimed the pandemic was over.

While I waited, wondering if Trig would show, I did a sketchy search on my phone. Trig was forty-seven. He'd been a student at the University of Kansas but apparently had dropped out halfway through his third year. He'd left school, but he couldn't tear himself away from the town. There wasn't any record of a marriage or children.

I pay for information on things like arrest records. Trig had been picked up countless times for crimes against property—trespass, defacing storefronts— under his birth name, Irwin, but I couldn't find any history of violence. I don't have access to employment records unless people post their work history themselves, so I didn't know what jobs he'd held before Prairie State Recycling. The plant was eighteen years old, so even if he'd been there from the beginning, he must have been doing something before that. I also couldn't find a reason for his nickname.

I was about to close the search and do some paying work when a header caught my eye: GALLOPING GARRITY RUNS BACK HIS EIGHTEENTH INTERCEPTION FOR A TOUCHDOWN. Trig as a football player seemed improbable, but I opened the file.

Mark Garrity was the galloper, not Irwin. Mark had played for the University of Iowa, where he'd set numerous Big Ten and NCAA records. He'd gone on to a career as a defensive end with the Chiefs. The year Trig dropped out of school, Mark had been named defensive MVP in his conference. Dr. Freud could probably suggest a connection there.

The bio didn't mention Trig/Irwin, but both men came from Waterloo, Iowa. Both had parents named LeRoy and Patty. Mark, the football star, was the elder by five years.

I looked up Trig's site, Kansans4Freedom. As is true for every website these days, the first page was an invitation to donate time or money. Photos showed Trig in front of a belching smokestack, confronting a deputy in front of the Yancy school, nose to nose with an abortion foe outside a clinic, facing off with a group holding assault weapons. The sad thing was, he was alone in most of the pictures on his side of the protests.

"Can I get you another?" One of the waitstaff appeared in front of me. I'd been so absorbed in my reading I hadn't noticed that the crowd at the bar had grown to four-deep. I was occupying valuable real estate for someone nursing a single drink. In fact, I'd only taken a few swallows, but it was thick and sweet, not to my taste.

It had gotten to be six-thirty; it didn't seem likely Trig would show. I was edging around the table to get to the door when the young woman I'd met earlier at Trig's apartment appeared.

"It's you," she said, relieved.

"It is indeed," I agreed. "You made it to your class without your grade being docked?"

"By seventeen seconds." She grinned. "I was looking for you but couldn't see you in the crowd. Trig sent me. He hates this place, but he can talk to you at the apartment if you go over there."

I offered her a lift, but she was hooking up with friends. By the time I reached the street she'd disappeared into the mob at the bar, and someone else had grabbed my seat.

I'd hoped that Trig's apartment would be an oasis of

tidy calm in his angry life, but when he undid the chain bolt, after studying me through the gap, I walked into a paper factory. Posters, posterboard, paints for writing on posterboard, covered an old sofa and part of the floor. News stories printed from the Web were taped to the wall with key paragraphs circled in red.

The furniture was old, the curtains threadbare, but he had a new-looking iMac on the corner table that served as his desk. The desk chair was a good ergonomic model. He swiveled it around to face me but didn't offer me a place to sit. I shifted some of the posters on the couch. He muttered under his breath about pigs thinking they had the right to mess with people's private belongings.

I pretended I hadn't heard. "Clarina Coffin was a modern-day miracle. She had no existence anywhere on the net before she showed up here."

I waited a beat, but he was watching me warily, not responding. He might be a loose cannon but this wasn't his first interrogation.

"I'm guessing Clarina Coffin was a fake identity. There was a suffragist named Clarina Nicholls who lived in Kansas in the nineteenth century. Clarina Coffin claimed to be deeply interested in local history, so I'm wondering if she named herself after that activist. There are thousands of people in the country with the 'Coffin' surname. Did your Clarina ever talk to you about how she chose her name?"

"She wasn't 'my' Clarina. Just someone who understood the importance of the issues facing our country."

"When did she start joining the protests?" I asked.

"What does this have to do with her death? You think Brett Santich murdered her to stop her picketing his school?" He sat up straighter, expression hopeful.

"I don't think anything because I don't have data," I said. "I'm hoping you can help with that. Was Cady Perec's suspension the first time Clarina joined you in one of your actions?"

"How can I trust you to keep what I say confidential?"

"You can't," I said. "It's a murder investigation. If you tell me something that connects to her killer, I'm bound to act on it. But if you tell me something about trespassing or throwing paintballs at a building, I'll keep it to myself."

"Yeah, that's about the level I'm good at," he said bitterly. "I thought I could make a difference in the world, but trespassing and throwing paintballs doesn't change anything."

He watched me for signs of ridicule, perhaps, or judgment, but I sat still, not speaking, keeping my face neutral.

"It's not a big secret. Clarina first came around

last fall, when Santich and his lackeys suspended Cady Perec for trying to teach their children the truth about race and class in America. Zoë, the kid at the paper, wrote up the way the school board reacted to Cady's class on Kansas history. Clarina read the story. She said she'd been digging into Lawrence history and could shed some amazing light on hidden corners of it."

"What kinds of things did she think she could reveal?"

"Things like lynch mobs in Kansas, or the way the heroes of the abolitionist movement treated Indigenous people after the Civil War. She offered to help Cady improve her reading list. The Perecs go around with their damned noses in the air, acting like they're the people who created this town, so of course Cady told Clarina she didn't need her help.

"Clarina wasn't the kind to take offense. When Santich took things with Cady to the next level and got his lapdog board to fire her, Clarina came out to picket with me."

Trig breathed heavily, his fury at Santich boiling to the surface again.

"Anyway, I told her about the Yancy project when she was working with me at the school. Brett Santich farmed that land on top of the mound, and suddenly he gives it over to some company that wants to put in a fancy resort. Like, all the rich people in Kansas City will invite their friends here for skiing or whatever rich people do, instead of going to Aspen.

"High-and-mighty Perec, she was head of the planning commission when the deal went through, she says it's a private concern, not run by local government. But when I ask why local government doesn't have responsibility for environmental impact or safety, but this private concern has, she tells me to raise the question with the right authorities. And when I do that, they tell me I don't have standing. So I picket, because it's all I can do. I'd been out there Tuesday mornings, because Tuesdays and Wednesdays are my days off from the recycling center.

"Santich, he got the sheriff to come around with some kind of injunction, but I fought that one—it's one of the few times that Judge Bhagavatula took my side. I'm moving, I've got a sign. Yes, I have a bullhorn, but the only people I'm disturbing are the creeps working the site."

When his bitter avalanche ended, I tried to bring the conversation back to Clarina, asking if she'd mentioned specific documents she'd thought Cady should use in her class.

Trig looked at me blankly. "I don't know. I don't

know what she had, just that this was her life's work, research on displaced native people, that kind of thing."

"She tried to get the university press to publish her memoir, but she couldn't show them anything in writing. Still, someone tore her place apart, looking for something," I said. "You have any idea what that could have been?"

He shook his head.

"When did you last see Clarina?"

He thought it over, and finally decided it was the Thursday before she died. She'd joined him at the access road to the Yancy construction.

"She said it was probably the last time she'd be coming out to picket with me. I asked if she was leaving Lawrence, and she gave this kind of superior smile and said, maybe, if everything worked out the way she hoped."

I pushed a little, hoping he'd asked Clarina what she meant, where she was heading if she left town, but he said she did stuff like that all the time. "She'd throw out some crumb of information, see if she had your attention, then she'd act all mysterious and not say anything else. I appreciated her support, but I got fed up with her act."

"Why did you go out to the Dundee house Tuesday morning?" I asked. "Did you get a message from Clarina?"

He picked at his nails, finally said without looking up, "I have a scanner so I know where the cops or sheriff are going to be. I saw they were out at the Dundee place."

I turned that response over in my mind. "You knew the Dundee place was used for drug parties?"

He looked up at me, looked down again. "Not in so many words."

"You didn't go to parties out there?"

"You think I'm that stupid? Cops are on my ass twenty-four-seven and I tempt them by going to a drug house? Besides, I don't use anything. I hate that loss of control."

"Did you think Clarina would be at the house when you saw the police activity?"

"Not her. Someone I know," he muttered after another pause. "I worried whether they'd get caught in some kind of sweep. When I got there, the place was all shut down. I was going inside to look, then her majesty Queen Gertrude showed up."

"Was Sabrina Granev the person you were looking for?" I asked.

"Who? Oh, the missing college student. No. It was someone who shouldn't be there but won't stay away."

It was all he would say: he wasn't going to feed an innocent person to the cops.

"You must have been surprised when Gertrude Perec showed up."

"I was sure the cops had sent her. She's so tight with Everard's mom you'd think the two were doing a synchronized act—maybe looking down their noses in unison."

I hadn't expected that kind of mordant humor. He had depths, which meant I needed to watch my step around him.

"She had some story about looking for a friend, but she wouldn't say who, so I thought Everard's mother. Of course I didn't tell Gertrude why I was there, and I wasn't going to go inside as long as she was hanging around. I finally took off. Was Clarina—was she there then?"

"Yes," I said. "Dead, in the basement where I found her a few hours later."

Peter's student, on the floor with their face in pieces, blood and bone and the soft gray mass that had been their agonized mind, appeared before me. I dug my nails into my head. *You will not faint. You have never fainted and tonight will not be the first time.*

Trig was suddenly in front of me, forcing a glass of water into my hands. The glass was greasy, but I drank, anyway.

"You going to be okay?" he asked roughly.

I nodded. I would be okay. Maybe not tonight, but surely someday soon. I was exhausted but I still had some questions.

"The picture. The police have a picture of you and Perec outside the house. Who took it?"

He snorted. "If I knew that I'd be outside their house right now with a bullhorn. It's the only reason I'm telling you why I was there. Because of the picture. It wasn't photoshopped, I was there."

I got unsteadily to my feet and sidestepped the cardboard and paper on the floor. In the doorway I stopped to look at him again. He'd swiveled in his chair to face his computer.

The screen saver had come up, a boy with a mop of dark hair and a gap-toothed grin. A redhaired woman was bending over him, hands crossed over his chest. When Trig saw me looking at the picture, he pressed a key and his files came back up on the screen. He gave me a menacing look: I dare you to say anything about that picture.

I said nothing about the picture. I asked instead whether Clarina ever said anything about where she came from.

"I told you, no! No, every time you ask, so stop asking."

He started a routine rant about cops not caring

about the truth, no matter whether they were public or private, but something about me, maybe the lingering anguish in my face, caught him up short.

"There was this one time. It was—I was telling her—I have a brother. Football star. Me, I was the skinny nerdy one, but not nerdy enough to be a genius and win prizes." His eyes squeezed shut from decades-old pain.

"At school, teachers and everyone thought I'd be another star, so when I couldn't even catch a ball I turned into a joke. The jocks liked to—never mind what they did. My brother, he was on TV every Saturday running back touchdowns for Iowa. To my parents, I was the world's biggest loser. When I was beaten up in school, my mother told me not to be a crybaby.

"Clarina, I told her about it one time. It was that jerk Santich, he was taunting me outside the school. Somehow he'd figured out who my brother was. His nickname, Galloping Garrity, so Santich, he said he'd get the police to tear-gas me and see—see if I could run as fast as Galloping Garrity."

He looked at me sideways, to see if I was going to join the mockery. "Clarina said, she came from a place where the town name meant everyone in school piled on, making fun of her for being chubby."

"The town name?" I echoed, bewildered. "What— was it some kind of Indigenous word for 'fat'?"

"She didn't say. I didn't pay enough attention, I guess."

I made my way out the door and down the linoleum stairs. Outside I walked to the end of the block and back, sucking in the cold air. Parents shoot their children, they bully their children, children bully each other. Was there no end to the grief we cause each other?

20

Pissing for Justice

All nine hours from Kansas to Chicago, I'd been thinking happily of reconnecting with Mr. Contreras and the dogs, followed by a peaceful night in my own bed. That happy fantasy was crashed by reality. When I reached home, Mr. Contreras was agitated, almost in tears: someone had come this morning and searched my apartment.

"They had a warrant, doll, I couldn't hardly stop them. I stuck with them, me and Mitch, to make sure they didn't steal nothing or maybe plant some drugs or something on you, but they was hardly civil."

The searchers had been with the FBI. My neighbor had studied their credentials. "Told them I was old, needed time to make sure they hadn't got those things

out of a cereal box, and I wrote down their badge numbers, like you taught me, but I couldn't stop them.
There was three of them, but one, he never showed me
his badge, and the other two said he was an observer."

I asked if they'd let slip anything to say what they
were looking for. They hadn't said anything, but they'd
been searching through all my papers, including my
mother's music, which I hold sacred. They hadn't been
sloppy, exactly, but they hadn't used ordinary courtesy.
I spent my first hour home inserting loose pages back
in the proper folders. I even sprayed the collection with
Lysol to get rid of federal cooties.

They'd also been to my office, my leasemate reported. They hadn't taken it apart, not like the
searchers in Clarina's trailer, but as with Gabriella's
music, they hadn't taken pains to hide their footsteps.

On Thursday, the home news got even more distressing. I'd cheered myself with a long run up the lakefront
with the dogs, then stopped near Lotty Herschel's clinic.
She took an hour away from duty to have coffee with me.
After that, I'd seen Sal Barthele, who owns the Golden
Glow in the South Loop, to catch up in private ahead of
my upcoming night meeting there with Murray.

My happier frame of mind ended with my third slice
of Mr. Contreras's French toast. That was when Bernie
called.

"Vic, have you seen the news? I am so sorry, it is my fault they are saying these things about you!"

"Who is saying what things?" I asked.

"*Mon Dieu,* you haven't seen, then? It is the Lawrence *policier,* they arranged a press conference about this murder you found, and about Sabrina."

My neighbor has a tablet, which he mostly uses to keep in touch with his grandsons and his old buddies from his Machinists local. I found a video of Lawrence police chief Rowland McDowell's press conference.

McDowell and the county sheriff met reporters on a small plaza in front of the Douglas County Judicial Center. Cornell Stamoran, the FBI agent, was on the dais, along with a man who was identified as Frank Karas, the Douglas County DA. Deke Everard stood behind the chief and the sheriff.

The first questions had to do with Clarina Coffin: no one had come forward who claimed to be a relative, or know anything about her past, the chief said, so if anyone could help with that information, please call the number on the screen. They also posted a portrait, where they'd photoshopped out the blood and fixed up her matted hair.

Reporters asked about time of death, cause, weapon, suspects—all the usual. The chief said they didn't have any details to give yet.

A Wichita reporter asked about the drug house where both Sabrina and Clarina had been found. Another man, in a suit and tie, was next to Stamoran. He was never identified, but before the chief answered, the stranger stepped forward to murmur into his ear.

The sheriff nodded. "The owner of the property has promised to put better security in place. It's a historic house, dating back to the Civil War, and the owner is trying to get landmark status for it. He definitely doesn't want it used for drugs or murdered bodies"—a ripple of laughter at that.

Another person wanted to know about the Chicago detective who'd found both Sabrina and the dead woman.

"She's a person of interest," Chief McDowell said. "We've told her to stay in the jurisdiction until we're a hundred percent sure she's not responsible for either crime."

Zoë piped up. "The Chicago detective is V.I. Warshawski. She saved Sabrina Granev's life, Chief. Why does that make her a person of interest?"

I blew her a kiss while the chief waffled around.

Someone who identified himself as with the Kansas University newspaper said, "Warshawski apparently came on campus on Monday and accused Omicron Delta Beta members of selling drugs. Trevor Millay, he's the chapter president, said she was snooping around their garage. He thinks she was looking for drugs. Do you know if she's a user herself?"

The chief turned to Deke, who said, "We saw the post Millay made on the chapter's Instagram account. We don't believe Ms. Warshawski is a drug user, but we will take measures to make sure of that."

A red mist rose in front of my eyes. I looked up the Omicron account and their other social media. They'd picked up my photo from the Web and posted it over the caption: *Pretending to look for a missing student but really searching for drugs for herself?*

Trevor Millay was the name of the punk I'd seen in their garage on Monday. *"Don't cross a South Side street fighter, buster,"* I hissed, *"because I can make you sorry you ever drew breath."* I had just enough self-control not to post the threat on his feed.

"That's terrible, doll, terrible," Mr. Contreras said. "What can you do to shut him up?"

"I don't know," I said. "It's a lie, but these days, in-credible lies spread faster than Canadian wildfires, and they're harder to extinguish. I'll check in with Freeman Carter, and the woman in Kansas City whom Freeman found to represent me, but if I find Clarina Coffin's killer, that should quiet some of the more obnoxious creeps."

"How you going to do that?" he fretted. "You don't have any friends down there, and if the cops are fixing to frame you—"

"I do have a couple of friends, but my big advantage is an open mind. The cops are looking at me and maybe two or three other people. I'm willing to look at everyone in Kansas as a suspect. After that, I'm going to nail that frat boy's hind end to his Porsche."

A good speech, but we all know how valuable talk is. My troubles hadn't exactly peaked, either. I had a voice message from Deke Everard.

"We knew you were staying in Gertrude Perec's garage, but when I went by to talk to you, Cady said you'd gone back to Chicago. You were told not to leave the jurisdiction. The DA is issuing a subpoena. Unless you are back in Lawrence by ten Monday morning to talk to Karas, we will send sheriff's deputies to bring you back."

I forwarded the message to Freeman, who phoned me at once.

"You are not my client who's the biggest pain in the ass, but you are in the top ten," he said. "There is no good 'why' in this scenario."

"Freeman, I struggle to keep on top of your bill. I cannot afford to set up a separate household and office in Kansas. I'm here to collect my computer, my files, my clothes, all those things. I'll be back in Kansas by tomorrow night. I'm even putting on my red Magli pumps to seal the deal."

"You're not convincing me," he said. "Someone could mail you all those things. Meanwhile, you're adding another buck-fifty to your outstanding balance with me. Shipping your home to Kansas wouldn't cost that much."

Shorthand for a thousand fifty. Which went up to twelve hundred when he phoned again half an hour later.

"Someone in Kansas hates you, Vic. The LKPD wants a urine sample to prove whether you're an opioid user. They've agreed to let the Chicago cops oversee it, but this isn't negotiable. They have a warrant, Chicago will honor it."

Opioids don't stay long in the bloodstream, but you can find a trace in urine up to four days after using them. It had been about eighty-four hours since I'd found Sabrina. If they thought I'd ingested something in the Dundee house, they would need the sample now.

Peeing for justice is humiliating, and humiliation makes me angry, but I drove over to the police lab on Harrison.

The Chicago cops sent a sergeant I knew, Lenora Pizzello, who arrived with the warrant. Pizzello and

I had worked around each other several times in the past, sometimes cordially, even, but she never forgot her first loyalty was to the wide blue line.

While we waited for one of Freeman's female associates, who would be a witness for the accused, I tried to make conversation. "This seems like such an intimate moment, but so one-sided, only one of us getting naked. I could bring out a bottle, put on a record, so that you could get in the mood."

"I don't want to be here, Warshawski!" Pizzello's face was red. "This isn't my idea of police work. And I thought better of you than for you to be a user."

"Me, too, Pizzello, and I expect the lab to bear out our joint good opinion."

Freeman's female associate arrived, the two women watched me pee, both looking like stuffed owls to hide their embarrassment. I don't know how I looked, but I'm sure it wasn't happy. The lab tech sealed the specimen cup and dated and initialed it; Pizzello and Freeman's associate initialed underneath, also with the date.

"When I'm super famous, you'll be able to brag about this moment to your grandchildren," I said. "Like people who touched Elvis's dead body: I got to watch the astonishing private eye, V.I. Warshawski, pee into a cup."

"You're already famous," Pizzello said. "People from as far away as Schaumburg want to know why you aren't behind bars."

My clients were worried, too. The Millay kid's social media posts were getting a big play. Two of my accounts canceled during the afternoon. The other nine for whom I was doing active work all needed phone conversations that showed how assiduously I was handling their business.

"Oh, Bernie," I murmured as I packed my wardrobe, my toiletries, my computer, and Peppy's food and blanket. "You meant well, but I was so much better off sitting at home feeling sorry for myself."

21

There's No Place Like— Wherever

Peppy and I arrived in Lawrence late Saturday night. In between packing the files and clothes I'd need for a week out of town, I'd caught up with friends. My evening at the Golden Glow with Sal and Murray had been a great spirit reviver, but it made my lonely arrival in Lawrence feel more desolate.

The lights were off in the Perec house. I moved our things into the garage apartment as quietly as I could. Peppy was uneasy in the unfamiliar space, but when I took her for a walk in the park near the library, she relaxed. She'd been there with me two years ago. Dogs have some kind of mental scent library; she knew she was in a familiar space.

Sunday morning, I drove to a co-op grocery on the west side of town where I stocked up on enough basics to last a week. I hoped I wouldn't have to stay here any longer than that. I sent a text to Lou and Ed, letting them know the Camry and I had made the round-trip without an arrest, assault, or impoundment.

After unpacking, and parking some distance from Gertrude's, I took Peppy over to the river. The path led us past the Riverside Congregational Church, where Clarina had offended the women by acting as though she knew more about Lawrence than they did. The parking lot was full; I could hear a hymn trickle faintly through the stained glass windows.

As the dog and I walked the river path, I pondered again Cady's claim that she'd been down here early Tuesday morning when Clarina was being murdered. The path was well maintained and easy to walk in daylight, but tree roots and rocks would be hazards in the dark. Had she really been here? And if not here, had she been at the Dundee place, assisting her grand-mother in moving Clarina's body into the basement?

Trig claimed he'd been at the Dundee house early Tuesday morning because he worried that a friend would be caught up in a police sweep. Trig was such a loner, I tried to imagine who he would care about enough to try to protect them.

I wondered about the boy in Trig's screen saver. Perhaps that was a nephew, the son of Galloping Garrity. If he was part of Trig's life, I could see him going out of his way to protect the child, but I couldn't see the rage in Trig that this murderer had exhibited. Even his flare-ups with Santich didn't rise to that level of fury.

The church was perched on top of a ravine, with a steep path down to the river. I let Peppy off her leash. She ran ahead of me, exploring the underbrush lining the river path, and even jumped into the water for a few minutes. The river must be cold this time of year, but so is Lake Michigan. She's a dog who likes the cold.

The path we were on ended at the boathouse for the university's rowing teams. A disused boat trailer was sinking into the mud at the back, but the building was locked up tight and, par for the Lawrence course, there wasn't any litter on the ground around it. If I managed to clear my name and find Clarina's killer, maybe I'd move here permanently.

By then, Peppy was so filthy I had to take her to a DIY dog wash before I could go back to the apartment. While I was drying her, Deke Everard texted me. He hoped I was back in the jurisdiction: Did I remember the DA was going to interview me first thing tomorrow?

Of course Zoë had sent several messages, panting for another meeting in our supposed collaboration.

PAY DIRT · 227

I called Everard from the Hippo, where I'd become such a regular that they invited Peppy inside with me. My call went to voicemail, but I got a text from him almost instantly, asking for my location.

While I was waiting for him, a woman about my age, in skintight Lycra with her hair pulled into a ponytail, popped into the Hippo, asked if I was me, and handed me a subpoena. She bounced out the door, resuming her run. That would be a good gig: process server while training for a marathon. I photographed the subpoena and texted it to Faye Mitchell.

When Deke came into the Hippo, a couple of people greeted him by name, and the barista brought him a mug of black coffee.

"Your pee is clean," he said by way of greeting.

"Good to have my essential purity confirmed," I said.

"Your essence is not exactly pure. You're screwing around in an LKPD murder investigation, and that makes you look suspicious."

"Sergeant, I'm screwing around in your investigation because I'm a suspect and I don't want to be railroaded for a crime I didn't commit. I would be happily drinking espresso in my own home right this minute if your crew had searched the Dundee house from top to bottom after I found Sabrina."

His lips tightened and he looked away.

"The blanket that showed up in my car trunk was in the front hall at the Dundee House when I went inside. Which means most likely Clarina was already dead in the basement. I haven't been able to talk to Valerie Granev since she moved her daughter to some facility in Florida, but she told me Sabrina was screaming about seeing monsters. I don't have any subpoena powers but if a competent interrogator spoke to Sabrina, they might discover she'd seen the killers carry Clarina into the house."

He hadn't put milk or sugar in his coffee, but he stirred it around, so forcefully that some of it slopped onto the tabletop. "I won't argue about that with you. Hindsight is always perfect. But believe it or not, I'm trying to protect you—I don't think you killed Coffin any more than I believe Aunt Gertrude did. Or my mom, for that matter, but you and Aunt—and Gertrude both were at the crime scene the same night that Clarina died. The DA, the Bureau's guy Stamoran, and even the chief keep coming back to that point. The fact that Gertrude also showed up there is all that's keeping Karas from charging you and Trig."

"So Gertrude really was there? And Trig? Why?"

"That's the impossible part of the story," Deke said. "Trig refused at first to admit he'd gone there. When we showed him the picture of him by the back door with Gertrude, he claimed it was photoshopped. Finally, he said he got an anonymous call telling him he could catch Brett Santich selling drugs if he showed up without announcing himself. In fact, Trig's phone shows him *making* a call, to a pay phone—there are still a handful in Lawrence. But we don't have any evidence that he received any calls."

"What does Santich say about that?" I wondered if Trig had been lying to me, or to the cops, or maybe telling each of us a separate lie.

"Santich says he wouldn't invite Trig to leave a burning house, let alone out to his land at any hour of the day or night."

"What about Gertrude?" I asked.

"Gertrude says she had a message from one of the women in her book club, saying her car had broken down outside the Dundee place and could Gertrude come wait with her, since it was creepy out there at night."

"Can you verify that?"

"She did get a call just before three. From a burner. Someone wanted her in the frame. She rubs a lot of people the wrong way—she and her mother before her are steamrollers in this town, flattening opposition to their vision of Lawrence's future. If the killer resented her enough, he—or she, I guess—could have thought it would be a good joke to put her at the crime scene."

"In the same way they thought it was a good joke to leave the blanket in my car," I said, my voice very dry. "How are you coming with inspecting it? When can I have my ride back?"

"Our CSIs are being very thorough. Any misstep with any evidence now could endanger a prosecution when we finally make an arrest."

"And that's what you call trying to protect me? Trying to find any evidence against me in my car?"

"Don't be so damned touchy. How about, thanks, Deke, for making sure the prosecution can't try to prove we overlooked drugs or weapons or whatever? We did find traces of fentanyl in your trunk, but they seem to have come from the blanket. Our super extra care shows they weren't in your clothes, your carry-on bag, or in the interior."

Prosecution could take those traces of fentanyl and turn them into a drug habit, or worse, a drug dealership, so I didn't thank him. Instead I asked about the Omicron boys. "Any luck tracing drug sales to them?"

"The Omicron house is under the campus force's jurisdiction. Our patrol cars are doing sweeps of the bars, looking for action, but we can't search campus housing."

He got up. "Be very careful here, Warshawski. This isn't Chicago, where you have good friends on the force. A wrong step here, and you could be looking at some serious charges. Chicago's a big city and anonymity is easier than in a small place like Lawrence. You'll be surprised by how easy it is for us to find out if you're being—let's say, unorthodox."

I smiled at him. "I'm living above Gertrude Perec's garage. She and your mother are BFF's. Zoë Cruickshank is dogging my steps. So, no, I won't be surprised if you know what I'm doing before I've figured it out myself."

I reported the conversation in person to Faye Mitchell, the Kansas City lawyer Freeman had found for me. The Kansas men were playing basketball Sunday evening. Mitchell had a ticket. I learned that meant she had serious connections—it would be easier to see Taylor Swift live, she told me. She talked to me at the Perecs on her way to meeting friends for lunch.

Mitchell was in her forties, with auburn hair pulled up from her face by a couple of combs. She was dressed like everyone else on game day—in a Jayhawk sweatshirt—but she sported an impressive pair of high-heeled cowboy boots.

She made a face when she learned I'd already spoken to the police, or at least to a police officer, since getting

232 · SARA PARETSKY

back into town. "I know it won't be possible for me to be here with you every time you talk to the local LEOs, but keep it brief, and record everything. Deke Everard's a good cop, straight shooter, but the local DA is pushing on the LKPD to find enough evidence for an arrest, and you have that FBI agent hovering on the sidelines like a bad fairy at a christening."

I told her about Sabrina's monsters, and Valerie Granev's troubling behavior. "She said that she hadn't wanted to bring Stamoran into the search for Sabrina, that it was a decision of senior management."

Mitchell's carefully shaped eyebrows shot up. "Senior management at Tulloh Industries? Does that mean one of the family?"

"It's family owned?" I asked.

I should have looked them up when Valerie told me she worked for them. Another sign of slippage. Get your head in the game, Warshawski!

"Oh, yes," Mitchell said drily. "It's very much family owned, and the family in turn owns a big chunk of the state legislators in Kansas. If Matthew or his son Robert wanted the FBI involved, they'd have called the Bureau chief, who would have given them instant support."

"Valerie told me to lay off at the same time her husband got funding for a pet project of his," I said. "The gift for his outdoor wilderness center was anonymous, but I suppose the Tullohs could have been behind it. A bribe to persuade Valerie to ask me to lay off."

"Could be," Mitchell said. "It doesn't explain why the fed is trying to implicate you in a nonkidnapping, but it's a good point to follow." She looked at an outsize Breitling watch on her right wrist. "I have to run. See you here at nine tomorrow ahead of the depo. Rock Chalk!"

"Rock Chalk?" I was bewildered.

"That's how Kansas supporters ID ourselves. You've got to learn to think like a local if you want to beat them at their own game."

22
Rock Chalk

When she left, I looked up the Tulloh family. Matthew Tulloh was close to eighty. He'd started his business life with three grain elevators his wife had inherited, and parlayed them into an international business with tentacles in a lot of different industries. Their headquarters were in a town called Salina in central Kansas, where they were close to the natural gas wells that made up a chunk of Tulloh Industries' business. They apparently didn't try to compete with Boeing or the other big plane manufacturers; their aviation division specialized in the kind of electronics and avionics work Valerie Granev did.

Since Tulloh Industries was privately held, it was hard to get an idea of how big they really were, but the business press said Matthew, his two sons, and his daughter each could count their personal wealth in eleven digits. Digits—I'd have to grow an extra finger just to count their money. What a disturbing image.

It was easy to see why the FBI would respond to a command from Tulloh to get involved in Sabrina's disappearance. It was impossible to see why the FBI would try to implicate me in a bogus kidnapping. If Matthew Tulloh was calling that tune, why?

I couldn't do anything about it, certainly not on a Sunday, but there were other tasks I'd overlooked, like the three photos I'd found in Clarina's trailer. They'd been ignored by the cops and the robbers, but they'd been important to Clarina.

I'd promised Lou and Ed I'd bring Peppy out to see them this afternoon. There was time for a stop at the Lawrence library, where I showed the pictures to the reference librarian.

"I'm hoping they can shed some light on who Clarina really was, where she came from, and maybe even on why she was killed."

The librarian's face clouded. "That was a terrible thing, her murder. She came in here a few times, but I sent her to the Origins Library in Topeka—Kansas Origins Museum and Library. They have a significant archive of papers and artifacts from the state's first fifty years, much bigger than our collection. These photos date to that time frame."

She wrote the museum's address and website on a scrap of paper. "Are you the woman who found Clarina? That must have been a terrible shock. You're a detective, aren't you? I hope you can find her killer."

It was pleasant to have a local greet me with a vote of confidence instead of a snarl. I thanked her and drove on out to the country with the dog. The afternoon was cold but sunny. Peppy had a glorious time chasing rabbits through Lou and Ed's fields, then persuading the men that I kept her on starvation rations.

When we got back into town, the crowds were growing for pregame parties. Traffic was backed up, horns blaring. The fresh air on the hilltop farm had made me hungry. I climbed the stairs, picturing a bowl of pasta with the cheese I'd picked up at the local co-op grocer, but I knew as soon as I unlocked the door that something was wrong. It was the smell, hard to identify, but not there earlier. A faint whiff, a sweet tobacco, maybe, or even aftershave.

I turned on my cell flashlight and held it away from my body. Nothing moved. I stuck my left arm out and fumbled around until I found the light switch. No one was in the main room. I left the door open, stuck my phone in my hip pocket, moved around the space. No one behind the half-wall that separated the kitchen from the big room. Nothing in the bathroom. Nothing in the alcove for the bed.

Peppy pattered anxiously behind me.

I shut the outside door and locked it before inspecting the room in detail. Little things. The suitcase that I'd slid under the bed was visible, instead of tucked completely away. I opened it, felt in the lining. Nothing there. My computer wasn't where I'd left it. I opened it, inspected it to see if someone had put a physical tracer on it, ran my malware software. It seemed okay.

I flicked through the blind slats, wondering if the intruder had planted a bug. They're almost impossible to spot these days without special equipment, but I still tried to search. Strangers in your room, handling your things, it leaves you feeling vulnerable and even dirty.

The skin along the base of my skull prickled, but I finally put on water to boil for pasta. When I took the box from the shelf, though, I felt a revulsion—I couldn't eat food intruders might have touched. I threw out all the food I'd bought yesterday and tied up the garbage bag.

I pulled the bin out from under the sink to stuff in the bag. It was heavy. Much too heavy for cheap plastic. It took me a minute, but I finally realized it had a false bottom. I pried it open with a knife blade.

Underneath was a piece of industrial plastic, wrapped a few times around something I couldn't make out through the layers.

I put on my cotton running gloves and lifted it out, gingerly, in case it was a something that exploded, but it felt like a piece of heavy tubing.

I found a paring knife in one of the drawers and slit open the wrapping. A pipe wrench about fifteen inches long. Made of a heavy steel but rusted at the business end. Not rust, steel like this doesn't rust. Blood. My gorge rose, blood in my room, on my hands.

"Stop!" I shouted.

The dog looked up at me, startled. I put a hand on her neck, felt her warmth through the glove. "Sorry, girl, sorry. Someone is messing with us, trying to mess with us, but they can't, they won't."

This was the weapon that had killed Clarina Coffin, or someone wanted the police to think it was. They'd planted it, they would call the cops and get them to find it. If I reported finding it they wouldn't believe it had been planted; with the blanket it would be enough to put me in a cell.

"And then what would happen to you, my beautiful one?" I murmured to Peppy, but I was already rewrapping the tool as I spoke.

I noticed the letter *K* embossed inside a raised circle

at the holding end. It looked like the symbol you see on kosher food. This wrench is kosher for murder. The thought raised a bubble of hysterical laughter.

The dog was clinging to my legs, my fears oozing through my skin, worrying her. "It's okay, girl, we're okay," I tried to soothe myself as well as her.

I must not linger in the apartment, but I scrubbed out the bin under the bathroom shower and left it upside down to dry. I put the wrench inside a plastic garbage bag, then swept all the food I'd bought into a second one. I couldn't bear to eat anything the intruders would have touched.

The bathroom window opened on the Perecs' backyard. I leaned out and lowered the bags onto the bushes. I hated to leave Peppy alone in the apartment, especially since I'd caused her so much worry, but I didn't want her with me on this errand. I couldn't keep an eye on a dog and on traffic or possible tails.

I ran down the stairs and rang the Perecs' bell. Cady came to the door. "Vic! Do you need something?"

"Someone broke into the garage apartment while I was out today."

"Vic—no—that's terrible! Gram!" She shouted over her shoulder.

Gertrude appeared, the frown lines around her nose and mouth deeply grooved. "We're at dinner,

Ms. Warshawski. If you have something you must discuss, come back tomorrow."

"Gram! Someone broke into the apartment today. We need to call the police. What did they take? Did they break down the door?"

"They either had a key or some good lock-picking equipment: I didn't see signs of forced entry. They didn't take anything, but they went through my things, my clothes, the food I'd bought. I'm wondering if you let someone in?"

"Why would I do that?" Gertrude bristled. "I'm not interested in anything you might own."

I smiled at her, my death-dealing smile. "Someone could have told you they were with the gas company, or inspecting for roaches or rats."

"I did not let anyone into the apartment. Now, if you'll excuse me, I'll return to my meal." Ramrod back, military-style U-turn, and she disappeared into the reaches of the house.

"I'm so sorry, Vic," Cady said. "But it's frightening. We've never had to worry about break-ins or vandals or anything. I'll call a locksmith and get a new lock in the morning. If—I know Gram sounds fierce, but if you're afraid to spend the night alone up there, we do have a spare bedroom you could stay in until we get the locks replaced."

"I'd be more afraid of your grandmother putting an ax in my head if I was in the same house."

She smiled, but said she still thought I should call the police.

"They didn't take anything," I said. "Cops are too overworked to fingerprint an apartment because the resident says her stuff was moved around. For now, I'd like to leave through your garden."

Cady took me to the back door. "It's dark in the garden, though. Are you sure you want to leave this way?"

"I want to double back," I said, "see if anyone is watching your house."

The explanation alarmed her, but she shut the door. She'd parted the curtains covering the glass upper panel, peering at me in worry. I smiled, waved, crossed out of her sight line, and crept back to retrieve my garbage bags. When I had them, I went south, to a park a few blocks from the house. I didn't think anyone had followed me.

The park was a few blocks from the main downtown street where the pregame celebrations were growing in enough intensity to reach me here. Tip-off must be soon.

I didn't think anyone was watching me. I left the garbage bag with the food on a bench, but took the wrench with me. Tricky part. Disaster if someone stopped me now and found it on me, but I walked through the park to Sixth Street, one of the town's busiest arteries. Cars were parading up and down, horns blaring. A cop was furiously blowing a whistle at the intersection with the main north-south street, where most of the happy fans were ignoring the lights. I skulked along on the edge of the park, finally found a break in the flow, and slipped across.

On the north side of the street, the park led straight down to the river. This was the route Cady claimed to have taken to walk off her insomnia the night Clarina Coffin was murdered. A few streetlamps made it possible to keep the path in view. A few runners were out, a couple of cyclists, and, despite the weather, some heavily loving couples. Maybe Cady really had been here. Maybe someone else who couldn't sleep at 3:00 A.M. would remember seeing her.

Near the end of the path, I found the old boat trailer Peppy and I had spotted this morning. Fluid motion, no looking over the shoulder. I walked up to the trailer, thrust the bag well underneath it, walked farther up the path to another garbage can where I lost the gloves: if blood had leaked through the plastic wrapping, the gloves would give me away. I strolled back up the path and merged with the mob on Massachusetts.

23

Hands-On Care

Back at the garage, I crept cautiously to the staircase but didn't see anyone watching, didn't find anyone on the steps. Peppy was lying just inside the door, trembling and whimpering.

I took her outside with me and sat on the top step, petting her, crooning Italian lullabies to her, until we were both calm again. We walked east, past the student bars, where people had crammed in to watch the game, and found a place with outdoor seating and heat lamps. I lingered there with the dog, sipping wine and feeding us both bits of risotto.

When we returned to the Perec place a few hours later, Deke Everard stepped out of an unmarked car across the street. Men were hanging around on street corners, hoping to talk to me. At least, one man was, even if he was a cop. Maybe I'd text that to Peter, see if it would rouse a current of jealousy that would make him call me.

"Wondered when you'd get back, Warshawski."

"Sergeant, that's so touching. What are there, a hundred thousand people in this town? And you keep track of us one by one to make sure we're safe? Chicago cops would never be so caring."

The streetlamps gave enough light that I could see him make a swatting gesture. "Aunt Ger—Ms. Perec—told me you'd gone out a couple of hours ago. She said you claimed someone had broken into the apartment over her garage."

"I claimed it because it happened."

"Where did you go when you left here?"

"Whoa, Sergeant. It's one thing to care about a single visitor to the town, especially on game night when you have thousands of visitors. It's quite another to conduct an interrogation, especially in the dark with no witnesses."

"I have a witness. We can talk upstairs in the lamplight."

He called into his lapel mike. A woman emerged from the car and crossed over to us.

"There's nothing to talk about," I said. "If you want to

question me, I'll come to the station with you, after I've let my lawyer know we're having a formal conversation."

He pulled a piece of paper from a vest pocket. "I have a warrant to search the apartment. I showed it to Ms. Perec, but I wanted to wait until you got back to execute it."

So someone had been keeping an eye on the place, and had called the cops when I got back. I didn't like this, not one little bit.

"You got a warrant because I told my landlady I thought someone had broken into the apartment?" I said. "How can you search for missing items if you don't know what was there to begin with?"

"We're not—" he began, then cut himself short. "Take us up to the apartment, Warshawski. Hawks are up by three. I want to get done here in time to watch the finish."

I led them in silence up the stairs built onto the side of the garage. I unlocked the door and laid my arm out flat along the wall to fumble with the room switch. I looked around but didn't think anything had been disturbed since I'd left.

When we were all inside the room, I recognized the junior cop as the young woman who'd been smart enough to call Uber when we'd found Sabrina. Officer Rockwell, her name badge told me.

"Place doesn't look like it was tossed," Everard said.

"It wasn't. Little things were out of place."

In my own apartment in Chicago, where I live in chronic disarray, I might not have been able to tell. It was only here, where I'd barely settled in, that the room was tidy enough to see that a suitcase had been moved.

With Everard right behind me, I walked around the dividing wall to the bed alcove and pulled my suitcase out, slowly. Before leaving with my bags, I'd tucked two hairs into the frame, one of Peppy's next to the lock, one of mine by the back hinge. Both were still in place.

The cops put on the requisite blue gloves and began searching. It didn't take long in the small space. Officer Rockwell found the garbage bin upside-down in the tub.

"What was that about?" Everard demanded.

"Bad smell," I said.

I sniffed the bin, gingerly. A reassuring scent of bleach. It was still wet inside so I put it back top-down in the bathtub.

When they'd inspected everything, including the inside of my suitcase, and the clothes I'd hung in the freestanding wardrobe, Everard frowned, looking around.

"What were you looking for, Sergeant?" I asked. "And who told you to come hunting whatever it is?"

"Those are two good questions. I can't answer them."

"Can't or won't?" I said.

He shook his head.

"Okay, I don't know what you were looking for, but I'm betting the helpful informant was the same upright citizen who told you that Trig Garrity and Gertrude Perec were at the Dundee house the night someone hid Clarina Coffin's body there."

He gave a reluctant nod. "I'm betting the same thing. I don't really believe you came down to Kansas on a murder-kidnap spree, but when the information is so specific, I have to follow up on it. Where were you between when you went out through the Perec garden and when you got back?"

"Murder-kidnap spree?" I said. "What—is Coffin's death connected to Sabrina's situation?"

"They were both found in the same space. I thought you were a detective—doesn't that suggest a connection to you?"

"Of course. But is there any evidence that Sabrina and Coffin knew each other?" I thought of my earlier conversation with Faye Mitchell. "When Sabrina was healthy, she traveled the world playing matches. Could she and Clarina Coffin have met somewhere? Maybe Coffin in her real identity was a scout for women's pro teams."

Officer Rockwell gave a snort of laughter, which quickly turned into coughing. I smiled at her. "You're right—unbelievable along every vector, including the idea that women's soccer pays well enough to hire undercover scouts."

"All very funny," Deke said drily. "Now that you've sidestepped the question long enough to come up with a good lie, where were you between six-thirty or so, when you disappeared into the Perec garden, and when I met you out front."

"I was hungry. I needed to eat. I found a place downtown that was mercifully free of basketball fans." I gave Everard the name.

I'd also doubled back to the park for the bag of food I'd abandoned. Lawrence had a food pantry close to the park; I'd walked over to it and left my contribution outside the door. That information I kept to myself: it detracts from a good deed to brag about it to the police.

I turned to Officer Rockwell. "We met the night I found Sabrina out at the Dundee house. Did you get a statement on record from the Uber driver who took her out there?"

Rockwell looked at Everard, who nodded; she could answer. They didn't have a formal statement, she said, but Rockwell had recorded the call.

"I want the Uber driver formally on the record

before the federal guy who's creeping after me like Captain Hook's alligator, or even your own DA, persuades them to change their story."

"But Uber has a record of the ride," Rockwell said.

"File scrubbing is a wonderful hobby these days. I would love to know that testimony is safe."

Deke sighed heavily, but gestured at Officer Rockwell. "Find the driver, take a formal statement. Tomorrow."

"Yes, boss."

"Thank you," I said, voice dry. "Another thing I'd like to know is who is pulling all these strings that make the LKPD dance to my side on a night when every officer has to be on duty downtown. Maybe as an outsider I'm a convenient fall gal, but if it were my investigation, I'd be searching for a puppet master."

Deke's eyes narrowed. He was a good enough cop to resent being told his job, but he was also a good enough cop to know I was right.

The silence built, until he finally said, "Warshawski, if you've been lying to me, the consequences will be serious."

I looked at him steadily. "Sergeant, I have not told you a single lie tonight. Officer Rockwell has her recording. You can consult it if your anonymous caller gives you any more tips about me."

I had withheld information, I had implied false information, but that is not the same as lying.

He seemed ready to leave, when he said casually— the kicker that cops like—"What was in the garbage bag you took out of Gertrude's bushes?"

I blinked but didn't blurt out, *what garbage bag, what bush.* Gertrude must have watched me from the kitchen window.

"I threw out all the food I'd bought yesterday. I didn't want to eat anything the intruders might have touched."

Loud roars rose in the distance. The game must be over. Deke glanced at his phone, but said, "And where is that food?"

"Outside one of your food pantries." I looked at my phone and gave him the address.

He frowned some more, weighing my story. It was too easy to check, though, unless someone had already been to the pantry and taken the bag.

"Okay, Rockwell, you and me are on our way to our favorite part of policing, breaking up bar fights. The Hawks won by nine, the town is exploding, like it's the first time it happened."

When they left, I did what everyone does these days instead of resting or looking for something to read. I checked my messages. Still nothing from Peter in Spain. A bitter ache in my chest, maybe near the heart.

I would not, could not, sink into fulmination or self-pity. I would think, and act. Someone had been keeping an eye on my comings and had called the cops when they saw I was home. A window in the apartment overlooked Ohio Street. I lifted an edge of one of the blind slats. Rockwell was just taking off, her roof lights spinning, but Deke was sitting in his car.

The neighbors immediately across from Gertrude had a few small bushes around the edges of their lawn, but you couldn't conceal yourself behind any of them. A bit farther south, though, a house had a wrought iron fence lining the sidewalk, with a thick evergreen hedge between the fence and the house. Perfect cover. As I watched, a glint of light appeared. A cell phone screen turning on. Someone else was keeping track of Deke in his unmarked car, or was it of me at my window?

I turned out the lights in the big room, left on a table lamp in the alcove by the bed, and slipped out the door. I went down the stairs on my butt so that my shape wasn't silhouetted by the streetlamps. Pressing myself against the side of the house, I walked away from the street until I reached the neighbor's yard, where a large bush shielded me. I crossed the street and made a wide loop to come on the neighbor's house from the side.

The cell phone light was still on. I moved slowly, looking for an opening in the bushes that would get me close to the peeper. A floodlight came on and a loud voice demanded to know what the hell we were doing in his front yard.

"You have ten seconds to leave before I shoot," he thundered.

The peeper sprinted along the edge of the shrubbery. I followed, almost up with him, when I tripped on a root and fell hard on my chest. Got up in time to see him head down Seventh Street. I followed. And ran into a crowd of celebrating Jayhawk fans.

My guy bulldozed through the crowd. I had my elbows out, following. Cut through the mob and saw him disappear around the side of the Lion's Heart.

The Jayhawk fans had filled the street, dancing, shouting, spraying unwary passersby with beer. I pushed my way through the crowd to the sidewalk and moved cautiously around the building. The Lion's Heart back door opened onto a municipal parking lot, as full of people as the streets. It would be impossible to figure out where my peeper had disappeared.

Cars were cruising New Hampshire Street, honking in celebration. A Carrera was in the mix, with a couple of guys leaning out the windows yelling, "Rock Chalk!" High on life? Or on China Girl or whatever the Jayhawk street name was for fentanyl.

I stood with my hands on my thighs, catching my breath while the cold air froze the sweat around my neck. Tomorrow I would definitely start running again.

I straightened up. And came face-to-face with Deke Everard.

24

Periodic Table of the Body

W hy didn't you phone or text me when you realized someone was watching your place?" Everard demanded.

We'd walked to the Perec house, a short seven blocks. I was shivering, rubbing my arms, slapping my chest. I'd come out wearing a hoodie, no coat, so I could move faster, but cold air and fatigue had depleted me.

"I don't know if someone from the Bureau or the DA's office is spying on me, but someone is feeding you information about everything I'm doing, almost before I do it. Punk lurking in the bushes, maybe videoing me—could have been a setup by you to see what I'd do when your back was turned. And that is what you did, right? You parked around the corner and saw the whole story unfold."

He stared at me, his face angry under the lamplight, but he didn't speak.

"The peeper disappeared around the corner from the Lion's Heart, into the crowd in that parking lot. My Omicron Delta Beta pals in the Carrera were joining in."

"Were you stupid enough to confront them?" Deke demanded.

"Neither stupid enough nor strong enough."

"Then stay the hell away from them. We have a drugs unit. They are conducting an undercover investigation into who's supplying the downtown bars. If you screw that up, I will be the person cuffing you and I will be happy doing it."

"You told me you couldn't do anything about the frat boys because they come under campus jurisdiction," I objected. "Now you conveniently have an undercover operation you can warn me away from?"

"It's on the QT. The DA brought in a team from Kansas City, in the hopes no one will recognize them. Chief told me this morning so I could keep you from derailing our work."

"Good to know, Sergeant. Outsiders can frame me, but I can't step on their delicate little toes. If Millay's driving around town, one thing is sure: oxy and meth and whatever will be flowing like lava from Mauna Loa. I best not keep you from keeping the peace."

He stared at me, hands on hips, a long menacing cop stare. "All right. Go up, go to bed. Stay there."

He waited until I'd started up the stairs to the apartment before turning around the corner to his car.

My head felt like a balloon, its string barely keeping it attached to my neck. My legs were lead. My body was like a periodic table, helium head, lead legs. The balloon bounced dizzyingly each time I dragged my leg up a step.

I had the key out, ready to work the lock, when someone grabbed my arm. My head crash-landed on my shoulders. Instinct, whirl, twist the arm around close to my body, dislocate the shoulder.

"Vic, don't!" she shrieked. "It's me, Zoë!"

I released her, fortunately before I'd hurt her.

"Why'd you do that?" she was aggrieved, rubbing her shoulder.

"You jumped me. When I'm investigating a murder I don't stop to ask for a business card." I unlocked the outer door, turned on the light and paused on the threshold to scan the room. It seemed free of intruders, except for Zoë, who followed me in.

Peppy greeted me with whimpers of joy, weaving around my legs. I knelt to fondle her.

Zoë gasped when she saw my face under the apartment lights. "What happened? Did someone attack you? Is that why you're so fierce right now?"

I moved to the bathroom and stared at myself in the mirror. I had mud on my face from where I'd tripped going after the peeper. I had a scratch on my right cheek, and a tear in the forearm of my hoodie.

I bathed my face, with Zoë standing in the doorway behind Peppy. I went to the kitchenette and filled the dishpan with hot water, set it by one of the straight-backed chairs, and took off my shoes so I could soak my sore, swollen feet.

"Who attacked you?" Zoë demanded.

"No one. I tripped and fell chasing a Peeping Tom. What are you doing here? You're not spending the night, you know, or even more than the next ten minutes."

"I saw on my scanner that cops were at the Perec place. I was covering a shooting in Eudora, and by the time I got back to Lawrence the cops were gone. Ms. Perec treated me like something she'd stepped in. Cady wasn't home. What was going on? I saw Deke was with you. Have you found Clarina's killer?"

"Not even close," I said.

Zoë had her phone out. When I realized she was taking pictures of my battle scars, I snatched the phone and deleted the shots. She protested hotly, but I stuck her phone into my back pocket.

"I can't be a sideshow for your paper, not at this point in the investigation. Someone is following me, someone is trying to frame Trig, or Gertrude, or me, or all of us. I need them to keep guessing on how much I know, and how much damage I've absorbed."

"I need my phone to record your comments. I promise not to take any more pictures."

"Zoë, please don't run a story about today's events. Take all the notes you want, but putting too much information out could help keep the bad guys ten steps ahead of me. Right now, it's only five or six."

She bunched up her mouth, thinking it over, but finally gave a reluctant nod. "If you give me back my phone so I can record what you say, I promise I won't use it until you've found the killer. Or for a week, whichever comes first."

"Fair enough. If I'm still floundering after a week, I'll probably risk the Douglas County DA's wrath and go home."

"Is that why Deke was here? Because someone was following you?"

"Deke was here because someone told him I had

something on the premises that the cops would like to see."

The sparkle returned to Zoë's eyes. "Don't tell me I can't print this! What was it?"

"I don't know. If Deke does, he didn't share the news."

"You're hiding something. I know you are," Zoë protested.

"I'm trying to hide my eyes behind their lids, and you're in the way." I put a hand on her shoulder and marched her to the door. I just remembered to lock it before falling into bed.

25

The Long View

I slept, but restlessly, my dreams filled with chaotic images, mostly of Trevor the frat boy breaking into the apartment and brandishing a wrench over my head. I ran from him and ended up in the playground of my old grammar school. Peter was there, roaring with laughter. "I'm not fat-shaming you, Warshawski, I'm crime-shaming you. Get it?"

I woke at five, my sleep shirt wet with sweat. I took a hot shower and lay back down, hoping for more sleep, but the dream had unearthed old memories. Neighborhood kids used to circle me chanting "Christ Killer" because of my Jewish mother. They thought it hysterically funny that I would fight even when they outnumbered me five to one or so. My parents tried to stop me, my mother because my torn clothes and bruises distressed her, my father because I was distressing my mother.

"And because fighting is the least helpful solution to any problem, Victoria," he added. "What are you learning from your battles?"

"That I need to get stronger," I'd replied.

"No, *carissima*, you need to get smarter," my mother said.

Days like today, I didn't think I'd accomplished either.

I sat up and looked at my social media. Trevor the frat boy had reported my return to Lawrence. *Cops are all over Warshawski. We're waiting for the arrest report.* A dozen or so responses—"hotshots from Chicago get what's coming to them" was the most repeatable.

I wrote to Peter, a stone thrown into an empty well, trying to explain what was going on. The FBI's Stamoran or even the LKPD could be reading my mail, so I had to phrase everything carefully. *What's going on in Spain?* I concluded.

What was I going to do about the wrench? The longer it stayed by the boatshed, the more likely the evidence would deteriorate. Animals could crawl into the bag, attracted by blood—if there was blood on it. Maybe someone had been messing with me. Why would they have hung on to the murder weapon, anyway?

I decided the best way to get it to the cops was to have it turn up near the Dundee house. But what if it wasn't the murder weapon? Someone could have planted a wrench with animal blood on it to distract me, and the cops, from what was really going on. Maybe it was my short night and a feverish brain, but before I risked life and limb putting it on the Dundee place, I would find out if it had been used in an assault on a person. On Clarina, for instance.

I leashed up Peppy and took her to the park near the library. She nosed around in the bushes while I did a full complement of stretches and squats. The advantage of bad sleep—it wasn't quite seven-thirty when I finished.

We walked to the side street where I'd left the Camry. I put Peppy inside and went for a slow run along the streets, checking every few blocks for pursuers on foot or car, or even bicycle. When I was pretty sure I was clean, I went into the post office. Bought an express mailer.

Now came the trickiest part. Resumed my run, headed down to the river path and the boathouse where I'd parked the trash bag last night. The bag seemed intact. I slid it between the folded leaves of the box in my pack. Walked back to the post office and addressed it to my account manager at Cheviot, the private forensics lab I use. The post office wouldn't mail it without a name and return address, so I chose a bland name, Susan Hall, and used the street address for the Lawrence police. If it was returned, they'd have it.

Eight-fifteen now. I left my phone at the Perec apartment, where its signal wouldn't betray my movements. Changed into business clothes so I'd be ready to meet with Faye and the DA. Drove to the Buy-Smart on the west end of town for a couple of burner phones, paying cash.

If Cheviot reported blood on the wrench, I wanted to leave it at the Dundee house so the police would know it was connected to Coffin's death. But I had to believe there were cameras somewhere around the house—otherwise, how had they photographed Gertrude and Trig the night before I found Clarina? Someone had devices that operated remotely so they could be turned off when the party animals wanted privacy. I needed to locate those.

Assuming that the DA would keep me only a few hours, I could go out there this afternoon. Unless I was in jail, of course.

I used one of the burners to call Lou and Ed, to see if they could babysit Peppy.

"The DA wants to depose me this morning. I can't

leave her cooped up in the car all morning, especially if he decides to arrest me. Cady might look after her if I left her in the apartment, but I'd feel more comfortable if I knew she was with friends."

"Tricky, Warshawski, can't have her in the yard, too much sharp metal. But we'll figure something out. You have time to drive out with her now?"

"I'm meeting my lawyer at the Hippo, supposedly at nine but I'll let her know I'm going to be late."

When we'd driven the ten miles to the hilltop farm, the men were in their work coveralls, getting ready to head to the yard. Peppy was ecstatic, jumping on them and racing in circles across the open land.

"She definitely needs to be in the country," Ed said, bending to fondle her ears. "What were you thinking, trying to coop her up in a bitty garage apartment, or worse yet, this old Camry?"

"You're right," I said. "You have a 747 I can borrow?"

The day was cold, with a biting wind sweeping across the hilltop, but the air was clear. I could see the silhouette of the tallest campus buildings on their own hilltop, but they were so remote they looked like a mirage, a mythical castle. Closer in, the river wound its way north of the town and made a loop before winding west. I watched toy trucks and cars move along the thin line of the interstate. A power plant belched a few puffs of gray-white smoke.

"The city uses coal power?" I asked.

"Yep," Ed said, but when he saw what I was looking at, he added, "Not that plant. That one—it was for Wakarusa. Hardly anyone lives out there anymore, and the ones that do buy their power from Lawrence. Thought that old dinosaur was going into mothballs. Owners had a different thought."

He and Lou exchanged glances, tight, annoyed.

"So what do you need to do that you can't risk the princess here?" Lou asked.

I shook my head. "I can't tell you, not without making you accessories, which would be a mean-spirited way of thanking you for your support."

"How about that?" Lou said. "She knows we like to accessorize. Most people see us in our work clothes and imagine that's how we always dress. She pictures us in earrings and what-do, but she thinks we'll tell all to Five-O."

I squatted next to Peppy. "Why are two Black men willing to risk prison or worse for lying under oath? They must know I'm in mud up to my eyeballs. Why do they want to join me there?"

Ed tried to squat on Peppy's other side, but his knees gave out and he landed on his butt. He clicked his fingers, and she turned to look at him. "Tell Ms. Know-It-All that we figured out a long time ago that we're Black men who run a junkyard, and therefore barely have the brains to tie our shoes."

Peppy licked his face, then turned and licked mine. I guess that made Ed and me spit siblings.

I told them about the pipe wrench, and Deke showing up uncomfortably quickly. "If the game hadn't drawn those big downtown crowds, he could have caught me red-handed."

"Someone doesn't like you," Ed said.

"Someone sees me as expendable. I don't think it's personal. I've sent the wrench to a lab I use outside Chicago, but if their analysis shows that it does have blood on it, I want to get the wrench onto the Dundee place.

"I need to scout the landscape first. From the time I found Sabrina Granev out on Yancy, I've been puzzled by how the cops got there so fast. They said a neighbor called in a disturbance to 911. And then, there's the photo of Gertrude Perec and Trig Garrity meeting on the Dundee kitchen doorstep—thanks, again, to a supposedly nosy neighbor. Yet there are no neighbors closer than a quarter mile.

"I don't know why it didn't occur to me earlier, but there must be cameras set up along the perimeter. I'm not dropping anything anywhere until I find out about the surveillance."

"You need help shinnying up a tree to look for them?" Lou asked.

"I figure I can park in the field I used before and come at the house from the back, but in case I run into trouble, I don't want Peppy with me."

Lou looked at me in disgust. "You are a moron, and that's a polite term for it. We'll keep the dog and you'll sashay around the property and then climb back in the car—which *we* are responsible for—and collect your dog?"

"She's crude, insensitive, but not a moron," Ed said. "That's harsh. She trusts us to babysit the princess, who is way more important than her, so it doesn't hurt that she won't ask us to drop her off and pick her up."

My face turned hot, but after arguing the point I was glad to concede. I would call them when I finished with Frank Karas, and they would collect me downtown.

26
Law and Justice

The deposition had its entertaining moments, especially because my attorney had been in law school with Frank Karas, the DA.

"Small communities," she said when we met over coffee. "We all rub up against each other. Frank has big ambitions, governor of Kansas, maybe, White House, maybe. Getting a Chicago felon behind bars would look good on his campaign literature. You have a reputation for mouthing off. Don't get cocky and we'll be okay."

"Right." I grimaced. "I always told my PD clients the two most dangerous emotions are anger and arrogance. Maybe you can mutter 'AA' if I'm getting off track."

"You'll be fine." She clapped me on the shoulder. "You know what you're doing."

We walked over to the Judicial and Law Enforcement Center. Inside the building, I put on a mask. None of the guards were wearing them and only a handful of the people putting their belongings on the security conveyor belts had them on. Mitchell nodded approvingly, putting one on herself.

She knew two of the guards by name and joked with them while we waited our turn to go through the body scanner. "You trying to disguise yourself, Faye, with that mask?" one of them joked. "People'll see those boots and know you in a second."

Like me, she'd dressed professionally for the meeting, but she was still wearing yesterday's high-heeled cowboy boots, black suede festooned with giant silver stars and crescent moons.

I let Faye handle all of the logistics, checking in with a clerk, what room we were in, how to find it. We were outside the door at 9:59, but Karas kept us waiting until almost eleven, to make sure I knew he was in charge of my life.

When he finally strode down the corridor, frowning, flanked by a clerk and the FBI's Cornell Stamoran, the sight of Faye and me in our masks drew him up short.

"Hey, Faye, no mask mandate in Douglas County, unless the libs in Topeka put one in place overnight."

"No worries, Frankie," she said. "My client. She's got medical sensitivities and can't be in a small room unless everyone is masked."

"It's Frank, and you don't set the rules in this court-house," Karas said.

"I know I don't, Frankie. Frank, I mean. And I don't want to inconvenience you at all. We can do this by Zoom. Just let us get back to an open space—"

"Remote is not a good option," Karas said.

"Of course not, Frankie. Frank, sorry! But if that's the quickest way to get this over, let's do it."

Stamoran tried to insert himself into the argument, but Karas was smart enough to know he wasn't going to win this fight. The clerk on his team went downstairs to find masks. While she was gone, Faye commented chirpily on the weather. Karas ignored her, scrolling through his phone.

When we finally settled around the table, the mood at the prosecution end was not cordial. We went through the usual preliminaries, me spelling my full name—including "Iphigenia"—and various other demographics.

Over our morning coffee, Faye and I had worked out the best way to answer the predictable questions, about why I was in Kansas, and how I'd come to be involved in Sabrina Granev's disappearance. Keep it short, no long explanations about Angela's basketball career or Bernie's pleading.

Karas probed into my career, into occasions where I might have been considered reckless. Why had I insisted on confronting Earl Smeissen or George Dornick or Robert Baladine?

"I acted in a way to protect the lives of the people around me, as well as my own." We went through about a dozen of my cases, including one where Mr. Contreras had taken a bullet. I curbed my impatience. They wanted to goad me into a misstep, and I could not misstep.

We finally got to the events of February 14–15 of this year.

Karas's main focus was on how I discovered the Dundee house, and how I'd persuaded Sabrina to go there.

"I don't understand the question, Mr. Karas," I said.

"It's simple: How did you persuade Sabrina Granev to accompany you to the Dundee house?"

"I still don't understand."

We went back and forth, until he finally broke it down into when did I talk to Sabrina?

When I found her in the Dundee house at midnight Monday night.

When had I talked to her previously?

I had said hello to her at dinner Sunday night.

What else?

Only hello.

Did you talk her into going to the Dundee house?

No.

Did you drive her or hire someone to drive her to the Dundee house?

No.

He wanted to ask about my drug use, and we went through a similar rigmarole where he finally had to break the query down into small pieces.

"Trevor Millay says he saw you ingest drugs at the Omicron Delta Beta garage."

He is mistaken.

We went through that three or four times, until Faye interrupted. "My client passed a drug test. Her car has been inspected, her home in Chicago has been inspected—"

I thought of the chaos I'd come home to last week, but I kept a tight clamp on my anger.

"No drugs have been found in her possession. Get over it, Frankie, I mean, Frank."

We were about an hour into the interrogation when a white man came into the conference room. He was wearing the kind of suit Armani cuts for you on Via

Monte Napoleone out of a fabric that is never seen in retail stores. The Armani man looked vaguely familiar, but I couldn't place him. I looked at Faye, but she shook her head slightly.

Stamoran scribbled something on his yellow pad and Karas nodded. When we got to the end of questions on the Dundee house—how had I known where it was, how had I known Sabrina was there, hadn't I really been searching for drugs?—the stranger shook his head, not happy with the proceedings. He beckoned to Agent Stamoran, and the two of them left the conference room.

Frank announced a short break and followed the others out to the hall. His clerk stayed behind to make sure we didn't read any of the prosecution papers.

Faye cocked an eyebrow at me. We went into the hall, where the DA was huddled with the Armani man and Agent Stamoran. They stopped speaking when they saw us. Armani man clapped Frank on the shoulder, said he'd call him later, and headed for the elevators.

Faye muttered at me to stay put and went over to speak to Karas. I began a series of wall push-ups, my back to the trio. I heard her murmuring with Stamoran and Karas, but I focused on my workout. I'd reached thirty-seven when Faye tapped my shoulder.

"Looks like the wall's in good shape, Warshawski—you haven't even made a dent in it. We're done here, right, Frankie? Sorry, Frank."

I turned around. Stamoran was on his way to the elevator. Karas said he guessed they had all they needed today, but he reserved the right to call me back if more questions arose.

"You do that, Frankie," Faye said. "The truth is a beautiful thing and we're happy to show you enough examples of it to make you realize when you're looking at the stupefying ugliness of your buddies' lies."

27

Power Ranger

Faye didn't know who the Armani man was. Since we'd had to leave our phones in a lockbox during the deposition, neither of us had been able to photograph him.

"Frank is not happy; he's going to be looking for you to violate laws and ordinances. Please do not go one mile over the speed limit while you're in Douglas County," she urged me.

"Absolutely," I promised fervently, even though I was already planning my next infraction, trespassing on the land behind the Dundee house.

I phoned the scrapyard. Lou said Ed was tied up, but he would meet me behind the public library in an hour.

I wandered downtown. The streets were still full of the detritus of the night before—beer cans, whisky bottles, Styrofoam. A couple of homeless people were picking through the remains, sucking the last mouthfuls from cans and bottles. Someone had abandoned a full head mask of the ever-present Jayhawk on a bench. It looked tawdry next to the cigarette butts and half-eaten meals.

I started visiting souvenir shops. The third place I came to had a head mask. When Lou and Peppy picked me up, I was sporting a Jayhawk hoodie. I waited until we were on the road south before putting on the head-dress.

"You know how stupid that makes you look?" Lou said.

"It also makes me look anonymous. Just one more idiot trying to recover from last night's victory dance."

He dropped me at a crossroads half a mile from the Dundee house. "You find yourself up the proverbial creek, signal us ASAP," Lou said.

I typed "Help" into a text box, ready to send if need be. Lou said he would circle back every half hour or so. To avoid possible cameras, he wouldn't stop at the Dundee place, but would wait five minutes by the nearest crossroads.

I left the road and walked up the hill to a stand of

trees that separated a plowed field from the under-brush surrounding the house. I walked in their shadow until I was about two hundred yards behind the house, then headed into the thicker shrubs and trees that I'd encountered ten days ago.

The trees were bare of leaves, which meant I couldn't get too close to the house without being seen if someone was inside. I paused behind a brake of thorny bushes. The back of the house looked sullen, hostile, as if it resented any human approach. I skirted the property, crouching behind the undergrowth. I spotted a camera over the kitchen door, angled to photograph faces at the door. Another was mounted high in a tree at the mouth of the driveway, two more facing the house, attached to trees at the edge of the woods I'd just walked through.

Someone, somewhere, watched activity at the Dundee place on their screens. It wouldn't be Brett Santich. He was out and about in the world, without the leisure to monitor activity at a drug house—assuming he was as involved in the operation as Trig insisted. I liked to think it was the Omicron boys, laughing in their frat house over how clever they were to frame me, or Trig, but I didn't see them doing grunt work—they were in this for kicks. They'd graduate and move on to hedge funds, legally sanctioned larceny.

Santich or whoever was running the Dundee house

parties was probably using local muscle. I wondered if that included the man with the gun who'd threatened me on top of Yancy. The construction site up there would be a convenient place to house surveillance monitors. Santich had been in a heated conversation with the gunman. Maybe he'd been using the Dundee place without Santich's knowledge.

I'd seen all I needed. Time to slide away. If Cheviot labs confirmed human blood and/or hair on the wrench, it shouldn't be too hard to place it near the house.

As I started to retrace my steps, a dusty SUV pulled into the drive and a man got out. With my bright red-and-blue Jayhawk head I was easy to spot inside the stand of trees. I dropped to the ground, pulled the headdress off, and tucked it under me. Lay completely still, heart pounding thick in my throat. Had I overlooked a camera? Had someone spotted me on a computer and come to tackle me? The dead leaves tickled my sinuses. Don't sneeze, you mustn't sneeze.

I turned my head slowly, just enough to see what the man was doing. He was turned away from me, watching the drive, so I couldn't see his face, but he was obviously looking at his wrist, checking the time. He pulled a phone from his hip pocket, stared at it, put it away again.

He turned his head in my direction. Brett Santich. I

listened as hard as I could, worrying whether the hard hat from the construction site was coming down behind me, but Santich turned back, watching the road.

The ground was cold and I was getting a cramp in my left thigh. No you don't, I warned my body. Everyone behaves well right now, including you, tight muscles.

Perhaps ten minutes passed. Santich took his phone out again, but put it away when a black Range Rover roared up the drive, potholes negligible to a beast designed to cross the Serengeti.

A white man climbed out. I was so astonished I almost cried out: it was the Armani man from this morning's deposition. He'd shed his suit for outdoor clothes, buckskin jacket, jeans, cowboy boots, but they, too, had been cut for him by hand. He strode over to Santich and began a heated exchange.

I inched my phone from my hip pocket up to my face, careful not to lift face or arm. Took pictures that I hoped included the stranger, since I couldn't afford to peer at the viewfinder.

The pair argued for some minutes, then went inside. I didn't risk getting up even then—if they looked out the back windows I'd be too visible. When I was so frozen I thought I'd risk sliding backward into the woods, they came out. Santich took off at once with a great roaring of engine: he'd been chewed out and was taking it out on his machine.

The stranger climbed into his Range Rover, where he sat with the engine running for several more minutes. The tinted windows made it impossible to tell what he was doing.

My phone had been dinging. I cautiously moved my arm down and looked at the screen, keeping my head flat to the ground. Lou, wanting to know where I was. I phoned, since I could keep my head down while I spoke. I explained that I'd been pinned behind the house.

"I thought that was Santich scooting past in his dirty Kia," Lou said. "When the other dude leaves, call me—we'll come for you."

I warned him about the cameras, then lay still for another long while. Finally, the Armani man kicked his Rover in the ribs and galloped down the rocky drive.

I sat up, massaging my thighs until enough blood was flowing that I could get to my feet. I stuffed the Jayhawk head into my jacket pocket and hobbled through the woods on the fringe of the property to the road. Lou was waiting near the mouth of the drive, away from the camera.

I stumbled trying to gain a foothold on the running board. Peppy was in the front seat. She grudgingly moved enough to let me in, but rested her head on Lou's lap.

"You are one fickle dog," I told her. "I'm the one who's been out in the cold and could use a warm puppy."

Lou grunted. "You look a mess, Warshawski. Even so, I prefer the leaves and mud and so on to that fright you had on your head going in."

"It's a Jayhawk," I said. "You're local; you must know they are sacred to the town of Lawrence. Come to think of it, I haven't seen one at your place, either the yard or the house. You and Ed must have to pay some kind of steep fine."

He flashed one of his rare smiles. "It's why we live so far outside of town. What'd you learn, besides where the cameras are?"

"More questions than answers." I described Brett's and the Armani man's interaction. "I'll have to look up the sale of the land to the consortium that's building the resort. Maybe Brett held the house back for sentimental reasons, or because he was making a bundle from his cut of the drug parties."

"You say it looked as though Armani was chewing out Santich," Lou reminded me. "Might have something to do with that pipe wrench. Maybe the Range Rover was the brains behind putting you in the frame, except you slithered out.

"Could be nothing to do with the Coffin woman's death at all, some fight over land or business that has nothing to do with her. You can't rely on Trig's version—dude chases so many shadows he can't tell what's real anymore.

"Santich, for instance. Trig calls him a billionaire, but Ed and I, we deal with him strictly on a cash up-front basis. Too many bills he's ducked out on. Santich hasn't been smart about his land. That's how he lost it to this resort company. He works part-time for an insurance agency in the town, and it's not because he loves the work."

I digested that. "It's a strange site for a resort. When I went to look at it, they'd poured foundation for some smallish structures, so it's hard to know what the end product would look like."

"They let you onto the property? They act like it's so secret their left hands don't know what the left fingers are doing."

"They didn't let me on. I was exploring the area, wondering if the hilltop might house a drug lab or something. A guy with a big weapon chased me away—making sure I saw the weapon. Santich was in the middle of an argument with him when I arrived. That seems to be my cue in this play—Santich fighting with someone and I stumble on the fracas but can't figure out what's going on. I saw him at the field house my first night here, you know, fighting with Cady, with one of the basketball moms and then with Trig."

Lou laughed, but said, "There's so much money in drugs, I wonder if the resort is a cover for building an opioid factory."

"They've put up one pylon and were building the tower for a second," I said. "It didn't register with me at the time, but a resort wouldn't need a grid, just the usual utility poles. How much power does it take to run a fentanyl factory?"

"So that's it," Lou said slowly. "That's who wants that old power plant back online. The one you asked about this morning. That Range Rover that you'd been waiting on, I know it, at least, saw it one time before it sprayed me with gravel just now."

He drummed his fingers on the steering wheel. "No reason not to tell you, I guess. Just that it still rankles."

He paused again.

"Ed and me, we've got plenty of contacts in the valley, we've been in business thirty-plus years, so we heard when the old Wakarusa power company decided to mothball the plant. Made an appointment with the manager, Clete Rotherhaite, to look it over, see what salvage we could handle.

"We arrived on time, but your Range Rover drove

up before we'd done more than shake hands with Clete. Another SUV pulls in behind him—big old Lexus. Suit gets out of the Lexus, Power Ranger steps out of the Rover, cowboy boots, takes off a Stetson and puts on a hard hat, new, YANCY HILL on it in black. The Ranger asks what we're doing. 'After you,' Ed says. 'We're talking to Clete here.'

"Clete says we operate a scrap metal yard, but doesn't say who the Power Ranger is. Before we can ask, the Ranger says, 'Boys, don't go taking apart the turbines. There's life in this old girl.' Suit laughs, like he's the chorus."

Lou's hands on the steering wheel were steady, but his throat worked. "'Boys.' He saw our truck and talked to us like—well, we've swallowed worse. He wouldn't give his name, although we asked. Just said, 'Meeting's over, boys.'

"Clete didn't say shit. Stood there looking like a scarecrow in a minefield. We'd been knowing him a lot of years, so we called when we got back to the yard. We wanted to know what in sweet fanny's name was going on. He didn't answer, didn't call back. We tried the next day, and the same nonanswer. We were getting to be spitting mad, wondered if we should talk to a lawyer—that plant had been promised to us, but not in writing, so we decided to let it lay."

He shook his head. "His wife called us maybe a week after that. She said something in Clete's meeting with the Ranger upset him, made him feel he couldn't work the plant anymore. That same day we'd gone out there, he called her to tell her he was resigning, that he'd explain it all when he got home. Only he never got home. Went for a walk along the river to cool off, she reckoned, and fell down dead."

"That must have been a shock," I said.

"Doc told her his heart must've given up on him, anger and stress and so on."

"A heart attack? Was she surprised?"

"What are you?" Lou said, irritated. "A damned ghoul? Not everyone who dies in Kansas has been murdered."

"No, of course not," I agreed. "It just seems like such a convenient coincidence."

We'd reached town while we'd been talking. When Lou pulled the truck up in front of the Perec garage, I took out my phone and opened it to the photos I'd taken earlier.

"Yeah," Lou said. "That's the guy, the Ranger. You can kind of hear him. Turn up the sound."

I'd been shooting blind and had hit the video button. The mike had better ears than me. We got words, interspersed with bird calls and rustling leaves.

The Ranger was angry. "Goddamn idiot! . . . now cops . . . Dad . . ."

Santich, also angry ". . . your sister . . . she wanted . . ."

Ranger. "always resent . . . told Dad . . . bitch the whole deal . . ."

A minute where I couldn't make out any words, then Santich, fed up, "to investigate my house?"

Ranger laughs. ". . . freezing my nuts off."

That was when they went inside.

Lou and I listened to it several times, but that was the best we could make out. "Ranger has a sister who could bitch the whole deal, whatever the whole deal is" was his best guess.

"And a dad who's still in the picture. I don't suppose the suit in the Lexus could have been Dad?"

Lou shook his head. "About the same age as the Ranger. . . . About your other matter. Now you've seen the cameras, how are you going to get your, uh, accessory onto the Dundee place? Wouldn't it be easier to drop it at the cop shop?"

"Only if I want to be arrested. Besides, I want the cops to tie it to the crime scene. There are two camera problems—the ones the town has strewn around checking on traffic, and the ones at the Dundee house. If I could find a boat, canoe, something to get me across the river to the north side, then I could go upriver—it winds around Yancy Hill. I could go from there cross-country—"

"That Jayhawk helmet boiled your brain, Warshawski. The Kaw may look mild but it has a strong current. You some kind of wilderness genius?"

"I have rowed a boat," I said with dignity.

"In the dark on a strange river going to a strange place? Get a grip."

I climbed down from the cab and persuaded Peppy to join me. "Unless you'd rather stay in Kansas, roam those wide-open spaces?" I said to her.

"She's a smart girl," Lou said, when the dog finally jumped down. "Be better for her than some city apartment." He gave two quick beeps on his horn and drove off.

I was starting to build a long to-do list, but the first thing on it was a bath and a nap. I was cautious going up the stairs to the apartment, but no one was waiting for us. Whatever the Ranger and Santich had agreed on this morning hadn't led to any attacks that I could see. Nothing was hidden in the kitchen garbage or under the bed.

I leaned back in Gertrude's tub. It was small, to fit into the small nook created for the bathroom, but I still soaked for a good twenty minutes, drifting, ignoring my phone dinging to tell me people were texting.

When I got out of the tub, I called Deke Everard.

"What is it, Warshawski?" He was brusque.

"Something puzzling, Sergeant. I was out at the Dundee house today—"

"Doing what?" he snapped. "That is a crime scene—"

"Which I respected. I was curious about the cameras out there." I paused, to give him a chance to say, oh, we know all about them. When he didn't, I explained my theory, cameras that someone operated remotely.

"I found them placed in trees around the property. Great blackmail opportunity for someone hard up for money, as we know Brett Santich is."

"*We* does not include me. Get to your point, if you have one."

"Brett was there. He didn't see me, but he did see a guy in a Range Rover, dressed like a cowboy-wannabe, who was chewing him out. Same Range Rover showed up at the Wakarusa Coal Plant the day Clete Rotherhaite died."

Deke was breathing heavily. "Now you're going to tell me some guy who can afford a Range Rover killed Clete."

"Just questioning why the same rich-looking man is interested in the coal plant and the drug house."

"You keep wondering, but don't bother me. Unlike

a private detective, I can't waste my time investigating imaginary crimes."

He hung up. I'd been going to share my scratchy video of the two men, but he'd forfeited that opportunity. Anyway, maybe he was right. Maybe Armani man meeting with Santich had nothing to do with Clarina's murder.

28

Illuminators and Bookbinders

Zoë called. She told me my pals at Omicron were insinuating that I was committing murders and dealing drugs all over Douglas County. Did I have a comment?

"I wonder if that's what Trevor Millay's mother thought when she first saw his entitled screaming face: I hope my baby grows up to be the biggest troll under the bridge," I mused. "I don't have anything to say about the frat brat's libel. But one question I'm wondering about: it looks like this resort is going to be a mega-power user. They're putting up huge pylons, and they may be getting ready to bring the old Wakarusa coal plant back on stream. The plant foreman, Clete Rotherhaite, died a few weeks ago, supposedly of a heart attack. Can you sniff around that?"

"You think he was murdered?" Unlike Lou or Deke, she was excited by the suggestion. More big stories.

"Stranger things have happened."

"What will you be doing?" she said, suddenly suspicious. "Something more exciting that you're hogging?"

"This afternoon, I will be working for my Chicago clients, the ones who pay me," I said with as much emphasis as possible. "Tomorrow I am driving to Topeka, to visit the Kansas Origins Museum and Library. I want to see what light they can shed on the three photos I found in Clarina's trailer. Does either of those rouse your journalist curiosity to a fever pitch?"

She laughed and hung up. I actually did buckle down to some paying work, and finished two projects for my real clients. I went to bed in a glow of virtue.

In the morning, I drove to the Origins Museum, a Romanesque monster with a glass extension tacked awkwardly onto the back. A helpful guard directed me to Abby Langford, a tall brisk woman, perhaps in her fifties, who was working the reference desk.

I explained that I was trying to identify some pictures but I knew nothing about where or when they'd been taken. "I'm a private investigator, and I feel it's akin to someone asking me to find a missing person whose name or age they don't know."

"Let's see them. I'm betting they're a little more re-velatory than you think," Langford said.

I'd stopped at an office supply store for some file folders. I opened these on the counter for Langford's inspection. When she saw the scene at the railway station, her eyes widened.

"Where did you get these?" she demanded.

I told her how I'd found them in Clarina Coffin's trailer. "I was third in line, behind the cops and who-ever tore her home apart. Coffin was murdered—"

"I know." Langford cut me off. "I read about it. I knew her, and so the news—"

"You knew her?" I interrupted in turn. "Do you know her real name, then, or what she was doing in Lawrence?"

"So it wasn't her real name," Langford said. "I won-dered about it, but she had a state ID; she had a right to use the collection. That's where these two photos come from."

She tapped the two reproductions. "Clarina said she was writing a history of the Lawrence area during the years immediately after the Civil War, and I helped her find contemporary newspapers from that era. This one"—the railway station scene—"was a fight between some Black families who were leaving Lawrence and white townspeople."

I wondered if she remembered all her patrons so clearly.

She made a face. "I'm afraid Clarina was the kind of person that we took turns avoiding. She was like the Ancient Mariner, telling you more than you ever hoped to know about what she was working on. She claimed she was going to rewrite Kansas history to refute the story of Free State heroism."

"She supported slavery?" I was astonished.

"Not at all. She was zealous about racial justice. She boasted she was going to show up the Kansas elites who didn't share her insights. I shouldn't be speaking of her this way, now that she's been killed, poor soul, but when I read about her murder, I wondered if she'd pushed too hard on a descendant of one of Lawrence's revered founders."

I thought again of Gertrude Perec and her annoyance with Clarina. Gertrude's story about the night before I found Clarina's body sounded bogus—she'd gone to the Dundee house in response to what she thought was an SOS from a friend. Maybe she'd gone there to confront Clarina in secret and had bonked her with a wrench—one lecture too many on the evils the abolitionists had committed.

According to Deke Everard, his mother and Gertrude were tight. Gertrude saw she'd killed Clarina and called Pat Everard. The two dragged Clarina down the stairs to the basement. Possible but improbable.

I asked the librarian if she could find the original news story where the railway fight occurred. She explained that librarians were honor-bound to protect the privacy of their patrons. "This means we don't keep a record of what anyone looks at. I know I can find the story, but it'll take me a little bit to track it down."

She took my phone number; she would text me when she had an answer. I set up shop in the reading room with my laptop and worked on my own caseload. I kept checking my messages, hoping against hope that Peter would get back to me, but only Zoë, Cady, and Murray wanted me. I let them ride.

I'd brought Peppy with me, since I was uneasy about leaving her alone in the Perec garage, with skilled B & E people planting weapons on me. Around eleven, I took Peppy for a walk around the museum.

Abby Langford texted me as I was putting Peppy back in the car. With a look of justifiable triumph, when I returned to her station she handed me a print-out of a newspaper story about the fight at the station.

"I couldn't trace the burned building. In the 1850s and '60s, the Missouri scallywags, as they were called, often came into Kansas, especially to Lawrence, to burn and murder, so it would be hard to pinpoint exactly when this building was torched or what it had been originally."

She hesitated. "The photo of the woman, the one that's an original, would you be willing to entrust it to me for a day or two? I want to see if our conservator can bring up the detail more clearly."

"Is there something in it?"

Langford smiled. "I don't know; the print is too faded to be sure of anything. But the conservators work miracles."

"You must have seen something," I urged.

She shook her head. "It's a shadow. I'm not going to build a picture out of a shadow."

Maybe there'd be a faded message from the picture's subject, telling her name and her connection to the abolitionists of Kansas. A ghost message, directed at her unborn great-great-granddaughter, telling her to head to Lawrence.

"Did Clarina ever say anything to you about where she was from?" I asked. "Someone in Lawrence who met her a few times said she came from a town whose name was used to fat-shame her."

"The town's name was used? What does that mean?" Langford said. "The town was called Fat City and she belonged there because she was fat?"

"I don't know," I said. "I was hoping she'd dropped a more useful hint in something she said to you."

Langford shook her head. "She was full of what she

knew and what she could do, including this story"—
she pointed at the printout she'd given me. "But she
never talked to me about her own life."

Maybe Coffin had been a fugitive from justice. She
was far too young to be a 1960s radical on the run, and I
couldn't see her as a January 6 insurrectionist, not with
her insistence on teaching race history. Perhaps she was
in a witness protection program, but that didn't make
sense, either: federal marshals would have descended
on Lawrence as soon as her murder was publicized.

"I hope your conservator can work quickly. The
longer we go without a lead on her identity, the harder
it will be to find her killers."

On my way out of the building, I passed a wall filled
with tribute plaques, listing the people who had supported the library financially. They were divided into
categories based on size of donation, with fanciful titles
from the medieval manuscript tradition.

Top donors, who gave north of a quarter million,
were Illuminators, followed by Scribes, Calligraphers, and Bookbinders. There were three Illuminators, Matthew, Robert, and Pauline Tulloh, another
six Calligraphers, who'd given a hundred thousand
or more. As the donations got smaller the numbers of
donors increased. There were a lot of them; this was a
well-loved museum.

29
Among the Dead Bones

From the *Kanwaka Courier*, June 21, 1867

While we join with Rev. Hamer in offering prayers and condolences to Amelia Grellier, we deplore the recklessness that led inexorably to the death of her husband, Frederic. Many in our community spoke to him of the unwisdom in running a school for members of the Negro race. They are savages, unable to benefit from the kind of learning Mr. Grellier sought to instill in them. He even taught them to speak his native French language, which made them hold themselves above the white people in town, as if speaking the language of an effete and debauched nation could do anything other than increase debauchery among the savages!

Now we see the result of all this imprudence, to use the tamest word. His school has burned to the ground, taking his life with it. His widow grieving, his daughter—we will not further harrow the mother's feelings by referencing the daughter!

And the remaining Negroes who rose above their station by going to that school showed their true nature last night, in scenes of the vilest destruction at the train depot. They fought with officers of the law who were escorting them to the train, assaulted the respectable of the town who came to make sure they departed, and even smashed their own furniture in their efforts to use tables and chairs as weapons against the custodians of law and order.

We hear that Mrs. Grellier is returning to her people in Skaneateles in New York State and hope she can persuade her daughter to accompany her. Sophia Grellier living on her own is an affront to every decent family.

The article included the photo of the train station I'd found in Clarina's trailer.

I read the story at the table in the Perec apartment. The language was like a thin icing over a cake made of worms and fecal matter. I had to sit with it for a long time before I started thinking about the questions it raised.

The first was the easiest: the Grellier name. If Clarina had searched out this article, maybe she was related to Frederic Grellier. I found a number of Groellers and a handful of Grelliers, but none of them matched Clarina's age or sex. None lived in Kansas.

I tried to dig into the Grellier history in Lawrence, but aside from the newspaper account of the school's burning, the only other mention I found was of baby Charles. An 1886 history of the town mentioned his having been the first burial in the new town. He'd died in 1855, aged three days, as his family was traveling from Kansas City to Lawrence, part of a convoy of antislavery emigrants.

Perec was Gertrude's married name, but it was French. I called Cady and asked if she could come up for a few minutes.

I took her over to the table and handed her the printout. "I found this going through some of Clarina's things. I know she was harassing you about the history you wanted to teach—did she show you this article?"

Cady took it reluctantly, looked at it, and nodded. "She was showing this to a lot of people, even to Gram at the women's breakfast she bullied her way into. What does it have to do with her death?"

"What do you know about the Grellier family?" I asked.

"Nothing! I never heard of them until Clarina tried to stuff this article down my throat."

"Your grandmother is descended from the original settlers, isn't she? Since 'Perec' is a French name, I thought perhaps she knows the history of other French abolitionists who came out in the 1850s."

"Her ever-so-greats did come before the Civil War, at least some of them," Cady agreed. "But her husband was the Perec. Gram's family were English to the core on both sides and proud of it. She thought she was a rebel marrying a Frenchman. Although he wasn't French, of course, by the time they got married."

"And she never talked about his family?"

"Not much," Cady clipped off the words as if they were toenails.

"Your grandmother's so proud of her ancestry, she surely told you family lore," I persisted.

"Meaning what?"

"Meaning big events, fires like this, or fights at the train station, they get handed down with the story of what the ancestor was doing at the time. The day Germany invaded Poland, my grandmother's father was trying to get his cow out of the neighbor's pumpkin patch. He stopped with his hand on her horn. My grandmother said he repeated the story a thousand times.

"I'm sure your granny told you a thousand stories about Lawrence history and what your family was doing at key moments."

Cady stood motionless for a moment, her eyes big in her pale strained face. "Whatever Gram's people did, or didn't do, that was a long time ago," she finally said.

She turned on her heel and fled the room.

When I heard her reach the bottom of the stairs I leashed Peppy up again. "We're going grave hunting, girl. I bet there are rabbits."

The dog grinned: "rabbit" is one of the human words she responds to. She scampered down the outside stairs and ran in circles around me while I looked up the cemetery location. The oldest cemetery in town, historic, was on the east edge, entrance on Fifteenth Street. The same route I'd followed to Eudora to beard Trig at the recycling plant.

Clouds were moving in when I found the Grellier plot. The thin stone grave markers were so weathered the names were hard to read, but I rubbed dirt away with my fingers and saw a heart-breaking array, six children, the youngest the three-day-old Charles, the oldest only nine. Placed behind them, like a sentinel, a bas relief of the Liberty Bell dedicated to Frederic. Born in Chambon-sur-ligon France, July 17, 1820, died Lawrence, Kansas, June 13, 1867, followed by the Liberty Bell motto: *Proclaim liberty throughout the land and unto all the inhabitants thereof.*

Amelia had returned to her home in New York state. Sophia, the daughter whose life was an insult to the decent people of Lawrence, wasn't buried with her siblings. Maybe she had followed the urgings of the *Kanwaka Courier* and joined her mother in New York.

Peppy had been running around among the graves, hunting rabbits, chipmunks, squirrels, but fortunately coming up empty. I called her to heel and drove back into town.

I had neglected the issue of who owned the Dundee house. The county building was open for another half hour. I found the recorder of deeds office and presented the Dundee address.

I apologized for not knowing the plat identifiers, but the clerk shook her head. "You're about the fourth person checking on that place. I can find that volume in the dark."

She brought out the large plat volume and opened it to the Dundee house. The adjacent lands on Yancy Hill were on the neighboring pages. The first registered title to the land had been in 1870 to a Theodore Wheelock. He claimed the land that the house sat on, and the wooded land behind it leading up to the top of Yancy Hill. The houses in the woods weren't men-

tioned. Maybe they'd already collapsed before Wheelock claimed the land.

Over the next three decades, Wheelock sold off
chunks of the property to other people. These days the
only part of the land still in Wheelock hands was one of
the fields near the house. The house and one adjacent
quarter-section between the woods and E. 1450 Road
were owned by Brett Santich. The rest of the land going
up the hill were now owned by a trust managed out of
the Pioneer State Bank and Trust.

The entries were written in a flowing copperplate
on parchment, which moved stiffly. I carefully turned
the pages back to the beginning of the book. The first
entries were in 1861, after Kansas achieved statehood.
They were for houses and businesses in the part of
town where Gertrude Perec lived.

The pages seemed to have been cut by hand. The
first page, in particular, had a rough jagged top, as if
the original clerk hadn't been able to hold the scissors
steady.

I returned to the Yancy lands. Theodore Wheelock sold off sections of them to other people. I traced
the history forward as best I could. In the 1870s, after
Wheelock made his claim, he sold or gave parcels of
land to other owners, including the Everards. The
Everards still had a little land there, but the Wheelock

fortunes had sunk in the 1930s, during the Great Depression.

That was when the Santich family acquired the hilltop and several thousand acres along the sides of the hill. The Santiches had prospered for a time, but fell in turn. I read a history of mortgages, sales, refinancing, and, finally, six years ago the selling of the top of the hill to a hedge fund managed by Pioneer State Bank and Trust in Topeka.

The clerk came over to the table I was using to tell me she was closing the office for the day. If I needed to consult the book further, they opened at nine in the morning.

I thanked her and got up to go. "One thing that puzzles me. The Dundee house—you probably saw it on the news—I guess that was built after Theodore Wheelock bought the land, but there are the remains of three or maybe four houses in the woods behind the house."

I showed her the plat and the woods where I'd found the remains of the chimneys. "The title starts with Wheelock, but it looks as if someone was building there before him. The drug house out there is called the Dundee place, but I don't see a Dundee anywhere in the title holders."

The clerk laughed. "This was the wild west back

then. People built on land they didn't legally own. Dundee could have been one of those—he left, but the name stayed. There were a lot of land disputes in the early days of the town. Some people think my job is boring, but when I look at some of the title fights that went on, it's every bit as exciting as CSI. If I could write, I'd do a murder mystery out of these files."

I thanked her and headed into the night. It was almost five-thirty, not late, but dark. This time of year, waiting for spring, the early hours when night closes in drag down the spirits.

The library stayed open until eight. I left Peppy in the Camry while I did some deeper digging through local history and genealogy files. These were housed in the basement, in the Osma Room. I hunted through their catalog, looking for more on the fire that claimed Frederic Grellier's life. I couldn't find anything. I looked for the Wheelocks and found a number of small stories. They'd been early immigrants, coming from Auburn, a town in western New York State. When Theodore Wheelock died in 1897, the paper gave him a long obituary, with a list of his contributions to Lawrence, and the names of his numerous children and grandchildren.

The funeral had been held at Riverside Congregational Church, newly built on a bluff overlooking the river. The original church (oldest in Lawrence, the paper announced) had sat right on the river and been destroyed in a flood. Theodore had been one of the most important donors to the new building. The writer dwelt on his bravery in leaving a comfortable home in western New York State to serve the cause of those in bondage, especially because his family claimed descent from the earliest English immigrants to Massachusetts Bay.

The obituary also praised Theodore for beginning the "civilization and cultivation of Yancy Hill, which had, until his leadership, been a lawless wound on the body politic, home to Indians, coloreds, and every variety of sin and debauchery."

I thought of the remnants of the chimneys I'd seen in my first daylight trip to Yancy. Maybe they'd belonged to people committing sin and debauchery. Had he driven them away and destroyed their buildings? Or had they been so thoroughly debauched that they burned their own houses down around themselves?

I looked up the Everards, Deke's family. They were early immigrants as well, from Lynn, a town near Boston. Like the Wheelocks, their stature as early arrivals meant the papers covered their weddings and funerals, and even Deke Everard's graduation from the police academy eleven years ago.

What would it feel like to be so rooted in a place that everyone knew your family and your family's family, going back 175 years? I had no idea what the Warshawskis were doing in 1856, or even if they'd been doing it in Słonim, the town my grandparents had emigrated from. And the Sestieris, my mother's family? Had they been harmlessly minding their own business in Pitigliano, until the locals decided that Jews were purveyors of every variety of sin and debauchery, and needed to be eliminated? I felt a knife twist of grief for my ancestors and the turbulent lives history had forced them to lead.

30

Armagnac to the Rescue

I restocked my pantry after leaving the library but couldn't face cooking in the tiny kitchen. Even after I scrubbed the pots, I still could feel the intruder's hands on them.

I went back to the gastropub I'd found on the east side of town. I kept Peppy with me, along with my laptop. Trig had said that the construction on top of Yancy Hill had been approved by the county planning commission. I searched Zoë's paper. There was a brief comment under the heading, *Your Government at Work.*

The county planning commission approved the application for commercial construction on Yancy

Hill. The project will include a resort, condos, and small retail shops. We're all curious about what kind of retail shops will be interested in a hilltop location outside of town, but the lawyer making the presentation said the shops would support resort activities.

I thought again of the pylons I'd seen under construction. Perhaps generating power was the development's real business, with a resort and shops as a way to sidestep environmental and construction permits. If the investors were expecting the Wakarusa coal plant to be their moneymaker, they could produce a lot more power than they needed, and sell it throughout the region. But why coal, with the push we all knew we had to make for greener energy?

Zoë texted. She'd had a painful interview with Clete Rotherhaite's wife; could she see me in person? I sent her the restaurant name.

I was drinking Armagnac tonight—its rougher edges brace me when I'm feeling rocky. I was on my second when Zoë arrived. She ordered a local brew, as befit a young local professional.

She gulped down half the beer, then told me about her visit to Rita Rotherhaite. "He died only three weeks ago, so she's still pretty much in shock. You know, they kissed goodbye and he went off to work and then he called her to say he was resigning, but he didn't come home. She thought maybe he'd done something stupid like gone off to get drunk, even though he wasn't usually a drinker. See, his dead body wasn't found for two days, when some runners came on it. So she had forty-eight hours of worry and fear and then disaster."

Her vivid face was filled with anguish. "I wish you'd been with me. It was so terrible and I didn't know what to say. You know, two days by the river—animals—" She took my Armagnac glass and emptied it.

I was glad I hadn't had to face Clete's wife. Not another horror on top of all my own horrors, but I took Zoë's hand and pressed it.

"They must have done an autopsy," I said after a time.

Zoë made a face. "He'd been a heavy smoker, he worked in a coal plant, so his lungs were shot. Mrs. Rotherhaite begged them not to cut her husband open, not after all the other damage he'd suffered on the river path. So they did a CT scan, but not a full autopsy. Deke let me see the police report. The pathologist said there wasn't much reason to say it was anything but a heart attack. Deke said he showed it to me because you were peddling conspiracy theories. He said he wanted to make sure I, at least, had my head screwed on straight."

"Yes, keep your head screwed on," I agreed.

"Don't be like me, unscrewing it at the least provocation and leaving it lying around in drug houses or places like that."

Zoë stared at me. "Vic—don't—I didn't mean—"

"You're right. That was mean-spirited. I'm getting so much unpleasant feedback these days that I'm becoming unpleasant myself.

"Clete Rotherhaite. Working around coal doesn't do your lungs a lot of good. A heart attack is sad but likely. Was his wife surprised that he resigned?"

"Yes and no. He'd been overseeing the plant shutdown. He figured his job would end by the end of the summer, so she was surprised that he quit on the spot. He said he'd explain why when he got home. All he told her was that the plant had a new owner who he didn't see eye-to-eye with. They wanted to bring the plant back on stream. Clete said he was past wanting to manage an active plant, and why hang on to be miserable when they could do like they'd always wanted, buy an RV and drive around the country."

Zoë's face crumpled with grief. "I don't know why this hits me so hard. I talk to a lot of people who've lost their loved ones."

I signaled to the waitperson for two more Armagnacs. Zoë protested that she didn't want more, but when they came, she drank hers, again too quickly.

She put on a determined smile and asked what I'd been doing. I told her about the cameras I'd found around the Dundee house. "They could be operated from anywhere, not necessarily from the Dundee house. I didn't see a control room either of the times I was inside. Whoever is controlling the feed can turn them off if they don't want their pictures showing up in a file someplace. But where are the controls?"

"Maybe up at the construction site?" she echoed my earlier thought. "You saw Brett up at the worksite. Maybe they gave him a deal when they started construction. Gosh, if that's true, Trig will have a nuclear explosion."

"It's a possibility," I conceded. "Santich has to know about the drug deals, but he seems like such an ordinary harassed man, taking his daughter to basketball games, selling insurance to support his family—if he was making a bundle from drugs why would he do that? People who know him tell me he doesn't like the insurance work."

I found a cash receipt in my bag and wrote down names on the back. Sabrina. Valerie. Power Ranger. Brett Santich. Trig. Clarina. Gertrude Perec. Cady. The Wakarusa plant. The Yancy project. The Omicron boys. The Dundee House.

"You can't believe Cady or her grandmother killed Clarina!" Zoë cried when she'd read the names.

"They have a connection to her, for sure, but how does Clarina tie into the Dundee house? For that matter, I have no earthly why Gertrude went out to the Dundee house the night Clarina's body was found. It feels as though there's a puppet master at work here, who didn't like the slow pace things were moving and decided to speed them up."

Zoë shook her head. "I wanted this to be my big breakthrough, but it's such a mess I don't know if we can figure it out before you have to go back to Chicago."

"I can't go back to Chicago until I clear up Clarina's death, so don't lose hope. And any day now, the local DA may arrest me, so you'll have a super-big scoop."

She smiled reluctantly. "I know you said you're second-guessing yourself, but you always seem to know the right thing to do. What will you do next?"

"I'm wondering how the Wakarusa plant connects to Yancy. I think I need to visit it myself, see if the guys will talk to me. A rich-looking cowboy was at the Dundee house today, fighting with Santich, and apparently this same cowboy was at Wakarusa the day Clete died."

Zoë interrupted, excited again. How did I know? When I told her I had a confidential source she tried to force me to reveal the name.

I wouldn't budge but showed her the video I'd shot.

It was fuzzy and the angle was bad, since I'd been on the ground, shooting surreptitiously, but Zoë studied them under the flashlight from her own phone. In the end, she shook her head.

"If he was a power player from around here, I think I'd know him, but I don't."

I asked if she could find out whether the same people applied for a permit to restart Wakarusa as had applied for the permits to build on Yancy.

"I know the Yancy project came before the board two years ago, but do you have any notes on who presented the project?"

Zoë drooped. "There are so many meetings, so many committees. With me as the only reporter in the county, I can't keep on top of all the things that go on. It was right after I joined the paper, anyway, so I was still trying to figure out what meetings to go to."

"Really? Did your editor go? Your paper printed a couple of lines about the commission approving the construction. How did you know?"

"My editor?" Her mouth twisted in contempt. "His idea of journalism is checking Google News twice a day. No, I got it from Pat Everard and Gertrude Perec. Pat was chair of the planning commission that year. I asked them for a report."

"They didn't tell you who had applied for the permit?"

She shook her head. "I asked, but they said the application was handled by the Topeka office of a big national law firm, and that the commission thought the numbers were good and the paperwork showed the applicants had checked the right boxes for environmental quality, with a permit from the state EPA. Maybe I should have checked with the EPA myself, but—" She flung up her hands, despair, drowning, some signal of distress.

"Like you said, it was just two lines in the paper, but Trig saw it and went completely bonkers. He wrote a gazillion letters, claiming Santich had taken bribes to fast-track the application so he could get rid of his land at a profit, and that it would be an environmental disaster. I asked Trig how he knew, when he hadn't seen the plans, and he said, destroying the natural springs on Yancy, for one thing, and that anyway, if Brett Santich was involved it would by definition be a disaster. We ran two of his letters, but the rest were so libelous we couldn't risk printing them. And then he attacked me for being a chicken-shit. His words."

I finished my brandy and signaled for the check.

"This is hard, trying to work on this investigation

and cover all the other stuff that's happening in the county," Zoë burst out. "Readers love disaster stories, like big car wrecks, and they also want to know about weddings and funerals. No one really cares about the library board or the county planning commission. I feel like I must miss big stories all the time because I'm covering the little stuff."

"You're wrong there. Local people covering local events is a big and dangerous hole in today's journalism. All these book bans, for instance, they happen at the local level, but all the small-town papers and radio stations have been swallowed by the big sharks, so people don't have any way of finding out what's happening in their own backyards. You're not missing the big stories; you cover a lot of ground. Your only problem is that you're doing it on your own."

Kind of like me, trying to run this investigation. At least I had Zoë helping out. And she had me. We were both understaffed.

31

Ladies Who Breakfast

I'd grown up in the shadow of Chicago's steel mills, when the U.S. steel industry was booming and the plants ran three shifts a day. I'd helped my mother wash the windows and windowsills every morning, but by night they always had a thin layer of soot over them. I was lucky that my dad was a cop, working in a district far from the mills. Fathers of my girlfriends hacked and wheezed into handkerchiefs they covered with blood and tarry mucus. That's what Clete Rotherhaite's lungs had probably looked like.

No one wanted to cause his widow additional grief by performing a thorough autopsy. It was only me, wondering what the animal bites had covered up.

In the morning, I called Deke Everard to ask him again about Rotherhaite's death.

"No you don't, Warshawski. Little Zoë was already in my face about it yesterday. Rotherhaite's death was sad but natural. There is no cover-up going on."

"I didn't say there was. Just wondered what the guys at the plant had to say about it."

"The guys at the plant were like people everywhere—some were upset, some were cynical, some were resigned. Rotherhaite wasn't loved or hated, he was just a guy doing his job. You want to stir things up at the plant, see if you can create a conspiracy where nothing existed before, don't come crying to me if you find a thousand hornets stinging your ass."

"Copy that, Sergeant."

I hung up without mentioning my plan to talk to the guys at the plant, after I spoke with the gals at the Riverside Congregational Church—this was the day a group of them met for breakfast.

At eight, I saw Gertrude Perec come out of her house. She was bundled against the cold in a puffy jacket, but she had on dressy slacks and well-polished ankle boots. Her head was bare, so I could see that her faded blond hair was pulled into a chignon, and she'd put on a dusting of makeup. I wasn't going to match her for elegance, but with clean jeans, a knit top in my favorite rose, and a wool blazer, I looked respectable.

It was an easy walk from the Perec house to the

church, but I drove so that I could leave Peppy in the car. Gertrude had been early, I guess, because knots of women were coming up the walk as I arrived. I followed them to the community building on the church's south side. A woman at the door smiled in welcome and introduced herself, Lucy Porter.

"Are you new in town?"

"Just visiting," I said. "I'm staying in Gertrude Perec's garage apartment."

"Oh! The detective." She eyed me avidly.

I agreed that I was the detective.

"Are you investigating our women's group?" Porter said.

"Just investigating breakfast, and a chance to talk to Gertrude. She's so busy . . ." I let the thought trail off.

"Yes," Porter said drily. "She is very busy with a great many things. I'm surprised she thought she needed a detective, she's so assiduous herself in conducting investigations."

"I understand she works with Pat Everard on a lot of committees?" I said.

"Oh, yes," Porter said, even more drily.

We'd reached the room where the breakfast was held. I asked Porter to point Everard out to me.

"Next to Gertrude, by the coffee urn. There's a goodwill offering—five dollars." She turned away, putting an arm around another woman in another warm greeting. I followed the crowd to the food table.

Pat Everard, with her head of graying curls, wasn't as elegantly groomed as Gertrude, but she possessed a similar authoritative air. When Gertrude saw me, she didn't seem to be filled with the charity one associates with church gatherings.

"What are you doing here?" she demanded.

I fished in my wallet for a five. "I want to talk to you and Ms. Everard. This seemed like a good place to do it."

"This is a church women's breakfast. It's unbearable that you think you can attack me here."

"Attack?" I poured a cup of coffee. It was thin and smelled bitter. Too long in the urn. "I want information that the two of you possess. I don't think asking for it is an attack."

"What is it you want to know?" Everard demanded.

"The planning meeting that gave approval to the project on Yancy Hill. When you reported on it to Zoë Cruickshank, you told her the application had been for a resort, with some condos and small shops."

"That was at least two years ago." Everard looked at Gertrude, who nodded. "I don't remember exactly what we said."

"This seems to be an enormous project. Since you chaired the planning committee, I hoped you might remember more details. How much did the applicant's lawyer spell out about the resort's power needs?"

"I just said, the meeting was years ago. I couldn't possibly remember details like that on short notice." Everard's dark brows rose in hauteur.

"Do you remember the firm the lawyer was with? It's not in the online minutes."

"The questions you're asking have nothing to do with Clarina Coffin's death," Gertrude said. "And even if they did, Ms. Everard's son is fully capable of following up on them."

"Has Deke talked to you again about what you were doing at the Dundee house?"

"*Sergeant* Everard knows everything about that unfortunate incident," Gertrude said.

Conversation in the room had died down. We were putting on a show, and everyone wanted to hear the dialogue.

I smiled so the audience could see I was the cool, relaxed member of the trio. "The whole project is so interesting," I said. "Have you been up the hill to look at the construction site?"

"Of course not," Gertrude said brusquely. "If this is your idea of an investigation—"

"But the Everard family owned land there, for generations," I said, eyes widening in astonishment. "I'd think at least Ms. Everard here would have some curiosity about what's happening to it. And then there was the sad death of Clete Rotherhaite. Not on Yancy land, at least I don't think it is. But on the river path right by the coal plant."

Gertrude and Pat exchanged glances—worried? Angry? I couldn't tell. They'd been friends a long time; an outsider couldn't read their cues.

"That was a natural death. It was unfortunate that it happened where it did, so that the poor man's body wasn't discovered for several days, but his death is not a police matter," Pat said. "I know Chicago is awash in unsolved murders, so that may have made you think all police forces are incompetent, but even before my son joined the force, the Lawrence police were able to solve local crimes without a hotshot private eye's help."

Gertrude nodded and brushed past me to face the room, smiling, holding out her hands. "I'm so sorry for the delay. A mix-up with the woman who's been staying in my garage apartment. Pastor Tracy, could I prevail on you to lead us in a blessing?"

Behind me, Pat Everard murmured, "Well done, Gertrude," and found a place at one of the tables.

The youngest woman in the room got to her feet to offer thanks for the thin bitter coffee and the sweet rolls, with a special thanks to Ashley and Judith, who'd done the baking this week. I'd paid my five dollars, so I took a muffin and some fruit and found a seat at the same table as the woman who'd accompanied me into the room.

"She's the detective," Porter said, when the rest of the women turned to stare at me.

There was a mixed flow of greetings—*Do you work with Pat's son? We think he does such a wonderful job; we heard Gertrude had a detective living with her. Her life isn't in danger, is it?* But Gertrude cut the flow off with a reading of the minutes, the agenda, the good works the group was doing with Bring Lawrence Home, the book they were discussing at tomorrow night's book club meeting, a fictionalized account of Henry Wadsworth Longfellow's love affair with a woman named Fanny Appleton.

Gertrude smiled. "You know I feel a connection there—one of my great-great-grandfathers was a cousin to the Appleton family, so of course I was enthralled by the story, but I'll look forward to everyone else's reaction."

"As long as we don't spend too long on our important family connections," one of the women at my table muttered.

A woman at another table raised her hand to say she thought the group should invite me to speak—it wasn't often they had a chance to meet a real investigator—but Gertrude shut that down with a firm hand. She assured the room I wouldn't be staying in town much longer.

"But two murders!" the woman said. "We'd all like to know if our lives are in danger when we walk along the river path."

There was an assenting buzz, which Pat interrupted. "This is how fake news takes hold. The man who died on the river path was not murdered; he had a heart attack. But if people want to hear from detectives who actually know what they're doing, I'll talk to Deke and see if he can send an officer over next week to speak to us. They have some bright young women on the force these days."

The meeting ended soon after, but several women came over to me, asking if I knew who'd killed Clarina. One bold soul brought up the trolling Trevor Millay was conducting. She wanted to know if it was true that I'd been to a drug party at the old Dundee house.

"I went to the Dundee house to rescue a student who'd taken an overdose," I said. "As Pat Everard just pointed out, it's so easy for facts to get garbled these days, but you can definitely check that one with Deke Everard. Or if you know Brett Santich? I understand he owns that house. Maybe he can shed some light on what's been going on there. As far as walking the riverfront—it's always good to let a friend know where you're going to be if you're out alone."

Everyone bused their own plates and flatware, while two other women packed up the leftover muffins and fruit. These were destined for a homeless shelter, someone told me.

I strolled over to Pat and Gertrude, who were trying to end a conversation with Pastor Tracy. "Pastor, I'm sorry to interrupt. I have a few more questions to ask Ms. Everard and Ms. Perec while they're together."

"Of course." The pastor looked at me curiously, but moved away from the pair to speak to someone else.

"There's nothing to discuss," Gertrude said.

"Just one last thing." I kept smiling—the only way to keep from shouting at her. "Yesterday I read an obituary in the *Kanwaka Courier* about a guy named Theodore Wheelock, who staked the first claim to the land. The paper praised him for—"

I unlocked my phone and found the photograph I'd taken of the story. "Yes. Until Theodore began plowing and planting on Yancy, it had been 'home to Indians, coloreds, and every variety of sin and debauchery.' Clarina read that and came to see you about it, didn't she? And that's what she wanted Cady to include in her Kansas history curriculum. That must have seemed like a terrible assault to the sense you both have of being descended from Lawrence's founders."

Gertrude stood frozen, like one of those plastic ice cubes with an insect inside. Pat put an arm around her.

"That's enough. You can't come into a church, pretending to be a detective, and hurl accusations like that. I'm calling my son to see what action we can take to make you leave town."

"The tried and true tar and feathering? I don't think the LKPD would countenance that."

"You need to be out of my house by the end of the day today." Gertrude choked out the words. "Pat, can you drive me? The shock—I need to sit down."

"If Ms. Perec suffers from your words, I will hold you accountable," Pat Everard spat over her shoulder as she tenderly escorted Gertrude from the room.

Pastor Tracy hurried to their side and took Gertrude's other arm.

"What was that about?" Lucy Porter asked me.

I was staring after them. "Genealogy," I finally said. "Their roots in this town are very important to them."

What was it Cady had said when I'd asked about French settlers in Lawrence? *Gram's family were English to the core.*

I'd bet my meager IRA that Gertrude's birth name had been Wheelock.

32

Urban Cowboy

It was early afternoon when Peppy and I drove across the bridge to the path on the north side of the Kaw. I should have been hunting for housing, after Gertrude's ultimatum, but I had an urge to see if I could stir up the thousand hornets Deke had threatened might come for me if I went to the coal plant. The day was gray, chilly, with a threat of drizzle in the low-hanging clouds.

The south side of the river, where we usually ran, was parkland, with a well-kept trail surrounded by trees and benches. The north side also had a trail, but heading west it was surrounded by industry. Dump trucks and semis rocked the roads. A train with sixty or so coal-filled hopper cars ran near us, its horn sounding like a cow in anguish.

We passed a salt mountain, a yard filled with school buses, a couple of cement plants, some motels, a light industry park, and then suddenly we were in open country. The Wakarusa power plant stood out in the near distance, its main stack a rusting orange sentinel keeping watch over farmland.

The state had created a two-hundred-mile-long trail on this side of the river. The trick was finding a way from the road down to the Kaw. The roads had been laid out by someone with a mania for squares. Every time I thought I was getting close, the road made a ninety-degree turn and led me deeper into farmland.

I finally came to the plant's access road, the one Lou and Ed must have taken the day they thought they were going to bid on the plant's scrap. A blinking red light in the distance marked the gates and guard station.

I didn't try to drive to the guard station but returned to the main road and pulled over to one side. There was no shoulder; the Camry was uncomfortably close to the drainage ditch between road and field. We were about a quarter mile from the river, on the edge of a field plowed for the winter. I let Peppy out, and we crossed the field. That makes it sound simple. Washington crossing the Delaware, yes, piece of cake in a small boat on a tidal river that bucked and heaved under him. V.I. and Peppy crossing the field. Piece of cake on foot over large clumps of dirt mixed with straw.

Peppy wasn't bothered—she ran in hunting mode, crisscrossing the field as if it were smooth grass, periodically returning to me with a big grin. Yellow-breasted birds skimmed the furrows, whistling to each other as they found insects in the earth. I was the creature who was out of place, stumbling my way through the heavy clods.

When we reached the river, my thighs and knees reminded me that I hadn't done any squats for months. Something else for my to-do list. I shared a peanut butter sandwich and part of a water bottle with the dog while I caught my breath.

Peppy was eager for a swim after her run, but the water surface here was oily and iridescent with coal dust. I leashed her up. "You'd come out a black lab if you went in," I told her, "and you'd have enough carcinogens in your system to poison a city block."

Now that we were close to the plant, I could see that the stack was periodically belching clouds of gray smoke, like an elderly smoker trying to blow rings.

The river made a number of tight bends here, so that while the plant was close, it was maddeningly hard to reach. We could hear machinery, which also sounded elderly, going *ka-thunk*, and then pausing to wheeze as it worked its way to the next *ka-thunk*.

As we followed the trail around the river's tight loops, I realized that apart from the plant noises, the nearby undergrowth was quiet. The whistling birds who'd flown around us while we crossed the field were keeping away from the dirty water and contaminated bushes.

Around one loop, we came to a place where the bushes and grasses were flattened by tire tracks from all-terrain vehicles. I guessed this was where the cops and ambulance team had driven to reach Clete Rother-haite's body.

Runners had come on him lying on the side of the trail, but that had been three weeks ago. I couldn't see any remnants of his death, but Peppy sniffed uneasily around the spot.

"Anything in the undergrowth, girl? A pipe wrench? A rock with skin on it?"

The two of us hunted but didn't find any possible weapon. Of course if he had been murdered, the river was right there to take care of the evidence.

The plant appeared suddenly around the next bend. It was enormous, covering an area that might hold a couple of football fields. Despite its age and the crust of grime covering the buildings, the complex held an air of menace: I dare you to try to get rid of me.

A fence surrounded the plant, but it, too, was old. Especially down here by the river, sections of it were so rusted that the prongs had come away from the metal posts. We were standing at the back, so I couldn't tell how many people might be at work, but we were at the end where the coal came in. A half-dozen hopper cars stood on the siding.

The noise had been growing as we'd gotten nearer. This close in, it was ferocious. Peppy whined, pawed the ground, looked pleadingly at me. I hated to torment her further, but I pushed away one of the rusted sections of fence and crossed into the yard.

Someone was overseeing the hopper cars, but his back was to me. He didn't see the dog and me as we passed. When we walked across the tracks a thundering noise shook the ground. One of the cars had released its load into an underground shed. The train engine blew its horn and begin inching forward, moving another hopper into position over the shed. I took out my phone to photograph the scene.

With Peppy clinging to my legs, I circled the plant and reached the entrance. A trio of men in hard hats and safety vests was sitting at a card table inside the plant's open doors, eating doughnuts and drinking coffee. Two of them were smoking. They all had phones out. Every now and then, one would lean across the table to shout something at his friends, but in that racket you couldn't carry on a conversation.

I walked up to them, smiling happily, Little Miss Sunshine, bringing joy to the jobsite. I tried to say, "Hi, guys," but the machinery swallowed my words.

The men looked up at me, taken aback by my arrival.

One of them stood so he could bellow in my face, "Who are you, and how in hell did you get into the yard?"

I put a couple of my cards on the table. "I'm an investigator; I walked up the river trail with my dog, looking for the place where Clete Rotherhaite was found."

The two men sitting looked at my card, looked at the standing man, waiting for his reaction. The last of the hopper cars must have dumped its load because the noise dropped enough that we could hear each other.

"You investigating Clete's death?" the standing man said. "That was a hard way to die. Hard on Rita, for sure, but, hell, we'd worked together going on twenty-five years. Hard on all of us. We'd just as soon let him rest in peace."

"I hear you," I said. "Insurance, you know, companies have all the sensitivity of a blast furnace."

"What?" the man was indignant. "They threatening not to pay his life insurance?"

"Workers' comp," I said. "They'll pay out if he was still employed when he died. That's the problem. Some suit in Chicago said he'd quit, that he wasn't on the Wakarusa payroll when he died."

The man spat, aiming about an inch from my foot. "You working for the company?"

I didn't flinch or move my foot. "Neither the insurer nor the coal plant. I'm independent, trying to get the facts so that Rita Rotherhaite can at least get the indemnity payment she's entitled to."

The three men looked at each other again, nodded infinitesimally. The ringleader took us inside, past giant boilers and pipes, conveyor belts and heavy fans. A scene from Walter Mitty. *Pocketa-pocketa.*

We crossed the floor and went into a room in a far corner that was sort of soundproofed. Peppy remained glued to my legs, whining at the noise, the heat, the smell of sulfur.

"That whole day was fucked, if you'll pardon my French," the spokesman said. "Clete, he was like a cat on hot bricks from the moment he walked in the door. Then Lou Arata and Ed Lyndes came by. They thought the place was being mothballed, they were going to bid on some of the pipes, things easy to dismantle that a two-man crew could handle. Arata and Lyndes, they were in this room here with Clete.

"I'm the day shift foreman so I'm down in the yard, when this dude drives up in some hundred-thousand-dollar ride. You can tell he's a suit even though he's wearing boots, jeans, the whole western look, all brand-new, like he opened the boxes this morning. Right behind him another suit drives up in a white Lexus, this one with a jacket and tie, carrying a briefcase.

"'Good news, fellas,' the cowboy says, like he can make us think he's one of the boys. 'Your jobs are safe for another few decades. This plant is a good cat with nine lives, she's got a whole bunch more in front of her.'

"The cowboy wants to look around. Suit works for him, so he has to follow him into the plant floor with his leather shoes. Would have been funny except they weren't a funny pair. Suit is tapping his wrist, time's a-wasting, cowboy draws out the tour just to be ornery, asking questions about the boiler, the pressure, whatever.

"Finally he gives us a wink, he's had enough fun with his flunky, and asks to see Clete. I point to this room but say Clete is meeting with a couple of guys interested in buying scrap. The cowboy just barges on in, suit at his heels, like your dog here.

"About ten minutes later out come Lou and Ed. They're usually an easygoing pair, take life in stride, but they were mad enough to fire up engine number two." The foreman pointed toward one of the boilers.

"I went in to see what the hey was going on, and I hear Clete yelling at the suits. 'How much do you know about coal? Yeah, you got all those papers, Tulloh, you're the owner now, but how much do you know about coal, how it works, what it does? You showing me these papers means you know jackshit.'"

"Tulloh?" I interrupted. "Like Tulloh Industries?"

"I suppose," the foreman said. "Heck, maybe they bought the plant, although why anyone that rich wants something this old beats me. I guess that was Clete's point, too.

"Cowboy was grinning all over his face, like he's pulled a fast one the rest of us are too slow to notice. Anyway, the sidekick says to Clete, 'He owns the joint, he can do what he wants.' And Clete says, 'Of course you can do what you want. Just not with me. I'm out of here.'"

"He left there and then?" I asked.

The men shook their heads, almost in unison. "He stayed to take care of the payroll and stuff. The cowboy and the suit took off, leaving it up to Clete to notify the crew that everything was about to change.

"You know, we got just a skeleton in place waiting to see what management was going to do about the plant. Now it looks like we're coming back on stream, start-ing to bring in new coal, but that's been since Clete died. After the cowboy left, Clete called everyone out into the yard, about twenty of us, explained there were new owners, they'd have to talk to the union about seniority, job security, so on, but that he, Clete, wasn't going to be back."

"And he went off for a walk along the river?" I said.

The foreman eyed me narrowly. "He worked his full day, and anyone who says otherwise is a goddam liar. He drove off at four when the shift ended."

"Did he do that a lot?" I asked. "I mean, walk by the river when he needed to think things through?"

One of the other men laughed. "Clete? His idea of thinking things through was a beer and a football game. Told him he should have got a job in Oklahoma, where the teams win more than they lose, but he was Jayhawks and Chiefs through thick and thin, and with the Jayhawks, that's a lot of thin."

"Him and Rita, they liked to garden," the foreman said, "but I wouldn't say he wasn't big on nature."

"So he didn't say anything to any of you, like I'm going to miss this sad old plant so I'm going to walk down by the river and take some pictures?"

They stared at me. "Are you trying to say he was trespassing, and Rita can't collect?" the foreman said.

"Oh, no," I said. "Just trying to make sense of it. He worked the full day, the full shift, he died essentially on the premises, so he was on the payroll and at work. That's what I'll tell the workers' comp board, anyway. I wouldn't want to confuse their tiny brains with all this talk of coming and going."

"Tiny brains, that's a good one." The foreman spat again, this time aiming away from my foot. We were buddies, I guess. "Let's not confuse those tiny brains."

They saw me to the exit. Yep, that proved we were pals.

Peppy refused to go back the way we'd come. The earth quaking as the hopper released its load had unnerved her. I led her away from the plant toward the gate with the blinking red light. She broke into a flat-out run. My shoes were too heavy with mud to keep pace with her, but I found her on the far side of the gate, sides heaving. We walked at a sober pace to the car.

33

Out of the Mouths of Babes

I had mud inside my socks as well as clumped to my shoes. Next to high heels, my running shoes were the worst choice for hiking through farmland. Peppy was panting, thirsty from running, and from the fear she'd felt at the plant.

When we reached the shops near the bridge, I pulled into the lot behind the Boat Yard and walked down to the river's edge. Close up, I could see the strong current Lou and Ed had talked about. I let Peppy go in swimming, but kept her leash attached in case she got into trouble. I took off my own shoes and socks and stuck my feet into the current. Big mistake. In seconds my bones were aching from the cold.

I rinsed the worst of the mud from my shoes and put

them back on. Horrible. Clammy wet rubber on bare feet. Fortunately, the strip mall where I kept buying clean clothes was behind the Boat Yard. I'd stop for socks on my way out.

Claiming to be a workers' comp investigator had gotten me a nice amount of information about Clete Rotherhaite's last day at the plant. His last day alive, probably.

If Tulloh Industries had bought the old Wakarusa plant, they must believe there was a fortune to be made on Yancy, doing something that required a power grid. Maybe they'd found valuable minerals, lithium or something, that would take a lot of power to dig up and refine.

Clarina had trespassed. The Yancy foreman had referred to Trig's "harassment brigade," coming onto the jobsite. She'd stuck her nose in many places where no one wanted to see it—the Congregational women, the Yancy jobsite. Maybe she'd visited the coal plant, too. She'd discovered something about the Yancy project that Tulloh needed to keep secret. He got Santich, or perhaps the gun-toting project manager, to kill her.

I could call Deke and tell him I'd solved the case: one of the Tulloh family had killed Clarina because she was trying to shut down the resort. She was the one Santich and Tulloh complained "would bitch the whole deal." It would be very nearly worth all my pain and trouble to listen to him erupt.

How does coal work? You set it on fire, you bring water in those big boilers to steam temperature, the pressure drives some turbines that somehow connect to a power grid and make it run. Presumably the owners knew that same minimum amount, so what did Clete Rotherhaite think the Urban Cowboy didn't know? And why did that mean Rotherhaite had to die?

A small boy with a shock of dark hair falling over his eyes wandered down from the Boat Yard parking lot. "Your dog is a good swimmer."

"Yes, she is."

Peppy came out to see who was accosting me and sprayed water over the child, who shrieked with laughter at the shower.

"Does she bite?"

"Nope. She's a mellow girl." I showed him how Peppy could take a treat from my mouth without biting me, which made him shriek again.

"Does your mom or dad know you're down here?" I asked.

He made a vague gesture. "Mom and Auntie Holly are talking, talking, talking."

"Then let's go see what they're talking, talking, talking about."

I stuffed my filthy socks into one of the bags I use for the dog and squelched up the hill, Peppy in tow.

Holly, the waitress who'd told me about the Dundee House, was in agitated conversation with a redheaded woman. Holly had a cigarette in one hand, which she was waving so furiously I thought she might stab the redhead with it.

I'd seen the other woman before. She'd been emptying the recycling bin at the University Press building. And Trig had her picture on his screen saver, bending over the boy with the dark hair.

"Are you Ivy?" I said. "I'm V.I. Warshawski. I was sitting down by the water with my dog when your kid came down."

"The dog can swim real good," the boy told his mother. "And she took food from the lady's mouth. She didn't bite."

"Ivy, you take Timmy on home. I need to go in and start my shift," Holly said.

"Before you take Timmy on home, can we talk for a minute?" I said. "I saw you at the University Press building. And your picture on Trig's computer."

Both women froze, but Timmy said, "Trig, he took me to the zoo."

"He sounds like a good friend," I said. "A super good friend who wants to make sure your mommy doesn't get hurt. He even went to a haunted house in the middle of the night to make sure your mommy didn't find any ghosts or zombies."

I smiled at Timmy while I spoke, to make sure we both knew a haunted house and ghosts weren't real. He tugged on his mother's jacket, wanting to know if she saw a ghost, if Trig killed a ghost.

"Who are you?" Ivy demanded. "What do you want?"

"I'm a detective, private, who found Sabrina Granev in the Dundee house. A day later, I found Clarina Coffin's dead body there." I spoke softly, directly into her ear, hoping Timmy couldn't hear me.

"Trig and I are leading suspects in Coffin's murder. I'm trying like mad to find her actual killer before the DA gets tired of waiting and charges me. Or him."

Ivy looked at her son, who was staring anxiously at us. I'd brought trouble to his mother, but I had a cool dog. Hard to figure out whether I was good or bad.

"Timmy, I need to talk to this lady for five minutes. Auntie Holly will let you play with my phone, okay?" She handed her device to her sister, who took Timmy to one side—out of earshot but close enough to leap on me if I threatened her sister.

"Trig knows you clean up after those parties," I said, "so he came out to the Dundee House when he saw cop activity there on his scanner. He didn't want you walking into the arms of the law."

"How do you know Trig?" she demanded.

"I met him because of this mess," I said. "How do you know him?"

"You think he's Timmy's father?"

I shook my head. "I think he wants to be Timmy's father. The birth father isn't in the picture?"

She gave a shout of laughter, raw, harsh, humorless. "He's in the picture, he got me the job cleaning the damned house."

"Not the Omicron brat—kid—Millay?"

"You're half smart, half clueless," she said.

"Santich?" I was even more incredulous.

"Brett Santich. The usual stupid story. Married man lonely and hurting, cruising without his ring. Used to come in here Friday nights. I worked here then, like Holly. Then I'm pregnant, and he reveals all. Wife, kid, mortgage, no money for another kid. So what does he do for me? Gets me odd jobs, like cleaning that old house. It is haunted. You go in there, you feel the spirit of all those drug ODs, but it's an extra hundred bucks once or twice a week. What a good daddy!"

"So that's why Trig hates Santich so much," I said slowly. "How did he find out?"

"He overheard me shouting at Brett about a year ago, out at the Dundee place. Timmy was starting school, he needs stuff. He needs a dentist, he wants the toys the other kids have. I need money, Brett doesn't have any. I told him to sell another damned acre of land. Two thousand would take care of the kid for a year. He's whining what would he tell his wife, when Trig pops out of the darkness—he was there to post one of his stupid signs on the house."

She stopped, panting. "I swore him to secrecy, but he likes to help out, takes the kid to the zoo, gets him presents for his birthday. You're right—he'd like to be Timmy's daddy, but Trig! He's so—creepy! It's like walking on broken glass, being grateful for what he does for us but not so grateful that he thinks he can, you know—"

I nodded sympathetically. "When did Brett start using the house for the drug parties?"

"What difference does that make?"

"Brett needs money, so he's letting people use the house, no questions asked. Meanwhile, he had to sell the family land on top of Yancy. I'm wondering if the people running that project also get a cut of what he does with the house, and how it connects to the Omicron boys."

She hunched a shoulder. "I don't know. The deal for

the land went through when Timmy was born. I thought Brett would have cash to burn, there'd be money for Timmy, but it turns out he had a triple mortgage to pay off and so he's *still* in debt. Asshole. I really know how to pick them. As for the Omicron boys—they're creeps but they're not in charge. They do it for kicks, I guess, to see how much they can get away with."

She paused, dialing back her bitterness for a moment while she thought. "The parties were something Brett worked out privately, during the lockdown, I guess. The Omicron boys got wind of them and pushed in, but someone else must be involved. On account of the cameras. They only went in about six months ago, and Brett, he's super careful about them. I have to go clean up exactly when he says because he can turn the cameras off, but he doesn't always have access to the master switch."

"I don't suppose you know where that is?"

She shook her head. "Along with everything else. I must have been born stupid. Holly's the smart one."

"Timmy's a lively kid," I said. "I know you're on a hard road, but you're doing a good job, or he wouldn't be so confident and outgoing."

"You think so?" She brightened a little and straightened her shoulders as she walked back into the bar.

34

On Top of Old Yancy

The Rotherhaites lived in Lecompton, a few miles up the road from the Wakarusa coal plant. I hated to bother Rita Rotherhaite, especially after Zoë had already been there, but I wanted to see if her husband had said anything to her that would clarify what he meant when he said the Power Ranger didn't know anything about coal.

The visit was as painful as I'd feared. The couple had been married for thirty-four years; Rita didn't know how she would sleep through the night without Clete snoring next to her.

"The men at the plant were surprised that he'd gone walking by the river," I said.

"It never would have come into my head," she said.

"First when he didn't come home, I thought maybe he'd gone out to get drunk. He only ever did that one time before, when our boy Milo died in Afghanistan, but then when two days went by—I thought if I called the sheriff Clete would never forgive me for making a fuss—but while I was still making up my mind, up came one of the deputies with the news."

"When your husband called, did he say why he was resigning?"

"The new boss said Clete should be happy they were reviving the Wakarusa plant because he'd get to keep his job. Clete, he said he explained the Wakarusa was so old it couldn't produce power safely. They had three accidents last year, which is too many, especially when you know the plant is only at quarter capacity. That's what they fought about. Clete, it was safety first with him. I'm not risking any more of my men's lives, that's what he said he told the boss. And of course he was right."

"Did he mention the new boss's name?" I asked. "Was it Tulloh?"

She shook her head slowly, tears shining on her face. "You'd think I could remember every word of my last conversation with my own man, but I can't. You don't know it's going to be the last time, and you don't do more than stand there while you've got the vacuum in one hand, thinking, maybe make him pork chops for dinner. Pork chops, and him about to go off and die."

I waited while she went through that terrible litany we all recite, regrets and remorse, things undone or unsaid, the things we wished undone or unsaid. When she was calmer, I apologized again for disturbing her, and offered the conventional hope that she had family or friends to help her through this hard time. She brightened; her girl Tara was coming to visit with the baby. Maybe she'd go back to Independence with her for the summer, help with the older kids.

The sun was setting when I got back to the Perec house. I sent a text to Cady: Haven't had time to hunt for new quarters. One last night here and I promise I'll be out in the morning. She wrote back with an apology for her grandmother's harshness and said morning would be fine.

When I'd looked up the Tullohs earlier, I'd only read some articles in the business press. Now I called up images. They weren't a family that relished being photographed, but I found Matthew, the patriarch, with Emmaline, at a reception for their fiftieth wedding anniversary seven years ago. They did not spend their billions on high fashion. He wore a suit that had been through many meetings; she had on a flower-print dress that could have come off the rack at Target or JCPenneys.

In contrast, their daughter, Pauline, was shown laughing with the senior senator from Kansas. She had on a navy cocktail dress that looked like couture work, while the sons were dressed in the modern version of evening wear—collarless shirts hanging over the trouser waistband, and box-cut jackets.

I even found a YouTube clip, a segment with Matthew Tulloh's mother, filmed by someone who called her "Auntie." Mrs. Tulloh had been 103, sharp-featured, her voice quavery with age but perfectly clear, and surprisingly vindictive.

"Everyone said Emmaline Wilton married beneath her when she said 'I do' to my boy," Mrs. Tulloh chortled. "She had those three grain elevators, and he had a pocketful of dirt. Look at the Wiltons now, all of them charity cases Matthew puts up with for Emmaline's sake."

The videographer panned the room and settled on a cluster in a remote corner, a weedy morose man perhaps in his sixties, and two younger men in ill-fitting sports jackets and khaki pants. "Yep, that's Emmaline's brother's boy and his sons. He squandered the elevators their pa left him. He didn't think my Matthew knew how to count to five, so he wouldn't listen to

Matthew's advice, and look at him now." Mrs. Tulloh laughed again.

The party had been seven years ago. Matthew's mother died not long after the event, a happy woman, I guess.

An article in *Kansas Business Today* had a reporter at the party who wrote, "There are reports of feuding between the two Tulloh sons, as well as between the cousins, but all we saw at the party was a family that supports each other and the Salina community that they call home."

I didn't know if the brothers were feuding or supporting each other in Lawrence, but they were definitely playing a role here. I'd seen them both. The older, Jacob, had been standing next to Agent Stamoran in the press conference the LKPD chief had held after I found Sabrina. The younger, Robert, was the man I'd seen arguing with Brett Santich outside the Dundee house yesterday morning.

Robert was the urban cowboy Lou and Ed had run into at the Wakarusa power plant. The man who'd laughed off his foreman's concerns about the plant's safety and forced his subordinate to tour the plant in a business suit and loafers. A man who loved using his position and his money to humiliate others.

True, that, but it was secondary to the question

about what was going up on top of old Yancy. If Tulloh Industries was reviving a dying coal plant, it wasn't because they were building a resort. I see pylons that size when I drive the route into Chicago past the area's nuclear reactors: they are feeding megawatts into the Chicago grid. What on earth was Tulloh building that had the power needs of a city?

I went back to the corporate website and read it with greater attention. Tulloh Industries had nine major subsidiaries, some of them doing things I couldn't understand even when I read the descriptions a half dozen times. The dropdown menu of countries where they had factories, mines, or cloud services included most of the globe.

They were ruthless in putting down strikes by workers in Africa and South America. Famous for exacting tax concessions from governments both foreign and domestic. Funders of various petroleum industry think tanks aimed at combatting climate change information.

I thought of Sherlock Holmes's description of Moriarty as a spider in the center of a web with a thousand strands. Moriarty knew what every strand connected to. I wondered if the patriarch, Matthew Tulloh, kept similar watch over his thousands of subsidiaries and factories. Not that Tulloh was a criminal enterprise, at least not in the narrowest definition of the word, but definitely not an outfit to tangle with.

Matthew Tulloh had brought the FBI in to oversee the investigation into Sabrina Granev's disappearance. His son Jacob had been right next to Agent Stamoran at the Lawrence police chief's press conference two days later. If the FBI jumped when Tulloh snapped his fingers, a county's judicial system might turn somersaults.

I felt sweat beading on my neck. If Frank Karas, the DA, told the LKPD to arrest me, that would be easier to deal with than if the urban cowboy and his daddy decided my body should join Clarina's and Rotherhaite's in some remote corner of the county.

I tried phoning Valerie Granev, but again my call went to voicemail. I left a message asking after Sabrina's health, telling her that I was on the trail of whoever ran the drug parties at the Dundee house. I finished by asking, *Do you know what the company is building on Yancy? Are you under orders not to talk to me?*

I texted Deke Everard. No hornets buzzing around me yet, but that may happen soon. The new Wakarusa owners have a lot of muscle in their power plays, both in the physical plant and in the county's planning board. You told me I was making your job hard because you didn't know what I was doing. Shoe fits both feet. I don't know what pressure the Tulloh family is exerting on your team, but it's making me nervous.

Murray called as I was staring at a plate of risotto, trying to talk myself into eating it. "Guess where I am, Warshawski."

I wasn't in the mood, but I played along, anyway. "The second moon of Jupiter?"

"Albuquerque. You owe me a plane ticket and a night in a hotel."

"Is there some reason I should be—" I cut myself short. "You went down to talk to Sabrina's father."

"Valerie is such a strong presence we were forgetting that the girl—strike that," he said hastily. "Young woman has two parents. I figured Ramir Granev might not talk to the fourth estate, but he opened up to a worried dad who wondered if Ramir's wilderness camping would be a good thing for his daughter. I caught up with him at the outdoor store where you told me he worked."

"Murray, I hate to stroke your already outsize ego, but that was genius," I said. "What issues is your daughter facing?"

"What so many entitled kids are dealing with these days—opioids. My ex-wife and I agree on hardly anything, but our girl's health scare brought us back together. We got LiliBeth into a good rehab program, but, dang, she's sixteen, going back into school is like sending her into a drug factory. Ramir shared his grief over his own girl. He and his wife didn't even know she was addicted until she went down to Kansas and some crazy woman lured her to a drug house."

He paused, but I declined the bait.

"Sabrina's in Florida," I said. "Is Valerie down there with her?"

"Valerie had to go back to work. Ramir spent the weekend with Sabrina, but both parents are scared for her future. 'Don't make your child's success your happiness,' he warned me. Made me feel a heel for inventing LiliBeth, but not such a heel that I stopped asking questions. The monsters you said Sabrina was seeing—I asked if she was strong enough to look at a photo lineup. That was a major blunder—why was a worried dad worrying about some other kid looking at a photo array?

"I said, sorry, the cops were hounding LiliBeth to try to ID her dealer and I wondered about his kid and her dealers. He said every time he or Valerie tried to mention that, she got hysterical again.

"I congratulated him on getting the funding for his wilderness camp. He said basically the same thing we saw on the news—it had been a goal for many years but was hard to enjoy with his daughter so ill.

"I asked if he thought his coworkers had clubbed together out of sympathy for Sabrina. He said his coworkers didn't have that kind of money. He wondered if that billionaire woman who makes mysterious gifts had heard about him on the news and decided to fund his program. Or maybe Valerie's coworkers—they had more money than the people he worked with."

"Most likely it's Valerie's bosses." I told him about IDing Robert Tulloh as the man who'd taken over the Wakarusa power plant. "Sabrina gets into an expensive rehab center, Ram gets his wilderness camp, all the parents have to do is tell me they don't want me investigating."

"It's that kind of story?" Murray sucked in a breath. "You think the pressure on that Bureau guy—what's his name?—Stamoran? You think Tulloh is pushing on Stamoran to arrest you?"

"No, just to get me to back off. But this coal plant—the foreman who thought firing it back up was a safety risk was conveniently found dead on the river path. Local LEOs assure me it was a heart attack, but you know the saying—if it quacks like a killing.

"The plans they filed with the county were for a resort and some ancillary shops, but the day I went up to the construction site, I saw pylons, big things that would be good for bringing power from this coal plant to something needing more watts than a resort. A resort on an out-of-the-way Kansas hilltop."

"What are they building?" Murray asked.

"Today's top question," I said drily. "Kirmek, the construction firm working on the Yancy site, also needs some attention. The foreman is armed, although who isn't, these days? My second day here I climbed Yancy Hill and saw Brett Santich in a heated discussion with the guy."

"I'll shake a few trees, see if they're connected," Murray said, meaning Mob ties, "but this definitely means you're paying my airfare."

"To Albuquerque, but not for your hotel. I know you didn't stay at Motel 6."

In the years he'd worked for Global Entertainment, Murray chafed at the company's slipshod journalism but had enjoyed their lavish travel allowances. That was one of the reasons it took him so long to go free-lance. That and the fact that no one is earning a living doing real journalism these days.

When we finished dickering, I'd agreed to cover a coach ticket, not the first-class he'd shelled out for ("I'm six-two, Warshawski, you can't expect me to fold up like a piece of laundry in one of those tiny seats." I was unmoved).

When we hung up, I caught up with Lotty, Sal,

and, of course, Mr. Contreras. Angela and Bernie had brought him up to the Northwestern campus yesterday. Angela had an afternoon game, Bernie a nighttime hockey match. He'd watched both matches, probably the loudest voice in the bleachers, then taken them out for pizza.

Everyone was happy, except he missed me and Peppy and he was sure the dog walker wasn't giving Mitch enough exercise.

35

Pants on Fire

Zoë called as I was getting ready for bed. She'd gone to the Lion's Heart this evening with some of her besties as cover. She'd stumbled into the kitchen, pretending she thought it was the bathroom, and saw the dishwasher dealing out the back door.

She'd taken a surreptitious picture, wondering if he was the guy who'd been spying on me from the bushes Sunday night. I shook my head—I'd never gotten a look at the peeper's face.

"But here's the interesting thing, Vic," Zoë added. "The bar almost went under during the pandemic. One of my girlfriends, she works for Pioneer State Bank and Trust, where the Lion's Heart owner banks. He's a guy named Don Wilton, he lost a lot of money during the pandemic. He couldn't get a PPP loan, he couldn't pay his mortgage on the bar, and he was having a going-out-of-business sale, like, all you can drink for twenty dollars or something, when suddenly he was back in business."

"So he found an angel. Interesting," I said. "Your friend say who?"

Zoë laughed. "She went all Banking Act on me, even though she'd broken a million regulations telling me as much as she had. So I think she doesn't know."

I told her what I'd learned out at the Wakarusa plant, and from Rita Rotherhaite. "If you have time, can you check the EPA filing the Yancy project made when they applied for planning permission? Gertrude and Pat claimed not to remember when I bearded them at the church breakfast yesterday. The plant foreman said Rotherhaite was worried that the new owners plan to run the plant either above its capacity, or without making the repairs and upgrades and so on that it needs."

"Lois Lane is all over it, Wonder Woman. What will you be doing?"

"Finding a new place to stay. Gertrude gave me the boot."

Over my second cortado the next morning, I tried to sort out my housing options. I should never have roomed in the Perec home to begin with, so getting the boot wasn't a bad thing, just a time-eating inconvenience. I found a website where people advertised for roommates, but none of the furnished places would let me bring a dog.

We were inside the Hippo, where the barista brought Peppy a small dish of milk. Even if it had been selfish to bring Peppy to Kansas with me, she was making friends.

I ran through my short list of local acquaintances. I could camp out in the Dundee house, I supposed, seat of the action. Peppy would have the woods to roam in and we could play hide-and-seek with Brett Santich and the Yancy man he'd been arguing with.

That sardonic thought reminded me of Clarina's trashed trailer. I finished the egg sandwich I'd ordered and headed west, toward Yancy, toward the Prairie View Mobile Home Park. Mignon Travers was still in her padded desk chair, still focused on her device.

"Yes?" She didn't look up.

"I'm looking for a week's rental furnished," I said.

"Month minimum," she said to her screen.

"I just need a base for a week, two tops, to sort out Clarina Coffin's murder. Is her place available?"

Travers turned her attention to me reluctantly. "Oh. The private cop. The Coffin woman's place is still a mess. Unless you want to spend a fortune on a new stove and everything, you don't want to live there. The park owners are fighting with the police over who's responsible for cleanup, so it may never be fixed. You want a week? Just you?"

"And my dog. She can catch both mice and cockroaches, so I wouldn't need to shoot them." Not that I'd seen her do either, but Peppy comes from a long line of hunting dogs. Not one that stretched back to the Pilgrims in 1620, but respectable, nonetheless.

Mignon snorted: my joke was not very funny. "I guess. Long as she doesn't pee or crap inside. She does that, out you go, but you pay to replace the carpeting. Got someone who's coming back from Florida in ten days. They'd be glad of the extra rent. Three hundred for the week. Includes electric, but butane for the heater is fifty extra. You provide your own linens."

She ran my credit card, told me she'd get Al to bring over a bottle of butane when he came this afternoon, then reached above the desk for the key. Peppy and I walked down the gravel lanes to 1422 Bluestem. The unit was a double wide with an electric cooktop, a refrigerator under the counter, a modest shower, and a big bed. It was cold, with a musty smell from being shut up all winter, but it was clean; it would do.

I drove back to the Perec house to pack. I put the towels and bedding into Gertrude's washing machine, but yesterday's coal-laden clothes I stuck in a garbage bag to take to a Laundromat. I had been tempted to run them through Gertrude's machine, to leave black grime caking the inside, but that pettiness was adolescent, unbecoming an adult detective.

As I packed, I inspected each garment, each toilet article and piece of paper, for any signs of Friday's intruders, but didn't spot drugs or trackers or bloodstained tools.

Peppy was yawning anxiously, uncertain because I'd put her food and bed and toys into a box. I took her down the stairs with her box and put both into the Camry.

I finished carting everything to the car, then rang Gertrude's front doorbell to return her key. Deke Everard came to the door.

I was preparing to tell him about Clete Rotherhaite and the unnatural exercise he'd been taking before he died, but Deke forestalled me.

"My mother says you came to the church women's group and accused Gertrude Perec of murdering Clarina Coffin."

"I'm sure your mother is too honorable a person to lie, especially about so serious a matter. What did she really say?"

His face was stern. "Maybe the Chicago PD has the resources to let you waste their time, but we're thirty percent understaffed here. You don't get to spin me around. Tell me why you made this accusation, and I will decide whether to ask the DA to file charges against you."

"Is your mother here now, comforting Ms. Perec? Let's go in and talk together, so you're not playing telephone tree, delivering messages that get garbled in transmission."

I didn't wait for his reply but brushed past him into the house. Gertrude and Pat were sitting together on a sofa. Cady was standing near a window, running the cord to the drapes through her fingers.

Gertrude straightened her shoulders when she saw me. "Have you moved out?"

"Yes, ma'am." I put the key on an end table near her. "I put my used linens in the garage washer. I can stay to dry them if you want."

"I'll take care of that." Cady's voice was low, affectless.

When none of the women said anything else, Deke said, "Mother, you called me here to lodge a complaint against V.I. Warshawski. Can you repeat it, please?"

"I said you accused Gertrude—Ms. Perec—of murdering Clarina Coffin."

I pulled up a straight-backed chair so that I could sit facing the two women. "Ms. Everard, could you please repeat my exact words?"

"I don't remember the exact words, but you implied—" Pat Everard glanced at her son. Whatever she
read in his face made her stop talking.

"Let me help." I turned the chair so I could see Deke
as well as the women. "All the events I've been involved
in, from Sabrina Granev's disappearance through Clarina Coffin's death, have centered on Yancy Hill. Sabrina and Clarina were both found at the Dundee
house on Yancy land. Gertrude Perec and Trig Garrity
were caught on camera at the Dundee house the night
Clarina's dead body was discovered."

"You were at the house that day as well," Deke said,
a pulse throbbing in his neck.

I stared him down. "Yes, indeed I was. When I
found Sabrina Granev, Clarina Coffin was probably
in the basement, dying if not dead. If I had known
her life was in the balance, I would have alerted your
emergency crew and told them to go down there. I am
paying a heavy price for saving Sabrina Granev's life."

"Yes, all right," Deke muttered.

I was angry, but I made myself put my bitterness to
one side. I shut my eyes, slowed my breathing, until I
could speak levelly.

"About six years ago, Brett Santich sold land on
Yancy to an anonymous developer. Trig blames Santich
for all the troubles around the land, the school, and so

on, but word on the street is that Brett sold because he's overleveraged, not because he's sinking money into a development on the hilltop. Someone told me he had three mortgages. I guess when you're a homeboy, the banks give you extra leeway, but it probably wasn't a good thing, because the sale supposedly didn't help him with the third mortgage.

"Monday I did a title search. The first registered claim was to a man named Wheelock, in 1870. A little later, Henry Everard claimed land out there as well. Clarina did this same search. Like me, she came on Theodore Wheelock's obituary. His contemporaries praised him for getting rid of Indians and what the newspaper called 'coloreds' that were making Yancy an undesirable place on the outskirts of this highly respectable town.

"I asked Ms. Perec whether Clarina had shown her these documents. She had. I said Ms. Perec must have felt this was a terrible assault on her family's good name. She told me to get out of her garage by the end of the day. Which was a good idea. I shouldn't have been living there, anyway, given how hostile Ms. Perec is to my involvement in the investigation."

"She's not the only one," Deke said. "The LKPD has enough qualified officers to solve crimes without your help."

"Not five minutes ago you told me the force was thirty percent understaffed. I won't say you need my help, but my help means I'm focused on this one situation, not the dozen or twenty new ones that crop up every day."

"That's not the point," Deke said. "You may think you're doing good, but you don't file reports, we have no idea what you're doing, you could recklessly destroy months of surveillance, the way you did by confronting the Omicron House guys."

"Is there someone at the LKPD I can put on speed-dial to check who I can and can't talk to?" I said, voice low and mean. "I am tired of being blamed for everything that is wrong in this county. That house in the woods was being used for drug parties before Sabrina Granev and I came to Kansas. If I had the time and interest to take on those frat rats, I would bet one or all of them have parents who are major donors to the university, and so the investigation proceeded slowly, hoping the boys would graduate before they had to be confronted."

I knew I was being reckless, speaking without counsel present, but I was too angry to care. "And you know *damned* well that I am no more responsible for killing Clarina Coffin than your mother is. On top of that, Clete Rotherhaite's death. I was out by the Wakarusa coal plant this morning—"

"You have a hell of a nerve! I told you yesterday not to come to me with imaginary crimes. Not content to screwing up one murder investigation, you think you can turn every unusual death in the county into a murder? And then investigate it on your lonesome to show up me and my force, with no other resource than a dog who couldn't find a steak in a butcher shop?"

I squeezed my eyes shut, took a steadying breath. "When you stoop to attacking my dog, it shows how far in over your head you are. Honestly. Go after me all you want, but I assure you, if Peppy were left in a butcher shop for three minutes, there wouldn't be a bone left."

I got up. "Ms. Perec, going back to the actual murder the sergeant is investigating, your reaction to Theodore Wheelock's obituary was so intense, it makes me wonder if he was your ancestor."

Gertrude stood as well. "I am proud of my family and with good reason. We helped build this town. My ancestors left a comfortable home in Skaneateles to make sure this state came free into the Union. We drained swampland and turned it into productive farmland. We helped write laws that have kept this town and this county safe for almost two centuries."

I stood still in the middle of the room. "Where did your family come from? Skinny Atlas?"

"Why do you care? Do you want to go there and harass any of my relations still living there?" Gertrude spat. "My mother fought against segregated housing both here in Lawrence and at the university. My family resigned their memberships in the private clubs that excluded Black people. None of that meant anything to Clarina. She wanted to turn us into cartoon figures who talked and acted like rednecks. Yes, she got under my skin, but I wouldn't murder to stop her making her pathetic woke videos. Now you may leave."

"Videos? Did the LKPD find these?" I asked Deke.

"She put them up on Instagram and TikTok," Cady spoke in the same listless voice. "The Yancy school board watched those videos the night they voted to fire me. At least that's what I've heard. Clarina had footage of herself with Trig picketing the school, but she also secretly videoed me when she was trying to argue me into letting her put what she called true Kansas history into my syllabus."

"She tried to video us at the breakfast she came to," Pat Everard said. "She wanted to push us into saying something she could make a fuss about in the social media world."

She smiled, a tight triumphant twitch of the mouth. "We got our friends to sing a hymn, and so she finally put her wretched phone away."

Cady followed me to the door, her face a study in un-happiness. "I'm sorry, Vic, sorry I invited you to stay here. Sorry I tried to get you to help look out for Gram."

"Murder investigations take a toll on everyone. Me included, so it's better that I stay someplace more private. One last thing, though—the town your grand-mother said your family came from. She called it 'Skinny Atlas'?" I spelled out what I thought I'd heard.

Cady gave a tired smile. "It's one of those trick words, like 'Ptolemy,' that don't sound like they're spelled." She spelled it out for me: Skaneateles. "You're not really going to go there to bother any Wheelocks still living there, are you? Gram took me to visit once when I was twelve so I could feel connected to my roots, but we didn't know any of the Wheelocks or Entwistles who still lived there. And they wouldn't know anything about land deals in Lawrence from a hundred fifty years ago."

"I'm not going to bother the Wheelocks of Skan-eateles," I said. "But if you were a creep who thought your town's name gave you license to bully a chubby girl, maybe you'd think it was funny that your town was called Skinny something."

36

The Agony Column

As I was getting into the Camry, Deke stood inside the car's door so I couldn't close it. "What is it you think you found out about Rotherhaite?"

"He quit after a heated argument with the new owners at the Wakarusa coal plant. Rotherhaite said he wasn't going to work for someone who knew nothing about coal."

"So now you're going to get local industry involved in your crap. You don't know anything about coal, either, do you?"

"My crap? A drug house I discovered is now my crap? A dead body I found is now my crap? Was it my arrival that caused Clete Rotherhaite to quit his job in fury with his new management?"

He knew he was wrong, and so he sensibly kept quiet. I wasn't quite so sensible. "Clete Rotherhaite supposedly went for a walk to cool his head after he resigned. He was someone whose idea of exercise was lifting a beer can."

"Just leave Rotherhaite and the plant alone. If you can't, I will lock you up for obstruction."

"Yes, you do hold the power cards here. If you could kindly move your law-enforcing body away from the door, I will get out of your auntie Gertrude's line of sight and thus prevent another heart attack in the making. And if you would release my Mustang, and me, then I'd be glad to abandon all my crap and go back to Chicago."

He moved away from the door but came back as I was pulling it shut. "I need to know where you're going from here."

"To the library. What else have I done that you should know about? I told you about Brett meeting some heavy outside the Dundee house, right? Is that on Everard land?"

"Don't push me, Warshawski. Everards don't own anything out there anymore. I don't know what the Wheelocks own, if anything. I need to know where you're staying."

I gave a tight smile. "In case Karas finally signs an

arrest warrant? I usually start the day at the Decadent Hippo. Or you can look at your tracking data—you must be following my phone these days, or those CCTV cameras that are perched on top of so many of your town's streetlights."

He put his hands together, parody of a prayer. "Could you, as a personal favor, make my job a tiny bit easier and tell me if you've found a place to crash?"

He was a good cop, and not usually this confrontational. It dawned on me that he was attacking me because he was caught between what he thought was right and what his chief and the DA said he should be doing. And on top of that, I'd attacked his mother. I told him where I was staying.

"What? You think you can solve Coffin's murder by being right on the spot there?"

"And you think I should cooperate with you when you challenge or criticize every step I take?"

I slammed the door. That's what you get when you cooperate with law enforcement.

I made a face as I gunned the engine. I sounded like Trig Garrity: they're all pigs whether they're public or private. Thinking of Trig made me remember the wrench. I hoped it had arrived at Cheviot. I hoped it held some conclusive evidence of Clarina's murder. I felt as though my head might split into pieces, like the jagged veins of a pomegranate, my brains spilling out in little red seeds.

A truck convoy from Kirmek Construction was bouncing along Sixth Street, spewing gray exhaust over my windshield. They were hard at work up on Yancy. I pulled off the road until the trucks belched past.

I'd landed in a strip mall, which reminded me that I needed to supply my own linens at the trailer. At the Buy-Smart outlet, I bought cheap bedding and towels.

When I got to the trailer, Al, whoever he was, hadn't been around yet with the butane, but I was too tired to mind the cold. I was too tired to mind anything. I made up the bed but crawled in without undressing, beyond shoes and blazer. Peppy curled up next to me, as exhausted as I was.

A warning bark from Peppy woke me a few hours later. It took a minute for me to remember where I was, but I heard banging on the side of the trailer and stumbled to the door.

A heavy-set man in a lumberman's checked shirt was attaching a cannister of butane to a nozzle. "You're just about set here, miss. I've switched on the electricity, too. Turning on the heater is pretty straightforward, but if you have any problems, talk to my mom and she'll give me a call."

I switched on the heat. The butane ignited, and the

trailer's baseboard heaters came to life. I heated up some canned lentil soup on the two-burner cooktop and set up my computer. The trailer park boasted Wi-Fi, but I thought it prudent to use my personal router. I sent messages to both lawyers—Freeman in Chicago and Faye Mitchell in Kansas City—along with Murray and Zoë to let them know I'd moved.

I called Lou and Ed to tell them where I'd landed, and also to report on my visit to the Wakarusa power plant. "They were unloading a half dozen hopper cars of coal. The day shift foreman and two of his buddies were pretty cooperative; they just don't know much. But what they told me has left me with a lot of unanswerable questions about how Rotherhaite really died."

I told them what I'd found out. "He seemed to think the plant would need a lot of upgrading before it could be fully operational again."

"He was right about that," Ed said. "Place is inefficient, and it doesn't have any computer controls. Should be sold for scrap. I'd think the Power Ranger outbid us for the scrap, except they wouldn't be bringing in new coal if they were going to scuttle the plant."

"What does it take in coal and human power for a plant that size to be running full capacity?"

"Depends," Lou said. "Maybe a hundred, hundred-fifty people spread over three shifts if they were going twenty-four-seven. If you didn't see a lot of activity, sounds like they're just doing a maintenance level of firing."

"Except six hoppers?" Ed said. "Sounds like they're gearing up for more action."

"I wondered if the resort was a side hustle, with the power plant being the main action," I said. "If they bought it cheap, maybe they figure they can turn a big profit on selling excess energy."

"Be careful around that plant," Lou put in. "People don't like you snooping, they could put a world of hurt on you that you'd never recover from."

"Mr. Sunshine," Ed said. "Don't try to scare her off. Number one, she's doing righteous work. And number two, you should know by now, lady don't scare easy."

That was comforting, even if not accurate. When we hung up, I called Zoë. She was predictably cross that I hadn't taken her with me to look at the coal plant, especially when I told her that Rotherhaite's body had been found nearby.

"Thank goodness you came down here to investigate. Otherwise, no one would know anything. How can I get to the place where they found his body?"

"You need to be on the river path. That's easiest to reach if you get on it in Lawrence, by the bridge. Otherwise it's a mess going across country from the road.

If you bike along the path, you'll see where the grasses and bushes are all beaten down by the emergency response crews, but you'd have to go soon. Any more rain or snow will obliterate the traces."

"You want to go out there with me tomorrow morning?"

"It's time I talked to Mr. Brett Santich," I said.

Zoë knew the name and address of the insurance company where he worked part-time. Once again, she bartered local knowledge for a seat at the interview table. I assured her she had a big career ahead of her— as a Mob enforcer.

My conversation with Cady, Gertrude, and Deke had been so fraught this morning that I'd overlooked one crucial point. If Clarina had come from Skaneateles, someone there would know her real name. When Sherlock Holmes was trying to find someone, he'd post an ad in the Agony Column of the *Times*. I guess Facebook and Instagram are today's equivalent. I drafted an ad, using the clearest of the pictures of Clarina that Zoë had taken for the *Herald*'s story about the Yancy school picket.

Skaneateles, NY Natives: Do you know this woman? She was using the alias "Clarina Coffin" when she was murdered in Lawrence, Kansas, ten days ago. If you know her, or know anything about her, please get in touch with private investigator V.I. Warshawski @viwarshawski-investigates.com.

I found Skaneateles on a map. Syracuse was the closest big city, but Skaneateles was also near Auburn, where Harriet Tubman had lived, and Seneca Falls, home of the first women's rights convention. Just the place to produce committed abolitionists, or today's woke equivalent.

I paid to target the ad for all those places, then took Peppy for a long run, all the way to Yancy Hill and back. For the first time in months, the first time since Taylor's killing, despite my disturbed sleep, I was moving freely through space. I had a plan, I was making connections out of all the data I'd been uncovering. My investigative skills were reviving.

Fishing without a Line

The Great Plains Agency was in a new building in a strip mall on the west side of town, not far from the trailer park. I'd looked at their website before driving downtown to pick Zoë up at the *County Herald*'s office. The five agents on staff had posted their photos with short bios. Santich said he was a fifth-generation member of the Douglas County community, committed to its economic well-being. He could assist with farm and farm implement coverage in addition to regular personal lines.

I'd only ever seen him looking angry. In his online photograph his tanned, square-jawed face looked reassuring, like the old Marlboro man: *You can trust me, ma'am, to take care of you and the little ones.* It wasn't impossible to think he could attract someone like Ivy.

A woman in her forties was staffing the front counter when Zoë and I arrived. She smiled hopefully—new business walking in the door. Her name was Patsy, she was here to help.

We asked for Brett. He was in but busy. Did Zoë and I have an appointment? We said we were happy to wait: he had been recommended as the best agent for our unique needs.

Patsy phoned him, then apologized. "He has an appointment off-site that he's just about to leave for. Any of our other agents would be glad to assist you gals, at least to take your information until Brett can get back to you."

Zoë started to say we had questions only Brett could answer, but I shook my head at her and said, "Tell him he's been recommended as someone who understands special coverage, especially when older, more rural property is involved. We're looking at a location that had been a drug house and we're wondering what we need to do to make it insurable. Ask Brett who else in the agency could handle this."

Patsy looked puzzled, but insurers bend over backward to win clients, so she relayed the message. After a brief chat, Patsy asked for our names. An even briefer chat and she told me Brett would be out to get us right away.

"That was cool, Vic," Zoë said when we'd backed away from the counter. "Now I know why you're the star."

I was expecting an instant eruption, but a good five minutes passed before the door behind Patsy's counter opened and Brett came out. He looked as he had on my other sightings: face set in harsh lines. The Marlboro man was going to drive me out of Dodge.

When he saw Zoë holding out her phone, ready to record, he snapped, "Zoë, put your damned phone away. I have nothing to say to the media, or to who-ever your sidekick is, about drug houses. No reputable agency would insure them."

I put on my most professional smile. "Mr. Santich, I'm sorry we're intruding. I'm V.I. Warshawski. Not exactly a sidekick, more like a private investigator looking into Clarina Coffin's murder. You and a buddy went into the Dundee house yesterday. The security cameras were turned off, so I had to assume you were the owner, or at least knew who operated—"

Santich cut me off hastily, with a nervous look at Patsy, who was practically levitating in her eagerness to eavesdrop. "We'll continue this conversation in the parking lot. Patsy, I'm on my way to the Schapens, to talk about covering their new spreader."

He tried yanking the outer door open, but the hydraulic arm didn't allow for violent gestures. Zoë and I followed him into the parking strip.

"I'll give you five minutes, but, Zoë, if you try to record this conversation I will smash your phone."

"That's a little excessive, and even pointless," I said. "Two of us here are witness to everything you say. What I'd really like to know is what you and Robert Tulloh needed to talk about that was secret and urgent enough to be at the Dundee house yesterday morning."

"What makes you think I was at that place?" Santich demanded.

"It's strewn with cameras. There's a record."

He curled his lip. "No record of my presence that I know about."

"So you are in charge of the surveillance," I said. "However, you didn't shut off my own camera."

I pulled up the video I'd shot while lying behind the trees. The resolution wasn't great, but Santich was recognizable.

Beads of sweat glistened at his hairline. "You were trespassing," Santich hissed, "which means you have a hell of a nerve trying to ask me questions about people I talk to."

"Why was Tulloh so angry? Was it about the drugs, or about the murder? Or about a connection between your house and the Wakarusa coal plant? He's been seen at both places."

"We were having a private conversation. That is my house, on my land, and the people I talk to are none of your business."

"It is your house," I agreed. "It's also where significant crimes have been committed—murder being the most serious, but America is suffering from such a horrific opioid epidemic, I can't believe you could host drug parties and take them lightly."

I paused, but he didn't speak. "When I saw you on the Yancy jobsite, in another argument, I thought maybe the construction crew had been using the house without your knowledge. I imagined you might be a hero, taking them to task, but after seeing you yesterday with Tulloh, it's clear you're involved with all the key players. Did you cut someone out of their share of your drug sales? Does Tulloh have some hold over you?"

Santich's Adam's apple worked, but he prudently kept quiet. I saw Zoë had surreptitiously pressed the record button on her phone.

"Going back to the surveillance cameras nailed to the trees and the back door and so on, I've been trying to figure out where the controls are. Surely not here at the agency, where Patsy is listening to every word you speak. I suppose you could do them from home. The lazy criminal often takes the easiest route, but you've got a wife and daughter who could find their way into the computer controls at any time. You wouldn't want them to see what happens at the Dundee place. Of course, you're not quite so finicky about what Ivy or Timmy might stumble onto."

A pasty pallor appeared beneath his tan, making him look like a painting where the colors were running. He was rocking on the balls of his feet, and he gave off a sweet, sickly odor. I wondered if he might faint. If he cracked his head on the asphalt, that wouldn't help Ivy, his wife, or either of his children—or the investigation.

"You need to sit down." I looked around for a bench, but this wasn't a scenic spot; no one wanted to sit watching the traffic on Route 59.

He ignored the suggestion. "What do you want?"

"So many things," I said. "Justice, mercy, peace for starters, but from you, mostly I want knowledge. I want to know what they're building on top of Yancy."

"A resort," he said thickly. "Everyone knows you were harassing Gertrude Perec and Pat Everard about the planning permits, but they were legitimate permits, and what they specify is a resort and shops."

"There's a particle accelerator west of Chicago," I

said. "They have a ring a kilometer around with magnets that whip particles into racing almost at the speed of light. That accelerator needs the kind of power they're getting ready to bring onto Yancy. Tell me what kind of resort needs that much energy."

"How should I know?" he muttered. "Maybe they're building a physics lab."

"What a great idea," I said. "That will be a nice surprise, a present from Tulloh Industries to the University of Kansas. Why call it a resort, though, unless old Mr. Tulloh likes giving people fancy surprises. Is that why Clarina Coffin was murdered? She was going to spoil the surprise?"

The pasty pallor was fading, but he was still sweating in the cold February air. "Just because your ass is in a sling over the Sabrina girl's OD and the Coffin woman's murder, you think that's on the top of everyone's mind. You're fishing and you don't have a line."

He was trying to speak contemptuously, but it didn't quite come off.

"I'd think crimes of that magnitude in your house would be at the top of your mind, too," I said. "Let's see what knowledge I've been able to fish up even without a line. Two nights ago, someone broke into the apartment where I was staying—someone with sophisticated lock-picking skills who could get in without leaving a mark on the lock plate. Maybe they were looking for something they thought I had, maybe they were trying to plant something on me. I think it was the plant, because they called the cops, and told them I had something hot and juicy for the law to find.

"However, nothing showed up, despite a diligent search, which must have annoyed the would-be planters. If your buddy Robert Tulloh was calling that shot, he must have been furious. I'm picturing the text or voicemail: *Meet me at the Dundee house.*

"When you got there, he screamed and yelled. *Why were you holding drug parties there*, I imagine him bellowing. *We don't want attention paid to Yancy because we're building this secret physics project or whatever it is, and drug parties and dead history buffs bring all kinds of attention.* Did he add, *Can't you do anything right?* Is that the insult you've been hearing your whole life?"

Santich was plucking at his throat, but he didn't speak.

I turned to Zoë. "What did the planning commission tell you about the environmental impact statement?"

Zoë said promptly, "The commission chair said the lawyers who filed the plans had submitted an environmental impact report that showed they'd had the site inspected and approved for the use on the application, namely a resort and an unspecified number of stores."

"So if the builders are doing something else, something naughty on that site, they'd want to keep it on the down-low, wouldn't they?"

"For sure," Zoë said vigorously.

"I can guess that the Tullohs, or whoever the investors are, would be seriously annoyed about drug parties near the hilltop. They don't want anyone nosing around until it's too late to backpedal on what they're actually doing. By the way, a present to the physics department, that was inspired thinking."

Santich's jaw worked. He was still off-color, and my praise didn't seem to boost his spirits.

"Was Clarina killed because she was poking around the physics resort and threatening to go to Douglas County's de facto bosses, Gertrude Perec and Pat Everard, with what she was seeing?"

At that Santich gave me a contemptuous smile. "You don't actually know anything. You think you have some fancy skills that will get me to tell you secrets I don't know so you can look important back in Chicago."

It was a good shot, but I ignored it. "What about Trig? Is he as big a nuisance as Clarina? Is his life in danger now?"

"Garrity?" Santich said. "He was born useless. No one takes him seriously."

"Then why did he have to be lured out to the Dundee house along with Gertrude Perec the night that Clarina died?"

"What I heard, he showed up, wanting to break in. Who knows why he went in the first place, unless he thought there'd still be drugs on the premises and he could help himself."

"That's a good storyline," I said. "Not as good as the physics lab, but still credible. Wouldn't you agree, Zoë?"

"I would if I didn't know Trig doesn't touch drugs," she said. "He's been arrested a gazillion times, and they've done a bunch of drug tests, but he's always clean."

I turned back to Santich. "I know you have to get out to the Schapens to talk about their—shredder, was it? No, spreader. I won't keep you. Just one more question. The construction on top of Yancy, when they made their application to the planning commission— what was the name on the project?"

"I wasn't involved in the application. It would have been a conflict of interest." His words came out slowly—his throat was dry, his voice constricted.

Zoë spoke up again. "I went into the planning

committee minutes for that date before I came over here. The applicant was Yancy Project LLC. Yancy Project LLC took me to Pioneer State Bank and Trust in Topeka. They're the trustees. Right now the only name on file for whom to call with questions is Pioneer's trust department, so I called them, and they referred me to their lawyer, who wouldn't answer questions."

"It's looking like all those layers of secrecy are shielding the Tullohs," I said. "Are the Tullohs in turn shielding you? Is that why Frank Karas is looking at me and Trig instead of you for Clarina's murder?"

"No one wants to arrest me because they know I haven't broken any laws."

"The drug parties?"

"The fraternity asked my permission to use the house so they could hold barbecues out there. They paid me rent, they kept the house clean, I didn't have any reason to check up on them. Of course, now we won't be renting it out to them anymore."

"You have an amazingly fertile imagination, Mr. Santich. I understand Marvel is always looking for talent. Gift-wrapped particle accelerators, frat boys holding barbecues, Ivy cleaning up after those s'mores—they do leave a gooey trail everywhere they go, don't they?"

Santich shifted his weight from foot to foot. "You

don't live here. So nothing that gets done here is any of your business. And you are not part of my life, so nothing I do is any of your business." He turned away.

"But I live here, Mr. Santich," Zoë said. "And I'm responsible for getting news to the hundred twenty thousand people in the county. A big construction project is big news. It could mean jobs, after all, which is always good news. It could also mean water and air pollution, which is always bad news. Whether it's good news or bad, I'll dig it out and report it."

Santich looked at her, then me, hands clenched into fists as they had been yesterday morning. And as they had been yesterday, hanging at his side, longing to punch someone but knowing he couldn't, at least not in full view of his office.

"You do that," he said thickly. "You report it. As for you—" He looked at me, jerked his head toward the parked cars.

I followed him to his SUV, the old, dusty Kia he'd been driving the night I'd first seen him at the field house. "What do you know about Ivy and Timmy?"

"Only what she's told me. I wondered why she would take on as scutty a job as cleaning up after one of those parties. It's a kind of hard way for her to get child support, isn't it?"

"How'd you even find her?"

"I'm an investigator," I said. "I investigate."

"Don't go investigating Ivy. You won't find the clear-cut victim story she wants you to believe."

He stumbled over to the Kia. I rejoined Zoë, but as we got into the Camry, Brett still hadn't started the engine. Before turning out of the lot, I looked back at the agency. Patsy was standing at the window, watching the end of the drama.

38
Marlin Fishing

Of course, Zoë wanted to know who Ivy and Timmy were.

"Ivy is someone who may have loved Brett too well, but not wisely. I can't tell you anything about her—I don't even know her last name. I met her by chance. She cleans, or used to clean the Dundee house after their parties."

Zoë digested that. "And Timmy?"

"I said she may not have loved wisely."

"Oh. She had a kid. Brett's married with a kid. He really is deep in quicksand, isn't he. Mortgages, dead bodies, angry investors, a second family."

"I still don't understand why local LEOs aren't paying close attention to him," I said.

"Maybe they are and they're playing it close to the chest. You'll figure it out though; I'm counting on you to make this a complete story."

"Get in line," I said harshly. "I feel as though a thousand people are counting on me. I'm tired of it."

My dad, talking to me earnestly after my mother's death, when I ran wild through South Chicago and his pals in the Fourth District picked me up and brought me home, instead of booking me. *I'm counting on you to honor your mother's memory by acting in a way that would make her proud.* Bernie counted on me. Clients counted on me. Peter's student Taylor had counted on me, and they were dead. And who could I count on? Not Peter, who wasn't even returning my texts.

"I'm sorry, Vic," Zoë said in a small voice. "You seem so cool and knowledgeable, like you can figure out anything, but I didn't mean to make you mad."

I forced a smile. "You didn't make me mad, I did that to myself. The words you used, they're a trigger for me these days. You can't count on me to make this a complete story—it's more responsibility than I can handle."

She didn't speak again until we reached the newspaper offices, then said, "Can I ask advice when I'm stuck? Will you keep sharing your discoveries with me?"

I nodded. "We have to keep working together. We're

all each other has right now. You know those photos of people fishing, where it's some giant marlin or shark that pulls them off the boat into the water? Tulloh Industries, Clarina's murder, the drugs, the Yancy construction, Clete Rotherhaite—they're a giant fish that's trying to drown me. If I go under, you save yourself."

"No, Vic. If you go under, I'll win a Pulitzer writing it up."

I couldn't help laughing. "That's the spirit. You do that."

I dropped her at the newspaper office and drove on across the river. I was on the far side of the bridge from the Boat Yard and the strip mall where I kept replenishing my wardrobe. On this side, there were sandbars and rocky shallows. I walked down to the edge and let Peppy splash around while I sat, trying to collect myself. Deep breaths, singers' breaths that Gabriella had tried to instill in me. I found myself weeping, as if my mother's death had happened three days, not three decades, ago.

After a time, the light on the water changed from brown to silver to black. I got stiffly to my feet, called Peppy to heel. On my way to the trailer park, I stopped at a wine shop, where I found a bottle of Terre Nere, a Sicilian red I've recently come to love. It's hard to find; maybe it was a sign that my luck would change.

Back at the trailer, I lay down. Peppy lay beside me, licking sweat from my neck.

"We're okay, girl," I said. "We'll make it through. Not clear how or when, but we will."

I forced myself to think about my open investigations in Chicago. First, though, I checked on the ads I'd placed this morning on social media. Five people recognized Clarina under five different names. When I wrote back, asking for particulars, it turned out only one of the five was missing, and I found her readily through a voter registration database. She'd moved to Arizona eighteen years ago and had cut herself off from her family.

Maybe my luck wasn't turning after all. However, I settled down to work. With the butane heater turned on, the trailer was warm enough, but it felt like a cold and lonely place. I was grateful for my dog's presence. I kept a hand on her neck, her warm soft fur a comfort as I verified details on the résumés one of my clients had sent me: both candidates looked too good to be true, including one who claimed to have been a navy SEAL. Maybe not the most common lie in the English language, but a recurring cliché on today's pumped-up résumés. I was tempted to dismiss him out of hand, but I sent a request to the Navy.

I resisted the impulse to drive into town for dinner

in a clean well-lighted place. I had my bottle of Terre Nere. I stirred up a mushroom risotto from the supplies I'd bought and made myself eat a large serving. Back in the saddle, V.I., back in the saddle. Client work, regular meals, regular workouts, soon I'd be ready to join the SEALs myself, or at least be able to pay my bills.

At eleven, when I got ready for bed, I studied my reflection in the bathroom mirror. Not so many ribs showing, but what I focused on was a gold pendant Peter had given me, made to his specs in his Institute's Conservation lab. Inanna, goddess of life and death, childbirth, and war, brushed my breasts.

"Your avatar, V.I.," he'd said when he placed it around my neck a year ago.

Inanna was a warrior goddess, he'd explained. When she went into the Underworld to be a goddess to the dead as well as to the living, her shepherd-husband cavorted around on her throne. She made him take her place in the Underworld so that she could return to the land of the living.

"Can you do that?" I asked the small amulet. "Can you return me to the land of the living?"

I sent Peter a text. I never thought of you as the kind of person who would ghost me instead of telling me directly that you were through with our relationship. My words for you: conscientious, wryly humorous, razor intellect, responsible. But that was before Taylor's father shot you. Maybe the shooting, the anguish over your student, reconfigured your character. It did mine. I'm easily depressed, second-guessing myself in ways I never did before. But I am still wearing Inanna. Xxxx V.I.

Right before I turned out the light, I got pinged by the U.S. Navy. My candidate had, in fact, been a SEAL; he'd lost a leg in combat and was transitioning to civilian life. It pays to do your best work even when you think there's no point. What a bundle of wholesome self-advice I was producing. Maybe that would be my new career—creating those little front-of-the-store books that tell you how you, too, could be perfect with a minimal amount of work.

I rechecked responses to my social media ads for Clarina Coffin and again had harvested a handful of duds. I was drifting off to sleep when my phone rang. A handful of friends are allowed to breach my silencing settings. My heart beat faster, imagining Peter, responding to my text. I couldn't find the light switch in the strange room, but I picked up my phone.

Not Peter. Angela Creedy. A stab of disappointment, but Angela wouldn't call at eleven-forty-five on a whim.

"Vic, I know this is a strange time to be calling, and

a strange thing to be calling about, but do you have another phone? Can you call me back?"

She hung up before I could answer. I found the light switch and sat up, bewildered, even frightened, fearing she or Bernie must be in trouble.

Another phone. I found a burner in my backpack and called.

"This is crazy and even creepy, Vic, but—but Sabrina's mother is here. She wants to talk to you but she's afraid her calls are being monitored. Bernie's in a match in Ann Arbor, that's why it's me calling."

She handed the phone off to Valerie Granev.

"Ms. Warshawski? I have the engineering skill to tell that someone has planted spyware on my phones. I have three, and they are all contaminated. I need to be quick, before someone figures I'm using this phone and starts monitoring it.

"I'm in Chicago to collect my daughter's belongings. Sabrina is—she is recovering, I think, I hope, but slowly. She won't be back in school, or anyway, not this school, not for a long while, if ever."

Her voice quavered, holding back tears. She stopped for a beat; I heard Angela urge her to drink something.

"Sabrina is in the best institution in the country for dealing with addiction and brain impairment. We—Ram and I—we couldn't have gotten her in on our own, at least not so quickly, and we couldn't afford to keep her there without help. I—I was asked—told—not to communicate with you, to fire you—after you agreed to help me—us. I told the FBI you had not kidnapped my daughter, that you saved her life, so I hope they're not charging you with a crime.

"Angela told me you have to stay in Kansas because they suspect you of a murder in that same house where you found Sabrina. I'm sorry, sorry my daughter's troubles brought all this grief to you, sorry I can't talk to you directly, but for me, Sabrina comes first."

"Of course your daughter comes first for you, but I also know the Tullohs made a handsome gift to your husband when you fired me. I'm cleaning up a giant mess involving drugs and at least one, maybe two, murders as the thank-you gift I got for saving your daughter's life. I want you to show some gratitude."

"I can't—Sabrina—"

I cut her off. "Tell me what the Tullohs are building on Yancy."

"I don't know. Honestly I don't know. It's nothing to do with avionics, so I'm not on the distribution list. All I can tell you is that the brothers are arguing over it. No one knows what Matthew thinks. Sometimes he talks to Pauline instead of the sons."

She hung up abruptly.

I called back, and spent some time talking to Angela, who was understandably worried by Valerie's behavior. The whole time we were speaking, I could hear Valerie in the background, urging her to hang up before someone traced her to the house.

I turned off the lights, but it was a long time before I went back to sleep.

39
Fermented Cabbage

Sometimes Matthew Tulloh talked to his daughter instead of his sons, Valerie had said.

The sons both lived in a gated community with their father near the company's Salina headquarters. Of course, being billionaires, they had plenty of other homes. New York and London to be close to financial centers. Palm Springs for golf, Mont Blanc for winter sports, Sardinia for peaceful getaways.

Pauline's main residence was in Mission Hills, a wealthy enclave in Kansas City. Pauline had been married and divorced some years ago. There wasn't any mention of children, while the brothers both had three each. She'd separated herself geographically, at least a

little; maybe she'd separated herself enough emotionally that she'd confide in a female PI.

"What should I do?" I asked Peppy. "Cold-call on
the phone, at the front door, or a text?"

Peppy pawed at my knee.

"Try her in person, right you are."

It was possible that she was in the family enclave in
Palm Springs or the one in Sardinia, but Peppy and I
set off for Kansas City in a hopeful spirit. The sky was
an eggshell blue, a color that made me feel young and
optimistic: spring would be here soon; I would solve
Clarina's murder; I'd hear from Peter; I'd figure out if
I wanted to end my life as an investigator and take up
something new and amazing.

Pauline's mansion was set well back from the road,
surrounded by a high iron fence with movable spikes
along the top. The road itself was a discreet ribbon
in the middle of a large parkway, barely noticeable
for the creek that ran alongside it. I let Peppy splash
in the creek and chase rabbits across the parkway
before shutting her back in the car.

I left the Camry on a nearby cross street and walked
back to the Tulloh place. When I buzzed an intercom
set into one of the gateposts, a man answered. I explained I was a detective working on the crimes around

the Tulloh family's Yancy project and hoped to speak to Pauline.

The man who spoke to me was waiting at the top of the walk. He escorted me around the side of the house to a glassed-in porch overlooking a garden with a pond and ornamental fountain. Pauline Tulloh was inside, sitting cross-legged in a white wicker chaise longue. She was in leggings and an oversize shirt, and her toes in her braided leather flip-flops had been groomed and painted turquoise. The sun picked out a range of colors in her hair, from a dull gold to a glossy brown. It was so expertly painted that it ended up looking fake.

When the man, whose name I learned was Mellon, ushered me inside, Pauline didn't get up, but waved me to a wicker basket chair. Mellon left me at the doorway, but returned almost immediately with a tall glass holding a greenish liquid, which he put on a round table next to Pauline's left hand.

"It's my ten A.M. pick-me-up. Do you want one? Grass, lemon, a little fermented cabbage as an immune booster."

It sounded revolting. "My body would collapse under so much health," I said.

"You're a private detective. Does that mean you want bourbon or rye?"

Mellon's expression remained bland, but he murmured that they also had Sardinian fizzy water or coffee. I was eager to try a billionaire's coffee.

When Pauline lifted her immune boost to drink, I saw a ring, gold, covered with small red stones, on the traditional wedding ring finger.

She saw me staring and laughed. "Such a beautiful ring. When my husband and I parted, I saw no reason to resize it for another finger."

She drank some more fermented cabbage. "What's the Yancy project?"

"I was hoping you could tell me," I said. "Yancy is a hill outside the northwest border of Lawrence. The Kaw makes a loop there and creates a kind of embrace around the hill. A hedge fund owns a big chunk of the hill. Two years ago they got planning permission to build a resort and some shops, but they are putting in an eye-popping power grid. I'd like to know what they're actually building."

Pauline looked into her glass. "I see, yes, I see a power grid, I see trucks. I don't see the Tulloh name."

"Tilt the glass," I said. "Look a bit farther north, to the Kaw and the old Wakarusa Power Plant. It now belongs to your brother Robert."

She held the glass out. Mellon materialized to take it away, returning a moment later with coffee in a small porcelain pot, a porcelain mug, and a little pitcher of cream. I drank some coffee, black. Mellon or whoever staffed the kitchen did a nice job. It wasn't any better than the Hippo's, but the porcelain elevated it to something special.

"And is Robert also in charge of the construction on this hilltop?" Pauline asked.

"I don't know," I said. "He keeps popping up in the area. The FBI was having me deposed for my involvement in saving the life of a young woman whose mother works for your family's company. Your brother showed up in the conference room and ended the interrogation. It was an interesting display of power, a private citizen derailing a federal interrogation.

"Two days ago, your brother Robert showed up outside an old house at the bottom of Yancy, a house that still belongs to one of the original owners of the hill. Robert was chewing out the owner, a man named Brett Santich."

"You think that proves that my brother is the secret owner of the hedge fund?" Pauline asked. Her husky voice was languid, almost mocking.

Being rich means you can ridicule the people around you to derail a conversation you don't like. Being a detective means staying serious and straightforward.

"Your other brother is also interested in some aspect of the Yancy project. Two days after I found Sabrina

Granev close to death in that house at the base of Yancy, Jacob seemed to be coaching the Lawrence police chief during a press conference on Granev's health."

"Jake and Robert do like to boss people around," Pauline said. "Mellon, what's Jake's connection to the Lawrence police chief?"

Mellon had been hovering just inside the door. "Jake and Chief McDowell were fraternity brothers at Wichita State thirty-three years ago."

Pauline nodded. "So it's not surprising the chief would welcome Jake's support at a press conference."

"When your brother Robert was arguing with Brett Santich, I overheard part of the conversation. I confess that I only caught a few words, so I may be filling in the blanks wrong, but he thought somebody's sister might 'bitch the whole deal.'"

"Real-life detectives actually do go listening at keyholes." The mockery was more pronounced.

"We're like everyone else—electronic keyholes, and mine wasn't very sophisticated. My recording suggested you resented your brothers and that might lead you to kill the deal."

"Resent? I try not to think about them that much. Daddy didn't want me working in the company. Mother was never involved; she let Daddy make all the decisions, turning her grain elevators into Tulloh gold. He thought that was a good model for me to follow.

"I married one of his rising executives so I could play the good daughter/wife role, but when my husband saw that no outsider would ever have a top job at Tulloh, he left for a start-up. And he left me. And then Daddy bought the start-up and shut it down.

"Since then, I try to pay no attention to anything any of them are doing, but sometimes Daddy still comes around whining because Robert is impetuous and stupid, and Jake is too cautious and also stupid." Her voice hadn't changed pitch or cadence; she might have been talking about what a nuisance it was to clean the birdfeeders that dotted the garden outside the sun-room.

"And has he come around whining about Robert and the Yancy project?"

Pauline studied her fingernails, which, like her toes, were perfectly manicured. "In a general way, he wants the boys to know how important it is to clear the ground of obstacles before you start building. He might have meant there were unexpected problems with the build-ing site, but it could have been metaphoric, of course."

"You know a woman was murdered and left to die in that house on Yancy land."

She gave a sardonic smile. "You think that she might

have been an obstacle to the building site? Robert killed her to show Daddy he could remove obstacles?"

"If she was in the way of the project, I expect he would have had someone do it for him."

At that she laughed. "That would be Jake. Robert loves getting his hands dirty."

"Murdering a woman would leave a lot of dirt on your hands. Not all the perfumes of Tulloh Industries could sweeten them. If you could bitch the Yancy project, would you?"

"I don't know what I could do to derail it, assuming it is a Tulloh Industries thing."

"If your father confides in you, I expect you could tell him your brothers are making serious mistakes over in Lawrence."

"Such as?" Her voice hadn't changed, but her face looked alert, cautious.

"The planning commission approved plans for a resort and some shops. But it looks as though they're installing a big power grid, which is perhaps why they bought a coal plant. It would be a resort on the scale of the country of Monaco to require that much power."

"I expect Daddy knows about that," she said. "He likes old coal plants. Coal makes him feel connected to the ground, and the ground is where his fortune comes from—coal, gas, but wheat and sorghum are where he started. He's suspicious of financial instruments that are separate from the land."

"But he must have a huge investment portfolio," I objected.

"Of course. He has a whole building full of portfolio managers. But he likes them grounded in reality. No crypto for him."

"Does your mother have a role in his business decisions? I gather he started with her grain elevators."

"Daddy turned her into a billionaire, while her brothers lost all their land and the elevators their father left them. Why would she regret it?"

"That's definitely what your grandmother Tulloh believed, isn't it?" I said. "Someone recorded her at your parents' fiftieth anniversary party. She was quite gleeful about how badly your mother's family had fared."

"Mother doesn't like conflict. She let Grandmother Tulloh say a lot of things that were hard to listen to. She won't fight with Daddy either, so she sometimes asks me to support—charities—he might not like."

Her hesitation before "charities" made me ask, "Is Brett Santich one of your mother's charities?"

"Santich? Oh, the man you saw Robert arguing with. If Mother knows him, she hasn't shared that knowledge with me. No, there are other people in Lawrence she cares about, but not him. Mellon."

She didn't raise her voice; he appeared at once.

"The detective and I are done here. Can you make sure she leaves the premises, maybe get Johnno to escort her out of the village?"

I got to my feet. "You don't have any role in the company?"

Her smile reappeared, but it was brittle. "I do have a role. I cash dividend checks and admire the boys."

40

"A" Student

I collected Peppy and walked with her along the creek bed, trying to decipher Pauline's comments. She had been strangely revealing of her family's dynamics, all delivered in a cool tone that made it sound as though she didn't care. Was I supposed to think we'd been intimate, and so I wouldn't question anything she or her family did?

Then there were comments about her brothers and their different ways of dealing with obstacles. Did she know that Robert had killed Clarina, or was she saying he was capable of doing so? And what about her statement that she gave money to her mother's—charities?

The dog and I had walked as far as a small commercial strip. While I waited in line at a coffee bar, I looked up Mellon on my phone. Geoffrey Mellon, forty-seven years old, had studied social psychology and homeland security at Wichita State University, had worked for a private security firm, then joined Tulloh Industries nine years ago. Doing what was impossible to discover, but he'd clearly proved himself worthy of bringing Pauline her fermented cabbage.

I shared a bagel with the dog as we walked back to the car, but I poured out the coffee. Three dollars and undrinkable. At least I could expense it.

We were just getting into the car when a text came through from Abby Langford, the archivist at the Kansas Origins Museum and Library. The museum's conservator had finished studying the photo I'd found in Clarina's trailer. He wanted to deliver his report in person; could I come in this afternoon?

The museum was seventy-five miles away, but those were Kansas miles, not Chicago. I was in the museum parking lot a little over an hour later.

Abby Langford greeted me at the reference desk with a worried frown. Before we met the conservator, she needed to talk to me about something truly serious that she'd learned only after her earlier message.

"I asked one of my coworkers if there were other materials Clarina looked at which might show what she was working on. I know I told you we protect our readers' anonymity, but in this case I decided to bend that rule.

"We have diaries belonging to dozens of early settlers; Clarina went through many of them during the fifteen months she used our collection. All of us in reference agreed she seemed most interested in one of the last collections she came on. These were the diaries of a Lawrence woman, a Mrs. Florence Wheelock. We were fortunate that the family gifted us with the diaries because Florence wrote in them for close to sixty years."

I made enthusiastic noises. "Fabulous. The Wheelocks were the first people, at least the first European settlers, to claim land on a place just outside Lawrence called Yancy Hill. Yancy is where Clarina's body was found. A current-day Wheelock descendant was at a drug house on Yancy the night Clarina's body was found there. Maybe the diaries can give some background on the Wheelocks' relationship to Yancy. I'd love to see them."

"We'd love to see the diaries, too." Langford's smile was thin-lipped, tight. "There are seventeen volumes altogether, starting in 1858, when Florence was thirteen, and ending in 1919, when she was seventy-four. The three volumes covering 1864, when she married, to 1877, are missing. We believe Clarina Coffin smuggled them out of the library. You didn't see anything in her home that could have been these diaries, did you?"

My heart sank. "If she had them, whoever tore her place apart found them and took them. What do they look like?"

Langford called to a young man sorting books in an area behind the reference counter. He disappeared into the stacks and returned with a trolley holding a collection of old books.

Langford took a box from the trolley and removed a cardboard binder tied shut with string. She opened it to show me a stack of paper, pieces of all different sizes, some with type set on them, some flimsy pages torn from mail-order catalogs. She let me look closely at one of the pages, as long as I didn't touch it. The immature handwriting was full of spelling mistakes.

"When Florence started her diaries, the family had no money, so she wrote on whatever she could find— bills of sale that she picked up on the town streets, things like that. She explains where she's getting the paper, and the paper itself is historically interesting. This carton represents 1859 and 1860, and it's fascinating for what she shows us of daily life while the border wars over slavery and statehood were in full sway.

"Then Florence began making a little money sewing for people in the town, and she bought journals. The first ones were accounting ledgers. I suppose that was what she could find, or what was cheap. She was passionately invested in her own education. She did odd jobs for a local schoolteacher in exchange for personal tutoring in the man's home at night. A lot of her entries from those years are school exercises, practicing her handwriting, composing little essays on U.S. history."

Langford opened one of a trio of large books to show me the accounting headers. The pages were marked off in squares for easy computation. Wheelock had written over the lines, but the ink was faded now, and the squares made it look as though her words were behind bars.

"When she married, and married a man of wealth, she started buying Italian leather-bound books. It's three of these that are missing."

She patted a row of books bound in a soft red leather. The skin had cracked with age. Langford explained that the family hadn't kept them in a controlled environment. She seemed almost as upset by that as by the disappearance of three of the volumes.

Langford wouldn't let me handle them, but she did measure them and let me photograph the fronts, with my flash turned off. The books were about six by eight inches, and perhaps an inch thick. Wheelock hadn't written every day, and as time passed, her entries grew shorter, but it was still an impressive record.

"You think Clarina stole the missing volumes?" I asked.

"She's the only person who's used them in the last five years."

"Could they be mis-shelved?"

Langford clicked her tongue impatiently. "Of course we thought of that, and we've done a thorough search, since my colleague told me they were missing. I'm hoping you can look at the Coffin woman's personal effects. Perhaps she took the covers off to make it easier to smuggle them out."

"In that case, you'd have found the covers here, surely?"

"She could have taken the covers to the women's washroom and put them in the trash there."

"I went through her trailer a week after her death, and the only things I found of interest were the pictures I brought in. As I said, whoever searched her trailer when she died got to them long before I showed up. It's possible the Lawrence police have them—they wouldn't share evidence with me, but they'd talk to you if you called and described what's missing."

Langford nodded and made a note.

I prodded the conversation away from the diaries. "You said your conservator had found something interesting?"

"Of course. And it is interesting. The loss of these journals has me rattled; sorry." She made a phone call, and a few minutes later a short, round man trotted in, carrying a cardboard folder fastened with a string around a button.

"Is this the detective? V.I. Warshawski? Have I pronounced that correctly? I'm Tommy Gellman. Your photograph is unique in my experience, I would say. It's a great pity it wasn't properly preserved, a very great pity." He looked at me sternly.

"It's a great pity that the woman who owned it was murdered," I said. "Thugs who trashed her home are responsible for the damage."

"That is sad. I was hoping you could give me more of a provenance. When you looked at it, what did you notice that was unusual?"

I felt I was back in Ms. Ruttan's high school English class, trying to cover up the fact that I hadn't read *Return of the Native.* "I did wonder about the flowers in her hair. She looks as though she's in mourning, so the wreath seemed odd. But I don't know anything about fashion history. Were flowers a part of Victorian mourning?"

He beamed. I might get an A after all. "When Queen Victoria ordered her court to mourn Albert's death with her, she decreed that jet was the only jewel that could be worn in court. After that, the demand for jet boomed not just in Britain, but in the States as well. Victoria spawned an industry for mourning jewelry in both countries. Another mourning token that people loved was jewelry made from the beloved's hair. People wore hair rings and brooches as a sign of love, not merely mourning, of course, as you must know if you've read your Austen—" He looked at me severely, and I nodded, pretending I had read my Austen.

"But what Abby thought she saw I've been able to verify. The wreath this woman is wearing is made of hair entwined with artificial flowers. But the hair is from a person of African heritage. A white woman sporting a Black person's hair—likely a man, since you can see the signs of a pregnancy in her waist and in her face—that is extraordinary." His face shone with excitement.

He showed me a magnified segment of the wreath, made as clear as his technology would allow.

I had to take his word for it. I couldn't distinguish the threads of hair from the faded stems of dried flowers.

"You don't have any way of identifying where the picture was taken?" I asked.

He shook his head regretfully. "I'm guessing it was taken by an amateur, a family member, someone like that. Professional photographers usually had their names somewhere on the print, and there's no trace of that.

"The dress looks to be from the 1870s, when the fashion was for hoopskirts to be flattened in front, as this dress is. That's what makes it possible to see the outline of her pregnancy." He used a paintbrush to trace a barely visible bump in the front of the frock. "Any middle-class woman of that era would have owned a dress like this for special occasions, so it's possible she isn't in mourning. Women of ordinary means wouldn't have owned a great many dresses, so this could have been what she wore to any special event, even church services. In those days, getting photographed was a special event."

Abby Langford had mentioned that Florence Wheelock had done sewing to make money. I asked if the picture could be of Wheelock.

Langford said, "We don't have a record of any photographs. Perhaps Coffin found it inside one of the diaries and didn't let us know."

"In which case it's the museum's property," Gellman said.

"We don't know anything about Clarina Coffin," I said. "She hid her identity amazingly in this age of constant surveillance. This could be a picture of one of her own ancestors. It's not mine to gift to you. Until we find out who Coffin is, what brought her to Lawrence, and who this woman is, no one can lay a claim to it. I want it back now so that I can show it to people in Lawrence who may recognize the woman in the picture. I'm also going to put it out on social media."

"Let me keep the original for safety's sake," Gellman pleaded. "I'll give you a high-res copy that you can show around without harming this. My lab can also restore the damage where that little tear is in the print."

I gave a reluctant agreement, demanding a written signed receipt, with the proviso that if I found someone with a legitimate legal claim to the print, the museum had to get their permission to keep the picture. Gellman took me to his office, where he produced the receipt. He also gave me three prints of the woman with the wreath in her hair. He clearly had already planned to keep the original.

Before I left, I asked Abby Langford if Gertrude Perec had used the collection recently. "She's a descendant of Florence Wheelock. If there was something scandalous in the books, perhaps even a reference to who this pregnant woman was—an ancestor whose misstep would sully the good Wheelock name—Ms. Perec might want to hide it."

Langford shook her head. "I double-checked that to

be certain. Clarina Coffin was the only person to request these diaries in the last five years."

On my way out, I stopped to look at the donor wall. Gertrude's name was there among the Bookbinders, people who'd given the museum between one and ten thousand. She was listed as Gertrude Wheelock Perec.

41

Gertrude and Cady

Smoke but No Fire?

Now do you understand why it was a mistake to involve that Chicago detective in our affairs?" Gertrude said.

"But, Gram—Frank Karas told her she had to stay in Lawrence."

"He didn't tell you to invite her to live with us. Even though she's moved out, she seems to think she has some kind of special right to barge into this house." Gertrude's lips had almost disappeared, the line of bitterness was so pronounced.

"Because she came around with that picture?"

Cady said. "Do you know who it was, Gram? Was that Florence Wheelock?"

Gertrude massaged the sides of her face. Tension had her clenching her jaw so hard that it was painful to move it.

"I don't know who it was. And neither does Pat Everard."

The detective had gone to the Perec house first. Gertrude had told Cady not to answer the door, or at least to tell the detective they had nothing left to say, no more patience for any insults the woman might spew out. Instead, Cady had spoken to her on the doorstep, and then invited her into the foyer.

Cady thought the photograph was exciting. A white abolitionist ancestor six generations back who perhaps had had a relationship with a Black man was remote enough to be romantic, not problematic.

"You know I have several photographs and even a daguerreotype of Great-grandmother Florence. I've shown them to you. This picture the detective is waving around doesn't look the least bit like her," Gertrude said fiercely, after she'd finally forced Warshawski to leave.

"Do you know the diaries Vic was talking about?" Cady asked. "They sound interesting, something we should try to publish."

"My mother gave them to the Origins Museum while I was away at college," Gertrude said. "One of the professors in the history department at the university here had been reading in them for some book he was working on. He persuaded Mother that they were falling apart because we couldn't keep them dry and cool or moist enough or whatever it was. So she gave them to the museum.

"There were many better ways to do it—a loan, for instance. Even if it helped preserve Florence's diaries, Mother lost control over an important part of our family's history by letting that historian into our lives. Once they're inside your house, your life, outsiders think they have a license to control it.

"And sure enough, this Chicago detective came trampling right through our privacy. She dared to ask if I'd gone back to Topeka to take charge of the diaries, if they mattered so much to me. A polite way of asking if I'd stolen them."

"Do you know what ever-so-Great-grandmother Wheelock wrote in the volumes that are missing?" Cady asked.

"Unfortunately, I wasn't interested when I was a teenager. Over the years I've gone to Topeka sometimes to read in them, especially around important celebrations in our town's history. The diaries aren't of universal interest, unless you are wondering how people celebrated marriages or did their housework."

The words were innocuous, but her look was so fierce that Cady didn't ask any more questions.

Pat Everard had come over to commiserate: the detective had gone to her house after she left Gertrude. "Did Ms. Chicago ask you why the Coffin woman would have stolen the books?"

"Oh, yes." Gertrude sighed. "I told her I thought as little as possible about Clarina Coffin when she was alive and wouldn't think of her now if people like this Warshawski didn't keep rubbing my face in her affairs. Anyway, I asked her what those diaries had to do with Clarina's death. She said until she read them she had no idea, but she was checking to see if Clarina came from Skaneateles. She wondered if I was still in touch with relatives there—after almost two centuries!"

"She asked me the same—and she knew my people came from Lynn," Pat said. "It reinforces the argument that what she's doing is simply harassment, not investigation. In fact, after she left my house, I called Deke and told him that he needed to get Frank Karas to either charge her or send her home. He said I made it sound like training a dog: *Go home, Warshawski!*"

Cady suppressed a giggle.

"Then he asked if I could imagine the outcry if he

tried to force her or anyone to leave town for the crime of asking two older women questions about their families."

"But he could make it unpleasant for her to stay here," Gertrude argued. "You know, routine traffic stops, searching her car, checking her insurance. Tickets every time she goes a mile over the speed limit."

"Gram! You can't be serious," Cady cried. "Those are all the things we protested the police doing to African-American and Indigenous drivers after Michael Brown and George Floyd! You were one of the strongest voices in that struggle. And, anyway, like Aunt Pat said, Vic didn't ask to stay here. The cops told her to. Or the DA did, at any rate."

Gertrude bit her lips and turned her head.

After a pause, Pat said, "Deke did suggest we get an order of protection. That would force her to stop harassing us. I'm talking to our lawyer in the morning about filing for one. You should, too, Gertrude. And you, Cady."

After Pat left, Cady said, "Gram, I know Clarina talked about those diaries with you and Aunt Pat the morning she came to the women's group breakfast. I was there that morning, remember?"

"Of course I remember," Gertrude said. "She'd been reading a number of different diaries. The Fremantle women kept them, the Entwistles, even Arnie Schapen's great-grandmother, not just Florence Wheelock. The Coffin creature wanted to show me some photocopied pages, but I was too angry with her for inciting the board to fire you to pay attention. I very much doubt if my responding to her inuendoes that morning would have kept her from being murdered. She liked to hint and wink her way around scandal, but it was all smoke if you pressed her."

Cady agreed with Gram—Clarina had shown her photocopies of some diary entries when she was trying to butt in on Cady's syllabus. Not Great-grandmother Wheelock's, but one of the other pioneers, Augusta Fremantle, who wrote contemptuously about Amelia and Sophia Grellier for not keeping their linen freshly washed and ironed. Maybe worth killing over in 1856, but not today.

More troubling was what neither Gram nor Aunt Pat had said this afternoon, either to each other or to Deke, let alone V.I. Warshawski. Aunt Pat had come over the Saturday before Clarina's death, an event so commonplace that Cady didn't linger downstairs after letting Pat into the house. She'd forgotten her phone, though. When she walked back down to the kitchen, Aunt Pat was exclaiming, "She didn't!" and Gram was saying, "I assure you, she did. I told her no one would pay attention to such a ludicrous claim. She said, 'Everyone loves a juicy story, especially one about people who think—'"

Gram paused, then said, "There's no nice way to repeat this. She said people like me who think their shit is clean enough to eat."

Cady's lips had pursed in a silent whistle.

"She said she knew how you and I looked down on her, but by the time our history was splashed all over the internet, we wouldn't be so high and mighty."

And then, three days later, Clarina was dead. And Gram had been at the Dundee House when it happened.

42

Auntie Kalina's Treasure

Before making dinner, I checked my ad again. I had another four responses, but again, when I looked up the names, I found the missing people relatively easily. Depressing.

Back in the trailer, I looked into Gertrude's claim that her family had fought for civil rights in Lawrence. Her mother, Maris Clover Wheelock, seemed to have been as involved a citizen as Gertrude. Among other activities, Maris's name appeared in the 1950s and 1960s newspapers for taking part in discussions of segregated housing and public facilities.

Gertrude's own name began popping up in the late 1960s, when the county and university were in the same throes over civil rights, abortion access, and the Vietnam War as the rest of the country. I saw a picture of Gertrude and Maris dedicating the Clover-Wheelock Women's Health Clinic in old East Lawrence.

After her mother's death, Gertrude created a foundation in Maris's memory, which chiefly supported the Clover-Wheelock Health Center. Gertrude gave the town sweat equity by helping run a food pantry, an after-school program for low-income girls interested in STEM, and the town arts council, along with service in elected offices, like the county planning commission.

Gertrude and Pat had received every conceivable civic award available in the county, and many state ones as well. I couldn't imagine any revelations from a nineteenth-century diary that would make them want to kill Clarina Coffin.

But what had brought Gertrude to the Dundee house the night Clarina died there? I couldn't begin to figure that one out, so I went back to my ad. Eleven new responses had come in. Ten were false alarms, but I had a feeling the eleventh was the right one. Lucia Bednarek wrote that she hadn't seen or heard from her sister for almost two years.

"You say she was found dead. If you think there's a reward for finding her, there isn't, but if it's her, I guess I need to make arrangements for her funeral, unless she got married or had a kid, which means she has a closer relative than me."

She'd attached a snapshot of a stocky woman with dark curly hair who stared aggressively at the camera. It was clearer than Zoë's shots in the *County Herald*. Although the woman in the Dundee house cellar had been pale, drained of life, I was pretty sure Clarina was Lucia Bednarek's sister.

I wrote that to Lucia, adding, "I'm not expecting a reward, I'm just trying to establish her identity." I included references, people who could vouch for my not being a scammer, including Deke Everard. "It would be good if we could have a phone conversation, but if you're more comfortable talking to the police, here's the main switchboard number for the Lawrence Department."

I attached a link to the stories Zoë had run about Clarina's death. After a few minutes, Bednarek agreed to a phone call. She was at work; she'd phone in the morning.

I spent a restless afternoon, trying to stay focused on Chicago client reports and not on the clock. I wanted to share Clarina's identity with Murray and Zoë, but I couldn't let that genie out of the bottle until I had complete certainty from Lucia.

I finally took Peppy for a long walk, down to the

river, passing the boathouse where I'd hidden the wrench. Why couldn't Lucia Bednarek talk tonight? I fumed, spinning rocks into the river.

Of course, she could be doing the prudent thing, checking my credentials. I walked back to the trailer, stopping for sushi at one of the little carryout places that dotted Sixth Street. I ate it while I watched Mike Shepherd use amazing intuitive leaps to solve crimes in Brokenwood, New Zealand. He was like so many other modern detectives who solved crimes in an hour or so without a lot of evidence. I wondered if they went to a special detective school where I could take a refresher course: the Zen of detection, something like that.

At ten, as I was getting ready for bed, Lucia called.

"I'm at the Kansas City airport. I thought maybe I should come out in person to see Rickey, or see if it's Rickey, but I don't know where you are or how to get to you."

I was going to suggest a rental car, or perhaps a bus service, but she sounded dejected, maybe scared. I told her I'd pick her up, but to wait in the terminal, since I was fifty miles away.

She called again as I pulled onto the interstate, wanting to know where I was, and yet again fifteen minutes after that. Clarina had annoyed everyone she met; I wondered if that was a genetic trait.

Lucia Bednarek was pacing the sidewalk in front of the terminal when I pulled up. She was a thickset fair woman, very like the snapshot of her sister except for her lighter coloring.

"Finally!" she greeted me. "I've been waiting so long I thought you'd gotten lost."

She was carrying a large suitcase and wearing a puffy coat that doubled her circumference. It took some doing to get her and the coat into the front seat. Peppy, eager to help greet her, didn't make it easier, but Lucia said she didn't mind dogs, she had a dachshund at home.

"My neighbor, she's agreed to come over and feed Jippy and walk him while I'm away. How long do you think I need to stay here?"

"I expect not more than two days. Where did you book a room?"

"I've never traveled like this before," Lucia said. "Not on the spur of the moment, just getting on a plane, like I was in a movie or something. But if Rickey was murdered—I didn't think they'd have gangs in a place like Lawrence. When I read about the town, it didn't sound like a violent place."

"Her death is strange for anyplace," I said. "She wasn't shot, though. Someone hit her on the head."

"She must have made them mad. She was always getting our dad totally pissed off. She made everyone around her mad at her, me included, but especially our dad. She wanted him to change his name, can you believe that? She said 'Bednarek' made people tease her more at school than they already did. They'd yell 'Who wants to take a fat girl like you to bed' and instead of fighting back she'd come home bawling that it was all Daddy's fault, and he should change our last name. Of course he wouldn't, but she changed her first name. Not that I blame her for that. They called her Ulricke, for Pete's sake, after our grandma. She changed it to Rickey."

"Did kids at school make fun of her because your town was called Skaneateles?" I asked.

"Yeah, that, too. She was always kind of stocky, not fat, built pretty much like me. No one ever bothered me like they did her, but in seventh grade, God, makes you glad you only have to be a teenager once! This gang of girls started telling her she should move to Fatty-atlas!

"So then she started telling people she was adopted, and her real family was named Bradshaw and came over on the *Mayflower*. It was embarrassing. She always had a different story about who she was and who her real family was. Sometimes they came over on the *Mayflower*, sometimes they were British aristocrats who had to go into hiding after the Revolution, and so they hid out in the hills around Skaneateles.

"The worst was the time she claimed she was Black, that we had adopted her and wouldn't tell her. See, she was kind of dark-complected and the rest of us Bednareks are blondies. She made a fool of herself at one of the Black historical society meetings. I wished she really had been adopted, it was excruciating.

"Not that I wished her dead, but I didn't miss her when she took off. She'd done it before, been gone once for three years, and then came back because she couldn't keep a job."

"What about the rest of your family?" I asked. "Didn't anyone miss her?"

"It was just the two of us. Daddy's family are mostly in Michigan, and Mother, she only had her own mom and our auntie Kalina. Mother and Daddy are both dead. And no one was friends with Rickey, she was just so weird. Every now and then someone at church asks about her, but no one really noticed she was gone. Or if they did, it was a relief not to listen to her conspiracies about the way Mother and Daddy lied to her about her true identity."

I could feel how embarrassing it must have been to see her sister make a spectacle of herself. Even so, I felt sympathy for Rickey, who felt so different from the people around her that she kept trying to create an alternate version of her life.

"Did she ever claim to be a navy SEAL?" I asked, thinking of the job candidate I'd been vetting.

"What? Why would she do that? She wasn't interested in the navy or physical fitness or any of that stuff."

"What about social justice?" I asked. "The one person in Lawrence who she connected to is a guy who leads protests over environmental issues. He joined her in picketing a school where a teacher was fired for having too woke a curriculum."

"That would be Rickey all right." Lucia sighed heavily. "That summer George Floyd was murdered, it was like Rickey invented Black Lives Matter. She took part in every march, and she filled the living room with posters and literature. Then she started worshipping at this Black church in Auburn."

"Do—did—the two of you live together?" I asked.

"I still live in my folks' house. Whenever Rickey was in Skaneateles, she'd stay there."

We had reached the Lawrence exit of the turnpike. I asked Lucia again where she was staying.

"I didn't know where I was going, I didn't know how to find a hotel. All I was trying to do was figure out how to get to Kansas. And then I had to pay a fortune for traveling at the last minute. I thought they had compassion fares for bereaved people, but can you believe? The airline wanted to see Rickey's death certificate. How could I show them a death certificate when I didn't even know if she was dead? Can't you put me up?"

"I don't live here," I said. "I'm renting a trailer with one bed and no spare sheets. There are a dozen motels in the area; we'll find one with good rates."

"Just for tonight? If there's a couch or something?" Her voice trailed off plaintively. "You're the person who told me my sister is dead. Probably is dead, I think you could give me a little support."

You'd think a private eye with a reputation for toughness and recklessness could put her foot down, but I thought of the journey she'd made. Seeing the dead body of a sibling, even an unloved one, was going to be a shock.

"Just one night. Tomorrow we'll book you into a motel."

When we got to the trailer I asked Lucia if she needed to eat. I half expected her to demand a meal, but she said she'd found food at the Chicago airport where she changed planes. "They had this huge food court. Chinese and Mexican and everything."

She dropped her coat on the couch next to her suitcase. She tossed underwear and a sweater onto the floor, found some pajamas decorated with owls and penguins, and a toiletry bag. She didn't bother to pick up her clothes, just demanded the bathroom.

"I'm on New York time. Beddy-bye for me."

I had left my papers out on the kitchen table and was pulling them together when Lucia put a hand on my arm. "There. That proves it's Rickey."

She was looking at the photo of the woman wearing the floral-hair wreath.

"You know her? Is she one of your ancestors?"

Lucia gave a derisive bark. "In Rickey's dreams. That's what started her most recent outburst. When Auntie Kalina died, Rickey, she thought she'd go through all the papers in the attic to see if there was anything valuable. She found a box of letters and diaries and photos going back to eighteen-hundred-something. Rickey said they were letters and newspaper stories and so on about abolition and slavery. This picture was one of them. So, of course, Rickey got it in her head that we must be related to these abolitionists."

Lucia was gesticulating wildly, slapping her forehead for emphasis. Her pajamas and toothbrush fell to the floor.

"I tried to tell her that our family was still in Kielce, in Poland, during the American Civil War. Auntie Kalina moved into that Skaneateles house when her and

Uncle Jarvis came to live in Skaneateles, and all those papers were probably in the attic when she moved in, but once Rickey made up her mind to some fairy-tale story, nothing could change it."

"I don't suppose you brought any of those papers with you, did you?" I tried to sound casual, not like Peppy with a rabbit in view.

"Rickey took them all when she left. She showed them to me when she first found them, but when I wouldn't believe they belonged to our family, she said she was going to take them someplace where she could prove she was descended from the women in the letters."

Lucia's lips tightened with remembered anger. "She said since I couldn't see the papers for what they were, I'd lost any right to read them. She grabbed them away from me and left the house. I thought she was taking them back to Aunt Kalina's place, but when I didn't see her for a week or so and went over there, the house was locked up.

"Some real estate company in Syracuse was putting the house on the market for this distant cousin who Auntie Kalina left it to. I got the agent to let me in to see if Rickey had left a message or anything, but she hadn't. And all the old papers were gone, too."

"What about the distant cousin—did you ask them if they knew anything about your sister?"

"Please. This is some guy in Arizona who we never heard of. I guess Auntie Kalina looked at how crazy Rickey was and decided to leave the house to someone as far away as possible. She knew I didn't need another house, since I already own the one that belonged to our parents."

Something in her voice made me think Lucia was pretending to take the high road. She may have thought Auntie Kalina should have left the house to her.

I prodded Lucia back to the papers Rickey had found in the attic, to see if she remembered anything from her brief chance to study them.

"The writing was so faded you could hardly make it out, but some woman named Carruthers had been murdered at a school along with the man who ran the school. Whoever was writing the letter said the murders upset her mother so much that the mother was going back to Skaneateles.

"Why Rickey thought that proved anything about our family tree beats me. I'm kind of surprised she didn't call herself 'Carruthers,' since that was the dramatic part of the story. Rickey always wanted the most dramatic role. But Coffin was her favorite pretend great-great-grandmother."

"Why Coffin?" I said.

"There was this woman, Martha Coffin, who lived

in our area back during the Civil War, and Rickey was obsessed with her, her and her sister Lucretia. They both had a million children, so Rickey pretended she was descended from them. 'They knew how sisters were supposed to act,' Rickey would say, like it was my fault we couldn't get along." Lucia's face turned red, then she remembered her sister was dead.

"I don't know where this Clarina name came from, unless Rickey stumbled on some other Coffin sister who was called that."

"I think Clarina was a Kansas suffragist and abolitionist." I picked up Lucia's pj's and toothbrush and steered her toward the bathroom.

While she was noisily brushing her teeth, and then showering, I stuffed her sweater and underwear back into the suitcase. I saw she'd packed a black dress and heels, anticipating a funeral.

I opened the couch into a bed. I'd only bought one set of sheets and I wasn't in the mood to share, but I did bring a blanket out for her.

When Lucia saw the sofa bed she was dismayed. She wanted a pillow, sheets, a better mattress.

I gave her my Death Eaters smile. "All those things are available at any of the motels in the area. I'll be glad to drive you to one of them right now, or in the morning as soon as we've been to the morgue."

"Oh, all right," she grumbled.

When I went into the bathroom, I had to remind myself to be thankful that Lucia had answered my ad. She hadn't closed the shower door tightly, and there was a quarter inch of water on the floor.

When I emerged, carrying towels heavy with water to the kitchen sink so they could drain overnight, Lucia said, "It's freezing in here. Can't you turn up the heat?"

"It's as high as it will go. Socks will help. And your coat."

43

The Sergeant's Softer Side

Despite her complaints about the couch, Lucia slept heavily, and loudly. I shut the door between the bedroom and the living area, but the walls were thin, and Lucia's snoring kept jerking me awake. The first time, around one in the morning, I sent a text to Deke Everard.

I've found someone who thinks she can identify Clarina Coffin. Is Coffin's body in the Kansas City Medical Exam facility? Do you want to ride over with us in the morning?

I switched my phone off; Deke would call as soon as he read the message and I wanted as much sleep as Lucia's saw blades allowed.

In fact, Deke, or actually Peppy, woke me at eight. He was pounding on the trailer, which sent her into a frenzy of barking. I pulled on a pair of jeans under my sleep shirt and staggered to the door, Peppy at my heels, keeping up her warning.

Lucia was sitting up on the couch. "Can't you shut up that dog? I'm trying to sleep."

"You'll have a better time tonight when you're in your motel bed." I opened the door and let in the sergeant.

He was wearing the frown that had become his permanent greeting to me. "This had better be on the level, Warshawski."

"Good morning, Sergeant. I'm glad to see you, too. Come in and meet Lucia Bednarek, who thinks Clarina may be her sister."

I stepped aside to let him enter. Peppy, uncomfortable with the tension in the room, was growling softly, hackles raised. I kept a hand on her head. "Easy, girl. He can't help himself, but he isn't going to hurt us."

"You can't let a man in here," Lucia screeched. "I'm not dressed."

Deke walked over to the couch. He crouched next to Lucia and spoke in a soft warm voice that I'd never heard.

"My apologies, Ms. Bednarek. I'm Deke Everard.

I'm a sergeant with the Lawrence police. Warshawski here texted me that she'd found you, but she wasn't answering her phone. I didn't know I'd have the pleasure of meeting you first thing this morning. If Clarina Coffin was your sister, I'm sorry for your loss. I'm sorry, too, that we have to ask you to identify her body."

Lucia blossomed under his tender manner. "That's okay, officer. I'll just be glad to have some closure with my sister. And I'm grateful to this other detective tracking me down. Like I told her, my sister was always making up stories about herself and using fake names, but her real name was Ulricke Bednarek, except she changed it to Rickey."

"Of course until you see her, we won't know for sure the dead woman is your sister," Deke said. "Why don't you put on some clothes so we can drive over to Kansas City and get this ordeal out of the way. Warshawski, you come outside with me. We'll chat in the car while Ms. Bednarek is dressing."

"Sure, Sergeant." I produced a Little Miss Sunshine smile. I was carefree and openhearted, not frowny and mean like Deke. "I just need shoes and socks."

And to brush my teeth and wash my face. I did all these things at a leisurely pace. Deke's frown deepened and Lucia cried out to hurry it up, she needed to get into the bathroom.

When I finally went outside, Peppy came with me, sticking close to my legs. A fine freezing mist was blowing. Deke's unmarked car had a grille between the front and back seats, which didn't allow room for the dog to get in with me. I insisted on staying outside with her, which didn't improve the sergeant's temper.

"How did you get on to this woman, what is her name? Bednarek?"

"It was an inspired guess." I told him what Trig had told me, about Clarina's having been bullied over her weight and her town name. "There was a newspaper article Clarina had studied, dating back to the 1860s, about one of the abolitionists coming from Skaneateles, but until I heard your aunt Gertrude say the name out loud, and say that her own family had come from there, I didn't know how to pronounce it. I ran an ad on social media; Lucia Bednarek responded. She decided to fly out on the spur of the moment yesterday evening."

"And you couldn't tell me you'd made this Skaneateles connection?"

"I figured you knew all these things, since you grew up hearing these stories from your mom and Aunt Gertrude. As for the guess to try Skaneateles, I could see you roll your eyes if I asked you to believe something Trig said."

He bit his lip and looked away.

"I was pretty sure she was Clarina's sister," I added, "but I wasn't going to notify you until I was convinced. I didn't want another lecture on hotdogging or wasting police resources."

"I'll bite: What made you believe her?"

"When she came into the trailer last night, I had a photo on the table that she recognized."

"Photo of Clarina?"

"No. It was one that Clarina had found in a great-aunt's attic, supposedly with a cache of documents that dated to the Civil War. The sisters had argued over their provenance—Clarina thought they were papers from her family, Lucia says they belonged to whoever originally owned the house.

"When Clarina took off for Lawrence, she seems to have brought all those papers and photos with her—she kept making veiled hints to Cady and to your mother and Gertrude about evidence she had of Lawrence's history. Anyway, I found the photo in the trailer where Clarina had been living."

Deke slammed his right fist into his palm. "Why am I only hearing about this photo and the attic and crap for the first time? What did you do with all the papers you found? Concealing evidence in a murder investigation is a crime!"

Peppy gave a warning bark: *Don't slug V.I.* I thought

uneasily of the wrench I'd sent to the Cheviot lab in Chicago. My excuse to myself was that I wasn't sure the wrench was evidence of a crime. Plus Deke had impounded my car, as if he thought I really was a criminal. I stayed confrontational.

"It's okay, girl. He's frustrated that I figured out something he couldn't. Sergeant, I was third in line at Clarina's trailer. Someone had searched it with a violent hand. Then your crew went in. And then me. This photo, which was an original, not a copy, was there, along with blurry printouts of newspaper photos dating to the 1860s. These were the scraps you and the intruders left behind."

I paused, still smiling, to give him a chance to acknowledge his crew had been sloppy. He didn't say anything.

"Either your crew or the first intruders had taken all the other documents. I had only those three pictures, so that's where I started. At the Origins Museum and Library in Topeka, they dug up the newspaper article for me, the one Clarina had found. They couldn't identify the photo, but they gave me some provenance for it. I showed it to your mother and to Ms. Perec yesterday—didn't your mom tell you about it?"

"I do not consult with my mother on active investigations."

"You just show up when the water is getting a little hot? Your mother and Ms. Perec are sitting on a secret. Do you know what that is?"

"A figment of your imagination," he said grimly. "You're harassing them because you can't justify—" He cut himself short, remembering in the nick of time that I had probably identified Clarina Coffin. "My mother wants to file an order of protection against you."

"Right. That will help protect her and Ms. Perec from me consulting with them as I uncover more information about Clarina's death. Rickey, I should remember to call her."

We were both getting wet. And cold. The dog was, too, but she didn't seem to mind. Deke wasn't going to show any weakness, such as admitting that standing in freezing rain is not pleasant, so I suggested he might like to look at the photo.

"Hopefully Lucia is dressed by now, but you can wait on the step if you're worried."

He followed me in without saying anything, but once we were inside, his professional manner returned. He smiled at Lucia, said they'd stop for something to eat on their way to Kansas City.

I handed Deke the print that I'd left on the table. "Does she look familiar to you?"

"She's old, Warshawski, not someone I would have met before."

"In a family photo album, I'm thinking."

"Unthink it. I have not seen this picture before. Tell me about it, Ms. Bednarek. This was among your sister's possessions, right?"

Lucia started the same saga I'd heard last night. Peppy followed me into the bedroom where I changed out of my wet clothes.

Lucia had used the bedroom to dress. Her penguin pajamas were on the floor, along with the socks she'd slept in. I kicked them to the door. I'm not much of a housekeeper, but it annoyed me that Lucia thought her role as chief mourner entitled her to fill up my space.

I hung my own damp clothes over the baseboard where the heat came into the room and put on dry ones before checking my phone: it had been dinging with incoming texts while I'd been outside with Deke.

Leo Knaub, my account manager at the Cheviot forensic lab, had left five messages, demanding that I call ASAP. I have company, I wrote back. Give me ten minutes.

When I went back to the main room, Lucia had gotten as far as Great-aunt Kalina and the papers in her attic, and why Rickey thought she had a right to stuff that belonged to them equally.

Deke was saying, "You said no one in your town liked her much. Would someone have followed her out here to kill her?"

"After she'd been gone two years?" I said. "I suppose it could have taken that long to track her down. She seems to have been quite skillful at avoiding surveillance."

"She rubbed people the wrong way with all her make-believe," Lucia said. "People didn't want her around, but it's not like she threatened them. At least, I don't think she did. . . ."

Her voice trailed off uncertainly. "Do you think she was maybe blackmailing someone? And she ran away under a fake name to keep them from killing her?"

"Before we worry about killers from Skaneateles, why don't we drive to the morgue and make sure that Clarina really is Rickey Bednarek," I said.

"We aren't driving to the morgue. I'm taking Ms. Bednarek. And I don't want to see you in my rearview mirror. If Ms. Bednarek wants to tell you about it when I bring her back, that's her business."

"I'm sure Lucia is going to want to give media interviews," I said. "And she's going to want to be someplace more comfortable than this trailer, with its one bathroom, and a shower that floods the floor if you don't close the door just so."

I stuffed Lucia's pajamas and socks into her suitcase, found the ziplock bag for her toiletries, and put her toothpaste and makeup into it, and forced the case to close.

Lucia watched me, squawking. "Those are my things! Now my pajamas are going to get all wet. And my funeral outfit!"

"Sergeant Everard will help you check into a motel when you get back from Kansas City. It will be so much easier if you already have your case with you."

I took her picture and forwarded it to Zoë. Lucia Bednarek from Skaneateles. Probably Clarina's sis.

Zoë replied instantly. Is she with you? I'm coming straight over.

I wrote back, Deke's here, about to take her to KC to see the body. I'm disinvited.

Even before they were out the door, Deke's phone rang. He looked at the screen, then back at me. "You sicced Zoë on me? Do you need to win every confrontation you're in?"

"Only when my expertise is disrespected."

44

Wrenching Problems

The trailer felt more depressing than ever. Between my damp clothes and the towels Lucia had soaked, the place smelled like a wet sheep. I took everything to a Laundromat and left them to wash while I went on to the Hippo.

I sat in my favorite spot, on a stool in the window, and drank my first coffee while staring at nothing. My shoulders relaxed; at my feet, Peppy curled up around her empty milk bowl and fell asleep. We'd both been too stressed lately.

When I'd ordered a second cortado, I called Leo back.

He got straight to the point. "There's a DNA match between blood traces and hair on that wrench, and a

DNA request filed two weeks ago by the Lawrence Kansas police. If this wrench is evidence of a crime, our lab can't hold on to it. It needs to be with the police or the FBI ASAP. In addition to the hair, we found microscopic traces of scalp tissue. If you're not going to take care of reporting these items, Cheviot will."

"Did you find fingerprints on the wrench?" I asked.

"Nothing usable. The surface doesn't hold prints well, and too many hands had been touching it, some in gloves."

"Leo, I found this wrench underneath a garbage can in the apartment I was renting. It had been put there in the hopes that the cops would find it and arrest me for Clarina Coffin's murder. I was hoping it was a red herring, but sent it to you to find out one way or another."

"Now you know. And that means you act now. If not, Cheviot will terminate our relationship with you."

"Do you want to send it directly to the Lawrence police?" I asked. "I have the address here."

"Of course—" he started, then stopped, imagining the legal headaches if they sent this out of the blue to the LKPD. Cheviot investigators spend half their lives in court, testifying on forensic evidence. It wouldn't do their own reputation a lot of good to explain why they'd had the wrench in their possession for the better part of a week without notifying the cops. They could blame it on me, but that would not only add to their days in front of a judge, trying to exculpate themselves, but it would also end my relationship with them. Other, more important clients would hesitate to send them confidential projects when word leaked out through my connections that they'd screwed with me.

"You are a piece of work, Warshawski," he finally said. "Do I send this to you or your lawyer?"

"I'm in Kansas, Leo. Give me five minutes to get an address for you."

I called Lou. "You know how you told me you and Ed like to accessorize?" I asked, after a hurried catch-up. "I'm ordering accessories online. Could I have them delivered to you?"

"What are we talking about?"

"Mmm. Something like punk metal jewelry."

"That's what I like to hear. Me and Ed, we've been eating our hearts out, longing for that heavy-metal look, and we're the guys who can carry it off. Send it to the yard; we're there in business hours more than we're home."

When I called Leo back with the scrapyard address, he told me I'd have the wrench Monday morning. "If we don't see a report that it's in law enforcement hands by Monday night, you and I will be having a very serious conversation."

"Copy that," I said. Forty-eight hours, roughly, until I needed the wrench in the LKPD's hands, with proof I could share with Leo. Piece o' cake.

I was gritty-eyed from my short night's sleep, but too restless to go back to the trailer to try for more. Although the sky was still overcast, the drizzle had ended. I walked with Peppy back to the Laundromat to put my linens in a dryer.

Before turning to my Chicago clients, I remembered another distraction: I had to let Murray know I'd discovered Clarina's identity—he wouldn't forgive me if he learned it from the wires first.

Murray was impressed by my investigative skill, but asked if knowing Clarina had been born as Ulricke Bednarek gave me a reason for her murder.

"I suppose it's possible," I said. "If her sister can be believed, everyone in Skaneateles despised Clarina. I'm focusing more on Lawrence. Do you want to go to New York and track down whoever she'd most annoyed?"

"If you'll pay first-class airfare," Murray said.

"I'm not paying any airfare at all. This case has already put me several grand in the hole just for legal fees."

I told him about my meeting with Pauline Tulloh. "She discussed her family's dynamics in a cool impersonal way. I wondered if that was a deliberate distraction—you know, show the audience how the billionaires bicker, keep their attention away from the important acts on the other side of the stage."

"Those being?"

"Whether her brother engineered Clarina's, or Rickey's, death. The most genuine thing she said was that her mother asks Pauline to support charities that she knows her husband won't approve of. It sounded as though charities might mean indigent friends and relations."

"You know, Warshawski, you should hire yourself out to a pest management company. People want to know if they have rats or roaches or whatever, and you just stand in the middle of their living room. Pretty soon, every vermin within a mile will come charging out to get you. No one in Lawrence cared about that hill or that house or even the drug sales until you came along."

I wasn't sure if that was a compliment or the most unpleasant criticism I'd ever endured, but when we hung up, I finally buckled down and cleared up the skimming that one of the partners was doing to the accounts at a law firm I work with. Put the report and a bill in an email. I entered my time sheet against the four thousand dollars Valerie Granev had paid me. I was about sixteen hundred down.

Zoë called as I was on my way back to the Camry to

collect Peppy. She had made it to the morgue in Kansas City in time to intercept Deke and Lucia in the lobby.

"Clarina is Lucia's sister, all right. They look amazingly alike, even though Clarina was dark and Lucia is so blond, but it's not just that, it's that they have the same whiny-aggressive attitude."

She hesitated, then said in a rush, "I know you feel too many people are counting on you, but you are amazing. You figured out Clarina must have come from Skaneateles. And, guess what, Ben Pike, my two-fisted tightwad of an editor, agrees that the story will sell, so he's paying to send me to New York to get background on Clarina. Ulricke. I don't know if I'll ever get used to calling her that. Anyway, if I were in the room with you, you'd get the biggest hug you ever got in your life."

I laughed. So much better to hear than being called a pest magnet. "When do you leave?"

"First flight to Syracuse tomorrow morning, by way of Chicago. Want me to stop and say hi to any of your friends during the layover?"

"Call them all and tell them that thanks to me, you're the next Martha Gellhorn."

The dog and I walked down a side street to my favorite sandwich shop. I was going to take lunch to a park so I could eat outside with her.

The air was cold but not unbearable; I had my

heavier coat over a hoodie, and Peppy was wearing fur. As we crossed Massachusetts Street, a Porsche revved its engine and turned in front of us, rubber squealing, missing us by a hair. I pulled Peppy against my legs and watched the Porsche go down Seventh Street, past the Lion's Heart, then turn the corner toward the municipal parking lot.

Peppy and I followed. The Porsche was in the lot, close to the Lion's Heart back door. The engine was running with that deep thrumming good sports cars make when they're idling. I put the sandwich down so I could use my phone to take his picture. The weedy-looking kid whom Zoë had photographed dealing out the back door emerged. He looked furtively around, didn't see any cops, and handed over an envelope. Trevor gave him one in return.

I walked over as he was getting into the car. "Trevor!" I cried in a hearty voice. "Good to see you again."

He looked up, startled. He'd posted my photo on his trolling messages, but he was the kind of jerk who didn't actually register women's faces, probably not women his own age, let alone someone old enough to be his mother.

"We keep meeting in parking lots," I said. "First at your fraternity, and now down here. I have a nice video of you and your buddy at the Lion's Heart. I'll be sharing it with Sergeant Everard at the LKPD."

He took a step toward me, fists balled, expression ugly, but a cluster of shoppers passed us on their way to their cars. He climbed into his ride, slamming the door hard, made a great show of gunning the engine.

I pulled Peppy away as he roared out of the lot and saw she had her nose in my lunch bag. I yanked her head out of it.

"Is this your payback for taking you far from home? Stealing food?" I asked.

She wagged her tail doubtfully.

"Yep. My bad, leaving it on the ground."

I walked back around the corner, past the bar again, on my way to get another meal. It was the lunch hour, and more people were starting to show up for noon-day drinks. I was crossing the street to keep the dog away from the crowd when someone else I recognized went into the Lion's Heart. Brett Santich. I was tempted to tell him he'd missed young Trevor, but decided it would be more interesting to see if he was meeting someone. I trotted back to the library so I could leave Peppy in the car while I checked out the bar.

The room was full enough when I got there that no one paid special attention to me. My prey was at a corner table near the kitchen where he could see the room. He seemed to focus on each newcomer for a few seconds, deciding on friend, foe, or neutral, so I didn't stare but wandered to the bar to order a drink. I don't much care for beer, but it seemed the easiest way to blend in. I ordered a Free State, since that was the local brew Zoë had drunk, and took it to a corner where I could stand looking at my guy without seeming to.

Don Wilton, the Lion's Heart owner, came out from the kitchen and sat down with Santich. The two men didn't seem to be talking as much as waiting—every time the front door opened, they'd look over and then shrug. After ten minutes or so, their party arrived: they both sat up straighter, and Wilton gave a half wave.

They were joined by a tall tanned man in pressed jeans and cowboy boots, wearing a Stetson and a fringed leather jacket over a sweatshirt that advertised Wichita State University basketball. Not Robert Tulloh. The other brother, Jacob.

Jacob Tulloh with Don Wilton. I felt like one of those cartoon characters whose hair stands on end after an electric shock. The Wilton family, those losers who lost their share of the family grain elevators while Matthew Tulloh turned his wife's into a massive fortune. Grandmother Tulloh cackling over the losers at Emmaline and Matthew's fiftieth anniversary.

The Wiltons were the charity Pauline Tulloh supported for her mother, her hapless siblings and nephews. An angel bailed out the Lion's Heart in the depths of the pandemic. Grandma Tulloh would have forbidden any money going to the Wiltons, but Pauline helped her mother help her cousins.

Jacob Tulloh and Lawrence police chief Rowland McDowell were old pals going back to their college days. If Santich was useful to the Tullohs in their Yancy dealings, Jacob would see that he wasn't harassed by the local law.

The trio headed for a narrow staircase rising behind the kitchen door. I hadn't noticed it before and went over to look.

The barman appeared at my side. "What are you doing here?"

I smiled. "Admiring the architecture."

"You've admired it long enough. Pay for your beer, which you haven't drunk, and get out."

I paid for my beer and left, the bartender close behind me. I closed the door slowly so that I could check the lock mechanism. Unlike the upper floor, Wilton used a standard keypad lock, easy to bypass. The bar had an alarm system. Harder to bypass, but not impossible.

45
Rookie Mistakes

I texted Deke the videos I'd made of Trevor with my peeper at the Lion's Heart. "Not saying they were dealing drugs. Just envelopes, maybe love letters. Hope you had a meaningful trip to the morgue with Lucia."

I was whistling a little under my breath as I reached the Camry, feeling smug. My finger was on the key's unlock button when I was jumped. Arm around my neck, chokehold. Reflexes: stomp on the foot behind me. Hit steel-toed boots. Drop arms and head. Elbow into rib cage behind me, teeth into arm, snarl of "fucking bitch," and a sharp pain, back of the head, on my hands and knees, unable to resist the thick arms lifting me, slinging me into an SUV.

I never completely lost consciousness, but by the

time I recovered enough to know what was happening, we were on the interstate, moving fast. My wrists were crossed in cuffs underneath the seat belt. I smelled of sick, a dribble down the front of my hoodie. I hadn't eaten lunch, not much to throw up.

Two figures were in the front, separated from me by a plexi panel. The high headrests meant I couldn't make out their shapes.

Peppy. My dog, locked in the Camry, she would be so scared. I had abandoned her, I'd brought her to Kansas with me, and she would die in the car while I died on a remote river path. Helpless tears trickled into my nose and made me sneeze.

"She's awake."

I knew the voice, struggled to put a name to it. The driver grunted.

"You hit her too hard."

"Bitch had her teeth in my arm."

"Tell Mr. T that when he can't get sense out of her."

Geoffrey Mellon. Pauline Tulloh's perfect Jeeves, doubling as a hitman. The car hit a pothole, jolting me; the figurine of Inanna bounced with me, hitting my breastbone inside my clothes.

Warrior goddess, life, death in her hands. No sniveling. Use the weapons you have, the strength you have. Do not die without a fight. I slid my cuffed hands to my left and unlocked the seat belt. Slowly. The driver could see me in the rearview mirror. Quick and sudden moves would catch his eye.

I leaned back in the seat, eyes shut to slits, moaning softly. Caught his gaze in the mirror. He watched my head lolling with the car's motion, a satisfied nod, back to watching the road.

My phone was in my hip pocket. I slid my hands around to the right side. Edged it out. Text to Lou and Ed. *Dog at library. Kidnapped.*

The driver stood on the brakes with a great screeching. I was flung forward, managed to turn sideways, got my knees to take the hit.

"Bitch has her phone. You worthless moron, why didn't you search her?"

"You're the one who shoved her in the car, said we had to get going," Mellon said.

The driver came around and wrenched the door open. I put every muscle I had into my kick, getting him square in the belly. He wanted my phone, he was not going to have my phone. He leaned over me and I jerked my cuffed hands up under his chin. His head whipped back. I kicked again. Mellon came at me from the other side, grabbed my phone.

A car stopped behind us, a woman's voice worried: Was anything the matter? Should she call for help?

The doors slammed shut on my outcry.

"Sick dog, getting her to the vet, she's pretty wild," Mellon said. "She got herself tangled in her collar back here but we're okay now."

We took off again. The driver was furious about his neck; he was going to be in a brace for a week, for sure. The bitch, meaning me, was going to pay for sure. "And we're behind schedule as it is with all this crap going on. Jacob is having fits, wants to pull the plug."

"Robert will keep it going," Mellon said. "Jacob is so cautious he won't cross the street on a green light. Pauline is twice the man he is, but the old man won't see she's the one who should be on the board."

Bitch was going to pay, all the crap going on. I recognized that voice. He was behind schedule. When he bent over me, I'd seen the .358 in his belt. The crew chief I'd encountered on top of Yancy.

I shut my eyes, rocked with the rocking of the car, tried not to focus on my throbbing head, my longing for water, tried not to worry about Peppy. Someone would see her in the car, someone would trace the car to Lou and Ed, she'd be okay. Would a runner find my bones while they could still be identified? Would Peter be grief-stricken when he heard about it?

We rocked and rolled for more than an hour before

the car came to a gentle stop. I braced myself for battle again. The driver opened the window.

"You have a permit for this lot?" a woman asked, sticking her head in, and then, "Oh, Mellon, didn't know it was you."

Mellon exchanged a few good-natured words with the woman. She released a barrier and we passed a sign saying we were entering the private parking lot for Tulloh senior staff, permit required. The sun was setting, glinting an orange light from the building directly in front of us. It felt like fire to my aching eyes.

Mellon seized my right arm, yanked me out of the backseat, undid my cuffs and refastened them behind my back. The driver came over to face me, hand turned flat. I pulled my chin to my chest a nanosecond before he delivered an upward chop. He hit my nose. Blood spurted out on his hand and jacket. He swore, swung his arm to hit me again. I went rubber legged and he chopped the air.

"Enough, Chet," Mellon said. "The old man is waiting, and you look a mess now, covered in blood."

Chet swore, called me a list of tired insults, grabbed my left arm and propelled me forward at a pace close to a run. I pounded along next to him. Each footfall felt as though my head were being hit again.

We jogged past the Tulloh campus, rows of long

low buildings fanning in a semicircle around the main structure, the glass building that was sending out orange sparks in the setting sun.

We landed inside, stopping at a lobby counter whose curves mirrored the lines of the front of the building. The woman sitting there greeted Mellon by name.

"This is the woman Mr. T wants to talk to?" she said. "What happened to her?"

"Chet got a little carried away," Mellon said. "He may have broken her nose."

"Fucking bitch tried to break my neck," Chet said. "And now she's bled all over me."

"They're expecting you on the bridge," the woman said. "Chet Bezory, you should clean the blood off before you go up. Mr. T doesn't like his employees to look scruffy."

"Scruffy is okay for me?" I asked her.

She looked at me for the first time. Her lips curved in a sneer. "You'll do just fine."

"The bridge?" I said to Mellon. "As in on top of the warship overlooking the expanse of empire?"

Mellon grunted and urged me forward with a hand between my shoulder blades. Only James Bond starts a successful fight in the heart of enemy quarters. I let him get away with it. "You'd do the same, right?" I said to Inanna.

"I'd do the same what?" Mellon demanded.

I'd spoken out loud. Careful, Warshawski. You cannot lose your wits, not when you're about to meet Mr. T.

"As Pauline," I said. "You'd help your mother, save her from your father, right? Help her fund one of her loser cousin's bars? Did you report that little subterfuge to Mr. T? Does Pauline know you don't respect her privacy?"

"You talk too much."

We'd reached an elevator. He swiped the control panel with a card from his back pocket. There were two possible destinations, G and 4. We were going to 4.

The bridge covered the front third of the building, as nearly as I could tell. An amber glass box set against the back wall was apparently Tulloh's lair. Mellon shoved me onto a straight-back chair and went into the box.

The floor in front of me held open-plan cubicles. Even though it was a Saturday afternoon, most of the desks were taken. I wandered over to see what people were working at so hard.

The cubicles didn't have ceilings, but the walls blocked noise from other parts of the floor. I peered into one filled with monitors that showed security prices from Shanghai to Rio. Pride of place went to the

Chicago Board of Trade. That wasn't surprising, since Tulloh's chief business was in commodities. It made me homesick, though, to see the CBOT logo on the screen.

Another cube held a squad of young people doing something intense at computers. Along one wall, a bank of monitors showed the premises, flashing pictures from the different outbuildings, including the cafeteria and the chapel.

After staring at the screens for several minutes, I realized I wasn't looking only at the Salina headquarters, but at Tulloh operations around the world. I saw a couple of men taking a cigarette break in what the monitor identified as west Texas. A loudspeaker adjured them to get back inside and back to work. A couple in Riga were caught embracing. It was sickening, terrifying. Did employees not know they were under constant surveillance?

Coworkers spoke in low murmurs if they spoke at all. No music was piped in, but most employees sported earbuds. I wondered if that let them listen to their own music, or if it was to make them constantly available for phone calls.

I found a woman's toilet tucked in behind Mr. T's amber box. It was a difficult business, pulling my jeans down with my hands behind my back. A woman came in as I was struggling to hoist them back up.

"They're looking for you!" she cried. "What are you doing in here?"

"Peeing," I said. "I didn't think they'd appreciate it if I squatted on the office floor."

"Don't you know how big a mistake it is to keep Mr. T waiting? Get out of here now."

"I know you're nervous, but it would be such a good deed if you'd get my pants up for me before I scurry in to face the terrifying Mr. T."

She made a face, wrapped her hands in paper towels, and nervously yanked my jeans into place and did up the zipper. She tried to hustle me out of the room, but she didn't have Mellon's upper body strength. I stopped to look at myself in the mirror over the sink.

My face was shocking. Blood from my nose had splashed up onto my cheeks and into my hair from the speed walk I'd been forced to do. I'd been hit on the back of the head; it had bled into my hoodie. Real blood. Taylor's blood, Clarina's blood, blood everywhere. I swayed, room swooping black.

You will not faint, you will not be weak in front of these monsters.

Yes, warrior queen. Upright into battle, battle until the end.

46

The Want Bone

Matthew Tulloh was sitting behind an old-fashioned wooden desk, the kind with two sides and lots of drawers and pigeonholes. He was dressed for the range in cowboy boots, an open-necked shirt, and jeans. His face was sunburned, except for the top inch or so of his forehead, which looked almost white in contrast. Presumably he wore a cap in the sun, but it was disconcerting to look at him, as though he'd started to put on clown makeup and stopped partway through.

He stared at me. "Don't like to see blood on a woman's face. Unfeminine. You been fighting my men, huh? Not feminine at all."

"I got my period on the drive over," I said. "Nothing more feminine than menstrual blood."

His mouth twisted in disgust. "Potty-mouthed, too. Hate that in a woman."

"Bullying," I said. "I hate that in everyone, including you and your vassals."

"You're not in a position to hate anything about me, missy. You're here by my orders, you'll leave if I say you can and when I say you can. You talk to me respectful, or Mellon here will make sure you do."

Old-fashioned wicker chairs were grouped around a table to one side. I moved over and sat in one of them.

"Didn't say you could sit, either," Tulloh snapped.

I didn't try to respond. My arms were aching from having my hands cuffed behind me. My head was aching, I was seeing double. I couldn't waste energy sparring with Tulloh.

He brooded for a few minutes, then said, "You've been looking into that Coffin woman's death, right? Except her name wasn't Coffin."

I didn't say anything.

"So what have you found out?"

"She was hit on the head. She died."

"You've been at it for two weeks. I know you've found more than that."

"I'm sure you know everything I do and more besides, Mr. Tulloh. Her birth name was Ulricke Bednarek. She was a history buff and a gadfly. She died in circumstances stranger than her name, in the cellar of an abandoned house at the bottom of Yancy Hill."

"Come, come, Ms. Warshawski, don't pretend to be stupid or naïve. You discovered her name when the Lawrence police were stymied."

"News travels quickly," I said.

"Small towns, everyone knows everything quicker than you can say Google," he said. "What's your interest in her death?"

"With news traveling so quickly, I'd think you could answer that already."

"I'm hearing a lot from Lawrence these days. You've riled up some leading ladies in the town, suggesting they're hiding secrets about the project on top of that hill. What's it called?"

Mellon supplied the name.

"Right. Yancy. The police say you're snooping around a mothballed coal plant, and asking about that project on top of Yancy. I know those things, but no one can tell me why you're poking so many rattlesnakes."

"You told me not to be naïve, Mr. Tulloh. Don't you act like a senile fool when we both know you're not."

Behind me I heard Mellon's quick breath—I was poking the king of all rattlesnakes.

"You keep track of everything happening in Lawrence. You have a pet FBI agent who tells you what's happening on the justice side, and your son Jacob's buddy, the Lawrence police chief, fills you in on the law side, on how the investigation is going. No one knows why Clarina-Ulricke was murdered. She claimed she knew things about the land your company is building on. She claimed she knew things about the families that used to own the land. If the police have found any evidence that backs up those claims, I'm sure they've told you. They haven't told me."

"But what have *you* found?"

"Your wife's nephew is dealing drugs out of his bar," I said. "He maybe helped supply the drug parties out on Yancy land."

He breathed faster, his face contorted in angry lines. "Pauline propped up that loser, thought she was doing her ma a favor. Well, Emmaline knows what a bunch of blood-sucking leeches her brothers and their spawn are. She tried talking sense into Pauline, but Pauline keeps bailing them out because she knows it raises my blood pressure. Same reason she went to that pinko school in Lawrence instead of Wichita State like her brothers and most decent people. And she wonders why I don't want her hands on the company controls!"

I looked at Mellon. "So whatever Pauline does, you report back to Daddy. I'm sorry I fought against coming out here: this is fascinating. A company doing business in a hundred and four countries, worth hundreds of billions of dollars, and the owner still is crawling around in the details of his daughter's life."

"Of course I am." Matthew was contemptuous. "You never had children yourself. One marriage you couldn't handle, and a bunch of lovers you can't commit to, a woman like you can't begin to understand the importance of family."

My mother, fierce, protective of me after losing most of her own family to the death camps. My father's love spread around me like a warm cloak. My cousin Boom-Boom and I, going to the wall for each other. I wasn't going to sully my family's memory by saying all this to Tulloh.

"The Coffin creature bragged she had some documents," Tulloh said. "She told everyone who listened, but no one knows what happened to them. Do you?"

"She had a great imagination," I said. "I expect she invented them to make herself interesting."

"She brought family papers with her to Kansas. They disappeared. If you know where they are, I want them."

"You want them because you share her interest in Kansas history?" I asked.

"If I want them, that's all you need to know." His eyes almost disappeared into the white stripe of his face. It had been a long time since anyone questioned his appetites, his wants.

Mellon and Bezory, they were the ones who'd searched Clarina's trailer before the cops got there. They'd searched the apartment over the Perec garage. They'd planted the wrench, but they'd also been hunting. They'd engineered a search of my home and my office in Chicago.

I'd learned about these papers last night. Deke had learned this morning. I could not—would not—believe Deke was one of Tulloh's secret reporters. But he'd have mentioned the papers Clarina supposedly took from the house in Skaneateles in his report about the trip to the morgue. Besides, Lucia was telling everyone about them. She probably told Zoë when they met at the morgue this morning. The story might already be on the *Douglas County Herald*'s website.

"Where are the papers?" Tulloh insisted.

"I don't know," I said. "I've never seen them."

"That dead gal, what I'm hearing is she was claiming she could shut down the Yancy project. What have you found out about that?"

"Nothing. She gave a lot of people a nod and a wink about secrets but none of them has surfaced."

"You've been detecting all this time and you've

detected nothing? Your reputation and all, I find that hard to believe."

I leaned forward and spoke earnestly. "I've learned the best espresso in Lawrence is at the Hippo. Brett Santich's little girl is a basketball fan. Your daughter is hurt that she isn't part of your operation. Lawrence wine stores carry some sophisticated Italian reds. Clete Rotherhaite questioned your son Robert's judgment about the safety of the Wakarusa plant. He's dead. I wouldn't call that nothing after a mere ten days in the town."

"Rotherhaite was the kind of hard worker America needs. His death, that was a great pity."

You could take that to mean Tulloh had chewed out his son Robert for killing the plant manager. Or maybe the rattler really thought it was a pity Rotherhaite had died. Unlikely but not impossible.

"Why is that Yancy project so important?" I asked. "Your hundreds of billions of dollars and thousands of plants and what-do, why do you need that plant on Yancy."

"Because I want it!" he snapped.

"I guess if that reason has worked well for you all these years, there's no need to abandon it now."

"I think you know where those papers are," Tulloh

said, "or you know who knows. You hand them over to Mellon, you could get back to Chicago and leave all this Kansas trouble behind you."

"A dream come true, in fact," I said.

I didn't say what we both knew: if I found the papers, I'd be dead in the first ditch we came to. As it was, I could hardly believe I was leaving the building alive, but he told Mellon to drive me back to Lawrence.

When we got to the SUV, Mellon locked me in the back with the cuffs still on. Chet Bezory didn't join us.

When we pulled into the library garage, he undid the cuffs and let me out.

"Mr. T wants those papers. He figures you're the person who can find them, but if you do find them and try to hide them, Mr. T will know. You watch your step."

"Always," I said. "Watching my steps is the core of my fitness regimen."

He took my phone from his pocket and tossed it at my feet.

47
Crashing

I sat on the garage floor cuddling my dog. She was frenzied after all her time alone in the car. She'd raced around the garage, zooming past me, until she'd worn herself out, and finally collapsed in my arms. This could not go on. Tomorrow I'd see if Lou and Ed could take her until I was ready to go home. If not, I'd drive her back to Chicago myself.

Peppy started licking my face, working at the crusted blood.

"Not your job, girl, not your job." My arms were stiff and swollen, but I pushed myself standing.

It was only twenty before six, I saw when I looked at my phone. I felt as though I'd been in Oz and back, but it was only five hours ago that I'd been carelessly whistling, thinking about Don Wilton's ties to the Tulloh family. The unsent text to Ed and Lou was on the screen. I erased it, stuffed the phone into my hip pocket, took Peppy to the park behind the library.

It was hard to coax her back into the car. As we were driving toward the trailer, I remembered that my towels and sheets were still at the Laundromat. I collected them, went back to Bluestem Lane.

I stood under the shower, washing the blood from my face and my clothes. That was another outfit going into the dumpster, another shopping trip behind the Boat Yard on the horizon. They should start giving me discounts.

I ate some cold risotto while I checked my voicemail and texts. Lucia Bednarek had left a long rambling message.

"That was poor Rickey, all right, lying there dead. Even though she could be a pain sometimes, she was my sister, she was my only living relative, and now she's gone. I want to take her home and have a proper funeral, but that policeman, the nice one with the beautiful manners, he said they keep the body until they find the killer. Can you believe that? What if they never find the killer, I asked, but he says they always do. I was hoping to stay with you again tonight, but when the nice sergeant drove me out here the place was locked up and no sign of you, no answer to your phone, so he took me to a motel."

I hadn't thought I could be grateful to Mellon and Mr. T for this afternoon's abominations, but at least they'd spared me another night with Lucia.

I had a message from Deke, telling me I'd better not have left the jurisdiction without checking in. He also said he'd looked at the pictures I'd sent him of the Omicron kid dealing with someone at the Lion's Heart back door.

"Do not think you are the cowgirl who can gallop in and solve Lawrence's drug problems. You will be in way over your head, and you will upend months of careful investigation here."

Zoë wanted a confab before she left for New York. Lou and Ed were double-checking Monday morning's accessory delivery. I sent them a quick thumbs-up. I was too exhausted to reply to anyone else, certainly too beat to talk to anyone.

All I wanted was my bed and eight hours of solid sleep. Which meant making sure Mellon, Chet, or any of their pals didn't jump me.

"What are we going to do, girl? They've put trackers on my phone, for sure, and probably the car as well."

I thought it through as carefully as I could for the blanket of fatigue that enveloped me. Finally, I tucked my phone into a paper bag, in case Mellon had put in malware that videoed me, and left it on a counter. I collected some basic supplies—hoodie, dark wool cap, some of Peppy's food and bowls—into my backpack, rummaged in the trailer's drawers, where I found a palette knife and some WD-40, because you never know, and drove back into town. Left my smartphone at the trailer where it could tell everyone I was in the trailer.

Seven on a Saturday night, the main downtown streets were packed, despite the cold weather. The Lion's Heart had a line at the back door. I drove a few blocks farther east and seemed to be in a different town and a different era. Small houses with crooked roofs lined the brick-paved walks and streets. I picked a parking spot at random and set out with Peppy, circling the block to make sure no one was with us.

It took us twenty minutes to get to Trig's apartment on Vermont Street. Seeing Peppy and me flustered him. He was appalled at the thought of giving us a place to sleep.

"Trig, you know all those protests you've tried outside the coal plant, and the development on Yancy, and so on? There is a real, genuine billionaire who bought the coal plant: Robert Tulloh. I think he also owns the Yancy project. You see my face? The crew chief up on

Yancy did that to me this afternoon, while he was driving me out to talk to Robert's daddy."

Trig stared at me. "Robert Tulloh? He did this?"

"One of the people who works for him and his father, Chet Bezory. Clarina apparently told them she had a document that could upend the project. They want that paper, they think I have it. They let me leave the Tulloh headquarters alive because they're hoping I'll lead them to it."

"What, you've come here so they can follow you and beat me up, too?" He tried to shut the door, but I moved inside with Peppy.

"I walked here. I made sure I didn't have company. I left my phone behind because they probably installed trackers in it while they were threatening me. No one knows I'm here. I'm on your side on this, Trig, the side trying to stop whatever is happening out at Yancy, the side trying to find Clarina's killers. They beat me badly today, as you can see. I need to sleep. Help me, tonight only. I'll crash somewhere else tomorrow."

"Do you have the paper they want?"

"Nope. I'm not even sure it exists. Or did she show it to you?"

He shook his head, slowly, nervously looking around. "She never showed me anything, just kept hinting that she had dynamite. I got tired of hearing her brag about what she would do when she never did anything."

"She might have bragged too many times to the wrong person," I said. "You know I found out her real name. Her sister says Clarina, or Rickey, I guess we should call her, she always was living some fantasy life."

He nodded. "I read Zoë's story. So now you're a hero."

"You led me to it, telling me that kids had fat-shamed her with her town's name."

He couldn't help preening a little.

"Here's your chance to show you're willing to back up your talk with a little walk, a short walk. I'm a sitting duck out in Clarina's trailer park if the guys get trigger happy."

He'd spent so many years carrying signs and ranting in the editorial pages that he was startled at the thought of real action, even an act as passive as giving me a place to sleep. He glanced around, saw his computer with Timmy and Ivy on the screen saver.

"I met him a few days ago," I said quietly. "His mom was visiting the Boat Yard the same time I was. He's a bright, active kid—I know you're making a difference in his life."

Oh, V.I., low blow—do this for Timmy. However, it tipped the balance. He had a small side room, a glorified closet, really, with an inflatable bed that he'd bought for Timmy. I could crash there.

He dug a cleanish sheet from a drawer and draped it over the inflated mattress, showed me the bathroom, which was surprisingly immaculate, watched me fill Peppy's water dish, and shut the closet door on us. It was just after seven-thirty when I collapsed onto the mattress, Peppy wedged alongside.

It was a little after three when I woke. My nose was sore and swollen and my shoulders ached from having my arms cuffed behind me, but I had slept for eight restful hours, with no dreams of blood or guns despite my broken nose.

"Peppy, I'm going to leave you here with Trig. You'll be safe. Either I'll be back or Lou and Ed will come to get you."

I moved silently into Trig's front-room-cum-office. He was asleep in a room beyond, or at least someone was snoring loudly there. I took one of his pieces of poster paper and wrote a note: *Off to try to get evidence about Santich's involvement in this mess. If I'm not back by 8 a.m., call this number and explain to the man who answers why you have my dog. He'll come to collect her.*

48
Second-Story Woman

The Lion's Heart door was locked when I got there, but there was still a light showing in the second-story window. I walked on for another block, came at the bar from the back, where the municipal parking lot lay, and sat on a concrete slab behind some bushes. I could see the square of light projected onto the ground even though I couldn't see the window itself.

As I waited, I began hearing the sounds of the night. Even in town, small animals rustle about. The wind blew papers across the parking lot. Near me, someone was groaning in their sleep. As my eyes adjusted to the dark, I realized that I had invaded a communal bedroom. I saw three people sleeping on the ground near me, including the groaner, but one man was sitting up, watching me.

"You a cop?" he asked.

"Nope. I'm a robber."

"You're in the wrong place if you want to rob anyone. No one here has the price of a night's sleep, or we'd be in a bed somewhere. I could use a drink, though, and a smoke."

"When I've finished my robbery, I'll come back and help you out," I promised. "As long as you don't call the cops on me."

He made a sound that might have been a laugh. In the dark, as I waited for the second-story light to go out, he ended up telling me his story, three tours in Afghanistan, too much anger when he got home, couldn't hold a job, his wife left him, taking their child with her. "Randy's eleven now. Every now and then I get myself shaved and bathed, go see him for a few hours."

It was past four when Don Wilton came out the back door and drove off. I waited another ten minutes, waited out a patrol car making a sweep of the parking lot, and then walked to the east side of the building.

Underneath the bottom of the fire escape, I took the time to ground myself. The bottom rung was almost three feet above my head. When I stretched my arms up, a stream of pain ran through my triceps.

V.I., the Candace Parker of the detective team, moves through traffic, squats, times her jump, leaps above the guards, whacks her hand on metal but can't grasp it. This time my traps screamed at me.

"Tough it out," I muttered. "You want this body to go back to Chicago alive, you play through the pain."

Flex the hands, squat, jump, hold on to a bar. Yes. Biceps trembling, hoisting the weight up, getting a second rung, swinging the feet, finding the wall, bracing myself, scooting crablike up the wall until my arms found the fourth rung and there was room for my feet on the ladder.

Sweat was running down my neck. My thighs were quivering along with my arms when I was finally next to the window, but I was there. A triumph.

I sprayed the palette knife with WD-40, slid it between the upper and lower frames, moved it slowly until I could push the knife handle partway through the gap. Sprayed the area with more WD-40, slid a finger in behind the knife and pushed at the catch until the paint and grime gave way and it moved. Pushed up the bottom sash, hooked a leg over the sill.

"Spiderwoman!"

The hoarse voice beneath me startled me so much that I let the sash come down on my butt.

"Could have used you climbing up from the irrigation trenches in Kandahar," he called.

My vet friend. It was oddly comforting to have his ghostly voice keep me company. I made a circle with my gloved left thumb and forefinger to let him know I'd heard him. Pushed the sash back up, slid into the upper room.

The window I'd come through didn't have shades or a curtain, but I needed to risk turning on a light. My flashlight would provide only a slow and uncertain way of exploring the room. Anyway, a bobbing pinprick of light might arouse more cop suspicions than a block of light from the window. After all, Wilton himself had been here late. People would be used to it. I hoped.

When I switched on a table lamp, I found myself in a Jayhawk memorabilia store with modern office equipment scattered around it. The KU flag hung on the windowless north wall, with the U.S. flag next to it. Jayhawk posters, trophies, framed laminated team pictures and newsclips were on the other walls and shelves.

A couple of computers faced the flags, sitting on a metal worktop that ran the length of the south wall. Papers taped above them looked as though they might be work schedules, or possibly delivery schedules. They could be innocuous—an active bar requires a lot of deliveries.

They could also be schedules for drug deliveries.

After all, Trevor Millay was still dealing at the bar's back door. The relationship between drugs and the Lion's Heart could go deeper than one frat boy looking for thrills. Don Wilton had a heavy clout: the wife of the state's biggest billionaire was underwriting his bar. Santich was an associate, supplying the Dundee house for drug parties. Maybe that wasn't his only location—perhaps Santich was augmenting his child support by running a chain of drug houses around the county.

I hit a key on the keyboards for both machines. One brought up a screen needing a password, but the other came to life with surveillance footage. These weren't as sophisticated as the surveillance videos I'd seen in Tulloh's headquarters, but the shots included the bar underneath me—the cash register, front and back doors, the corners where waitstaff might be pocketing money from the table or doing their own deals.

However, when I tried to look at archival footage, the machine demanded a password.

I wished I were a DA who could subpoena the records from the computer. I wished I'd had the forethought to bring a thumb drive with me, because when I looked closely at the keyboards, I saw that Wilton had been careless with his passwords: they were taped to the countertop next to the keyboards. The password for both was Go-Hawks!

49

The Kindness of Strangers

I kept my gloves on, which made typing cumbersome, but I was able to log in to the computer that was playing the surveillance images. I was looking for the Dundee house history. After a tedious half hour, with half my attention on any sounds of anyone entering the bar, I realized Wilton was a sloppy record keeper. He didn't keep separate archives for photos from the bar versus the Dundee house. He didn't label anything, so that when I finally found a folder, it contained pictures of the bar, porn movies, and the occasional snapshots from Yancy.

I had to open each file to see what it covered, but I finally found the Sunday night where Sabrina went missing. The cameras had been on early, showing first Trevor with a group of guys who I assumed were his Omicron brothers carrying cartons of supplies into the house. The motion detectors were sensitive; as the night darkened, the occasional fox or raccoon triggered a shot.

Around nine-thirty, guests started arriving at the house. They were young, for the most part, perhaps college students, perhaps people from the small towns that dotted the county. The faces weren't in great focus, but good enough that a cop or a blackmailer might make use of them.

A little after 11:00 P.M., Sabrina Granev arrived, a ghostly, skeletal figure, stumbling up the kitchen steps. At eleven-thirty, lights in the house flashed off and on and the partygoers suddenly burst outside, moving so fast that several tripped and fell down the kitchen steps. They picked themselves up and streamed quickly to their cars.

The cameras went black. This had to be when the killers were carrying Clarina into the house. Don Wilton was here at the Lion's Heart, looking after his bar and turning cameras on and off in response to orders from Robert? Santich? Maybe Mellon as Robert's lieutenant?

The cameras stayed black until after I arrived. They were switched on in time to photograph me with Sabrina. They showed the first responders and stayed on until three, when they recorded Gertrude Perec's and Trig's separate arrivals. These were the photos that had made their way to the LKPD's doorway.

At that point, the cameras went dark again, which meant they missed my finding Clarina the following day and calling for the cops.

All that confirmed what I already assumed, but it was frustrating that I couldn't find footage of the killers arriving with Clarina's body. They'd ferried her in during the interval between the end of the party and my own arrival, since I'd stumbled on the blanket she'd been wrapped in. I guessed they'd come through the woods, not by the road, because of Sabrina's screaming about monsters, but I couldn't find any pictures to prove that.

I opened the second computer, which held more files. They were as disorganized as the surveillance footage, but they seemed to contain Wilton's financial records. Receivables, payables, more porn, emails to liquor distributors showing proof that the bar could meet its obligations.

I could hear seconds ticking away in my head. I needed to find something more concrete while I was here. Proof of what was really underway on Yancy, proof of where Clarina died, better still, proof of why she died.

And then, by luck and not skill, I stumbled on some audio files. The most recent was from yesterday, when Wilton was meeting with Jake Tulloh and Brett Santich.

"I spoke to McDowell. The Coffin woman's sister has no idea what evidence the Coffin broad claimed she had hold of. We didn't find a trace of secret papers in her trailer, or at the Dundee house. We know she went up to the Dundee place a few times, we got her on camera, but she apparently just liked to be lonely in the woods.

"Daddy's going to talk to the Chicago dick, dickette I guess"—Wilton and Santich snickered obediently—"this afternoon. I know you went through her things when she was at the Perec place, Chet, but you go to her trailer and give it another once-over. Mellon will take care of searching her car and looking through her phone."

My stomach churned. I'd been right, they'd been pawing through my private space. I'd have to get a new phone, new malware, new everything, and even then I'd feel the slime of those slugs on me.

"So are you going ahead with the installation?" Santich asked.

"I don't know. Daddy hates to give up; we've put in upward of a hundred million, what with the plant and all the equipment we've already bought, and of course Robert is ready to go torpedoes and full steam ahead. I'm not so sure myself. We'll see at the end of the day.

"But, Santich, your fucking head is on the block if this goes under. If you hadn't been trying to make a few bucks on the side with your asshole drug sales, no one would have paid any attention to the Yancy project until it was up and running."

"If your father wasn't the richest man in Kansas, you'd be selling insurance or shoes to make ends meet," Santich said. "You don't have any vision. At least Robert does, even if he likes to jump off the high dive."

"What's that supposed to mean?" Jacob's voice was ugly.

"It means if this whole business comes crashing down, it won't be because of the Dundee house, it'll be because you thought you could skate around the environmental impact statement. You think your money is some kind of force field that protects you from stuff ordinary people have to face. I warned your lawyer, when he made the presentation to the county that you can't hide a project this big by pretending it's a resort—"

There was a sound of glass crashing. Jacob must have thrown something, or swept the table clean. I looked from the computer to the floor. Chunks of glass still lay under the far counter, as if Don had brushed them out of the way.

"Clete Rotherhaite thought he knew better than us, too," Jacob said.

Below me, I heard my vet's hoarse voice calling, "Spiderwoman."

"In a minute," I called back, intent on the audio.

My vet called "Spiderwoman" again, and then another man spoke, the same twang I'd just heard on the recording.

"What are you doing here, dirtbag?"

"Hey, man, you don't own the sidewalk."

"I own the building and you're turning it into an eyesore."

There was the ugly sound of someone being kicked, someone crying out, and then footsteps going around to the back of the building.

I closed the file, went to the window. Slid out as I'd slid in, closed the sash, climbed down the fire escape, and jumped from the bottom rung. Pain ran up and down my body like voltage through the Yancy pylons.

My vet was on his side, knees drawn up to his chin, rocking in pain. I crawled over to him. I was holding his hand when a squad car pulled up and shone a spotlight on us.

"What are you two doing?" The officer spoke on the bullhorn instead of getting out of the car.

"Resting," I called.

Wilton heard the bullhorn and hustled around the side of the building, looking from us to the squad. He beetled over to the car, yelling that we were breaking in. While he blocked the cop's view, I casually stuffed my palette knife and WD-40 into a crack between the foundation and the ground.

Wilton came over to us with the cop. "They were breaking into the bar," he huffed. "I caught them in the act."

"Oh, please, Don," I said. "You caught my friend here resting against the side of the building. You kicked him so hard he's having trouble getting to his feet. I was walking by. I heard you."

"Who are you?" Wilton demanded.

"One of your less-satisfied customers," I said. "The one who found Sabrina Granev dying of an overdose out at the Dundee house."

"You!" Wilton swore. "You goddam cunt, I'm going to—" He remembered the cop before he issued the whole threat.

"Going to what?" I asked.

Next to me, the vet started to laugh but was overcome by a coughing fit.

The cop demanded an ID. I dug my driver's license out of a zip pocket in the hoodie.

"Oh, the Chicago detective," she said, making "Chicago detective" sound like "pizza-peddling pedophile." "What were you doing here?"

"As I said, I was walking by. Don here was kicking an Afghan vet." I was careful not to say I'd seen him.

"Every damned homeless freak in this town claims they were vets," Don said. "You use it as an excuse to guilt students into giving you money for drugs."

"Which you conveniently stock," I said.

"It's five in the morning," the cop said. "All three of you, knock it off, unless you want me to take you to the station and book you. And you, Chicago detective, how did you happen to be just walking around?"

"Sorry, officer," I said, contrite. "As you pointed out, I'm from Chicago. I don't know all the local ordinances in Lawrence. If you're not supposed to take walks early in the morning, I won't do it again."

My vet coughed again, covering another laugh.

The woman debated making more of an issue of it, but Wilton was insisting that I'd been breaking into the bar, that a light on the second floor was on, which proved it.

"You forgot to turn it off yourself, man," my vet croaked. "Watched you leave, saw the light was still on, figured you're rich, it don't matter to you if you burn electricity twenty-four-seven."

Wilton said that was a lie, but the cop was tired, her shift was close to ending. She told the vet and me not to move, that she was going to check for signs of forced entry.

Although it was clear that none of the doors had been tampered with, and that the alarm hadn't gone off, she gave in to Wilton's demand that she search me for my lock picking or alarm bypassing tools. When she found only my flashlight and my phone, she told all of us to go home to bed.

Wilton grumbled that he was going to file a complaint, but she was smart enough to ignore that. She got back in her squad, watching to make sure we didn't hang around.

Wilton went into the bar. I squatted next to the vet.

"Let's find a place where you can bathe and get some sleep. Can you walk a few blocks?"

He pushed himself upright, clutching my arm to keep his balance. "I'm not going to a shelter."

"I won't take you to a shelter. If you'd like, I'll pay for a room at a motel for you. I owe you that and a lot more for saving my butt just now."

He was limping, and we stopped several times on the four-block walk to the car while he caught his breath.

When we got to the Camry, he sank into the passenger seat, exhausted.

"You said you were a robber, not a cop," he said. "But that cop back there said you were a Chicago detective."

"I'm a private eye, not a member of any government force. I live in Chicago, but I'm down here helping out a friend. Right now, I'm not sure which side of the law I'm on. I'm going to collect my dog, and then take you to a clean bed. You rest here; I'll be back in twenty minutes."

At Trig's place, I used my picks to let myself in. Trig was still asleep, which was a mercy. I'd worried that Peppy might bark out her indignation at my abandoning her yet again.

When we got back to the car, she sensed the vet's troubles. She leaned over from the backseat and laid her muzzle along his neck.

I drove him to the motel where I'd hoped to park Clarina's sister Friday night, clean, but spartan and therefore affordable. Gave him a couple of twenties.

"You need to see a doctor," I said.

"You're a good-hearted Spiderwoman, but what do you know about life on the street? Where am I going to find me a doctor?"

I took a moment to open a search engine on my

phone. "There's a VA clinic here in town." I wrote the address on the pad of paper by the motel bed. "If you still have your dog tags, they'll see you for nothing."

"Maybe." He bent down to say goodbye to Peppy. "Been a long time since a beautiful lady gave me a kiss. Take care of Spiderwoman."

50
Cover Story

My muscles were screaming at me to get to bed. I drove on west of town, past the turnoff to Yancy, and found another anonymous motel, like the one where I'd taken the vet, bare bones but clean.

A sign by the front door told me dogs weren't allowed. The dawn was plastering its rosy fingerprints on the night sky as I smuggled Peppy in through the rear entrance.

No toothbrush, no nightshirt, but a shower, a clean bed. I just remembered to hang the DO NOT DISTURB sign on the door. I was asleep by the time I'd pulled the covers up to my chin.

It was past one Sunday afternoon when Peppy woke me, urging me to let her outside. I got out of bed, legs stiff and swollen from my long day yesterday. Weight work, which used to be a regular part of my workout, was another thing I'd let slide lately.

I stumbled outside with Peppy. A man collecting used bedding from one of the rooms saw me with the forbidden dog but shrugged and looked away.

The motel backed onto a field ploughed for winter. I let Peppy run free and did a standing workout, twenty minutes of lunges, squats, nerve glides, taking it slowly, until my arms and legs felt less like swollen sausages attached to my torso and more like usable limbs.

As I stretched I could see the tops to the grimy orange smokestacks of the Wakarusa power plant. We weren't far here from the river walk where Clete Rotherhaite had died.

The audio file I'd stumbled on held staggering revelations. The Tullohs went into the Yancy project using a proposed resort as a cover for something that required power on a massive scale.

Clarina had tried to stop them, using her tried-and-true method of pretending, maybe even believing, she knew secrets about local history that would derail the project.

In a way, Clarina-Ulricke had died from an overdose of make-believe. But just as she'd tried in Skaneateles to claim that she was Black, or descended from

Mayflower Pilgrims, she had no proof. She had only the desire to make herself seem important, and she'd chosen the wrong theater for that particular drama.

There were plenty of questions about Clarina-Ulricke's murder—where and why had she met her killers, besides who had struck the fatal blow—and even what she had said that made them strike her. But even if she'd stolen diaries from the Origins Museum and Library, she apparently hadn't given Tulloh's team any believable proof that she could derail the project.

The wrench would arrive tomorrow. I'd get it to Deke Everard. If it proved to be Clarina's murder weapon, he'd take care of hunting out the killer. Or Chief McDowell would oblige Matthew Tulloh by burying the wrench under a pylon. Perhaps they would bury me next to it.

I wished I could go home as soon as I offloaded the wrench to the LKPD, but that wouldn't get rid of the bullseye Matthew Tulloh had painted on my head. Maybe I could make some use of the recording I'd heard in Wilton's office, if I could copy it before he erased it.

I called Peppy to heel. I found the man who was collecting sheets and towels from the rooms and gave him a five. I drove to the trailer to change clothes and pick up messages.

On Wilton's audio, Jake Tulloh had mentioned his

crew were searching my trailer and the Camry while I was with Matthew. Putting on clothes those vermin had touched made me squirm, but I couldn't keep going to the Laundromat, let alone buying new outfits every other day. I packed clean underwear and toiletries in my backpack, inspecting them for signs of trackers. I went through the Camry and found an Apple tracker in the spare tire well. I left it in place—I'd remove it when I needed to get someplace I couldn't afford to be seen.

I had to get Peppy out to Lou and Ed. If I put her in harm's way, I would not be able to live with myself. I also needed to find an anonymous place to spend the night myself. I couldn't jeopardize Trig's safety by crashing in on him a second time. I'd been lucky they hadn't followed the Camry to the motel where I'd spent the rest of the night.

Knowing that Tulloh's grasping fingers had been invading my phone made it hard for me to touch it, but I needed to read my messages. I drove to the Buy-Smart on Sixth Street and bought two more burner phones. Over coffee at the Hippo, I manually entered phone numbers for the people I most needed to be in touch with, including my clients for whom I had active projects.

I sent out messages to them from the burner, telling them my main number was compromised and to use this one until further notice. I listened to the messages on my smartphone, sickened again by knowing other ears had heard them first.

Mr. Contreras had called, as had Lotty, Sal, and Bernie. Deke Everard wanted to hear from me ASAP. Cady Perec had seen the news about Clarina's identity and wanted to talk to me.

Her message made me search my news feed. And there was young Zoë Cruickshank's byline, picked up by Reuters and the AP, reprinted all over the world. She was in Skaneateles, New York, she'd interviewed people who'd known Ulricke "Rickey" Bednarek as a child, people who had no use for her, people who knew she was a brilliant woman who just needed to find her niche, people who told how her father had beaten her, people who said she'd driven her mother to an early grave with her carryings-on.

"Those two girls never got on," one neighbor said. "The father favored the older one, the mother liked Ulricke better, and when they got to be grown-ups, it was like they channeled those parents: Lucia, the older responsible one, Ulricke like her mother, whining, not able to face life with an adult attitude."

Zoë had looked up the property records for the house their aunt Kalina had lived in. She learned it had been built for Elias Entwistle in 1830, and passed from him to his daughter, Amelia Entwistle Grellier at his death. It had been inherited by Sophia Grellier Carruthers, and passed down through that family until 1993, when Louise Grellier Carruthers sold it to Kalina Bednarek.

The papers that Rickey Bednarek found in the attic when her aunt died may connect the family to the Grelliers who went to Kansas as abolitionists in the 1850s. Until we locate those papers we'll never know the full history of what Clarina-Rickey was doing in Kansas.

Zoë included a link to the story I'd seen in the 1867 *Kanwaka Courier*, about Amelia Grellier returning to Skaneateles after her husband's death, and concluded her first dispatch by writing,

Did Frederic Grellier's death in a terrorist attack in 1867 cause Rickey Bednarek, aka Clarina Coffin's, death a hundred fifty-seven years later? We have a private investigator looking into the details in Lawrence, Kansas, while I'm exploring them in western New York. The *Douglas County Herald* has a hotline for anyone with information about those papers that Rickey took away with her. And, of course, if you have information about Rickey Bednarek's murder, we will pass it on to the Lawrence police for you if you wish to remain anonymous.

The hotline was Zoë's cell phone. Very enterprising of her. As was making it sound as though the *Douglas County Herald* had the funds to hire me as their investigator. I sent her a congratulatory text and called Lou and Ed. They were delighted to take on dog sitting "the princess." I promised to be at their farm by six—"unless I've been kidnapped or arrested or knocked out."

"You could *say* all those things happened, and they're good excuses, but how could you prove it?" Lou said.

When I'd hung up I sat back and thought again about the Yancy project. The resort was a cover for—what?

I put Peppy into the Camry and drove to the library, to use their computers. Looked up revived coal plants, and found they were a pet project of people building bitcoin mining companies. I couldn't follow all the technical specs, but cryptocurrency requires tens of thousands of high-speed computers, and they in turn required thousands of megawatts of power. I read about one bitcoin facility in Kentucky that was operating with four coal-fired power plants.

I couldn't make my poor dog spend more time locked in the car. I walked down to the river with her and sat on a bench while she explored the underbrush and dabbled her feet in the shallows.

If the Tulloh brothers were putting up a crypto mining operation on top of Yancy, the Wakarusa coal plant was ready-made to generate the power. Pat Everard and Gertrude Perec would never have approved a bitcoin mine, but they'd given a pass to a resort. But what about Matthew? Was he on board with bitcoin mining?

I called Pauline Tulloh. I was prepared to leave a message on her voicemail, but she surprised me by answering herself.

"I met your father yesterday," I said. "He had Mellon and Chet Bezory beat me up a little and drive me to the headquarters in Salina."

"Oh?" It was her usual cool drawl.

"I wondered whose idea it was."

"Not mine," she said.

"Not just the kidnaping, and the threats—your father will have me killed as soon as I lead him to a crucial piece of evidence he wants. I wondered if he placed Mellon with you to spy on you for him, or if you and Matthew agreed Mellon was on loan to you, but his primary allegiance was to Matthew."

She didn't speak for a beat, then said in the same cool voice, "Everyone connected to Tulloh owes Matthew their primary allegiance. What evidence is he looking for?"

"Whatever Clarina Coffin claimed to have found that would derail the Yancy project. You said your father hates crypto, but I think that's what your brothers are building on top of Yancy. A data-mining facility."

"Daddy doesn't want any of us speculating in crypto, but if the money the boys make from it comes from coal power he'd be glad to take part. Coal comes from the ground, that's what he thinks is reliable. What evidence is Daddy looking for?"

"My private opinion, it doesn't exist. My public opinion? I'm hunting for it like mad in the hopes I'll live long enough to keep him from killing me."

Another short silence, and then she said, "I see," and hung up.

51

Troubled in Mind

Deke texted me as I finished talking to Pauline. Warshawski, this is my 4th message. We need to talk. Don't make me put out an APB.

I called him and said he could meet me at the library if he wanted to see me. I went out to the car to give Peppy some attention until I saw his unmarked car pull up.

He was wound too tight for ordinary niceties. "What were you doing at the Lion's Heart at five this morning?" he demanded.

"Protecting a homeless veteran. Don Wilton had kicked him pretty hard for using his building as a backrest."

"Don't fuck with me, Warshawski. Officer Helios

reported that you claimed to be going out for a walk. Randomly, outside the same bar where your Chicago college students were drinking two weeks ago."

I backed away to calm myself. The person who loses their temper loses the battle. "Yesterday, after you took Lucia off to view her sister's body, I wandered downtown. First, I saw young Trevor Millay dealing at the Lion's Heart's back door. I sent you the photos."

"And I'm repeating my response. Leave the local drug scene to us," Deke said. "Besides which, I wouldn't arrest Vladimir Putin based on those pix. It is not a crime for two people to hand each other envelopes in broad daylight in a public parking lot."

"I did think they were amazingly brazen. Almost as if they had protection." I eyed him steadily.

"Do not slander this department. I will not stand for it!" he cried so loudly that everyone in the lobby stared at us.

"Your chief and Jake Tulloh are frat brothers. They share their secrets, so presumably the LKPD knows that Don Wilton is Jake and Robert Tulloh's cousin. Their sister, Pauline Tulloh, bailed out the Lion's Heart during lockdown, so you can bet Wilton is ready to do whatever the Tullohs want, including handling the computer feed for the cameras out at the Dundee house."

Deke sank back in his chair, his eyes squeezed shut. He was trying to make sense of things he knew and things he didn't want to know.

"That still doesn't explain why you were at the Lion's Heart at five this morning," he growled, eyes still shut.

"I was like Bluebeard's wife," I said. "I wanted to see what was behind the steel door that leads from the bar to his office. I hoped Wilton left things unlocked so I could take a look."

"And had he?" He sat up, frowning fiercely, daring me to lie.

"Let's just say I was able to look inside without breaking his door locks or security codes," I said.

He stared at me for a long moment. "The window. Son of a bitch. I went and looked the place over after I read Helios's report. You went up the fire escape. He doesn't have an alarm on the window, I take it."

"Climb up and check it out. I can't confirm."

"Or deny. Right. When I talked to Helios, she remembered that the drunk you were helping called you Spiderwoman. When you looked inside Don's office, what did you see?"

"If I had access to the criminal justice system's legal machinery, I'd get a warrant," I said. "If I had access, I'd wonder if drug supply routes and schedules were taped next to the computer monitors. I'd look at the footage from the cameras spread around the Dundee place, because I'd wonder if Don was the person who controlled those cameras."

"So now you're not only Spiderwoman but Wonder Woman," Deke jeered.

I smiled. "Wondering woman, more accurately. Because I'd also wonder what conversations Don secretly recorded."

"You'd have to have grounds for a warrant, and the speculations of a wall-climbing private eye don't constitute grounds."

I bowed my head, acknowledgment. "You're right. One thing that actually happened, I'll share with you for nothing. Matthew Tulloh's daughter Pauline has a bodyguard-cum-butler, man named Geoffrey Mellon. He's really on Matthew's payroll.

"Yesterday, Mellon jumped me, together with the crew chief from the Yancy project. They stunned me and carted me off to Tulloh's HQ in Salina. Matthew Tulloh is a scary guy. He and his sons think that Clarina really did find a document that would derail Yancy. He's keeping me alive until I lead him to it.

"On another topic, Cady Perec is worried about your mother and her grandmother. You remember those diaries that disappeared from the state Origins Museum? Cady thinks Gertrude may have stolen them and given them to your mother to hide."

"Is she infecting your brain or you hers? Those two women work hard and do nothing but good for this town. And you think they're capable of theft of some ancient history books? And killing that strange woman over them?"

"If there is an explosive document, I'm betting it is connected to those ancient history books. I don't know what your team found in Clarina's trailer, but we know she had a photograph of a riot at the local train station over some Black settlers leaving town in the 1860s, along with a mourning photo from that same era."

"If I was killed tomorrow, you'd find Patrick Mahomes's photo in my bedroom," he said. "That wouldn't mean my death was connected to the Chiefs."

"I don't know—a jealous fan from Chicago might resent all those Super Bowl trophies and take it out on you."

He couldn't quite hold back a smile, but said, "Clarina was obsessed with Kansas history from the 1860s. I had an earful from Lucia all the way to KC and back. I know Matthew Tulloh is a billionaire and I'm just a sergeant getting by on my paycheck, but I think he's wrong about there being any evidence. Clarina *wanted* to find a document that would make her famous, but it doesn't exist."

He got to his feet. "I guess I should thank you for IDing the Coffin woman. Not that it helps ID her killer or a motive."

"I'm pleased you feel grateful. That will keep me going in the dark watches of the night. You are a good and dedicated cop, but you have a chief who is close to the Tulloh family. I am not making up what I heard on a recording in Don Wilton's office: Chief McDowell is reporting on what you and your team discover to his old fraternity brother, Jake Tulloh. You don't want to believe this, but you need me here."

"The LKPD does not need you—"

"Not me specifically," I said, "but someone outside the chain of command who can keep a secret and also keep asking uncomfortable questions."

He stared back at me, his expression bleak. After a long moment, he turned on his heel.

52
Juggling Chain Saws

It was a relief to reach Lou and Ed's hilltop retreat, a relief to sit with a drink around their fire pit and tell them everything that had happened in the last few days, including climbing into Don Wilton's office.

"When I was a boy, my dad took me to a fair they were holding outside Topeka," Ed said. "Little thing, suitable for a colored neighborhood, rides that could've fallen apart if they went too fast, a sad pony carrying us around a circle. There was a man who juggled chain saws. That's what really stuck with me. Chain saws.

"That's you, Warshawski. Those are going to come crashing down on you. You want to cut off your head, your choice, but the princess here doesn't have a vote. You leave her here with us until you get this business done."

Lou nodded. I didn't argue. It helped to know I didn't have to worry about Peppy's safety, although I warned them that my chain saws included the probable bugging of the Camry. "I found an Apple tracker in the spare tire well, which I left in the library parking lot, but they may have put other devices in harder places to find. In which case the mad billionaire may send his vassals to call on you."

"You are a lot of fun to know," Ed said. "Good thing you've got a cute dog. And where are you spending the night?"

"Crashing at Zoë's while she's living it up in western New York," I said. "I'll meet you at the yard tomorrow when my accessories come in."

I drove back into Lawrence and parked in the visitors' lot at the new police station, leaving my infected phone in the trunk so that Tulloh would know where to find me. If someone decided to blow up the Camry, the police would surely investigate it there. I rode the free bus back downtown. It let me out near the library. I crossed the street and sat on a curb, watching people getting off and on the buses that pulled in there.

When I was reasonably sure no one was waiting for me, I walked down to the *Douglas County Herald* building near the river. Zoë had told me she was the only person who regularly spent time there.

I could hear the river nearby while I worked the lock, heard the murmur of voices from the homeless camp underneath the bridge, metal plates on the bridge surface clanking as they bounced under the passing cars.

I was working in the dark, but it was an old lock that needed touch, not sight. In a few minutes I'd jiggered the tumblers into place.

I switched on my flashlight and saw a cadre of gray tails slither under doors as I walked along. How good to know I wouldn't be alone in the cold damp building.

In one of the disused offices, I found an array of mismatched furniture, including a couch. It was dusty, but the cushions were reasonably firm. A quilted tarp was draped over a pallet mover. It was dusty, too, but it was heavy. I lay on the couch, fully dressed except for my shoes, the tarp pulled up to my chin. I sneezed for a while, but my sinuses adjusted and I drifted into sleep.

I was warm enough under the tarp, but I woke often, wondering about the rats, about Peppy, about whether I'd left Lou and Ed exposed to danger, and how good the surveillance on me was. At six, I got up for good. There were toilets at one end of the hall. The women's room was reasonably clean—no doubt Zoë's work— and even had warm water for my dusty face and heavy eyes. I brushed my teeth, combed my hair, and looked like a woman who hadn't slept much but who at least had a clean face.

I walked across the river to the Boat Yard, which was already open, doing a brisk business with truckers and work crews heading to the industrial sites along the river's north bank. There were a couple of Kirmek trucks in the mix, one laden with more phone pole–size logs. Women with kids in tow were crowded at a front table.

At first I kept looking around nervously, wondering if some Tulloh hireling had followed me to the paper's offices and then to here, but no one was paying attention to another exhausted, ill-kempt customer. I sat at the counter, building up my strength over corned beef hash with an egg, reading Zoë's latest dispatch from Skaneateles.

The yard where Lou and Ed brought new life to old metal was another half mile up the river from the café. They hadn't arrived yet; the gates to the yard were still locked. I found an old car seat lying outside the fence and lay in it drowsing, watching the eagles pass overhead.

A sharp wind was blowing from the north, from home, but I was too tired and achy from my poor sleep to do jumping jacks or anything that might keep me warm. I was glad when the FedEx truck pulled up to the yard gates. I hoisted myself out of the seat and lumbered over to meet the driver.

Lou and Ed pulled in while I was signing for the box. Cheviot wanted to see my signature on the form, so it was good that I'd shown up in person.

Lou unlocked the gate. "You want to look at your accessories in the shop, come on in," he said.

I shook my head. "Anything that gets on them will be analyzed and can be traced back to the metal or dust in your shop. I'm going to take them to the library and use one of their sound rooms; they're not sterile, but they're pretty clean."

The box wasn't heavy, but it was cumbersome. The men looked at each other as I started out of the yard.

"Someone sees you walking across the river with that, even if they shoot you first, they're going to figure we know you. Get in the truck, Warshawski."

I got in the truck. Peppy was there; they weren't going to leave her alone on the farm. She greeted me with a polite thump of the tail but I was not forgiven for leaving her alone in the car too many times the last few days.

At the library, no one questioned me when I signed up for one of their sound studios. I opened the box and found the wrench, wrapped in a clear plastic evidence bag, labeled with the chain of custody, from me to Cheviot and back to me to deliver to Deke.

I had not thought this through. I cursed myself, but repacked the box. In the Osma local history room, I tucked it carefully behind some outsize atlases.

I rode the free bus out Sixth Street to the Buy-Smart outlet where I bought latex gloves, a box cutter, and some two-gallon clear plastic bags.

Back in the library I made sure I had on gloves, opened the box again, and removed the wrench in its evidence bag. I couldn't remove the chain of custody label from the evidence bag. I cut open the bag. Careful not to touch the wrench, I dropped it into one of my two-gallon bags.

As it lay there, I noticed again the embossed *K* in its circle. I'd been looking at that *K* every day for the past two weeks. Kirmek Construction. I wanted to scrawl on the bag in red ink, "Look at Chet Bezory's tool box, see if his fourteen-inch pipe wrench is missing," but that would not be smart.

I put the bag with the wrench in it inside a second two-gallon bag and wrapped that into a ten-gallon black garbage bag.

Now the scary part. I found a bus that took me within half a mile of the Dundee house. I walked up

1450 Road until I was close to the house, then cut across the field on the Dundee house's north side. Crouching down to make use of what cover I could, I went into the woods behind the house. I wished I'd felt safe going back to the trailer—my boots would have been a boon on this rough terrain. Two consecutive nights' sleep would have been welcome. A companion. A message from Peter.

My mother had hidden alone in the hills near Livorno, waiting for a signal that a dilapidated fishing boat was waiting to take her to Lisbon. Her father had just been arrested. Italy was no longer safe for her. She was eighteen. She had hiked the 160 miles to the coast at nights, carrying her cardboard suitcase with her grandmother's red Venetian wineglasses wrapped in her few clothes.

How much sleep had Gabriella had in those eight nights? How had she found help in Lisbon, where she knew no one and didn't speak the language? And then she'd ended up in Chicago, imagining her glorious voice would find her a paying job in one of the rough bars on Milwaukee Avenue.

Gabriella, help me find some of your courage, your indomitable spirit. I began singing one of her favorite Mozart arias, my voice rusty and scratchy. Along with my triceps, I'd abandoned my vocal exercises these last five months. When I returned to Chicago all would be different.

"Porgi, amor" brought me to the fringe of bushes on the perimeter of the Dundee house. Pale green buds were emerging along the branches, but it would be some weeks before they provided cover between the woods and the house. I pushed the bags deep into one of the densest clumps of undergrowth, estimated it was in a direct line about seventy-five yards from the far edge of the house.

I was starting back the way I'd come when a black Jeep Cherokee bounced up the Dundee house drive. Chet Bezory, the Yancy project foreman, jumped out without taking time to turn off his engine and headed toward me.

My throat pulses choked me. Had he seen me from the hilltop? Or despite my care, had I shown up on the Lion's Heart camera feed?

I crouched low and started to run up the hill, where the tree cover was thickest. I'd gone about thirty yards when a bullet whined near my head. I dropped to the ground and began crawling at speed.

"Whoever you are, come out or eat lead," the voice boomed through a megaphone.

I couldn't suppress a nervous giggle. *Eat lead*, language from an old cowboy movie.

Another shot whined overhead, hitting a thick tree branch. It cracked and fell, briefly blocking the route behind me, giving me maybe a fifteen-second edge. I reached the remains of the trail I'd followed three weeks ago and picked up speed. The ground had been muddy a week earlier, but it was cold enough now that the soil was packed; I wasn't leaving footprints.

Just as I reached the first ruined house, it started to snow. Now I would leave a trail. I looked around wildly for cover and squeezed myself through a gap into the remains of the chimney. And made myself a sitting target. V.I! You used to have good instincts, what happened to them?

I squatted, patting the ground, seeking anything that could be a weapon, and felt—empty air. I risked a quick look with my flashlight. A hole, partly filled from years of leaves and branches, but bricks jutting from the inner wall offered a makeshift ladder.

Hand over hand, feet flailing, losing my grip and sliding the last six feet to the bottom. Tree roots and bricks cut into my jacket. I chanced another quick light.

I was in an old root cellar. A light shone above me. I stuffed the flashlight into my pocket. Backed into the cellar against one dirt wall and looked upward. A hand had come through the gap I'd used, then a head. The light played along the old chimney wall, pointed at the branches and leaves along the outer wall, missed the opening down to the cellar.

The hand and head withdrew. Dimly I heard two voices, men, impossible to tell whose. More faintly still, renewed crashing through bushes and branches. And then quiet, sudden, enveloping, as if the air were a velvet blanket folding around me.

I collapsed on the ground, muscles weak from relief, sweat soaking my hoodie. After some time listening until I was sure my pursuers had disappeared, I shone the flash again to look at the cellar. And sat still, dumbfounded. A small table, a chair, a metal chest placed on a trestle. Best of all, a battery-operated lantern. I switched it on.

The dirt walls held shelves that must date back to the house's origins. Hand-printed labels were still stuck to some cans, with lettering so faded that it couldn't be read. Some of the cans had exploded, but so long ago that the contents had dried past identification.

The chest had a padlock, but the chest itself was made of a light metal. Using a stick as a lever, I pried the top open. The padlock held, but the metal around it peeled back.

I brought the lantern over to inspect the contents. Most of what lay inside was paper. The top document was a notebook with the University of Kansas logo on it. Inside the front cover, Clarina Coffin's name was printed, with the address of the Prairie View Trailer Park. "Reward if found and returned," she'd written.

The notebook seemed to be Clarina's journal, which included an autobiography called "Following in My Family's Footsteps," along with notes she'd made about documents she'd read in various libraries. She'd also felt free to help herself to some original material. Tucked between two pages in her notebook was a yellowed piece of newsprint, so fragile pieces fell from it when I tried to lift it. I could see the header: YANCY LEDGER, KANSAS OLDEST NEGRO NEWSPAPER, June 28 1867.

A binder held more original documents, including telegrams and letters from members of the Grellier family and people named Entwistle. Zoë had mentioned that name in her first report from Skaneateles. Elias Entwistle had built the house where Clarina found the old letters and papers that prompted her move to Kansas.

Beneath the binder were three books bound in red leather, which had faded with time. I opened one to the elegant script I'd seen last week in Topeka. Abby Langford and Tommy Gellman, librarian and conservator at the Kansas Origins Museum, would be horrified to see Florence Wheelock's precious journals down in this damp cellar.

An additional journal, in a different hand, bound more simply in mildewing cardboard, lay at the bottom of the chest, next to some packages of dried fruit and yogurt chips.

I barely had feeling in my hands. The latex gloves I'd worn to keep from leaving prints on my evidence bag were no protection from the cold.

I thought about leaving everything in situ, but I was afraid Tulloh's team would come back to the chimney when they didn't find me in the woods. If they really started searching, it wouldn't take long to uncover this hideout.

I needed to save the journals. If my pursuers found them, they'd either destroy them outright or leave the paper here to disintegrate.

Florence's three volumes fit into my daypack, although I couldn't zip it completely shut. Clarina's notebook I tucked into the waistband of the jeans I'd been wearing since yesterday morning. The cardboard-bound journal was too big, its contents too fragile, to risk wearing it. I carried it in my left hand over to the brick ladder.

My shoulders and arms were still throbbing from the battering they'd taken on Saturday. Those same battered muscles needed to hoist me up the chimney stack, one-handed to protect the binder. Inching up, leaning into the brick stack so it took my weight, fumbling for each handhold, pushing up with my quads.

When I reached the top, I stuck my head cautiously around the chimney stack. My sweat froze in the harsh wind.

The snow had stopped, leaving only a thin cover on the ground, but enough to show that my pursuit had gone back to the Dundee house. I would also be leaving prints, but that couldn't be helped. At least I knew which way not to go.

I moved as quickly as I could, ordering my body to ignore the cold, ignore my swollen legs and trembling arms, repeating my old basketball coach's mantras. *It's not the size of the dog in the fight, it's the size of the fight in the dog. Quitters never win; winners never quit.* That was before St. Cecelia beat us 98 to 40, but we never quit.

I'd planned on walking in the road when I got there, easier terrain in my running shoes. A few yards from the edge I tripped on a root. I was clutching the cardboard journal and so I fell awkwardly, hitting my right shoulder hard. I lay still, catching my breath. A black Jeep Cherokee cruised by, slowly, Don Wilton in the backseat peering out the open window into the woods.

When it passed, I counted the seconds until it reappeared. About three minutes, and then five more as it made a return trip. I could lie here until the weather warmed up, when flowers and bushes would grow high enough to mark my grave. Or I could get back in motion.

Crawling, latex gloves in tatters, fingers bleeding, shoulder pounding. Lying flat every time I heard tires on gravel.

And then a crashing through the undergrowth, a short sharp bark, a man's grunt. "Got her."

53
Beauty Treatment

Peppy was licking my face, whining. Lou scooped me up. Compared to a car door, I apparently didn't weigh much. Ed had the engine idling. Lou dumped Peppy and me into the backseat; the truck was in motion before Ed shut the door.

"What in the name of anything holy are you trying to prove, Warshawski?" Ed said. "You're a dog person, not a cat, you don't have nine lives to squander. When I said there were corpses better-looking than you, I didn't mean you should go for it as a beauty treatment."

"Ease up, man," Lou said. "You got her started with your chain saw juggling. She figured she had to do something better than that to keep your attention."

Waves of fatigue were carrying me away. I struggled awake. "How come you two were on that road just now?"

"Remember, Warshawski? Back when you told us about your accessories, you said you needed to have them on Dundee land so Five-O would connect them to the Coffin woman's murder. You went silent for so long we thought we'd better take a look. Princess here, she was all for letting you rot in the woods so she could stay with us, but Ed had a moment of softheartedness, he insisted we come out.

"Not much we could do without jamming ourselves up, but we saw the Yancy project foreman driving up and down in that Cherokee, so we knew he was probably hunting you. I dropped off the princess and Lou. What were you doing there?"

"I found Clarina's hideout. I have her papers. Here with me."

I must have fallen asleep midsentence, because the next thing I knew, Lou was slapping my face; we were at the mountaintop house. I was in a point beyond exhaustion, but I had to get a message to Deke about the bag of evidence. My smartphone, with his mobile number, was in the Camry trunk near the library, but Lou said he wasn't going to risk his license by driving a corpse around downtown Lawrence.

"Give me the keys. Give me your phone passcode so I can look up the number. I'll text him from this doodah. And then it will go into the compacter."

It's hard to text from a burner keypad, so I kept the message short: CC murder weapon in bush 75 yards east Dundee house.

54
Library Privileges

A long bath, a long nap, a vegan dinner Ed created from the produce in his and Lou's greenhouse, and I was more or less ready to face whatever had built up during the day. They drove me to the trailer so that I could pick up my smartphone. I opened it to a truck-load of messages.

Deke had phoned and texted, six messages that escalated in fury, ending with, You are not leaving the jurisdiction until you explain that wrench to me.

Murray wondered why I'd gone dark. Mr. Contreras wanted me to come home. My erstwhile client, Valerie, wanted to talk to me. Zoë had sent an urgent text, Call, I've found the original owner of that house.

I wrote down my messages; I'd answer them from

a different phone when I was outside both the trailer and the Camry. An exhausting way to spend time but essential until I got back to my Chicago computer experts, who could clean my phone for me.

"You going to sleep here, or you want to hunker down with the rats again?" Lou asked. We'd gone outside to talk.

I made a face. "Tulloh is keeping track of me, I'm sure, either through his contact at the LKPD or through whatever tracers they have on my phone and the Camry, but so far they don't seem to know I've found anything. I should be safe for another night, anyway."

Ed moved the door back and forth. "Door's okay. Be hard to remove. But this lock isn't worth the price of the key."

Lou nodded. "Got an ABUS padlock at the shop. Length of 100 chain. Even if they have the right bolt cutters, the noise will wake you long before they get in. Back in thirty. Anyone comes looking for you, hide under the couch."

"That's a hell of a way to leave the princess's ma. I'll stay here and tell her my life story while you collect the hardware."

Lou grinned. "Thought you'd man up. Be sure to tell her all the different ways chain saws have figured in your life."

Ed grunted and made a flicking motion. When Lou had left, we inspected the furniture and the bathroom fittings for booby traps. Ed disconnected the cooktop electrics and made sure they hadn't been wired to electrocute me.

When Lou returned with the chain and padlock, we moved the bed so that if someone threw something through the window, say a Molotov cocktail, I wouldn't be under it, and would have a clear path to the door. They made sure their numbers were on my speed-dial.

I walked back outside with them.

"You're carrying a load of dynamite on you. You going to keep it here?" Ed asked.

We'd packed all the journals into the lining of one of Lou's old jackets. It was oiled leather, and heavy, but it had a lining buttoned into it where I could pack my documents. I moved with the lumbering gait of a woman close to her due date, but on a dark February evening I hoped no watcher would be suspicious.

"They searched this place on Saturday. They searched me, they searched the car. I think the papers and I will be safe here for one night." I spoke with more confidence than I felt, but these documents had cost me too much trouble to want to separate myself from them.

I dreaded being alone in the trailer, but I kept up

a bright face while the men packed Peppy back into the truck and took off. When they'd disappeared, I walked over to the building the trailer park advertised as a common room and gym. This was a double-wide unit with an old treadmill and some arcade games for children. No one was there, so I sat on a stationary bike to call Zoë.

Her eager voice vibrated the phone's speakers so loudly that my ears were hurting. I slid the volume bar down and still could hear her over the wind banging on the door.

"Vic, you're not going to believe this, but I found the family that used to own the house, you know, the one where Clarina or Rickey found all those papers? Their name is Carruthers. They were a prominent Black family in Skaneateles, but in the nineties— 1990s, I mean—there was only one immediate family member left, and she got a job in the Clinton administration, something in the State Department, then she stayed on in DC, teaching at one of the universities there."

"She sold the house to Elise and Clarina's aunt when she moved?"

"That's right. Well, here's the creepy part. I mean, I tracked her down, it wasn't hard—Louisa Carruthers, her name is, but Rickey also tracked her down. Professor

Carruthers—she's eighty-something now, she's retired from teaching but heads a foundation.

"Anyway, Professor Carruthers said this strange woman wrote her, claiming her name was Martha Carruthers, that she'd been adopted at birth by a Polish family, but that she was a cousin to Professor Carruthers, only she needed the professor to give a DNA sample so she could prove it. Of course, the professor refused. She had her secretary write back to say she did not respond to such letters, from white people who imagined there was glamour in being Black and not to bother the professor again. Only, guess what?"

"Martha Carruthers was a name Clarina-Rickey was using?" I asked.

"Yes!" Zoë cried, triumphant. "I talked to the neighbors who knew Clarina and they said she kept claiming she was Black and descended from this family who were important in the civil rights movement. I guess when Clarina-Rickey heard back from the professor, she retreated and decided to be descended from white abolitionists."

"That's great work, Zoë," I said. "Did the Carruthers family have a Kansas connection?"

"The professor didn't want to talk much about her own family, but she said her people had originally gone from the Auburn area out to Lawrence, and then come back to Skaneateles after the Civil War. 'It was not a hospitable climate' was how she put it."

"So at least we know now what made Clarina come out here," I said. "This is great. When do you publish?"

"Someone from the *Washington Post* showed up in Skaneateles today, so if I'm going to scoop, I have to publish in time for the morning cable feeds. Ben Pike is even giving me more money to stay on." She hung up, beside herself with excitement.

The Camry was still in the police parking lot. I decided to leave it there one more night and rode the free bus downtown to get some dinner, the journals weighing down the coat, giving me practice in rebuilding my muscles.

My skin prickled all the way through supper and on the bus back, not knowing if anyone was watching me, or where they were watching from. Life in a surveillance state must feel like this, constant exposure, constant vigilance over what you said and who you said it to.

55

Pranking the Sergeant

B ack in the trailer, I checked the windows and the perimeter a half dozen times before settling down with my trove. I started with Clarina's notebook.

Her handwriting was big and sloppy, hard to decipher. I'd gotten as far as following the footsteps of "my Grellier ancestors" from Skaneateles to Kansas Territory in 1855 when a car pulled up outside the trailer's door.

My heart went cold. I stuck the notebook back behind the lining of Lou's coat. I switched off the living room light and pressed myself against the wall next to the door.

A pounding on the door, and then Deke Everard said, "I know you're in there, Warshawski. Open up before I get a bar and pry the door apart."

I called out that the door would be open in two minutes. Police—especially angry frustrated police—don't wait long before busting down doors. I got the lights on, picked up the key from the kitchen countertop, and got the padlock undone.

I went outside, pulling the door shut behind me—standard advice every defense lawyer gives their clients. Only let them in if they have a warrant. Invite them in and they can make themselves at home.

"I've been trying to reach you since one this afternoon. Where have you been? What's the meaning of your text about finding evidence of Clarina's murder in the woods behind the Dundee house?"

Every nerve in my body was on high alert. Lou and Ed told me they'd put the phone through their compacter. If Deke had had a warrant to search the yard, they would have told me. I was grateful for the dark, which hid any nervous twitches I might be making.

"My text, Sergeant?" My voice came out light, steady, annoyed. "Was someone pranking you, sending you on a wild goose chase after evidence? Or were they pranking me, claiming I was texting you?"

"Don't push me, Warshawski, because you'll be pushing yourself into a holding cell. We have a photograph of you at the Dundee place yesterday."

"Do you, now," I said. "Sent to you by the same

helpful people who provided you with photos of Trig and Gertrude there the night Clarina's body was found?"

"Do you deny you were there?"

"I wasn't at the house," I said. "Interesting that you got a picture of me there. Must have been photo-shopped. Maybe that's what happened with Gertrude and Trig?"

"Not at the house, in the woods behind it."

If he hadn't been a grown man and a police officer, I would have said he sounded sullen.

"Yes, I was in the woods. I wanted another look at Yancy, at the woods, and the remains of those old houses behind the Dundee place. I was hoping for some hint about what connected Clarina to that property."

I spoke to him earnestly, innocent, not knowing why he was so agitated.

"You're in the woods at 9:03 A.M. and at 1:16 P.M. I get an anonymous text telling me there's evidence of Clarina's murder in those woods. And then a SOC team finds the wrench—where you stashed it."

"Wrench?" I said blankly.

"You're not a good enough actor to go on Broadway," he snapped. "You know about the damned wrench."

"Even if I knew what you were talking about, I

wasn't hanging around in the woods for four hours waiting to text you."

"No, but you were there dropping off a plastic garbage bag that contained evidence of a murder."

"It's time for Faye Mitchell to join this conversation. You are making wild accusations and I am not listening to more of them without my lawyer present."

I hit her speed-dial icon but got her voicemail. "Deke Everard is with me at the Prairie View Trailer Park. He claims he found evidence of a murder in the woods behind the Dundee house and is blaming me for it. If we move to the police station, I'll let you know."

Deke walked around in a circle, venting steam, came back to face me. "I'm not booking you, not yet, but one fingerprint on that bag, on that wrench, and you will be in a cell so fast your feet won't have time to hit the ground."

He turned to go.

I said, "By the way, Sergeant, someone shot at me, more than once, in those woods, and I ran. Does the photo include that?"

"You're making that up!"

"Not for one second. You should find evidence of where I landed flat on the underbrush. And a branch fell on the trail when the shooter hit a tree instead of me."

He stared at me for another long minute, face tight

with emotion. Not anger, I thought, but frustration. He turned on his heel and got into his car, leaving with a great spinning of gravel. I went back inside. Collapsed onto a chair, muscles too weak from stress to hold me up. He was almost certainly recording me. If he'd asked me directly about the evidence bag, I could not have lied on the record.

56

Family Stories

After Deke left, I sat up in bed reading through Clarina's spiral notebook. It was a jumble of details from her archival research, her fantasy history, and her grievances, first against her sister and then, as she spent more time in Lawrence, against the Perecs and Pat Everard for not paying appropriate attention to Clarina's knowledge of Kansas history.

She'd done impressive research in the Lawrence and Topeka libraries. At first I jotted down notes about the Wheelock, Entwistle, and Everard families as she recounted some of their history, but she tangled together nineteenth-century history with twenty-first-century slights. It became impossible to figure out which century she was writing about.

Her list of grievances expanded to include staff at the University Press.

> You'd think a press in the same spot where John Brown led freedom fighters into battle against slavery would be eager to publish books set back then. I showed them a proposal, and even made the mistake of letting them see one of Sophia's letters. That won't happen again! They wanted the letters but not my historical writing.

Her proposal wasn't in the notebook. Maybe I'd overlooked it when I was nervously cleaning out her trunk, but she might have handed Kayla Huang a handwritten paragraph torn from this notebook.

Elsewhere in the notebook, Clarina wrote about Cady Perec's course, how Cady "didn't have the spine God gave a goldfish." Clarina said she'd fought for Cady's rights at Yancy school and Cady repaid her with disrespect.

I flipped through the pages, hoping for something more substantive. If this was what Matthew Tulloh thought could derail the Yancy project, he was spending time and money chasing a chimera, and chasing me in the bargain.

The last entry in the book returned to her grievance

with the University Press. She'd found something that would let her tell the truth about Yancy to the world. "I can't wait to see Queen Gertrude's face when I tell her. And the snobs at the Kansas press! They're wrong if they think I'll let them publish my work. I'll go to a real university, like Harvard. They'll make these Kansas people look like the hicks they really are."

This entry was dated February 7. Whatever she'd found out, she'd given some inkling to the Kansas hicks, because six days later she was dead.

57
Love Story

B ut what did you find?" I demanded out loud,
before remembering the trailer might be bugged.
Clarina maddened everyone around her in life; I tried
to curb my annoyance with her in death.

I put her notebook into its protective plastic bag. I
slipped it behind the lining of Lou's coat and carefully
extracted the cardboard-bound journal.

"Sophia Grellier, her book" was written on the inside
cover, with "Carruthers" inserted sometime later.

The early pages dealt with the Civil War, the struggle Sophia had to look after the house while "Mother
continues poorly after Baby's death and Papa is absorbed in his important educational work."

In an 1860 entry, I found a first mention of the Carruthers family. This was the family Zoë had located, whose only living descendant was the professor in Washington.

Sophia described the Carruthers as a free Black family who had come from Auburn, at the suggestion of Mrs. Tubman, to help establish a settlement for freed Black people on a hill outside town.

> They are calling it Yancy Hill, for they tell me that in the Hausa language of Africa, Yancy means freedom. Miss Anna Carruthers, who was highly educated at Oberlin College in Ohio, assists Papa in the school, which he has renamed as Yancy School. Miss Anna's father is dead, but her brother Nathan looks after house and farm with manly zeal. Three other families are joined in this small settlement, all working for one another in the most noble cooperative spirit.
>
> In Anna I find the first true bosom friend I have met since we first moved to Kansas territory.

In February 1863, Nathan joined the First Kansas Colored Infantry Regiment. Sophia wrote about her and Anna's fears for his safety, about the bandages they rolled, the uniforms they made and mended, and the quotidian, responsibility for growing food while the men were all away at war, christening presents for babies born despite war.

In 1865, Nathan returned to Yancy. After that, he appeared more and more often in the diary, with Sophia uncovering more and more instances of his remarkable gifts and sweet personality. Late in 1865, he and Sophia were married by the local white Congregational church minister, Louis Hamer.

In a ceremony only Papa and Anna Carruthers could attend, for fear of the increasing violence in the town against Negro people. We spent our wedding night secretly in the schoolhouse, where Anna laid out for us a cold feast, including a cake, and spread blankets and cushions on the floor.

Clarina had underlined this section in red, and written "SHAME ON YOU, LAWRENCE!!!" in large red letters in the margin. "These are my people, I'm sure of it, and the town treated you vilely."

Clarina must have written Professor Carruthers in Washington after reading the journal. Clarina's need to be important, to be a player in big historical events, felt painfully embarrassing.

Through the end of 1866 and into the following spring, Sophia wrote of her and Nathan's longing to find a place they could move to where they could live together openly as husband and wife without the fear of mob violence. They were considering moving to a Black settlement in Canada, or perhaps back to the Auburn district.

And then came the attack on the school and Frederic Grellier's and Anna Carruthers's deaths. I'd seen the *Kanwaka Courier* story about their murders when I was at the Origins Museum. The newspaper article had been written in a cruel spirit, blaming Frederic's support of Black education for his murder.

The *Courier* hadn't mentioned Anna Carruthers's death in the conflagration. I suppose as a Black woman she was considered beneath their notice.

For Sophia, the murders created a trauma that must have been unendurable. In the days leading up to the murder, she recorded the ugly letters her father received, accusing him of sex, "consorting" with Anna. The letters ordered him to close the school or pay with his life. Sophia quoted one in her journal as saying, "We don't need n- here, and edicated n- is the worse."

2 July 1866

The day of the murders I was approaching the school with a supply of milk and bread so that the children could have a nuncheon, when I saw the cowardly demons throwing kerosene on the building and setting it ablaze. I screamed and ran, scattering milk and bread. The monsters fled, but by the time I reached the school it was a bonfire. Father and Anna were heroic, sacrificing themselves to move the children to safety. As the children emerged, I smothered their smoldering clothes in my skirts, which fell to rags around my legs by the time we were finished.

Nathan saw the blaze from where he was working on the riverfront and came running but by then the inferno blazed with such heat we could not enter the building. As soon as the flames had died near the entrance, we saw the bodies of our dear ones, charred and contorted from the fire, along with two children they had not been able to save.

Nathan took the surviving Negro children to their homes on Yancy. Kind Mr. Schapen appeared with his wagon and drove the white children to their parents.

I could not bear to leave Father or my sister Anna's bodies, although I knew I must find the strength to break the terrible news to Mother. If there is a God, I pray he reward Mr. Schapen for his support and friendship throughout that terrible day, for he went to Mother, came back with more men and a wagon to carry the bodies to the undertaker to be fitted with coffins, and then stayed with Mother until the worst of her overwrought nerves could be calmed.

My cherished Nathan's grief surpasses my own. The sister with whom he shared every hardship, every grief—my love cannot salve those wounds. He has gone to stay with his mother on Yancy Hill. We agreed that I must not attend his sister's funeral—a white woman at a Black person's funeral would incite the mob to greater violence. And if they learned that Rev. Hamer had married us! My only consolation is the small life growing inside me. I hadn't wanted to tell my beloved until I knew with more certainty, but I told him before he left my side, and it did, indeed, bring him some measure of relief. If it is a girl we will call her Anna in honor of our beautiful sister. A son we will name for Papa.

Once Papa's funeral was over, Mother announced her intention to return to New York state. She needs more support than I can provide, alas. It is a sad reversal of roles, her need to return to the Auburn district. Twelve years ago, she was alight with a different kind of fire, kindled with the desire to loose the bondsman's chains. It was I, eight years old, who cried bitter tears at leaving my grandparents, my friends, my little bedroom hung with white muslin curtains. But poor Mother—she lost one babe on the journey to Kansas, and five more little bodies are now joined by their Father in this prairie cemetery. She can take no more sorrow, no more hardship. Grandmother Entwistle may purse her lips up in displeasure, and cry that Mother has her reward for marrying a man with more ideals than common sense, but she and my aunt Hypatia will nurse Mother back to health.

I helped her pack her trunk, and saw her safe into the cars taking her east.

And then went to pay my respects to Mrs. Carruthers and to see my beloved, whose face, whose strong arms wrapped round me I sorely needed. But when I arrived in Yancy, I was greeted by new horrors.

In the place of the tidy houses in the woods were their charred remains. The only house still standing was Mrs. Carruthers', but when I went to the door, a strange white man, reeking of alcohol, and missing so many teeth I could barely make out his speech, cackled in a horrible way and said, "The n-'s had all made tracks, and a good thing, too. They'd a disappeared in the night afore we could burn them down. Got rid of that big black buck who we all seen eyeing the schoolteacher's girl. Good riddance to the teacher, traitor to his race, good riddance to the n-. And if the girl shows up, good riddance to her, too." He waved a shotgun in my face. I stumbled through the grass, and somehow made it home before I fainted.

I sat back in my chair. The woman in the mourning photo Clarina had brought with her from Skaneateles had been Sophia Grellier Carruthers.

Pogrom on pogrom, is there no end to the hate and violence we bestow on one another?

58

The Dundee House Gets Its Name

I read through Sophia's journal to her final entry in 1875. She finally moved to Skaneateles when her child—Nathan Frederic Grellier Carruthers—was five.

I thought I could outmatch the Wheelocks and the Everards and the rest of them, and let my boy grow up where his father and I had been happy, but after they forced Rev. Hamer to retire I felt I had no friends left in this valley. Here in Skaneateles Mother and the Entwistle relatives are almost as cold and rude as Florence Wheelock, but I have the comfort of Mrs. Tubman and Mrs. Wright and their circle.

It was past three when I finished Sophia's journal. I hoped whatever secret Clarina had uncovered lay in Florence Wheelock's journals, but my eyes and shoulders ached from leaning over the faded script. I needed to lie down for a time.

I packed Sophia back inside Lou's coat. I made another circuit of the yard around the trailer and finally fell into a jumble of dreams, where the rioters fighting open housing in the Chicago of my childhood grinned, dancing around Clarina Coffin's murdered body. Sophia Grellier Carruthers watched from the sidelines, hands folded over her pregnant stomach. She was talking to Peter, saying you're right to keep your distance.

It was a relief when I came fully awake again a little after nine. I stood in the shower until the hot water ran out, trying to wash the dreams and turbulent thoughts out of my head.

I couldn't face more time alone in the trailer. I took Florence Wheelock down to the library to read.

Wheelock, Gertrude Perec's ancestor, had performed an Eliza Doolittle transformation on herself, from illiterate child of a poor farmer to wife of one of the town's top citizens. Somehow her own experience of poverty, and being an envious outsider to the lives white middle-class girls were leading, hadn't made her sympathetic to other outsiders, such as the town's Black or poor white populations.

Instead, she looked scornfully at them, even her own sisters. She often wrote witheringly about them doing the back-breaking farmwork she'd escaped, enduring multiple pregnancies. She wrote that they could have followed her example, but they preferred "to remain in the mud."

The three volumes Clarina had filched covered the years 1865 to 1872. As was true with Sophia Grellier's journal, Clarina had defaced Florence's writing with her own comments. I started by looking for those.

She and Theodore Wheelock belonged to the Riverside Congregational Church. He was one of the church elders, a group that seemed to make up the church's management committee. He and some of his pals disliked the minister, the Reverend Louis Hamer, who kept trying to ram sermons on racial equality and justice down their throats. When people learned that Hamer had married Sophia and Nathan, Florence wrote so angrily that sparks leaped from the paper.

In the margin, Clarina had written in red ink, "Queen Gertrude's racist supercilious heritage on full display!!"

Finally in 1869, Wheelock controlled a majority of the elders, and they forced Hamer to retire. It was then that Sophia left Lawrence for New York State.

An 1870 entry explained how the Dundee house got its name.

November 18, 1870

Mr. Wheelock was finally able to lay claim to the rich farmland on Yancy Hill. Rev. Hamer had his supporters in the congregation as well as his detractors, and one such has always been Simon Booth, who used his position as county recorder to oppose Mr. Wheelock's claim. But with the November election behind us, and Henry Everard now installed as the county recorder, Mr. Wheelock had smooth sailing.

Nine years ago, when the school burned down, Mr. Wheelock installed a Cyrus Dundee in the Carruthers house, the only house in the colored settlement still standing. Dundee has a slattern of a wife and five or perhaps six raggedy children, but he has a shotgun. Over the years he has shot at any coloreds trying to sneak back onto the property.

At least now I knew why the drug house was called the Dundee place. It seemed heartbreaking, the house that Nathan Carruthers had built with his mother and sister first handed over to an illiterate drunkard, and then made the site of Brett Santich's drug parties. Perhaps some shaman or priest could perform a purification ritual.

I turned back to Florence's journal. And in the next paragraph found the hand grenade Clarina had tried to lob at the Yancy project.

Mr. and Mrs. Everard joined us tonight to celebrate the liberation of Yancy. Mrs. Everard and I suggested changing the name Yancy to something more Christian, since the word is a heathen one, bestowed by the riffraff who used to camp there, but Mr. Wheelock advised against it.

He has given me the old, illegitimate record for safekeeping, and what safer place than here, where only my own eyes look.

I read the entry a half dozen times, trying to take in the meaning. Theodore Wheelock had finally been able to claim the rich farmland on Yancy. He had given Florence the old illegitimate record, and she had kept it in her journal, where only her own eyes looked. The illegitimate record. Wheelock had laid claim to the land, he'd been turned down by the county recorder, but with a new man in office, he'd been able to push his claim.

Wheelock had claimed land that belonged to the Carruthers family. This meant that all the subsequent sales of the land—to the Everards in the 1870s, to the Santiches in the 1930s, and the Santich sale to the Yancy project two years ago—were invalid. Assuming the original title still existed. And that it was valid.

I imagined Clarina hinting to Gertrude, to Brett Santich, to anyone in her radius, that she had proof that the title to Yancy land belonged to the Carruthers family, in fact to Professor Louisa Carruthers in Washington.

Gertrude would have hated the world to know her ancestors had stolen the land, but the legal implications were explosive.

Fifty years ago, even ten years ago, courts would likely have ruled that Wheelocks, Everards, and so on had de facto rights to the Yancy property. Today's courts were starting to recognize the rights of African-Americans to property that had been forcibly seized from their ancestors.

I went back through the diary, trying to see what I might have missed. It was four o'clock, and my eyes were aching from the strain of a day reading words handwritten so long ago. I moved to a table with a magnifying lamp on it.

And saw, in the margin of the November 1870 entry

where Wheelock was laying claim to land on Yancy, faint remnants of dried glue, a patch an inch or so wide, that extended to the bottom of the page.

I took out Clarina's scrapbook of photographs and newspaper articles, went through it page by page. I finally found it: a piece of parchment, roughly an inch wide by perhaps a foot long, torn around the edges where it had been removed from the recorder's book, folded in half to fit the size of Florence's journal. It had slipped down behind a plastic cover in Clarina's KU notebook. I pulled it out slowly, protecting the edges from further damage.

When I laid it on the page in Florence Wheelock's journal, patches of dried glue on the parchment strip exactly fit into the glue traces in Florence Wheelock's journal.

It was a record, created in March 1861 by the Douglas County Recorder of Deeds. Even though the ink was faded, the recorder had written carefully in a fine hand; it was easy to read the text.

The recorder had proclaimed: "Know All Men by These Presents" that land with plat numbers 1594-632 to 1594-660 on Yancy Hill was registered to Phyllida Carruthers and her son Nathan, that they owned the title free and clear of all encumbrance, that the property included five brick houses, a barn, a section of farmland and a section of timber that stretched to the top of the hill.

The recorder hadn't been able to refrain from exulting in the margin, "We are truly a state now with a freely elected government. Our first recorded deeds in Douglas County!"

59

Pressing Business

I needed someone else to know what I knew. Someone who would act quickly, and who would make sure that the Carruthers family was recognized as the legitimate title holder to the land on Yancy.

I didn't want to keep carrying these diaries around with me and yet I was terrified of leaving them where they could be damaged or destroyed. I finally went back to the Osma Room, where I'd briefly stored the wrench.

Before I put my fragile hoard behind the outsize atlases where I'd left the wrench, I photographed the pages, moved them to a text, and sent them to Zoë. You know what to do next, I said.

I walked to Gertrude Perec's house and rang the bell.

Gertrude came to the door and told me to go away, that we had nothing to discuss.

"But we do, Gertrude, either on the street or indoors—your choice. We can discuss what Clarina Coffin said that got you to go to the Dundee house in the middle of the night. Did she tell you she'd learned that your Wheelock ancestors stole the land on Yancy from the Carruthers family? Did she offer to show you the proof if you'd meet her at the Dundee house?"

Gertrude's jaw worked. "She claimed so many different things it was impossible to believe any of them."

"But you couldn't be sure. You wanted to see what she'd found."

"Gram!" Cady had appeared behind Gertrude in the foyer. "Is this true? Did you see her before she died?"

Gertrude swayed, looked as though she might fall. I pushed my way into the house and put an arm around her. Cady took her other arm and led her into the living room. Settled her in an armchair.

"Gram, what happened? You have to tell me the truth now. What did Clarina say to you?"

"She came up to me at church that Sunday," Gertrude whispered. "She said she wanted to see how I acted when I wasn't queen of Lawrence any longer. I asked what she was talking about and she wouldn't say, just smirked all over her nasty face and said 'wait and see.' I wasn't going to give her the satisfaction of watching me beg for information. I turned and left her standing there smirking."

"Of course you told Pat Everard," I said.

"Of course," she agreed. "Pat had watched her, anyway, and wanted to know what was going on. Then, Monday, I got a message to meet Clarina at the Dundee house at three in the morning and she'd show me proof."

"She phoned, or texted?" I asked.

Gertrude shook her head. "A typed letter through the mail slot. I went. I told Pat, she thought it was dangerous, so she followed me out there, and waited in the road. No one came except Trig. I thought Clarina had sent him, they worked together like a couple of deranged people, but he didn't seem to know anything about what Clarina knew. Finally I left."

"Did you keep the letter that was dropped through your mail slot?" I asked.

"I burned it. I wanted nothing to do with Clarina or her hints and insults. I want nothing to do with your hints and insults, either."

"Of course not," I agreed. "It's a pity you burned the letter. There's no way to prove whether Clarina wrote it."

"Of course she wrote it," Gertrude said.

"There's no 'of course' about anything in Clarina's life or death," I said. "I'd thought maybe the killers wrote it, trying to implicate as many people as possible in her death, but of course they thought her body would lie undiscovered in the Dundee house basement until it was a skeleton. They didn't know I'd find her."

"And what about Trig? Why would Clarina want to meet him in the middle of the night?" Cady asked. "They were such buddies, or at least, it seemed that way."

"He went there for a completely different reason," I said. "Nothing to do with Clarina. But where was she killed? Did she go up to Yancy Hill and taunt—"

I cut myself off. Of course. Her note about the snobs at the Kansas University press. She had tried to peddle her story there. I stood abruptly and headed for the door.

"But where are you going?" Cady asked. "You can't just run off like that in the middle—"

"Gertrude needs to confess everything to Deke. Get her to do that, and it will clean up one part of the investigation."

Cady called after me, frantic with questions, but I hurried back to the bus stop near the library. A freezing rain had started to fall. I was still wearing Lou's jacket, a couple of sizes too big for me, now that I wasn't carrying a load of books, but the oiled leather kept me dry until a number 10 bus arrived. I rode it out to West-brooke Circle, to the University Press.

Kayla Huang was in the lobby, chatting with the receptionist. The pair stopped mid-laugh when they saw me. "You're the detective, right? I'm sorry I don't remember your name," Huang said.

"V.I. Warshawski. I have an awkward question, so I'll ask it bluntly. Yesterday I stumbled on a notebook Clarina Coffin was keeping—part journal, part fantasy autobiography."

The burner camera didn't offer the clarity of my iPhone, but it showed the text well enough. I scrolled through the pictures I'd taken of the diaries and of Clarina's notebook until I found her incensed comment about finding a real university to publish her book.

"You told me it had been a long time since you'd seen Clarina. She apparently found—or thought she found—startling new information about Yancy a week before her death. And it implies she showed it to someone at the press here."

Huang shook her head, puzzled. "Not to me. Graham?"

"I guess she could have come while I was on break," he said doubtfully. "She was so recognizable, I'm sure I would have noticed her even if she didn't stop at the counter here."

Out of the corner of my eye, I saw red hair and a blue smock come into the reception area and then scurry down the hall. I darted after her.

"Ivy!"

She broke into a run. I caught her as she was opening a rear door.

"Ivy, did Clarina talk to you here, the week before she died?"

"Mind your own damned business. Thanks to your interference, I have less money for Timmy than I did two weeks ago."

"You are not nearly as stupid as that remark makes you sound," I snapped. "Thanks to Brett and Don Wilton you got money to clean up after drug parties. You are incredibly lucky you were never arrested in a police raid. Were you here when Clarina came in the week before Valentine's Day?"

"You're not going to frame me for her murder."

I sighed. "Only if you committed it. Clarina came in, she was full of herself, you were the only person in the lobby and she couldn't help gloating over her find. What was it?"

"She didn't say, just that all the high-and-mighty people in Lawrence would be shown up for the bigots they've always been. She had something that would blow Yancy Hill sky high. She said she wanted Kayla

Huang to know she could beg and plead to publish her but it wouldn't do her any good."

Huang and Graham had appeared behind me, but I signaled to them to stay back.

"Did you tell Kayla any of this?"

"Oh, please. Clarina was so full of herself. Everyone who hung anywhere near Trig knew that. I wasn't going to look as stupid as—whatever it was you said, that stupid—by telling Kayla or any of the other editors."

"But you told Brett," I said, tone conversational, taking it for granted.

She hunched a shoulder. "Maybe."

"And then—" I started to say. Stopped. The letter, that fragment I'd found in the woods behind the Dundee House.

"You and Brett had a laugh about it," I said. "She was pathetic. She thought she'd make Kayla crawl to her, now that she had identified Yancy's original owners, but poor Clarina! She wanted recognition more than anything, and Brett, or at least Robert Tulloh, understood that. Brett asked you to get him a piece of the Press's letterhead. Do you know what he did with it?"

Ivy's eyes were wide with fear. "He said, a practical joke."

"It was very practical." My voice, harsh with judgment that I couldn't suppress. "He invited her to come to the Press for lunch to discuss her findings with an eye to a book contract. And then I suppose he jumped her, or Chet, the Yancy crew foreman, yes, with his Kirmek pipe wrench, a good tap on the skull on a wintry day, no one notices her fall, into his arms and then into the back of his truck."

"Ivy!" Kayla Huang gasped. "You didn't—you couldn't!"

"Wait until you have a child to support before you say, oh, you couldn't!"

Before I could react, she bolted out the door and into a pickup. I was on foot with no way to follow.

"Is that right?" Graham said. "She really helped lure Clarina to her death?"

My shoulders sagged. "I expect she's right, I expect she didn't know why Brett asked for letterhead. And he probably didn't know, either—he was doing whatever the Tullohs asked of him so he could keep on trying to pay down his debts, look after his wife and daughter, throw the occasional bone to his girlfriend and son."

"You said Clarina found proof of who originally owned the land on Yancy," Kayla said. "What is it?"

"The title was originally filed by a Black family named Carruthers." And now Ivy was on her way to Brett, Brett would tell Tulloh and Chet that I'd seen the proof. I needed to get to the recorder's office. As soon as Tulloh understood that Clarina—and now I—had proof of the original title, he could destroy that first volume of Douglas County titles and deeds, and with it proof that the Carruthers title had been cut from the book.

It was four-thirty now; half an hour before the office closed.

60
Book Report

The clerk was tidying her papers for the day. She gave me a look that was half-humorous, half-exasperated. "You do know the office opens at nine in the morning, don't you? It isn't necessary to wait for fifteen minutes to closing to look at a record."

I apologized, but said, "I want to look at the very first deeds registered here, after statehood."

"Yancy doesn't figure in the records until 1870," she said.

"You said this place was like the wild west back when people were first filing claims. I want to see how wild the west was."

She cocked an eyebrow, her attention caught. I followed her into a side room where the older volumes were stored. She rolled a ladder over to the corner and pulled the first volume from the top shelf.

"All these have been digitized," she said, "but we're keeping the first volumes for historical reasons."

She laid it open on the big table in the front room and watched me, forgetting that she was eager to get out of the office.

We bent over the book together, looking at the first titles filed in Douglas County in the winter of 1861.

"When I came in here last week, I noticed that the top of this first page had been cut so that the first entries are lower than in the rest of the book. I thought perhaps the parchment had been cut by hand and they hadn't done it evenly. What really happened is that someone cut that first entry out of the book. The first title filed in Douglas County after Kansas became a state had been removed.

"No!" she cried. "That isn't possible. No one is allowed alone with these books."

"Not now, maybe, in the twenty-first century. In 1870, though, when Henry Everard was the recorder, and a close friend of Theodore Wheelock, he was happy to let Wheelock cut out the original title. Wheelock registered the Yancy land in his name in 1870 and shared some of it with Everard as a thank-you gift."

I turned to the 1870 registration I'd looked at on

my first visit. The clerk read it, then returned to the first page.

"What was there originally, then?" she asked.

I had put the registry of the Carruthers' title into a plastic sleeve. I pulled this out of my daypack now and removed the title to the land on Yancy. The strip of paper exactly fit the gap on the page.

I had photographed the pages from Florence's journal where she boasted about getting the title registered and showed those to the clerk. The woman frowned over the page.

"This is—I don't even know the word. Staggering. Shocking. If it's true, it completely undoes all the titles to Yancy plats that flow from the 1870 registration. I—we have to get an expert to study this. Lawyers—what do we do if you're right and the Wheelocks and the Everards stole the land? Unless they didn't know they were stealing?"

"The diaries Florence Wheelock kept make it clear they knew exactly what they were doing. But even if they didn't know, these records don't show any transfer of the title from the Carrutherses to the Wheelocks—just that Theodore Wheelock staked a claim to the same plats deeded to the Carruthers family nine years earlier.

"I agree, it will be a huge legal mess. Particularly

since Tulloh Industries is building on top of Yancy now, in the belief that they own the property."

An outfit like Tulloh has a legal department with thousands of attorneys. They could probably mount a successful defense for claiming the land, or at least tie up claims in litigation for so long that they'd build their crypto farm or whatever it was before the case was settled. They really hadn't needed to kill Clarina-Ulricke.

The clerk looked at me helplessly. "I need to talk to Amos—Amos Clapton—he's our recorder."

I put the fragment back into the plastic sleeve and returned it to my backpack.

The clerk said, "If that was cut from our deed book, then it belongs here."

"If we establish its authenticity, and prove that it was cut from this original volume, of course it stays here. But anyone could walk in and take it away with them while you were busy assisting someone else."

"No one could go into our book storage room without my knowing they'd been here," she said. "When I leave the office, even for five minutes, I lock the door. You really mustn't carry that title around with you— it's—what if you were mugged and someone stole your backpack?"

"You could be right," I said. "But I believe Clarina Coffin was murdered by someone who wanted this scrap of paper. It needs to be with the police or the FBI until it's authenticated, and the chain of ownership on Yancy has been established. I'm going to keep it safe until then—it goes into a bank first thing tomorrow."

She eyed my pack, as if debating whether she could wrest if from me, but finally picked up the 1861 deed book and took it back to her inner room. I was on my way out the door when the landline on the counter rang.

The clerk answered, and then said sharply, "Yes, she was here."

I left the door cracked open and pressed myself against the wall.

"The FBI? Oh, goodness, I wish I'd known. I should have guessed she was a criminal, she acted so wild. You should have called five minutes ago . . . She'll have to go out the east door, the rest of the building will be locked by now, but does she have a weapon? Am I safe? Yes, I can lock myself in my office. You'll call when you've picked her up?"

I skittered down the hall, looking wildly for an escape route. The west door had a chain and padlock across it. Stairs going down or up. I ran up. At the top of the second flight, I almost ran into a guard talking to a man in a suit. I slowed my pace, just a working person on her way to her office, not someone wanted by the Faux BI.

"Don't think they'll make it pass the Elite Eight," the guard was saying.

"Don't be a killjoy, Dree, I know they don't have last year's depth but my crystal ball says repeat."

The men's basketball team's chances in the NCAA tournament. No one cared what I was doing.

I walked to the far end of the hall and found Judge Bhagavatula's chambers. The door to the courtroom wasn't locked. I walked behind the bench and knocked hard on the door on my left.

"Judge Bhagavatula?" I called, not too loudly. No answer. This door opened as well. The judge's law books filled several shelves. I picked *Kansas Statutes, Courts to Domestic Relations.* I pulled the Carruthers title record from its plastic sleeve and placed it near the beginning.

When I moved back into the hall, the guard and the man in the suit had left. I peered over the railing. Mellon and Don Wilton were in the lower hall. Somehow they'd acquired vests that read FBI, and they were escorting the few people still in the building toward the east exit.

I shut my eyes briefly. Breathe, don't panic, don't abandon your training, find a secondary stairwell. Clinging to the wall to avoid being spotted, I skidded around a corner, found the fire EXIT sign I was looking for, moved down the stairs to the basement, found a door to the janitors' room, beyond it an exit to the parking lot. One step at a time, push the door open.

I was almost home free when my phone rang. I pressed the switch to silence it, but a hand came from above me. I kicked out furiously. A terrible pain along my skull and then darkness.

61

Coal Dust

I was cold. I knew my mother was near, but when I tried to open my eyes to look for her my head felt as though it would splinter from pain. My throat was raw. I smelled vomit and something harsher. Steel mills.

I was sitting on something rough. The ground by the mills. What were we doing there? Had Gabriella gone to complain about the coal dust? *Cappotto. Aqua.* Coat, water, I begged her, but my throat was so raw I couldn't get the words out.

"Did the bitch say something?" a rough voice asked. English. This wasn't South Chicago.

I felt someone leaning over me. Kept my head bent down, breathed through my mouth, produced a half snore.

"She's still out. Why'd you hit her so hard? We need her conscious and talking. She stinks, by the way."

I knew that voice, thin baritone. It was agony to think, to concentrate. They'd hit me, too hard, and so my head hurt. I'd been running. Escaping. I had to move my mind to the other side of its mountain of pain, figure out where I was, who was with me.

I wanted to stand, to get away from the men, from the pain. My feet were tied together. There was a metal pole at my back. I was tied to that as well.

"What about the reporter, that nosy bitch hanging around the detective?" The first speaker, the rough voice.

"She's still in New York. No chance Warshawski handed it off to her. Anyway, the courthouse has been sealed off." The thin baritone, impatient with under-lings.

"Maybe she ate it," a tenor suggested.

The rough voice laughed. "In that case, put a bullet through her and dump her by the river."

"No bullets," the baritone said. "Natural causes, just like Rotherhaite."

Rotherhaite. Coal. The smell that made me think of steel works. I was at the Wakarusa coal plant. The thin baritone, that was the urban cowboy who'd bought the plant. Robert Tulloh.

"Cops have the wrench," the tenor said. "Cunt here managed to hide it when Chet put it in her room. She planted it in my woods. Another dead woman with a head wound, not even Big Matthew's friends can make that go away."

Robert Tulloh laughed, ugly sound. "You're underestimating his powers, Santich. Like you underestimate everything, including your debt load. Bezory, you'd better do a more thorough job than you did with Rotherhaite, hide her deeper in the bushes."

I opened my eyes a slit. We were on the floor of the coal plant. What had they done with the afternoon shift workers?

"Wake her up," Tulloh said. "This is getting boring. We need to get going."

A bucket of water over the head. That did wake me up. Flushed the vomit from my jacket. Protective reflex, arms to face—except they wouldn't rise that high. They were bound to my sides at the elbows. Feet tied, arms bound, wits gone a-begging.

Tulloh pulled a chair up right above me and straddled it, chin resting on the back. "You've been a busy little cunt, haven't you? Snooping around in things that don't belong to you. Time to turn over that scrap of paper you found. It isn't yours."

I let my eyelids droop, through the veil of lashes saw

his arm sweep toward me. Let my head fall. He hit the metal pole behind me hard, swore, stood, and kicked me in the stomach. No protection from that.

"You think you found something valuable, but you didn't. Any more than the stupid Coffin woman did. The girl at the recorder's office said you showed some bogus piece of paper, claiming some Black family a thousand years ago squatted on Yancy, but we own the land. We'll do what we want with it."

"Then why kill Clarina?" my voice came out in a croak.

"She was a pest, a nuisance, a cockroach. We don't tolerate vermin at Tulloh, and you're a bigger piece of it than she was."

"A lot of people know I found the Carruthers 1861 title to the land on Yancy. I sent a photo to the nosy reporter bitch. Editors at the University Press have seen the title. Your daddy will—"

He backhanded my face. He was wearing a ring. Blood on my lips, in my mouth.

"What did Clarina tell you she found? The title? Or the diary where the Wheelocks boasted about stealing the land?"

"She told that useless piece of shit Trig she'd found something that would blow Yancy sky-high. She didn't tell him what, but Trig told Ivy, trying to impress her, or warn her to stay away from loser Santich," Tulloh said. "We knew Coffin had something we needed to see."

"Loser Santich knew how to get her to come out to the Press," Santich snarled. "The real loser is your hulking Neanderthal who hit her too hard and killed her before we could get her to talk."

"Not a problem this time around." Tulloh grinned, showed perfectly capped teeth. "We're not letting him hit this one."

He ran his fingers around my jaw, a caress. I bit him, hard. He laughed, punched me again. "Hellcat. Good. We'll have more fun all the way around. But in the end, you will tell me what I want to know. Where is that title?"

I didn't speak. I had no clever remarks left in me, no questions I wanted answered, nothing to say, nothing to hear.

Tulloh told Santich to take off my shoes and socks. He lit a cigarette and knelt to hold it to my instep.

Bezory smacked his hand away, grabbed the cigarette, dropped it and stood on it. "Fucking moron! You don't light a fire in a coal plant."

"You don't call me names, Bezory, you work for me." Tulloh stabbed Bezory's chest with a finger, backing him away from the cigarette.

"I'm not one of your lapdogs like Santich here, or that creep of a houseboy Mellon. You want to blow up the plant, I'm out of here."

I put my left heel on the floor, wriggled the right foot out of the rope, then the left foot. Santich was watching the other two men. Ten seconds, roll as far as possible to my left, retrieve the cigarette, roll back. The cigarette was still glowing. I held it against the rope around my left wrist.

"Afraid of fire?" Tulloh jeered, flicking his lighter in Bezory's face.

Rope fraying, left hand burning, left hand free, pull the rope away from the pole, leap up. I ran across the floor toward the doors. Skidded on an oil slick. Tulloh was on me. Hands around my throat, he dropped the lighter into the oil.

In the nanosecond between the flame and the fire he lost his hold, bellowing with fury, fear. I slid away, ran out the door, to the river, into the blessed terrifying cold.

62
Rowing Practice

Lou's coat filled with water and dragged me under. I wrestled myself free of it and stood, feet in the muddy shoal, choking out oily water. Onshore I heard Tulloh and Bezory shouting but not what they were saying.

I couldn't stay in the cold water, didn't have the strength to swim across the river. I grabbed at the bushes close to the shore and was pulling myself out when I heard voices on the river.

"Hey, guys, look at that! Fire coming out of the stacks!"

"Pull!" someone shouted. "This is practice, not a sightseeing trip!"

"Help!" I screamed, louder than Callas at La Scala.

I screamed again, and again, and the boat turned toward me. A racing boat, eight oars. I flopped into the boat, landing on someone's knees. Outcries: *what the fuck was I doing in the river on a winter night, mind your knees, I guess practice is over for tonight, huh? And look at those flames. The place is on fire.*

"Running from the fire," I gasped out the words.

"Anyone else there?"

"Don't know," I said.

One woman thought we should go ashore and check, but the person I'd landed on said I was wet and frozen and needed emergency care; best call the fire department.

An ambulance was waiting when we reached the boathouse. I stayed awake just long enough to give my rescuers Lou's phone number.

63
Homeward Bound

W e saw the fire shooting from the stacks up at the farm. Should've guessed it was you. How'd you make that happen, anyway?"

"My warm personality," I said.

Ed air-punched me.

I'd been moved from the ICU to a regular bed, but I was still fragile—broken ribs where Tulloh had kicked me, more damage to my nose and upper teeth. One or both men had been with me ever since they got the call from the rowing team.

"Tulloh is a mean rattlesnake even when he isn't cornered. You bested him in the plant, big-time, and he isn't likely to forgive and forget."

The fire had burned for over a day before the

firefighters got it under control. They'd kept it from spreading to the underground coal storage, but there was enough coal dust in the air that it blew out the windows and melted joins in a number of the pipes. It would be a long time, if ever, before the Wakarusa plant could come back on stream. Which meant that even if Tulloh Industries made good on their claim to Yancy land, they wouldn't have a dedicated power supply for the crypto farm.

The first week after the fire, once the doctors discharged me, I spent at the Hilltop Farm. Lou and Ed were reluctant to allow any officers of the law on their land, so when Deke Everard wanted to interview me, we did it at my third favorite spot in Lawrence, behind the Hilltop Farm and the Hippo—the public library.

Faye Mitchell, my Lawrence lawyer, was with me, to enforce an agreement that the entire conversation was off the record and that I had immunity from any charges in connection with unauthorized entry into Don Wilton's office above the Lion's Heart.

I gave Deke the same story I'd told Faye. He took the information to Brett Santich, telling him they could get him dead to rights on running a drug house, on kidnapping me, and a bunch of other charges unless he was willing to cooperate. Santich was the weakest link among the coconspirators; he apparently revealed enough of the drug operation to get the LKPD to apply for a warrant to search Wilton's office and his computers.

Frankie Karas didn't want to issue one, but Deke's application coincided with a story Murray ran, showing evidence of unreported payouts by Tulloh Industries to Karas's campaign chest. Zoë and Murray had been working in tandem. Zoë had been reporting the history of Yancy, the role of the early Anglo settlers in killing the Black residents and seizing their property. Murray decided to go after the present-day power brokers.

Of course, the police chief should have made the decision about applying for a warrant, but Chief McDowell had announced a leave of absence. Zoë, inspired by Murray, had dug up evidence that the chief and his wife regularly took vacations on Matthew Tulloh's yacht, the *Prairie Schooner*. Zoë was using FOIA to apply for the chief's phone records, to see how often he'd called Jake Tulloh.

When the story of the payouts broke, Karas backed down and issued Deke the warrants he was requesting for the Lion's Heart computers. It's one thing for a billionaire to bankroll Supreme Court Justices, but a county DA has to face voters every few years. Revelations that Karas was giving Tulloh's subordinates favorable legal treatment in exchange for financial favors had a number of local lawyers ready to challenge him in the upcoming primary.

After Deke and I finished, I agreed to talk to Gertrude Perec. She wanted me to come to her home, but as with Deke, I insisted we talk in the library. Pat Everard and Cady came with her.

"My mother gave those Wheelock diaries to the Origins Museum when it first opened in 1960," Gertrude told me. "They made a big deal of it—daughter of one of Kansas's founding families donating family treasure. I was a sophomore out at Wellesley—Wheelocks had been sending their daughters to Wellesley since the college opened. In the 1870s Florence Wheelock made sure her daughters had the same education as their Massachusetts cousins. A hundred-forty-year tradition broken by little Missy here—" She patted Cady's knee.

"Kansas," Cady said. "My girlfriends and I all went to KU."

"I hadn't bothered with the diaries, growing up," Gertrude said. "The time or two I tried to read them, I couldn't decipher the handwriting. But I think my mother did. I think she gave them away after she read about how the Wheelocks took possession of Yancy. That was when she started agitating for civil rights and so on here in the town. Of course I thought it was noble: 1960, the sit-ins started that year, and then the Freedom Riders, Freedom Summer. I didn't have to go south like some of my college friends, I worked with my mother right here in Lawrence.

"But then Clarina showed up. First she was criticizing Lawrence history in general, saying we thought we were special, abolitionists and so on, but we had just as much blood on our hands as any southern town. She got on everyone's nerves, but she never had any proof.

"Then she started harassing Cady and the Yancy school about teaching woke Kansas history, and that made me angry."

Pat Everard nodded. "The day she showed up at Riverside, determined to lecture us on our history and on our duty, I asked her, 'Were you ever on the front line of getting a university to integrate its dorms? Did you ever make sure your town, whatever it was, offered Blacks and whites the same economic opportunities? Did you ever fight your local bank over punitive mortgage rates? Don't come lecturing to us until you show you took risks yourself.'"

"Clarina said, 'My whole existence is a risk, which you will never appreciate.' If Cady or her mother had ever said something like that to me, I would have smacked them," Gertrude put in.

"And then, about a week before she was killed, she started in on the 1860 Wheelocks, how they pretended to be for freeing the enslaved, but were just as bad as any southern lynch mob. She said she could prove we'd never had a right to Yancy land.

"The night you found that college student in the Dundee place, I had a call—I thought it was from Clarina. Ulricke. Saying she'd show me the proof if I'd come out to the Dundee house. I don't know why I lied and told you she'd put a letter through my mail slot. Anyway, I guess you know that part—how I showed up at the Dundee house and found Trig."

"Why did Trig go out there?" Cady asked. "Did the same person who tricked Gram tell him Cady was there?"

I shook my head. "He has a police scanner. He saw there was activity out there and he—well, he was trying to look after Ivy and her little boy, Timmy. He knew she cleaned out there after the drug parties, and he wanted to make sure she didn't walk straight into cop arms.

"Which she did anyway," I added sadly. "I don't know if they're going to prosecute her for her role in Clarina's death, but she did blindly do whatever Brett Santich asked. Including giving him some Press letterhead to entice Clarina to show up where it was easy to kidnap her. The building is in the middle of a kind of park, without much traffic unless people are going to the Press. It was easy for them to ambush Clarina."

Deke had been a silent member of my conversation with his mother and Gertrude. He followed me out to the street, where my Mustang was waiting—freshly detailed at the LKPD's expense.

"I hope you'll accept my apologies," he said. "I was getting tied in knots by too many different interests. I worried that my chief was not—let's just say upholding the law equally for everyone. I worried about Karas. The FBI creep was jerking my chain. And then you— you may be right a lot of the time, but you can be pretty hard to take, galloping in from the outside like you know stuff we hicks don't understand."

"That's not my intention at all," I protested. "I had a terrible fall and winter. I was questioning my judgment on things as simple as ordering dinner, let alone figuring out a series of crimes in a jurisdiction where I didn't know anyone or anything."

"Yeah, maybe. I'll just say every time you were proved right, it made my blood boil. I so wanted you to be wrong about something." He laughed self-consciously. "Including Clete Rotherhaite. By the time we finished listening to all Don Wilton's audio files, it was clear that Rotherhaite was murdered, by Mellon and Bezory—they did all the muscle work for the Tullohs. I don't think we'll ever get anything to stick to Matthew or Robert. They're shelling out big-time for legal counsel for Bezory and Mellon, so we may never get anything to stick to them, either."

"But why did they kill Rotherhaite?" I asked. "He didn't have any power to stop their data farm."

"He did, though. Tulloh was still in the room with him when he called the Kansas EPA about the plant being too old to handle the power demands Yancy was going to put on it if the data farm went up. And also that Tulloh's lawyers had lied about the purpose of the project in their filings with the planning commission. What you didn't hear was the next part of Wilton's private recordings: Tulloh called Rotherhaite back and said he'd thought things over, cooler heads prevailed, a walk by the river where they could be private, work it all out. Only it was Mellon waiting for him there."

He handed me the Mustang keys and walked me to the car. "Do me a favor, Warshawski. Even if your closest friend in the universe is playing the Jayhawks for the national title, watch her on TV, okay?"

I was glad to part from him on good terms. He was basically a good cop, just one in a bad spot.

As I got ready to return to Chicago, to friends and responsibilities, I kept wondering if, or maybe how, the Tullohs would exact their revenge on me. My last full day in Lawrence, a sleek Mercedes convertible came up the drive to the Hilltop Farm.

The men were at work. I walked out with the dog,

every muscle braced. It was Pauline Tulloh who got out of the car.

I raised my eyebrows. "I can't offer you fermented cabbage, but there's coffee or tea."

"I won't be staying. Tulloh Industries is undergoing some structural changes, and I thought you should hear about them from me. Robert will be going to Lagos to oversee our African operations. Jake will be taking over as chief operating officer, and Daddy decided I should be a financial officer. He thought I showed good judgment, trying to warn him that Robert was dabbling in crypto, even if it was the computer end, not bitcoins."

Her voice was as calm and arrogant as it had been when I saw her in Mission Hills in February.

"He agreed that we shouldn't try to revive the Wakarusa plant. We'll sell it for scrap. He says in hindsight you showed good judgment and that he was too hasty in accepting Robert's interpretation of your actions. Mother agreed. She asked me to see that you got compensated for your time and trouble."

Perhaps a more moral person would have ripped up the check Pauline handed me. However, it seemed like the right amount, a hundred thousand for six weeks of travail and lost income, for the expenses of life on the road, for Faye Mitchell's fee. Mitchell wasn't running a charity, she said, and she billed accordingly.

I'd been cleared by the local doctors to drive, but they advised local trips only for another week or so. Ed and Lou said it had been years since they'd been in Chicago. Ed drove the Mustang. Peppy and I followed in the truck with Lou.

Mr. Contreras was beside himself with joy when we arrived. I'd warned him that the men were vegetarians, so out of his trio of specialties he served up spaghetti with the sauce he makes from his home-canned tomatoes. Because it was a festive occasion, he followed up with his home-distilled grappa.

After the fourth shot, Mr. Contreras began singing one of his grandmother's folksongs. Lou said he'd had a grandmother, too, and began belting out "Froggie went a-courtin'." Ed said he'd also had a grandmother who also sang. Around midnight, Mr. Sung from the second floor was at the door, almost weeping because we'd woken the baby.

Unfazed, Lou said, didn't he have a grandmother? And didn't he want to honor her memory? To my astonishment, after downing a steadying shot of grappa, Mr. Sung produced a song from his Korean childhood.

After that, I couldn't resist singing "Il fervido desiderio," my favorite of the Italian songs my mother used to sing for my father and me.

64

Happy Ever After—Or at Least for a Few Days

My bruises healed. A plastic surgeon got my nose more or less back to where it had been in January. I started working out, started eating, started spending more time with friends.

Was it my triumph over the billionaires that cured the anguish and self-doubts that had deviled me the last six months? Nothing is ever that simple. The murder of Peter's student would stay with me for the rest of my life, but recovering from my own injuries, seeing justice done to Clarina Coffin's memory, helped bring an end to my self-torment. I'd pushed myself, been pushed, almost past the limit of my endurance, and I had endured.

Mr. Contreras joined Bernie, Angela, and me when we went to Kansas in late April to celebrate Yancy Day. Louisa Carruthers, the George Washington University professor who was the last living descendant of Sophia Grellier and Nathan Carruthers, came out for the celebration.

The Dundee house, named for the illiterate white drunkard whom the Wheelocks and Everards had installed there, was renamed. Professor Carruthers chose to call it Yancy House, since her ancestors had named the hill Yancy, meaning "freedom" in the Hausa language.

Zoë had been working with Gertrude and Cady Perec to publish excerpts from the Wheelock diaries in the *Douglas County Herald*. Professor Carruthers gave her permission to publish sections from Sophia Grellier Carruthers's diary as well. This history fired up public imagination. Zoë appeared on Colbert and all the other big shows, sometimes alone, sometimes with the professor. Books, streaming shows, movies, all were in the works by the time I returned to Lawrence.

Pauline Tulloh had made an unexpected investment in the *Herald*, with the proviso that Zoë stay on for a minimum of three years.

Valerie Granev came to Yancy Day, without her daughter or husband. She apologized again for abandoning me to the challenges I'd undergone.

"My daughter's health and safety had to come first," she said. "My husband says I could have figured out how to protect her and stand up publicly for you, but that's easy to say in hindsight."

Sabrina was finally showing signs of recovering from her own brain traumas, Valerie said, which made Valerie all the more certain she'd made the right choices.

I didn't say anything, let silence build, until Valerie said, "Can't you acknowledge my apology, and understand why I had to act as I did?"

I gave a half nod. "I saved your daughter's life and you hung me out for bears to eat, but I acknowledge your apology."

A week after we got home from Kansas, I returned late from the office. As I came up the walk to my building, a man got out of a car parked in front. He was thin and pale, and although he called to me, I didn't recognize him.

"Perhaps you think I don't deserve to be remembered," he said quietly.

"Peter?" I was too dumbfounded to say anything else.

He came up to me. "I have a short story and a long story. Will you let me tell them to you?"

We walked up the street, not speaking, until we found a bench. The sun was setting; the semidark made it easier to talk.

"When I left Chicago—when I left you—I knew you were suffering as much or more than I, but I didn't have the strength to give you the support you needed. I didn't have the strength to get myself through the day, let alone to help someone else. I fled to the place I've always gone when the world around me has been too much—I ran backward, into the past."

"Yes," I said, just to show I understood.

"As you know, ancient Sumer and Syria have made up my professional life. I'm a newcomer to the Phoenicians. I'm useful on a dig because I have decades of experience in examining potential sites. I know careful but efficient ways to approach them. I also have decades of important contacts among people who fund archaeological digs, and among government officials who decide whether we can dig, but I'm a junior member of the Mediterranean group.

"However, I was not a helpful member of the Malaga team. I was still recovering use of my shoulder. Spanish physical therapists have been most helpful in many aspects of my recovery. Especially a Syrian refugee, who was glad to work with someone who could speak her form of Arabic, but that came later." He lifted his arm and moved it in a wide arc; he was recovered, at least physically.

"Yes," I repeated, wondering if he was about to confess an affair, and how I might feel about that.

"I took to driving off down the coast by myself. Very much not a good team player, but the international group cut me a lot of slack. My reputation, you understand, and my years of being director of the Institute—many of them have known me a long time.

"Quite by chance, I found a place some ninety miles away from the main dig that seemed to have a strong Phoenician stamp in the place-names of the nearby hilltop settlements. I began some preliminary explorations on my own. I acted completely out of character, as if I were Lawrence of Arabia, whom I've never admired. But I hired some local people, and we began to dig in what seemed the most promising spot."

He stopped speaking. Sitting next to him in the dark I could smell his sweat, the sickly smell of someone who was afraid. I took his hand, held it gently.

"We found a children's burial site." He spoke in a rush, so quickly I had to strain to follow the words. "Hundreds of small bodies, all buried in a mass grave. There's controversy over the Phoenicians, whether they practiced child sacrifice. I don't know what those small bodies were evidence of, but—they merged with Taylor, with my student, sacrificed by their father. I couldn't face myself, the world, the horror of millennia of parents murdering their children.

"The past where I sought refuge seemed as if it had

betrayed me. I fled. I was driving so wildly that I drove over the side of a cliff. My body was flung free, the car crashed to the bottom and was destroyed.

"People who witnessed the crash set up a rescue operation, but I had no identity. My phone and passport had been in the car. After a week or so in a coma, word trickled around about the injured American. My Spanish colleagues came to the hospital in Algeciras where I'd been taken and identified me.

"My recovery was slow, but the therapists, as I said, were splendid. I got a new phone, I saw your texts, I followed what you were doing in Kansas as best I could from your young journalist's reports, and from Murray's, but I felt so much shame I couldn't reach out to you."

"Shame?" I echoed.

"You had been as badly damaged by Taylor's death as I, but you kept on doing what you do well, doggedly looking for some measure of justice in an unjust world. I had fled, and then fled again. How could I face you?"

I thought back to all the months of self-doubt, self-torment, loss of weight, loss of acuity. "I have a long tale of my own, but I won't tell it tonight. I'll give you the short one, instead."

I undid the top three buttons of my shirt, and held out the little figure of Inanna, just visible under the streetlights. "My avatar did not desert me."

Interlude III

13 October 1935

Auburn, New York
To: Mrs. Eleanor Roosevelt
The White House

Dear Mrs. Roosevelt

I do not have enough words, or the right words, to thank you for appearing at the funeral of my mother, Sophia Grellier Carruthers, and for the words you spoke about her. Hers was a strong and dauntless spirit in the cause of Equality for all. Your recognition of her work and her gifts has been the greatest possible consolation to my wife and me.

Yours most truly
Frederic Nathan Carruthers

Notes and Thanks

Chicago has been my home for more than five decades, but I grew up in Lawrence, Kansas, and have a strong attachment to the land of my youth. The land and its history keep speaking to me, drawing me into stories both real and imagined. *Pay Dirt* is the fourth of my novels to be set there.

My family moved to Kansas from upstate New York when I was four. We spent our first nights in the Eldridge Hotel, which had been the headquarters for the antislavery forces in their battles with the slavers who crossed the Kaw and burned down homes and buildings to try to terrorize the abolitionists into leaving the state.

I grew up proud of our antislavery heritage, proud that Kansas came free into the Union in 1861. I grew up ignorant of the fact that well into the twentieth century the town was segregated, that Black students couldn't live in student housing at the University of Kansas where my father taught, that the town had real estate covenants that dictated where Blacks, and Indigenous people, and Jews could own homes. Knowledge of injustices in my home state has come to me slowly.

Pay Dirt was inspired by two books which I read in 2021, *The Agitators,* by Dorothy Wickendon, and *This Is Not Dixie,* by Brent M S Campney. *The Agitators* recounts the friendship and solidarity among three women in the Auburn, New York, area: Harriet Tubman, Martha Coffin Wright, and Frances Seward. The two latter women were white, they were committed both to abolition and to racial equality, and they provided material support to Tubman, who settled in Auburn partly as a result of their support.

This Is Not Dixie tells a very different story, that of active and widespread anti-Black violence in Kansas in the decades after the Civil War, including rape, lynching, forcible seizure of property, and mob action in driving Black residents from various communities.

I had the germ of an idea involving the violent seizure of land from Black settlers in the 1860s and

1870s, and how that might play out in contemporary America. It took me a very long time to figure out the right narrative arc for this story. I started the novel by creating many pages of nineteenth-century diaries and letters among my fictional antislavery families. In the end, I didn't use most of them, which was a sadness, but the right decision for the shape of the book.

Along the way, I incurred many debts.

I have also taken liberties with the Lawrence landscape.

Contrary to popular belief Kansas is not flat. Eastern Kansas has the same rolling hills you see in Ohio or Missouri, and the University of Kansas is spread out across the top of a large high hill—people who work at the university are said to be On the Hill.

Yancy is a fictitious hill on the outskirts of Lawrence, just southeast of the Kaw River.

I have also taken liberties with Lawrence and Douglas County law enforcement.

Lawrence has an outstanding police department, with a true commitment to community and to building coalitions with community social service organizations. I am grateful to Chief Rich Lockhart and his team, Investigations Commander Major Trent McKinley and Deputy Chief Adam Heffley, for taking most of a day to step me through their operations. Thanks, too, to Laura McCabe for making all this happen.

Unfortunately, it is the nature of private eye novels for the PI to be at loggerheads with the police. Every officer mentioned in *Pay Dirt* is a complete fiction and bears no resemblance to anyone at the LKPD. Chief McDowell in particular might be more at home in Chicago than in Lawrence—perhaps that's where he'll appear next.

In practice, because Yancy is outside the Lawrence city limits, the Douglas County sheriff's department should have been investigating crimes there, but involving the sheriff would have meant bringing in another cast of characters; keeping track of them would have ground the story to a halt.

I have a loving connection to the Lawrence Public Library, where I learned to read and where my mother was children's librarian for many years. I'm proud of my hometown for its strong commitment to this library at a time when many public libraries are under attack. This is where V.I. Warshawski finds a home from home in *Pay Dirt*. Thanks to Kathleen Morgan and the library team for suggesting the Osma Room when V.I. needed a place to sequester some of her own documents. Mrs. Osma was the reference librarian when I was growing up. She had a formidable knowledge of the library's resources. She might pretend to consult a card catalog, but it was all in her head.

Angela Wilson gave essential advice on criminal law at the state level. Danielle Cassel spent an afternoon talking me through titles and deeds; I have an uneasy feeling that I may not have followed her advice carefully enough. In addition, the recorder's office in *Pay Dirt* is completely a creation of my own imagination.

Martha Swisher suggested "Il fervido desiderio," which V.I. sings when she and her friends are having a late-night semidrunken songfest.

Kathy Arata Lyndes and Louis Lyndes Arata kindly let me use their surnames for Lou and Ed. I admire the way Kathy and Louis changed their names when they married to entwine their lives with each other.

Tom Laclair helped identify the muscles V.I. injured during the perilous late chapters in the novel.

Federica Caneparo helped me learn the traditional songs Italian mothers, including Gabriella, sing to their children.

Many people provided support and advice during the long process of creating this novel, in particular Erin Mitchell, Jolynn Parker, Marzena Madej, Jonathan Paretsky, Barb Wieser, Jo Anne Willis, Eve Paretsky.

Above all, I owe an enormous debt to Lorraine Brochu. I wrote and discarded seven drafts before arriving at the storyline that makes up the book. Lorraine read them all, with care, with thoughtful comments, and without a complaint. I am most grateful.

Any mistakes in this novel—and there always are some—are down to me, not to the many people who gave so generously of their time and knowledge.

Postscript

V.I. Warshawski—How She Got Here, Where She's Going

Pay *Dirt* is the twenty-second novel I've written about my private detective, V.I. Warshawski. When she and I started, I didn't imagine such a long career for either of us. My goals with my first novel, *Indemnity Only*, were both simple and grandiose: I wanted to create a woman private eye, and I wanted to change the narrative about women in fiction.

When I began my writing career, U.S. cities were just beginning to admit women to their regular police forces. Up until the early 1980s, women had been on the margins as matrons in women's or juvenile prisons. We had our first U.S. Supreme Court justice the year before *Indemnity Only* came out. Our first women in senior cabinet offices were still in the future.

Crime fiction, indeed, much fiction and a lot of historical writing described women's characters basely on our sexual activity. Women with active sex lives were wicked, trying to get good boys to do bad things. They were properly punished for their efforts. If they were chaste, they were saccharinely virtuous, but so unable to act that they could barely tie their shoes without adult supervision. The exception were nuns, who had a luminous authority. Even Harriet Vane and the combined female intelligences of Shrewsbury College needed Peter Wimsey to rescue them.

The most common role for women in crime fiction was as victim of murder or sexual violence.

V.I. was neither vamp nor victim, but a woman like me and my friends, doing a job that hadn't existed for us when we were growing up. She was cocky, she was resilient, she became a PI because she was convinced she'd be good at the work, and she saw a need for her particular outlook and skills. She also had a sex life that didn't define her moral character: her moral compass was, and is, centered on questions of justice, of voice, of making sure that those whom the world seeks to silence get a hearing.

It took me eight years and a lot of false starts to

create V.I. I have never had her self-assurance, even if we share the same sardonic sense of humor, and the same regrettable tendency to leap before we look.

Publishers were cautious: forty turned down that first book, one explaining that a novel set in Chicago had regional interest only, and not enough Midwesterners read to make it worthwhile to publish a book set here. But V.I. found a home at the Dial Press—thanks to Nancy van Itallie, and to Juris Jurjevics, whose passing I mourn.

V.I. also found a home with readers. I'm grateful to those who feel at ease with her particular brand of humor and of stubbornness. I'm grateful to the readers who wanted to read more of V.I.'s adventures.

In the years since that first book came out, the mystery has changed dramatically. Whereas it took a year to find a publisher willing to take a chance on a woman detective, especially one in Chicago, we now have so many novels by women, and novels with women heroes, that I can't keep up with them all. That's a luxury I didn't imagine when I started, when Marcia Muller, Sue Grafton, and Linda Barnes joined me in redefining women in fiction.

V.I. is tougher, braver, and cleverer than me, so much so that she even ages more slowly; she's about fifty to my seventysomething. Even so, the strange world we inhabit these days has taken a toll on her. She is more prone to self-doubt, less cocky. She needs some time off. While I work on a new venture, she'll be recharging, perhaps tracing her family roots in Poland and Italy, or hiking the Canadian Rockies with her dogs. She and I are grateful to all the readers who've followed her on her many adventures; we both promise she'll be back, ready to look danger in the eye and take it on.

About the Author

Hailed by the *Washington Post* as "the definition of perfection in the genre," Sara Paretsky is the *New York Times* bestselling author of twenty-four novels, including the renowned V.I. Warshawski series. She is one of only four living writers to have received both the Grand Master Award from the Mystery Writers of America and the Cartier Diamond Dagger from the Crime Writers Association of Great Britain. She lives in Chicago.

Praise for
PROPHET

"A perfect blend of twisty, high-stakes scenes that a reader expects from a sci-fi thriller, along with a strong narrative voice."
—*Book Riot*, **A Best Book of the Year**

"I could not put this book down and nearly threw it across the room when I finished it!"
—**Brianne Kane,** *Scientific American*, **A Best Book of the Year**

"An ambitious first novel from this duo—I can't wait to see what they come up with next."
—*Wall Street Journal*

"A surprising and unexpected blend of surreal science fiction, action thriller, and slow-burn queer romance, character-driven with a depth I rarely encounter in SFF . . . I've never read anything with quite this combination of elements, and Blaché and Macdonald balance the mix superbly."
—*Locus*

"The authors hit all the expected sci-fi notes—an ill-fated experiment expanding into a quantum field of love and loss—but resist the containment of a single genre. *Prophet* is a page-turner in which object-oriented philosophy sits comfortably alongside military acronyms—and with a handful of familiar horror tropes to boot." —*The Telegraph* (UK)

"Instantly enticing . . . A freaky, touching horror story that explores, among other things, the nature of nostalgia and how it can be weaponized by an otherworldly adversary . . . This is the debut collaboration for Helen Macdonald and Sin Blaché, but here's hoping it's not the last. *Prophet* is a trip." —*Philadelphia Inquirer*

"Striking in its originality and its capacity to instill unease, even terror. It evolves over time, with the consequences of its use growing ever more disturbing and incomprehensible . . . A chilling speculative thriller in which some suffer, and others profit, from idealizing the past."

—*Foreword Reviews*

"A fast-paced techno-thriller, with a high body count, zippy dialogue and an intriguing central mystery . . . The novel is immense fun, a work of exceptional storytelling skill and stylistic panache . . . The writing is high-spec, lively, vivid. The dialogue is sharp, often funny . . . Without letting the pace slacken, Macdonald and Blaché manage to fold in powerful reflections on loss and trauma . . . H Is for Highly Recommended."

—*The Guardian* (UK)

"Mind-bendingly absorbing."

—*Marie Claire* (UK)

"Redolent of such small-screen favourites as *Twin Peaks*, *Stranger Things* and *Lost*, this sci-fi novel is entertaining, erudite and eerie."

—*The Scotsman* (UK)

"*Prophet* is a blast."

—*The Times* (UK)

"I had heard *Prophet* (accurately) described as a genre mash-up, blending the best of techno-noir, dystopian sci-fi, and espionage procedural (with a dash of queer romance). And while it is all those things, at its heart Helen Macdonald and Sin Blaché's tightly wound (yet somehow tender?) mystery-sci-fi-thriller is a philosophical novel . . . What is life without mystery? And at what point does nostalgia grow so strong it derails our lives?"

—*Literary Hub*

"The authors' most irresistible achievement . . . is their odd-couple pairing of the Dionysian Rao with the fastidious Rubenstein, who bicker and banter contentiously despite their fondness for each other. The well-matched authors make good on their audacious premise."

—*Publishers Weekly* (starred review)

"Intriguing and deftly plotted . . . pulse-pounding, philosophically fascinating, even blackly funny . . . A crisply written, inventive, complicated brew of a novel." **—*Kirkus Reviews***

"A beautiful, tense, strange, and heartfelt first collaboration from a duo not to be missed." **—*Shelf Awareness***

"Unlike many sci-fi titles, the focus of the book revolves around the two main characters rather than on action sequences or futuristic technologies. This allows for plenty of mystery and drama as the story shifts between the present and the past, intertwining the two men and a substance that is making time essentially irrelevant."

—*Library Journal*

"Fabulous . . . Present day science fiction that feels like the best sort of spy novel with real people you can care about. And it's a page-turner. So good." **—Neil Gaiman, author of *American Gods***

"*Prophet* is a crackling, shape-shifting romp with big ideas and a bigger heart. Blaché and Macdonald take a no-holds-barred approach to manifesting the ways in which individual desires are exploited by the systems we live under, and ask the necessary question of whether escape from that cycle is possible. This is a display of sheer inventiveness, and a delight." **—C Pam Zhang, author of *Land of Milk and Honey***

"Absorbing, fast-paced and febrile, *Prophet* takes you through the world at an angle, exposing cracks in the reality we think we inhabit. An exhilarating and surprisingly tender trip."

—G. Willow Wilson, author of *Alif the Unseen*

"Sin Blaché and Helen Macdonald have turned nostalgia—'the trash of hearts'—into a world and a trap. Prophet promises to bring back everything you lost and now yearn for. Is it a drug? Or is it a new state of matter? Whatever it is, it's proper science fiction—self-aware, funny, ruthlessly propulsive, full of invention, parodic yet perfectly serious about its underlying issues with contemporary retro culture, and ending with a complex, emotionally satisfying extension of the personal into the sublime. I loved it."   —M. John Harrison, author of *Light*

"*Prophet* is a wildly fun, inventive, funny, and terrifying book, with a superb mystery that gets ever more compelling and weird and, horrifyingly, familiar. This book finds the nightmare in the comforting lies we tell ourselves about our pasts, and how they inform our present."
—Phil Klay, author of *Uncertain Ground*

"A hyperkinetic headrush of a novel that proves its organic bona fides by getting you drunk with ideas before casually and cataclysmically breaking your heart."
—Paraic O'Donnell, author of *The House on Vesper Sands*

PROPHET

A NOVEL

SIN BLACHÉ
AND
HELEN MACDONALD

Grove Press
New York

Printed in the United States of America

Lyrics from "It Was a Very Good Year" by Ervin Drake
used by permission of Songwriters Guild of America.

This book is set in 11-pt. Janson Text LT Std
by Alpha Design & Composition of Pittsfield, NH.
Designed by Norman E. Tuttle at Alpha Design & Composition.

First Grove Atlantic hardcover edition: August 2023
First Grove Atlantic paperback edition: July 2024

Library of Congress Cataloging-in-Publication data is available for this title.

ISBN 978-0-8021-6340-0
eISBN 978-0-8021-6203-8

Grove Press
an imprint of Grove Atlantic
154 West 14th Street
New York, NY 10011

Distributed by Publishers Group West

groveatlantic.com

24 25 26   10 9 8 7 6 5 4 3 2 1

The ultimate hidden truth of the world is that it is something we make and could just as easily make differently.

—*David Graeber*

PART I

CHAPTER 1

The room she ushers him into smells of stale cigarettes and air freshener. The decor is '80s mil-spec Holiday Inn. Dark-green carpet, striped armchairs, a smoked-glass table, a print of two F-15s trailing vapour set high in a gilded frame. The scream of their engines outside has been softened in here to a dark, low-frequency roar.

Miller pulls off her jacket, drops it over the back of a chair, winces at the half-drunk coffee cup on the table, and looks apologetically at Rao. Her eyes are the colour of airmail paper, the wrinkles at their corners attest to years of sun. Her hair is bleached, tousled on top, very short at the sides and back, and her business suit hangs far too perfectly on her spare frame to be worth anything other than a fortune. There's a Cartier tank solo on her left wrist, gold studs in her ears, and she is trying so hard to be friendly Rao feels his teeth ache.

They sit.

"Can we get you anything?"

"A drink."

"Mr Rao," she chides. "I can offer coffee, tea, or soda."

"Water," he says tightly. "No ice." She's amused by that—and for the right reasons. She can read an insult even when it's placed gently in front of her. Not a lot of Americans possess that talent, in Rao's experience.

"There's a cooler in the corner."

She doesn't expect him to get up. He doesn't.

"I expect you don't know why you're here."

"Why I was escorted from prison by two MoD AFOs and driven to an American airbase in the arse end of England? No. I don't. They didn't want to tell me."

"They didn't know. Do you want to guess?"

Ugh. Rao stares at her day-for-night reflection in the top of the smoked-glass table between them, the curve of her jaw, the interrogative tilt to her head. "Respectfully, fuck off. Tell me what you want, and please attempt to do so without vague requests for me to perform for your amusement, or I'll find my way back to my cosy remand cell and get on with the rest of my life."

"It's like that?"

"Yes, it is."

"Ok," she says mildly. She reaches into the bag at her feet, pulls out a file, flips it open. "Sunil Rao, thirty-six years old, born 1974, Kingston upon Thames, UK. British citizen, OCI cardholder. Parents Himani and Bhupinder. Mother works for Christie's. Father's family business, fine jewellery." She reads on, raises an eyebrow. "*Very* fine. Educated St Elgin's, BA in art history at St John's College, Oxford. Six years at Sotheby's, fraud and attribution, then MI6." She glances up, smiles. "Very patriotic."

She's definitely looking for a rise. Which could mean she's not in possession of enough information to push him in any other way. More likely it means she's purposefully testing his patience. Both possibilities make it less likely they're going to put him on a plane back to Kabul in the next twenty minutes, but that doesn't make her strategy any less exhausting.

"Eight-week joint operation in Central Asia, last fall." Her voice softens. "Your partner at the DIA spoke highly of your abilities."

"Did he. I've quit."

"We're not unaware." She frowns at the file. "Then Afghanistan. Where things went less well, I see. It says here you became unreliable."

"Highly."

"It says here there was an overdose in a hotel room."

"There was. It wasn't a cry for help."

Her response to that is silence, but not the kind he'd wanted to provoke. It's thoughtful. "Could you tell me about the incident in rehab?" she tries, gently, after a while. "It's not in the file."

"Isn't it?" He holds her eye. "I punched an obnoxious cunt in group therapy who was lying through his teeth."

"I heard it was far more than a punch."

Rao spreads his hands flat on the tabletop, breathes in once through his nose, exhales.

"Why am I here?"

"Are you fit enough to work?"

"I doubt it."

She lays the file on the table between them, pushes at a corner to straighten it. Drags a finger down the cover—a slow, considered movement. "We think we need you, Mr Rao." She doesn't sound happy about it. "We've no one with your skill set."

"Yeah," he snorts. "I guessed."

She raises an eyebrow. "Guessed?"

"Yes."

She walks him down a corridor to an empty conference room where a Stars and Stripes hangs limply by a projector screen. Set out along the length of the long central table is a line of cups, mugs, plates, and bowls. Miller runs her eyes over them, looks at him expectantly. He knows what this is now. Rubs the back of his neck at the familiarity of the setup. Recalls the light slanting from the windows, cigarette smoke rising through it, his father's question as he gestured to the trays of jewellery on the desk. *Which, would you say, is the most interesting of these, Sunil?*

"Kim's Game, is it?"

"No, Mr Rao," she says.

A radiator ticks and hisses. Rao buries both hands deep in the pockets of his jeans and waits to be asked to do what he knows he'll be asked to do.

"I'd be grateful if you could examine these objects and tell me if any seem unlike the others."

"Third from the left," he says. "White mug."

"That quickly, by eye? Could you tell me what's different about it?"

"It's wrong."

"Wrong?"

"Simplest way I can put it in the circumstances."

She brings the pad of her thumb to her closed mouth, rests it there for a few seconds, pulls it away.

"Mr Rao, we'd like to show you something. I think you'll find it interesting. If you could follow me, there's a vehicle waiting outside."

The urgency of whatever this is is suddenly so apparent Rao stops in the corridor to read a random noticeboard. *Baseball practice, commissary tours, missing dog, zip-lining trip, garage sale, pizza night, motorcycle competition.* He glances over at her, registers her clenched fists, her silent agitation, and with a burst of pettiness reads it all again.

Their steps echo on wet tarmac. Suffolk is buried in fog: thick, inconstant air that glitters and shifts around the base lights in the dusk. Miller drags a parka from the back of an unmarked Land Cruiser, hands it wordlessly to Rao. Inside, their driver is tense. He tries to start the ignition while the engine's already idling, hits the indicator far too early for the junction. It's not Miller's presence. He's spooked. Rao splays his hands on his thighs, looks down at his fingers, and knows that he is too. There's a lie to all this that isn't the usual bullshit dissimulation, and the taste of it is beginning to press on his mind. He looks out the windows to push it away. Lights in the mist. Passing bulks that are barns and chicken farms, smears of headlights over roadside hedges. After half a mile they turn up a potholed farm track. A few hundred yards later they halt at a high-security fence set in concrete blocks. A guard steps forward with a torch. After a brief negotiation he opens the gate; the rutted track behind it veers back towards the base.

The driver slows, cuts the engine. Miller gets out and opens Rao's door, informing him it's a three-minute walk. He clambers out into dank, still air and follows her, trudging over rows of fleshy leaves that squeak underfoot. Wet clay clumps on his Converse, making each step a little slower, a little more effortful than the last. He has no idea what this is. Wonders what he's being taken to see. A crash site, a corpse, a cache of arms, a burned-out car. No. None of those. Perhaps a pub? Yes. Let Miller be taking him to a pub. A pub with an unexpectedly fine selection of single malts and a blazing log fire. He knows she isn't, but he's imagining that blessed, forbidden idyll when they reach the crest of the rise.

He stops.

"The *fuck*," he breathes.

Below them, stranded in fog, right in the centre of the field, is a small, one-storey building with a panelled facade of shiny sheet steel. A circle of floodlights haloes it in soft, candescent air. The scale of it is peculiarly uncertain. For a fleeting moment it seems to Rao no bigger than a matchbox, as if he could just reach down and pick it up. There's no doubt what he's looking at. It's an American diner. Not only does it look like the most generic roadside diner ever built, but there's also a red neon sign over the entrance that reads AMERICAN DINER. The lights are on inside. But no roads lead to it, there's no parking lot beside it, and no sign of disturbance in the crop growing around it except the narrow, muddy trail that runs from their feet straight to its double doors.

"Not right, is it," says the voice next to him.

"No, it isn't," he says. He rocks on the balls of his feet in the mud, licking his lips at the sight below. "Not the usual at all, this."

"Is it like the mug?"

"Yes. But—" He blinks, finds himself unable to finish the sentence. Looking at the diner is like watching water swirling down a plughole, and he balks at chasing the intuition any further. In his peripheral vision there's something that could be a smile.

"The mug you identified came from inside. But you already know that, I think. Want to take a closer look?"

"Lead on."

"It's seventy to eighty hours old," she announces as they walk downhill. Her voice is easier now. This has become a briefing, the nature of which is to turn a thing into someone else's problem. "To clarify: that's how long it's been in this location. It's weathered and aged in a way that would date it, ordinarily, as a midcentury building. But we don't know how old this structure is."

"It's seventy to eighty hours old."

"You're sure?" she says.

"Call it a hunch. The lights?"

"It's not connected to utilities. And there's a zone around it that's apparently of interest."

"To whom?"

"All of us."

"It's an us, is it?"

"I hope so, Mr Rao."

"And who are we, exactly?"

"I can't lie to you, can I?"

"You can lie as much as you like. I'll just know you're doing it. You want me to go inside?"

"Go ahead."

He walks to the door. The air smells of fried onions and behind that the faintest hint of diesel. He stretches out a hand, brushes the chrome with two fingertips. The metal is cold, bright, beaded with water. When he pushes, the door swings easily. He steps in. Looks down at his muddy sneakers on the black and white tiles, hears Miller behind him.

He tried to describe it, later. Said that it felt like getting into a hot bath. Not the temperature change but the suddenness of the alteration, how deep it hit, the welcome of it. He's never been inside a fake before. He's never experienced a fake like this before. His skin itches with wrongness. But warring with the wrongness is a surge of elation running up his spine, a quickly unfurling warmth in his chest. After a few seconds, he's surprised to find himself close to tears.

There's no one inside. It's deserted.

It feels full of people.

"It's lovely in here, isn't it?" he says.

She's not sure how to respond. Her arms are folded, her expression complicated. "Look around, Mr Rao. Take your time. The griddle is hot. I wouldn't advise touching it."

He sees a turquoise counter faced with checkerboard tiles. An illuminated jukebox in one corner. Red banquettes, steel chairs with padded seats and backs. Framed photographs across the cherry-coloured walls. Elvis, Sinatra, Marilyn, Bill Haley, the Everly Brothers, a *Gilda*'d Rita Hayworth. These, Rao realises, after they snag on his eye more than once, are wrong in a very specific way. The more he looks at them, the less recognisable their subjects become, and isn't *that* interesting. He walks up to the nearest. Blinks. Diner lights reflected in his eyes against a face that isn't quite Sinatra's. It could all be in his head. He knows he's not right. But he doesn't think so; he doesn't think that's what it is. He looks over his shoulder at Miller. Judging by the stance she's taken by the door, he's not going to be given all night in here. He decides, reluctantly, he has to let this particular mystery wait.

The more Rao looks about, the more wrongness is revealed. Behind the bar, the griddles are indeed on full—he holds a palm just above one to check—and gleaming with oil. There's a row of torn paper orders stuck along a narrow steel strip on the wall—*eggs over easy* scrawled on each one—but there's nothing else. No sink, no grill, no plates, no cooking implements. Scores of coffee mugs, flasks, no means of making coffee.

"And no bathroom," she says, watching him. "What do you think?"

"It's like a model. A full-size prop. What's this thing about the zone outside?"

"There are no foundations. It sits on exactly six inches of sand. And exactly six inches of sand extend from it on each side before it meets the soil of this field."

"What kind of sand?"

"We've not had time to analyse. It's only been here for seventy to—"

"Eighty hours." He's looking at the ruby cursive glow of the neon sign over the counter. SERVICE, it says. There are no wires. None at all. "So, you've shown me this, and before you'll tell me anything more about what it is, you'll need me to sign an NTK declaration, yes?"

She nods.

"In blood."

"It's cold tonight, Mr Rao. Let's eat. They can bring us food from the Officers Club, and I'll do my best to be helpful."

Miller picks at a Caesar salad while Rao devours a plate of chicken fajitas. When he's done, she picks up her coffee, sits back in her seat, and looks at him speculatively.

Here we go, Rao thinks.

"So, the term your former employers used about you, Mr Rao, and they were very keen to explain how off the record it was, was 'fucked.'"

"Just Rao will be fine."

She considers her cup for a while, swirls the coffee a little, watches it circle.

"It must have been hard."

"What?"

"What you've been through."

He closes his eyes. "Let's not, shall we? I've had an awful lot of that lately. If you want to play 'let's make friends,' let me ask the questions."

"Go ahead, Rao."

"What's your department?"

"Defense."

"Job?"

"Investigator."

"Ah," he says. "Columbo."

"No dog, no wife, and I loathe cigars."

"Where did you grow up?"

"Wyoming."

"Where did you get your watch?"

"That's none of your business."

He grins. "No, it isn't. Does this thing scare you?"

She blinks, twice. "The diner? Yes."

"Good." She's looking at him very seriously. He wonders what she sees. She's treating him less like a live grenade now, more like a terrible liability, which is more than fair. He wonders if she has a son somewhere. A difficult one. Something in her expression tells him she might. Yes. He pulls at a loose thread at the hole in the cuff of his sweater, rubs it idly between finger and thumb. "You can get your need-to-know form out now. I'll sign it. Do you have a pen, or should I open a vein?"

"I have a pen."

He signs. Doesn't bother reading it. He's signed them before, and none of them mean shit.

"So what's the deal?"

"There's no *deal*, Rao," she says. "This isn't transactional."

"Not literally. Figure of speech. What's going on here?"

She bites her lip, speaks carefully. "There's been a death on base. Surprising and suspicious circumstances. I'm here to act as liaison between UK and US investigations."

"But you're really here for the diner."

"My liaison role's not cover, Rao. But we're not solely concerned with the diner. I've been tasked with assembling a small team to investigate other recent events at this location. They might have some connection with the diner, maybe with the death. You were recommended highly."

"By whom?"

"You'll be working with Lieutenant Colonel Adam Rubenstein."

"Fuck, is he not dead yet?"

A wry smile. "No."

"What's the point of this team, if anyone asks?"

"Investigation. There's a body, and a lot of people need answers."

"And what's its actual role?"

"Investigation. Just a touch more complicated. A series of objects have turned up around this site. Mostly inside the wire. No one knows where they came from. Base operations assumed they were a practical joke. Then the diner appeared."

"What kind of objects?"

"Various. A surprising number of children's toys. The first was a Cabbage Patch Kid doll picked up on the main runway during a routine FOD walk. The last was a ticket stub for a performance of *The Philadelphia Story* at the Arlington Theatre.

"Awful play."

"Deflection isn't a helpful strategy," she says, "but I agree with you. I should note that this particular production was from 1982."

Rao yawns. It's a stress response. She misinterprets it, looks at her watch, and frowns. "It's late. You were denied bail because you were assessed as a flight risk, Rao, so I'm afraid there'll be a guard outside your dorm. But we're not placing you in the confinement facility, and you'll be more comfortable here than in Pentonville. Do you need anything?"

Rao shakes his head. He doesn't need anything. He wants several things right now, but none would be good for him and none will be given to him. He watches her nod at the uniform sitting three tables away, watches him rise, waits to be escorted away.

CHAPTER 2

See, the main problem with the way Sasha's life shook out is that she hadn't really planned for this to happen. Truthfully, speaking from the heart and all that crap, she hadn't really planned for a lot of stuff, but this really took the cake. She could have probably handled the loss of a limb better than her uptight older brother getting some poor woman pregnant. Not that disappearing for five years and losing her brother's number after she got the happy news could really be counted as handling anything well.

What was she supposed to do with that information? Grab his wife's shoulders, shake her carefully, scream at her to get the fuck out before the baby dropped? It was too late for that. If Sasha had wanted to do something for her, she should have done it before they got pregnant. Should have done it before the damn wedding.

They weren't really a family equipped with healthy coping mechanisms. Growing up like they did, they'd learned early that if they had a problem the best thing to do was to keep it to themselves. Bottle and bury it.

Then she'd kind of forgotten about the whole pregnancy thing during those years. She'd gotten into her own shit, bottled and buried too deep to remember that she was supposed to keep her head aboveground. So, five years later, with an impressive array of gambling debts and a few scars nobody needed to know about, Sasha found herself at her brother's doorstep. Funny thing about family, right? No matter what happened, neither of them could ever manage to fully burn that bridge down. There was always enough left over to cross.

He didn't even say hello when he opened the door. Just looked at her, looked at the suitcase leaning against the back of her legs, watched the taxi drive away. "How long do you want to stay?" he asked.

"How long you got?" she answered.

"I'll get the spare room made up," he told her and stood aside. Never offered to take the bag, but she wouldn't've let him anyway. "Lunch is nearly ready, I think. Go meet the family."

That's about when Sasha remembered about the pregnancy and how cruel she'd thought the whole thing was. Locking his wife up in a prison made of something she guesses he'd call love. "Yeah, lunch sounds good," she said.

"This is your aunt Sasha."

Do you offer to shake a five-year-old's hand when you meet them? Probably not, but there was something about the kid's eyes that made Sasha want to. She fought it.

"Hey, kid. Wow, you're like a whole person these days, huh? Last time I saw you, I don't think you were fully cooked yet." She grinned down at the little boy sitting at the table with a perfectly square PB&J in front of him. He didn't respond. Nobody in the kitchen did. Her brother, his wife, the kid all just looking at her like Sasha just spoke Italian at them and danced a jig.

"The last time your aunt was in town was when I was pregnant with you," her brother's wife explained.

The kid nodded. "Oh."

That's all he said. He ate his sandwich in silence while Sasha avoided answering questions about what she'd been up to for the last few years. He sat quietly, watching with big brown eyes while the adults in the room skirted around how long Sasha was going to stay. As far as she could tell, they landed on "indefinitely" with some underlying threat of that being yanked away as soon as there was a whiff of bad behavior.

Bad behavior, with her brother, was sort of a gray area. Smoking inside the house, talking about her artist friends, playing music he considered subversive: all those were Bad Behavior. But if she sat outside on the porch even though all his neighbors could see her smoking, which she kind of assumed would freak him out, that was okay. If she brought him and the wife to an art gallery in the city, managed to score them some comped passes, then that was culture. That wasn't bad behavior at all. And if some of Sasha's favorites happened to come on the radio, well, what was he going to do about it?

It was a lot like living with their dad again. People cope in their own ways. Sasha went crazy and moved to the city way too young. Her brother went crazy and turned into a slightly softer version of their father. Shit happens. She never blamed him for how he turned out, anyway. None of that was their fault. Sometimes, and only sort of, Sasha wondered if her brother knew that he wasn't to blame. There was no way she was ever going to find out, though. Easier to bottle it all up. Way better to bury it.

CHAPTER 3

"**D**id you get breakfast?"

Rao nods as they walk. He didn't. He probably should have. He's certain he'll die if he doesn't find coffee in the next ten minutes.

"I've got a meeting, so I'll leave you to it. In there," Miller says, halting in the corridor and indicating an unmarked door to their left. Rao hesitates. He's learned a few lessons over the years about walking blindly into rooms like these. "Rao, please get something to eat," she adds, smiling wearily, gesturing again at the door.

He pushes at it. Walks into an open-plan office. Fabric cubicle dividers, worn grey carpet, mesh desk chairs. People staring at screens. Some wear suits, others BDUs. Four of the latter are frowning over something on a breakout table nearby. Porn, maybe. *No.* He looks about. Has he been assigned a desk? Has Miller stuck him in here so people can keep an eye on him?

No to both. He's looking for a spare desk with a screen to hide behind when he feels a tiny, sliding dislocation in his sinuses and chest. Something's not right in here. It'll be something he's dragged his eyes across but not properly seen. An item from the diner, he guesses.

It's not. It's Adam.

Lieutenant Colonel Adam Rubenstein, bent over a file at the far side of the room. Just another dark-haired man in a cheap suit. There are at least five of those in here. All just like him, none of them anything like him.

He looks the same, Rao thinks, but seems somehow unfamiliar. Perhaps he shouldn't be surprised. There was a Rao before Afghanistan, but Rao's not sure how much of him still exists, which makes the Adam he's looking at now seem a souvenir from an impossibly distant past. The shoulders of his jacket still sag. His hair is just as short and ostentatiously poorly cut. The collar of his shirt is tight, the knot of his tie too snug against it. Adam has always dressed as if he's trying to stop himself from giving anything away. The scruff on his jaw is a worrying sign. This must be a serious situation if Adam's not found time to shave.

He remembers Adam's last words to him. Late afternoon in Tashkent, just under a year ago. Bright, landlocked light beating through plate glass into the departure hall, dragging like sandpaper on Rao's appalling hangover. Weak black tea in paper cups. More than a little awkwardness. "Take care," Rao had said as he rose to walk to the gate. He'd judged it the safest bet, but as soon as he'd said it, he knew it sounded as if he were doubting Adam could look after himself. Adam had nodded once, then lowered his eyes to the cartons of cigarettes under Rao's arm and raised an eyebrow. "You know those are fake," he'd said. Not a trace of a smile, but Rao'd been cheered. Adam's peace offerings, on the rare occasions they're given, have always had something of the nature of knives.

Rao doesn't say a word as he approaches. But Adam wouldn't be as good as he is if he hadn't noticed Rao long before he reached his desk. He doesn't look up.

"You look like shit," he says flatly.

"Yeah, thanks," Rao answers. "You look nondescript."

That makes Adam raise his eyes from the file. They're dark, schooled into the usual faint hostility he uses to dissuade conversation. Rao thinks back, recalls the very few times Adam's smiled at anything he's said. There's a sense of humour behind those eyes: that's an immutable fact. He's made Rao laugh in the past. His habitual impassivity, his immunity to jokes and jabs—it's a control thing, Rao's always assumed. The man is wound up tighter than those intricate Black Forest clocks, and Rao is reasonably sure that Adam himself did the winding. Intelligence officers like him hold their own keys. That's the point of them.

He gives Rao a once-over. He'll have already taken in everything he needs, but now he's decided to extend Rao the courtesy of being involved with his assessment. For Adam, this is an act of consideration bordering on generosity. "Glad to see you standing," he says. He probably means it, Rao decides, looking down at the file Adam's holding, the faint, black-inked fingerprints decorating its edges. Writing implements rebel in Adam's hands. Rao suspects he affects their ink like he does most people's blood pressure. "I didn't mean it literally," Adam adds. "You can take a seat."

Rao sits. "Are we just going to talk about my current state of being or are you going to tell me about that file you're ruining?"

"This is a copy," Adam mutters, pushing the papers over to Rao. "Doesn't matter what happens to it so long as it doesn't leave the room."

Here we go again, Rao thinks, feeling the vague headache he's had for days blossom into deep, bruising pulses behind his eyes. He pushes his fingernails hard into his palms. It'd be good to ask Adam what he knows about Rao's state, his place in all this, and so many other things, but there's no way he can do that without a sickening amount of vulnerability. Later, Rao decides. Maybe. When his head isn't pounding so badly and his eyes can focus properly. He picks up the file, opens it, flips through it helplessly. "Adam, I might look like shit, but I feel far worse. Just tell me what it says."

"Three days ago, a civilian contractor working grounds maintenance found the body of an SNCO in an unscheduled bonfire in the southeast sector of the base. Senior Master Sergeant Adrian Straat."

"Dead before the fire?"

"No."

"Cause of death?"

"Fire."

"Is that in the file, or are you fucking with me?"

"Both, maybe. That's a separate file. Miller's told you about the objects. They appeared about the same time as the corpse over a four-hundred-meter radius. No one admits to placing them or seeing them being placed. They've been bagged and inventoried. Miller wants you to take a look at them after this. They're all in the evidence room except a 1950s jeep that turned up behind a munitions bunker and a 28-gauge Browning Citori in the weapons store."

"That's a shotgun."

"Yes, it is. Specifically, a Citori White Lightning Over and Under, hand built in Japan circa 1983. I'm leaving out a lot, Rao. There are details here that can wait for when you're more able to take them in."

"You're handling me."

"And I'm doing it well."

"Fuck off. Is there any coffee around here?"

"You want *coffee*."

"Don't start."

Adam gets up, returns to the desk with two mugs, sets them in front of Rao. Tugs at the file, extracts two stapled pages, and hands them over. The top sheet is an outline map of the base. Across it is a scattering of numbered crosses, concentrated in some areas, sparse in others.

"These crosses are where the objects were found?" Rao says, gulping down liquid so vile it's like a slap round the face.

"Yes. The circle is the fire."

"Should I be seeing something in the pattern?"

"Do you?"

"No. Do you?"

"No."

"Have you been to the diner?"

"Not yet."

"Surprised at you, Adam."

"Rao, I got in at three a.m. off a flight from Dulles. I didn't have time."

"Sure, yeah."

"I'm telling the truth."

"*Sure*, yeah."

Rao feels the grin on his face, marvels at it. He turns the page, scans a few lines. It's as if a yard sale exploded over the base and someone had itemised the fallout.

29 *Motorcycle jacket (black leather)*
30 *Plush dinosaur (yellow, worn condition, missing one eye)*
31 *Recliner chair (burgundy, leather)*
32 *Toolbox (varnished pine)*

33 *Bunch of roses (red)*
34 *Connect 4 game (assembled frame with complete set of counters)*
35 *Beanie Baby (bear, black, worn condition)*

"Santa?" he suggests. "Maybe all the personnel have been good boys and girls."

"Santa is not a plausible delivery system," Adam murmurs. "Security cameras showed nothing except several bursts of static between zero six forty-eight and fifty-one. Before them, nothing. After them"—he nods at the map—"this." He hesitates. "I don't want to get *Twilight Zone*, but I can't account for it."

"I've always assumed Rod Serling taught you how to knot your necktie, Adam, but no, let's—" Rao stops. Reconsiders. "Yeah. Well. I've been in that diner, and it was full *Twilight Zone*. A guy died in a mysterious bonfire and weird shit appeared all over the shop. Why shouldn't we go down the freaky rabbit hole? Do you have a time of death?"

"Approximate." Adam pulls another file towards him, opens it. "There are photos of the scene, if you—"

"Not now, thank you."

"Zero six forty."

"So when was the first one of these objects picked up?"

"Six fifty-one."

"The Cabbage Patch doll?"

"From the flightline, yes."

Rao sees the doubt in Adam's eyes. He drains his mug, picks up the second, takes a gulp, and winces. This one's even worse. He's pathetically grateful for it.

"The diner's mental, love. I've been inside it. And when we look at this Santa shit, it's going to be mental too. There's going to be some kind of logic to all this but I'm pretty sure it's *Twilight Zone* logic and we're just going to have to deal with that as it comes. Keep our minds open."

"Don't patronize me, Rao. I don't care if it's elves. I just need to know why and how it's elves."

It's a three-minute walk, Adam informs him, to the evidence room. Hands stuffed deep in his pockets as he steps over puddles on the footpath, shoulders hunched against the worsening rain, Rao decides he's sufficiently caffeine fortified to broach the subject of how Adam's been.

"So, Adam."

"Rao."

"How've you been?"

"How have I been."

"Yes."

"Busy."

"Busy good or busy bad?"

"Busy."

This, Rao recalls, is what it is like to converse with Adam. "*Classified* busy?"

Adam gives him the barest frown. "More desk work than before," he says after a while.

"You have a desk, Adam?"

"Technically, everyone has."

"Technically?"

"It's more of a concept."

"The fuck does that mean?"

"If you live long enough, you'll end up at your desk."

"Ah, this is a case of there being a bullet out there with your name on it, is it? A bullet, a desk, a grave?"

"Always waiting."

"You're one dramatic cunt."

"Yes, Rao."

"A *desk*," Rao breathes. "Did you fuck up?"

"No, I didn't fuck up."

"No escándalo? Got caught in a compromised position in an embassy broom cupboard?" Rao represses a snicker: it emerges as an almost inaudible squeak. The very idea of Adam having a fumble somewhere. Impossible.

"No."

"Don't tell me you got tired of shooting people? Fucking hell, Adam. Did you find god or something?"

"Rao, you asked me how I've been. I've been busy."

"Of course you have. Christ. Catching up with you is like trying to break into Fort Meade. Don't know why the fuck I bothered asking in the first place." Rao grins. A pair of F-15s passes low overhead, both bristling with ordnance. "Well?" he says when the noise allows.

"Well what?"

"Aren't you going to ask me how I've been?"

Adam shakes his head. "You'll tell me."

The evidence room is in a squat, redbrick building at the far end of the base. Two sad-looking laurel bushes flank its entrance door; the black-painted guttering above gurgles with rainwater. A leftover from the war, Rao surmises. The old RAF operations block? *Yes*.

Adam leads him to the basement and marches straight to a door at the far end of a corridor still decorated in wartime cream and green. Flashes his ID to the guard outside, who straightens, snaps a "sir," unlocks the door, and stands aside. Striplights flicker on.

Rao wrinkles his nose. The air in here smells odd. Aromatic hydro-carbons off-gassing from plastic, he supposes. *No*. Whatever it is, it's redolent of jasmine and mud. Rainwater, sandalwood. He shivers. The room is narrow and deep. Steel floor-to-ceiling shelves stacked with transparent plastic bags run along the walls, and at the far end of the room a number of bulkier bagged items rest on the floor. Rao sees leather upholstery pressed unpleasantly against taut plastic, a Yamaha 50cc.

Adam's businesslike. "OSI forensics said there were no fingerprints on any of the items they looked at except the people who picked them up. Miller wants anything else you can give us."

Rao pulls a pair of nitrile gloves from a box on a steel examination table, puts them on. "So far, all I know is they're all incredibly wrong. Chuck me one?"

"Which?"

"Whatever. Doesn't matter."

Rao takes the bag Adam hands him, squints through it. "I think this is a Care Bear," he decides. "It is a Care Bear."

"It's Funshine Bear."

"Adam, how do you know what a Funshine Bear is?"

"Television." Adam's attention is focused on another item he's pulled from the shelves.

"Bollocks. You definitely had a Funshine Bear," Rao says, then stops dead in wonderment. "Shit, Adam, I never thought about this before. You must have had toys when you were small. What were they? Teeny plastic army men? Retractable daggers? AR-15s?"

Rao expects Adam to greet this with the usual classified silence. Unexpectedly, he answers. "Models," he says flatly. "Scale models. From kits. Mostly aircraft."

"I adore scale models," Rao says. "You still have them tucked away somewhere? Can I see them?"

"No. You should look at these," Adam says, extending his arms.

It's a bunch of red roses.

"Appreciate the sentiment, love, but I've always preferred mimosas."

"Rao."

Rao takes the bag. The blooms are deep scarlet and highly scented: as he unzips the closure, their fragrance hits the back of his throat. He slips them out onto the table. They're a little wilted. He peers at the card attached to a length of red ribbon wrapped around their stems. A message in cursive script, blue ink. *To my Millie. Forever, like we said.*

"There's a date. Ah. The flowers are trying to tell me they're from 1973, Adam."

"Are they. Could you just look at them, Rao."

They look like a bunch of roses. Although there's something about the space between the flowers that isn't quite— Rao frowns, pushes his fingers between the blooms, careful, exploratory.

Holy shit.

They're roses on the outside. But inside the bunch is a monstrosity, a clumped mass of curled, soft, velvety-red vegetal tissue smeared with patches of glossy, veined green, as if leaves and flowers had melted together. Staring at it, Rao remembers a textbook photograph of a plant that had been exposed to gamma radiation and wrought itself into a growth of exuberant and incoherent horror. When he pulls his fingers back, the bouquet snaps shut strangely.

It looks like a bunch of roses.

"Are they roses?" Adam asks slowly, as if the question were not only surprising but unpleasant.

"Well. What's a rose? Look, I did a lot of reading a long while back about the metaphysics of identity. That's not the kind of question that comes in true or false. But there are other things I can test. Like, these flowers were cut from a plant."

"Were they?"

"No. They weren't. *Shit.* Give me something else. Something," he says, thinking carefully, "in a box. There was a toolbox, wasn't there? No, Scrabble. Find the Scrabble box."

"There are two," Adam says, peering at the inventory.

"Give us both."

The first is an old-style set. The board is unremarkable: grey green, dotted with squares of pink and pastel blue. Wooden tile rests. Wooden tiles. The other box can't be opened. When Adam pulls a knife and slices through one corner it turns out to be solid all the way through: fibrous, grey matter that the blade works through with difficulty. Afterwards he spends more time than Rao thinks necessary wiping the blade of his knife on the fabric of his pants, an expression of disgust on his face. He brushes at the spot on his thigh with his fingers several times, looks at Rao.

"They're all going to be like this, aren't they?"

"Yeah, love. Probably. Yeah."

CHAPTER 4

"**W**here?"

"In England. RAF Polheath. It's a fighter base, an American one, the name is, uh, misleading."

"I know Polheath."

"Hello? Are you still on the line?"

"Loud and clear. I was thinking. This is deeply suboptimal."

"It's not ideal, no. But, you know, the proverb. Every cloud."

"Every cloud?"

"I was thinking of Dennett. You know Dennett? Daniel Dennett."

"Philosopher of mind, yes. What about him?"

"He holds that making mistakes is the key to making progress. I think this complication could turn out to be quite, quite serendipitous."

CHAPTER 5

"Leave the dishes to me," Sasha told her brother, and the whole family cleared out of the kitchen like magic, not even pausing to talk her out of it for appearances. Now she's alone. Which is exactly right, really, since she offered, and she doesn't mind doing the dishes. It's payment, sort of, and that's what Sasha had planned when she offered, knowing it would be her role for the entire time she stayed with her brother. There were worse things she could've been stuck with, and she'll definitely pick up a few more chores as she goes. No rent, after all. Not even he's so much of an asshole that he'd hound her for a monthly check, probably.

It's suddenly obvious that someone has come into the room, like there's a shift in the air somehow, and Sasha makes a safe guess. "Listen. You can trust me with your china, okay? I'm not a butterfingers like some people I know—" And she's this close to dredging up some old childhood fight just for the fun of it as she turns to face her brother, when she stops.

It's not him. It's his son. He's standing at the door, watching her with those big eyes. "Huh. You're real quiet, kiddo," she says. "Like a ghost."

He shakes his head seriously. Sasha lifts an eyebrow.

"No? Not a ghost."

He shakes his head again. She leans against the edge of the sink, ignoring the wet as it seeps into her shirt and onto her back. It's fine. It's lukewarm and weirdly homey. All the grime and discomfort that comes with a family home. Little things she'd forgotten about while couch surfing with her bum friends. "You want to tell me why you're not like a ghost? Because I'm not seeing any other options here."

She doesn't think he's going to answer. He stands there in silence so long that Sasha shrugs and turns around again. Sticks her hands into the soapy water. Searches for the mug she knows is in there along with the plates and utensils. She'll never know why mugs are more fun to wash, and maybe it's just a lie she tells herself to make the cleaning job easier, but she searches all the same.

The kid talks, so quietly, as her hands find the handle.

"Not real," he says. He's beside her now. Moved from the doorway to the counter right by her side. Neck craned, looking almost painfully tiny, just to see her from where he's standing. "Ghosts aren't real."

Maybe this is the result of a serious family talk, she thinks. Maybe the kid was scared one night, and his parents had to curl up with him and explain that ghosts aren't real. Sasha smiles at the small face looking up at her, thinking about that imaginary scene, all its unlikely domesticity. It doesn't fit her brother or his wife, and it doesn't fit in this house. Like it's too small to stretch over them all and too big to fit into the house. She knows that ghost talk would never have happened, but it's cute to think about. Especially with those big eyes looking up at her.

"Okay. So ghosts aren't real. You got me, kid," she admits. He frowns a little at her, confused. "It's not really a lie when it's part of a story. You get that, right? Like sometimes people tell stories about their days and not everything is all the way true, but they're not all the way lies. You ever hear someone say that it's raining cats and dogs?"

He nods.

"And that just means it's raining a lot, huh?"

He nods again.

"So, saying you're like a ghost doesn't mean that you're fake. Not fake like a ghost," she says, carefully avoiding the topic of death. Maybe that's not a talk she's supposed to have on the first day the kid meets her. "But you're quiet, and you move like it's a secret. Like ghosts. Get it?"

He thinks about it. He really thinks about it. Sasha wonders if maybe it's too much. How old is he again? She's gone too fast and too much. But then he hums at her. A tiny copy of her brother, serious and all straight lines, and far too young to have lost all the laughs inside him. Shit. She needs a smoke.

"I get it," he says.

"Cool. You want a glass of water or something?"

"Yes."

She pulls a glass from the suds, cleans it quickly. "We'll get you to talk more than three words in a row one day, kid. I'm gonna promise you that," she mutters.

CHAPTER 6

Miller listens intently to Rao's report. "Noted," she says. "Rubenstein, anything to add?"

"No, ma'am."

She nods. Her manner is brisk, her equanimity unnerving. "I'd like you to talk to Ed Gibbons," she announces. "The civilian contractor first on the scene at the fire."

"Where is he? In a cell somewhere?"

"No, Rao. He's at home in Brandon with his wife and two dogs. He's been off sick for three days with a migraine. But he's well enough to"—she purses her lips—"have a chat."

"You want us to have a nice chat with the gardener?" Rao asks.

"That's what I want you to do."

Adam glances at Rao, who sends him a sharp side-eye. A wordless *Yes, Adam, I know there's a quicker way to do this.*

Rao remembers that night eleven months ago, driving between Khujand and Tashkent. Tense with the upcoming border crossing, rattled by a desert road littered with broken concrete and ridges of impacted sand, they'd got into a fight about an impending rendezvous.

"He's not going to turn up."

"He'll be there."

"He fucking won't. How did you get to be so *trusting*, Adam? Don't they beat that shit out of you at Langley?"

"I never went to Langley. And it's not like we need to meet him. In fact, I'm pretty sure we don't need to be here at all. Because I worked it out, Rao. I know you're not a polygraph. They think that's what you are, but you're not. You just somehow know what's true and what isn't.

I could write a list of likely possibilities on a piece of paper, and you just point to one. We don't have to be here. We could be in Ohio."

The silence had stretched like molten glass into a thread impossibly fine, impossibly brittle, waiting to break.

"We need to be here," Rao said eventually.

"We really don't."

He'd clutched at Adam's arm. "Adam. Listen to me. *I need to be out here.*"

Puzzled, Adam stared down at Rao's fingers until he let go. Turned his gaze back to the road ahead. It took him five seconds to work it out. Rao counted each one.

"They'd never let you out."

"That's the size of it, yes. They'd lock me up, throw away the key, feed me paper. I'd really rather they didn't know."

Then a long and perilous silence. After a while Rao unwound his window, fragrant night air flooding the cabin. Stuck his head out, craned his neck to watch bats dipping over the UAZ to snatch moths drawn in by the headlights. "The asset'll make the rendezvous," he'd said, finally, settling back into his seat.

"Yeah. He will."

Another mile.

"There are limits to what I can do," Rao began, certain that saying any of this was a terrible course of action, but it was happening, and it was happening like an apology happens, and Rao has never been a fan of those. "Exceptions. Like emotional states: there's a lot of vagueness with those. Can't track them. What I *can* do is judge the veracity of propositional statements about the world. Written or spoken, even implied. And no, I don't know how it works."

"What does it feel like?"

Rao shakes his head. "Knowing what's true and what isn't? Fuck, Adam, that's like trying to describe what breathing feels like. You know when the air you inhale is cold or hot. You know how to draw breath and let it out. It's automatic, part of you. It's like that, for me. A sensation. It isn't something I can describe, it just is."

"Did you learn to do it?"

"Nah, it's always been there."

"How far back can you go?"

"What d'you mean?"

"In time. Historically."

Rao rubbed his cheek. "With enough specificity, as far back as you like."

Adam considered this for a while. "Abraham and Isaac? Did that happen?"

Oh that is adorable, Rao thought. "That's impossible. Neither of those people are real enough to track, you know?" He'd glanced across. Adam appeared genuinely disappointed, and Rao felt bad about his lie. Abraham existed, and so did Isaac. As for whether God demanded Abraham kill his son—well, he just didn't want to have to get into the complication of explaining why the "that" of Adam's question was a problem. If statements about gods were testable, Rao'd be in an entirely different line of work than *spy*.

"So, you should probably know. There's one other exception."

"Which is?"

"You. I never know when you're lying."

Rao watched Adam's face harden. An entirely reasonable response, considering. "I'm not fucking with you, Adam. It's been that way since the beginning, and I don't know why."

"The *questions*. So that's why you were like that when we met."

"Like what?"

"Like you were on uppers."

Rao scratched at the corner of an eye. "Erm, to be honest, love, I was. But yes."

Adam nodded slowly. "And you don't know why? Really?"

"I've thought up a fuck ton of theories. But I can't tell if any of them are true. It's a thing, Adam. It's a fucking bizarre thing, and I'm telling you about it now for a reason."

"Which is?"

Rao sat back, heart hammering.

"You're going to keep my secret."

"Of course I am."

"I'm very relieved to hear you say that. I can't know, you see? And cards on the table, it's much weirder than that, because it's not just you. It's anything about you. First time they mentioned you in a briefing my skin crawled. When they ran through your operational history it was like white noise." Rao frowned. "No. Not white noise. What I think of, when people talk about you, it's more like a roulette wheel."

"A roulette wheel."

"Yeah, but not the bit when the ball skips in the pockets. The noise of it circling the rim. Before it falls." He snorted. "I freaked out quite a lot when you told me you grew up in Vegas."

"Outside Vegas. And I could have been lying."

Rao rolled his eyes. "I know. But I've seen you play cards, Adam. And I've seen your file."

"No you haven't. So, you work with me because I made your skin crawl when you first heard my name and because I'm a freak?"

"Yes. Also they told me I had to."

Rao hadn't even caught Adam's name, in truth, only the end of the sentence his name had been in. He'd been staring at his own reflection in the deep shine of the tabletop, letting his mind wander. *French polish. Shellac*, he'd been thinking. *Shellac and denatured alcohol. Layers of it, set one on top of the other. Chatoyancy, the proper name for the way the lustre works light like that. Like in chrysoberyl, like in tiger's-eye*—and he'd been musing on the optical phenomena certain gems display when they're cut in particular ways when he'd heard the phrase "commendable record, six years at the DIA," and his head emptied with a sickening flash of heat. Like magic paper, a conflagration collapsing instantly into absolute vacancy. He'd closed his eyes, and they kept saying things about this Lieutenant Colonel Rubenstein, and all of them were nonsenses, and the sensation in his head bloomed and grew and was so unlike anything he'd ever felt before that for a long while Rao had to grip the edge of the table in terror, convinced he was having some kind of neurological event. The feeling shifted and flickered as the seconds stretched, slowly turning itself into something halfway between a sound and an image. A spinning roulette wheel in that uncertain moment before the ball drops to the pockets below. The moment that's nothing but potential, whose meaning is its own inevitable end. But it refused to end, the entire time they talked about Rubenstein. And there was Rao, trying to follow what they were saying, trying to understand what was happening when they spoke of him, trying to comprehend what could be different about this man and grasping, finally, the point of the entire discussion. They wanted Rao to *work* with him? *Fuck.*

In a black cab en route to their first meeting Rao had wondered if he should have made more of an effort with his clothes. He'd been nervous, and nerves make Rao kick, hard. He'd decided on his oldest, shittiest jacket, threadbare, with a cigarette burn on one sleeve. Vaguely odiferous trainers and a pair of conker-coloured corduroy trousers his mother had once pronounced too short in the leg. A bag slung over his shoulder: laptop, pens, notebook, two packets of Marlboro Lights, a dog-eared 1980s spy-themed Mills and Boon novel called *Cloak of Darkness* he'd stolen from a B&B in Brighton and had become something of a lucky talisman.

A little heavy with the Terre d'Hermès that morning, perhaps, but it separates the men from the boys. Maybe the bump of coke before he left the house had been a bad idea—he was expending a degree of effort in the back of the cab trying not to talk with the driver about *everything*, but he wasn't going to worry about it unduly. They'd seen him worse.

The meet and greet had been in the kind of room Six loves to use when it does performative Britishness for Americans. Magnolia walls, Axminster carpet, leather armchairs, a muddy sub-Landseer oil of a stag above the fireplace, elaborate plaster cornices blurred with layers of white gloss paint covering decades of cigarette smoke.

As soon as he walked through the door, Rao stopped in his tracks, his usual disarming smile dying on his face.

Rubenstein.

Huh, one part of Rao thought. *Cute.* But the rest of him recoiled, like he was seeing something against the laws of nature. Rubenstein wore a dark grey suit, black tie, white shirt, stood at military ease. His eyes were dark and expressionless, but Rao understood they'd very rapidly assessed him from the way Rubenstein tilted his head, just a little, before saying hello.

Baritone. Unplaceable American accent, entirely without emphasis. Hearing it was like trying to climb a sheet of glass. Rao had no purchase at all.

"Hi," he said back, looking a little desperately at his handler on Rubenstein's left. Morten Edwards twitched his nose, smiled back. On Rubenstein's right, a white-haired man in the well-pressed blue shirt and red tie that is something of an unofficial uniform for unofficial elements in the American government nodded at him.

Edwards cleared his throat. "Well here we are," he said cheerfully. "Lovely. Shall we run through everything?"

They sat, and for almost two hours Rao listened to red-tie man— who remained unnamed—run through their upcoming op. Eight weeks in Central Asia, primarily in Uzbekistan, assessing the reliability of intelligence sources and assets in place. A lot of talk of FVEY and interagency cooperation. Rao's lips twitched a little whenever he heard that. He knew he was being loaned to the Americans as a favour, part of some tit for tat. Whatever. Red-tie guy took him through some of the less classified highlights of Rubenstein's career—*Yeah, that's what I've read*, Rao thought helplessly, *but I still don't fucking know?*—and emphasised that he would fulfil a personal protection role in addition to being Rao's operational partner.

Over those eighty minutes, Rubenstein spoke for less than three minutes in all. Everything he asked was acutely to the point, and Rao, struggling to make sense of things using methods quite alien to him, eventually decided that he might be the sharpest man in the room. Also, he thought, considering the blankness of Rubenstein's face and the tone of his voice, he's going to be the most boring man alive to spend time with. Eight weeks. Eight weeks of mission-mandated shared hotel rooms. He's going to drive Rao up the wall. He's going to go absolutely fucking mad.

CHAPTER 7

He learns a lot of things without lessons. He learns by watching, without asking questions, without being sat down and told. If he asks questions, that means he's stupid. If he has to be told, that means he's in trouble. He learns by watching where his mom keeps the wine for Friday, and that it's different from the wine she drinks during the week. He learns that no one is supposed to touch the lighter in the cabinet unless his mom is lighting candles. He learns the words of his dad praying. He knows all the words for what they're doing, but he can't remember when he was told them.

He can't remember figuring out that it's better to watch than to ask. It's just how things are.

Now he's watching and nobody notices him, and his parents are talking about his aunt staying in the house. How his dad thinks she's a hassle, but she's family. How his mom thinks that it's great timing that his aunt turned up when she did, since they have an important dinner and now they don't have to get a babysitter.

That night, after his parents leave for dinner, his aunt smiles at him. Says that they have the house to themselves, that they can do anything that he wants. He can't think of anything, but his aunt doesn't get mad. She finds a pack of cards and starts teaching him games. He doesn't talk much, and he doesn't ask her questions, but it's okay. She's telling him the rules to the game, but he's not in trouble for not already knowing them.

She asks him what they do on Fridays. He tells her. Says the right words. Tells her where the wine is. She doesn't ask, but he tells her that he doesn't like how it smells.

"Like if vinegar could be too sweet, huh?" she says, and she's agreeing with him, and they're both smiling, and everything is fine.

She lights the candles but not like his mom does. She waves her hands to him, gesturing for him to come closer. Places both hands on his shoulders. He cranes his neck to look up at her, but her eyes are closed. And when she prays, it's not the words he's used to.

He listens. He watches. Tries to memorize the words she says.

"What is it?" she asks when she's done. Her hands are still on his shoulders. "Did I get it wrong?"

He shakes his head, but he doesn't know if she did or not. He stays quiet. Doesn't ask questions. He has a lot of them, but he doesn't want her to think he's stupid. But she guesses.

"Your mom and dad don't do that one," she says. It sounds like a question. He shakes his head again. "That's okay, kid. That'll be the one I say, if you want."

He isn't sure why his opinion matters, but he doesn't tell his aunt that. He's not supposed to argue. "Yes," he says. He doesn't move after that. He barely breathes. She's still holding on to his shoulders, but she's not holding him in place. He could move away from her if he wanted to.

He doesn't.

He's the only kid in the house, she tells him, so that means that prayer is just for him. "My lips," she says, "to God's ears, if he's paying attention." Says that it's all about God keeping an eye on him. Shining a light on him.

Peace, she says, and she takes one of her hands from his shoulder. Rests it on his head. The one she'll say on Fridays makes sure he gets a little peace. He's not sad, but he wants to cry.

CHAPTER 8

E d's house is a 1950s bungalow at the far end of a rural cul-de-sac. Purple violas bloom in a planter shaped like a pair of cowboy boots next to the yellow front door; there's a motorbike under a tarp, a square of well-kept lawn. The man who opens the door is in his fifties, open-faced and weather-beaten, with thinning fair hair, a checked flannel shirt rolled to his elbows, and faded tattoos of playing cards dancing up one arm. He's wearing a pair of dark-blue 501s, a belt with a silver rodeo buckle.

Rao apologises for calling on him like this out of the blue. Says, as he always does in situations like these, that his name is Ray. Explains that he and Adam are journalists working on a story about spooky happenings in Suffolk. Ed's face is all caution when he hears the word "journalists," but as soon as Rao says they've heard Ed knows something about this *diner* that's turned up in a field, he perks up. "I might," he says.

"Can we have a chat with you about it?"

"Yeah, why not? Lucky you found me at home. I've been a bit under the weather the last few days. D'you want to come in and have a cup of tea? Roz's just put the kettle on."

Rao knows this is the place.

He knows it as soon as Ed walks them through the hall, and he sees the photo of Roy Rogers, the framed Polaroid of a younger Ed leaning against a pink-and-white Oldsmobile and the metal license plate fixed below it bearing the slogan: HOME MEANS NEVADA. In the lounge a movie poster for *Western Jamboree* on the wall above the TV catches at him almost viciously. He stares at Gene Autry's off-register face for so long, Ed asks if he's ever seen the film.

"No," he says. "Maybe I should."

"It's mad," Ed says. "Absolutely mad. It's about a gang of outlaws trying to steal helium from under Autry's ranch."

"Helium?"

"The gas. There's a blimp and everything."

Rao struggles a bit with this. "And songs?" he says, recovering.

"Of course!" Ed says.

Sinatra is playing on the stereo in the corner and motocross on a muted TV. There's a leather sofa with a Navajo-pattern fleece throw, a lurcher sprawled across it, and a wiry, steeped-tea-toned terrier that jumps onto Rao's lap as soon as he sits in the armchair he's offered. It circles a couple of times, lays its head on his knee, and sighs. Outside, Rao can see ferret hutches, more violas, the woody stems of some kind of climber trained on wires along a fence.

Adam refuses a seat and stands by the door. He's not at ease in domestic spaces. Rao's given him shit for it any number of times, has more than once suggested he was raised in a forward command base, not a family home.

Roz appears.

"This is Ray and—"

"Adam," Rao says.

"They're journalists, want to talk to me about *you know what*."

"What?" she says. She starts collecting mugs from side tables.

"The diner."

She shakes her head, looks sidelong at Rao. "He knows sod all about it. Either of you want a cup of tea? Milk? Sugar?"

Ed is gleeful. He pulls out his Nokia. Clicks through, holds it out to Rao. On the screen, silvered and foggy, is a photograph of the diner, taken at some distance, its leftmost side obscured by the shadow of a thumb.

"Is that it?"

Ed nods and grins. *Ed*, thinks Rao. *Oh, Ed. You're so eager to please.*

"How did you get this?"

"I know the guy who found it," he says, lowering his voice conspiratorially. "Tomasz. He's Polish, that's Tomasz with a zed, but he lives in Thetford. We were on JCBs together back in the day. He was spraying off the field, came over the hill and there it was, and he sent this to me 'cause he knows I'm into Americana. It's amazing, isn't it. Can't stop looking at this photo."

Rao stares at the phone, shakes his head, says with some wonderment, "No one we've talked to knows how it got there."

Ed laughs. "Well it wasn't the farmer. Garnham's already pissed off at the acreage of sugar beet he's lost, and he hasn't got the imagination to come up with something like this. He doesn't even watch TV, can you believe that? John at the Bells says it's an art installation, but why would someone come up from London and do it here? Waste of time. Then the Yanks came and walled it up, so it's got to be something to do with them. Roz thinks that too. Right, Roz?"

"Yeah. We don't know half of what goes on in there. It's not bad living this close, except the noise. You think you'll get used to it, but you never really do."

Ed nods. "You don't. We've been here fifteen years," he adds. He adores her. Rao's prickling with the weight of emotion between them; it's not right. He already knows why.

"They're alright," Roz says. "Some of the Americans are a bit up themselves, but most of them are nice. We had one next door for a bit. He went off to another base in Idaho, somewhere called Mountains Home."

"*Mountain Home*," Adam corrects.

Ed's eyebrows go up. "You're one, are you?"

It's one of Adam's tightest smiles. "Not by choice."

Ed nods thoughtfully.

Fuck's sake, Rao thinks. "This is a good song, Ed," he says. "Who's this?"

"You don't know who this is?"

"Why would I ask if I knew?"

"The best of the Rat Pack!"

"That's subjective."

"Alright, yeah, ok, if you want to be like that about it." Ed grins. "It's Dean Martin."

"No. Really? I don't think I've ever heard this one."

"One of the best."

"Of the Rat Pack?"

"No, his *songs*."

That kicks off an animated conversation about the Rat Pack that segues quickly into all the things Ed knows about Sinatra and the Mob. "So, this Americana," Rao says, "how did you get into it?"

"He's always been into it," Roz explains. "His dad was as well. I think it's infectious. Few years with Ed and I even got into line dancing."

"She's *really good*," Ed says seriously before launching into a disquisition on the gloriousness of America. America back then. The cars, the music, the clothes, the movies. Ed's trip to Graceland. All Ed's favourites. Sloppy joes, '50s jukeboxes, diner coffee. Diners.

Then Rao says softly, "I love diners, Ed, but I've never been in one. What are they like, inside?"

"Well," Ed says. "They're all the same, basically."

"Tell me. Describe one."

Ed's eyes shift left, shift up as he conjures one inside his head. "Well," he says, drawing it out. Right now Rao knows Ed's thinking of him as something like a stage hypnotist, is thrilled at being in the spotlight, and Rao feels the heavy weight of all his unwarranted trust.

And then it happens. He and Adam sit in the room with the hissing gas fire and the muted TV, the terrier and the sleeping lurcher, and they hear Ed describe the interior of the diner in the muddy field. They hear him describe it *exactly*.

They're quiet driving back.

"How?" Strain in Adam's voice.

"I can't even start to think about tackling that question right now." Rao grimaces. "Also, his wife's having an affair. And he sort of knows it."

"Is that relevant?"

"Fuck knows."

They hit a squall line, water battering the windscreen, blurring the road between each sweep of the blades. "Miller's going to pull him in," Rao says. The knowledge sits sour inside him, a chestful of curdled milk.

"It'd be stupid not to," Adam says, glancing across to the passenger seat. "But they won't be rough with him. It's not like that, here."

Bullshit. Rao looks at twisted roadside pines and runs through all the definitions of "rough" that apply in these cases, all the ones he knows, all the ones he's seen, until Adam, registering the silence, starts complaining about how much he hates driving in the rain. They're almost back at the base when Rao swivels in his seat. "You're babysitting me again," he observes. "But this time they think I'm a lost cause. So, what are you going to tell Miller in your one-on-one?"

Adam flicks the indicator, turns in to the gatehouse lane. "That you're better than I thought you'd be."

"We'll bring him in," Miller announces after they brief her on their visit. Rao swallows past the lump in his throat. It's not just the thought of Ed in one of those rooms. It's the betrayal on Ed's face.

Ray, you said you were a journalist.

"Ed?" he says lightly. "Nah. Leave him for us."

"I understand your position, Rao. But he has to come in. I want to talk to him and I can't be seen leaving for this. It's complicated."

"Ok, but first— Look, I think me and Adam should take him to the diner."

"Your rationale?"

"Ed's got an attitude. Stick it to the man. Bit of a poacher vibe. He thinks we're journalists. We can work with that. Get conspiratorial and sneak him into the site, see how he reacts. Have a chat. We'll get more that way than by shouting at him over a desk."

"Shouting isn't my style," she says. "But I'm willing to permit this. Rubenstein, you want me to send someone else with Rao? Anything to finish up in Washington?"

Adam shakes his head. "No, ma'am. I'll see this through, if that's alright."

"Ok, good. Call Gibbons. Be persuasive."

At eight, a clean-shaven Adam turns up at Rao's dorm with takeout from the base McDonald's, tells him they're picking Ed up at 10:00 a.m. For a while they sit in silence picking at fries tipped out upon a torn-flat bag spread out upon the tiny desk. The smell of grease and salt is overpowering. Rao knows it'll probably turn his stomach later when he's looking to sleep, but right now the heavy olfactory blanket feels welcome. Safe. The silence, on the other hand. The sound of paper rustling and quiet chewing. That feels like a small death with each bite. Can't hack it. Can't stand it. It's going to turn him feral soon, and he won't like who he'll become out of sheer annoyance, hot frustration. He has to fill the silence.

"Adam?" he begins, submerging a chicken nugget in BBQ sauce, munching on it.

"Rao."

"Riddle me this—"

"The Greeks," Adam interrupts. Doesn't look up. Picks another chip from the pile.

Rao blinks. "What?"

"Nothing. What were you going to ask?"

"Right. I was wondering, as I tend to do, but have never actually got round to asking, what you get up to when you're not working."

"I'm always working."

It's what Rao expected him to say. Entirely automatic. *Everything's always work, everything's a job, Rao. I'm always working.* Rao's willing to take a chance on it being a deflection; what spurs him to enquire further is partly curiosity, mostly a desperate need to stop hearing himself chew.

"Legally, you must have downtime."

"Officially, of course I have downtime. Operationally, however, no, I don't."

Rao snorts. "Fucking hell. That might be the most depressing thing you've ever said to me."

Adam frowns as he reaches for the stack of napkins. Wiping his fingers, his eyebrows pucker more deeply. "Is it?"

"No, probably not," Rao allows. Adam says a lot of shit that would be heartbreaking to hear from anyone else. But Adam exists in a weird little covert reality. And he isn't anyone else. Half the time he doesn't act like other human beings. Rao sometimes forgets he's in the room until he moves or speaks. Barely human, Rao's informed him, many times. "Whatever. Answer the question. What do you get up to?"

"On my downtime, which does not exist."

"On your downtime, which does not exist." Rao grins. "What do you get up to?"

Adam peels back the lid of a waxed cardboard cup, inspects the liquid inside, passes it over. "I don't have an answer that's going to satisfy you."

"Try me," Rao says, punching a straw into his Sprite.

Adam looks at him evenly. Chews. Rao can't hear him do it, so it's fine. It's all fine. This is just Adam looking for the simplest route to say something. He's not a voluble soul.

"I watch TV, read books. Go for walks."

"Yeah, you're right." Rao's amused by how disappointed he is at this predictably vapid answer. "That's shit."

"Told you."

"You can't be this boring, love. You can't. No one is."

"Maybe I am."

Rao flicks the hard end of a french fry at him. Adam doesn't even look at it, just snatches it out of the air. If anyone but him had pulled a move like that, it would be remarkable. There'd be astonished laughter. Awe. But it's not anyone. In absolute silence, Rao watches Adam place the fragment back on the flattened bag.

"But you're not, though," Rao tries. "Are you? You're one of the scariest men on America's payroll. Am I wrong?"

"You could be. That could be a lie. Who told you that?"

"No one told me that. But a lot of people have intimated it."

"Mm." That's all the fucker says, but he lifts an eyebrow and passes Rao his Filet-O-Fish. He's laughing, Rao realises. The bastard's laughing at him.

"That's funny, is it?"

Adam unwraps a burger from its now-sheer paper, inspects it. "A little," he admits and takes a bite.

Shithead. He's *such* a shithead. Rao snorts again. Can't help it. "Ok. Here's another question."

"Shoot."

"How many weapons do you have on you at any given time?" Rao doesn't expect Adam to answer this at all. But he might. They used to have nights like this in the field: a shitty dinner and beers, Rao firing off questions, Adam answering them, or more usually not, and somehow never, not once, pissing Rao off in the process. Rubenstein's far too much of a government weirdo for Rao to take his silences personally.

"Depends."

"Depends on what?"

"A lot of variables."

"Name one."

"Carry laws of the state or country I'm in," Adam answers flatly. It sounds true, and Rao's sure it isn't.

"Currently?"

"Currently . . ." He sits back in his chair, looks off to one side.

"Fucking hell. Are you counting?"

A flicker of amusement. "Currently, I have my service weapon."

"Ah yes, your beloved M9. Anything else?"

Adam inclines his head again. "Knives."

"How many?"

"Why are you asking this?"

"Just tell me," Rao says. But really, why is he asking this? He wants to know. And he'll never know for sure with Adam. And it's just fun, talking with his old partner again like they're normal—even if they are talking about how many blades one of them is lugging around at any given time.

"Calf, boot, waistband."

"Three? Bloody hell. I didn't know they were there."

"That's good. That's what you want from concealed weapons."

"No, but— Adam, you don't even move like you're armed."

"Yes, Rao. Because if I did, then people would know that I am."

"See, you are a scary fucker."

Adam hums before taking a bite out of his burger. He thinks while he chews. "You're not scared," he observes eventually.

"No, love," Rao says, rubbing his cheek with the flat of one hand. "But in all honesty, these days I'm not exactly sane."

CHAPTER 9

He keeps hearing things he doesn't mean to. Yesterday he was in the yard, the window was open, and his mom was talking inside the house. First, he heard her say it was just a phase. Then she said Judy's daughter was obsessed with a book last year, but she'd gotten bored with it after a couple of months. That crazes were things kids just go through. Then he heard his dad saying it was something he'd better grow out of soon, that his son was carrying that book around like it was a goddamned teddy bear, and he was too old for that shit.

He shouldn't have heard that. His dad cursing makes him feel inside like when you put your hand into water that's way too hot. He'd looked down at the book he was holding. It was true he had been carrying it around, but he didn't know he wasn't supposed to.

The next morning his mom asks him about it. "Where's the book your aunt Sasha gave you?" she says.

He puts his spoon down into his bowl of Cheerios, looks at the floating Os, tells her that it's in his room. "You read it a lot," she says. He nods again. Then she asks him why he likes it. He's not sure how to answer, so he tells her it's educational. To begin with this seems the right thing to say, but after a bit he's not sure it was.

"What's your favorite story in it?" she asks him.

He explains that it isn't stories; it's all one story. Because the book is about a Greek Hero called Hercules and how he has to do a series of labors. Those are all different though. He thinks about what he's just said, then tells her that he guesses you could call them stories.

She is doing that thing now where she is looking at him but somehow it's like she's thinking about something else. Then she asks him another question. "What's your favorite?"

He thinks fast. He's not going to tell her the one he reads over and over again is not one of the labors. It's the ending. When Hercules puts on a shirt that is soaked in the blood of the Hydra, and it burns him, but he won't take it off, even though he knows he's going to die from it. And when he is dying, Hercules wants to get burned on a fire—because that's what happened back then, people didn't get buried—but there was nobody there who would light it. So the gods—the Greeks thought there were lots of gods—take pity on him and because he had been very brave, they burn him all away with lightning and make him into a god, too, and take him up to where they live, a place called Mount Olympus.

He's read that bit so many times he can see the page in front of his eyes sometimes when he's dreaming. He doesn't dream of Hercules; he's never done that. He dreams of the page the words are on.

"The lion," he decides. "There's a lion called the Nemean Lion." He's not sure if he's said that word right. "And it is . . . impervious to weapons, but Hercules strangles it with his bare hands and then he skins it by using one of the lion's claws to cut through the fur and then he wears the lion's skin as armor afterward. To protect him."

She looks at him. She's really looking at him. He said the right thing.

CHAPTER 10

"**D**o you like her, Adam?"

"Miller? She's good people. Checks out. Doesn't get in your way, doesn't want to control you. You, specifically, Rao, is what I'm saying."

"Yeah. About that . . ."

"In my experience, she's trustworthy."

"Fucking hell. Now I can't know that for sure."

"Why would I lie?" Adam pulls up outside Ed's house, leaves the engine idling. Grips the top of the steering wheel tightly, taps at it with his thumbs. Something's agitating him. Rao doubts it's the prospect of the diner.

"What is it?" he enquires evenly.

"We're in a different vehicle."

"It's exactly the same make, colour, and model. You think he took our number plate last time?" Rao snorts. "This is Brandon, we're not in the Red Zone. Toot the horn. Let him know we're here."

"What's funny?"

"Nothing. I just. I don't know how you manage to make a car horn sound like a hacked-off drill sergeant."

When Ed appears, grinning and waving, he's clad head to toe in camo. Adam lets out a short, sharp sigh. "Fucking hell," Rao breathes. "He's gone full Raoul Moat."

They've been driving for a while now and Ed's still bouncing about on the back seat like a nine-year-old on a school trip. *Calm the fuck down*, Rao thinks at him, hard. "Ed, we had no idea you found a body the other day," he says. "Rough. Are you doing ok?"

"Used to work lairage for an abattoir, years back. Seen a lot of dead stuff. Doesn't bother me. How did you find out about that?"

"Adam knows someone who knows a guy at the base. What happened?"

"Is this for the paper?"

"No," Adam assures him.

"Good, I don't think they'd like me, you know, talking about it."

"Completely off the record," Rao says.

"Off the record," Ed says, grinning. "No one's ever said that to me before. Yeah. I'll tell you. I'd come in that morning and I was heading over to the workshop, turned the corner by the munitions bunkers and got a faceful of smoke. Smelled like barbecue, which is grim, looking back on it. Then I saw this bonfire. Flames were about six foot high, and right by the doors of a weapons store isn't an ideal place for a fire so I grabbed an extinguisher off an outside wall and started putting it out and then I saw a boot and a leg sticking out."

"Bloody hell," Rao says.

"Yeah. I pulled him out." He screws up his face. "Then I reported it. They asked me a load of questions, took me into the base hospital, they said it was smoke inhalation, but what a load of fuss over nothing. I told them I'd done worse on Guy Fawkes. I didn't know the guy. Might of seen him about, but they all look the same in uniform." He sighs. "I hope his family are ok."

"They'll be looked after," Adam assures him.

Ed looks speculative. "So you going to ask me if I think it's murder?"

"Is it?"

"Yeah," Ed says. "Has to be. No one's gonna off themselves like that. But I don't know what whoever it was was thinking. Can't think of a worse place to dispose of a body, and that fire would've taken ages to build and get going. What I'd have done is stuck him in a car, taken it out to the forestry, torched it." He drops his voice. "But you know the best way to get rid of a body? Pigs."

"Pigs?"

"Yeah, they'll eat anything."

"He's right, Ray," Adam says, eyes on the road. "They're efficient. And in this area? Lots of farms. I'm sure no one would look too hard at a pig farmer."

"Teeth, bones. Crunch up everything."

"They can't digest teeth," Adam says. "You need to remove them first."

Rao makes an agonised noise. "Adam. Ed. Please."

They park up on the far side of the hill, strike out up a muddy track that runs alongside a plot of adolescent pines. Spiderwebs are everywhere, slung between branches and stalks, the sky turned blank and gold. Rao watches the hems of Adam's suit trousers darken as they drag through grass and herbage still wet from yesterday's rain. He looks absolutely fucking ridiculous in this environment, Rao thinks, amused, before glancing down at his own sodden hems and yellow Converse high-tops and deciding he might be in no position to judge.

He wiggles his toes. They're cold. Wet. He wonders if he'll get chilblains. He's not had chilblains for years. Then he stops dead. Feels ice blooming in his veins, pushing up his spine. The thought of chilblains—it's so ordinary. And nothing else, nothing else is. None of what's happened here, what's still happening, makes any sense at all. A theory has just occurred to him, and it's a pretty fucking convincing one. All of this could easily be the last, florid kick of his own dying brain in creative overdrive. If this is a dying fantasy, nothing'll be real and testable. He's probably still there in his hotel room in Kabul; his exit plan had worked after all. He wonders how much longer it has to go on for.

He's staring dully at his toes when Adam appears by his side.

"Rao? You ok? Need to wait one?"

"Got a bit dizzy all of a sudden," he says slowly. "It'll pass. Where's Ed?"

"Over there. Are we sure about this?"

"A little fucking faith, love," he says. Takes a deep breath. *A little fucking faith, Rao.*

Ed's eyes widen when they reach the top of the hill. His face lights up and crumples into an expression of tight and painful longing. Then he runs. Runs downhill towards the diner as if he were running into the arms of someone he'd thought lost. Twice he stumbles, nearly falls. He disappears through the doors. Sun flashes from them, sharp, as they swing back into place.

Adam halts, stares. "That was unexpected," he observes.

"*Shit.*"

They jog down to the diner and find Ed perched on a stool at the counter, forearms stretched flat across turquoise melamine, fingers spread wide.

"Alright, Ed?" Rao tries.

No reply.

"What is this?" Adam says, like there's a bad taste at the back of his mouth.

"No idea. It isn't one of those 'it's because he's British' things."

Ed's staring straight ahead, eyes unfocused, an expression of such palpable bliss on his face Rao feels uncomfortably like a voyeur. Whatever this is, he thinks, it's deeply private. He's speculating on the nature of Ed's connection to this place when there's a sharp *clunk*. Deep, metallic, coming from somewhere on the far side of the room. He jumps in alarm, sees Adam reflexively uncoil into a combat stance, then moves his eyes slowly along the slide of Adam's pistol to the source of the noise.

It's the jukebox. It's on. On and *moving*. Mutely, he watches the record selector travelling slowly behind glass, watches it halt with a second solid *clunk* and pull a record from the rack. A flicker of something mechanical, a damp *bump*, a hiss, then a high oboe melody and a floating harp arpeggio. The music's loud. Feels as if it's playing inside Rao's skull. He shakes his head, trying to dislodge it.

And Adam? Adam's still got a bead on the jukebox. Adam's got a bead on Frank Sinatra's voice.

When I was seventeen
It was a very good year

"Are you hearing this too?" he whispers.

Adam holsters his Beretta, face grim. "Yeah," he says. "I hate this song." He looks at Rao expectantly.

"What?"

"This is your department."

"Sinatra?"

"Catatonia."

Rao supposes it probably is.

"Ed?" he tries again.

Nothing. He should be doing something. Adam gives him a vaguely impatient look, then slips two fingers under one of the wrists on the counter. Frowns after a while. Leans in and drops a hand over both Ed's eyes, waits a few seconds, pulls it away. "No reaction to light," he concludes.

Rao winces when Adam brings the base of a ketchup bottle down sharply on Ed's left thumbnail. Numbly, Rao watches the nailbed turn from shocked white to deepest rose.

Still nothing.

"Ok, let's get him out," Rao says.

And it came undone
When I was twenty-one

They pull Ed from his seat and carry him supine, Rao gripping his ankles through thick woollen socks, Adam locking elbows under his armpits, walking him backwards through the swing doors into the open air. Fifteen feet from the diner, he wakes. Wriggles convulsively, shouts. Kicks Rao in the shins, breaks free, falls, scrambles to his feet, and runs inside. They find him back at the counter, hands covered in mud, as unresponsive as before.

It poured sweet and clear
It was a very good year

"Don't slip this time," Adam says.

"Fuck *off.* You take his legs."

Ed wakes again as they carry him over the deep, muddy troughs he made in the field the first time he broke free. This time his waking is more violent. He wails wordlessly, eyes wide and wet with panic, back arching, fingers clutching at the air, stretching his arms back towards the diner. Rao swears under his breath, a litany of soft curses in time with the music in his head that's louder than ever, lodging itself even deeper, a slowly driven nail. He's sweating now with the effort of keeping Ed's writhing, not inconsiderable weight off the ground and the contagious terror of the noises Ed's making. Rao's back aches now, his knees too. It's a struggle to keep moving. He stumbles, catches himself, keeps going.

Forty yards from the diner.

Fifty.

Sixty.

Silence.

Abruptly, Ed's quiet. He's stopped resisting their hold, arms fallen slack, muddy fingers curled. *Thank fuck*, Rao thinks, relieved. But when he glances down, Ed's face is ashen, eyes rolled sickeningly up and back, and Adam's already lowering his feet to the ground. They lay him down on mud and sugar beet. Rao loosens his collar, Adam his belt. They listen to Ed's gasping breaths, hear them turn to desperate hauls. Hear them rattle and stutter, then stop.

Rao can hear himself calling Ed's name. Fruitlessly, pointlessly, stupidly. Rao is watching Adam administer CPR, thinking dully, *But that's not what Adam's for.* And all the time Sinatra, growing fainter now and turning far too slow, as if the voice is slipping, pulling him under, and Rao knows the truth of what this is, knows exactly when it happens, sooner even than Adam does.

After a while Adam sits back on his heels. His expression is glacially cold. He checks his watch. Pulls out his phone, calls it in. The music is distant, now, like it's back in the diner, and Rao sits on the ground hugging his knees. Breathing is an effort. The air stinks of sewage and crushed beet leaves. He doesn't want to look at the diner. He doesn't want to look at Ed. He doesn't want to look at Adam, and he's sure as shit not going to look at himself. He raises his eyes to the heavens. A flock of birds is passing overhead, making noises far too much like Ed's last, ragged breaths. He watches their slow and shifting constellations and screws his eyes tight, knowing the darkness won't help, won't make any of this go away.

Halfway along the corridor to Miller's office, Adam slows and stops. "You're not needed in the debrief."

"Miller's orders?"

"Mine. I told her you wouldn't be there."

"Thank you, Adam. I'd entirely forgotten the delights of you deciding what's best for me," Rao replies, because sarcasm is easier than gratitude. But as Adam nods and turns to leave, he's gripped with panic. "Wait, what am I supposed to do while you explain to Miller this is all my fault?"

"I'm not going to do that." Adam tips his head to a couple of soft chairs and a low table. "Sit."

"Oh, wonderful. Back issues of the *Stars and Stripes*. Go on. I'll be here."

He sits. Picks up a newspaper, opens it, stares moodily at a photograph of smiling assholes standing by a gunmetal-grey drone. A new DOD contract with Lunastus-Dainsleif, the Pentagon's corporate fuck-buddies in Sunnyvale, California. Money to be made, people to kill. Same old same old.

Bile rises. He tosses the paper back onto the pile. Snaps his fingers compulsively to fill the silence. Stares at the skirting boards and door-frames, watches feet walk past, counts them, counts the chips in the paint by the side of the chair, the snagged threads in the orange fabric of the chair he's sitting on and the one next to him too. Ed's death is right there waiting for him if he puts a foot wrong in his mind. It's on a perpetual reel. Ed's face in the diner, the smears of mud on his hands after their first attempt to get him out. The sounds he made as they carried him. The colour of the inside of his mouth as he gasped for air. That stupid, stupid fucking camouflage jacket. Rao knows his defences are crumbling fast. He thinks of a number. Four. He says *four* in his mind. Repeats it. Imagines the word, the shape of the letters. It's like holding up a crucifix to a vampire. It keeps it at bay, but only barely.

Sweat's prickling in his armpits, in the small of his back. He wants to throw up but his head doesn't hurt, and that's freaking him out too because he doesn't know why. His head has no business being clear.

Ed's death wasn't his fault, Rao knows. But it was, all the same.

It's like that time with *the cold*. He'd been small when that happened. They'd been out in the West End on a frozen winter afternoon. There were lights, Christmas lights, he thinks now that's probably what he'd been taken to see. His mother was pointing them out, and yes, they were pretty, but his hands hurt from the cold and his feet hurt worse, he'd wanted to cry, and he'd looked at all the people passing by in big coats, all kinds of people, some of them looking up at the lights, most of them not, and a thought had lit on him out of nowhere. *One day I'm going to die.* And then he'd whispered it, because he needed to test if it was true. And the truth of it, spoken, had grabbed him like a cat grabs a sparrow in its jaws, and then everything inside his head ballooned outwards and upwards until it seemed to fill all of London, and everything inside the rest of him crushed itself down and constricted to a point so fine and cold it trembled on the edge of not existing at all. It's there, still. He can still feel it, or whatever it did to the places around it, the burn of the hole it made.

Rao knows the story isn't a special one. There's a moment in everyone's childhood when the great and terrible secret makes itself known. But Rao's particular relationship with truth, he thinks, might have made it different for him, because after all that he'd fainted, right there on the pavement, and he'd woken in the London house with the family doctor and his parents by his bedside and the light from his Transformers lamp making his hands gripping the covers look like they were made of metal, and he'd been looking at his hands when they'd asked him about what happened, and he'd thought again about how after he dies and his soul's reborn in another body he won't remember himself. He won't be *him*. And he'd looked at his mother then and known he couldn't lie. He said, because it was simple, *I just got cold inside.* And that was true enough.

Adam's face is blanker than ever when he reappears in the corridor. As he draws nearer, Rao sees it's more than the aftermath of a difficult debrief. Adam's exhausted. The pallor, the darkness below his eyes, his blink rate, the faint tremor in his hands: seeing them, Rao feels an unexpected burst of compassion. A weird compulsion to tell Adam to fuck off home and let someone else deal with this shit. Whatever this shit is, wherever home is for Adam. DC, probably. Or some condo outside Vegas, maybe. Home gym in the garage. Knives in every drawer.

"She's taking the guard off your door."

"Why?"

"She's putting me in with you."

Of course she is. Adam'll be there to stop him going out and getting fucked up. No. Not that. Adam's on fucking *suicide watch*. Rao lets the complicated, heavy mess of gratitude and outrage wash over him and ducks out the other side.

"Roommate?"

"Suitemate."

"Sleepover. Lovely. Will you want me to do your hair?"

"Sure," Adam says. "I want French braids."

"Yeah, and I want a handful of oxy and a blow job, Adam. Life is cruel."

CHAPTER 11

He's so tired. The only sounds he can hear are his own breaths, the beating of his heart, the sharp echo of his wrist snapping in his ears. Time doesn't always work the same, he thinks dully. When he fell from the tree, it felt like forever before he'd hit the ground. It feels like seconds since he sat on the porch steps but also it feels like days. It took him twelve minutes to get a grip, stop crying, and start walking home after it happened. He checked the time on his watch. The watch in his jeans pocket. The watch with a cracked face. He had to take it off his wrist. That took forever too.

He knows his arm is broken. He knows it's all his fault.

The crack when he hit the concrete was scary, and the pain was worse, but the only thing on his mind walking home was what his parents would say. How he should have been more careful. How he shouldn't be crying. How he's torn his shirt. Cracked his watch. How this is just what they need. How he's ruined their nice evening. He was feeling cold all over by the time he made it to the porch. He was sitting before he knew what else was happening.

Time isn't always the same, he thinks. He doesn't know how long he's been sitting here, waiting for the shakes to go away, waiting to warm up, waiting to get brave enough to knock on the door and tell his parents what happened. When he thinks about his aunt, about how she never seemed to get mad at him, it feels like someone else's thought. He blinks it away, but even that feels like he's pulling the strings of himself to make it happen. He's not there with her, and it wouldn't help even if he were.

He doesn't mean to sleep. He doesn't know if he does. All he knows is that when he comes back down to himself it's because his mother is saying his name and his dad is pressing a bag of frozen peas into his hands, right where he has his wrist cradled against his body. He starts crying, starts apologizing. His dad tells him to shut up, to keep it to himself, so he stops saying the words. But he can't stop the tears. The pain is bad, but the crying is worse. He hates it.

He hates the tears more than anything.

CHAPTER 12

"Ah, the usual five-star accommodation," Rao grumbles. "So, which room of this delightful suite do you like best, Adam? The one with the bald eagle print or the one with the old aeroplane?"

"It's a P-51 Mustang."

"Of course it is. I'll rephrase. Which room do you want, Adam?"

"I think this room is yours," Adam says, staring down at a bed. "These are."

Rao pads over. Two plastic bags from the base PX have been dumped on the covers, SUNIL ROY printed across each in black Magic Marker. He sighs, tips their contents out, rifles through the clothes. "What the fuck is this?" he demands, holding one up to Adam.

"It's a Union Jack T-shirt, Rao."

"Ugh."

He showers, pulls on a checked flannel shirt and a navy sweater, a pair of beige chinos. Stares dubiously at his reflection in the narrow mirror bolted to the wall. Swivels to take in all angles.

"I look like I'm having a midlife crisis. Just not the one I'm actually having," he mutters. Then he perches on the side of the bed, looking down at the wine-coloured, horribly patterned carpet. There are stains on it, tidelines running out from the wall. He hopes they're water. Mostly they are.

Adam is staring into space from an armchair. They sit in silence for a while.

"Alcohol's off-limits?" Adam asks.

"It is, yes."

"Want me to turn the TV on?"

Rao shakes his head. "No, I don't. Adam, have you ever been to India?"

"Yeah."

"Jaipur?"

"No."

"It's a good place, you should visit. So. Listen. There's this thing happens there. In the evenings, the sky's full of kites. Everyone goes up onto the roof to fly them. It's competitive. You show off your moves and you're trying to cut other kites down with yours. And to help them do that, a lot of the kite lines are coated in glass dust."

Rao thinks of the dancing mosaic the kites make of the sky as it tips to dusk, notices himself breathing. It's always strange when you remember that's what you're doing, what you're doing *all the time*. "I was flying one once, I was eleven, they're not big, these kites, this one had the glass *manjha*. And a bird flew into it. Cheel, a kite, that is, same word but a bird of prey. They're everywhere in the city, really slow wingbeats, look like little eagles. Graceful. This one was gliding fast on its way somewhere and it hit my line. It sheared through one of its wings. It crumpled up midair, fell out of the sky." The words are just spilling out. Rao doesn't hate them yet. "I ran down to look for it."

"Did you find it?"

"Yeah. It was huddled up against a wall, covered in blood. I picked it up and it sank its talons into me. Dug them right in. Tore at me. Don't blame it for doing that. I mean, it's what I would have done. I've still got the scar." Rao turns his arm, points at the faint, pale line across the back of his right wrist.

"You rescued it?"

Rao shakes his head. "It died."

Adam nods thoughtfully. "So, in this story you're the bird."

"No, Adam. Of course I'm not the fucking bird. I was the kid with the kite."

Ed's death—it wasn't his fault the same way everything in Afghanistan wasn't his fault. He can taste Kabul in his mouth right now, vinegar and rust and radiator water. He feels suddenly vicious. "How much do you know?" he demands.

"About what?"

"Kabul."

"Some."

"You'll have found the intel like a ferret scenting blood. *Some* isn't enough."

"Ok. They had you ground-truthing interrogations. British citizens only, to begin with. Then you got loaned out. CIA pushed you too far and it all went to shit."

"It did. Have you seen these places?"

Adam shakes his head. "I'm glad," Rao says. He's surprised to hear himself say it, but Adam doesn't seem surprised to hear it. He looks unhappy. Wipes his mouth with the back of one hand. Gets up, walks to the kitchenette, returns with a pack of Marlboros and a mug. Sets the mug on the bedside table for an ashtray, passes the pack to Rao, who extracts a cigarette and lights it. Doesn't quite get round to smoking it. "I'm not going to talk about what they were doing in there," he says slowly. "It was obscene. Still is. It's happening right now. There's a cabal of sadists in possession of the conviction that they're saving the world running that shithole and its redacted fucking city."

A long drag on the cigarette, a longer exhale, both of them watching smoke threading its way through the close air of the room.

"Should we be smoking in here?" Rao asks.

"Probably not," Adam says. "But if you trigger the alarms, I'll take the rap."

"Colonel Rubenstein. Always looking out for me," Rao says a little sourly. "You know what happens to you if you're tortured, day in, day out for months? You start to give the people hurting you gifts. You tell them things you think they want to hear. A plan, a map, a bomb, some HVT. There'd be a cousin in Islamabad who knew someone who knows where bin Laden is, some fissile material coming in from Iran, something *sexy*. The interrogators'd look at me to truth it, and I'd shake my head. They hated me for that. And the people coming up with the stories? They hated me even more."

"You were everyone's problem."

"I was."

Another long silence. In it, Rao realises he's going to tell it all. "They put me in a hotel in Kabul for the duration. One night, there was a guy in the bar. There were a lot of guys, Adam. This one was American. Ex-marine. I was—at this point it didn't really matter who. I remember him being taller than me."

"And that's relevant?"

"No, but not all of us are short arses, love. Taller doesn't happen often. Didn't, back when it happened." Rao's viciousness has receded; he feels a little violent flutter of skittishness. It comes out as a breathy giggle. "Can you even handle this? Listening to my hot man-on-man action stories?"

"I don't understand the question."

"Most straights can't handle it."

Adam frowns. "Oh. No, I'm—it's fine."

"So. This marine. He had a very beautiful smile. I can't remember much about us getting off," Rao lies, "but afterwards he pulled out a bag and some foil and we smoked. I'd never done brown before. He was surprised about that. Really surprised. Anyway. That happened, and I lay back on the bed feeling good for the first time in forever."

Adam's watching him carefully, now. Cautiously. He'll be memorising all this for his next debriefing and Rao doesn't care. "He was there again the next night. And two nights later, when he said he was shipping out. But by then I'd managed to sort myself out, easy, because one thing Afghanistan is very good at, Adam, is heroin. Famous for it, you know?"

"Does it—did it—work like your fights do?"

Rao smiles. "Ah, that's a clever question, love. No, it doesn't. Get hurt enough and the world disappears. No truth, no untruth. You can't tell what colour the room is when the light's off, right? Opiates are different. They don't stop me reading the world. They just put the world *over there*. Which turned into a couple of months of me sitting in the corner of the room listening to pain like I was looking into a glass case at a museum. Didn't fucking care."

"But something happened."

"Adam, questions like that are going to make me think you keep a therapist in a cupboard back home."

Adam's laugh at that is sudden, pained, apparently genuine. "No. I don't do those."

"This does not surprise me. Yes. Well. Something happened."

Rao pulls the cigarette from his mouth, taps it on the side of the mug, holds it horizontally in front of him. Blows carefully on the coal. It glows fiercely. He watches little petals of spent ash grow around the incandescent core. Lets his breath die; smoke curls into his eyes. He widens them and blinks it in for as long as he can bear, screws them tight and grimaces. Wipes water from his cheeks, takes another drag.

"They broke people in there, Adam. Took me too long to work out torture's got fuck all to do with innocence or guilt. I watched them carry a body out once. *Oh, that one got wet somehow overnight, was he naked in that cell, oh well, cold night, shit happens. Must have been the guards, they're locals, we don't get involved. Whatever, one less to worry about.* They brought this new guy in, and he was so fresh, Adam. They picked him up in Birmingham. Not Birmingham, Alabama. England. He hadn't a clue. Went to the wrong mosque. He was an apprentice heating engineer. I told them, *This guy knows fuck all.* Less than. I kept telling them. They decided I was lying. They decided I'd got unreliable. They didn't take me out of the room, though. Everything this guy said was true, and I told them, and they didn't stop. They were rough with him with me right there. Slapped him first, then threw him against the wall a dozen times, and I think most of that was punishing me. And they put him back in his chair and he looked at me and he hadn't looked at me before, and he said, *Brother, I'm not getting out of here alive.*"

"Which was true," Adam says slowly.

"Turned out to be, yeah. And that was the *something.* I wanted out. Made myself an exit strategy. Thought it was a good one, at the time. Didn't work. As you can see. And here we are again, happy as can be. With you on suicide watch."

"That's what they asked me to do."

"I'm not going to."

"I know that, Rao."

"And just how the fuck do you *know* that?"

"Don't be an asshole to me for being in your corner. I *know* because I figure it's going to take a hell of a lot more than today."

Rao thinks about that for a while. "Not much more."

"Get some sleep."

He tries. At three in the morning he's frowning at the ceiling wondering if Adam's following his orders to the letter. Ten minutes of idle speculation evolves into an insistent need to know, so he throws back his blankets, swings his legs to the floor, and sneaks across the room to the connecting door. There's enough light through the curtains to confirm that Adam is indeed asleep, which is always a wonderment, because sleeping Adam looks like an eleven-year-old *this* close to asking for hot milk. Not quite: the analogy doesn't fit the long scar along his right collarbone that according to Adam may or may not have been something he'd picked up in Iran. He's on his stomach, face pressed to the sheets, one hand curled over the edge of the bed, pillows stacked neatly on the floor beside the frame. Seeing him, Rao's hit by a wave of exhaustion so total he reaches for the wall to steady himself. Some part of him, he supposes, understands that if Adam's sleeping, he's safe. He staggers back, falls atop his covers, is almost instantly out. When he opens his eyes again Adam's standing over him, looking blank and impatient at once.

"Get up. I'm taking you to breakfast," he says.

"Ugh, no. I can't cope with the whole DFAC thing right now."

"Good, because we're going to IHOP. How's your mental health?"

Rao rolls his eyes. "Fucking outstanding, Adam."

They perch on padded vinyl by an expanse of rain-streaked glass. Looking up from the laminated menu, Rao sees a badge on a red shirt that reads MADDY. She's tiny, with blonde hair scraped from her forehead and an expression of such obvious boredom Rao knows she's English before she opens her mouth.

"Short stack buttermilk," Adam says. "Rao?"

"Give me a sec—"

Adam gives him five. "He'll have the Split Decision Breakfast."

"It's *not* called that," Rao protests.

Maddy looks at him pityingly. "Yes, it is."

When Adam pours an obscene amount of syrup over his pancakes, Rao stares, fascinated. "Are you a bee, Adam?"

"What? Oh. No. This stuff doesn't get graded. It's not maple syrup. Just corn syrup with colour and flavouring. It's pretty bad, but some people prefer it. Reminds them of their childhoods, I guess."

"Like Angel Delight," Rao suggests.

"Sure."

"You have no idea what I'm talking about."

"No."

"Good. I shouldn't have mentioned it. State secret." Rao's rambling on autopilot watching Adam dissect his stack. The cuts he makes are neat and precise, but the quantities of syrup involved make the process of eating the result teeter on the edge of uncontrollability.

"You should eat."

Rao looks down at the food in front of him, makes a face. "I'm not hungry."

"Doesn't matter. We have a ten a.m. with Miller."

"That information is not improving my appetite."

"Eat your breakfast, Rao."

Miller doesn't ask Rao how he's feeling, which raises her greatly in his estimation. So do her earrings du jour: pink gold brilliant-cut Cartier Diamants Légers.

"Lot to get through, but I'll keep this short," she says, pulling a sheet from a file. "Straat's autopsy gives cause of death as thermal injuries from the fire. Apart from a stomach ulcer, he was in pretty good shape. There was no antemortem bruising. Which makes me think, in light of preliminary findings from Mr Gibbons—"

"He ran into the fire," Rao says and discovers it's true.

"You think? Mr Gibbons died from what's called takotsubo cardio-myopathy. I called the pathologist just now to get a clearer summary. It seems he experienced a sudden, massive surge of stress hormones that first stunned the heart then ruptured the left ventricle wall. She told me it's very rare and happens mostly in postmenopausal women. She also told me it's called broken heart syndrome."

"Ah," Rao says.

"You have a theory?" she asks.

"No, just thinking what you'll be thinking. These objects have some kind of intense attraction for some people. For Ed, it was the diner. The bonfire for Straat. Don't know what they have in common."

"They were both fifty-two-year-old white men. But that doesn't seem much of an explanation. There are a lot of those around."

"Mind-altering drugs?" Adam offers. Rao snorts. Miller shakes her head. "Toxicology came back clean. Or at least nothing they could detect."

She sits back, contemplates Adam and Rao for a while, then looks down at the watch on her wrist. Licks a thumb, rubs at its crystal face. "Everyone," she says softly, "needs this to be suicide. Unfortunately there's no evidence that Straat wanted to kill himself. So it's likely we're heading for an open verdict, which is suboptimal. There are a few financial irregularities, an ex-wife, child support. Things could pan out. Depends on the coroner. But you should both hear this. Straat's last leave is very much of interest. He spent the first twelve days of it on base. Golf. Two trips to London. Then he hopped on a transport from Mildenhall to Nellis and dropped off the map."

Adam sits up, listens intently. *No*, Rao thinks. He was doing that before. He's just somehow giving the impression he's doing it *more*.

"Phone?" Adam asks.

"Bricked. I assume a burner was in play. When he reappeared, he went around telling everyone who'd listen that he'd spent a week with friends on a camping and fishing trip in the Jarbidge Wilderness area, and he talked a lot about trout when he got back here. A lot. In a very spiritual way."

"Eventually, all things merge into one," Rao observes portentously. "And a river runs through it."

"That's not a bad Redford," she says.

"Thank you."

Adam frowns. "There wasn't a fishing trip."

She shakes her head, looks disappointed. "It was terrible cover. Fishing trips generally are. But we have a possible lead. It concerns the contents of his laptop."

Rao sits up. "You want us to watch his porn? I'll do it."

"You don't want to watch his porn, Rao. He was a commanding officer," Adam says quickly.

"Oh. Missionary only, huh?"

"Aggressively heterosexual," Miller confirms in passing. "But that's not what I meant, Rao. Straat had been in contact with a lecturer at the University of Cambridge. A Dr Katherine Caldwell. I've asked forensic IT for copies of their correspondence. Should have been here by now, but you can pick them up from"—she checks her notes—"room 26, building 832. There's not much there. I'm told it's mostly concerned with scheduling a series of telephone calls. So, I've talked to Caldwell, told her we're investigating Straat's death, exploring all avenues, and set up a meeting this afternoon. Three p.m. Go speak to her."

CHAPTER 13

He knew he would be taken to the playground after the cast came off his wrist. *It'll be good for him*, he'd heard his dad tell his mom. *Soldiers need to retrain after injury.* His mom replied that he wasn't a soldier, but it wasn't an argument. She wasn't fighting. They never fought.

Two days after his cast came off, his dad took him to a quiet playground and put him on the monkey bars. He hadn't been good at this before the break, and now he was even worse.

"What's taking you so long?" his dad asked, standing on the far side of the bars.

He hung there, pain shooting up his arm. He knew better than to show it. "It hurts."

His dad looked at him.

"It hurts, sir," he corrected.

His dad shook his head and took out a soft packet from his shirt pocket. Tapped out a cigarette. Lit it with a match as he spoke. "Pain's one of those things," he said, like everyone knew what *one of those things* was. "It's all in your mind. If it's in your mind, then you can think past it."

The whole memory is blue, like he can only see it through a thin film of grease. Like he's looking at it from far away or underwater. It feels hazy even though he can hear every single one of his father's words to him clear as a bell in his head. He'll always hear them.

He only managed to get to the third bar before it felt like progress was an impossibility. He hung there in silence, watching his dad finish his cigarette. Willing him to look over. To notice. He didn't want to say anything. He didn't want to speak first, but he had to. His dad wasn't just not noticing him. He was looking away. He didn't want to see.

"I need help," he said quietly. The pain was getting too much, and he was going to drop soon. Not that it was all that high from the monkey bars to the dust and scorched grass underneath him, but the thought of falling again so soon made his stomach feel cold.

His dad didn't look at him. He tried again.

"I need help, please." No response. He tried again, with urgency. "Sir."

His dad finally looked up. Shook his head so minutely that— Did he imagine it? It's hard to remember. He remembers the look on his father's face, even through the haze. His expression stays with him like the words.

His dad wasn't just disappointed. It was worse than that. He looked sad about being asked for help. His dad, in that moment, looked just about as helpless in disappointment as he felt on the bars.

"Help yourself," his dad said. Flicked the cigarette away. "I'll wait in the car."

It was after his dad had left him alone that his arms finally gave out. He dropped, but it wasn't as bad as when he had fallen from the tree. He didn't hurt himself. His wrist hurt again, inside, but he hadn't hurt himself.

CHAPTER 14

The rain has stopped and the sky has no colour at all. Rao sniffs the air as they walk. He can't smell kerosene in it anymore. It feels like a personal failing.

"We should do a truth run," Adam says.

"*We?*"

"You. Why haven't you?"

Rao shrugs.

"Answer the question, Rao."

"Are you pissed off with me?" Rao asks.

"I'm not pissed." Adam still sounds tired, though Rao knows he slept. "Miller's on my back. Someone's on her back, and someone else is on theirs."

"Ah, so this would be a personal favour, would it?" Rao doesn't wait for an answer. "I need a fag. You can go on if you want. I'll find the place." He halts by the corner of the accommodation block and lights up. Adam stands at ease and watches a golf buggy labouring across the green of the base course a few hundred yards away. An F-15 screams low overhead on its final approach. Rao glares at it, leans back against the wall, waits for the noise to subside.

"Look, you know they think I need a real live person to work from," he sighs. Adam isn't looking at him. His head is tilted up, watching a second Eagle coming in. "I can't just go in and give Miller the answers."

"But you can find them."

Rao nods. "Some, maybe." He drags on the cigarette he doesn't want. "Brute force it. But we'd have to keep whatever I find to ourselves, and the way I am right now, I don't know if I'll be able to do that. So I've been inclined just to follow the mood, you know? Work to rule."

Eyes still fixed on the now-empty sky, Adam's expression turns sour. "But if you'd done it before we took Ed to the—"

"Don't you *fucking dare*," Rao splutters. "You want the reason why I've not done a run? Here it is, Adam. The truth. I'm not inclined to do one because I'm not looking forward to what I'll find out. This shit isn't right. It really isn't right, and it's doing my head in."

Anger is a weakness, he remembers too late. A vulnerability. Which is why, he realises with a flush of fury, Adam must have said what he did, and *it fucking worked*. "It feels like I'm standing outside an extremely haunted house," he spits out. "And pardon me if I'm not particularly thrilled about the prospect of walking up the path and knocking on the door."

"You won't be walking in alone," Adam says.

"It's a *metaphor*, not an actual building," Rao hisses. "Not that you know much about houses, homes, or the kinds of people who might live in them, Lieutenant Colonel 'vat-grown in a government facility' Rubenstein."

"It was air force housing in Vegas."

Rao's eyes widen. "What?"

"Housing for personnel on base for a term or two. Temporary accommodation. We always stayed. My dad wasn't constantly there, obviously."

"Obviously?"

"He hated anything that wasn't work," he says tonelessly.

It sounds more like a tape recording than human speech, but—this is personal information. From Adam. Rao's astonished. He wants to know more, but he's not going to ask. No fucking way. He hates, absolutely *hates* how much he wants to. "Military workaholic, was he?" he snickers instead. "Now I see where you get it from. Like father, like son."

"Rao, could you . . ." Adam rubs both eyes, one after the other, with the heel of one hand. "Could you *not*, right now?"

Rao tosses his cigarette to the ground, grinds it beneath his heel until it's flat and frayed on the tarmac. *Fear is the mind-killer*, he thinks. He's always hated that quote. He's always hated that fucking book.

"Whatever," he mutters after a while. "I'll do you a run. When we get back from this thing."

Persuading a Cambridge college porter to open the gates to a Cambridge college car park is at least 80 percent harder than getting into GCHQ without a pass, Rao decides: it takes two minutes of crackly negotiation over the intercom and a call to Dr Caldwell before the porter admits defeat and lets them through. They follow the narrow road past a rugby pitch, park up under a bruised-looking chestnut tree. "All you need to know about Cambridge," Rao mutters, pulling his jacket tighter around himself as they walk to the Porters' Lodge, "is that it's awful. My world, Adam, for my sins, so leave this to me."

Caldwell's rooms are at the far side of a three-sided court of yellowed wisteria and honeyed stone. The outer door is open. Rao knocks, and the inner door swings wide.

"Dr Caldwell?"

"Kitty, please. Come in."

Rao stares. He'd expected a patrician, middle-aged Englishwoman in tweed, someone with whom he could forge an instant and mutual dislike. But Kitty is not that person. She's Black, has a New York accent, a soft plaid shirt, and a burnt-orange jacket, and is so instantly likable Rao's surprised to find himself vaguely cross they're not already friends. Her rooms are warm and spacious, with arched Gothic windows, oak bookcases, and—Rao's eyes widen—a flood of *things* spilling over and across shelves and tables and sills. Stacks of board games, an ant farm kit, a lava lamp, figurines and statuettes from *Star Wars*, *Spy vs. Spy*, *Mars Attacks!*, the Sinclair dinosaur, a full-size plastic Canada goose. There's a jackalope mounted on a trophy shield hanging by a Caesars Palace mirror, a pile of *National Geographic* magazines on the floor by Rao's feet, and in the far corner is a mannequin dressed as fucking late-stage Elvis.

"I was sorry to hear about what happened to Adrian," Kitty says. "I was told he was in the air force?"

"He was a master sergeant," Adam says.

"Huh. Ranked," Kitty replies, looking Adam up and down. "He always called himself Mr Straat."

"You never met?"

"Not in person. I don't think I'm going to be much help to you," she says. "And I don't have long. Thirty minutes before my next supervision. But until then, I'm all yours. Please, sit. Coffee? Tea?"

"No thank you, ma'am." Adam shakes his head. Kitty's mouth twitches momentarily before she resumes her expression of respectful solemnity.

"So." She gestures again at the brocade-covered armchair. Rao sits. "What can I tell you about him? He contacted me just over a month ago. An email, a couple of follow-ups, then a series of phone calls. I don't normally work with independent researchers, but he was an exception."

"Why?"

She looks shamefaced. "He *paid*. I'd have farmed him off to a graduate student, but he paid *well*, and I want a new kitchen."

Oh Kitty, Rao thinks. *That's not why you wanted the money.*

"What did you talk about?" Adam asks, while Rao silently determines that Kitty's screwed herself with credit card debt.

"He'd read one of my books and wanted to discuss the subject."

"Which was?"

"Nostalgia."

"Ah," Rao says. "Could you elaborate?"

Kitty shrugs, turning one hand palm up, letting her eyes close for the briefest of moments. "You could read the book."

"An executive summary would be very helpful, Dr Caldwell," Adam says.

"I was joking. I can lend you a copy, though." She looks up at the clock on the wall, her face shifting into an expression so familiar to Rao that he prickles with angry guilt at having somehow failed to write another essay. *Oh god*, he thinks, suppressing a horrified laugh. She's going to give us a tutorial.

"Do you know the history of the concept?"

"Of nostalgia? No, ma'am," Adam says.

"It was a military disease. Back in the eighteenth century, Swiss mercenaries in France and Italy started falling ill. They lost all interest in life, pined for the mountains, had hallucinations, saw ghosts."

"Ghosts," Adam repeats, so quietly it's hardly a word at all.

"A medical student called Johannes Hofer coined a term for it: 'nostalgia.' It was a kind of homesickness. From the Greek *nostos*, meaning a return to home, and *algos*, meaning—"

"Pain," Rao says.

"Yes," she says. "Or longing. Classicist?"

"Art history."

"Where?"

"St John's."

She nods, looks intrigued. "You know Tom McAlister?"

Kitty, Rao thinks. *You are sharp as a fucking knife.* "Can't recall," he says, with a moue.

She grins at him, continues. "They hit on a couple of cures. Pain and terror, that worked. Or opium." Rao glances at Adam. His face is as impassive as ever but he'll be thinking it, the fucker.

"Much later it evolved into a more Romantic concept, got tied up with nationalism." She pauses. "The problem with imagining a home you want to return to is, of course, that you tend to exclude people from it you don't want there with you." She lets that thought breathe in the open air before continuing. "Anyway. One model of nostalgia sees it as a psychological response to trauma and discontinuity. A defence mechanism. Big social changes can conjure it. Wars, revolutions, 9/11. People feel dislocated, so they conjure an imaginary past they long to return to. This fantasy place of safety. So nostalgia is emotional and psychological, but it's also political. Highly manipulatable, either politically or in the marketplace. And that's what my book's about. Specifically, on how material history and nostalgia and politics coincide." She waves her hands around the room. "All this stuff, you know?"

Rao nods, frowning. "So if nostalgia is a defence mechanism, something like a Mr. Potato Head can feel to someone like a safe refuge from harm?"

"It's complicated, and we could talk about transitional objects, but yes. There's some pretty convincing work by Starobinski and Roth on how nostalgia got privatized and internalized in the twentieth century, on how the longing for home got shrunk into the longing for one's own childhood. So childhood toys or things associated with your childhood memories tend to feature pretty high up on the list, yeah."

"Kitty, can I show you something?" Rao says, pulling a file from his bag and holding it out. "We'll get back to Straat, but I'd really value your thoughts on this collection of things."

She takes it, flicks through the photographs of the objects picked up at the base. Rao sees her linger on a toy rifle, a red velvet comforter, a plush rabbit, a rocking chair.

"Yeah," she says. "Beautifully curated. Makes me think of the Valley of Lost Things. There's a chapter called that in my book. It's a literary device, a place characters visit in stories and find all the things people have lost. These, though"—her voice turns speculative—"seem to me not so much lost things as things *made* of loss. Where are these from?"

Adam cuts in before Rao can answer. "Dr Caldwell," he says, speaking as delicately as if he were walking through a minefield, "can you tell us how an object can be made of loss?"

"I can try. Have you ever read Philip K. Dick?"

Adam nods. Rao's not proud of his surprise.

"The Man in the High Castle?"

Adam manages to smile without smiling. "Of course."

"Remember the scene where the memorabilia dealer is talking about historicity?"

"I remember it," Adam says. "Roosevelt's lighter."

She looks delighted. Then blinks rapidly. "Sorry," she says to Rao— and isn't. "It's a wonderful scene. The novel is set in an alternate universe where the Nazis won the war. A memorabilia dealer shows someone two lighters. One was in Roosevelt's pocket when he was assassinated, so it's worth a fortune. The other one wasn't, so it's not worth anything. The dealer points out that you can't tell them apart. There's no mystical aura; you can't detect which is which. It's impossible. *The* line comes later in this scene, when the dealer talks about a gun that's been in a famous battle. He says it's just the same as if it hadn't, unless you know it has been through the battle." She taps her head. "It's in the mind, not the gun."

"Not entirely," Rao says.

Adam's expression shifts to solid, Rao-directed remonstration.

"Well, that's a position," Caldwell says.

"It is," Rao agrees, scratching his beard. "Ignore it. I get carried away, sometimes. Devil's advocate, terrible habit. And I hate to interrupt," he lies, "but time's marching on. I'll be happy to give Adam the rest of his Semiotics 101 later. Can we get back to Straat? What did he want to know, specifically?"

"To begin with, he kept asking me about the neurological basis of the nostalgic experience," Kitty answers. "I told him I was the wrong person for that. We talked some more, and then he wanted to know about how loss and nostalgia relate to homesickness. There was a lot of general discussion, we had two hour-long calls, but it seemed to narrow down, for him, to the question of whether people who are geographically far from home experience nostalgia in a different way."

"Do they?"

She shrugs gracefully once more, an upturned palm. "Depends. First-generation immigrants often refuse nostalgia completely. Second-generation sometimes get lost in it. Imagined homes, imagined places can have a power far greater than real ones."

"Like an imaginary American diner?"

She looks at Rao closely. "That's a very specific example."

"It is."

Adam speaks up. "Do you know why he was asking you these questions?"

"No. He just said he was interested in the subject."

"Did anything he said suggest a motive to you?"

"Nothing I can remember. I'll let you know if I do. Is there a way to contact you if I think of anything else?"

Adam gives her his phone number. She gets up, walks to a bookcase, pulls out a book. "Here. Keep it as long as you need. This conversation hasn't been what I expected, and I've got a feeling I'll be seeing you again."

Adam's deep in thought as they walk back to the vehicle. "What was all that about Tom McAlister?" he asks, eyes on the worn flagstones beneath his feet.

"Yeah, I couldn't believe that. She's fucking on the ball, Kitty is."

"Who is he?"

"Oh. History professor. Talent spotter. Not me, obviously, he wouldn't have touched me with a barge pole. They sent someone else for that when I was at Sotheby's. Apparently one of my cousins-in-law got expansive after three bottles of Lynch-Bages at one of those dreadful dinner parties in Chipping Norton and told everyone at the table I had this miraculous ability to detect fakes and frauds. Word got out, and after a while Morten Edwards appeared. Blond with a deep Welsh accent and a spectacular suit. Came in asking me to authenticate a Sebastiano. You know him, for fuck's sake. He was in that meeting, the first one."

"I didn't know he was Welsh."

CHAPTER 15

Before

You can get a lot about a person from how they present themselves. Sunil Rao was the type of mess he'd seen a bunch of times before in cryptanalysts. Guys like that get cut a lot of slack because of what they can do. They push back. Make a point of it. The file he'd been given suggested Sunil Rao wouldn't be easy to handle. The meeting confirmed it. Rao talked incessantly, told unrelated anecdotes and jokes. The jokes were pretty funny, considering, but wildly inappropriate in context. Adam quickly put most of this down to him having taken some kind of stimulant. His pupils were dilated and he found it hard to sit still, kept brushing the arm of his chair with his palms, drumming the desk with his fingers. Half an hour in he took out some gum and chewed it for so long and so energetically Adam's own jaw started to feel uncomfortable.

After the meeting, Rao came up and told him, conspiratorially, that he didn't have to believe all the stuff in his file.

"I have to take it on trust," Adam replied.

Rao laughed. "Trust, yeah. Very, very important concept, Adam."

"It is, Mr. Rao."

"So it's very important, you know, you don't lie to me."

Adam blinked. "I don't intend to."

"Good. Good. How old are you?"

"Thirty-five."

Rao shook his head in wonderment. "Fucking hell. Have you been to London before?"

"Yes."

"Are you in London now?"

Adam frowned. "I am."

"Am I?"

He hadn't answered that, just stared at Rao, and Rao had laughed, high and hysterical. Which was when Adam reassessed his previous assessment. Slotted this operation into the category *potentially very difficult.*

It was, and it wasn't.

Several weeks in the field proved Rao was as chaotic and uncontrolled as Adam had predicted. He waved his arms a lot, scratched his head compulsively. Always laughed at his own jokes. It always looked like he was wearing someone else's clothes. He was uncomfortable with silence. Had to fill it with words, hummed tunes, snapping fingers. And there was a degree of oppositional behavior. It wasn't directed at Adam, but sometimes that made it worse.

Operationally, however, he was superb. First, he was a natural at soft interrogation. It was fun to watch how quickly people trusted him who shouldn't. Adam knew the mechanics, but there was more to it than tone, word choice, body language. There was something intangible involved, a form of *Fingerspitzengefühl* that couldn't be learned if you didn't already have it. Adam never had. Second, Rao's Russian was flawless, and from the pace of the conversations he heard, his Uzbek nowhere near as bad as Rao insisted. Third, no matter how much vodka he'd drunk, Rao's reports were admirably clear and concise. One evening, Rao had told him the trick, smugly tapping one temple. "I'm cursed," he'd said. "With perfect recall and a photographic memory. It's *awful.*"

Most of all, Adam had been impressed by Rao's specialism.

They'd informed him Rao worked like a polygraph, but his numbers were better, said he was near infallible. Which sounded bullshit. Predictable bullshit: Adam had long been entertained by how much of a hard-on certain sectors had for supernatural intel. It'd be so much cheaper, if they could ever get it to work. They never could. Like those phonies holding their temples in Fort Meade back in the sixties, trying to put Soviet missile silos on bits of unexposed film.

But the evidence stacked up, day by day, and eventually Adam couldn't deny it. Rao could tell when assets were lying, when DOD personnel and embassy staff were lying. Waiters, taxi drivers, receptionists, anyone. But maybe he needed to concentrate to do it, because he wasn't infallible, and it wasn't all the time. Adam had lied to Rao a bunch of times and he hadn't seemed to notice.

On a Bukhara backstreet, listening to Rao complaining bitterly about how some cruel fluke of fate had deprived him of the excellent driving skills that everyone else in his family possessed, Adam tested him again. Informed him, deadpan, that their vehicle had gone.

"Gone? As in stolen? Shit. Shit. This isn't good. What are we going to do? We have to be on the road in—" Rao stopped, then glared. "You're fucking with me."

"I am."

Adam was very familiar with the kind of person who could dish it out and not take it. He hadn't thought Rao was among their number, but he must have been wrong, because Rao was suddenly furious.

"You're just another tool in the kit, is it?" he spat out.

"What?"

"I just can't tell how you're doing it, that's all. I need to know."

"Years of training in marksmanship, close quarters, and hand to hand?"

"No, not the creepy stalker hit man stuff."

"I'm not—"

"How are you doing it?"

"Rao, I'm afraid I'm going to have to ask you to talk in full, complete sentences. Please attach as much information to these sentences as you can."

"Get fucked," Rao said. "Seriously."

CHAPTER 16

"What culinary delights are the American air force offering us this evening, Adam?"

"Specialty oatmeal night."

"What? Is that a— Oh fuck off." Rao squints at the DFAC menu on the wall. "What the shit is turkey spaghetti?"

"What it says," Adam says, pulling a tray and walking down the line.

"BBQ Beef Cubes?!" Rao calls after him. He opts for fish and chips, dumped on his plate by a server with a fixed smile and doubtful eyes. Rao smiles back. *Good evening to you too*, he thinks. He likes his terrorist beard. He's not shaving it off. He looks over to Adam. He's sorted himself a plate of mac and cheese. If he didn't know Adam, he'd assume it was comfort food. They sit. Rao forks up some chips.

"This place is like the diner," he observes. Adam looks up, alarmed. "Not like that," Rao says, gesturing at the faux-Tudor beams, the tabard-wearing mannequin, the heraldic shields on the walls. "It's Olde England. Like those American movies from the 1950s, you know. *Robin Hood. The Flame and the Arrow.* Old America's version of Old England. The thing being that it feels fake, but actually . . ."

Adam's still not eating, is waiting for him to finish, and Rao's already tired of what he's saying. He's relieved when Adam starts chowing down again, having evidently decided that none of what Rao's saying is operationally relevant. It's his usual metric, one that means that most of what Rao says most of the time can be safely disregarded.

"Hm," Rao grunts. "What's on the docket for the rest of the day?"

"No more meetings."

"Thank fuck."

Twenty seconds later Miller appears in the room, catches sight of them, walks over. Rao mouths "meeting" at Adam, gets a flicker of irritation that's sufficient to count as a win.

Miller politely asks the airmen sitting with them to fuck off, then sits. "How did it go?" she enquires.

"Caldwell doesn't know anything," Adam says. "Their discussions were on the subject of nostalgia and homesickness. She says she'll contact us if she recalls anything that might relate to the reason behind Straat's interest. And she's loaned us a book she wrote on nostalgia. Rao's going to read it."

"Good. Rao, let me know if it's useful. I'm sorry to disturb you both while you're eating, but this is new." Miller slides a photograph across the table. "It was found in the fire. It was missed in the initial search." She glances at Adam. He blinks, nods minutely.

Rao puts his cutlery down, wipes his hands on his trousers, pulls the photograph towards him. It shows a small, scorched, broken glass vial by a millimetre scale, the label curled and burned.

"What was in it?" he asks, handing it to Adam.

"We don't know. It's gone to the lab."

"Anything on the label?" Rao asks.

"A few letters. An *e* and an *o*. Possibly a *p*. We'll run the ink, too, but there's no reason to think it's anything other than a standard label."

"Except it being found at the site of a master sergeant's self-immolation."

"That doesn't mean the label ink is going to be unusual," Adam says.

Rao gives him a weary look. "No, it doesn't."

After dinner they make a detour to the base food court Starbucks, where Rao loads a venti Pumpkin Spice Latte with shedloads of nutmeg and cinnamon. Back in the room, he sets the cup on the table. Places the photograph next to it. Picks up a legal pad and a pen, hands them to Adam, sits.

"Right, let's do this, Adamski. Truth run time. Can you keep tabs?" Adam nods, pulls up a chair.

Rao takes a breath. "Straat was murdered." He shakes his head. "Straat's death was accidental," he says. "Ok, that's true. Straat brought the vial to the base. *True*. The substance in the vial was involved in the appearance of these objects on the base," he says. "*True*. Humans were involved in the appearance of these objects on the base. *True*."

"Not aliens?"

"Shut up, Adam. The substance in the vial created these objects. *Unclear*. How about . . . people created these objects. *Unclear*." He tries again, selecting his words with more care. "Exposing people to the substance in the vial caused the objects to appear. *True*."

He sits for a moment. "The fuck is this stuff?"

Adam's dark eyes are on his, expecting the truth of what this is, if Rao can reach it. For the benefit of the American government. Does Adam see Rao as anything more than a sentient ticker tape spooling out intel? Times like these, he's not sure.

"I don't know," Adam says.

"That was a rhetorical question," Rao snaps. "But thank you for your contribution." He shakes his head, goes on. "The substance was in the smoke from the bonfire. *True*. The objects that appeared around the base were a consequence of people inhaling the substance in the smoke. *True*."

He's quiet for a while.

"How did—"

Rao waves a hand in dismissal. "I'm thinking."

"A single person was involved in the creation of each object. *True*. These objects contain the substance. *False*."

He breathes in, breathes out. "Ok. The objects are . . . memories. Ugh. Not quite. *Maybe*. The objects have psychological significance to the individuals who created them. *True*. The significance of the objects is related to safety. *True*. The significance of the objects is related to a sense of refuge. *True*."

"Can I ask something, Rao?"

"What?"

"Caldwell said that nostalgia was a kind of knee-jerk response to psychic trauma."

"She didn't say knee-jerk, Adam, or psychic trauma, but good point. How about this: the substance causes psychic trauma to people exposed to it. *True.* That's a definite yes. The effect of the psychic trauma is to make people nostalgic." He tilts his head, listens. That one is a very near truth that isn't quite the right shape, exerts a pressure like the feeling in his sinuses when a plane ascends, and he's still not sure why his brain thinks that listening will take him any closer when this occurs. It never does. He thinks the word "nostalgia" isn't the right one. But it's close enough. He's going to put that one down as true.

Vagueness and indeterminacy are sensations that Rao can worry at until they scratch at him unpleasantly, even when he knows that a statement he generates can't be reduced to truth or falsehood. On a run like this, he constantly falls into the trap of convincing himself that truths can always be found if he could just find the right way to ask for them. The longer a run goes on, the more he feels that his questions aren't precise enough, that the words he's choosing are the wrong ones. Sometimes he'll slip into Russian or Hindi or Dundhari, Spanish or French. Not because words in those languages connect more accurately with reality but because the sentences are angled differently, are new ways to engage with it.

Truth runs are always exhausting. He knows that someone brighter than him—someone with a clearer mind—could do them better. They always remind him of his inadequacies. They make him tired and frustrated. They make him hate himself. Right now he knows he's too much of a mess to go much further. Has a good idea where he'll end up if he does, and then he'll be no good to anyone.

He stretches, runs both hands savagely through his hair. "This is hard. It's a conceptual minefield and right now I'm too freaked out to think clearly. Let's get back to it in a bit. I'll take a look at the vial instead." He takes three long gulps of tepid coffee, leans to squint at the burned label in the photograph, mutters under his breath. "Two words," he says. "This could take a while. You can go and lie down or have a wank or whatever. Chuck me that paper and pen?" Adam hands them to him, then sits back, starts doing the expressionless sniper thing, behaving like he's not really there. It's one of Adam's specialities, making himself unremarkable to the point of invisibility even when someone's looking right at him. It should be infuriating, but it's surprisingly easy to ignore. Rao supposes that's the point.

It doesn't take long. Six minutes later he takes a fresh sheet, scrawls on it, pushes it across the table to Adam.

EOS PROPHET

"Shit," Adam breathes. Rao, fascinated, watches his face drain of all colour.

"The fuck, Adam. You look like you've just read your own death sentence. What is it?"

Adam's throat works a couple of times. "Us," he says eventually.

"What d'you mean, 'us'?"

"Sounds like a project nickname."

"A nickname?"

"That's the correct term."

"Correct for who?"

"Defense."

"So it's a military project. Can't you look it up, find out what it is?"

Adam meets his eyes.

"Ok, so it's a black project."

"Likely an SAP, yes."

"In English, love?"

"Special Access Program. There are," he goes on, speaking quietly and more hesitantly than Rao's ever heard him before, "various different categories of classified initiatives."

"Well, shall we find out what kind this is?"

Adam doesn't respond for a long while. Then he nods. "Worst case, this could be an unacknowledged Special Access Program."

Rao tests the supposition, nods.

"Yeah, that's what it is."

"Fuck."

Another long silence.

"Does Miller know?"

Rao whispers under his breath, shakes his head. "She hasn't a clue. Well. Isn't this exciting. Make yourself some coffee. I'll keep going."

"No, you won't. You'll stop right now."

"The fuck?"

"An unacknowledged SAP is a world of shit. The ramifications aren't pretty. I need time to think."

"Knowing more about what it is isn't going to stop you thinking, Adam."

"It might, Rao."

It's late. Rao is asleep, and Rao is dreaming. It's the usual dream, and it starts in the usual place, just outside the door of his great-uncle's business room back in the big house in Jaipur. The dream is a memory. In it, he's small and uncomfortably full of dinner. It's getting towards bedtime and this summons is unexpected. He's not been allowed into this room before, though he's sneaked in a few times just to thrill in the agony that someone might catch him. It's a dark room, the windows always half shuttered, and it smells of pomade and jasmine and, on one of his secret visits, strongly of perfume. It must have been a visitor's perfume because these rooms are where people come to buy things. Not the kind of people who go to the showroom but people who are very famous or very rich. That's what his father had said. And it was true. He'd even seen a man come out of the room once that he'd seen twice before, not in real life, but on the big screen at the Raj Mandir.

He knocks on the door and a voice behind it tells him to come in. The bottom of the door brushes a little against the rug as it swings. He approaches the desk where his great-uncle sits. He is as stern as usual, his collar buttoned tight. And his father is there too, sitting this side of the desk, which is a relief, but the atmosphere is forbidding, like it always is when his great-uncle is there. His father is smoking a cigarette, and Rao stands there watching the smoke climb through shafts of setting sunlight that have come through the bottom of the blinds. He can hear pigeons cooing just outside the window, traffic. He's worried. Has he done something? He must have done something to be called in here. He can't think of any particular thing he's done of late that would mean a big punishment, and he doesn't forget things. Sometimes he doesn't know that what he is doing is bad, that's true. But still he can't think of what it could be.

Then his father smiles at him, so he knows he is not in trouble. But the smile is odd, like his father's worried. Rao feels a new tug of anxiety. Maybe he's not doing this right. He links his hands behind his back and stands even taller.

His father nods at his great-uncle, and then turns and spreads three padded trays across the mahogany desk. They're display trays, like the ones in the showroom in the city. They're full of assorted jewellery, which is strange, because usually, he knows, they are all one thing. All rings, or all bracelets, or one kind of other thing.

Then his father turns back to Rao, his face very serious. His voice is low. Almost a whisper.

"Which, would you say, is the most interesting of these, Sunil?" he says.

Rao's not sure what he means. He thinks he should be, but he isn't. He whispers back. "You mean beautiful, papaji?"

"They are all beautiful in their different ways. I mean, which is the most interesting because it is different?"

Sunil nods. Points. It's easy. There it is, on the second tray, a sapphire pendant whose gleaming stone isn't a sapphire at all.

"This one?"

He nods. And he sees, then, his father and great-uncle trade a significant look. He didn't know what it meant back then, but in these dreams he does, because that was the moment they discovered that Rao could ascertain fakes by sight alone, and things after it were not the same as they had been. Which is why, Rao presumes, he has this dream a lot. Sometimes he knows he's having it, is aware and lucid inside it. When that happens, he always tries to point to a different jewel, but the dream never lets him. It's a horrible feeling, his inability to change the narrative. The dream runs always like the dream always runs.

But this time it doesn't. This time the dream veers off its usual course. Instead of nodding gravely, his uncle laughs. Hearing it, seeing him do it, is a shock. So much so, Rao wakes, all his senses tingling. The whole dream felt far more real than usual. He feels like he's just been dragged back here from thirty years ago. Then he hears a low murmuring from the room next door. Adam. Adam's talking. He must be on a call. And then, blinking in the dark, Rao hears it again. It's not his uncle. It's Adam. Adam is *laughing*.

CHAPTER 17

"What's this?"

His dad kicks the box across the floor to him as he walks into his room. He winces because the impact could knock the optics out of alignment, maybe break the lenses. That's his first thought: the telescope, the impact of his dad's foot. Then he catches up with the scene.

There are worse ways to find out his dad searches his room.

"It's a telescope," he answers.

The telescope was his. It was his before he bought it. It was his the second he saw it in the faded print of the mail-order catalog. It was his the entire time he was saving for it. He mowed lawns. He did extra chores for his mom. He stood dutifully nearby while his dad worked on the RV, ready to pass whatever tool he needed. He spent so long outside doing things, working, finding chores and little jobs that his mom told him he was getting a tan just like normal kids.

His parents never asked why he wanted to work so hard for the money. They were distracted, he supposed, by the work ethic. That was the most important thing to them. He was showing dedication to something, putting in the time, and he wasn't complaining about the tasks they laid out for him. All that showed something. Character, probably.

He'd ordered the telescope when his dad was out of town. It wasn't planned, but it was better that way. He didn't want to answer any questions, like *Why a telescope?*

Why *not* a telescope?

When it arrived, the box was a lot larger than he thought it would be. His mom stood on the porch with him, both of them staring at it.

"Did you tell your father that you were spending your money on something big?"

Of course he hadn't. He should have. His aunt liked to say it was better to beg forgiveness than to ask permission, but she never sought either from his dad. The former was infinitely worse to beg for than the latter.

"It'll fit under your bed," his mom said. Looked at him evenly as she lit a cigarette with a match. "But I don't know when you'll get to use it."

"I'll figure it out," he told her. Sounded like he believed himself.

"Good."

He figured it out. He got to use the telescope twice while his dad was away. His eyes watered the first time he used it, which messed with his ability to focus. He was crying, but somehow that wasn't bad. There was so much more above him than he'd expected. It wasn't even the stars, more the darkness between them. Looking up there, seeing what there was, it made the band around his chest go away. Felt like being lost, but somewhere he wanted to be.

"That's a telescope," he answers.

"Don't give me back talk."

Back talk is answering questions when he isn't supposed to, or knowing things too early, before his dad has a chance to teach them to him, or not wanting to do something his dad wants to do, or wanting to do something his dad doesn't. Back talk is saying anything that isn't right. He's usually smarter than this, usually knows to shut up when he's asked a question, especially when his dad is this mad. Why is he so mad?

"Who gave you this?"

He waits. Doesn't answer right away. Isn't going to be stupid again. Opens his mouth only after his dad gives him a nod, a go-ahead. "I bought it myself."

"With what money?"

"I worked for the money, sir."

They look at each other. He watches his father remember. He'd pressed bills into his son's hand. Hadn't thought about it at the time.

"Why are you hiding it?" his dad asks.

Good question. Because his mom told him to. Because he was scared about asking for permission and terrified to beg for forgiveness. Because he'd wanted to avoid this anger that came from nowhere and made no sense.

He doesn't have an answer to give his dad. That's enough.

"I hope it wasn't expensive," his dad says, picking up the box like it weighs nothing. "No one hides anything from me in my own house. Do you understand?"

"Yes, sir."

They look at each other again. A beat of silence. An unasked question.

"The searches are random," his dad tells him on the way out of the room with his telescope under his arm. "No secrets from me in my home. I'll always know."

A threat, a simple fact. Flat and absolute. He'll always know.

CHAPTER 18

Back at IHOP for breakfast, Adam's pouring coffee in a peculiarly talkative mood. "Do you know why IHOPs keep a pot of coffee on every table?"

"I see you're making conversation, Adam."

"So you don't."

"Come on then, out with it."

Adam tears open a pot of vanilla creamer, dumps it into a mug, inspects the result, adds another. "Back in the fifties, there was a guy making films for the Federal Civil Defense Administration about surviving atomic attacks. Logistics, delivering essential emergency provisions. Coffee was one of the necessities. He got thinking and it ended up with him opening this place." He pushes the mug across to Rao.

"Huh," Rao says, picking up a sachet of sugar. "That can't possibly be true." *It is.* "Are you working right now, Adam?"

Adam regards him blankly. "I'm talking to you, so yes."

Rao taps the sachet and tilts his head to watch the sugar fall. "No, besides all this. Are you on a job? Go on, tell me. I can help."

"If I were, then you might help. That's true. But I'm not."

"So what was all that last night?" Rao says, stirring.

"Elaborate," Adam says.

"All that laughing at two a.m. I heard you, Adam, so you can stop lying to me."

"Laughter proves that I'm working because . . . ?"

"Because you don't have any friends."

Adam shakes his head. "I have friends, Rao."

"With a sense of humour?"

"Some of them. This one does."

"So what does this funny friend do?"

"Combat controller."

"What's that?" Rao knows what a combat controller is, but there's no satisfaction in admitting it. There is considerable satisfaction, however, in the precise and irritated diction of Adam's reply. "AFSO CCs are the MVPs in pretty much any theatre. Their training's the most rigorous in existence. The instructors spend fifteen weeks pretty much trying to kill the recruits. They use CS gas for negative reinforcement. The washout rate's over eighty percent. Survive that and you're the best. Period."

"Better than the SAS?"

Adam stirs his coffee. "Yes, Rao."

Rao narrows his eyes, recalling all the times he's heard the USAF dismissed as the lamest branch of the American military. Decides not to raise this particular point with Adam. It never goes down well. "So who is this guy?" he asks.

Adam rolls his eyes. "She's not a guy."

"Well fucking *sorry* for not working out that this friend is a woman. You can't tell me that's a piece that fits in the grand puzzle of Lieutenant Colonel Fucking Rubenstein."

"Explain your logic."

"Don't women hate you?"

Adam twitches his lips. "No, women don't hate me. Everyone dislikes me. There's a subtle difference."

"So what's this guy who's not a guy's story?"

Adam drinks his coffee, considers. "We go back a long way. She's just back stateside."

"From where?"

"Afghanistan."

"And what was she doing over there?"

"Rao. I wouldn't tell you even if I had the specifics."

Rao waves vaguely. "Not specifically. *Generally.*"

"CCs are attached to special ops," Adam explains. "Delta, SAS, all sorts. They do everything special ops do and simultaneously provide terminal guidance and control for fire support."

"So your not-guy calls in air strikes."

"She directs air traffic for that purpose and others." The fondness in his face shifts to something nearer awe. "The role's complex as hell, Rao. Like playing chess, only—"

"Yeah, yeah." Rao cuts Adam short. "So she's an air traffic controller."

"She's qualified, yes."

"What's her name?"

"Hunter."

"Just Hunter?"

"Hunter Wood."

"Like Dr. Quinn, Medicine Woman."

"Rao."

"Hunter Wood, ATC."

"You don't want to call her that."

"If I ever meet her, I will certainly be calling her that."

Adam's eyebrows rise. "Your funeral. She's a master sergeant. She called because a guy who went through training with her has gone AWOL."

"That's what Special Forces do, Adam. They disappear. Like we need more problems right now. Your friend's mate vanishing has nothing to do with what we're working on." He feels his jaw drop, slack. "What's his name?"

Adam narrows his eyes. "Why do you need to—"

"Humour me."

"Flores. Danny Flores."

"The disappearance of Danny Flores is related to the substance in the vial. *Shit*. Adam."

Outside Miller's office, Adam gives Rao a warning look that resembles a straight razor made into a facial expression. Rao sighs, lifts his eyes to the ceiling.

"I've been briefed on the matter of deniability, love. Extensively, by you. I won't mention the thing."

"Because it's crucial that you don't."

"You've made that exceedingly clear. Stop nagging."

Miller's arms are crossed. Her perfectly annealed surface manner is intact, but her hair is a little wild and there's a chaotic intensity to her stare that makes Rao suspect she's about three seconds from imploding.

"How are you?" Rao says, with genuine concern.

"I'm good."

"No, but really," he insists.

"It's nice of you to ask," she says, surprised. "I'm quite tired, Rao. But things are getting done. You have an update?"

"No. A theory. And it's going to sound insane."

She looks at Adam. He looks back. What passes between them is opaque. She turns her eyes to Rao. Periwinkle blue, the faintest shadow above their upper lashes. *Such a striking colour,* Rao thinks. Evening sky. They're wonderful. He watches them narrow.

"Try me," she says.

"Right. Ok. Yes. So, I think the substance in that vial got into people and made them create the objects."

"Create them?"

"Yeah, I know. The physics makes no sense at all. But it fits. Look, let's say Straat was carrying the vial, brought it back from his covert holiday, and it breaks by mistake. He gets contaminated and creates the bonfire. Right in front of him. Runs straight into it."

"But—"

"Like I said, it makes no sense. Bear with me. The substance in the vial boils off, gets carried in the smoke. Ed gets a huge hit, makes the diner. A way away, for some reason. Then the smoke drifted downwind—"

To his surprise, Miller nods, finishes his sentence. "Base personnel breathed it in, and they"—she flexes her fingers in front of her—"*made* everything else we found. The dolls, that theatre ticket, the board games."

"Exactly."

"Which is why the objects seem wrong to you."

Rao makes a face. "It's the best word to describe what they are. 'Fake' isn't right. They just don't have histories." He scratches his beard, rubs his knuckles over his mouth, decides to go for it. "I think they're made out of feelings. Not memories, though memory is part of what they are. They're constructions. A blend of things. Like the diner, right? Ed made that out of things he felt should be in a diner, how he felt a diner should look and feel and smell. It isn't a memory of any particular diner he's visited or seen. But it has absolute phenomenological fidelity to what diners are in Ed's mind. So there's no way of making coffee in that place because that wasn't relevant to him. The coffee was, though. He didn't think of toilets when he made his diner, so they're not there."

Adam nods. "Same with the Scrabble box and the roses."

"Exactly." Rao lets out a long breath and wishes he'd not used the word "phenomenological." "And I'd keep people away from that storeroom."

Miller stares at the desk for a while. "Well, boys," she says, finally, with a weak smile. "This isn't the working hypothesis I'd hoped for." Again, she wipes at the face of her watch with a thumb. It's one of the most delightful tells Rao has ever seen. "You know there's a department that deals with stuff like this?"

Rao's eyes widen. "There's a real *X-Files*?"

"Mulder wouldn't last a week. The Extranatural Incident Office employs actual professionals, Rao. But yes. Turning it over to them might be inevitable. But . . ."

"They're assholes?"

"Legendarily so. I wonder if we could—"

"We have a lead," Adam cuts in.

"What is it?"

"Sensitive source. At present, I'm not in a position to—"

"Rubenstein," she says warningly.

"Allow it," Rao says. "If we can wrap this up for you, you can present it as a fait accompli to Mulder and Scully."

"To the EIO. Are you trading on my professional ambitions, Rao?"

"He's not, ma'am," Adam says.

"I totally am, Adam."

"So what *can* you tell me?" Miller asks.

"We need to be in Colorado ASAP. There's a transport to Peterson tomorrow. Can you authorize?"

She looks at them both for a long second. "I'll need to speak to the UK authorities to take the flag off Rao's passport. I'll action that now."

"You have my passport?"

"We have your passport. How long will you need over there?"

"Fuck knows," Rao says. "But Adam'll give you as many sitreps as you need."

Miller closes her eyes briefly. "Don't make me regret this, Rubenstein."

"No, ma'am," Adam answers.

"Rao, go and pack. I need a word with your partner."

Rao hangs around outside. When Adam emerges a few minutes later, Rao's surprised to see him looking almost cheerful. "Adam, she *said it*," he hisses.

"Said what?"

"'Don't make me regret this.' I thought that was only in movies."

"It's not only in movies."

"So? What did she say?"

That's definitely amusement in Adam's eyes.

"A few things. She was very clear on one matter. She says I have to keep you safe."

"Well, listen to her, Adam."

"I'm thinking about it, Rao."

Rao stomps his feet beside his loaned kit bag and swears in several languages, breath clouding the air. The morning smells metallic, like snow or blood, and despite his numb fingers and toes, he feels a shiver of grudging delight. Last night's freezing fog transformed the base into Fairyland. Fence wires, asphalt, spiders' webs, the leaves of the car park shrubs—all are furred with delicate, geometric threads of frost. He rubs his fingers across the top of the bollard by his side, watches the crystals melt away in front of his eyes.

When their car draws up, he and Adam stow their bags and are driven to Mildenhall in silence. Twenty minutes later, he's trying to place the atmosphere inside the passenger terminal as he thaws. Decides it's a late-night Walmart, maybe a haunted parking garage. The floor is so highly polished he jumps when he glances down at check-in and makes eye contact with his own reflection. Leaving Adam at the desk, he wanders off to find a seat, stopping to stare at a flowerbed tucked under a staircase: fleshy houseplants bordered by the fakest fake rocks he's ever seen, amateur dramatic props in a village hall production of *Dracula*. He finds a bank of five chairs already occupied by an older couple, sits.

"Hi," he says. She has an ash-blonde bob, a cream gilet, pearl-templed rimless varifocals. He's bulky with a thick neck, a brown cowhide jacket, an Omega Seamaster, a copy of *Newsweek* folded in one hand. All-American. Apple pie. "You off on vacation?" he asks.

"Kind of," she answers hesitantly. "We're visiting our son." Their son is called Gary, she explains, a first-class cadet at the Air Force Academy majoring in space operations. They're an air force family, he says, and Gary makes them very proud. Rao knows a thing or two about family traditions, says a few words about carrying on legacies. She beams at him.

"Rao," he says, extending a hand.

"Heather," she says, shaking it. "This is my husband, Bill."

A photo is pulled from a wallet, passed across.

"Looks like he's born to it," Rao says.

Bill nods. "He loves it there. Duck to water. So what takes you to CONUS?"

"Work," Rao says with a significant wink.

"Ah," he says, pleased. "Good for you."

Adam reappears, looking askance at them all. "Also," Rao announces, "I'm going to meet my friend here's girlfriend for the first time, which will be nice."

Adam hands him a bulky puffer jacket. "Showtime," he says, ignoring Heather and Bill. "You'll need this. C-17s get cold at thirty thousand feet."

CHAPTER 19

Before

Adam cursed under his breath as he drove back to their Tashkent hotel. The last thing he needed was a stop from Uzbek police at two in the morning with a bloodied and bruised man in the back of the vehicle. Keeping to backstreets, he recalled what had happened at the end of that first London meeting, just after Rao had left the room.

"So," Morten Edwards had said to him, not quite making eye contact, "that's Rao. There's something you should know about him, and I thought it might be politic to wait until he was out of the room before discussing it."

"The drinking?"

"Well, there is that, yes." An awkward smile. "But that doesn't affect his particular skills, so we don't worry too much about that side of things. It's more that Rao's a little"—Edwards hesitated—"I suppose you might call him punch-happy. Fighting's fighting, as I'm sure you know, but we really don't want any trouble on the books. So if you could keep an eye on him, don't let it get too out of hand, we'd really appreciate it."

Adam nodded. Sunil Rao was a savant with an attitude problem. He had to keep him clean without losing him. Sounded about right.

"Understood," he answered.

Rao got into a fight three days after they arrived in Uzbekistan. Adam didn't catch what Rao said to the guy who punched him, but he'd obviously earned it, already bloody-mouthed, swaying, drunk in his chair. Adam considered stepping in immediately, but he'd wanted a fuller understanding of what this was. Why start a fight at all?

———

Rao stayed upright. Impressive. Sometimes he was on his feet, sometimes fallen back onto his seat, but he took every blow like he didn't feel it. He ended up laughing at the big guy he'd chosen to fuck with, out of breath and frustrated by Rao's passivity.

Adam didn't get it. He didn't even really have to break up the so-called fight; mostly he just pushed past the guy beating bruises into Rao and called it. "Whatever he said to you, he's sorry," Adam informed him. Rao laughed at that, high and wet, continued laughing as Adam dragged him away from the bar.

Adam didn't see the next fight. Rao had sneaked out late one evening. Impressive again. Not many people would have been able to get away from under Adam's nose like that. He got a call from a dive twenty minutes from their hotel. The bar was a bitch to find. He parked two blocks away, followed the smell of shashlik smoke and rowdy Russian voices. Found Rao laughing, bleeding freely, sitting in the dirt outside. "There he is!" Rao shouted, pointing at him as he approached. He took a breath and looked at his partner. He could have done a better job than this. He'd been told Rao liked to look for trouble, and he'd known what that meant. But over the years, Adam had learned not to care about all this. If someone was going to get their ass kicked, and if Adam wasn't doing the actual kicking, it really shouldn't involve him at all. It was very rare he'd been told outright to stop it from happening, however. He definitely could have done better.

He sat on the curb next to Rao. "Bored, huh?"

Rao dabbed at his split lip, examined the blood on his fingers. "Let me ask you something, Adam," he said, tonguing at the wound as he spoke, sounding close to laughter with every word. Adam suspected he was high as well as drunk, but in this light—two strings of dim light bulbs between the front of the bar and a tree—Adam couldn't see his pupils clearly enough to tell. "You don't really talk to people."

"That's not a question," Adam replied.

Rao laughed, a little hysterically. "That's *true*, isn't it?"

"It's true you didn't ask me a question," Adam observed. "And it's true that I don't talk to many people. We're working, as you know, and considering my role, contacts are limited."

"That's the most you've said since we've met," Rao pointed out.

Adam had never known how to respond when people told him things like that. *Is it everything you hoped for?* Too sarcastic. *That's factually accurate.* Too cold. "Mm," he said.

Rao considered Adam through the eye he could still open. "You don't say fuck all to anyone, and that's how you block them out," he continued. Adam was struck by how clear and cutting Rao's speech was. No trace of slurring at all. This could be a learned skill or just a natural one, he mused, if it could be called a skill at all. "We all have our things, yeah? Yours is being a dickhead."

"That's my thing, huh?" Adam sighed, pulling Rao's arm around his shoulder.

"Yeah. Your armour," Rao insisted, doing his best to stand as Adam pulled him up. "Yours. This is mine."

Adam didn't follow this reasoning. He considered the merits of continuing with this conversation. If he understood Rao's justification for finding his way into fights, he might be able to predict his moods. Good enough.

"Getting pummeled every other night isn't the best armor, Rao."

"Depends, doesn't it? Whether the armor's to protect or whether it's there to block," Rao answered, chuckling low and thick like he had a bubble in his throat, but at least the hysteria was gone. Adam made a mental note to check for bruising around Rao's neck when they were back at the hotel.

"You're precise with your words when you want to be," Adam observed. He'd known for a while that Rao preferred statements to questions. It didn't matter if he was doing his focused shit on them or not. He liked statements. Facts. Liked having them in the air. Adam supposed that it was something they had in common.

Rao raised a hand. "Precision, love, always throws people off. You've noticed that, surely? I reckon you notice a lot of things." He tried to waggle his fingers. It was probably meant to be a playful gesture, but the attempt failed. He grimaced and aborted the action. *Funny*, Adam thought and didn't laugh. The whole night was sort of funny in its own way, in the Rao way, which was something he was still getting used to. It was when nothing made sense, when the words were precise and evasive at the same time. Frustrating more than anything else. But pretty funny too.

"I'm sure I don't know what you mean," he replied evenly.

Rao considered Adam sideways. "Fucking hell," he murmured, shaking his head enough to quickly shut his working eye. *Concussion check*, Adam added to his list. The list grew longer as they walked to the truck. Rao's habitually uneven pace had become a limp. His hands would need examining too. More than likely bruised rather than broken, but he needed to be sure.

The streets were quiet. Lines of whitewashed tree trunks in the dark. A white Moskvich 2140 slowed as it approached; Adam put himself between Rao and the car. Private taxi, he decided, as the driver reconsidered his speculative stop and accelerated away.

As Adam watched its taillights recede along the street, Rao seemed to realize he didn't have all his attention and started on some godawful, deeply inappropriate drinking song. Sung it right into Adam's ear, trying to get a rise. Rao had no idea how easy it was for Adam to shut everything out while making a list. How easy it was for him to turn his focus elsewhere. Check out.

"You're no fun," Rao grumbled as Adam dumped him in the back seat.

"Is that true?"

"Fuck off. Of course it fucking is," Rao said, wincing. "Fuck."

PART II

CHAPTER 20

It's cavernous inside the cargo bay: grey paint, stencilled signs, pipes, alcoves packed with steel hardware. Strapped-down boxes, pallets and crates, passenger seats along both sides of the fuselage. It's bright outside, but as soon as the bay door closes it feels like the end of a long night inside the plane, everything foggy and tired and old, the light strange, as if it were tipped on one end.

Rao buckles himself in, asks Adam which inflight movies are showing today.

"I don't know, Rao," Adam says patiently. "Ask the flight attendants when they come around with champagne."

Rao smirks. He knows he's easily bored. It's one of his worst qualities. Well, no, it's far from his worst. But flying has never bored him. He adores the dissociation it brings, the mild hypoxia, the way it picks you up and hides you from the world. And it meant family, for years. Home to home on his school holidays. London Heathrow to Delhi, onwards to Jaipur, up on the top deck of the 747 where the upholstery was the colour of apricots and candlelight, and small Sunil rejoicing in all of it, tracing the murals on the walls with his fingers, poring over the route maps, transfixed by the cabin crew. The Air India Girls. When he was a child, they'd been *everything*. He'd told his mother he wanted to be one once. She'd nodded gravely and told him she absolutely understood why. There was laughter in her eyes, but Rao had heard the truth behind her words and basked in the joy of being known.

His last plane journey had been on an aircraft like this one, but Rao doesn't remember much of it. He'd been barely conscious. It returns to him in disconnected images, like damp newsprint photos, grimy halftones adhering to his skin. And the one before? An ancient TriStar from Brize Norton. Dirty side-eyes from scores of Royal Marines and bouts of nausea from what the pilot had called heavy chop. But the worst recollection of that journey was how excited he'd been throughout, grasping the knowledge that he was going out there to help as tightly as he had his mother's hand back when he was a child, slowly, determinedly, climbing the steep steps to the cabin.

Heather and Bill have taken seats opposite them on the far side of the bay. Rao nods at them, opens Kitty's book as the engines spool up. He always feels guilty reading books like these. Having perfect recall and an ability to discern truth in things made his university career a case of outrageous academic fraud. "You're a smart guy, Rao," Adam had said once, and Rao had grimaced. "I'm educated, Adam. People regularly mistake the two."

Two hours into the flight he's munching on chocolate-covered pretzels and deep in a chapter called "The Valley of Lost Things." Lots of writers have conjured such places, he discovers. Have filled them with things long forgotten and things still longed for. He reads that L. Frank Baum made it a valley filled with pocketbooks, shoes, toys, and clothes, just over the desert from the Land of Oz, and that P. L. Travers put lost things on the moon: Mary Poppins escorted children through the clouds to reach it. And four hundred years before Mary Poppins, the moon was also the home of lost things in Ariosto's *Orlando Furioso*. Things lost in error, lost through time or chance. Ruined castles, lost towns, lost reputations, lost loves, lost fame, people's wits stoppered tightly in jars. *Sanity sealed into vials*, Rao thinks, frowning, and reads on.

These are places, Kitty tells him, that you can only visit if you're accompanied by a guide. *Like the underworld*, Rao thinks, pleased by his analogy. He recalls the *Inferno* and Doré's etchings for it, and these bring Piranesi's *Carceri d'invenzione* to mind. He closes his eyes and wanders about inside Piranesi's impossible spaces of chains and walls and wheels and stone. There are lost things in these prisons, too, he muses, and with a jolt exactly like expecting a step underfoot that isn't there, he realises with horror that what he's done is put himself right back in Kabul. He opens his eyes, grips the book tightly. Tries to read on but can't resolve the words. His concentration's gone. Everything has, except a visceral, desperate need to use. *Fuck.* Could anyone on the plane help him out? He looks at Bill and Heather doubtfully. But the pilots? Surely. Those assholes get handed drugs by the kilo. Rao is thinking about getting out of his seat to go see when he feels a nudge against his shoulder. His whole body tenses for a punch. *How does Adam know?* he thinks, outraged. But the nudge doesn't stop. It becomes a weight. And it's not an admonition, he realises. Adam's head is on his shoulder.

Adam has fallen asleep.

He's astonished. Then gleeful. He's going to give Adam *so* much shit about this. The prospect makes him grin. He's still grinning when a burst of turbulence hits the plane. The seats shudder, there's a low swoop in his stomach, the head resting on his shoulder shifts slightly, and so does Rao, and suddenly he's feeling the prickle of Adam's shit crewcut right against his cheek and the corner of his mouth. And he's overtaken all at once by a wave of dreadful longing. It fills him so completely he shuts his eyes and drifts in it for a while, lost in the sensation, the scent of cheap shower gel. He shouldn't be feeling this. But he is. It's not arousal—well, it is a little bit, for fuck's sake, of course it is, this turbulence isn't helping—but *Adam*? Fuck.

Maybe he should cut himself some slack. It's been a wretchedly long time. Plus, Adam looks out for him. In fact, these days, Rao muses, he's probably the only person who does. He deliberates on this pathetic fact for a while and decides that he'd look out for Adam, too, if that were ever required, which it won't be, of course, and none of this would mean shit to Adam anyway because Adam doesn't need anything. Rubenstein is the most self-contained, emotionless bastard in existence. Rao feels a peculiar burst of self-pity at the thought. Pulls his head back and does his best to ignore the continuing weight on his shoulder. *You know what,* he thinks, looking down morosely at the book spread over his lap, *I really need to get laid.*

When Adam shifts back to his seat, apparently unaware of his transgression, Rao masters himself sufficiently to read. He reads. Adam sleeps.

Then Rao sleeps. When he wakes, Adam's still asleep. Two hours before landing, he blinks back into consciousness. Rubs his neck, stretches, checks his watch, looks surprised. "I missed the flight," he says.

"You left me alone with my thoughts, you bastard."

"Won't happen again, Rao."

CHAPTER 21

Before

The morning after the bar fight, Adam watched Rao angle his head in front of the mirror, touch the swelling around one eye, tentatively massage his jaw. "You've been lucky with the police," he observed.

"Uzbek police can always be bribed."

"Lucky," Adam repeated, sharp and weary. "There's redundancy in our schedule. But not much. And it's not just what this is going to look like when we meet the people that count. Those bruises are a liability on the road."

Rao fussed about in his wash bag. Brought out a small bottle and a sponge. Wet the sponge, squeezed it into the sink. Shook the bottle. "Keep your hair on, Adamski," he said, uncapping it. "Stop worrying. We'll be fine."

"We."

"I will. You will too." He upended the bottle onto the pad of one finger, dotted the finger across the bruise on one cheekbone, then dabbed at the place with the sponge. "Concealer hides a multitude of sins."

Adam didn't respond. Sins weren't a topic he wished to raise with Rao. He walked closer, looked at the bottle, then up at Rao's face in the mirror.

"You carry this around with you."

"Just in case."

Adam began to calculate exactly how much more fucked up that was than Rao getting himself fucked up in the first place, but he stopped, because this was fascinating to watch. Like an actor preparing for a role. He'd never thought about makeup. His mother used to use it.

Sometimes thicker than other times. This was different. And not different, because Rao was putting it on with the same short, assessing glances at his face his mother had used that time he watched her from the bedroom door when he was small and snuck away feeling he'd seen something he wasn't supposed to.

He forced himself to keep looking, watched the paint slowly cover Rao's bruises, hiding his damage, making it disappear.

"Is makeup a lie?" he said without thinking.

Rao paused, sponge an inch from his face.

"Now Adam, why would you ask a thing like that?"

Adam felt an obscure sense of shame then, and it must have shown on his face because Rao kept talking, smoothing over the cracks with ease. "Depends on the makeup, depends on the person. This? Yeah. I'd say this was a lie the same way you telling people you're an international freight coordinator is. It's cover."

But it wasn't. It wasn't a lie. Adam stood there somehow knowing it wasn't but lacking the words to articulate how or why. He looked away, troubled.

"You've never messed about with makeup, have you?" Rao said.

"No."

Rao frowned at something that wasn't quite right under one eye. Patted at it with his little finger. "Not even for a school play?"

"I'm not good at drama."

"Could have fooled me, love. Anyway, you'd look killer with a subtle wing on those eyes. Want to give it a go? You can always wipe it off."

"No."

"Go on."

"No, Rao."

"I'll get you someday."

Adam didn't reply. What was bothering him, watching Rao in the mirror, wasn't Rao's freedom to indulge in his own brand of masochism. Wasn't even his fucked-up makeup routine. It was that Rao said things. Just *said them*. At first Adam had assumed this was a calculated act. He had a fine-grained knowledge of distraction techniques, knew how effective a strategy verbal chaff could be. But recently he'd figured out that usually Rao had no idea what he was going to say until after he'd heard himself say it. In fact, Rao regularly didn't seem to hear the words he'd been saying at all, because he was too busy doing something else, thinking about something else. What would it be like to live like that? Adam wondered, watching Rao cap the concealer, stow it back in his bag, fuss with his hair. What would it be like to be so unconcerned by the words that leave your mouth. To not wonder if they were the right ones or if they should have been spoken at all. To just *say them*, like Rao?

Lifting the heel of his hand to one eye, he rubbed at it so hard lights blossomed against the black. "Five minutes," he called, picking up the keys from the table and walking to the door.

"Someday," Rao shouted after him. "You'll love it."

CHAPTER 22

Another bloody hotel. This one has a lobby of varnished pine, rustic stone, cheap leather armchairs, and framed photographs of elks bellowing in snow. Rao hates it and is pathetically grateful for it. He needs to sleep. The silence that follows a flight is something he's habitually filled with alcohol, and he's hoping unconsciousness will claim him before the craving gets too insistent to ignore.

Adam gets them a second-floor room. Two single beds with dark-brown comforters, regulation Air Force Inn pub carpet. Rao unlaces and kicks off his sneakers, falls back onto a bed, laces his hands behind his head, and stares at the ceiling fan. After a while he turns his neck to watch Adam. He's already unplugged the TV at the wall and set the small radio he'd brought on the windowsill. Now he's pulling folded clothes from his bag and stowing them carefully in the wardrobe. Rao'll never cease to be bewildered by Adam's inability to leave his things in a suitcase like a normal human being. It's not like they'll be staying here long. There'll be another hotel. There always is.

"You should keep hydrated," Adam instructs, angling another white shirt onto a hanger. "We're over a mile high. You'll feel the altitude for a couple of days."

"Thank you, Doctor Rubenstein." He clears his throat. "Adam?"

"Mm?"

"Heather and Bill, our nice friends on the flight. They came into the lobby after us."

"Yeah, I saw."

"They told me they were here to visit their son. They aren't. And I don't know who the fuck they are, but they're not called Heather and Bill. They're tailing us."

"Yeah. That's why I rejected the first two rooms they gave us."

"Is that what you were doing? I just assumed you were being a dick. Are we in danger?"

"We could be, if we wanted," Adam murmurs. "Or we could get some sleep."

Jetlagged and itchy under his sheets, Rao sleeps fitfully, dipping in and out of dreams in which something obscure and massy is writhing inside him, dark and patently desperate. He wakes just before seven with a coughing fit. The dawn light is a surprise. The fact that Adam's bed is perfectly made up is not, nor that Adam is fully dressed. He's standing to one side of the window, gazing down through the net curtain, and his posture is highly professional. Something's up.

"What's going on?"

"Come and look at this," he answers with evident irritation.

Rao hauls himself from the mattress, walks over, and peers around the edge of the chequered drapes. There's a Dodge van pulled up on the verge of the narrow access road behind their room. Dark blue, a bit beaten up.

"Ah. A van. Good morning to you too."

"Watch."

"What am I watching?"

"Predictability. They're going to put the hood up like they've got engine trouble."

That's exactly what they do. Three clean-shaven guys in casual sportswear clamber out of the van, two of whom make a big show of shaking their heads at whatever the one who's stuck his head under the hood is saying.

"Ah. Heather and Bill have friends."

"Yeah. The van'll be there for the duration. I'll put the radio against the glass and close the drapes." He sighs. "They're shit, Rao. I'm insulted."

"Come on, Adam, don't take it so personally."

"How the fuck else am I supposed to take it?"

"It's nice to know we're wanted, love."

"Yeah," Adam says flatly. "Just like old times. I almost feel nostalgic."

Rao whistles along with "Bad Moon Rising" on the radio laid against the window and futzes with the coffee machine. Adam's at the desk setting up an encrypted remote meeting with Miller on his laptop. "Sorry about the diner logo," he announces, handing a mug to Adam. "Thanks. Huh. Ok, we're through."

Rao pulls up a chair, stares dubiously at the screen. The feed is tinted like a video transfer of an '80s sitcom. Intermittently it stutters and freezes. It's the hotel Wi-Fi, but Rao amuses himself with the theory that Miller's clipped, executive manner is simply too much for the technology to handle. Her right hand is laid flat on the papers in front of her, her left clasped around a vacuum-walled coffee mug. Perfect manicure on brushed steel. "Rubenstein?"

"We're being tailed. Skeleton team."

She nods. "Useful."

"Yes, ma'am."

"News here is that vial's gone missing. Disappeared before it got to the lab. I'm assuming someone's taken it. We'll work through everyone in the chain."

"Understood," Adam says.

Rao blinks. A sliding *thump* from the laptop speakers and Miller jumps in her seat. "Just files falling off the desk," she explains. She pushes her chair back a fraction, leaning down to retrieve them.

Rao feels a trickle of foreboding.

"Miller—" he starts.

She reappears with a snub-nosed revolver in one hand. The puzzlement on her face shifts to astonished recognition. "Oh! I had one just like—"

"Miller! Shit. *Shit.* Adam, call the base medics. Call them *now.*"

Adam's pulled his phone and is already dialling. Miller is cradling the gun like a doll now, pressing it tight to her chest with both hands, her face rapt, beatific, wet with tears. Rao can hear Adam requesting an emergency paramedic team to her office in a voice so impossibly calm he wants to scream. He waits until he can't wait any longer, grabs the phone out of his hands.

"Right, this is important," he says through his teeth. "Tell the paramedics. She'll be in a trance. And she'll be holding a gun. Yes. A gun. I don't know what— No. It's a revolver, why the *fuck* do you need to know? Don't take it off her. Don't even think about— If you take it away from her, she'll probably die. What?" He can barely hear the question down the line over the roar of blood in his ears. "Rao," he snaps. "R-A-O. Sunil. Yes. No. I'm not . . . Will you *fucking listen to me . . .*"

He exhales heavily. Turns to Adam. "They keep telling me to calm down—"

Adam takes back the phone. "Who am I speaking to? Ashley, hello. This is Rubenstein again. We've seen cases like this before. Under no circumstances should the medical team remove the revolver from her grip. Or attempt to. She can't and won't use it and taking it from her will lead to severe complications up to and including her sudden death. Clear?"

He listens for a while, furrows his brow.

"Yes. We're working on that, but it's complex. Results won't be immediate. What I need right now is a verbal confirmation from you that these orders will be followed."

Rao hears a "yes, sir" down the line.

"Keep me updated. And, Ashley, this is super-secret squirrel. I'll liaise with the DIA about forward options. Just keep her alive."

Another pause.

"Thanks." He cuts the call.

Rao can't drag his eyes from the screen. Miller's bent forward over the desk now, her face completely obscured. He stares at the pale curls on her crown, the wrinkled seam along the shoulder of her jacket, the clock on the wall behind. At milky coffee from her upended mug seeping slowly through paper, wetting the side of her sleeve. His heart hurts, his hands itch. "*Fuck*," he spits out.

He and Adam sit there in silence until the paramedics enter the room, administer to Miller, produce a stretcher—carefully avoiding the weapon in her grasp—and ferry her away. When the room is empty,

Adam cuts the video call, pushing at the screen and snapping the laptop shut.

It's then Rao glances up. Sees Adam's face. It's alight with rage. When Adam catches his eye, the briefest flash of something like panic races across his features before he adjusts them, fixing them back into their usual impassivity. Rao sees the effort this takes, the perfection of the result. There he is, as he always is. Or was. Adam Rubenstein: nothingness made manifest.

CHAPTER 23

They were having a great day. His aunt picked him up from his house in the morning, telling his parents that they were going into the city for the day for "lunch and stuff." She fed him, as promised, then she took him to one of the last locally owned ice-cream parlors in the city. He ate a bowl of pistachio with slivers of nuts on top and listened to his aunt talk about work and the people she worked with. *Artists*, she said, rolling her eyes. *Painters*. He doesn't know what his aunt does, but he knows it has something to do with art galleries. She isn't an artist but sometimes it seems like they must be the only people she talks to, because they are the only people she talks about. He doesn't think he's ever met one.

After ice cream, she takes him to her little apartment. It's not permanent, she tells him as she unlocks the door. She won't be in this place forever. But it's close to the family, and it's close to her favorite nephew. When he points out that he's her only nephew, she grins and agrees that he has an unfair advantage.

It's a great day. He ruins it.

He's talking about cars. He doesn't know that much about them, but not knowing much about things doesn't matter when he's alone with his aunt in her apartment. Here with her he doesn't need to know everything about a topic to speak about it. He can just like a car sometimes and say so.

"What car are you going to have when you can get one?" she asks. They're both acting now, he knows. It's all pretend, make-believe, that when he gets to have a car he'll have any choice to make about it.

"I want to fix mine up," he answers. He hadn't thought about it at all before she asked, but the words come out of his mouth, and it feels like he's telling the truth. "I want to get some old piece of junk and fix it up."

"You want a project."

"I've seen some cars that people say are beyond hope," he argues. "It's not true. It's just hard work, and they don't want to do hard work."

His aunt throws her head back and laughs. "You sound like your dad," she says. It's not an insult. He laughs back. Not because it's funny but because it's true. He sounds like his dad, but both of them know he's nothing like the man. His aunt gets up to get another drink from the fridge, walking around him to do so.

He turns to her, still talking. "Hey, do you think—"

There's a crash, and he forgets what he was going to ask because his brain turns white at the noise. It only takes a blink for him to realize what he's done: he wasn't paying attention, he'd been too loose, too careless, and his elbow had bumped one of the mugs on his aunt's table and knocked it to the floor. He hadn't even been aware enough of what he was doing to have managed to catch it in time. It's smashed into irreparable pieces, right across the kitchen tiles.

"Shit," his aunt says under her breath.

His heart kicks against his chest. Hurts him with the force of it. "I'm sorry," he says quickly, getting up only to kneel and begin gathering up the bigger pieces as fast as he can without cutting himself. It'll be worse if he starts bleeding on everything as well as making a mess of the kitchen.

"Sit down, kid," his aunt says, but he doesn't do what she says. He keeps cleaning. There's a broom in the corner, he tells himself. The bigger pieces pile into a ceramic pyramid in front of him as he tells himself repeatedly that there is a broom in the corner. He can clean this all so quickly. Like it never happened. The quicker he goes, the more it feels like he might be about to outrun his aunt getting mad about it. He's never seen her mad. The thought of it makes the world turn grayer somehow. She's not always smiling, and she's not always laughing, and he wouldn't classify her as a Happy Person like people always seem to be outside their family or on TV or in magazines. But that doesn't mean that she's angry. She's definitely not angry.

He's seen what angry looks like. His aunt's not that kind of person. And there's no way he's willing to risk making her into one.

She's saying something else to him, but he's ignoring her. Can't hear her. He says that he's sorry, again, and finishes cleaning up his mess. At least there wasn't a drink in the mug. He sits back down at the table and closes his eyes. At least there wasn't a drink in the mug.

"Okay," his aunt says slowly. She's got a fresh glass of orange juice in her hand. Very calmly, she sets it down on the table. "Are you alright, kiddo?"

"I didn't mean to do that," he tells her. "I wasn't thinking. I wasn't paying attention. It was stupid, but that's no excuse, and I'm sorry."

Her eyebrows go up, but she nods. For a second she looks like his dad: serious and pensive and unreadable. Then, without saying anything, she picks up the matching mug on the table. Meets his eyes. Lets a second pass between them. Then, with a grin that banishes all semblance of his father from her face, she lets the mug drop to the tiles.

It smashes worse than the one that he broke.

There's no breath left in his body.

"I hated those things anyway," she says, sipping her orange juice. "Thanks for doing me a favor. I never would have gotten rid of them otherwise."

There are broken mug pieces and dust everywhere. It's going to be dangerous to walk in here without a dedicated and deep clean. His mouth feels dry, but the white in his brain is gone, and he doesn't feel like he's out of place in the world.

"Do you have any more of those mugs?"

"Now you're talking."

CHAPTER 24

Before

"Uhh," Rao said, and froze.

He'd always taken personal pride in being open to the unexpected, in taking all life's switchbacks in his stride, but coming back from the Chorsu Bazaar to find his colleague pressing a gun to the kneecap of a terrified man tied to a chair in the middle of their Tashkent apartment? There are limits. There really fucking are.

The man was middle-aged and looked Russian. Patterned sweater, knockoff Levi's. Sweat shining on his face, he was looking down into Adam's eyes. And Adam, crouching, was looking up into his.

I'm interrupting a private moment, Rao thought, shocked into stupidity, tucking the bag of warm pastries he'd brought from the market a little closer to his chest. Adam turned his head to look at him then and—his expression. *Christ.* Whatever desperately deflecting bit of schoolboy humour Rao'd been assembling died in his throat, right there.

"What's going on?" he managed.

"Close the door."

A few seconds of silence while Rao tussled with the ambiguity.

"Which side," he asked carefully, "of the door do you want me on?"

Then the man with the gun against his knee started to talk. A long outpouring in Russian. Pleas for help, attestations that the man with the gun was crazy, a total psycho—*quite possibly you're right*, Rao thought, *now I've seen this*—interspersed with lavish protestations of ignorance and innocence and—

Ah.

Rao made no move to shut the door.

"You've zip-tied him to the chair."

"Yeah."

"So he's not going to fuck off if we have a quiet word, is he?"

The undeniable fact appeared to require deliberation. And Adam wasn't deliberating with his usual impassivity; something about the set of his jaw made it look as if he were taking on the pros and cons in close quarters combat.

"No," he said finally, rising to his feet. As he drew near, Rao clutched the pastries even tighter to his chest. Some visceral sense of self-preservation was screaming at him to get the fuck out of the way, and it took him a deal of courage to master it.

"You weren't supposed to be here," Adam points out in the corridor, low and deeply accusatory.

"I am. Who's this guy?"

"He's tailed us for two days. I concluded they're either amateurs, short of personnel, or I'd made a mistake."

"You've not made a mistake, have you."

The briefest of smiles. "No."

"Ok," Rao says. "You don't know who's running him."

Adam shakes his head.

"And you want to."

"Obviously."

"So before you start really hurting this guy, might I suggest I sit in?"

Adam's not dumb.

"Sit behind him. Blink twice if he's lying."

Rao jerks his head at the Beretta in Adam's hand. "I'll do that. Can you put that away?"

Adam opens his mouth to protest, stops himself. Nods slowly. "It's a problem."

"No," Rao lies. "I just think you've already made your point."

Rao wasn't assisting with this interrogation for solely humanitarian reasons. Felt like it, to begin with, but no. Occupying the moral high ground. Showing off, a little. Having a chance to do some real spy shit. And as the minutes passed it was gratifying to see how freaked out the man got when he saw Adam knew when he was lying. Maybe a little too gratifying. Gratification, if he was being honest, well on its way to being very fucked up.

After fifteen minutes and a lull in the proceedings, Rao became impatient enough to do some covert truth-testing on the sly: he left his seat, started whispering suggested questions in Adam's ear. Questions he'd tried to make sound like guesses. But he got carried away. Pushed his luck way over the line when he told Adam maybe he should ask about the guy's sick sister. A lurch of apprehension in his stomach when Adam frowned. Another after the guy had heard the question and stared at Adam in disbelief.

But the sister had been the key. As soon as she was mentioned, the man started talking, stumbling over his words like he was running too fast down a very steep hill. He sat there sweating, explaining that he wasn't good at surveillance, it wasn't his job, he was just a driver—a good driver, he drove the important guys—but their usual team was working in Termez because some VIPs were up there now. That he'd been told to follow them because there was a tip-off from someone, he didn't know who. He apologised for that. He apologised for a lot of things, for not knowing things, but he'd heard a lot of conversations, and he knew the names, he explained the Turkish connection, told them exactly where the goods came through from Afghanistan and then, his voice rising even higher, how worried they were getting these days, because the government was wiping out a lot of the smaller importers because heroin was lucrative, and the government wanted the trade. Nationalising it, that's what they were doing, under the table. Because, he went on, the government's very happy to have the Americans here, to help on their war on terror, and they're also happy to buy from the guys in Afghanistan, the ones that are killing the Americans, because that's what Americans don't understand about here, is that things don't work the way they do in the movies.

Rao sat there listening to it all. But all he kept thinking when the guy was finished, all he continued to think after Adam cut him free and set him loose, was: *Which movies?*

CHAPTER 25

When Hunter marches into the lobby through the doors of the Air Force Inn, the first thing Rao notices are her eyebrows. They're absolutely perfect. He's instantly envious. The eyes beneath them are the kind that veer between dry amusement and outright challenge. A khaki T-shirt, fatigues. Box braids, bitten fingernails, a bunch of woven and leather bracelets, a *lot* of tattoos. *She's not what I expected*, Rao decides, before realising he'd no clear expectations at all. She's hot. Shit. She's *very* hot, and she makes him incredibly nervous. This is a combination dear to Rao's heart; in any other circumstances he'd be all over it like a rash.

Seeing Adam, Hunter raises her chin a fraction and does the Adam thing, the frown that's a covert smile. She jerks her head at Rao. "Is this the guy? Your lie detector?"

Adam grins. There's nothing covert about it. "Yeah. And he's not."

"Not yours or not a lie detector?"

"I'm right here," Rao says.

"So you want to hear about this?" Hunter says. "I've got a room. But we can walk and talk if you want—"

"Secure?" Adam checks.

"Secure."

"Then inside's good. Rao wants to pick up a Starbucks first."

"Of course he does." She's looking at Rao like she's his bloody mother. How is she doing that. "Ok," she says. "Hi."

"Hi," he says.

"Pleased to meet you." She turns to Adam again. "He's exactly what I expected, Rubenstein. Let's get him a Frappuccino or whatever the fuck else it is he needs."

She leads them to a block of offices designated as a Distinguished Visitor Area and opens a door onto a room that's little larger than two king-size beds: cloth walls, no windows, a dark wooden table surrounded by high-backed chairs upholstered in cream-coloured leather. She sits. Adam drops into the seat next to hers. Rao pulls up a chair at the farthest end of the table and regards them both over the Americano he didn't really want. Adam sends him an enquiring glance and gently taps one earlobe. Rao shakes his head. No one's listening in.

"So," says Hunter. "Flores."

Danny Flores, Rao learns, was invalided out last year after taking a round to an ankle while doing something unspecified in an unspecified location in Afghanistan. Hunter maintains that Flores "knows his shit cold," whatever that means, and that he's reliable. "Reliable like Rubenstein," she says, looking right at Rao. He picks up his cup, works out he's only done so because he wants to hide behind it, puts it back on the table.

"Where was he living?" he ventures.

"Boulder. I just came from there," she says. "But he dropped off the map fifteen days ago."

Huh, Rao thinks. He's gone AWOL for longer than that without anyone getting even vaguely worried. His scepticism must show, because Hunter tells him about Flores's dogs. How he'd booked them into a boarding kennel for three nights but never returned to pick them up. This, in her opinion, means Flores is likely dead.

"Hunter—" Adam begins.

She cuts in quickly, vehemently. "Can't see it. That's not his kind of broken. And his mom's still alive. She's got dementia. She's in a care facility a few blocks from his house. It's why he moved back out West. I've heard him talk about her. No way he'll kill himself if she's still alive, even if she doesn't know him from a stone."

"He's alive," Rao says quietly.

She stares. "You can't know that."

Adam's looking at him, wary and surprised. *Yes, you bastard*, he thinks. *I'm willing to trust her because you do.* Which is nuts. He nods.

"Actually, he can," Adam says. "Rao can tell when things are true. Not just whether people are lying. It's a talent."

She rolls her eyes. "He's a goddamn psychic investigator? Jesus, what is this? Have you joined the EIO?"

"They wish."

"Don't fuck with me, Rubenstein."

Ten minutes later she picks her bottle of peach tea from the table, slaps the cap with the flat of her hand, twists it off, and drinks. Her eyes regard Rao very seriously as she does. She's tested him, provided him with a series of statements to verify. Some were personal; some were shading to classified. In this particular area she's not found him wanting.

"This is insane. So, he—" She stops herself, addresses Rao directly. "You know what's true and what isn't. Anytime, anyplace. Except when it's about *him*."

"Yes," Rao says. He's learning the less he says to Hunter the better. Using words in her presence is like putting out targets in a live-fire exercise.

"Insane," she says, again to no one in particular.

"It's not insane," Adam says. "It's just Rao."

She gives Adam a side-eye for the ages, drains the last of her tea, pushes the bottle across the tabletop, and leans back in her seat.

"Ok. So you said you had shit to tell me. Quid pro quo. I'm listening."

"It's connected with Flores, and we don't know how," Adam explains. "Yet. But we're pushing into full unacknowledged territory. Hunter, this is strict ears only. And it's going to sound crazy. You have to trust me that it's true."

She tenses at that. "I trust you," she says quietly. "You know this. Don't need to ask for it."

"Ok," Adam says. And he tells her. He tells her about the diner and the fire. He tells her about Straat and the roses, the proliferating objects, the static cutting in on the surveillance footage. He tells her what happened to Ed. What happened to Miller. She winces. He tells her about the vial and the vial going missing—she winces at that too—and Rao's conclusions about what the substance does. How Rao had found out that Flores's disappearance was connected. She listens with fierce attention, asks a bunch of perceptive questions, and she buys all of it.

"Huh," she says. Stares at the wall for a while, rubbing at the corner of her mouth. "Miller. Shit. I'm sorry, Rubenstein. Someone dosed her, yeah?"

Ugh, Rao thinks. That hadn't occurred to him. He's losing his touch. Lost it. He tests possibilities, exhales. "No, her contamination was accidental."

"Fuck." Hunter breathes. She gazes at Rao. "This is messy. Don't end up dead, Rubenstein."

Adam twists his mouth. "Not able to promise you that."

When Adam heads off to the bathroom, Rao sends Hunter his sweetest smile. Feels like the bravest thing he's done for a while. She meets it with a level stare. "What's the deal with you and Rubenstein?" she asks.

"You are aware we work together."

"Don't be a smartass. You know what I mean. How do you take him? You ride or die?"

Rao nods slowly. "Ah, we're talking professional bonding. Battle buddies."

"Sure," she says, like she's joking. But Rao knows she's not. She *knows*, now. She deserves the courtesy of a proper answer. What comes out of his mouth surprises him.

"I, uh, was going to die. Seems like ages ago now, but it wasn't long at all. And while it was happening, I thought about Adam." He frowns. "Actually, he was the last thing I thought about, which is weird. I've thought about that. Why, I mean. It's because he's unknowable to me. Which means he's just like death. Like what comes after, if it comes after. And . . ." He assumes a smile, aware he should lighten the tone. "I guess Adam's a bit inevitable too. You know what he's like."

Hunter mutters a low "Jesus" and shakes her head. Rao's gratified he's knocked her off-balance, but he's feeling off-balance, too, now, and the silence between them is strained.

Adam halts three paces into the room, regards them with suspicion. "Rao. Hunter," he says.

"Rubenstein," Hunter replies.

"How very formal," Rao observes. "I was just telling Hunter here that you'll probably be the last thing I see before I die, one way or another."

"That's not going to happen, Rao."

"Well." Rao grins. "Sorry to inform you, love, but it's kind of inevitable."

They arrange to meet for dinner at a nearby smokehouse grill.

"It's called *what*?"

"Racks 'n' Butts," Hunter repeats.

"Ok," Rao says eventually. He watches them both disappear around the corner of the building, stares dully at the space they'd walked through. Time, he decides, for a swift personal sitrep. He'd liked Miller and has likely just killed her. He'd kind of liked Ed and definitely killed him. Hunter's doing his head in. He's jetlagged, achy, getting seriously scared of this EOS PROPHET business, and is fighting a slew of silent, increasingly insistent cravings.

It's not optimal. He sets off on an aimless walk, staring for most of it at the few inches of asphalt or grass around his feet. Then he sulks his way to a local Denny's and eats his way through a Chicken Philly Melt, a double portion of fries, and a chocolate lava cake a la mode, which have the double benefit of upping his self-hatred and dulling the worst of the cravings to a level he thinks he'll be able to live with for a while.

He drags himself back to the Air Force Inn and throws himself full-length on his bed. He'd have a wank, but the surveillance van outside their window is a little off-putting; exhibitionism really isn't his thing. He doesn't want to think about why they've come here. So he stares at the ceiling and wonders what Adam and Hunter are doing. Decides, considering Adam's perpetual disinterest in having any kind of fun, that they're probably not having the dangerous sex he can't seem to stop imagining. He tells himself they're probably sitting in a room some-where comparing their respective knife and firearm collections, which, he realises gloomily, isn't any less libidinously confronting. *Fuck's sake, Sunil*, he tells himself. *Get over yourself.* He gets up, showers aggressively,

opens his kit bag. Stares moodily at the terrible suit and shirt and tie
that the Department of Defense saw fit to gift him with. Stretches out
on his bed again, shuts his eyes.

What he wants and needs is sleep. But he can't get near it. He's
remembering that last night in Tashkent, eleven months ago to the day.
By virtue of who and what he is, he recalls every second with agonis-
ing fidelity. He doesn't want to, but he has no choice. The memory has
found him and fallen on him entire.

They're in an old-style Soviet hotel, a vast brutalist hulk of stained
geometric concrete that reminds Rao vaguely of a monumental Triscuit.
Inside, dark, glossy wood and peeling corridors, light-deprived houseplants dying slowly by the lift doors. The city outside smells of lignite,
salt, and woodsmoke, but inside the lobby all is bleach and turpentine,
and Rao had felt a surge of grandiosity as they approached reception
and agitated for a whole suite. Adam, to his surprise, had agreed. It
turns out to be shabby and magnificent. Acres of brocade wallpaper,
tired ornate chairs, chandeliers holding half-blown arrays of tiny bulbs.

Rao's never seen Adam drink like this. He's never seen Adam behave
like this. He's rolled his shirtsleeves up, loosened his tie. He's eating
ravenously, black bread and cheese and pickles and beetroot-stained
Russian salad on a side table drawn up to the couch. He's found a pack of
cards in a drawer, is playing with them between mouthfuls of food and
shots of vodka. Rao draws near, fascinated. Adam looks up, still chewing.

"Adam, this is what I was talking about."

He swallows. "What?"

Rao waves a hand vaguely.

Adam grins. "That's a vodka answer. Try using words."

"Cards."

"Yes."

"What are you doing?"

"Just fucking around."

"Yes but . . ." Rao watches him. It's mesmerising.

"There are hundreds of different kinds of cuts," Adam says after
a while. "Thousands. They all do the same thing. It's just the same as

splitting the deck. Another kind of shuffle, always working towards random order. The whole idea of cards is that there's random order. It's the lie everyone agrees to."

"Everyone," Rao concurs, but he's not really listening. The cards, Adam's deft fingers, the peculiar combination of fluidity and decisiveness in the way both move: he's getting a little lost in it.

"Everyone. So you have a thousand legitimate cuts, a thousand legitimate shuffles. For every legit one, there's a false one. So *this* is a false cut. But it looks like . . . *this*, which is a legitimate cut."

Rao nods. "Where did you learn this stuff, Adam?"

"Around."

"Just around?"

"Just around."

"Is that classified?"

"Everything about me's classified, Rao," Adam says, deadpan.

"Including me?"

Adam gives him a quick, glancing look. His eyes meet Rao's for a fraction of a second, get pulled away like they've been scalded. *What's that*, Rao wonders. He sits down on the other end of the couch, eyes on the ever-moving cards. Finally he works out what the look had meant.

"Yeah. Fair. I know you know."

"Know what?"

"I'm not a real agent. Thanks for not giving me perpetual shit about it, actually. I appreciate that."

Adam stills the cards in his hands.

"What are you talking about?"

"You know what I'm talking about. You practically said it. Definitely implied it. I'm not a real agent. It's bullshit. I'm only here because I can do tricks. What I am is a bit of kit to deploy. You know"—he waves a hand—"Geiger counter, navy-trained whale, Sunil Rao."

Adam shakes his head decisively. "No," he says. "That's not what you are."

"Adam, do me a favour. You should know by now I'm the world's most fraudulent asshole. I'm not a proper intelligence officer. Never did the induction. I wasn't a real art historian. I conned them all at

Sotheby's. I've never been anything real." This is vodka and he should shut up. He should stop talking right now. "And it goes all the way down. I've never felt properly Indian and I'm certainly not English. Not quite a man, but not a woman either. I'm just . . ." He sighs. "Ignore me. Ignore this. I'm drunk." But one more awful sentence crawls out of his mouth. "It's not that I don't fit in, it's not that bullshit. It's that I'm not . . . anything real. I mean, I'm just *not*."

Adam shrugs as easily as if Rao'd asked him about the weather outside. "You're not *not*. I'm an expert on *not*, Rao. You're *all*."

"Right. Care to enlighten me further, or is this full Adam koan shit?"

Adam looks at him like he's in dire need of remedial education. "You're like this pack of cards. You can pull any combination. It's all there. You carry all of them at once, but you don't have to show anyone shit unless you want to. You get to choose. You're lucky."

Rao is a little blindsided. That was a hell of a speech from Adam.

It was a hell of a speech, per se. He thinks about that "lucky" and what it might mean that Adam said it. But his head isn't clear enough. He shakes it instead, says, almost angrily, "What the fuck do you know?"

Adam laughs at that. Properly laughs. Another thing Rao's never seen before. There are *dimples*. "True," he says, reaching across for the bottle. "That's true."

A few hours later, Rao walks carefully into the bathroom and succeeds in taking a piss without getting any on the tiles. *Absolute triumph*, he thinks, awarding himself a small imaginary medal and a round of imaginary applause. Zipping himself up, he spots his wash bag on the shelf beneath the mirror and remembers. Snickers out loud. Walks back into the lounge. Marches up to the couch that Adam is sprawled across in a way that in literally any other individual Rao would consider bewitchingly dissolute.

"It's time," Rao says.

Adam cracks an eye. "What?"

Rao brandishes his eye pencil. "I told you I'd get you someday. Today is that someday. It's today."

"It's not day. It's three in the morning."

"Don't deflect, Rubenstein. Take this like a man."

Adam sits up. He assumes an expression of intense resignation, then picks up his glass from the table, drains it, slams it back down. "Ok. Alright," he says. "Ok, do it. *Do it.*"

Rao's taken aback. "It's not like I'm going to throw a punch, for fuck's sake. Stop psyching yourself up, you complete and utter lunatic."

Adam, Rao suspects, has just worked out that this joke is not entirely at his own expense, because a flicker of something like wonderment crosses his features before they turn distinctly apprehensive.

"Don't worry, it's hypoallergenic," Rao assures him, waving the pencil, and this is sufficient to start Adam laughing. So much so that Rao's fighting a losing battle to grip his face to keep it still enough to apply the pencil. "Fucking keep still," Rao mutters. "Stop it, this is *serious.*" They're both cracking up now, and Rao's squinting in the low light of the room, focusing on where he's going to apply these bloody wings. Adam blinks. *He has stupidly long eyelashes*, Rao thinks. Stupidly. And his eyes are. Yeah. And that's when Rao jettisons his hypothesis that whatever sexuality Adam possesses has been entirely sublimated into government-sponsored violence. Forgets the eyeliner in his hand. Forgets himself. Because it's obvious now that they both know what this is. Rao looks down at Adam's fractionally opened mouth and thinks, *Fuck. Yeah. Why not.* He shifts his grip on Adam's jaw minutely and meaningfully, leans in, and is so buoyed on the longing he knows Adam is feeling, too, he expects Adam to meet him first.

Adam does not.

Adam flinches.

He looks away. He pulls back. Rao gets the full, awful trinity. He even raises a hand to Rao's chest. Doesn't touch him, just keeps it there between them. Rao looks down at it. It's trembling violently. Looks back up. Adam's eyes are a mess of refusal and panic.

"Fuck," he begins. He'd been so *sure*.

"It's fine," Adam says.

"Adam—"

"It's *fine.*"

CHAPTER 26

Wasn't nightmares that woke him. He's too old for those, and he never remembered having them anyway, even when he was told that's what they were. And it's not that he's away from home. There are kids in his class who still have problems with that, which is pretty fucked up, considering. He woke up because it's hot. The air in the RV is stifling because the generator's been off all night. He breathes in the dark, knows he has to get outside. He has to do it without waking his parents, but that is not going to be a problem because they're sleeping in the bedroom at the far end of the vehicle, and he is very, very good at being quiet. He gets dressed lying on the mattress, picks up his boots, and pads to the door. Eases the mechanism of the door catch open, slips outside, softly closes the door behind him, and releases the handle back into place so slowly there are moments in the process that feel like falling through space, like they'll go on forever. Outside, he puts on his boots, laces them tight, starts walking toward the shore.

It was a long drive to get here. His dad had been in the kind of mood that was red flags from the start. Kept talking about how great this place was, how much they'd love it, how it was a real American Riviera. He didn't need to listen too hard to what his dad was saying, because there wasn't any instruction in it and besides, his mom was listening, and she was starting to make the very blank face she makes when she's bracing herself against bad things. He knows what that face means because he makes it, too, sometimes. He didn't know until he caught sight of himself in a window once, and there it was.

She'd pretended to sleep most of the way. She always does. She's never really asleep. He'd sat between them in the front, and after a couple of hours he had felt her hand grip his. Secretly he was glad, because his dad's mood had been getting tighter by the mile, and he'd tried to look more interested in everything, and that had worked for a while but then there was a song on the radio that he hadn't heard before and hearing it was a bit like the feeling of falling asleep, like being hypnotized. It sounded English, and he thinks it was called *golden brown* but that could have been the chorus, and his father noticed him listening to it, and looked at him sideways and said, *You like this song? You know it's about foreign women?* Which made him suspect he shouldn't like it at all, and he knew that silence would be the wrong response but so would talking, so he nodded and said *mmm* and that's when his mom had taken his hand. Not for too long, and he didn't look down to where her fingers gripped his, but out at the shoulder of the interstate instead, where the palms were fat and dusty and sneakers tied in pairs were thrown over wires.

When they arrived, it wasn't what he'd expected. It wasn't what his dad had expected. The place was a ruin. People had been leaving for years, the only other guy at the RV park said. He was here to make a documentary, and he had told them about the history, everything about what had happened. He thought it was funny that they had come here for a weekend away, and his dad's face when the guy laughed was something he's trying to forget. But he remembers very clearly wanting to take the guy down and hurt him very badly, knowing there was no way he was going to try it. Nothing happened. Nothing was going to happen. This weekend was like a lot of weekends. It was going to be a thing to get through, is all.

It's a long walk. The sky's already lighter. He can make out birds wheeling and flapping overhead, hear them squawking. The air smells bad. Like rotten eggs. Sulfurous. He knows he'll get used to it. Takes deep breaths to make that happen quicker. When he gets close to the lake, each step sinks into something that's not sand and not dirt. Something in between. Sludgy and crunchy, like sugary cookie dough. The stuff doesn't get any deeper as he nears the waterline, but when he looks back over his shoulder and sees a dim trail of his own footprints pointing to where he stands there's a little kick of adrenaline in his stomach. He turns his back on the evidence of his movements. Keeps walking. Soon he's treading on what feels like scattered, grainy drifts of white gravel. But it's not stones. He crouches and picks up half a handful of the stuff. It's dry and light, and he stares in puzzlement at the heap on his palm before he figures out that he's looking at fish bones.

He looks at his watch. He's been out here a while. He knows he should be back at the RV.

He's not. He's here.

He brushes what looks like salt off the wood of a section of wrecked jetty and sits on it, facing the lake. After a while he pulls a packet of his dad's illicit smokes and a box of UCO matches from his pants pocket. He lights a Lucky Strike looking out at the water.

The sun's rising behind the hills on the farther shore. The sky is blue, then pale blue, then lemon, then gold. There are seagulls flying everywhere, and he sees, as the light increases, that the shapes on the palisades far out in the shallows might be pelicans.

He sits there and looks at the water glowing under the low California sun and thinks about this lake. How it was a mistake. How some engineers messed up a river diversion, and until they managed to stop the flow, all this water had poured into this place. And now there's nowhere for it to go. How it's full of salt and poison getting more and more concentrated under the sun. First all the fish will die, and then the birds, and the shoreline will shrink as the lake dries up, and one day everything in front of him will be desert again, dust. He looks at the water. Its surface is completely still, like a pool of mercury colored blue and gold from the sky above, and as he looks at it something happens. It's another stab of adrenaline in his stomach, but this one is joined by a weird creep up his spine.

He looks at it and realizes he loves it.

He loves it. It's showing him that everything will end. Everything he knows, all of it will disappear one day. It's the weirdest thing to think, because it makes him feel calm. It might be the most calming thought he has ever had, and he knows he hasn't seen much of the world, not yet, but he also knows this: this is the best, the most perfect place in it.

CHAPTER 27

Adam looks up at the night sky after Rao makes them stop so that he can take a piss around the side of a closed store. Hunter sighs and rests against the wall with him, leaning forward to swing a look at where Rao is. "He's a tactical liability," she mutters. Adam smiles a little. He knows what she means.

"You get used to him."

Hunter snorts. Offers him a cigarette. Shakes her head when he declines. "I don't think I want to. Seems like a hell of a lot of wasted effort."

"Wasted effort."

"Sure. I don't have the same patience as you do for these babysitting gigs, Rubenstein. I don't get off on this like you do."

"It's not like that." *That's not entirely true*, he hears himself think in Rao's voice. Watching Rao return from bar restrooms wiping his lips, hustling pool badly for attention, having to roll with the verbal punches whenever Rao is in a bad mood: none of that feels good. He doesn't crave it the way Hunter thinks he does. He knows it's not simple. Is fully aware that his role in this partnership doesn't allow for his fulfillment. But that doesn't bother him. It never has. He's not an idiot. He knows his odds in life. Knows that dedication doesn't have to be a two-way street for it to mean something.

"He's asleep," Hunter observes, leaning forward again. The smoke rises from her hand into Adam's face. He doesn't hate it. He should quit. He's quitting. He's not smoking right now. But the smoke is a nice bonus. "He fell asleep pissing against the wall."

Adam closes his eyes briefly. "He does that."

"How the fuck."

"He puts his forehead against the wall and closes his eyes. Either he falls over or he wakes up. Several points to inner ear function in that case. But it doesn't take longer than thirty seconds," he explains. Hunter stares at him, incredulous.

"How come you're always there to clean up this mess?" she asks. She must know the answer, but she wants to know if Adam does too. If he will say it out loud.

"I have nothing to say about that," he tells her. It doesn't work.

"How long are you going to do this? Have you thought about that? Because there's going to be one night when you aren't around to stop him from drowning in his own vomit."

Adam frowns. People get Rao wrong. "That won't happen."

"Rubenstein." Hunter sounds genuinely disappointed in him. Adam flips her the bird. She grins, but only briefly. "I'm serious. You're not usually the one to get suckered by optimism."

"This isn't optimism. This is being in possession of all the facts. You aren't aware of the intricate details related to the subject," Adam says simply, flatly, honestly. "You have surface intel, which only gives you an idea of a fraction of the field."

"Don't give me jargon just because you're cornered."

"Don't decide that I'm cornered just because you don't like the answer you're getting."

She looks at Rao against the wall. "By your count, he'll wake up soon."

"Or fall over," Adam reminds her.

"I know you see things to the end," Hunter sighs. "I know that 'do or die' is the Rubenstein credo. But I've never seen you like this about anything but work."

It's not an unfair observation, but she's a little off the mark. She thinks that he's dedicated to the cause, whatever that might be, once he has an objective. An airman down to the marrow. Adam knows that's not exactly an untrue observation, but being a good airman, being reliable, aiming to always stay standing until the last, that isn't dedication. That's inevitability.

He was always going to enlist. That was going to happen from the day he was born.

"I thought Rao was work," Adam deflects. "Babysitting."

"That's not what this is, Rubenstein."

Rao's head falls back by an inch and he startles awake with a snore. "Fuck," he mutters.

The conversation ends there. Adam's not sure if he's relieved. Hunter's known him best since they went through basic together, and she still doesn't really get it. She might not ever get it. Adam doesn't even know where he could start.

Rao likes to say that he's a tool in a box, like a James Bond gadget on the belt of international intelligence agencies, and he's accused Adam of being the same more than once. But he's never been right about that. Adam's only a gun to point at a problem. Even holstered, he's meant to be dangerous, and that's how he's always been used, from intelligence to target elimination to babysitting. He's a weapon—and a simple one.

Nobody's ever used a gun to finesse a complex situation.

"I don't know what to tell you, Hunter," he says. Makes his way over to Rao before he falls backward. "Rao just knows where to point me."

"Doesn't strike me as a man with a plan. Now you're saying he gives you direction?"

"That's not what I said."

"That's what I heard."

"Barely my problem," Adam responds and gets flipped off again. There's no malice on Hunter's face, just exhaustion. It's been a long night for all of them and, with some luck, maybe she's done trying to talk sense into him, whatever that means to her.

He gets an arm around Rao's waist and braces, pulling him from the wall. "Come on, Rao. Put your dick away."

"What? Oh. Right you are, Adam."

*

Rao wakes and immediately wishes he hadn't.

He wakes because Adam's turned on his antisurveillance radio, and right now KMFC: The Bullshit—or whatever the local station is called—is serving up Rick Astley. Rao feels so atrociously unwell he wants to die. No. No, he wants Rick Astley to die first, and he wants to watch.

Then he wants to die.

"You're alive," Adam says.

"Jury's out," he mutters. He tries to turn to bury his face in the pillow—it's appallingly bright in here—but the attempt is far too challenging, and he comes perilously close to throwing up. "For the love of god, close the curtains," he whispers. "Or shoot me."

Rao can't see Adam through the sickening patterns on the back of his eyelids, but he hears the ratcheting drag of a single curtain being drawn, then the sounds of a series of objects landing on the bedside table like heavy artillery at point-blank range. He groans.

"Tylenol, water, coffee. We have breakfast in forty minutes. Hunter's shipping out."

"Fuck. Forty minutes."

"I factored in the hangover."

"Can't you just leave me here to die?"

"I'm not doing that, Rao."

Through the near-opaque walls of his hangover, Rao slowly comes to understand there is a bit of an *atmosphere* at breakfast. He keeps his head as still as he can, chews slowly on dry toast, and listens to Hunter and Adam talking. In his fragile condition, Adam is the more bearable. His voice is lower, and he doesn't keep shooting him glares. Hunter doesn't like him, does she? Which isn't fair, considering.

Rao thinks about it a little more, decides it might be fair, considering.

"So," he says to her. "Last night."

She fixes him with a look that's remarkably like the pins entomologists use to stick insects onto plywood.

"Do you remember what happened?" she says.

Adam frowns. "Hunter . . ."

"No, I don't," Rao lies. "And I'm blissful in my ignorance, thank you."

She turns to Adam. "I'm going to tell him."

"Why?"

"Why wouldn't I, Rubenstein?"

"Fuck's sake," Rao breathes. "Listen. Could I finish my coffee first?"

"Finish it while I'm talking. I don't care."

"Patently obvious, yes."

She sits back, folds her arms. "I think we lost you during the pool game. You don't remember that? That's when you started to get messy, anyway. Told us that you were going to hustle some poor assholes. Ended up draping yourself on the first dude that would let you. Loudly asked him if he wanted to follow you to the restroom."

"You called it the loo at the time," Adam interjects, the fucking turncoat.

"Devil's in the details, Adam. *Cheers.*"

"You instantly ignore this dude as soon as you emerge massaging your jaw and licking your lips, by the way," Hunter continues. "Obnoxious."

"Sounds like he got the best result from the night, quite frankly."

"Then you spent an hour talking about, quote unquote, *amazing* things you've done while high. There was some shit about being on acid and discovering money?"

"Inventing the concept of currency from first principles," Rao supplies. There's something wrong with his voice as he speaks. No. It's Adam. Adam just said exactly the same sentence he just said at exactly the same time he said it.

Hunter's world-weariness increases by several tonnes.

"Jesus," she says.

"Got to that one, did I? You could've stopped me," Rao points out, reasonably.

She tilts her head at Adam. "That fucker wouldn't let me."

"It's better to let it play out," Adam says very seriously.

"I didn't go on about how I'm a god, did I?" Rao can't forget things, but sometimes he mislays memories on purpose.

"Do you want me to lie to you?"

"Fuck me," Rao groans.

"*That* came up a few times too. I'll tell you now what I told you then—"

"Adam," he whispers.

"Sorry, Rao."

"You're not my type," Hunter finishes.

"What *is* your type? You'll find me very accommodating when there's decent incentive."

"Shut up. You told us about how you were a god among men, alright. For some reason *this* is what made you go to pieces. What the fuck was that about?"

"I mentioned my mum?" Rao sighs, turning to Adam.

"You asked me not to tell her that you called yourself a god."

"I've asked that of you before, haven't I?"

"Haven't told her yet."

"Deeply appreciated, love."

Hunter's gaze has now turned baleful, getting on for full Medusa. She's not finished.

"We had to shepherd your ass out of the bar and back to the inn."

"*In?*" Rao frowns.

"Hotel."

"Ah."

"And that took fucking forever. You fell asleep pissing, at one stage. It's not funny, you shitheads."

"Hunter," Adam says, with the barest ghost of a grin, "I think we're done here."

"I'll tell you when we're done," she snaps.

"Yes, ma'am."

"Fuck you, Rubenstein."

They glare at each other. For a teetering moment, Rao thinks they're going to kick off. But then Adam snorts with open amusement and Hunter dissolves into giggles. "Were you fucking with me?" Rao demands irritably.

"I absolutely was not," Hunter says. "You were a pain in the ass. If you'd—"

"Hunter, you remember Tampa?" Adam cuts in.

What happened in Tampa?

Hunter rolls her eyes. "It was once."

"Last night was once."

"It felt longer than one night. Fuck." She shakes her head, turns to him. "Rao?"

She used my name, he thinks, alarmed. "Hunter?"

"When you've gotten over yourself, you're gonna put yourself on Flores's case, right? Find out where he is with your magic powers. I'm on leave for a while now visiting my folks, so keep me in the loop."

"Where are they?"

"Alaska."

"No they aren't."

"No, they aren't. Your battle buddy's got Flores's photo. Call me. No. Don't call me. He can call me."

At the door of the breakfast place she gives Adam a highly military hug that lasts, Rao thinks, a good four seconds longer than military hugs ought. She slaps his back to break it. "As you were, fuckhead," she says. Adam grins. *Dimples.*

Then she turns to Rao. She's hard to read, Hunter, but judging by how his skin prickles as she stares at him, under all that hostility and humour is someone truly terrifying. He's not going to get a hug. Possibly a punch in the mouth. But after looking him up and down, mouth downturned, she finally extends a hand. He shakes it firmly and is about to say something suitably lighthearted when the words turn to ash in his throat. He's met her eyes. Seen deep, deep resignation in them. *Ah,* he thinks, slowly. *She doesn't think I'm going to survive this.*

CHAPTER 28

Before

Adam had stopped the vehicle to let a small flock of turkeys cross the road, skinny, long-legged things shepherded by a small girl in a dress that brushed the dust. Rao was oblivious, slumped low in the passenger seat with both feet on the dash, continuing the complaint he'd started twenty minutes earlier. "Just because you don't eat, Adamski, doesn't mean other people don't get to. Come on, you must be hungry?"

Adam assured Rao again that he was not. But all this was moot. He'd diverted their route to the nearest town as soon as Rao started needling about lunch. He parked the UAZ in a leafy, shaded street. Explained that he needed to stretch his legs, so he'd come into the market too.

"Feel free," Rao muttered. "But I can buy food without getting murdered, you know. I do it all the time."

"Only takes once," Adam observed.

"Is that so? You're like the worst maiden aunt in existence. I keep expecting you to tell me to wear clean underwear, just in case."

"In case of what?"

"Doesn't matter. World War Three. Are you coming or not? It's a very exciting experience, watching me buy lunch. You won't want to miss it."

Sun-aged melons, bunches of greens, apples in piles, bowls of nuts, dried grapes, ash-coated apricot pits. Birds that hopped about his feet, chirruping through Persian pop, woodsmoke, pale-yellow sun. Adam kept his distance, but after establishing there was no sign of a local tail, he walked closer to Rao, overheard him telling the woman behind the bread stall that she was so beautiful he'd forgotten what he was here to buy. She threw her head back and laughed at him, and he grinned. She told him he'd better be wanting bread, because that's all she had, this being a bread stall, but it'd cost him more if he threw out compliments like that to a woman in her sixties—one married at that—and he arched his eyebrows at her in mock horror. Another line, this one in Uzbek, not Russian, conspiratorial and low. She laughed again, called him an idiot.

Rao's so dumb, Adam thought. Stupid. Look at him. The angle of Rao's jaw, the curl of his shoulders, the threads of silver at his temples, how he used his hands to help him speak, the shape of his mouth as he did. All familiar. But somehow not. Adam wondered, absurdly, if he'd ever seen Rao before. Then stood there, totally nonplussed. For a moment, he'd forgotten why they were here. Not just in this market. All of it. The tactical knives, the 9 mil at his back. The most reassuring things he owns. The express weight and presence of what he's for. But now the knives and pistol felt entirely insubstantial, like they were made of water. Hands would slip right through. He felt his heart contract, looking at Rao in the smoke, in the lemon-yellow morning light, staring at Rao's mouth as he spoke. And realized the fact, all at once.

Oh, he thought, astonished. *I'm in love with him.*

"You're being bloody quiet, even for you," Rao observed, back on the road. "You're not sulking because of the maiden aunt thing? Get over it, Adam. I've said much worse."

"I'm not sulking, Rao. I'm driving."

I'm compromised.

"Uh-huh."

Adam glanced down at the bags stuffed into the footwell around Rao's legs, at the two plate-sized rounds of lepeshka on his lap. Stamped, patterned decorations like needle marks, tiny black seeds scattered over glossy crusts.

"Break off some of that bread for me?"

"You *were* hungry. I knew it."

"You don't know shit, Rao."

"Shut up, you tosser," Rao said amiably, tearing him a section, handing it over. "I got cheese, roast chicken, samsas, gumma, pickles, fruit. Just let me know what you want when you want it."

"I'm all set," Adam said, biting into the piece, pulling a strip away, chewing it. He wasn't hungry.

The bread was good. He hated it. Kept his eyes ahead as he swallowed, staring as far down the road as the haze permitted, to where the Silk Route disappeared in a chaos of light and dust.

CHAPTER 29

B ack in their hotel room, Rao whistles as he unfolds the map.
"I've not done this for ages. Have you got it?"

"What?"

"The photo Hunter gave you. We've been through this before, love.
There are other Danny Floreses; the name isn't a rigid designator. Seeing a picture makes it easier."

Rao takes the photo, looks at it. Moves it a little farther from his
face, hoping Adam doesn't start his usual "you need glasses" routine. It's
a matte 4 x 6 print of a pine-panelled room, and it's a room in Afghanistan, because the man front and centre is wearing a pakol and a grey
wool waistcoat over a white shirt. No. It's Pakistan. He's got a tawny,
spec-ops fashionista beard, and he's giving the camera a half smile that
doesn't reach anywhere near his eyes.

Flores. Ok. Rao lays the photo down, mutters at the map spread
across the table before picking it up and folding it once along its vertical
axis. "He's not in the Rockies. Shame. Always wanted to visit." He lad-
ders his index finger up the sheet, dropping it on panel by creased panel,
asking each one if Flores's current position is within its bounds. "Ah,"
he says eventually. "He's in Denver. Denver-*ish*," he peers. "Aurora?"

"Aurora."

"Yeah. Ah! That'll be why it's EOS."

"What?"

"Aurora's the Roman goddess of sunrise, Adam. Eos is the Greek
goddess of sunrise."

"I know that, Rao. It won't be why. Project nicknames are generated automatically."

Rao ignores that after whispering it to himself, pushing past the usual weird resistance he feels when he's retesting one of Adam's statements and finding it's true. Rao scoots his fingers about, zeroing in on a location.

"Have you ever been lost?" Adam asks suddenly.

"Emotionally?"

"Rao."

"If I know where I have to get to or I've someone or something to find, no. How long will it take us to get to Aurora?"

"Who's driving?"

"Fuck off." Rao is an excruciatingly slow driver.

"Just over an hour. Hour and a quarter. But we should move base. I'll get us a motel."

"Yeah, good plan. Let's go full Bates. Find one with those vibrating beds."

"Magic Fingers."

"Yes, Adam. That's what I have, or so I've been told. Many, many times. Right. Fire up your laptop, we're taking this to Google Earth."

"So, Flores is in this block of buildings across the road from Buckley Air Force Base," Rao concludes a little while later, gazing at the screen, at the aerial view of long shadows falling from rooftops across a parking lot before losing coherence in a mass of summer foliage.

"That's Space Command," Adam says.

"You think he was retraining as an astronaut?"

"Unlikely."

"It was a joke, Adam. Let's find out who owns this place." He googles the address and blinks. "Fucking hell. Lunastus-Dainsleif BioScience."

"Huh," Adam says. He doesn't sound surprised.

Lunastus-Dainsleif, Rao thinks. Raytheon for the new millennium, the RAND Corporation in hipster suits. Big data and defense contracts, fingers in all the pies.

"So what's the plan?" he asks.

"We walk in."

"That's a terrible plan."

"We don't have time to recruit assets and we're in no position to SWAT team it."

"Adam," Rao says patiently. "They won't let us in."

"You can brute force sufficient intel to get us in."

"Right. Then they shoot us. Or dose us and make us make Furbys."

Adam's silence isn't reassuring. "What would you make?" Rao asks. "If you got, *you know*."

"What?"

"Dosed with this stuff."

"I've got no idea."

Rao narrows his eyes. "A knife."

Adam rolls his. "I'm not nostalgic about knives, Rao. They're kit."

"Bullshit. I've seen your knives. They're a bit flashy for kit."

"They're not flashy."

"They bloody are. Ok, not a knife. One of your airplane models."

"Stay on target, Rao."

"Al-most there."

Adam closes his eyes for a moment. "Give me my laptop. I'll book a car and a hotel."

Rao throws himself upon his bed, flings the back of one hand theatrically over his eyes, and lets out a self-pitying groan. For the last forty minutes he's been generating statements out loud and ascertaining the truth value of each one. He's found out that Flores is alive but incapacitated by the substance, along with fourteen others in that building, all but three of whom are ex–Special Forces. Volunteers.

After that, Adam handed him a pen and paper and asked him to run through the alphabet to find the name of the guy at the top of the hierarchy on-site, who happens to be someone named Montgomery. Adam intends to tell whoever this Montgomery turns out to be that they've come to conduct a spot check on project progress. Drop the words "EOS PROPHET."

Rao's not happy with this plan. "With a bit of time and a lot of paper, we can just find out the names and roles of everyone involved in the project," he'd pointed out quite reasonably, because it's fucking obvious that's what they should do. "You know, now you've decided I'm allowed to."

"Names don't get Flores out," Adam had said tightly. "We need to go in."

Rao had struggled with this statement. Adam's mission prep has always been infinitesimally granular, and it's disturbing how ready he is to go in on such limited intel. *Must be because of Miller,* he thought, remembering the rage on Adam's face. Or did he call Miller's boss and get explicit orders while Rao was having a smoke outside? Maybe. More likely.

He yawns. He's ok. Tired but ok. Agitated the way he always is after a run but ok. His hangover has been lessened by time, water, and Tylenol, but its diminishment has exposed all his self-recriminations, and those are far trickier to handle. All day he's been telling himself that last night's relapse was a one-off, but Rao's a past master at lying to himself. He's going to do better. He had been. He has to.

Adam walks back in from the bathroom. Rao hadn't noticed he'd gone, and startles slightly. "How're you doing?" Adam asks.

"Headache's gone, but my brain's leaping about like an ant on a hotplate." He waggles his brows. "Might go back to that bar and start a fight."

Adam snorts. "That won't be happening."

"You punch me in the face, then."

"Rao. Please."

"Adam, *please.*"

"I'd suggest we raid the minibar, but I think you already did that."

"Leave off. I get it. I went off on one. I'm not going to apologise."

"Wasn't asking you to," Adam says, pulling the chair from the desk to sit. He leans back and folds his arms; there's the faintest suspicion of a smile. Rao closes his eyes to shut it out.

"I was really awful though, yeah?"

"No. Hunter just doesn't know you. I had a pretty good night, considering."

"Considering what?"

"Nothing, never mind."

Rao's not going to let *that* lie. He props himself up on an elbow, fixes Adam with an enquiring eye.

"Fine," Adam acquiesces. "If you weren't giving me shit last night, then Hunter was. I'm not used to pincer manoeuvre ass kicking."

Rao grins. "I'd never be able to kick your arse, and I think it's alright if we both admit that."

"Mm. There's kicking someone's ass and then there's giving a friend an ass kicking."

"Ah," Rao says sagely. "It's all becoming clear now, Adamski. So what was Hunter's problem? You don't look at her during?"

"We're not a thing, Rao."

"But you have, though. Haven't you?"

Adam's mouth twitches. "Wow. No. Extremely no. She's a friend, and that's it. I'm not her type, and she's very much not my type."

"Out of your league?"

"Hunter's out of everyone's league."

"Alright, alright. So what was the problem, then?"

"I don't think you want to know."

"Fuck off, Adam. Stop being a wanker."

Adam shrugs minutely. "She thinks that you're taking advantage of my patience."

Rao laughs at that. "Fuck right the fuck off. Are you serious?"

Adam's covert smile hovers on the edge of being in the clear. "You asked," he says.

"Your *patience*?"

"Not her exact words, but yes."

"Does she *know* you?"

"Yeah, she does. Apart from you, better than anyone."

Rao's not sure he heard that right. He doesn't want the moment to pass unmarked. "I'm touched," he says eventually.

Adam frowns. "Don't."

"No, I'm being serious. You know I always sound like this, love. Can't help the sarcastic lilt to my tone. Social camouflage at school. I was surrounded by silver spoons, you know."

"Right. I know."

Liar, thinks Rao, amused. He can hear Crosby, Stills and Nash on the radio. Housekeeping in the corridor. The dopplering drone of transport planes outside. Adam's quiet, studying the floor.

"Would you believe me if I said that I feel similarly?" Rao offers.

"You don't have to do that."

"I don't *have* to do fuck all, Adam. Yet here I am, telling you the truth when I don't have to. Sober, too."

"Lucky me?"

"Fucking right. I trust you, you berk. Always have," he says. *No*, he thinks. *That's false.* "Well, not from the start, obviously, but it was a close thing. I had to, really. Trust you. If I didn't, I'd have gone mad with uncertainty and second-guessing. So that paid off, professionally speaking, pretty quickly. But, you know. Turns out I started trusting you as a friend as well."

"Rao—"

"I know, I know. Maybe I'm still hungover. All this sharing."

"You're not hungover. You'd be complaining more."

"That's true."

Adam looks up, eyes dark and serious. "I trust you, too, Rao."

"I should hope so."

"But I think you should be more careful about where you place your trust."

"Don't be a twat. I know you think I don't notice things, but I do."

"Do you."

"Yeah. I know it's always you that keeps us right when we're working. I'll wander off the second anyone gives me a chance, and I'll kick at any bastard who tries to stop me. But you manage it. Don't know anyone else who can do that. I see that, you know. I'm not an idiot."

"I know you aren't."

"You've probably kept me alive way more times than I know about, yeah? Just a hunch."

"There are some things you don't know about—"

Rao raises a hand. "Don't tell me, love. I really don't want to know about all the people who could have killed me if you hadn't been there.

I just hope you know that if I were of any use at all in that arena, I'd have returned the favour by now."

"That's not a concern."

"So what's this revelation?"

"It's not just your protection I've been tasked with when we're partnered, Rao."

"I know you're not just a bouncer with a gun because I was there, if you recall. You're a Defense Intelligence Agency officer. We met with your assets."

"Yes. But I've filled other roles." Rao waggles his brows. Adam rolls his eyes minutely. "*Roles*, Rao. Not *holes*."

"Was that a joke?"

"You know I'm not capable of jokes."

"Right. I say that a lot, don't I?"

"I haven't noticed."

"Stop lying, Adam."

Adam is staring at the floor again. He's thinking. "What?" Rao asks eventually. "What is it?"

"Are we still sharing?"

"I'm rather hurt you feel you need to ask. You know me better than that."

"I guess I do. I just wanted to say . . ." Adam starts, then hesitates.

"Spit it out, love."

"I do my best not to lie to you."

"Nice to know. You have an unfair advantage, after all."

"Lies would mess things up."

"Without a doubt."

"Lies by omission are worse than making things up, though. Aren't they?"

Rao feels a soft flutter of foreboding. "What are you getting at?"

It takes Adam a while to speak. "I was contacted," he says, "by some people, a few times, for advice on how to get you to focus on a job."

"And when was this?"

"You were in Afghanistan."

The air is cold, suddenly. "Is that so," Rao says. Precise diction. Each word honed to a point.

"Yes."

"Go on."

"I let them know that you're happier when you indulge and that it was in their best interest to let it happen. That your limits with that kind of thing are higher than average."

"*Indulge*. Right. I see. Better drug tolerance than your average bear, is that what you told them?"

"Not word for word."

The coldness is now so searing Rao half expects his breath to fog the air when he opens his mouth and speaks. "No. You don't get to joke. I get to joke. You get to shut the fuck up."

Adam raises his eyes briefly to Rao's, drops them to his feet.

"Well? Go on. Tell me what you're not saying."

"They misused that information."

The ice inside Rao spreads and ramifies. Reluctantly, he recalls the details. Sees them for exactly what they were. What it was. How much of a setup it had been. And now the coldness inside him isn't cold anymore. It's molten metal, it's magma, incandescent, and Adam's still talking. "You said something about meeting a guy at a bar—"

"Yes, thank you. I'm capable of following the bread crumbs of shit you're trailing around. Fucking hell. This tall fucker, too. Did you tell them to use him too? Do you keep a file on my sexual preferences, Adam?"

"No. I don't."

"CIA, I suppose. Nice little chat. You'd be happy enough to open up to them. Everything's a job, right?"

"They already had the reports I wrote on you after our time in Central Asia."

"Reports. Fucking *wizard*, Adam! What else? Been calling my mum each time I piss on the toilet seat?"

"I—"

"Don't fucking answer that," Rao hisses. It's astonishing how difficult he's finding it to breathe. It hurts. Feels like he's inhaling scalding steam. It's astounding that he's not already beating six shades of shit out of Adam. He knows from his face he'd let it happen. And it'd be happening right now if it weren't so very hard to move.

"It's not just your advising the cunts it'd be a good idea to get me hooked on heroin, is it," he says slowly. "Your reports were why they wanted me in the first place."

Adam doesn't respond. Rao sits. Rao waits.

"Well?" he says finally.

"Well what? That's all of it."

"You're shitting me."

"That's all, I swear."

"No, you prick. You're not even thinking about apologising, are you?"

Nothing. Silence.

"You wrecked my life, Adam. And you can't even fucking apologise."

Rao watches Adam inhale and exhale slowly before he speaks. "What's done is done."

"There. That. The *arrogance* that oozes from you, deciding what matters from someone else's past just because you never pay in sanity or blood like the rest of us. And no one can see it, because you're so boring and god-awful to be around. But now—would you like to know what I have now?"

"You're going to tell me."

"Yes. That's true. I am going to tell you. I have my wits about me now. My eyes are open. I know what you are. You're broken on the inside and that's why I can't tell with you. There's nothing even remotely human in there. It's just all the missing parts from every other soldier on the roster jumbled into the cage you call a body. Under your shitty, *shitty* suits." He takes a deep breath, trembling with rage. "Say something," he says. "No. No. On second thought, don't say anything. Don't talk to me. Don't fucking look at me. Fucking *trust*. That's it. That's me taught."

They sit in silence.

"Rao," Adam says eventually. "You should go home."

"Home."

Adam nods.

"What the fuck would you know about home? Yeah, an evasive look, what a surprise. Home's a meaningless concept to a military shit like you. Also," he spits out, "home for me isn't a nice house in the country, if you recall? What's waiting for me back in Blighty is prison. Sorry. *Jail*."

"I'll talk to some people. Write up a report on—"

"Fuck you and your reports, Adam."

"Rao, please go home."

"Care to tell me how? I've got no wallet. I've been spending *your* cash. My passport's locked in *your* bag. What do you want me to do? Suck off a trucker for a ride to an airport, walk up to check-in, and beg?"

"I can get you to Andrews, then—"

"I'm not some faceless goon like some people. I can't just plug in at any charging station at any fucking military outpost, you cunt."

Rao killed Ed. He's probably killed Miller. All those poor bastards in Kabul. Guilt, sour, stacked high, wet paper in his chest. "I'm coming with you tomorrow," he continues, voice like it's held in a vice. "No matter how much you'd rather I didn't."

He is. Mainly because he's gripped by an inchoate desire to find whoever's responsible for this and beat the shit out of them. That would be satisfying. While it lasts. Considering the scale of this project, what it's already done, he has no illusions about how an encounter like that would end. Maybe Adam'll watch him die. Yeah. That works.

"Rao—"

"Conversation's over."

CHAPTER 30

His parents are gone for the day. They've been leaving him alone in the house since he turned ten. Now that he's nearing his fourteenth birthday it's barely worth mentioning he's home alone to a neighbor or anything. Nobody will poke their head in. It's fine. Only, that day, his aunt comes to visit.

"Got the house to yourself, kid?" she grins as she walks in. Her voice is scratchy from the cigarette she's just stubbed out on the porch. He smiles back at her but doesn't answer. He doesn't have to. She never minds if he is a little quiet or slow to warm up to a conversation. "Are we having a party or what?"

"They're back at midnight," he explains. He isn't going to have a party, but that wasn't the question she was asking.

"So you have some time to breathe, huh?" She nods.

Aunt Sasha gets it. He never has to say the words to her. She understands. She knows how sometimes being in his parents' house feels like being held underwater, and no matter how hard he wants to kick and buck against it, he is always going to go under. He tells her how his dad has needed to get out of the house. How he's said he's been having trouble looking at his son lately. How he needs to go out and be normal with his wife. Talk out some things.

Then he tells his aunt about the camp. About how some friends of his dad's had sent their sons there. Their sons were older than him, already enlisted now. Tells her how, when they came back, their dads kept talking about how disciplined they were.

He isn't sure why, but that's when he tells her about Mark.

He knows it'll be fine to tell his aunt about Mark. She's safe. He knows she'll always be safe. Whenever he's messed up, she's never cared.

And this? This was a big one. Several clicks past messing up. Mark, and being caught with Mark, wasn't messing up. It was a fuckup.

She listens to him like she always does. Asks him if Mark was his first kiss or just the first boy. First everything, he tells her. She smiles like she's proud of him. It doesn't matter how much he messes up. She always smiles at him like that in the end.

"What's the name of that camp?" she asks.

He doesn't know. He's never listened to the details because there's no point in fighting his dad about it, he tells her. She knows how he is.

She nods and speaks slowly. Carefully. "How about, instead of that camp, you come live with me for the summer?" They look at each other in silence. She shrugs. "Or forever. Get away from your dad. Get away from that camp."

He thinks about it. It's not a real option. He'll never be allowed. Doesn't get a chance to say that to his aunt before she starts talking again.

"We gotta get you out of here, kid," she says quietly. They're the only people in the house, but she speaks quietly like there might be someone listening. "All I need is a few days and I can get us tickets to somewhere else, anywhere else, and your mom and dad won't find us."

"He'll kill me," he tells her. It isn't a no.

"He's going to kill you if you stay. One way or another, kid, he's going to kill who you are. You know what that camp is, right?"

CHAPTER 31

The building is a smoked-glass corporate pile set behind trees just off the air base perimeter road. Rao steps out of the car, brushes the lapels of his stupid suit jacket, pulls at the knot of his tie. The parking lot is half empty. Movement catches his eye. A vulture, flying past the mirrored facade of the topmost floors, reflection following it tilting and flickering frame to frame to frame. He stares at the bird's double until it winks out of existence, then shifts his eyes to the living vulture as it flexes its wings and soars higher.

"Rao."

"What."

"You ready for this?"

Rao hunches his shoulders, starts walking towards the doors.

Reception is a built guy in a black shirt whose sternocleidomastoid muscles are so outsized that when he opens his mouth Rao half expects him to ask him how much he can press.

"Good morning," he says. "How can I help you, gentlemen?"

"We're here for Montgomery," Adam replies.

"Misters Rubenstein and Rao?"

Credit to the asshole, but Adam doesn't blink. He nods. When reception guy looks down at his desk, he shoots Rao a tense look. It's a question. Rao doesn't dignify it with a response. Maybe they'll both get bullets in their heads once they're through those shining walnut doors. He doesn't fucking care.

Reception guy pushes a confidential visitor book across the desk and Rao watches Adam print in capitals across the black panel that says: WRITE YOUR NAME HERE. When Adam offers him the pen, he doesn't take it. Waits until it's laid back down on the page before grabbing it and filling out the form. When the passes are slid across the desk, Adam picks them up.

"Take a seat," built guy says. "I'll call him now."

They sit.

Adam's going to say something. Rao waits for it with infinite weariness. When it comes, it's even more absurd than he'd predicted. Even more maddening.

"Does this feel right to you?"

"Now that's important, is it? Suddenly my feelings on the matter are important."

"I'm serious. They know our names. We just walked in."

"No shit."

"This is weird, Rao. You should—"

"If you finish that sentence I will honest to fuck break your nose. Leave it. Shut up."

They sit in silence for another six minutes until a harassed-looking white man in his late fifties with close-cropped receding hair and wire-rimmed glasses walks through the doors into the foyer. His smile is speculative and hopeful: the kind Rao's always read as hoping for a punch in the face.

"Hi. Welcome," he says, opening his hands. "Look, I was given your names, but I wasn't told much about this visit, so I don't have a working brief—"

"Well, we've only just been brought on board," Rao says and shudders. The unexpected truth of that statement sets up a runaway physiological panic. He collects himself with difficulty. "We're here for a site tour, a rundown of the project history, and a progress report, if you have time."

"Sure. There's time." Montgomery smiles. "Dr Rhodes is managing day-to-day. She's our clinical research associate." He looks at his watch. "Let's go to the boardroom, I'll get you up to speed, and then we can head down to the clinical floor."

It's the worst boardroom Rao has ever seen. Futuristic art deco lit in Cherenkov blue and cotton candy pink, it's like a team at Industrial

Light and Magic had got fucked up on K and designed a grotto for a cruise ship.

"Wonderful, isn't it?" Montgomery enthuses.

"It's impressive," Rao agrees.

The vast glass tabletop rests on cubes of crushed automobiles. It's awful. The coffee brought to it by an urgent young man with pomaded hair is, however, sensational. Rao pops a Godiva chocolate in his mouth, then another. Glances at Adam. He's being worse than fucking useless. Rao might as well have brought a Care Bear and propped it on the table opposite him. Would have been more fun to look at.

Montgomery's eyes dart from Adam to Rao and back again. He looks down at the space in front of him as if expecting an agenda to magically appear. "Right," he says. "Yes. I don't know how much you—"

"Assume we know nothing. Start at the beginning."

"Ok. Yes. Twenty-two months ago a materials lab at Duke University synthesized a novel high-temperature superconductor. Shortly afterward, there was an incident. An outbreak of psychological instability. Started when one postdoc became convinced he'd lost something important under the refrigerator in the break room and kept pulling it out to look underneath it."

"Did he find it?"

"There wasn't anything there. He wouldn't leave the fridge alone. EMTs got called and they had to sedate him to get him home. The PI didn't come in the following morning because she'd spent the previous night throwing all the furniture in her bedroom out of the windows into the yard. Said she needed to re-create her childhood bedroom. They had to sedate her too. One of the lab technicians vanished. Wyoming state troopers picked him up nine days later on a ranch near Sheridan, dehydrated and delirious, raving about how he was a cowboy. They're all still unable to work."

"How unable?" Rao asks.

Montgomery swallows. His professional expression shifts to something more haunted. "The tech still thinks he's a cowboy, and the PI's marriage collapsed. Psychologically, she's regressed to a seven-year-old. They're both doing ok, though, considering."

"Are they," Rao says. "What about the postdoc?"

"He's not doing so well. Stopped speaking. Doesn't eat. Has to be tube fed. And he's still trying to look for what he thinks he's lost. He's—"

"DOD flagged the lab," Adam interjects.

"Well, yes." Montgomery looks at Adam. "Turned out there was a thin film of an unknown substance on the sample in the vice. Defense considered it a potential battlefield incapacitant. You with them? Thought so. I can tell. And you"—he turns to Rao—"I mean, you're a creative. Lunastus, right?"

Rao smiles thinly, reaches for another chocolate. "Very recent hire."

"And Defense reached out to us." Montgomery gives Rao a shy, conspiratorial grin. "You know how Lunastus-Dainsleif was a CIA start-up. A natural home for a project like this. We put materials scientists and neuroscientists on the case, looking at the structure of the substance and its affective mechanisms. We got some results. Then . . ."

"Then?"

Montgomery frowns. "It started growing."

"Growing?"

"Yeah. It increased in volume. Also in complexity. It's still doing that, actually. But how and what it used—uses—to polymerise, we've not yet been able to determine. And the effect it has on those exposed to it, that's changed too. Early iterations, exposed subjects got obsessed with things they'd lost or thought they'd lost. Later, they stopped getting upset about things they'd lost—"

"And started making them," Adam says.

Montgomery nods.

"How?" Rao says.

Another frown. "What kind of how? There are—"

"The physics of it. Conservation of energy, for one thing. Where does the matter come from?"

"Yes. Well. Our physicists are pretty freaked out. No one's got any idea."

He's not lying.

"And now?" Rao says.

Montgomery's looking a little uncertain. "You're here for the manifestation program?"

"We are. How's it going?"

"Mixed results," Montgomery says. "Look, it's an elegant idea. We want it to work as much as you do. We've recruited the right volunteers and put them in a hostile VR environment. But so far, none have generated defensive weaponry. We expose them to a virtual firefight and they . . ."

"Make Care Bears and get incapacitated," Rao offers.

"Not all of them," Montgomery says.

"I think you should show us," Adam says.

The elevator doors are glossy Kubrick white and open into a roomy elevator with scuffed yellow walls. On the lower floor, Montgomery leads them down a corridor and through two sets of airlock doors into a clinical lab. A petite woman in a white lab coat turns to them as they enter.

Hello, Rao thinks. She looks almost exactly like the house rigger at a fetish club in Berlin he used to kick about in back in the day: the same simultaneously welcoming-and-unwelcoming demeanour, the same straight-cut auburn bangs, narrow chin, and wide grey eyes. She has the kind of face that gives nothing away and a mouth—wearing what he's pretty sure is Rouge Dior 999—*yes*—that hovers disconcertingly close to a smile.

"Dr Veronica Rhodes, clinical research associate," she says. Cut glass RP. She extends a slender hand.

"Hi. I'm Rao."

She glances enquiringly at Montgomery.

"They're here for the manifestation program," he says.

Her mouth twists a little as she takes them in. Adam doesn't appear to interest her at all. Her eyes slide off him, return to Rao. Excellent judge of character, he decides. She looks at him curiously. When he finally takes her hand, she smiles warmly. It's like the sun's come out. Winter sun, for sure, but still Rao can feel it on his skin.

"A pleasure to meet you," she says. "What might your particular expertise be?"

Rao winks, lets her hand drop. "I'll tell you mine if you tell me yours."

Adam clears his throat. "He's an expert at spotting fakes and forgeries."

Rao's mood instantly plummets back to the pit it was in. Fucking Adam and his long history of cockblocks. *Fucking who asked you?* he thinks venomously.

Veronica's eyes haven't left his face. "How interesting," she says. The smile's still there, but a little fixed. The merest furrow has appeared on her otherwise perfect forehead. Rao's fascination ratchets up a few notches. She's a fake. He's just not sure what flavour yet. "And where does one learn to do that?"

"Long story. Spent a few years in fraud and attributions at Sotheby's."

She nods, turns to Adam. "What about you, Mr . . ."

"He can't talk about it," Rao says firmly.

"Can't or won't?"

"He's constitutionally unable."

"Defense," Montgomery explains.

"Ah. In which case I'll refrain from further questions. I'm about to head down to the ward," she says, gesturing to the door and smiling her pale sunlight smile. "Shall we start there?"

Rao's heart drops, skips, and swings into a too-rapid rhythm as they enter a large clinical space. Sallow light, lemon-scented air with an undertow of shit and bleach. Serried sounds of heart rate monitors, light refracted through pouches of saline. Submerged memories surface sharply: his stomach churns and sweat prickles under his arms. He takes a series of deep breaths, counts the beds. Thirty. Fifteen occupied.

Two nurses in white rush up. Veronica hastens forward and draws them a little away. Rao can't hear what she's saying—it's hurried, sotto voce—but from the looks on their faces as they leave the room, she's just told them to fuck off. She turns back to Rao and Adam, bringing one finger up to tuck one curled end of her fringe behind her ear, though not a single hair is out of place. The gesture is an obvious act, and Rao finds himself charmed by it. "We've had some issues with sores," she says. "Placing even a partial physical barrier between skin and object generates poor outcomes. But I'm happy to say that with our current regimen they're all doing very well."

In his peripheral vision, Adam is scanning the rows of unconscious bodies. He moves towards a bed, considering its occupant for a while before turning towards Rao. Rao, who's ignoring Adam so thoroughly that he knows exactly where in the room the fucker is and exactly what he's doing. He tries to listen to Veronica, but he can't parse what she's saying because Adam is looking at him and Rao knows that look. It's one of Adam's *significant* ones. He tries even harder to listen, hears the phrase "memory-reward coactivation," then gives in and joins Adam and his fucking significant looks.

"*What is it?*" he hisses, making his way over. Adam's looking down at the bed. It's Flores. Clean-shaven, a tube through one nostril, a bruise on his forehead, but Flores all the same. He's gripping something small in both hands, tucked tight under his jaw, and his expression is a rictus of such manifest bliss Rao feels a tug of unexpected envy.

"So, tell us about this one," Rao asks Veronica.

"It's a cassette tape. Specifically, a cassette single. 'On Our Own' by Bobby Brown, taken from the *Ghostbusters* soundtrack. It's one of the easier objects in terms of patient management."

"Not the object. The subject."

"Oh, yes. One of our first. Invalided ex–special ops, like most of our volunteers. This one"—she frowns—"Flores. We had high hopes for him."

High hopes. Rao's skin crawls. Flores is trapped in a moment of absolute emotional truth: looking at him makes Rao tight chested, like his lungs are packed with sugar. Dread ticks under his skin. He still wants to punch something, and even though that urge isn't going anywhere while Adam Fucking Rubenstein is in the same room, he knows he has to focus. For Miller. For this faded Flores. For Ed. He drags his eyes away from the corner of the cassette pressing into Flores's reddened jaw, looks down at the bed to his left.

This patient's face is pressed against a wooden box. An old-style radio. Oatmeal grille cloth, a rose-and-gold dial. It's the source, Rao realises, of the soft, sibilant noises he's been hearing under the hum of climate control. Whispered squeals and hisses, snatches of barely audible voices, as if someone were searching for a station. He listens. The hissing whispers, the static highs and lows all loop back to their starting point every four breaths. He can't tell if the radio is syncing with the breathing, the breathing with the radio, or if there's any meaningful causal distinction to be made between breathing and radio at all.

"This one's notable," Veronica says. "It's a 1952 Raytheon tube radio. We've ascertained it wasn't a feature of the subject's childhood environment, so it doesn't possess the usual autobiographical affect. Our working theory is that this EPGO, that's Eos Prophet Generated Object, is the manifestation of a more generalized cultural nostalgia." Rao nods. The radio is a tiny version of Ed's diner. "And secondly, it's the first that's emitted sounds."

Adam looks up from Flores's chart. "You've had others?"

Rao's very close to snapping, *Of course they fucking haven't.* He doesn't. He recognises that covert, enquiring glance he's getting, and he's not going to fall in line. Adam's working. Adam's on mission for the military, like he always is. Always was.

Fuck him and fuck them.

He stares dully at the rows of beds, the racks of monitoring machinery. Thinks of what this is. How it works. How it's always fucking worked. Thinks, *complicity.* Thinks, *Kabul.* Thinks, *naïveté.* Thinks of Adam's betrayal. Feels a fresh, rolling wave of outrage.

He needs to ask. Turns to Montgomery, and despite the bile in his throat, keeps his voice low, soft. Manages, even, to sound impressed. "How on earth did you get this past an ethics committee?"

Montgomery makes a small, private smile, shakes his head. He looks like John Denver, Rao decides. An amoral, balding, asshole John Denver.

"There isn't an ethics committee. Very technically, the manifestation program isn't classified as medical research, so the Declaration of Helsinki doesn't apply. Any adverse effects on test subjects fall under the category of nonoperational casualties."

Rao wonders who taught him that fluid little speech. He didn't quite follow it. Adam, apparently, did. "It's a military training program," he says slowly.

"Indeed," Veronica clarifies. "No limits on training if the ends justify the requirement."

"Deaths?" Adam asks.

"Two," Veronica says. "Before we developed our current postinfusion protocols. A pity, but these things happen."

Adam opens his mouth to respond, but Rao cuts in, addressing him directly. "Well, you know how it goes with these things, Adam," he says, voice like silk. "What's done is done, after all."

He watches that land. Detonate. Adam's face is expressionless, but there's agony in his eyes. *Good.* Rao needs to see more of that. Adam should suffer. Because, as people have always been so fond of telling him, there should be consequences to one's actions.

Adam struggles back into the conversation. "You're working on fixing this?" He looks to Rao again. Unbelievable. He's still working. Still trying to generate statements for Rao to read. Still fucking using him.

"Fixing?" she says.

"Waking the subjects. Getting them out of their comas."

"They're trance states."

"Getting them out of their trance states," Adam corrects.

Everything she's said so far has been true. Everything except the line about her patients doing well. That was a barefaced lie. And, considering the supine bodies surrounding them, an impressively ballsy one.

"Oh, yes. A priority," she says. "We're making progress."

And that's two more.

Adam is giving him another look. This one's even more hopeful.

"Adam, fuck off," he says flatly. He couldn't give a shit about the questioning looks. Couldn't give a shit about anything. Fuck this horror show. He sees how it works.

What Adam is leads to all of this.

And what all of this is leads to Adam.

Adam, who's standing there looking at the floor.

He's not evil, Rao thinks. He's a blank cassette, a wet clay tablet. Lieutenant Colonel Tabula Rasa. Something they could write on. Train. Make. Use. Or maybe that's not true. Maybe he is an evil bastard. Absolute psychopath. No feelings, no blood, never gave a fuck. Yeah. *Because he gave me up for what? For work*. Because it's his job. Because CIA asked him and Adam's the Rao expert. Better at handling Rao than Rao is. All those times Adam's done things for him. Water and Tylenol on the nightstand. All the times he's bought him cigarettes. Checked his vision with a penlight after Rao'd let off steam. The time he laid out that asshole who threw a slur in Rao's direction. Even that. All of it was work. Adam, babysitting. Rao's astounded by the extent of his naïveté. Even after Kabul. Feels like he's grown up, wrenched into the world. Curtain twitched away. Plato's fucking cave. Now he's behind the—

"Mr Rao?"

It's Veronica. She's been trying to attract his attention for a while.

"I was saying, perhaps you'd be interested in viewing the test footage?" she asks.

Rao shrugs. "Sounds good, yeah."

CHAPTER 32

His dad taught him how to pack. Told him the key was practice. Repetition. Like stripping and reassembling a weapon. Do it enough times and you won't waste any mental effort on it. It's more efficient in the long run. Plus, if you pack and unpack and repack a bag a bunch of times, then you get to know where all the items are inside, which makes them easier to find when you need them. First you need a staging zone, where you can lay out the contents and organize them. Then you pack in reverse order, so the things you need last are the things that go in first. You have to break the pack into thirds. Bottom third is medium weight, middle third is heavy, top third is light. And the heaviest things always go closest to your back.

He knows this is a good go bag, but he also knows that if he messes up and doesn't pack something important, he'll never get another chance to pack it.

Nothing inessential, his dad always said, when you pack a bag. He looks down at the things arranged neatly on his bedroom carpet. Some of them aren't essential. The Swiss Army knife is. The buck knife really isn't. But he's packing it anyway. He thought about taking books to read but decided they weren't necessary. His aunt has a lot of books already. But he's bringing the book she gave him when he was a kid. He hasn't read it for years, but he doesn't want to leave it behind.

Two shirts, three tees, two pairs of socks, three pairs of underwear, two pairs of pants.

Sneakers. He'll wear his boots.

Jacket.

Wash bag.

His passport. Social Security card. He went into his dad's den while his parents were out and picked the lock of the filing cabinet, which was easy—he's done it before—and pulled out the file with the family passports and cards. He flipped his dad's open. *Joseph*. His name is Joe. Nobody calls him Joseph except his aunt. But nobody calls his aunt Alexandra except his dad, so he guesses that's fair. He opened his own and looked at the photo. Blinked at it. It's an old photo and he looks different now, but he's not good at recognizing himself in photographs anyway. Even in mirrors he never quite gets who it is looking back. This photo, though. He looks like a dumbass in it. Doesn't matter.

He finishes with his backpack. Slips the passport with his SS card tucked inside it into the secret pocket at the back. Then he undoes the top and looks in. Pajamas rolled up and fitted neatly on top. He closes it. The tightness is happening, the band around his chest, and he knows that if he took everything out of the bag and packed it again that would help. But he doesn't. He's already done that twice. He sits on the carpet and holds his knees instead. He wants to do the thing, but maybe he won't have to this time. Sometimes it goes away on its own without getting really bad.

Not always.

There's got to be something wrong with him. Something wrong with his heart, probably, because he can feel it beating in his throat, times like this, and that tight feeling is what people talk about when they talk about heart attacks. He hasn't told anyone about it. Never will. Especially his dad. If there's something wrong with him, they won't let him enlist. And he doesn't like to think about that, but he's thinking about that now, and it's making his heart worse, it's beating stupid fast now, thumping in his ears, and it's a bad one, he knows it is, because he's getting that shivery, trickling feeling, and he's sweating, and when he lifts a hand from one knee it's shaking.

He's going to do the thing because he has to.

He gets up and goes to the bathroom, blinking because the world is dark. He doesn't turn on the light. He shuts the door, locks it. Steps into the bathtub, sits in it, curls up over his knees, closes his eyes, takes deep breaths, and waits.

CHAPTER 33

Veronica leads them to a dark, luxuriantly carpeted room that smells of expensive hotel. Montgomery hovers by the door. She takes a seat before a wall of monitors, pulls a keyboard towards her, and brings up time-stamped footage on two of the screens. When she presses Play, both run synchronously.

The first shows a moving landscape. It could pass for real. It isn't. All digital. A hillside, crags. Bare trees, stretches of dry grass pushed by breeze. Midday glare, gullies in deep black shadow. Rocks. No truth to the flocks of birds in the sky except the algorithm that's making them wheel and turn.

The other footage is a man in a white-walled room. He's wearing a white singlet, sweatpants, and laced-up boots. Flores.

Veronica moves into view beside him on-screen. She wrinkles her nose fondly at him, her mouth moves—there's no sound—and he laughs, shoulders easing as she speaks. She's flirting, Rao sees, and she's good at it. He watches her hand Flores a virtual reality headset. The manner in which Flores puts it on, his ease as he walks about to test his orientation: the routine is familiar to him, and as he turns and walks, the landscape on the other screen shifts to match his movements.

He nods. She takes his hand, guides him back to the centre of the room. Picks a syringe, a vial, and a small packet from a surgical dish on the shelf beneath the observation window, walks back, tears open the packet, and wipes his upper arm. Then she draws Prophet from the vial, slips the needle into the muscle just below his shoulder. When she withdraws it, she speaks again.

He nods. She leaves the room.

"You'll need sound for the cue," Veronica says, pressing a key. Wind, sifting grass, and birdsong fill the room. She fast-forwards the video; when it resumes normal speed, three minutes have passed.

Then something like the crack of a whip, loud and unmistakable. Rao hears Adam inhale, sees the subject's head turn, then realises it's the sound of a round passing far too close. Flores drops to the ground—perhaps less fluidly than he would have done back in the day, that right ankle is definitely off—but he's prone, on his elbows, and there's another crack, rippling into an intermittent fusillade.

"As I said, we had hopes for this one. You can see he puts a hand to where he expects his rifle to be."

Rao blinks. He doesn't want to. Doesn't want to miss any of this. But he blinks despite himself, watching Flores reach for the rifle that isn't there. In its place, the cassingle. Flores raises it to nestle it under his chin, his face bright with joy.

Veronica cuts the video. Brings up another. "That was subject three. This is six."

The same setup but a different man. Shorter than Flores, wirier. Same outfit. He's treated to the same flirting as Flores, though this time it doesn't seem to land. The same goggles are handed to him; they show the same arid, virtual scene. Veronica administers her dose. Time passes. Same crack of ordnance, same response. But no object. Nothing appears. A little while later, the virtual scenery cuts to slowly flashing red text: PLEASE REMOVE HEADSET. And the guy pulls off the goggles, gets up, and grins.

"What's the difference?" Adam says.

"Prophet appears to provoke flash memories of objects with deep psychological salience to our test subjects," Montgomery explains. Rao doesn't jump, but it's a close thing. He'd entirely forgotten about Montgomery, though that's probably a regular occurrence for the man. "Some people don't have those." He glances at Veronica.

"Have what?" Rao asks.

"Emotional memories," she says. "The combination of flattened emotional affect and less-than-vivid autobiographical memories is found in approximately one percent of the general population, but individuals of this type are overrepresented in our test demographic."

Rao suspects she's trying to lose him in the jargon, but he's hanging on with glee. "Veronica," he breathes with mock horror. "Are you telling me that Special Forces hire *psychos*?"

She gives him a dangerous smile. "That's not a term recognised in the *DSM-IV*."

"Well," Rao says. "Whatever you call it, this is good news for you, Adam."

"I'm not a psychopath, Rao."

"Is he?" Veronica asks.

"Yeah," Rao says. "Full Tin Man. No heart. That bastard'll be immune."

He waits for Adam to kick back after that. Expects something properly vicious. To prove him right, prove him wrong, do fucking anything at all. He gets nothing. Just a mute mask and downcast eyes. It's *enraging*.

Montgomery coughs a cartoon *ahem*. "Mr Rao, individuals with limited empathy are essential to this project. The substance aerosolizes readily. Infusions can only be carried out by people who are immune."

Veronica's beaming at Rao. Ah. *So* that's *her flavour of fake*, he thinks. Of course. All that flirting. He sees it for what it is. Doesn't care. She's good.

"I don't think I've ever met a psycho that isn't a bloke before," he lies.

"I'm sure you have," she says sweetly. "We're just much better at keeping it under our hats."

Next stop on the tour, Montgomery informs them, is the test suite. En route, Rao keeps his eyes trained on the art on the corridor walls. It's dreadful: corporate always is. But he'd rather stare at shitty sub-Rothkos than look at Adam, who's matching his pace, walking inches from his side. His skin itches with that unwelcome proximity, right hand bunching into a fist. He imagines the swing, the force he'll put behind it, the satisfaction when it connects.

"Rao—" Adam begins, voice low.

"Whatever it is you feel you have to say," Rao spits, "keep it to yourself. I can do this on my own. I don't need you. You're entirely fucking pointless."

They file in, silent, through a pair of airlock doors into a room so fiercely ventilated a breeze tugs fitfully at Rao's hair. The steel wardrobe near the entrance hums softly: a refrigerator or freezer, Rao assumes. *Refrigerator.* Three chairs, two workstations, three screens. It's spotlessly clean. Rao rubs at one wrist, feeling grimy. Out of place. Pathogenic.

"Observation room. The test room is through there," Montgomery explains, gesturing at the wide window next to a door on the far wall. Rao walks up to the glass, peers into the space beyond. Complicated ceiling ductwork, plasticised floor, wall-mounted cameras, everything white, wipe-down, a whole Michael Crichton vibe. It's dimly lit, far smaller than it looked on-screen. *They're going to be fucked,* he muses, *when some poor bastard re-creates their childhood house in there.* Would the created house push all this out of the way into rubble, or would it manifest itself right through it? He imagines being trapped in that impossible architecture. Rooms cut into dead-space angles by facility walls, bisected by sheets of glass.

No. Everything in the ward upstairs was small. Nothing bigger than that bulky radio. He remembers the diner, clouds over beet fields, sun on wet clay. Maybe it's—

"So where do you keep the substance?" Adam's bastard voice, breaking his concentration.

"In the refrigerator," Veronica says. "Shall we take a look?"

"Are we—"

"It's perfectly safe."

She opens the door. Rao walks over to see. Bathed in white light and laid on wire racks are a score or so of syringes in separate, glass-like containers.

"That's it?"

"Yes, Mr Rao. That's Prophet."

Rao takes another step towards the fridge, hesitates.

There's impatience in her voice. "It's safe, as I said. We no longer use vials. The syringes are predrawn at the point of manufacture and shipped here in vacuum containment vessels."

"Prophet," Rao says, feeling the word curl on his tongue.

"That's what we're calling it."

Close up, the substance in the syringes gleams.

"It's a metal?" he says.

"No. It's a very unusual substance. Our physicists have begun calling it a supersolid. The infusion is a colloidal suspension. Point six percent by volume. It looks like that because it has very particular optical properties. Even at this concentration, it scatters light with phenomenal efficiency."

Rao blinks. The syringes are right there, right in front of his face. At the same time he has an unpleasantly compelling intuition that they're also *somewhere else*. Worse, the intuition feels true. The dissonance grates horribly. Glass paper in his sinuses, a low swoop of motion sickness. He's relieved when Veronica shuts the refrigerator door. But the dim reflection of his face in brushed steel feels precisely the same: somehow both here and somewhere else. Revulsion, suddenly, and Rao moves quickly to the far side of the room, dimly aware that he'd prefer to put a wall between himself and the stuff in the fridge. Turning his back on everyone, he looks again into the observation room. But he can't focus on what's inside, only the surface of the window, and when his eyes find his own reflection, they get stuck on it.

Somewhere else.

The last time he'd stared like this at his own face was in his hotel bathroom in Kabul. He remembers spending a long while before that pacing about his room, then slowing. Slowing to look at everything in it, the filled ashtrays, the clothes on the floor, the glass in the window, smoke in the sky outside, the spaces between all these things somehow more real than the things themselves, before he'd walked into the bathroom and stood in front of the mirror, drawn to commit his own face to memory, knowing that in a little while there'd be no memories left to have. Such a relief. So quiet, those long moments before he went back into the room to make it happen. So quiet. It's not that he'd expected his life to flash past his eyes. But the quietness of it all was still a surprise, his own eyes in the mirror looking back at him from somewhere else.

Another face joins his reflection. Pale, clean-shaven. Takes him a few seconds to work out it's not a ghostly hallucination. It's Adam, standing far too close, looking into the test room as if he's trying to comprehend exactly what Rao can see in it.

My death, Rao thinks. *Which was on you. All on you.*

He closes his eyes, hears Adam asking about the current status of the testing program.

"It's slowed lately," Montgomery admits. "As you can imagine, the pool of suitable volunteers isn't large."

Rao speaks then. Keeps his eyes shut and speaks. Every syllable is hot and vicious. "Being a cunt doesn't interfere with the test, does it? Because if it doesn't, I volunteer Adam. He's a *huge* fan of secret military drug programs."

Montgomery hesitates. "I'm not sure if you can volunteer your partner on his behalf."

"Don't worry. Literally no one will miss him."

Adam says something too low to hear.

"No," Rao says evenly, opening his eyes. He turns to Adam, stares him down. "If you've something to say, do me the courtesy of saying it out loud."

Barely a whisper. "I hate you, Rao."

What a fucking child.

Rao rolls his eyes at Veronica. "That's a lie, of course. He's bloody obsessed with me."

Adam looks at him blankly. Doesn't say a word. Turns his back and walks towards the door.

Good. Fuck off back to the car.

"Right," Rao says. "Veronica. Where were we? Questions and answers time."

"Questions and answers," Veronica repeats, her grey eyes holding Rao's. Then her gaze slips past him. Her eyes widen. A quiet sound then, an indrawn breath, a light bulb dropped. She reaches forward and pushes him. He stares down at her hands on his chest. She pushes him again, harder. Rocking back on one foot, he opens his mouth to protest when he catches sight of the floor by the door. Glitter of broken glass. A jacket.

Adam's jacket. Adam's jacket is on the floor. And above it, Adam.

Adam, head bowed low over his forearm.

Adam with his sleeve pushed up, needle sunk into his skin, and everything is moving sickeningly slow, but he's depressing the plunger appallingly fast.

He's saying something. He's saying, "I'll find an answer."

He's not looking at me, Rao thinks stupidly.

Even before Adam tugs the needle free, Veronica's hands are on him, propelling him backwards towards the test room. He yields to her insistence. No protest, not a sound. He still isn't looking at Rao, and this, more than anything, is what drives him. Before Veronica gets Adam through the door, Rao's already slipped through.

"Not you," she says tightly. "Get out." He slips around her, slams the door. "Foolish," she hisses, shaking her head rapidly as if ridding herself of him.

Adam's right arm has fallen to his side, the syringe still gripped in his hand. The fingers holding it are white. Blood on his fingers, a track running down his right wrist. He's looking at Rao now, eyes wide. Rao has seen eyes like them before in a mirror in a hotel room in Kabul at sunset, and for one impossible second, he's certain he's looking at himself.

The full weight of what Adam's done falls on him. *No. Oh no.* Mutely, he watches Veronica prise the syringe from Adam's fingers. She turns her wrist to glance at her watch, strides quickly to the far side of the room.

"How long?" Rao manages to croak.

"Radial artery? Seconds."

Adam's already looking rough. His eyes have lost Rao's. His skin is clammy, pale. He's breathing with effort. Rao steps forward, takes his face between his hands. Rasp of hair against his fingers, skull beneath skin.

"Adam, please," he hears himself say. "Get through this. Just be ok. Anything you want. I'll do anything."

Adam's mouth moves, once. Barely a whisper.

"Don't—"

CHAPTER 34

Rao thinks it's fear, at first. It's a scent, close, thick, wet, deep as blood, but it's not metallic and doesn't cut that way. Not blood. Heady as arousal, but not that either.

No. He knows what it is. Exactly what it is, but it shouldn't be here. He's smelled it in Rajasthan, in Uzbekistan, in every desert he's walked in after rain, fragrance rising from the ground after water hits dry soil. He's holding Adam's face in his hands in a room that smells of petrichor. And woodsmoke, now, threading through it, strengthening until smoke is all there is, hazy and sweet. Abruptly, an atmospheric shift: the room pales, lit like morning sun. Then noises, a quick succession. One ping, like an oven timer, makes him jump out of his skin. A scrape of something like a cry, a distant *burr* that might be jet noise, the drumming of heavy rain, charred toast, then that lemon-yellow light again and more woodsmoke and then the smell of a just-fired pistol and then Rao can taste vodka in his own mouth. Turpentine, gun oil, something sharp like grapefruit juice, a snatch of what he thinks is a song by the Seekers playing on a transistor radio. It's too fast. The sensations are being pulled over him like striplights in a freeway tunnel at top speed and over all of them, or under, is the growing tick of a metronome. Burned toast, again. Thickly acrid, almost makes him choke. Rao battens himself against the rising barrage of sensory information, turns his head to follow Adam's gaze and sees it fixed on the wall across the room. On it is a languid patch of brightness that's moving like sun on water, and the sounds are slowing now, the shifts of light, too, a dying zoetrope, the perpetually rattling roulette wheel finally coming to a halt, and the blank wall is no longer bright and glittering, it's no longer blank at all, because it's honey-varnished pine

panelling, golden with evening sunlight, and hanging on it, right at
eye level, is a clock, hands set at

5:45 p.m.

He was supposed to leave the house at six. It's a fifteen-minute walk to
the traffic lights at the intersection, the rendezvous his aunt had picked.
She said she'd be there, waiting. Motor running. Ready. He just had
to leave the house without arousing suspicion. That was supposed to
be the easy part. But it hasn't been so easy. Until recently his parents
hadn't cared where he was. They'd give him a time to be home and tell
him to stay out of trouble. They never asked questions. That changed
a few weeks ago. The reason was obvious.

He was supposed to just walk out. Dodge questions. Check his
packed bag. Open the door. Walk away. His mom was supposed to be
upstairs. His dad was supposed to be working. They were supposed to
be busy. Easily ignored, easily avoided.

This was supposed to be the easy part.

He wasn't supposed to be sitting at the kitchen table watching his dad
standing at the countertop fuming over the broken toaster. He wasn't
supposed to be watching the clock on the wall, waiting for a chance to
leave. He wasn't supposed to be here. At 5:45 p.m., he was supposed to
be double-checking his packed bag, opening the door. Walking away.

His aunt was going to be at the lights.

"Do you think you could fix this thing?" his dad asks suddenly, jig-
gling the toaster. There's bread in it. He can smell it burning. Smoke
is rising from the slots.

He's surprised. Why would his dad ask him if he knows how to fix
a toaster?

"I don't know anything about that right now, but I could probably figure it out," he answers, speaking as honestly as he can without
sounding like he's back talking. It's always a fine line to walk. "If you
gave me time."

Right now he's supposed to be double-checking everything.

Right now he's supposed to be getting ready to leave.

"You're a smart kid," his dad mutters.

The toast doesn't pop. It slides up after a soft *ding*. Burned, black crusts. Smell charring the air. Sharp. It's 5:50 p.m.

He isn't sure if his dad has ever said he was smart before. It shouldn't matter that he has. He knows he's smart. He just doesn't think his dad has ever said it out loud. Trust the man to drop that at 5:50 p.m. He doesn't reply because he doesn't think this is a conversation. But then his dad starts speaking again, so apparently it is.

"You're going to think all kinds of things about life soon, you know," his dad says, looking down at the toaster. He picks a single black slice out of it. Turns it in his hand. Doesn't do anything to it. Doesn't bother to get a knife to run down its surface. Doesn't bother scraping the carbon off. "You're going to come up with explanations about life, about growing up. About me. About your mom. While you're out of this house, you're going to be told all kinds of things. And you'll come up with more. You're smart."

He's talking about that camp again. He talks about it a lot.

"It's complicated, Adam," his dad goes on, sitting down at the table. He sets the burnt toast down on the table. No plate. Just rests it between them on the tablecloth. Neither of them looks at the other. They look at the toast. "It'll get more complicated as time goes on. That's life. That's what they don't tell you, but I'm telling you now. It gets more and more complicated. The only way to make it through life intact is to figure out your own way to think about it."

"And I don't think about it the right way," Adam says.

It isn't a question. He gets what his dad is saying. He usually does.

The sun is setting. Golden light is falling over the kitchen in pools that warm the parts of his leg it touches. His eyes catch on the tip of his dad's air force tattoo, just visible below the edge of his tan shirtsleeve. It would have been black once. Now the ink is kind of blue. He's never been sure what it is. He's never seen all of it. It's probably a bird.

He doesn't know.

He looks up. There's sunlit dust in the air. Little points of light, moving slowly, like stars.

The clock says 6:00 p.m.

He was supposed to be gone by now. He's not supposed to be here.

"You don't think about it the right way yet. That's all."

The clock ticks over to 6:01 p.m.

*

Adam mustn't, must *not*, *cannot* touch the thing on the wall. Rao isn't going to let it happen. He flings his arms tight around him, braces his feet against the floor. Takes a deep breath, grips harder, waits for the struggle. He knows this is pointless. He's seen Adam fight, knows he could kill him without breaking a sweat, expects to be thrown to the ground in less than a second. But there's no retaliation. No movement at all. Beneath his shirt, Adam's muscles are locked tight. It's like clinging to a statue. Blank. Inert. The only heartbeat Rao can feel is his own, wild and high in his throat. The seconds slip and drag and thicken until Rao feels a flutter of wild, uncertain hope. Unlike Ed, unlike Miller and those poor bastards in the next room, he realises, Adam isn't being drawn to the thing he's made.

He loosens his hold a fraction. Nothing. He loosens it a little more. Adam's legs give way. Taking his weight, Rao helps him down to the floor, where he sits, frozen in place. Rao gets to his knees in front of him to block his view. Takes both of Adam's hands in his own. Talks to him. Low and urgent, edged with hysteria. The words are nonsense. They're barely words at all. But it doesn't matter. He's pretty sure Adam can't hear him. He's certain Adam can't see him.

His fingers twitch, spasm weirdly, a painless cramp. Adam's skin is *hot* suddenly. No. *Cold.* Freezing. Something else. *Something—*

He turns Adam's left hand. Sees something like sweat beading on his palm. Something. Like drops of mercury. Metallic. Silvery. Palladium grey. They're hard to focus on, as if they don't want to be looked at, but he can't tear his eyes away. They're like the vulture. Like the diner. Like that small, cold night. And as he stares at them, the room, the building, the whole world flows smoothly, inexorably inwards, contracting into Adam's outstretched hand, taking Rao with it.

Helplessly, he drops a finger, soft, onto Adam's palm and stares, entranced, as the beads move towards it, tiny droplets coalescing into thin rivulets that run along the lines of Adam's skin into his own. He watches it soak into him like ink into a wick. Like capillary action, as if he's pulling it in. Feels it, senses it slipping into his blood. He shivers. A weird, weird hit. Yes. *Yes.*

He grabs both of Adam's hands. Laces their fingers. Presses their palms together. Screws his eyes tight like Dorothy—*there's no place like home*—and wills every single atom of the stuff into himself.

Fuck, he thinks. *Fuck*. This is new. *Holy shit*. It's like he's being bent backwards to the floor. He's not moving. Sprays of phosphenes bubble up in front of his eyes to obscure his vision and he blinks them away. He's falling through all the things that ever existed or will exist and now they are carefully pleating themselves inside him into something so fine and perfect he's not sure he'll ever need to breathe again. It—

There's a tug on his hands. Through his eyes he sees the man whose hands he's holding double up. Fold over himself. Hears coughing, a desperate hauling in of air. For an instant the room is his cell at Pentonville, his hotel room at Kabul, his flat in Clapham, his college set, his childhood bedroom, that suite in Tashkent, all at once, and he blinks their ghosts away and looks at the man who's now sitting back on his heels before him, swaying a little, trembling violently. He's so—

He's so—

Rao can't think of the word. It's important, it's crucial. He searches for it in vain, searching the man's face. It's perfectly expressionless. His eyes are closed. He's crying. Not sobbing, no noise at all, just water coursing down his cheeks.

Rao remembers a little more. Turns his head to the wall behind him. The clock's still there, light still gilding the pine boards behind it, shining on the curve of its metal case.

"Oh," he hears a woman say breathlessly. "This is *very* interesting."

"Adam?" Rao says, though it takes him a few tries to remember the name.

Adam's mouth opens and moves and shuts again. He furrows his brow, opens his eyes, tries again. "Rao," he whispers. "Can we leave?"

Unsteadily, Rao gets to his feet. As he does, the room snaps abruptly into a negative of itself and slips precipitously to one side, but he manages to tilt it back into something approximating normality as he hauls gently on Adam's hands to pull him up from the floor. It takes a while.

Rao slings one of Adam's arms over his shoulders, grips his wrist tight, and turns them both to the door. There's a woman in front of it. *Veronica*, he remembers. Her face shines as she speaks.

"You need to stay for observation. This is a highly anomalous result."

Rao shakes his head, works hard to assemble a sentence.

"We're leaving. Adam, love, can you walk?"

Another room. Rao remembers it. A mirror. Adam's jacket. He leans to pick it up as they pass. Broken glass crunches underfoot. Harmonics, high-pitched, like voices. A man rushes up. Rao can't remember him at all. He's agitated, fists clenched, eyes wide. "Are you ok? Is he ok? Was this a test?"

Rao ignores him, concentrates on getting Adam into the corridor.

It takes forever to get to the car. He leans Adam against the passenger-side door, drags the keys from his inside jacket pocket. Gets him in the seat, buckles him in. He's cold, shivering, shirt soaked with sweat.

Rao pulls the GPS out of the glove compartment, plugs it into the cigarette lighter. "Where's the motel, love?" he asks. He's scared he can't remember its name, can't remember where it is.

Adam looks at him blankly.

"Our hotel. We left our bags there. Can you remember what it's called?"

A long silence, then Adam manages some words. They're almost inaudible, but one, Rao thinks, might have been "King." Yes. He stabs at the GPS screen with a finger, flinching at each keystroke tone. The King's Inn. He drops the GPS in his lap, starts the engine. Judders out of the lot, merges with the traffic. At the first intersection, he looks over to the passenger seat. Adam's face is red with reflected stoplight. Bad grey underneath. Rao jumps when his face shifts green, is hit by another wave of disorientation. More amplitude to this one. Deeper, wilder. The car behind them sounds an impatient horn. *Lucky*, he thinks, as he gets the car moving again, that he's had comprehensive experience of driving while off his face. Lucky. *You're lucky.*

"Fuck's sake, mate," he breathes. "Psychos are fine with this stuff. Why couldn't you have been?"

Adam speaks so quietly Rao can barely hear. "I'll be fine."

CHAPTER 35

C hills, a cold sweat, the smell of his childhood kitchen, his father's burnt toast acrid in his nostrils, charred caramel of spent rounds, thick sludge of dread and self-loathing fresh and new in his stomach, everything balling up inside. He can't care. He won't care. He cares too much.

They're driving to the motel. Rao's talking. Rao's driving. Adam doesn't care. Dangerous to care. Rao's driving, he's talking, and he looks shaken. *Mate*, he's saying. Adam knows that there's a meaning behind every one of Rao's pet names, Rao's endearments. They're an arsenal. Needlelike, and every single one a weapon or a piece of armor. He's only ever heard Rao call people mate when he's worried about them. Armor, then. Much easier to bear than Rao's everyday velvet-wrapped bullet of "love."

Rao asks him a question. He feels the click of his own mouth opening, how much air he uses up to answer. He says he'll be fine. A violent wave of shakes hits him and he wonders if he's going to die. He considers asking Rao if he's dying—but what's the point? Rao won't know. The only thing they both know for sure is that he's a black hole. A cigarette burn in the fabric of Rao's tapestry of truth. Adam is the promise of a migraine without a trigger. No point in asking. He'll never get an answer.

The car halts. "I'll be back. Just stay here," Rao's saying. After some time, the vehicle's moving again, Rao biting his lip and pulling at the wheel. Where they park has windows in front. A door. Rao helps him out of the car and walks with him. It's not hard to walk. Adam can do it unsupported. He doesn't tell Rao that.

He learned the merits of keeping his mouth shut when he was young, but the way his aunt Sasha talked about him made Adam suspect that he was always kind of quiet. "You grow up around all that noise, kid, and you lose your voice," she'd said, once. Only once. He remembers the smell of her cigarette smoke in the air as she said it. How the sunset through the curtains hit her, made everything seem brightly colored and unlit all the same. He remembers her saying it and how it made him feel like he was a chipped cup in a set.

"Look, I know you're not talkative, love, but this is next-level," Rao complains from the kitchenette. Adam watches from the end of the nearest bed. Two queens, one large TV, good floorspace, a desk. Upmarket. Stakeout rooms. Recoup motel. "Usually I'll get at least a grunt from you to let me know whether you're ignoring or humoring me."

He has no idea.

"The problem is, if you don't say anything, I'll just keep talking," he continues. "Have to fill the silence." A pause. A frown. "Fuck me, Adam. That's true. I have to fill the silence? Compelled? Fuck. Wasn't ready for that little nugget of impromptu self-reflection."

Normally Rao's monologue would be entertaining. It's different in the recoup motel. Here, it's not funny. Here, Rao being Rao is prying Adam's chest open. Cracks into marrow. He can breathe but feels like he can't. His arms ache with an effort he doesn't understand.

"Please," Adam rasps and slowly lifts a hand to his face. Doesn't cover his eyes. Can't bring himself to. He has to stop caring. He can't.

Rao looks up from the fridge, eyes wide. "Didn't think that would actually work," he admits. He leaves the kitchenette, pulls one of the chairs from the desk, and drags it across the carpet to Adam's bed. Sits. His eyes dart around Adam's features, taking him in. Adam's ribcage feels weak. Might collapse at any second. He can't ask Rao if he's dying. He'll never know. "What do you need?" Rao asks.

Adam works his throat. Knows what he wants. Knows what he can ask for. "I need you to shut up," he says quietly. His voice. It sounds like he's been strangled. The bruised swelling that follows. The rasp and dryness of a healing throat. The constant ache of minor internal bleeding, tiny shards of glass inside his words. It'll pass. In a day. Maybe two. "Rao, please shut up."

Rao laughs. He laughs and the laugh blocks out the ticking of a clock somewhere in the room. Adam hadn't even noticed the sound until it was gone. Feels like he can't breathe again. Needs Rao to laugh again.

"Fuck off," Rao says, grinning, gripping his knee like they're friends. Maybe they are again. Some people, they just need to shed some blood together. But Rao telling him to fuck off sounds like he's saying something else. Adam doesn't know what those other words are. They just aren't the words coming out of his mouth. "So you're alright?" Rao adds.

"I'm fine," Adam lies. Looks around the room to find the clock he'd failed to notice. Locates it on the wall opposite the bed he's sitting on, to the left of Rao's head. He focuses on its face. Doesn't know if that's a good idea or a bad idea. Can't care. Probably should.

"Don't lie to me, Adam. It's a dirty trick."

Adam snorts humorlessly. It hurts. Like he has a cold. Sinus pain, throat pain: cousins, not siblings. "I guess I really look like shit, huh," he croaks.

Rao considers Adam carefully. Speaks gingerly. Might be the first time Adam's seen him so gentle in all their time working together. "Let's just say that you look fucking terrible and leave it at that."

Adam blinks at him.

"What? I'm not going to get into it. You know where I've been and what I've seen. Imagine all the comparisons I could make with my vast experience of just how ragged a human being can look and apply them. And don't get ratty with me because I'm choosing to be kind."

"Kind," Adam repeats. Hard to say. Makes his throat cut into itself. Rao talked about kite strings made to cut others before. Glass dust. Adam feels a sudden kinship with something he's never seen.

"Extraordinarily kind. And trust me when I tell you that right now you need to get something to drink and make an attempt at solid food."

Adam sighs. He could fight. The clock ticks beside Rao's head. He could fight it all. But he can't pin down if he should fight, if he wants to fight, or if any of this will matter in the long run. "So you're primary on this?"

"This isn't a job, Adam."

"Everything's a job, Rao."

"You're delicate right now, love, so I'll leave that morsel of innuendo on the table to enjoy later." Rao pats Adam's knee and gets up, walks back over to the kitchenette. Adam tears his gaze from the clock on the wall to watch him. Rao's standing by the fridge, making a face. "There's a Safeway a block away. I could get groceries. But I'm not a cook."

"No shit."

"We'll get takeout."

By the time he was thirteen, he could cook pretty well. His mom taught him. Told him there's no point in being in the world if you can't look after yourself. Told him he wouldn't be "one of those boys," a designation Adam wouldn't understand until he was living in barracks with scores of "those boys." His mom could cook, but she was also a practical woman. Most of their family meals came from cans or jars. They all knew that a homemade sauce was better, but who could find the hours in the day for that kind of dedication? She used to put different herbs in the sauces. Made it personal. It was fine. Adam still thinks nobody can cook up a box of mac like his mom. They didn't do takeout. "It's lazy," his dad told him. Lazy was the worst thing a person could be. "And you don't know who's making your food. They could put anything in it." Adam thought that realistically that could happen anywhere. Anyone could do that. Anyone. He never said that to his mom. He figured she knew already.

He watches Rao eat his fourth slice of pizza. Rao seems unfazed. That's good. Rao's the one with experience in situations like this one, so Adam has to assume that if Rao seems calm, then his own crushing feelings of doom are just his own. Maybe therapy would've helped him to figure out where to put these feelings. He has no idea what to do with them now. Never imagined he'd have them. Therapy's not a dirty word to Adam, not a sign of weakness. He's known a lot of people in the service who needed it, got it, came out the other side better for it. He's known a lot of people who needed it just as badly but did nothing about it. Once you know that type, you can see them everywhere: the ones who think getting help is a weakness.

He's never gotten help. He's dealt with everything himself. Coped. Driven on. The higher-ups would check in sometimes. Ask him if he needed to talk to someone. He never took them up on their offers. Didn't want to visit that kind of hurt on anyone else's head, especially when they meant well enough to offer him help. And because, realistically, where would he start?

Turns out, Prophet knew exactly where he would start.

"You've been giving me and this pepperoni the evils for a solid minute now," Rao observes. "Not hungry anymore?"

Adam isn't hungry at all. "I spaced out," he says. "Wasn't really looking at you."

"Fucking hell, Adam, you always know how to make a man feel wanted."

Rao sounds playful. Upbeat. What you're going through is normal, he'd assured Adam earlier. Wanting to die, wanting to scream, feeling like you're moving when you're not, feeling like you'll never breathe right again. It's all normal.

Adam doesn't feel normal. Adam's never felt normal.

He watches Rao deposit his half-eaten slice on top of a napkin. Pizza oil leaks and blooms into the paper. He blinks back a memory of blood welling through sand-dusted DCU.

"Did you space out on anything specific?" Rao says carefully.

Therapy, Adam doesn't say out loud, and how it might have helped him now. Not then. He still doesn't think he'd have been anything but disturbing to the people with the notepads at the time, but right now, after what's happened, he thinks he might like to possess the tools to hold a conversation at the very least. "I should get some sleep," he says instead.

It's not an answer, but it gets a nod. "Which bed do you want? I don't care which you pick," Adam assures him. "I just want to sleep."

"Then sleep. I'll put the telly on low."

"You need the TV on?"

"You know I do."

Adam nods. Radio, TV, the voices of strangers. Doesn't matter what language, doesn't matter where, Rao needs white noise to relax and sleep. Adam's never minded. It's standard countersurveillance. He's found scores of talk radio stations for Rao during jobs. Has always liked the way Rao's features ease after a few minutes of background chatter. How there's always this one split second before he gazes out the window or picks up a book when he seems honestly at peace.

CHAPTER 36

*U*nscheduled calls break unspoken rules, but Steven needs to know. *When he appears on-screen, Veronica's relieved to see he's at his Maine residence. The house resembles a nineteenth-century cabin, but as with so many of his things, this is merely an impression it's designed to give: there's a T1 line into the property and sufficient security to repel whole armies. Steven will be in Maine to search for heritage apple varieties in the woods, which is good because it means he'll be—as far as Steven ever is—receptive to conversation. He shifts in his seat, fiddles with the wick on the oil lamp; the light dims in the wood-panelled room. He doesn't like to be visible, even here.*

"Do we, uh, have a breakthrough?" he says in his familiar whisper.

"We had two visitors today, Steven. I didn't know they were coming. It seems Lane let them in: he'd passed Montgomery their names."

A pause, a sigh. He pushes at an unsharpened carpentry pencil on the desk, shifts it an inch sideways. A longer pause.

"I'll talk to him," he says eventually. He looks unhappy to be discussing this. It means nothing. He's never, in the years Veronica's known him, ever looked comfortable discussing anything other than apples.

"I'd be grateful, Steven. Were you aware of them?"

He wrinkles his nose. Another long silence. "I talked with Zachary two days ago. He, uh, notified me. Rubenstein and Rao. Said they might turn up at the Aurora facility. They were Miller's hires."

Veronica frowns. "I didn't like that."

"Like what?"

"How Lane used her."

He looks mystified. "Morally?"

"No, Steven. Unwitting agents aren't my favourite flavour. But in retrospect—" She rubs a thumb along the fingernails of one curled hand, shrugs minutely. "What's the state of play in England?"

"The coroner returned a favourable verdict. The, um, the objects have been removed from the base into level four storage and Miller's off-site and secure."

"And we're clear her exposure was accidental?"

"As far as we, uh, yeah. It was. We also have the vial in our possession. So that project's complete."

She nods, exasperated. That EOS PROPHET side project never got off the ground. It was a little gift for Steven from Lane, and like most of Lane's little gifts, an embarrassing one. It's highly irritating to her that Straat's death had such fascinating consequences.

"What do we have on Rubenstein and Rao?"

"One's at the Defense Intelligence Agency. Rubenstein. The other one is, uh, damaged goods. Ex-MI6. Miller got him out of prison. He's supposed to have some kind of extranormal ability to detect lies. CIA overtaxed him and he tried to kill himself. He's Indian, I think? I suppose he must be. The name."

"Rubenstein said he could detect fakes and frauds."

A snuffle of laughter. Steven doesn't laugh like any other person Veronica has heard. A high-pitched grunt, no facial levity attached. "Maybe those, too, yes, maybe, maybe. Lane was keen to bring him in. He thought he'd be useful, ultimately, but the odds seemed too long to me. He's apparently, uh, you know, quite unstable."

Veronica enjoys the ambiguity, says nothing.

"What's Rao's relation to the DIA operative?"

"Rubenstein's . . . a bodyguard? We couldn't get much on him. Lane said he wasn't interesting."

She sits back in her seat and smiles. "He is."

CHAPTER 37

Adam's propped up against his headboard staring at the motel wall opposite, at the unlikely blue-on-blue wallpaper printed with geese and flowers. He's blinking slowly, taking deep breaths he doesn't seem to ever exhale. Rao's been watching him for a long time. Knows he's barely registering on Adam's consciousness, is little more than a shadow on his periphery. Adam certainly looks like he's in a dissociative state, brain slipped into protective mode to unshackle him from himself and the world. Yeah. Well. Rao is familiar with dissociation. Knows the safety of that disconnect. He's looked down at himself and felt his body doesn't belong to him more times than he can count. But he's certain that's not what's happening here. There's something about Adam's stare, the way his right hand grips the coverlet. The way fear scents the room like rain the air.

No, Adam's not dissociating. This is the opposite. He's thinking and feeling too much. Inside his skull, there's a crescendo of white noise running in a terrible, screaming, silent loop. Rao knows this. He doesn't know how, but he does.

He has to get Adam out of it.

"Adam."

Another blink. Adam doesn't look over. "Yes, Rao."

"Can we talk?" Rao regrets his choice of words instantly. *Far too intense, Sunil. You're usually so much better than this.*

Still, it makes Adam look over. His eyes look black. "Is it a big talk or a little talk?"

"No, just a little talk."

"Ok. What do you want to talk about?"

"Anything at all. Tell me something about yourself no one else knows."

"You already know so much about me that no one else knows," Adam sighs, rearranging himself against the headboard. That's true. Rao knows it is, but it doesn't feel like it. It just feels like Adam.

"Yeah, well. I'm a greedy bastard, then. Tell me something new."

"I can't think of anything."

"You didn't try."

"Rao, this isn't as fun a game as you think it is."

"I'm not having any bloody fun! You're not telling me anything."

Adam closes his eyes, but he's smiling. It's barely there, barely a smile, but it's not a frown. That counts. "Ask me a question and I'll answer it."

"Alright. Give me a second," Rao instructs, suddenly desperate not to waste this chance. As if it were the only one. Yes, he has questions. Questions about the clock on the wall, what it meant. About Adam's family. Why he chose this career. What the real deal is with Hunter. Why Prophet didn't work the way they thought it would. He *really* wants to know why Adam chose to tell him about his involvement with those fucks from the CIA. But he wants to keep Adam from the white noise in his head. None of what he wants to ask will keep him clear of that.

Something easy. Softball.

"What was your first kiss like?" he asks with a bit of a grin. Easy. Softball. But real, and something he knows Adam would never talk about otherwise. "Let me guess first. Was she your high school sweetheart? Yeah, I can see that, with you. Apple pie shit. Probably kissed her cheek while an American flag waved behind the two of you."

Adam's eyebrows tick down in a frown. "Incorrect. Guess again."

"Piss off," Rao laughs.

Adam opens his eyes.

"Just tell me," Rao says.

There's a pause. A breath. Long enough for Rao to realise how much he's enjoying himself. Begin to worry that Adam's right, and this game might just be for him.

"For a start, I think I was still in middle school," Adam tells him, speaking slowly. Nice and careful. *Adam's like that,* Rao thinks with sudden fondness. Always takes his time when he's saying something more than a statement or rebuke. "There was a ball field near where my house was. My dad found us at the fence by the diamond."

"What was she like?"

Adam snorts humourlessly. "*Mark* was taller than me. I don't really remember a lot about him. I know he had green eyes. I remember keeping my eyes open. I saw my dad coming before Mark did. Man, you know—" He laughs, genuinely: a sudden shift in energy. "My dad made him piss himself. We were so scared."

"Wait."

"Yes, Rao."

"This isn't like, you know, a girl called Alex, is it?"

"No."

"Adam. I rather think that after everything, you should be honest with me. We're rebuilding trust here."

Adam takes a deep breath and sighs it out. Sits back against the headboard. Rao'd missed when he'd sat forward. Missed that entirely. The laughter is gone. Might as well have never existed. "I'm not lying to you."

This demands some thought. Adam in his early teens with a boy a little taller than him. Eyes open during the kiss, because of course Adam would kiss like that. Low sun, dust in the air, asphalt and dry grass. Rao can picture it so clearly it's like it's a memory of his own. Feels the ghost of a hand gripping his shirtfront. He shakes his head. None of this feels like a lie. It doesn't feel like anything. Feels like Adam.

"But you're straight," he continues to argue.

"I never said that."

The makeup. The eyeliner. They were so close, and Rao had been *so sure*. "That time, we didn't kiss, but it was fucking close—"

"Are you suggesting," Adam interrupts, exasperated, "that I must be straight because I didn't kiss you?"

"Yes."

"Rao."

"Well! Alright, maybe not that exactly." Only, *that*. Exactly that. "Are you bisexual?"

Adam rolls his neck to level a raised eyebrow at him.

"It's alright if you are, obviously," Rao says quickly. "I'd say that's what I am, if I ever stopped to think about it. I reckon I'm alright with anything, actually, if we're—"

Adam interrupts him again. "What's your obsession with me having sex with women?"

"What?"

"Why do you fixate on that?"

"I don't fixate on anything about your sexuality, Adam."

"That's bullshit."

I've never seen him like this, Rao thinks in some wonderment before correcting himself. He's seen him like this before, and he'd hated it. Adam is like this with Hunter; he laughs and he swears. Doesn't just roll with the verbal punches, doles them out too. Wait. No. That's wrong again, isn't it? Because he'd seen Adam like this before he knew Hunter existed. Adam with his sleeves rolled up unscrewing the cap of a bottle of Tashkentvino vodka, Adam sprawled on a couch, messing with cards.

"If you're not deciding that I'm making out against the flag or sleeping around with every female soldier at the base or just banging my friends, then you're declaring me sexless." Adam doesn't sound mad. He sounds tired. "It's one of your favourite topics."

"Do I go on about that?" Rao asks, his words feeling oddly pointless. Like all of this, somehow, was inevitable.

"You once told me that if I had any animal magnetism in my system, I might be considered handsome," Adam says, then laughs like he had when he'd talked about his dad finding him by the fence. It surprises Rao all over again. "And I think it was probably the nicest thing you've ever said to me."

"Bloody hell, Adam. I'm sorry."

Adam's face twists. "You don't have to do that. You were right. You're always right."

"You know how desperately I'd like to agree with you on that one, love." Rao lifts his chin, scratches his neck, sees Adam's wince deepen.

"But I did just find out that my extremely heterosexual best friend has, in fact, no interest in women whatsoever."

"I'm not your best friend, Rao."

"That seems to be a choice I get to make, Adam."

Adam frowns. "Make a better choice."

Rao clicks his fingers as he thinks. Weighs up his options. Decides he doesn't care about safety or stability. They were probably well beyond that already. "What if this were a big talk?"

"It's not a little one."

"No," Rao agrees. "Which means that I'm well within my rights to bring up the whole . . . well, you know."

"Ruining your life," Adam prompts, flatly.

"Ruining my life, yes."

Rao watches Adam gather himself up, far more slowly than usual, in order to present his mask of cold indifference. There sits Adam as he's always been before: a forgotten cigarette burn in the tapestry of the universe. Nothing tangible for Rao to hold onto, nothing ever true or false. A spinning wheel.

The only proof he has that Adam might still be hearing that white noise in his head, might still be a mess, is how his fingers tremble as he wraps them around his left wrist.

It's not just the straight thing, Rao realises with a start sudden as laughter. He's misunderstood everything about Adam the whole time.

"Ok. Let's talk about it," he says evenly. *Such a professional.*

*

Desk work after time in the field makes Adam's skin crawl. Low ceilings, fluorescent light, gray DC skies outside. He's good at it. But it always feels like a shackle. And it's thoughts like these that had been getting Adam through the day, snorting under his breath and thinking how Rao would call him a drama queen. *An incredibly boring drama queen, but we work with what we're given.* Because Rao was on his mind. It would have been easy to get pathetic about that, blame it on all the time he had to let his mind wander while he wasn't in the field, but the truth was that recently he'd been asked to provide a more detailed file report of their operations in Central Asia. He had dug up all his memories, stripped them clean of sentiment and camaraderie, packaged them up for another set of eyes, and passed them on.

So it made sense that he was thinking of Rao. Expected, after reliving all the moments that don't make it into reports. The jokes and quiet evenings. Stories shared. Market stalls. Dust and cologne and cigarette smoke. The way Rao always complained about the scratchy blankets, lumpy pillows, moldy couches with too-hard armrests.

He wasn't surprised when he got the call.

"A follow-up on your report." A male voice, a crackly line. Adam wondered exactly where this one was posted.

"You should have all the details you need," Adam sighed, acting like he had something better to do. What did he have lined up? Meetings. A 5:00 p.m. sit-in with a service chief, a four-star general, a politician with a thousand-dollar-a-day coke habit, and a diplomat fucking his au pair.

"We need to know about Sunil Rao."

Adam sat up. "What do you need?"

"We're working with him at the moment and we're finding his behavior . . ." A pause during which Adam smiled grimly at nothing. "Challenging."

"He's being an asshole."

"Yeah, he really is."

Adam nodded. "Fights?"

"Nearly every night. Grounding doesn't stick. He slipped out of cuffs. He drinks, gets his ass kicked, causes havoc," the man continued. He was off script already, but that's the whole point of knowing the right words to say. "I'd get rid of him but . . ."

He didn't need to finish the sentence. Adam got it, and so did the strung out officer. Rao's something else, even when being a pain in the ass.

"You're giving him what he wants," Adam said. "Something to kick against. You cuffed him?"

"Desperation."

"Obviously."

"I need solutions, Colonel Rubenstein, not a dressing down."

It was hard not to laugh. "I don't have any special instructions for you."

"You're the only person who's managed to work with him without punching him."

Adam grinned. "I've punched him."

"It didn't make it into the report."

"No, it didn't," Adam allowed, wondering how many people had included all the times Rao had goaded them into retaliation in their reports. He'd say he was immune, the way Rao told him he was, but that wasn't true. He wasn't immune like that. "I suppose I've already given you the best advice I can give you."

"Don't cuff him."

"Don't treat him like a prisoner," Adam corrected. "He's an asset. Treat him like he is. Whatever the situation—"

"Classified."

"Of course. But whatever the situation is, you need him. The fights are his way of letting off steam," he explained. It wasn't hard to talk about Rao. Never has been. What's always hard is getting people to understand. "Give him another outlet. Let him drink. Let him smoke. Let him go further than that if you need to. Encourage it. His tolerance is higher than you think, and he'll always bounce back, so long as it's done in moderation."

"You're encouraging recreational drug use."

Adam paused. Was he? Yes. But it's Rao. "If there are substances floating around, he'll find them anyway. It's in your best interest to be aware and in control of the situation if you want to work with him without the headaches, officer."

"Littlewood."

"Excuse me?"

"Officer Littlewood."

Poor bastard. No wonder he's having trouble with Rao. "I hope this has been useful to you, Officer Littlewood."

"Extremely."

The call clicked to an end and Adam sat for a moment, rapping his fingers on the desk, remembering the time he punched Rao, too early in their friendship to know he was doing exactly what Rao wanted him to do. Before he realized Rao was an asset.

The asset.

He got up from his desk, convinced for the first time in a long time that he'd actually done some good.

CHAPTER 38

Rao sits in silence after Adam recounts the phone call. Then, pursing his lips, he asks him if he wants to order in more pizza.

"I'm not hungry."

"Nor am I," Rao agrees. "They were shit anyway."

"You ate five slices."

Rao smiles bleakly at that.

"Why didn't you just tell me that they were cunts?" he asks seriously. "The way you said it before sounded like you just told them to hold me down and stick me with a needle to control me."

"That's basically what I did," Adam says. "If I had more intel on the situation, I would have been more careful." He's shaking his head. He doesn't believe what he's saying.

"This really doesn't suit you."

"What?"

"Guilt," Rao sniffs. He hates it. "I've never seen it on you before and it's not your colour, love."

Adam shoots him one of his not-frown smiles. "Like it's a hat I'm trying on."

"Yeah. Take it the fuck off."

"It's not that easy, Rao."

"It should be."

Adam stares at him blankly.

"I'm the injured party, and I'm expressly forgiving you," Rao says. "Which should knock that shitty guilt hat clean off."

Adam hums tunelessly. "And if you're wearing a shitty guilt hat of your own?"

Fuck. Trust Adam to be a total pain in the arse even in recovery from impossible experimental substances. "Leave my hat alone," he says.

Adam nods, slow and silent. He's thinking. They're having a big talk now, after all. All their guts on the table. All of Adam's guts on the table, anyway. Rao blinks, suddenly comprehending the power imbalance. Aware of it and hating it.

"You don't have anything to feel guilty about," Adam says eventually.

"That's bollocks. The shrinks kept telling me that when I got back. They didn't understand that everything in those rooms in Kabul was a weapon, Adam. Everything. And I was in the room," he insists. "I'm guilty as fuck."

"Yeah, all that is true." Adam speaks slowly. Eyes back down to his own hands.

Rao follows Adam's gaze. Remembers those hands holding a gun to the kneecap of a man in Tashkent a lifetime ago. The man who'd ended up telling them both, his voice tight with fear, that things in Afghanistan aren't like they are in the movies.

But they are, Rao thinks. They *really* are. Just the movie happens to be *Goodfellas*, not *Saving Private Ryan*.

Adam raises his eyes. "But . . . I don't think you have anything to feel guilty about as far as I'm concerned."

"It isn't that easy." Rao shivers, though he feels warmer. Doesn't hate it right this second. Hell of a ride. "This is my fault."

"What is?"

"This. You. Right now, you and now."

"You didn't make me do anything."

"Yeah, but—"

"Shut up, Rao. You didn't make me do anything."

A propositional statement that can't be read. But Rao knows it's a lie. Because he was pushing Adam in the facility, pushing as hard as he could. He wanted—

He doesn't know what he wanted. He knows exactly what he wanted. But what he got was something else, and he got it at Adam's expense. Rao looks down at his own hand. Turns it, regards the creases on his palm. Remembers the beads of Prophet climbing out of Adam's skin and slipping into his own. The unnatural heaviness behind his eyes that doesn't feel right, feels so right. Shivers. Lights behind his vision when he blinks. What he got was something else, and there's no going back. But it's Adam. Adam who's in recovery. Adam, who's looking at Rao closely now, leaning forward to get his attention, as if he didn't already have it, as though Rao weren't the most alert and aware he's ever been in his life. Everything's firing at once. He's feeling like he did when he was a kid, when he wanted to be able to do everything in one day and getting tired was a waste of time. Feels like he did when he tried coke the first time. Just that first time. Like he'd figured out how to do everything at once. It was a fleeting intuition and confusing after an hour, but insistent. He feels insistent. All of him feels insistent.

"What is it, Adam?"

"You look like you have more questions."

Rao suppresses a laugh. "Well, given the brand-new information laid at my feet about your formative years, not to mention a whole retelling of your narrative, I do indeed have quite a few more questions."

Adam blinks at him. Sits back. Seems disappointed.

"You want to ask me about my love life?"

"Now that I have something to give a fuck about, yes."

"You didn't give a fuck when you thought I was straight?"

"Neither of us want me to answer that, Adam."

One of Adam's eyes is twitching spasmodically. He's haggard as fuck. Exhausted. Rao should let him sleep. But he can't let this go. Not yet.

Adam laughs, low and tired. "I really hate you, Rao," he says.

"You said that before."

He'd whispered it before. Rao'd pulled it out of him before. Humiliated it out of him.

"Yeah, I did." Adam's eyes are closed again. Back against the headboard.

Two steps forward, Sunil. "Did you mean it?"

Adam opens his eyes to meet Rao's. That heavy feeling comes back, resting just behind Rao's ocular nerve like a migraine without pain. Pressure.

He shakes his head. "No," he mouths, voiceless.

He's spilled single malt on the table. It's right there, a splash of it the size of his little fingernail. If he leaves it there it'll eat through the varnish and scar the wood. If he leaves it longer it'll evaporate, rise into the air, alcohol molecules bumping around under the low ceiling, suspended in cigarette smoke. Rao leans down to examine the spill more closely, is reaching for it with a finger when it disappears. Which is not, he realises after a confused second or two, his doing. The bar's gone dark. Another power cut. Cheers and jeers from the surrounding tables. He waits to see if this time the hotel generator will cut in.

It does. He exhales. Lights another cigarette. His hand is shaking. That's the whisky. But if it weren't the whisky, it'd be not enough whisky. If he were sober right now, he'd have to listen to the room. International agency pricks bragging about how many war zones they've been in. Journalists swapping photographers and vehicles. Brittle expats being weird about everything. Everyone everyone else's best friend. Everyone loathing each other. Everyone mendacious. A rotating cast of lies and liars. Faces he knows, faces that come and go and return and go again. Faces staring into phones, arranging cars. Faces that most often greet him, as he walks in, with suspicion, with irritation, or the fixed smile that means fuck off. The usual. *When did this get to be usual?* he thinks. *When wasn't it like this?* He lifts his hand to his forehead to rub at the frown that's a pressure between his eyes. It doesn't go away. Drags his fingers lower to massage his cheekbone. It hurts, a bit. His skin's doing that thing where it feels like it's not his. Then he remembers that tomorrow will happen, and that's a sickening turn, like skidding on ice, the wheel going light in his hands.

Ash falls everywhere when he stubs out his cigarette. He stares at it on his fingers. How long has he been here? Good question. He looks up to the line of clocks showing different time zones on the wall above the bar and is surprised because none of them are there. Someone'll have nicked them, yeah. Because things go missing around here all the time. Clocks, minds, wallets, wills to live. He turns his wrist to find his watch. Stares at it for a while. The bastard face refuses to resolve, so he recites numbers. Discovers, to his surprise, that it's not even midnight, though it feels like four in the morning.

Then blankness falls on him, heavy and damp and far too stifling, and it goes on a while, until eventually a question hauls and heaves its way out of it.

What do you want, Sunil?

Well.

He wants to pass out.

There's a problem with that. Experience has taught him that the hotel staff aren't big fans of unconscious patrons on the floor. They don't like fights, either. He's not their favourite guest. So. Where was—yes. Somewhere upstairs is his room, and he supposes he's going to have to get himself there first. The mechanics of doing so are vague.

Adam, he thinks. Or says out loud. One or the other, anyway. Because he has a sudden sense of Adam's physical presence. It's odd, he decides after a while, how Adam never smells bad. Maybe it's the way the American government stamps them out. Maybe they put something in the mix like Twinkie preservatives. Because sometimes Adam smells hot and clean, like laundry, and sometimes more like vermouth and knives. Sharpest when he's angry, sometimes when he's tired. Iris root too. Hint of motor oil, but maybe it's not motor oil. Maybe it's C4.

He's thinking of Adam again.

That'll be because he's fucked, yeah? Times like these, sometimes he's blacked out and opened his eyes in the morning in a real bed with bottles of water within arm's reach, and that's all Adam. Rubenstein makes things easier. But it's not that. *Fuck*, Rao realises slowly. *I think I miss him.* Is that mad? He can hear Adam's tired sigh. *Yes, Rao*, he says. *That's completely fucking insane.*

Very carefully, Rao turns in his seat, looks about. No. Adam's not here. That's very strange. He should be. Wasn't he here, just now?

The air in the room is darker now. Maybe the generator's dying. No, it's just cigarette smoke. Darker than usual, almost black. He glances over to the blank space on the wall where the clocks should be. The wall's not right. It's not painted vermillion. It's wood panelling rouged with a patch of sun. And when he looks back down at the room it's empty and he's completely alone. There's never been anyone here. And the truth of what this is falls on him. It's death, he knows it is, opening inside him like a mouth, and he opens his own to scream—

He wakes into it. Sweating, constricted, tangled in sheets, one arm trapped behind his back. But the relief of it being a dream is torn away in an instant when he realises the scream he can hear isn't coming from his mouth. It's coming from somewhere else. *Still a dream*, he thinks, desperately, and his throat closes up because he knows it's not true. Can't move. Can't breathe. Couldn't scream now if he wanted to. Because it's Adam. This is Adam's scream. Adam is screaming.

*

"Adam?"

What wakes him isn't the tearing in his throat, the sound of his own shouts dying in his chest. It's Rao shaking him. Rao saying his name. Adam blinks up at his face.

The room's too hot. He's shivering. So is Rao.

"Are you alright, love?" Stupid question. Adam screws his eyes shut. He must take too long to answer because he hears a tap running. Then Rao's feet on the carpet. "Obviously you're not alright. But I mean—are you alright?" he clarifies, badly.

Adam cracks an eye to look at him. He's holding out a glass of water. He looks shaken. Worried. Rao almost never lets it show like this. Panicked and wide-eyed as he puts the glass on the bedside table.

"I'm fine," Adam lies.

Rao sits beside him on the bed. "Is that one of those 'I'm fines' where you're not fine at all?"

Once, not being able to read truth in Adam's words would have freaked Rao out. Lately, he's getting better at figuring him out on his own. Adam gives up on his lie.

"Yes."

"Is there anything I can do?"

So much. He could do so much to help. He could leave, but Adam doesn't think that would actually help. Wanting him to is instinct, some deep wound in Adam's gut crying out for quiet and safety. Rao's never embodied safety, not to anyone, including himself. But if he left, Adam would feel worse. And if he stays, then Adam will feel . . .

Doesn't matter.

"I don't know," he answers. Noncommittal. Another lie.

"Scoot over, then."

Adam acquiesces, giving Rao enough space to get properly into the bed. He stretches out, makes himself comfortable. Turns to face Adam. Streetlights outside. Everything is blue and orange. Rao can't have any idea what his face looks like in the half darkness. Rao's staying, and that seems better than him leaving, but Adam's skin aches like a bruise.

"What was the nightmare?"

"Aren't you supposed to ask if you can ask first?"

"What kind of rule is that?"

Adam sniffs. "One that allows me to run interference."

"Very funny. You don't have to tell me—"

"No, I'm just being a dick," Adam sighs. Trying to distract Rao. Crying out for quiet and safety. Maybe just one of those. "Would you believe me if I told you that I don't remember?"

"Wouldn't have any choice in the matter, love. I'd have to believe you."

"Not the first time you've said that."

"Not the first time it's been true."

Rao's voice sounds deeper when he's being serious. It's different from his regular lilting sarcasm, a distant relative of the biting tone his insults are laced with. Nightmare sweat is cooling in the small of Adam's back and it's making it very difficult for him to figure out if he likes Rao's serious voice or not. He might hate it. He feels strongly about it. He knows he does because he keeps replaying what Rao just said, turning it over and over in his mind.

Maybe he just wants to get away from Rao's voice on repeat in his head. Maybe he doesn't remember the details of the nightmare, but he knows what it was about.

He thinks for a while. Maybe he just wants Rao to know. Yeah. Of all people, Rao. If anyone, Rao.

"I think you would've liked my aunt Sasha. Or she would've liked you," he begins slowly. It's strange to say her name out loud. Feels like it's been years. Maybe it has. "She died when I was a teenager but I always kind of thought—"

Silence. He stops, surprised. He has, hasn't he? Always thought, somehow knew that Rao and Sasha would have gotten along like a house on fire.

"Thought what?" Rao prompts, nudging Adam's shoulder with his own. He leans against him, doesn't move away. It's a tactic. Rao deploys charm to get what he wants, never intimidation. But it's a tactic Adam appreciates right now. He'll take it.

"I was supposed to go live with her," he says. Rao's question is still there in the air between them but it doesn't matter. Has anything ever mattered? "We had this big plan to get me out of my dad's house. All I had to do was leave the house before six."

Adam keeps his eyes open. The clock that Prophet pulled out of him floats in his vision whenever he blinks. He keeps his eyes open in the half-orange-blue light.

"She was waiting for me at a junction near my house, and I was supposed to meet her. We were supposed to get out of the state before my dad even noticed that I was gone. I never found out where we were going to go. She was going to drive, or she got plane tickets, or something. I didn't have to think about it. She had it all planned out."

His eyes sting, dry. He has to blink. Hates it.

"What happened?" Rao asks, quietly. There it is again: the serious drop, that illusion of depth in his voice.

"You can guess."

"I can. But I don't think that's the point, is it?"

"No," Adam sighs. "She waited for me for too long. Didn't see an oncoming truck. Truck driver wasn't expecting her to be parked where she was. The coroner called it for just a little after six."

Rao doesn't say anything for a long time. Maybe it's not that long. Time doesn't always work the same way. Maybe it's just a single second stretched out forever in front of them. Pulled out into the silent wishes that Rao could have met Sasha, the questions Adam can feel bubbling under Rao's skin and into the other thing that can't ever be spoken. "That's what I saw. What I made was me failing to leave and go live with my aunt. Not a model plane. Like it probably should have been. Not one of my knives, like you predicted."

Rao swallows. Blinks in the half light. Adam woke him and he must be exhausted, but he's just going to have to suck it up a little longer. He's always wanted Adam to talk more.

"Well," Rao says quietly, unexpectedly gentle. "You know I'm a kinky bastard. I've always liked knives. Always liked how they work, you know? People are very much themselves when they're wielding a knife. People are very much themselves when they're underneath a blade."

Adam frowns. He's not following Rao's reasoning. "You're talking about lies again," he concludes.

"I'm talking about truth," Rao counters, shaking his head. "You made a moment like a knife."

"Oh." He knows what Rao's trying to say about him. "It must have confirmed some theories."

Rao exhales. It's almost a grunt. He's tired and he's frustrated. It's making him relax farther against Adam, press heavier against his side. "What *are* you on about?"

"Psychopathy."

"Ah. That was— You aren't, though."

"I'm not *not*."

Rao laughs softly. "No, love. That's me."

"What?"

*

It's hot in here. Stifling. Adam's shivering again. Affectless tears gleam on his cheekbones in this cinematic half light and the shadows under his eyes are so dark it looks like makeup. He's blinking back at Rao as he waits for an answer. His face isn't expressionless. It's disoriented, confused. Rao hates that it is. His own eyes ache. His sinuses hurt. Hurt like jet lag. Hurt like truth-run exhaustion. Hurt like compassion. He just wants Adam to be ok. So he doesn't bother answering Adam's question. Doesn't consider the manifest idiocy of what he's going to do. He just does it. Slips an arm behind Adam and gathers him up. Drags him down gently until Adam's head rests on his chest, and to his astonishment, Adam lets him do it. Absolute quiescence, unresisting passivity, and Rao is holding Lieutenant Colonel Adam Rubenstein in his arms and his own heart is beating hard. It's probably adrenaline. Probably.

It's just that—it isn't, is it. It's not adrenaline at all. Adam's shockingly heavy with muscle. There are hard biceps under Rao's palm, the faint tug of the scruff on Adam's jaw catching on Rao's stupid Union Jack tee. It's far past disconcerting. Shit. *Shit.* He should have thought this through. It's been a long time since he's felt the weight of a body on his own, this much sweat-soaked solid skin. He takes a deep breath and fights off a surge of desperate, overwhelming need, want so intense he can taste it. Tells himself a little hysterically that this is *Adam having a breakdown at 3:00 a.m.*, not *motel hookup round two*, takes another deep breath, lets it out shakily, shifts sideways a little uncomfortably, and after a few minutes of something like barely contained terror, gets over it.

Just about. A rolling wave of weariness hits him then, so sudden and entire he only barely registers the way Adam's pressing himself closer, has thrown an arm right across his chest to grip him tighter. Only barely registers all this, because Adam is falling asleep, is already asleep, and if Adam's asleep then Rao's good to sleep too.

CHAPTER 39

"**Y**ou don't have any idea, do you?" he blurts out as soon as Adam wakes. Rao's been sitting in the chair by his bed for some time, impatiently drumming his fingers. He has things to say. Things Adam has to hear.

"Rao?"

"Look, what happened in there was incredible. It came out of loss, obviously, I mean, that's what Prophet does. But you didn't conjure safety. You conjured something else."

"Failure," Adam offers flatly after a while.

"No. Well, yes. Bear with me."

He should shut up. Adam's a wreck and only just awake. But he can't. Because Rao's had a hell of a night. It's not just the revelation that Adam can cuddle. The death of his aunt and what that meant, the sudden apprehension of Adam having been an actual child, his sexuality, his whole— Rao frowns. Adam's got a heart. He's got a *fucking heart*. What's he supposed to do with that information? He's going to have to put it to one side. That's what he's going to have to do, because Rao's hell of a night started after he fell asleep. The dreams were—they weren't dreams. He doesn't know what they were. But he knows what caused them. The Prophet inside him might not have chosen to make doodhia wood dolls or beloved childhood bedrooms out of thin air, but it is very, very far from inert.

What's inside him is busy. It's doing things he can't describe or conceptualise because words weren't invented for things like it. The closest he gets is during the intoxicating shivers up his spine that hit him repeatedly last night, waking him each time. Each one carried with it a ghostly intuition, like a signal harmonic, and all were different. The first was like a chasm of stacked plates of glass, another seemed as if all the music that ever existed had bent back in on itself and become a single tone. In another, Prophet was working on him like a paper thread book he'd played with once at Sotheby's, a faded Zhen Xian Bao. Each page was covered in squares that unfolded into tiny boxes. If you closed them all, you could lift two adjoining squares at once, turning those into different, bigger boxes. Or you could shut them all if you wanted and make the whole of each page a box. And then? Shut those boxes, lay the whole book flat, turn it on its side, and pick up the corners to turn the whole book into one single hollow box. It's like that. Like that, but backwards. As if every inch there is, is folded inside itself uncountable times, and the boxes inside the inches go on forever.

He shivers again. He needs to talk about what he saw in the test room. Needs Adam to know. Needs him to know like he needs to breathe. He knows the truth of what he saw. He doesn't know it in his accustomed way, which is disconcerting. He knows that explaining it to Adam might be impossible. Words. All the trust people have in them, the worlds between them. The ludicrousness of them. But he's going to have to do his best.

"You conjured a choice. You brought a choice into existence, Adam. That's so much better than the things other people make."

Adam sits up. Rubs at one shoulder. "It wasn't a choice. It was a failure. Over and done."

"No. It's not. That's not how this works. Choices aren't traps, like the things regular people make. They're hinges. The world swings from them, you know?"

"Swung, maybe."

Rao can't do it. He can't explain. The frustration is so immense he wants to punch something. Takes a deep breath. "What you did in there, it's important."

"If you say so."

He tries again. "You're feeling like shit because what happened didn't lock you in a fake loop, like other people, it opened you up instead. It opened you up to—"

Adam raises a hand. "I'll take your word for it."

Adam needs him to stop. Which is fine. It's not like he can go much further. "I'm having trouble with words this morning," he admits, and the smile he tries then feels watery, like it's stuck on with paste. He knows he's being an arse. Having word trouble isn't in the same order of difficulty as Adam's full-on breakdown. But he really is struggling. It's not as bad as it had been in the immediate aftermath, when he'd forgotten so many words he'd wondered if Prophet had attacked the language centres of his brain. If it had done, it was temporary, because the words are all back, all there for him to use. It just feels as if none of them are working properly. None of them are talking about what's *there*.

Now he's watching Adam swing his feet to the floor. Push back the blankets. He's getting up. Rao watches the balls of his feet on the carpet, the crook of each toe, the bones of his ankles, the musculature of his calves and knees and thighs, aware of the actions of sinew and blood and lymph and all the vascular patterns that are somehow visible to him though they can't be seen. He knows the temperature beneath Adam's skin, feels the air in the room parting to let him pass through. For a moment he's astonished that Adam's alive. How impossible it is.

But as he watches Adam tuck a filter in the coffee machine, spoon coffee into the paper, fill the reservoir from the tap, something happens inside him. It's deep and final. It's something like a nod, an *ah*, an exhale, like the sensation of taking a seat. It's here, and it's him, but it's somewhere else, and it isn't him at all, and a memory is twisted into it. An ancient banyan in Ranthambore, a grove of trees that was all one tree, streams of evening light through crowded columns of roots. Roots that weren't roots at all, because they'd grown downwards from the branches above, dug themselves into the ground and thickened into trunks. Rao sits in the hotel room and pulls the memory right through himself.

When it's done, there's an intense feeling of relief. He can still hear the sound of one of those forest birds calling a slow metronome through motionless air. But whatever that was, it's over. Every hiss and glug from the percolator bubbles in his chest like laughter. It's going to be ok. It is ok. The chair is just a chair now. The room is just a room. He's come down from whatever Prophet did to him. It's all ok. And Adam's ok too. He's making coffee. He's not speaking, but when the fuck was that anything other than normal for Lieutenant Colonel Rubenstein?

Everything's smooth now, seamless. The coffee smells amazing. He stands, pulls back the curtains, and looks out of the window. His eyes catch on a tattered Jack in the Box bag flapping from the branches of a parking lot maple. The way the wind fills it and drops it over and over again: it's bewitching. Sirens in the distance. The just-risen sun painting the cloudy Aurora sky with swathes of gold and rose. It's fucking lovely.

"Rao."

Somehow Adam's dressed. Barefoot, tieless, but dressed. He's holding out a mug of coffee. Rao takes it. He should have made the coffee. He should have done that. He's not sure why he didn't. He's a fucking terrible friend. "Cheers, love," he says. "It's a beautiful day out there."

Adam looks vaguely amused. "Glad to hear it," he says and sits back on his unmade bed, taking uncharacteristically delicate gulps from his mug.

"How are you holding up?" he asks.

"Don't. I'm fine. I'm—a lot better. Thanks, Rao."

"Yeah, no problem."

"No, I mean . . . last night. Thanks for sitting up with me. And thanks for after. I don't know if I would have slept for very long if you'd left."

He's so *earnest*. "You ever had a cat, Adam?"

"What."

"A cat. You've seen them, right? Fur, tail, arsehole, retractable claws. You've never had one?"

"No."

"Me neither, but people I know do, and I'm hopeless at moving them when they fall asleep on me."

"I'm not a cat, Rao."

"Definitely not. But I still wasn't going to move after you fell asleep. Listen, I'm famished. Shall we go out for breakfast? You up to it?"

Adam thinks for a full two seconds, then nods.

Rao gets up, rests his coffee on the windowsill, retrieves his chinos from the floor, steps in and zips them up, slips on his sneakers, picks up his mug, takes another mouthful of coffee. "Going out for a smoke, won't be a sec."

Mug in one hand, he pulls a soft pack from his pocket, extracts a cigarette with his lips, stuffs the packet back in his pocket, takes the chain off the door, rests a hand on the handle, and what happens next—it's like the fucking Pamplona bull run. The door bursts open, bouncing off Rao and spilling hot coffee down his groin and thighs—he yelps—and then two men are standing in the room. It's the built guy from reception that first day and an even bigger guy with a buzz cut and a jaw like a cartoon anvil. Full G.I. Joe vibe. A proper heavy's heavy. Their eyes register Adam, still sitting on the bed with his coffee, face as blank as Rao's ever seen it. Now the two guys are looking at Rao for all the world like they're bounty hunters and he's a jail breaker. Rao feels a punch of laughter through the shock because he is. He fucking is, isn't he. He takes the cigarette from his mouth. "Can I help you, gentlemen?" he enquires.

"We're here to escort you to Dr Rhodes," says reception guy.

"Not Montgomery?"

"Rhodes wants to talk with you," anvil guy explains.

"I got that," Rao said. "But this isn't very polite, lads. I'm only half-dressed and we've not had breakfast. Why don't you fuck off back to Veronica and we'll think about dropping by later."

"She wants to see you now."

"You know what?" Rao says. "No."

"You're coming with us," anvil guy says. Rao can hear the edge he's put in his voice.

"No we're fucking not," Rao replies, hearing the glee in his. He's light as air, floating, adrenaline ballooning up his spine. So much so, he giggles when anvil guy steps forward, takes hold of his upper arm, and tugs him towards the door. And then. Then—

Rao's seen Adam fight. Or *thought* he had. There'd been a guy kicking about in Tashkent that Adam had trained with back in the day—*no, not at Langley*, he'd breathed wearily when Rao had enquired—and during a few days' downtime, this guy and Adam had arranged to spar in a basement backroom of the US embassy that was fitted out with mats and pads and punchbags. Which amused Rao greatly. Backrooms in British embassies tended more to faux gentleman's club libraries featuring week-old copies of the *Daily Telegraph* and moth-eaten Afghan rugs. He'd come along to watch because he had fuck all else to do, thought he'd heckle from the sidelines like a cunt just to piss Adam off, but that didn't happen. It didn't happen because Adam fighting was a revelation. His usual blankness was stripped away to reveal a being of aggressive fluidity and unholy grace. Rao watched the whole session in stunned silence, barely able to breathe, and when it was over, as Adam rolled his neck, sniffed, and walked back towards him, the expression on his face made Rao snicker. He'd looked so intensely *bored*. So yes, Rao thought he'd seen Adam fight. But right now, in a Colorado hotel room, he understands that wasn't what he'd seen at all.

It's not elegant. It's brutal, and it happens incomprehensibly fast. Adam throws scalding coffee into anvil guy's face. Brings an elbow—Rao thinks it's an elbow—down hard on the back of his neck. Once he's on the ground, a knee with all Adam's weight behind it is dropped squarely on his groin. The guy's making terrible noises now, fighting to breathe, and *shit* the receptionist guy has just put one hand on Adam's shoulder to pull him off, and that was dumb, that was *so* dumb, because Adam uncoils, punches receptionist guy in the throat, pushes him against the nearest wall, smashes his head twice against it, and then suddenly there's stillness.

Relative stillness. Because the guy on the floor is writhing and Rao's heart is beating a ridiculous tattoo against his chest. Right. Right. He's still holding his coffee. He looks down at the mug. His knuckles are locked around the handle so tight he might never be able to let it go. Right. Ok. He shuts his eyes. This is a situation. The situation is— What is the situation? He takes a deep breath, opens his eyes, and looks.

Ok, he might shut his eyes again. The receptionist's on tiptoe, struggling to breathe, head tipped back against the wall. And with good reason, because Adam's pulled a knife from god knows where and has lodged its point an inch to the left of his chin. The tip must be grating against his jawbone. Blood is running down the blade. Rao can't see Adam's face, but the other guy's eyes are wide, nostrils flared like a terrified horse.

Shit. Shit. Rao was only being a dick because it pleased him to be a dick, because he's always a dick. *It's what he does.* Of course they should go to the facility. Of course they should see that psycho Veronica Rhodes. All the answers they need are there.

Fuck.

The man on the floor interrupts his thoughts with a series of hoarse noises shaped a little like words. Rao looks down. His nose is broken. When did that happen? Sees him spit blood and try again.

"*Call him off,*" he croaks.

"What?"

"*Call him off, call him off.*"

It might be the most ridiculous thing he's ever heard. Rao splutters. "You think I'm the one in charge? Adam, love," he says. "Tell him?"

No answer. Rao takes a couple of steps to bring Adam's face into view. Freezes. *Christ.* All those times Rao's told Adam he's barely human. All those stupid jokes. But here it is. There it is. That's not a human face.

"Adam?" he says cautiously.

Adam twists the blade a little. Inhales. Exhales. Blinks a few times. Shifts his grip on the knife. His expression doesn't change, but maybe, Rao thinks, he's thawing, atom by atom, into something fractionally less remote.

"He's not in charge," Adam says, like he's just learned how to speak. "See?"

Adam's knife hand is wet with blood. It's soaked his shirt cuff, is spreading in terrible patches through the cotton of his sleeve. Rao can see drips forming at his elbow. One falls to the floor. *Shit.* He has to *try.* "Maybe stand down a little, Adam?" he suggests.

Adam frowns, turns his head towards Rao. The look in his eyes is almost too much to bear. It's like he's pleading for something, and Rao has no idea what. He nods.

"If he lets you live," Rao says to the guy against the wall, "you're going to back the fuck off, yeah?"

A strangled noise of assent. Adam steps back. Both of them watch the guy slide to the floor, both hands pressed against his jaw. He's coughing uncontrollably.

"Adam, you ok?"

"I'm fine."

"Did you hurt him anywhere else?"

That gets him a blank look. Rao bites his lip. "So look, I know . . . this sounds mad. But I think we should do it."

"What?"

"Go to the facility. I know it's not optimal. But we need to hear what Veronica has to say for herself." He grins. It's a terrible effort. Glances at the mug he's still holding. "Also the coffee there is great, and they might give us breakfast." He yanks his head at the man on the floor and continues. "And doctors, yeah? I don't think we should leave these poor sods here and I don't know about you, but I'm not too keen on calling an ambulance."

All the eyes in the room are on Adam now. All register his nod of assent.

Rao puts his coffee cup down on the table, massages his fingers. "Lads," he says almost sadly. "This could have been a bit easier if you hadn't come in all guns blazing. You could have just asked nicely. We'd have been happy to go see Veronica, but you had to be dicks about it."

CHAPTER 40

The smile Veronica gives him when Montgomery ushers them into her lab is no longer winter sun. It's hungry. Expectant. Her face is a little flushed, her fringe awry. Different lipstick today. Darker. Eyes a little wide. *She's fucking mad, isn't she*, Rao thinks, unfazed.

She purses her lips. "What happened in the test room?" she demands.

Rao steps forward, scratches at his beard, runs his hands through his hair, grimaces at the whole backwoods Elvis thing he's got going on.

"You wouldn't happen to know a good barber in town, would you, Veronica?"

She stares. "No."

"You have the resources to find out, surely. Care to send some more heavies to bundle one in the back of a van and bring them here?"

She catches on. "Your pickup? It seemed a wise precaution, now I know who you both are."

"Do you? Well done. Congratulations. Veronica, the men you sent were assholes. You could have tried calling on the motel phone and asking nicely."

"I was busy."

"Yeah, well. So was I."

Silence. Her face is that of a person who's never learned to smile. *There she is*, Rao thinks. *The real Veronica Rhodes.* "I'm told your colleague overreacted."

"No shit."

"Should we be concerned about his propensity for violence, going forward?"

Yes, you bloody should. "The fuck are you asking me for? Adam's right here." She raises a hand to her fringe, smooths it. Rao steps forward. "A word in private?" he murmurs. "I'll be fine," he adds, answering Adam's dubious look in the same breath.

Veronica complies. He knew she would.

"Right," he says when they're both in the corridor. "Let's talk. What's in this for me?"

"We need to understand exactly what happened in the test suite, Mr Rao. It could lead us to a cure."

"Could, yeah. Maybe. But that's not what I asked. I'm a cynical bastard these days, Veronica. Good of humanity isn't really my thing anymore."

"We can talk compensation—"

"We can certainly talk compensation. We very much should, in fact. But before that we need to talk about Adam."

"What about him?"

"You want me on board, don't fuck with him, don't test him, don't lay a finger on him. Don't bring him into this."

She's frowning now. "But he—"

"Terms. Take them, leave them, Veronica."

The frown deepens. "You're not in the strongest of negotiating positions, Mr Rao."

He giggles. Doesn't mean to, but *really*. "Of course I am. I know what happened in there, and you're going to need me onside to get more of it. It wasn't . . ." He searches for the right word. Finds it, after a while. Picks it up, wet paper from asphalt. "Passive. It wasn't a passive thing."

That piques her interest. "What do you mean, passive?"

He raises his eyebrows and waits.

"Ok," she says finally. "If you work with us, Mr Rao, we'll leave him alone."

She's lying, of course. Rao doesn't mind. It's enough for now, and he's pretty sure that however blank Adam can be, he's going to know if they lobotomise the fucker. Maybe.

Montgomery and Adam are gone when they reenter the lab, and Rao turns to Veronica, ready to kick off. She raises a placatory, perfectly manicured hand. "He's being taken to have a blood test, Mr Rao. That's all. It's nothing to worry about. We'd like you to have one too.

You both appear to be well, but we don't want to take any chances with your health, do we?"

If he weren't so weirdly antsy about Adam's whereabouts, Rao'd enjoy these ludicrous falsehoods, empty reassurances in primary school teacher tones. "Where is he?"

"Mr Rubenstein is in a treatment room off the main corridor. I'll be taking his bloods personally. Dr Montgomery is in the room next to it. He'll take yours."

*

Adam watches as Dr. Rhodes finds his vein and begins to extract blood with practiced efficiency. Doctors always have trouble finding Adam's veins, but not this one. She speaks first. Bright and pleasant. False. "Your reaction to Prophet suggests you aren't a psychopath, Mr. Rubenstein." She smiles, looking up from his arm. "But you're far from normal."

"No shit," he says under his breath.

"You aren't surprised?"

"To find out that I'm not a psychopath?"

"Mr. Rubenstein." Dr. Rhodes makes a complicated vial swap look as simple and routine as replacing toilet paper. Adam wishes he liked her like Rao seems to. "I've just told you you're not normal. Doesn't that bother you? Interest you?"

"Colonel."

"I'm sorry?"

"Lieutenant Colonel Rubenstein." He's too tired after the last few days to let her weak power plays slide. Too tired after the motel and Prophet and late nights and too much truth with Rao.

"As you like."

"Thank you. Where's Rao?"

"He's also having his bloods taken."

Another vial change.

"Mm," he hums, noncommittal. "What other tests are you intending on running?"

"What makes you presume we have other tests in mind?"

"Dr. Rhodes, you're drawing a lot of blood from me right now."

"It does seem a remarkable amount, doesn't it?"

They're locking horns. It's not about rank. Not about authority. Rhodes isn't trying to intimidate. They're both after the same thing. Apart from Rao's whereabouts, all Adam cares about is finding the avenues in front of him that will grant him as much information as possible. Tit for tat is an easy road to walk, but it's tricky to make it to the end with more intel than the other person. Still, it's the route Adam chooses.

"Fine. I'll play along for now."

"Appreciated."

He sighs, gives her what she wants. "What do you mean, not normal?"

"Ah, that *is* the question." Dr. Rhodes smiles again. This one is genuine, and it does nothing to change Adam's opinion of her. "Do you know what you made after your exposure to Prophet?"

"No, I don't. What was it?"

She shakes her head. "You misunderstand the question, Colonel. What did you make? What was it that you manifested? You didn't respond to it like our other test subjects."

Adam decides to leave the "test subject" designation on the table for now. It'll keep her sweet—or as sweet as she's liable to get.

"That was . . . a moment from my life."

"A happy memory?" She's removed the needle, is taping a wad of cotton over the puncture wound. He presses it with an index finger, eyes drawn to the bruise over the artery above his wrist. He's overtired, skin still jumping after the encounter at the motel. On edge, not knowing exactly where Rao is or what they're doing to him. Blood loss, at this stage, at this level, will only keep him going. Rhodes has stopped short of making him useless, but there is no way in hell Adam is going to let her know that.

"No, Dr. Rhodes," he answers. "It wasn't a happy memory."

"That makes you the first subject who appears to have manifested an object relating to an unpleasant past experience."

"Glad to be of service."

"And you weren't drawn to your . . . moment."

"No."

"Do you think you could replicate it? If you were exposed again?"

"No."

"No, you don't think you could replicate it?"

"No, I don't think that's going to happen."

"You're withholding consent."

"At present."

"Very well. I have more questions—"

"I don't think I have any answers you want."

"But I'll refrain from asking them for now."

She tilts her head. She's expecting more. She's not going to get it.

"Thank you for being such a good sport, Lieutenant Colonel Rubenstein," she says eventually.

"A sport."

"Indeed."

*

Rao massages his inner elbow with a thumb, stares at the tubes of his own blood on the desk. *Dark*, he thinks stupidly. *So dark. Blood's so dark.*

"So, we'll be analysing this," Montgomery says, picking up a pen to fill out labels for the vials.

"No shit," Rao snaps. He's surprised by the flinch that provokes. "Sorry. Sorry, Monty. It's been a bit of a morning. Why've you drained my arm, exactly?"

"We have to determine if you were contaminated in the test room."

Very much so, Rao thinks. *You have no idea.*

Montgomery pauses then, pen wavering. Rao lets the silence stretch. It's a promising one.

"You know, Mr Rao, we had a debrief after"—he clears his throat—"after. We viewed the footage several times. What happened in there wasn't clear."

"Veronica wasn't a happy bunny, eh?"

That gets Rao a nervous, conspiratorial glance. *Bingo*, he thinks. That's the fulcrum. Monty's shit scared of her.

"She . . . exhibited some frustration, yes."

"Fucking hell, Monty," he says seriously. "Don't envy you that experience. Veronica's quite terrifying, isn't she?"

"It's Kent."

"What?"

"Kent Montgomery."

"Ah. Right. Kent. So, Kent. You had a theory about what happened, yeah?"

"I did. I pointed out that her own psychological profile could have negatively impacted her experimental design. She didn't take into account the possibility that emotional bonds, relational attachments could inhibit the action of Prophet. She agreed with me." He smiles. Then the smile slips. "She brought in some volunteers. They weren't military. A couple." His face falls farther. He lowers his voice to a near whisper. "Between you and me, I don't think there was fully informed consent. She put them in the test suite together, dosed the man. He made an orange blanket."

"He's in the ward?"

Montgomery nods. "With his blanket."

"Where's the girlfriend?"

"She's there too."

"Bedside vigil?"

"She's sedated."

"How sedated?"

Montgomery shakes his head sadly. "I don't think Dr Rhodes will stop with these two. I asked her to give you some time to recover, and she was amenable to that. But I'm glad you're here now. I hope you can help."

"Help what?"

"We'll take whatever we can get at this stage," Monty says slowly. "But don't tell her I said that."

CHAPTER 41

Rao watches the door of the room Montgomery ushered him into. Windowless. Cramped. Feels like a holding cell. Maybe that's just how the room makes Rao feel. Maybe he's being horribly unfair to the room. A vending machine clicks and hums itself out of a nap beside him. Moodily, he remembers that he was supposed to be eating some godawful fast-food breakfast. Something too fatty and greasy and absolutely too perfect not to complain at length to Adam about. Because Adam had looked better this morning, and Rao's plan had been to carp about something banal until the man had regained his usual blankness. After all that time in the motel faced with an honestly, immovably, horribly empty Adam, Rao is sorely missing what he'd always assumed was his innate lack of emotion. He watches the door and thinks threats into the air. If they don't bring Adam back out soon, then he'll . . . He'll what, exactly? *Figure it out, Sunil*, he thinks, acid thoughts turning against him in the humming silence. They were supposed to be getting shitty McDonald's pancakes. Egg McMuffins. This day was supposed to be different. This all feels wrong. He's waiting, and he's staring at the door, and he's thinking very hard about not eating every last candy bar in that fucking machine.

*

Rhodes escorts Adam to a small room where Rao is perched on a table swinging his legs and looking bored. She tells them she'll return shortly. He half expects to hear the door lock behind her when she leaves. It doesn't. There's no need. There are eight doors between them and the parking lot, and likely all are controlled remotely from a room they'll never see. If Rao decides to make a break for it, he'll have to come up with a better plan than *run*.

After the door clicks shut, Rao stops kicking the air, starts snapping his fingers. "What did you talk to Veronica about?"

Adam hesitates.

"No one's listening," Rao assures him.

"Dr. Rhodes wanted to talk about what happened last time we were here," he says, pulling a chair up to the table. He sits, looks up at Rao, watches him frown out his thoughts.

"You didn't give her anything?"

"Not much. I told her that what happened, what got made—"

"What you manifested—"

"Was a moment."

"A moment. Yeah. Well. I guess that's true enough." There's something about how Rao says that, something a little *off*. Adam opens his mouth, but Rao doesn't give him the chance to ask his question before he's answering it. "No, I still can't tell with you, you paranoid cunt."

That's not it. That's never been a concern. In fact, sometimes Adam is happy Rao can't tell with him. "Happy" is the only word he has for the feeling. Happy that Rao can't just do a run on him and leave him unraveled like he does everyone else. Rao has no qualms about doing runs on people—and truth be told, neither does Adam. They've never talked about it, but it's clear to him that Rao's knack of zeroing in on a person's vulnerabilities, coupled with his extraordinary talent, his knowledge of the truth, makes Rao one of the most important intelligence assets in the world. Espionage rests on trust, on passing, on leverage, and on betrayal, and Rao's existence breaks the whole system. Nobody seems to get that. Drives Adam crazy. It should be obvious as soon as they find out about Rao.

"Does Rhodes know about you?"

Rao doesn't miss a beat, doesn't stop to test it. Which means he already has. "Yeah. She's had access to some official file or report. Very recently. It's probably one of yours."

Adam blinks a few times. "Probably," he agrees, voice tight. Rao sniffs, holds back from another blow. He's feeling merciful today. "I don't trust her, Rao."

"Of course you don't," Rao laughs. "Veronica's out of her mind. But she's alright."

"You just said that she's out of her mind."

"Quite a few people could say the same about me, love. And after this morning, I suspect a few people are saying the same about you."

Adam sits back in his chair. Thinks about Dr. Rhodes, her fake smiles and plyboard-thin lies. "You like her," he asks. Doesn't sound like a question, but it is.

"I really do."

Adam knows how much Rao enjoys liars. Once, drunkenly, he told Adam he considered himself a connoisseur of mendacity. He explained that he doesn't always know when people are lying. All he can tell is whether a statement says true things about the world. But with the right questions, he can usually find out. And that, he said with relish, is the art of the thing. The only times that liars get to him are when he decides their lies are stupid or messy or lacking in craft.

Adam can see that Rhodes appreciates "the craft." And she—well. Rao has a healthy appreciation for beauty, and Dr. Rhodes is objectively beautiful. Classically so. Silver screen beauty that out of Glorious Technicolor, in faded and muted reality, makes her look a little cruel. Brunette. Gray eyes. Carefully chosen shades of lipstick. She and Rao flirt when they talk, and Adam wonders if either understands the terms of their interactions. Likely both simply enjoy playing the game.

"Is it because she's English?" he deflects.

"You're fucking with me."

"I'm fucking with you."

"Glad to see you're in such a good mood after our highly eventful morning, Adam," Rao observes, a grin spreading on his face.

Adam looks down, picks at the dried brown on his left cuff. Blood is hard to get out of a light cotton blend. "Mm," he says.

"Adam?"

"Yes, Rao."

"Where did that knife come from?"

"Waistband."

"Looked like you pulled it out of thin air."

"I think that's what it looked like to the guy who grabbed you too," Adam says. The words tumble out of his mouth. Truth pulled out of him because he's tired, or is suffering transient anemia after his blood was drawn, or because now he owes Rao every truth he's carefully squirreled away.

Rao looks at him. Adam looks right back. He doesn't think Rao's scared or spooked, though the expression on his face looks like both at once. *He's got to know now*, Adam thinks. If he didn't before, he definitely got a clue after last night, after their talks in the dark, after how quickly he fell asleep when Rao did what he did. And if that hadn't been enough, he knows now. He *has* to.

They hold each other's gaze. Neither of them startles or looks away, but it's too much for Adam to handle. He takes a breath and picks himself up, goes to the vending machine. He's got a few loose dollars in his pockets, and he effectively ruined any chance they had at having a decent breakfast. "What do you want?"

Rao thinks about his answer very seriously. "Butterfinger."

Adam throws the chocolate bar to him, and Rao unwraps it, eats it ruminatively. "Veronica and Monty," he says, taking another bite, "don't know about our tail. They didn't put it on us."

"Who did?"

"Internal. Yeah. It's Prophet. This project has hands that don't know what other hands in the project are doing with themselves."

"Succinct," Adam comments mildly.

Rao ignores that, pops the last of the Butterfinger in his mouth, chews, and swallows. "Also, Veronica isn't related to Elise."

"Elise?"

Rao smirks. "Someone I knew in Berlin. Spitting image. It's uncanny."

"This isn't relevant, Rao."

"I hoped it might be."

Adam exhales. "Miller?"

"She's alive. Still in a trance. Veronica knows what happened in Polheath but wasn't involved. Monty doesn't know about it. Monty hasn't a fucking clue about much, if you ask me."

"Is Miller—" Adam begins but shuts his mouth as the door opens and Veronica walks in.

"Colonel," she says, looking at Rao, "I'd like to have a word with your colleague. Might you excuse us?"

Rao screws up the Butterfinger wrapper, drops it on the table. "Is there somewhere for Adam to get breakfast?"

"There's a canteen. It's on the third floor. I'm sure Montgomery will be delighted to take him there. I'll call him now."

"Rao, I'm—"

"Go on Adam. I owe you."

CHAPTER 42

As soon as Adam and Montgomery leave, Veronica leans across the table, picks up Rao's discarded candy wrapper, and walks it to the far side of the room. Dropping it into a trash can, she looks back at him, smiling brightly. *Mistake*, Rao thinks. He doesn't respond well to being treated like an errant child. But then he notes the professional interest in her eyes. She pulled that move specifically to provoke him. *Yeah*, he thinks. *She's good.*

She walks out of sight behind him to the far side of the table. A scraping noise as she draws up a chair. He considers staying put. Decides, on reflection, to hop off his perch and take a seat facing her.

"Cards on the table, Mr Rao," she says. "Montgomery is concerned with the possibility that you and Colonel Rubenstein are infiltrators."

"Infiltrators."

"Moles. Working for outside agents. He's worried about it."

"I expect Monty worries about a lot of things," Rao sighs. "Who am I supposed to be reporting to?"

"Montgomery suspects corporate espionage."

"And you?"

She purses her lips. "I'd say the most likely recipient would be the British security services."

"I'm not reporting to those wankers."

"And I should take that on trust?"

"I would," Rao says. This is tiresome. He sits back in his chair. "Look. We just came here following a lead. We were trying to find Flores. He's the friend of a friend. But I'm feeling inclined to stick around."

"Are you. I'm a little perplexed about why."

He snorts. "Because Prophet fascinates the ever-living shit out of me, Veronica. I can't stop thinking about it."

"So you're . . . sticking around in the spirit of intellectual enquiry?"

"One way of putting it."

"Better than prison?"

"Another way."

She considers him. "You've rather a difficult personality, Mr Rao."

"I'm being sweet as pie to you, Veronica."

"Your psych evaluations suggest oppositional defiant disorder."

That's bullshit, Rao thinks. Doctors invented ODD so they could diagnose it in patients who hate them. Besides, he's not in the habit of blaming other people for his problems. When things go wrong, it's always Rao's fault. He's just an asshole who's a maestro at fucking things up when he's just trying to *help*.

"You have those evals, do you?" he says.

"I do. I also have a police report relating to an incident at the Laburnum recovery centre."

Rao briefly closes his eyes. "Fucking reports," he sighs. It's not that he didn't expect Lunastus to have fingers in all the pies, but it's still disagreeable to discover how quickly they've got hold of this shit.

"They tell me," she says, "that you're a man capable of unprovoked violent assault."

"It wasn't unprovoked."

"Why don't you tell me all about it?"

"You sound like one of them," he says sourly.

The Laburnum. The group sharing session. The peach-hued walls, the velvet couch, and the marble fireplace. The chairs around the rug in the middle of the room. The black rug. Circular. Like a hole in the floor. Rao staring at his trainers, failing to get anywhere near serenity because his opiate eiderdown has been taken away and memories of Kabul have kept him from sleep for days. They're cutting, continual, snipped into sections like strips of celluloid film, looping backwards and forwards in nonsensical, nauseating patterns. It's not the lack of heroin that's slowly killing him here; it's the memories. It's the lack of sleep. It's the floral room fragrance that's making his throat close. The faux-orchid-scented air.

He focuses on the man opposite. Colonel Foster. It's his time to share. Tattersall open-necked shirt, a patrician mouth. A pair of red corduroy trousers. Brogues. Salt-and-pepper hair with a fringe swept sideways like he's still wearing a beret. He's here with a DUI. He's resting his hands on his knees, looking everyone in the eye, one after the other, telling them about how he started drinking heavily after the first death at the training barracks he commanded.

Well that's bollocks, Rao determines. *Didn't start then*. He's interested now. Listens harder. Foster is strangely at ease in this therapeutic space. It's because he grew up in a God-fearing Roman Catholic family. He's used to confession. How to do it. How to make it sound: everything he says rings with deep conviction. A little tremble in his voice here and there. A catch, sometimes. He's telling everyone how terrible it was as a commanding officer to have such things happen under his watch. The beating squads, the torturing of new recruits. He has tears in his eyes now, and his hands are shaking. His voice is a whisper when he tells the group that he had had no idea what was going on. How the bullying had been kept from him. How he should have known. How those suicides from the bullying were unacceptable, and he'll never forgive himself—

No, Rao thinks firmly. Not all those deaths were suicides. *No*. Foster had full knowledge. Foster is lying through his fucking teeth. And Foster is suddenly all of them. All the bastards who strung up naked men in Kabul and left them soaked through bitter nights, who assaulted them, humiliated them, pissed on them, threw them against walls, broke their souls to shards and ashes, and Rao isn't sitting anymore, he's up and retaliating, he's punched Foster in the face, tipping his chair back onto the carpeted floor, and he's kicked him in the face twice, the second time harder through the fingers that Foster brought up to protect himself, and he's doing it because he *must*. It's not just to stop this cunt talking, it's to obliterate every lie that ever was in the world, to obliterate the knowledge that such things happen in it, and he feels the searing pain in his toes as the kicks connect and usually that would clear his head but this just makes him go harder, there are people reaching for him and he pushes them off and he's on top of Foster now, punching him again and again and there's blood on that tattersall shirt and blood on his knuckles, and a siren is going off and Rao isn't sure if it's in his head or in the room, and then they drag him off and there's a needle and Rao laughs when he feels it and he just keeps saying thank you, because he's never before met unconsciousness with so much simple, desperate gratitude.

Remembering it, his knuckles sting anew. He won't lose it. He *won't*. Rubbing his eyes, he takes a deep breath, lets it out as slowly as he can. "It wasn't unprovoked," he repeats. "He was a lying piece of shit."

"You nearly killed him," she says almost cheerfully. It's calming, Rao thinks, how little she cares. Like she's balancing out how much he does in some cosmic ledger. Now she purses her lips, leans closer. "You should know I've been considering granting you both access to the project."

"As test subjects?"

"Subcontractors. Coworkers."

"Because you'd rather have us inside the tent pissing out than outside pissing in?"

"No. Not for that reason," she responds, unflinching. "Mr Rao, you were flagged as a potential asset to our project before you walked through our doors. I'm told you can detect fakes. Can you identify an Eos Prophet Generated Object, an EPGO, on sight?"

"Yes, as I'm sure you already know. Go on. Cards on the table, Dr Rhodes."

"My sources also say you're a human polygraph, a unique talent that could also be of use to us here." She opens her hands. "So, Mr Rao. Tell me. Using your special powers. Am I being straight with you?"

Yes. She is. And isn't. "Yes, Veronica. You are. Though there's rather a lot of lying by omission, isn't there? Most of your interest in us is medical."

"Could you be persuaded to join us?"

"I'll have to talk to Adam."

She nods. "If you did, will you behave?"

He sniggers. "Really, Veronica? *Austin Powers?*"

"Rao, could we please talk seriously?"

"Alright, alright. I'll talk to Adam. Be nice to us both, and I'll do my best."

"Is that an undertaking?"

"It's as much of one as you're going to get."

The following morning, staring at the TOP SECRET designation printed on the pages spread over the boardroom table, Rao is experiencing a small, silent crisis. He'd expected Adam to painstakingly read the small print, factoring in every possible consequence of them joining the project. Instead, he'd simply picked up a pen and signed everything Montgomery put in front of him. Rao'd never thought Adam capable of recklessness. But the clock had happened. That guy he'd pinned to the wall with a knife. And now this.

This is what Adam wanted, though. Wants. Rao'd quizzed him about it yesterday evening outside the motel, dogs barking fitfully, streetlights flickering on. While he'd sat on the low car park wall and smoked, Adam had informed him they were fine to sign up to the project.

"Fine in what sense?" Rao'd asked carefully.

"Miller's boss wants us embedded in the program."

Rao'd sighed. "They should bring in those assholes she told us about. The paranormal ones."

"I mentioned them. Got told there was no guarantee the EIO weren't involved already and could be antagonistic to our investigation. We have to stay under the radar as long as possible."

"You don't sound enthusiastic about any of this, love."

"They're orders, Rao."

So here Adam is. Here he is. Here they both are. Reckless as fuck. Still, the coffee continues to be great. He pours himself another cup. "We don't get chocolates now we've signed up as guinea pigs?"

Montgomery glances at Veronica. "We can call for chocolates," he says. "And you aren't guinea pigs. You're subcontractors. The forms are quite clear."

"They are. They say I shouldn't have access to this project at all," Rao continues cheerfully, counting on his fingers. "I've taken drugs, I've drunk to excess, I've been arrested, and I'm not a US citizen."

"Technically, neither of you should have access to this project," Veronica counters. "But I wanted you, so I made it happen. Let's move on. I believe Montgomery wants to run through some of our results, and then we can discuss ways forward that suit our needs."

"Whose needs?" Adam says.

"Ours. I'm assuming you want to discover what Prophet is, and why it does what it does. It's what we want too."

"Ways forward?" Rao asks.

"Investigative procedures."

"Vivisection's off the table."

"I've never vivisected anyone," Montgomery says hastily.

"Rather glad to hear you say that."

"Ok, so, let's give you a little more background on my background," Montgomery begins, voice shifting official. "Before this I worked with Dr Rhodes on another Lunastus biomedical project, based in . . . uh, based elsewhere. Before that I was at DARPA, where I was a program manager."

True, Rao thinks, *but so fucking boring.* "Kent, can we skip the CV? Just tell us about Prophet."

"Ok, ok, sure. What do you want to know?"

"What happens to it after it's got inside someone and fucked them up?"

"Near torpor," Veronica says. "Reduced heart rate, periodic breathing, metabolic rate suppression. The state is akin to hibernation. Physiologically fascinating."

"Does it break down over time?"

"Good question, Rao," Montgomery says. "No, it doesn't. After exposure, levels in the bloodstream remain constant. We can't detect any trace of Prophet or any potential metabolites in sweat, urine, faeces, or exhaled air. Once administered, it crosses the blood-brain barrier, concentrating in regions of the brain associated with memory retrieval and emotional regulation."

"You're employing scans? MRIs?" Adam asks.

"Yes," he says. "But we can only scan subjects with smaller EPGOs. Nonmetallic ones."

Veronica cuts in. "Functional MRIs don't directly show the presence of Prophet; they evidence the neurological activity it provokes. For finer structural analysis, we've recourse to histological samples." She smiles at Adam. "In layman's terms, we've been looking at samples of tissue to understand where Prophet collects in the brain."

"Whose tissue?" Adam says.

"Our previous principal investigator has made an important personal contribution to our understanding of the substance. Postmortem. We're very grateful to him."

"Fucking hell," Rao breathes.

She waves her hand. "It won't happen again. Not now we've robust postinfusion protocols."

"And you have Kent."

Montgomery gives Adam and Rao a miniature, self-conscious wave. Clears his throat after a few seconds of silence. "Moving on to test results. Rao, I'm afraid I have to inform you that you have Prophet in your blood."

Rao sits forward. Asks the question that's been burning away at him. The question that's remained bafflingly unanswered by every run he's made at it. "Why haven't I made something and got stuck to it, then?"

Montgomery shifts in his seat. "Well . . ." he begins.

"I'm not a psycho, Kent."

A watery smile. "Individuals with psychopathy show a characteristic pattern of neurological activity after being exposed to Prophet. We can put you through an fMRI and—"

"What about Adam?" Rao interrupts.

"Well. Mr—Lieutenant Colonel Rubenstein is a mystery. His self-administered dose was a full one. But there's no trace of Prophet in his blood."

"Samples got mixed up?" Adam asks.

"No," Veronica says. "Everything was labelled at source. But considering these results, more blood work will be required."

Rao groans. "You're a bunch of vampires."

"I'm a doctor," Montgomery protests.

"So was Renfield," Rao shoots back. Adam looks down at the table-top and smiles. Rao's not seen that smile for a while. He wants to see it again. "He's not going to start eating flies, is he?" he whispers.

"Good protein source."

"Fucking hell, Adam. Ok, Kent, fire up your MRI. I think you should give me a scan."

CHAPTER 43

Rao's voice comes over the intercom. "This is weird."

"How are you doing, Mr. Rao?" Rhodes checks. Adam watches her tap a key to change the image on-screen. Still Rao's brain. The scan isn't fully complete, but he understands what he's looking at. Rao's skull. His eyes. There his brain sits and sparks. "Looks fine here."

"No, I think I'm alright," Rao confirms. He's nervous in the machine, his voice wavering like he's on the edge of laughter. "I just wanted to say that this is fucking weird."

"Please don't move," she instructs. Rao responds with a huff over the mic and the line goes quiet.

Adam decides he hates the scanner. Which surprises him. Generally speaking, he doesn't mind heavy machinery. He understands engines. Aircraft. Cars. Doesn't understand people who feel intimidated by technology, by things built to do a specific job and do it perfectly. He grew up on base surrounded by the roar of jets, the noise of sirens and horns. But the machine Rao is in isn't making the kind of sounds he's used to. They're alien hums and tones that remind him of alarms. In the back of his mind, the Big Voice over base loudspeakers. *Scramble. Scramble.*

"I would like to take you to see the clock, Colonel Rubenstein," Dr. Rhodes murmurs, her eyes on the screen. "Your manifested object."

"I know what clock you're talking about, Dr. Rhodes," he says. "To what end?"

Rhodes smiles a private smile. "To see what happens."

There are a million reasons why he shouldn't tempt fate by going down there. One of them is the expression on Rhodes's face. Adam looks at Rao in the tube, hears the alien clunks. Thinks about how Rao simply wanted to talk through how *weird* it is in there.

"Alright," he says.

Dr Rhodes turns her head to look at him properly. She'd been expecting resistance. "Do you think you can handle it?"

"I suppose we'll find out."

"Told you there'd be aftereffects," Rao complains as the slab rolls out of the tube like a tongue rolling out of a mouth. "I feel fucking dreadful after that."

"The scan is entirely safe," Rhodes says. But once Rao is sitting up, she takes his wrist all the same. Old school. Eyes on her watch as she counts the beats. "You're fine."

"Dreadful," he repeats venomously. "I want to lie down."

"You're welcome to do so, Mr. Rao. There's a bed in the room next door. Take as long as you need. Colonel Rubenstein and I are going to take a stroll down to the testing labs to revisit his EPGO."

"The clock?"

"Correct."

Rao shakes his head, winces. Speaks with his eyes closed. "Adam."

"Rao."

"That's bonkers."

Adam's inclined to agree, but Rhodes speaks before he can reply. "Even when the object was manifested, Colonel Rubenstein showed no signs of wanting to connect to it. I'm confident revisiting it will be a risk-free experience."

Rao opens his eyes and looks at her. Adam knows that look. Rao's pissed that he can't tell if her statement's true because it's about him. Rhodes, he realizes, has no knowledge of that particular block.

"I'm coming with you both," Rao says eventually.

"I thought you wanted to lie down," Adam says.

"Yeah, but that was before I found out you were intending to be a dickhead today."

Adam hums. "Not the whole day."

Rao smiles, despite himself. "Piss off, Adam."

Rhodes leads them to the test room. It's illuminated by ceiling strips of harsh fluorescents, but the clock is lit up like the sun is hitting it just right in Nevada sunset yellow. Time frozen in place.

They stand in silence looking at it. Adam doesn't feel anything. He wonders why. The nothing he feels now is complicated. The loss of his aunt, the absolute failure of that day, the sheer drop of grief—all of it sits in the exact same place inside him as before. Might be sharper. The wound opened fresh again. Maybe. He can remember everything that happened back then more clearly now. There must be something about Prophet that seeks out the part inside you that yearns for safety and pieces it all together. Pulls it out like a lure forged by muscles you didn't know you possessed. The EPGOs are that, in the end. Some kind of lure. A light to entice, an escape. An escape that's a trap.

But he's looking at the clock in the test room, flush to a section of wall decorated like his mom's kitchen, and he doesn't feel a damn thing.

He turns to face Rao and Rhodes.

"You have no urge to get closer to it?" Rhodes asks. Adam shakes his head. "Are you feeling any revulsion at the sight?"

"I'm indifferent," he tells her.

"Remarkable," she murmurs, stepping closer to check his pupils. He hates her standing so close, but in only a second's breath she's moving beyond him to examine the clock for what he can only imagine is the fiftieth time. He watches her lift a pencil tip to the ticking, trembling second hand that will never move any farther. "Could you touch it?" she asks.

He walks to the wall. When he raises his right arm, his hand is pale with fluorescent light, though the clock and the paneled wall around it glow with evening sun. He isn't casting any shadow.

He reaches. Hears Rao take a breath.

The glass is warm, like evenings were. He feels nothing. Lets his hand drop.

"You're alright?" Rao says.

"I'm fine."

"Outstanding." Rao presses a thumb against the bridge of his nose. "I'm going to lie down. You'll find me."

"I will."

Rao grunts, leaves the room. Doesn't look back. Adam watches the door close behind him.

"I wonder if another dose might clarify matters," Veronica muses aloud.

Adam considers it. All of them were expecting *something* to happen when he came down here. His feeling nothing at all is a result of sorts, but it's not exactly thrilling. Funny, considering that the clock is an artifact of the most thrilling thing about him. He's not normal. The clock. Feeling nothing. Being a snowstorm in Rao's cacophony of truth: all point to him being abnormal. *Anomalous*, Dr. Rhodes would say.

"Let's find out," he says. "The scientific approach would be to repeat the experiment, correct?"

Rhodes's lips twitch. "Perhaps more of a military approach, but I'm not inclined to disagree. Intravenous, like last time. Shall we?"

Adam's already rolling up his shirtsleeve, thankful that Rao isn't around to try to talk him out of this. But this isn't like last time. Adam wants to see the other side.

Rhodes isn't prone to wasting time. It's one of the few things Adam likes about her. He waits for her to return with the single dose of Prophet with his back turned to the clock and the Nevada sunset. She doesn't speak again, remains silent as she wipes his skin and injects the dose. Not even the customary *you'll feel a pinch*. He recognizes that this doesn't come from mutual respect, only her desperation to find out something new about a substance she barely understands, but he appreciates it.

Once it's in his veins, she withdraws the needle. Stands back. They wait. Adam looks down at the injection site, expecting to see where the needle went in. It bit like hell. It should have left a mark. And there *is* a mark, but it's not red. And it's not a pinprick. It's black. It looks like a mole. He thinks he's imagining things when the mole starts to grow. He holds himself still, barely breathing. It's not a mole. And it's not black. It's dark gray, then silver. It's Prophet, and it's pooling out of him like he's an overfull glass of water. With every tick of the not-clock behind him, the bead doubles in size until a puddle of Prophet is sitting in the bend of his elbow. He looks up at Rhodes.

"That's . . . unusual," she says, eyes wide. She sounds like she's just seen something beautiful. Singular. The tone people use when they talk about the first time they see some natural wonder. Machu Picchu. Niagara Falls. Adam Rubenstein with a silver puddle on his arm.

"What am I looking at? What's happening?"

"It doesn't want you," she breathes.

Hard not to take that personally. "What does that mean?"

"I'm not sure," she says. Her voice is full of awe. Adam hates it. "Don't move," she adds.

She rushes out of the room and returns with a petri dish and another syringe of Prophet. Silver, like it's solid in there. Adam knows it isn't.

"Tip your arm, please. Carefully," Rhodes says. They both focus very hard on the task of letting the Prophet drip from his skin to the dish. It doesn't flow like a liquid should. Doesn't get caught in the tiny hairs of his arm. Isn't directed along the imperceptible lines of his skin. It drips onto Rhodes's dish like it's flowing over smooth metal. Adam thinks about all the times Rao's called him a robot.

"What is your plan, Dr. Rhodes?" he asks, nodding at her second dose of Prophet.

"I'd like to try again," she says. Doesn't try to hide her enthusiasm.

Adam thinks about that. Thinks about Rao with his headache, lying in another room. Thinks about how ready he had been, when they first arrived, to get Rao his answers or die trying. How much he'd been hoping for the latter. That had been stupid but only because he'd acted without a cushion in place.

Rhodes looks hungry. Adam thinks that she doesn't know what hunger is.

"Let's talk testing," he says.

Rhodes raises an eyebrow. "By all means."

"How far do you want to go?"

"Obviously we must stay within safety parameters," she says. Adam doesn't buy it. It's a line. He doesn't care about her script.

"And if we didn't?"

Her gray eyes darken. "May I ask why you have a sudden interest?"

"I'm wondering how much I should be asking for in return for compliance."

She smiles. "What is it that you want?"

Adam smiles back. "We were talking about you, Dr. Rhodes."

"Proximally, I want to know why Prophet affects you like it does. Ultimately, there is no limit to what I want to know. I want to know everything. And now, as is customary in a negotiation, I'd like to hear your demands in return."

"How deep does Lunastus-Dainsleif go?"

"You're talking about influence?" she asks. He nods. "Deeper than, I think, you currently comprehend."

"That sounds like dick swinging, Dr. Rhodes."

"It does, doesn't it?" She's smug. "It isn't."

Adam hums. "If that's true, then you already know about Rao's record."

"Correct."

"I want that cleared."

"Is that all?"

He shakes his head. He's got a lot more. "You'll employ him. As staff, not as a contractor. I don't care if he actually does a job or not, Rhodes," he tells her. "I don't give a shit. You'll have him on payroll and he will be entirely legit. I want him untouchable."

"To what end?"

"Stability."

"For only one of you?"

"You said there's no limit to what you want to know. Doesn't that imply there's no limit to the tests you want to run? Beyond safety parameters."

"You're willing to commit yourself to this course of action for—"

"Yes," he interrupts, suddenly aware of how little time they might have before Rao comes looking for them. "If I get confirmation, without a doubt, that all of this will be provided. I want certainty that it will go ahead."

"Of course."

Adam inclines his head. "Then we have the beginnings of a deal."

"Seems that we do," Rhodes concurs. "Would you be willing to take another dose?"

"I'll do it again," he nods.

"Now?"

"No. After I get everything we just talked about in writing."

"In order for this to work, you may need to be recategorized as a new hire," she says. "Working for the research department."

"I don't care how you make it work," he says honestly.

"I appreciate your directness, Colonel."

"Fine. Dr. Rhodes?"

"More requests?"

"Rao doesn't need to be in the loop from the beginning."

"You don't want him to know?"

"He will know, eventually," he tells Rhodes. No reason to lie. He doesn't tell her the truth, that he wants to control when and how Rao finds out. He has to be the one to tell Rao every part of the arrangement. Not Rhodes. Not Montgomery. Not any of their Lunastus lackeys. Only him. "He just doesn't need to be contacted directly with any of these details until everything is finalized."

"Ah. I believe I understand."

"I don't think you do, Dr. Rhodes, but I do think you'll do as I ask."

"Very confident."

There's no reason why that statement strikes Adam's last nerve. Could be the simple fact that he doesn't like her. Every smug comment out of her mouth feels like sandpaper against his skin. Then again, he feels closer than ever to snapping since that first dose and the clock, after everything said and unsaid in the motel.

Whatever. Adam gives her the truth again. He doesn't care if she doesn't like it.

"I'm a test subject with my wits about me and free access to a weapon. I could blow my brains out and ruin your chances to get what you want. Every hostage situation begins and ends with confidence."

She doesn't answer for a beat. Two beats. Eventually, she opens her mouth. "I sincerely hope that we get along, Colonel Rubenstein."

"You'll cope, Dr. Rhodes."

CHAPTER 44

Rao complains so incessantly about his headache and nausea that Rhodes sends them back to the motel for the rest of the day. "Fucking dreadful," Rao repeats in the car. Adam smiles tightly at the road but doesn't respond. It's difficult not to. There's a twist in his stomach that surprises him, and every time he looks at Rao, even glancingly, the twist gets sharper. Feels like when he saw Rao in Polheath for the first time in forever, feels like when he found out about the heroin, about Kabul. Feels like he just connected the dots between what he said about Rao that one time and what happened to him. Guilt.

At the door to their room, Adam's not so much struggling with the keys as hesitant with them. Doesn't want to go into a closed space with Rao. Feels like a trap. Hard to tell who's being trapped.

"Rao."

"Adam," Rao sounds exhausted. He's leaning against the wall beside the door, eyes closed, head turned toward Adam's voice. "What does that tone mean?"

"What tone?"

"The way you just said my name means there's a problem," Rao sighs, eyes screwed tighter now. "Are we talking about an external problem or an internal one?"

Adam hums. "Could you define 'external' versus 'internal' for me in this context?"

Rao opens his eyes, annoyed. "'External' as in there are snipers trained on us."

It's funny, but Adam doesn't laugh. "There are no snipers, Rao."

"Brilliant news," Rao says flatly. "In that case, could the internal problem wait a bit? This headache is the kind of monster that demands drugs before it'll leave me the fuck alone, and since I'm moderately sure there are none in my immediate vicinity?" He pauses, looking vaguely hopeful. Adam shakes his head. "Right. Then I'm going to go lie down. Can it wait?"

Adam thinks about that. It can wait, but he doesn't want it to. He rips off the Band-Aid. "Rhodes and I decided to dose me again." Rao pushes off the wall. Looks at Adam closely. "When are you planning to do this?"

"Already done."

"Fuck's sake, Adam." Rao grits his teeth.

"Let's talk about it inside."

"Fucking let's."

In the room, Rao sits down heavily on his bed. "What happened?" he demands.

"Nothing."

"What do you mean, nothing?"

"It means nothing happened," Adam repeats. "I didn't manifest anything. Rhodes administered a single dose." He shrugs off his jacket and rolls up his sleeve. Shows Rao the crook of his elbow. The injection site stings, and there's a dull ache there, like a bruise under his skin, but he's just showing Rao his arm. There's nothing there. "I guess it happened again."

"What are you talking about?"

"My blood work showed no Prophet. I'm not normal, Rao. It doesn't work on me like other people. It did what it did to me last time, then it must have just come out of me. Like today."

Rao blinks at him. "*Fuck off.*"

"What?"

"Are you *serious*?"

"I don't understand the question."

"Then fuck right off. It didn't just come out of you, last time," Rao says. He sounds incredulous. Insulted. Adam frowns, confused. "I took it out of you. I— Fuck, Adam, I *drew it out of you*. It was me."

"That doesn't make sense," Adam says. He feels stupid. Distant. He tries to remember the day. He thought he remembered everything. The injection, the manifestation. But the more he thinks about it, the more he realizes there are breaks in his memory. There was the clock. The clock, everything about it and everything it meant. All the grief he'd felt back then, all the grief he'd buried since, all of it out in the room for everyone to see. He could barely breathe through it. Couldn't think through it. And then—then he could. He knew that Rao was there. He'd asked to leave. They'd left. There were stoplights somewhere. In the vehicle. In the car. That's what Adam remembers.

"What about any of this makes sense?" Rao counters. Adam silently agrees. "What did Veronica say?"

Adam crosses the room, sits on the other bed. "She said . . ." He pauses. Hates that he does. Stupid. "Rhodes said that it didn't want me."

Rao crows with sudden laughter. "Story of your life," he splutters.

It's weird how quickly Adam forgot how to handle Rao saying things like this. The insults that aren't quite insults. It's the purest form of Rao familiarity: find the weak joint and pull until the structure groans into near collapse. Adam isn't ready for it, this punch to the gut.

Internal problem.

It obviously shows on his face. Rao winces.

"Sorry, Adam."

"It's fine," he says. It nearly is.

Adam's grateful when Rao goes to take a shower. He sits on his bed and stares at the chaos surrounding Rao's. Clothes on the carpet and discarded mugs and candy wrappers on the nightstand. He's gotten pretty good at ignoring Rao's clutter, but right now he can't. He picks up the mugs, brings them to the kitchenette, and washes them. Puts the trash where it should be. Picks the clothes off the floor, folds them, lays them on the bed, and he's squaring the books on the nightstand when Rao reappears wearing a waffle robe and hotel slippers. Every time Adam's cleaned like this before, Rao's given him shit for it. But now he looks amiably at Adam. "Cheers," he says. "I'm a messy bastard. Okay if I order in some pizza?"

Pizza's turning into their Big Talk food in the motel, Adam thinks as he chews slowly on a slice. He's going to have a Pavlovian response to pepperoni after this. He's going to order a Meat Lover's one day and start opening up to the server about his relationship with his mother.

"Alright. I've waited long enough, I think," Rao says, mouth full.

Adam blinks at him. "For what?"

"A thank you. I saved your life, Adam."

He's talking about Prophet. Drawing it out of him. Did he?

"Did you?"

"Yes, you prick."

But he can't tell. He can't tell with me. "Today, with Rhodes," Adam says, "you weren't there. It came out of my skin without you around—"

Rao holds up a hand to stop him speaking, looks away, mouth moving silently. He's doing a run. "Well. I obviously know fuck all about what's going on with you. But I can draw it out of people. Other people."

"That . . . changes a few things."

Rao exhales, puffing up his cheeks. "No shit. I think I can cure people," he says, then grins. "I can cure people."

"How?"

"Fuck knows."

"Rao."

"No, really. Adam, I don't know how to run that. I don't know what I can check. I have no idea about the mechanics of this shit, and I don't know why I can draw it out," he says quickly. "It feels right, though. When I did it for you, it felt—" He stops. Shakes his head.

"I have a fucker of a headache, Adam."

"I know, Rao. Do we tell Rhodes about this?"

"We'll have to. I have to," Rao says. He rubs his face. "I'm seeing her first thing tomorrow to go through my scans. I'll do it then."

*

Veronica's office delights Rao. It seems more like a prop-filled stage than a space a human uses for work. When she invites him to join her behind her desk, he takes a seat and looks up at her monitor. It's showing a photograph of a village in the Cotswolds. Honey-coloured stone houses, lush meadows, a ribbon of road climbing a hill. *Bibury*, he thinks. Back when he was a student, he'd visited it with his parents on holiday, staying near Cirencester in a country house hotel. Amiable political talk with his father over breakfast on the terrace, ragged peacocks dragging their tails across dew. Rao necking mimosas under a sky luminous with mist and the promise of a hot summer's day. His mother wrinkling her nose at the state of the peacocks here, she and Rao sharing one of those moments of laughter that punctuate all his memories like gold.

"How are you feeling?" Veronica enquires.

"Fine," he answers. *I miss my mother*, he thinks.

"No symptoms?"

He shakes his head. Trying to explain his episodic hallucinatory experiences would be tedious. Besides, they're private. "Let's look at my brain, Veronica," he says.

She taps at the keyboard and Bibury is replaced with his scan results. The image shifts and roils as she moves through sections of his skull. *Thunderclouds*, he thinks. The way they roil and rise on a summer's afternoon. She raises a pencil, taps the screen with its point. The minute click of graphite on glass as she moves it from place to place. "Frontal, limbic, paralimbic, midbrain regions," she says. "Increased activity in these conforms to previous research in the neurobiology of nostalgia. But your reward centres—hippocampus, substantia nigra, the ventral tegmental area, and ventral striatum—are all in an intense state of arousal."

Rao waggles his eyebrows.

"Not that kind," she says. "Many pointers for further investigation, Rao. For now, let's just say Prophet affects your brain differently than it does other people's."

Maybe, he thinks, *my brain is just different from other people's*. She's dropped the "Mr," he notes. Pity. He'd rather liked the formality.

"Perhaps now might be a good time for us to discuss the passivity you raised, in relation to events in the test room," she murmurs.

"Absolutely we should," he says. "That whole thing in the test room, that was down to me."

"You induced Rubenstein to dose himself?"

He freezes momentarily. "Not . . . not that bit. What happened afterwards. I physically drew the substance out of him. It came out of his skin, right out of the palms of his hands where I was touching them, and it went into mine. Like osmosis."

She looks hungry again. Leans forward. "Not like osmosis. Not at all like osmosis."

"I'm not a bloody biologist, Veronica. Capillary action, osmosis, whatever you want to call it. It came out of Adam, went into me."

"Did it affect you?"

He makes a moue. "A little bit. Got dizzy for a while."

This is by far the greatest understatement of his life, he thinks. He should get an award.

"Are you and Lieutenant Colonel Rubenstein romantically attached?"

He laughs, surprised. But of course she'd ask that. "No."

"You're close?"

"He doesn't really do 'close,' Veronica."

That gets a different smile. She's got a host of them lined up for every occasion, and they're all almost right. "I wonder if we might replicate this phenomenon," she says.

"You want me to take it out of someone else? Very happy to try."

Flores looks worse. Greyer, the smile on his face stranger, his cheeks appreciably more sunken, his skin angrier where the cassette tape is pressed against his jaw. Rao walks closer, sees now that the patch of white hair at his temple runs downwards across the centre of an eyebrow, how his bitten fingernails have grown during his trance. The mark on his face is faded but still visible. "How did he get that bruise?" he enquires lightly. Adam's looking at it too.

"Oh, an accident," Veronica says. It's a lie. "You're sure you want to attempt to extract Prophet from this particular subject?"

"It's Flores or no one."

"And you believe you can cure him?"

"I'm going to try."

"I'll call a porter. We'll take him down to the test suite and set up. It'll take about twenty—"

"We're doing this here. Here and now or not at all."

Veronica isn't happy about that. "Rao—" she begins. He shakes his head firmly, then looks down at Flores, feeling a little self-conscious. Is this a performance? Maybe. He's not worried about his ability to get Prophet out of him. He can do that. It's a fact. But he's less sure how Flores will respond to the process. It's complicated. Too many variables—physiological, psychological. Far too much resting on this.

What's resting on this?

Hunter, he thinks. He's not quite sure when it became important that he stayed in her good books, but life's full of surprises.

"Rao?" Adam's voice, just behind him. He sounds concerned.

"I think he'll be fine, Adam. Really."

Adam frowns.

Rao looks back down at Flores, considers him carefully. It isn't going to matter where he touches him. It just needs to be bare skin. But his arms or wrists don't seem quite enough of a show, and his neck and face don't seem right somehow. "Veronica, be a dear and expose his chest area for me?"

She walks forward, pulls at the cotton bow behind Flores's neck, tugs the blue cotton gown to expose a stretch of skin. Seeing it, Rao holds his own thumbs to steady his hands. They're shaking. A memory, out of nowhere. The morning six days after his seventh birthday when he'd seen what looked like a fat, furry grub clinging to a wall by an oleander bush at the back of his uncle's house. Stubby wings, tiny feet like grappling hooks on pale grains of sandstone. He'd come back to look again a few minutes later and was entranced: the stubby wings had turned to swept-back planes patterned with geometric greens and purples and pinks. It wasn't a grub after all. More like a jewel, alive, and so beautiful it made it kind of hard to breathe to look at. He found out by doing the questions that it was a moth. He wanted to touch it and knew he should not, but most of all he wanted to show his mother, so he went to find her. When he brought her back the moth wasn't just pinned like a brooch on the wall anymore. It was vibrating, wings shivering with a buzzing noise like electricity lines in a storm. His mother saw that he was nervous of it, and she told him that the shivering meant the moth was readying itself for flight, getting itself warmed up before it could leave, and that was true. Scales in his mouth, soft dust. History. Scintillating dots, just for a moment, in front of his eyes. He blinks, steps forward, and lays both hands on Flores's upper chest, fingers spread wide.

A sharp intake of breath. He's surprised that Flores is warm, that's all. Despite the steady rise and fall of his chest, that wasn't a thing he'd expected.

A few seconds tick past and the sensation begins, that hot-cold confusion across his palms and fingers. *Fuck*, he thinks numbly. He knows this feeling, and he's spent a lot of time doing his very, very best to make it go away. *Too late, Sunil*, he thinks. *But you're saving Flores.* And then the thinking stops. Prophet has seeped into his skin and all the thinking is just a dot, a dot smaller than the size of the dot over a letter *i* drifting in the open ocean and the ocean might be water, he thinks it could be, but it doesn't have depths, or tides, or waves, and it's not blue, or even the black of deep water, it's not got edges, either, it's not water, it's definitely not water, and he feels a twist of panic that picks him up and wrenches at him so hard he knows, for one screaming, yawning gulf of a second, that his brain is gone, that this is *madness*—

And then it's done.

He's back, for whatever given value of back this is, he knows he is, and he's looking at his hands. They feel a little unfamiliar, but they're his. And the skin beneath them is Flores. And the sound he's hearing is coughing, and that's Flores too. And the eyes that are looking back at him from Flores's face, between the coughs that wrack his ribcage, are the tiredest he's ever seen. They're trying to focus on his face. He drops his gaze, doesn't want Flores to meet his eyes. Because he feels ashamed of what he's done. Flores didn't ask for this. Flores didn't ask. And Rao swallows, turns his hands, stares at his palms. Nothing. They look normal. But it's in him.

"Rao?"

Rao stands. He feels a thousand years old. And then, a moment later he doesn't. Quite chipper, actually. "Adam," he exclaims, beaming. The expression on Adam's face is perhaps the most complicated he's ever seen it. He has no idea what it means. Obviously.

He bursts out laughing.

"You ok?" Adam asks.

"Yeah, I'm fine. And not the way you use that word, Adam. I'm honestly superb. Hunter's going to be psyched. Look at this Lazarus shit!"

There's a clatter. It's the tape Flores was holding; it's fallen to the floor. Flores is ignoring it, is trying to sit up, Veronica by his side. No, he's not trying to sit up, Rao realises. He's trying to get away from her.

"Veronica, think you should give him a moment, you know? And about twenty feet? Ta."

Rao turns back to Flores and this time looks him right in the eye. "Back with us?"

Flores blinks. Tries to speak.

Adam speaks first. "What do you remember," he says.

Orders, Rao thinks. Adam's good at giving them. Flores's haggard eyes track up to Adam's and stay there. When Adam asks again if he remembers anything at all, Flores nods. The horror in his eyes as he does is naked, unbearable. Worse than anything Rao saw in Kabul. Rao reaches down to take one of his hands, squeezes it gently. Keeps hold of it until Flores's expression slips back to hazy bewilderment. Then Flores rouses himself, tugs at Rao's hand, looks up at him again. Opens his mouth and manages something like a whisper. None of the words are audible, but Rao knows. He knows what gratitude is.

CHAPTER 45

Rhodes tells Rao three times to leave Flores to their nursing team. He ignores her. Now she's clenching her fists. Looks close to attempting physical persuasion. Adam permits himself a brief, therapeutic rehearsal of exactly how he'd take her down, then casts it from his mind. "Rao," he says softly, keeping his eyes on Rhodes. "Let them take over." He gets a weary look but Rao complies.

As Rao sits heavily on the examination couch in the treatment room Rhodes led him to, Adam decides he looks okay. Irritated, more than anything, as Rhodes takes hold of a wrist and examines his hand, telling him she observed filaments of Prophet extruding from Flores's skin into his own. She's speaking animatedly of possible mechanisms for this transferral when a nurse puts his head through the door and requests her attendance.

As soon as she leaves, Adam steps forward.

"I think you need some fresh air."

"What?"

"If you're up to it, we should take a walk," he says. "Outside."

"You think they'll let me out, after this?"

After what Rao just did in there, Rhodes would give him anything he asked for. She'd gift wrap it. Adam keeps that observation to himself.

"Yes," he says.

*

Adam brought him out here, Rao assumes, because he's got something to say he doesn't want anyone else to hear. But he's not speaking, shows no sign of wanting to speak, and it's been more than five minutes, and he's walking fast, and Rao's already bored with the scenery, the marked-up construction plots and rows of half-built townhouses, and he's tired after healing Flores—

"Ok," he says. "What is it?"

Adam slows and turns. His voice is deep and full of concern. "You're sure about all this, Rao?"

"Stop fussing. I'm fine."

He nods, once, after the briefest pause. "You could fix Miller."

"I can, yes."

Another nod. They pace another forty yards in silence. Eventually, Rao stops, exasperated.

"Adam. Why are we out here?"

"You tested if Miller knew about the project."

"Yeah. She didn't."

"What about Richard Clemson?"

"Who's he?"

"Civilian. Defense. Miller's higher-up. I've been taking his orders on this."

"Ah." Rao raises his eyes to the sky. Silver, matted with high cloud. He mutters quietly to himself. "*Shit*. Yeah. He's in on this project. Part of it. Miller didn't know. We should have worked that out. I should have worked that out."

"This is on me," Adam says.

"Fuck that. And fuck them." Rao scratches his beard. "So what are we now? You and me? Ronin?"

Adam smiles slowly at that. "If you like."

Rao looks at him carefully. "What do you want to do?"

"What do *you* want?"

"Heal more people. Find out what the fuck Prophet is. Work out how to fix this bizarro nightmare."

"Yeah," Adam says, face resigned. The expression is familiar to Rao. He used to love it, used to be a dick to Adam specifically to make it happen. He doesn't enjoy what it looks like anymore. "I know you want to fix things, Rao. But this might be too big to fix. You're one person. And in my experience, one person can't—"

"I'm not one person, Adam. I'm *me*."

Adam's resignation deepens. Rao grimaces, knowing what he's about to say will come out like the worst kind of sop. "Besides, it's not just me, is it? You're here. And you're important in this, love. All this. Somehow."

"You don't know that." Adam shakes his head. "You can't tell shit about me, Rao."

"I know. But I know this, and I don't know how. You're *important*."

Adam shrugs. "I'm an expert shot."

"No—"

"And I don't mind the sight of blood."

"It'd be beyond fucked if you did, love. But, no, shut up—"

"You heal people, Rao. I shoot people. Ok?"

"You're more than that."

"Only when standing near you."

"Fucking *stop* it, Adam," Rao says. "Just stop. You're important in this. I'm not saying that to make you feel better or *do* anything. It's just how it is, and it's true, and I don't know how I know it's true, but I do know this: if we're going to be ronin or knights-errant or rogue agents or whatever, then the first rule is not to fall out about stupid shit. I've seen a lot of movies, and that's always what fucks things up."

Adam's looking at him, evidently amused. "Movies," he says.

"Shut up."

CHAPTER 46

"*Tell me again.*"

Veronica raises a brow. De Witte so rarely asks her to repeat herself. He's speaking to her from the plant-filled private office in his sprawling Lake Tahoe home. Head tipped back, he's squinting at her now as if she's causing him pain.

"Sunil Rao has the ability to extract Prophet from our subjects," she repeats. "I watched him do it. Skin-to-skin contact, mechanism as yet unknown. And there's more, Steven. He metabolises Prophet. No matter how much he absorbs, his levels remain minimal."

"Your pet test subject continues to demonstrate his uniqueness," De Witte murmurs. "He remains asymptomatic?"

"Yes."

"And on board with what we're doing?"

"I've told him barely anything. But yes, he seems content."

"Say anything to keep him happy."

"Understood. I'm working on modelling the mechanism for his extraction and potential pathways for metabolization. We'll continue monitoring him in the meantime."

De Witte doesn't respond for some time. Eventually he clears his throat.

"You could," he says, "do more than monitor him, Veronica."

"I could. But I suggest we hold off from initiating more rigorous investigations."

He screws up his face. "You weren't so, uh, squeamish in Guantánamo."

"This is a different project. And it's a question of exigency, rather than concern for his well-being," she adds lightly. "He's very much the goose that lays the golden eggs, don't you agree?"

"Fairy tales, Veronica?"

"Quite so, Steven."

CHAPTER 47

Lunastus-Dainsleif's Aurora facility is nothing like the offices Adam has worked in. Government offices don't get this kind of money, not even Defense. He knew that Lunastus was next-level, but it's another thing to wander its corridors and experience this kind of corporate luxury for real. He and Rao have spent most of their time on the windowless lower levels. But right now he's walking a brightly lit corridor on the fourth floor on his way to Dr. Rhodes's office. There. A frosted glass door with her name on it. He knocks.

"Come in," she calls.

She's at her desk. The room is sparsely furnished. A dark-green filing cabinet. A vibrant monstera. A metal mechanical pencil and a fountain pen, a monitor and keyboard on her desk. She's holding her phone. It's very late in the day: Adam disrupted her plans, he's guessing, to make or take a private call. He doesn't care.

"I want a visitor's pass," he says.

She lifts an eyebrow, puts down her phone, gestures for him to take a seat. He shakes his head. She doesn't push the matter. Gives him a thin, brief smile, nothing like the wide ones Rao gets; they work on him. "And who might this pass be for?"

"Hunter Wood. USAF master sergeant."

"No," she answers. Simple.

Adam can do simple too. "I wasn't really asking."

"Are you threatening me, Colonel Rubenstein?"

"No," he says slowly, seriously. "I'm stating intention."

She likes that. The smile he gets this time isn't as thin or brief as before. He doesn't enjoy the change. "Who is this individual?"

"She tasked me and Rao with finding Flores," Adam says. He realizes his hands are resting behind his back, like he's delivering a verbal debrief. Muscle memory. Rhodes likes that too. "We found him. Rao . . . did what he did. My goal is to return Flores to someone who can care for him outside of the facility."

"And that someone is Sergeant Wood."

"Correct."

"What's your relationship to her?"

"That's not your business, Dr. Rhodes."

She looks at him in silence for a solid ten seconds. She's trying to make him feel uncomfortable. She watches him and he watches her right back.

"We still have tests to run on Flores," she says eventually.

"Run them on someone else. You have a lot of patients, Dr. Rhodes. Ask Rao to wake another one."

"Ah, but you and I both know that our eyes aren't set on that prize," she says, her smile sharpening.

So, that's what it is. That's fine. Makes sense.

"You have my blood already."

Rhodes nods. "I'd like more."

"What else?"

"A biopsy."

Adam frowns. "Of what?"

Her too-sharp smile slips. "Has anyone ever told you that you're far too clever?"

"No." It's the truth, not that anyone can tell.

"You slip under the radar quite often, don't you?" Rhodes says with a thoughtful frown. No, it's not thoughtful. It's considering. There's the slightest of differences, important intel when dealing with Dr. Rhodes. She thrives on people paying no attention to subtle tells. Adam grudgingly admits that he can only see what she's doing because he does it too. He's just better at it.

"Professional habit," he tells her.

"Perhaps." She studies him for a while, then reaches for her pen and opens a drawer. Produces a stack of pale-yellow Post-its, scribbles a note, sticks it to her monitor out of view. "I'll look into issuing

Sergeant Wood a visitor's pass and we can discuss possible procedures in the future."

If he leaves now, he'll be giving her carte blanche to do whatever she likes to him. It's not express permission, but at this point, he thinks, implied permission might hold more weight between them. He doesn't like any of this, but he needs to get Flores out of here and get Hunter through the doors so she can see some of the shit he's had to see. And if he doesn't make it out of Rhodes's tests, he needs Hunter to have some idea of what happened to him.

And he needs Hunter's eyes on Rao.

He'll have to tell Rao. But that can wait until Flores is out and safe.

"Always a pleasure, Dr. Rhodes."

She hums and picks up her phone.

"I'm sure."

Walking back down the corridor, Adam is about to push open the stairwell door when he stops. Stills himself. Something's off. He withdraws his hand from the steel plate it rests against. Backs himself against the wall and quiets his breath. He follows his combat instincts, looks and listens for movement. No obvious threat. No sound except the low grumble of air traffic into Buckley. He takes a breath, exhales. The light in here has changed. Looking up, he sees that the line of halogen spots that ran along the ceiling on his way here has gone. Instead there are eight lamps of a kind he's seen a hundred times before. Upside-down domes tipped with brass finials. Dusty, yellowing glass swirled like the top of an ice cream. The light inside them is soft, and all the lamps are flickering gently in unison. Around them, the plasterwork is the textured popcorn of the ceiling of his childhood bedroom.

Fuck. Adam could be responsible for these, but he can't know that for sure. He doesn't think he is. They don't make him feel anything, but the clock doesn't either. Not now. All he knows is that ten minutes ago the lights were modern, and now they're straight out of a rental from thirty years ago. He looks at his watch, notes the time. Rao told him about his fears back in England. Told him this operation made him feel like he was walking into a haunted house. But it's not really a haunted house, the way things are going. There's momentum to what's happening. It feels more like a ghost train.

Adam steps forward, pushes the door open. Doesn't look back.

CHAPTER 48

The morning is bright; a stiff breeze blows through it. Curling over the rooflines into Lunastus-Dainsleif's courtyard garden, it pushes so hard at the fountains they shiver, breaking intermittently into a host of ephemeral rainbows. Rao bows his head, cups his hands around his lighter, and tries once again to light a cigarette. Success this time. He takes a lungful of smoke and raises his eyes to the miles of blueness above. *It's good to be out here*, he thinks, exhaling slowly. After days of air-conditioned rooms and fluorescent light, the press of the wind on his face is a benison. Makes this mannered quadrangle of pools, fountains, shrubs, and lawn seem close to something real.

His cigarette burns away too fast. He's about to light another when he sees Veronica walking towards him. What the fuck is she doing out here?

"Veronica, is something on fire?" he calls.

"Not to my knowledge," she says as she nears.

"What's the problem, then?"

"There's no problem at all. I saw you and came to give you the happy news that Flores is doing wonderfully well. He's walking now, with the assistance of a nurse. We're about to move him to a private room."

She tilts her head expectantly. All this was prologue. She's about to start on another round of questions about how he did it. What it felt like. Couldn't even wait until he was back in the bastard building. His spirits sink. He's really not in the mood. He could walk away. Or—no. He gestures to the chair opposite. She sits, rests her hands on the table between them, studies him for a while.

"Happy, Rao?"

"Always. You know me. Life's an unmitigated joy."

"Are you experiencing tiredness?" she asks.

"Perpetually."

The wind catches her hair, fans it over her face. She strokes it back into place.

"Your blood shows negligible amounts of Prophet. There's less in your system now than in the first test we took," she says. "So—"

"Before you talk about more tests, Veronica, we need to discuss Miller. You know Elisabeth Miller. Department of Defense. Got dosed with Prophet at Polheath," he says. She widens her eyes with faux innocence. Wants Rao to drop the subject. No chance. "Why don't you tell me about what happened there," he adds. They lock eyes. Rao waits.

"That subproject," she replies tightly, "was not under my aegis. But a degree of compartmentalisation is inevitable in a programme of this nature."

"Whose aegis was it under?"

"That's not relevant." The wind lifts her hair again. Again, she tucks it behind one ear.

Rao waits out ten seconds of silence as she scans the garden. It's deserted. It always is. Despite the tables and seating, Rao's never seen anyone here except a man in a John Deere baseball cap and overalls lackadaisically sweeping leaves.

"Straat died," she says, "while scouting for volunteer test subjects on an overseas base. There was a theory that subjects far from home would experience a different form of nostalgia, provide novel data."

"But it all went tits up."

She nods. "He broke a vial."

"He broke a vial and died."

"His death was accidental and extraordinarily inconvenient."

"But useful. Without the accident, you wouldn't have me." She blinks at him. "Fucking hell, Veronica, I thought you were supposed to be good at faking it. Couldn't you try a bit harder?"

"Hooray," she says flatly.

"Straat was a twat to carry that vial about in his pocket," Rao says. "Accident waiting to happen."

"Well," Veronica says, "he died because his vial was manufactured over five months ago."

"Manufacturing issue? Dodgy glassware?"

"Far from it. At the time, subjects exposed to Prophet weren't creating EPGOs. Straat's vial was perfectly sound. It was foolish to walk around with it in his pocket, yes. But with that particular formulation, he would have assumed that inadvertent exposure would simply have made him sad or made him feel he'd lost something. Perhaps it might have made him miss wherever he came from. Which was Michigan, I believe?"

Rao remembers the diner glowing in the fog, the dreadful roses.

"You know Prophet changes, Rao," she continues. "And you know it isn't a gradual evolution; it's intermittent, saltatory. But what you don't know, what I'm telling you now, is that these alterations have been global in nature. By which I mean all of the substance, wherever it is, undergoes change at the same time."

"Everywhere?"

"Everywhere. But there's a fascinating exception. These changes don't seem to occur in Prophet if it is already inside a test subject. If it was administered before one of these shifts happened."

Rao thinks about that. "You're saying it all changes at the same time when it's on a shelf, but not once it's found itself at home in a brain. Which means," he adds, slowly, "that there are people walking around full of early stage Prophet who never got glued to teddy bears?"

"There are."

"Can I meet one?"

"Why?"

"So I can get it out of them, do my thing, and see what happens. They're walking about full of Prophet and so am I. Nothing might happen. But it seems interesting, you know? You'll get some data from it. Shouldn't be too expensive to set up, if that's what Lunastus is worried about."

"It's not. Very well, Rao. I'll look into setting up a meeting with one of our early test subjects."

"And get me to Miller. I need to heal her too."

"She's in England."

"I *know*. But if you want me onside, Veronica—"

"That will take some time to arrange, you understand."

"Never doubted it. But glad to hear it. And for that, I'll give you a pet theory of mine. It's a good one. You'll love it."

"What?"

"When I first saw your test room, I was surprised how small you'd made it."

She gets it instantly. "Because you'd seen the diner in Polheath."

"Exactly."

She ducks her head. "When we designed the program, we weren't aware that subjects could generate EPGOs of that size."

"You didn't think someone might make an evacuation helicopter."

"We did not."

"Flawed experimental design, Veronica."

"Noted, Rao."

"But I think I know why." Rao sits back, crosses his arms. "So, I reckon the size of the objects it makes maps to the size of the surroundings the test subject is in. If you're in a room, you'll make something that'll fit inside it. If you're in the open air, you could make something of any size, theoretically. The limit's in your head. It's not about how big Prophet can go. It's about our sensing the space available for it. Put someone in a box, they'll make something tiny. Put them on a mountaintop, who knows. Might make something that'll block a valley."

"What's your evidence for this?"

"Call it a hunch."

It's not a hunch. He knows it's true. He did a run on it late yesterday afternoon over a cup of Assam tea. Worked out that Ed could make a diner because he was dosed in the open air. That the smaller things at Polheath were made by people asleep in their dorms or working in rooms. But why they were scattered around the base rather than appearing in their subjects' arms is still a puzzle. He spent twenty minutes throwing statements at it, but all he got in return was a vague intimation of flowers, somehow. Made no sense at all.

She taps her lower lip, then nods. "We might investigate this theory."

"Will I be coauthor on the scientific paper?" Rao says.

"There won't be a paper, Rao."

"*Quelle surprise.*" The wind's dropped. He lights another cigarette. "So, Veronica, have you got any further with the big question?"

"The big question?"

"Why I don't make objects like other people."

"We haven't come up with an answer on that. But with time, we—" She's distracted by a message notification on her phone. "You can tell Colonel Rubenstein," she says, reading it, "that his request for a visitor's pass has been approved."

"What pass? Pass for who?"

Merriment in her eyes. "Out of the loop, Rao?"

"Apparently, yes. So, in the spirit of not being a cunt, you should tell me what's going on."

"The pass is for a Master Sergeant Wood."

Rao sits back, waves his cigarette. "Oh, her. Yeah. Doesn't surprise me. She hates me, you know. But between you and me I'm kind of obsessed."

Evening sun through the motel windows casts bright, burnished rectangles across the carpet of their room. Rao's in a lazy, contemplative mood; he's been lying on his bed watching them lengthen and slide for a while. The sun's now so low they're climbing the far wall. "Gorgeous light, isn't it?" Rao observes, stretching into a luxurious yawn as Adam pulls up a chair and sits. "Venetian, almost."

Adam looks at him but takes some time to answer. His face is faintly strained, almost sad, as soft as Rao's ever seen it. Maybe Adam's been to Venice. Maybe he's remembering a time there. Dusk over the basilica of San Giorgio Maggiore. More likely blood on marble floors.

"Venice," he clarifies.

"Yeah. I got that. We still clean in here?"

Rao sighs a yes. "Are we doing this now?"

"You want to wait?"

"No." Rao shifts himself up to sit, rolls his neck, regards the sunset light on the wall. "So, the staff are tight-lipped," he begins, "and I can't test silence. The facility isn't a happy ship, is it?"

Adam shakes his head. "Rhodes told them not to talk to us?"

"Yeah. Three-line whip. So much for us all being one big happy family. I got insinuations of fatalities from a couple of nurses and a strong sense that Veronica can be a vicious bitch, but that's old news. She's been quite happy to tell us all about turning people into microscope slides."

"What have you got on her?"

"She's a twenty-four-carat psycho. Vivisected the family cat when she was ten."

"Seriously?"

"Adam, you're asking for intel. This is the bit where I never lie to you."

"Personal life?"

"None. She's renting in Tallyn's Reach. She's untouchable. I've got nothing on her we could plausibly use, even if this weren't the blackest of deep black projects. She's a murderer, but a super-careful one. Not counting the deaths here, they were all work-related fatalities except one. A guy at Harvard who pissed her off. She put a hit on him, used a cutout."

"How many in all?"

"Five. I still like her, though."

"Good to know that murders don't put you off a person."

"We're best friends, after all."

Adam snorts. "All of mine are state sanctioned. Montgomery?"

"Yeah, he's the pivot, isn't he? Or would have been," Rao says, making a face. "Wouldn't have taken long to get him singing, but we missed the window. Veronica came down on him like a ton of bricks the day we signed on the dotted line. He did mention a visit by someone called Lane, five weeks ago. Seems to have been stressful for all concerned. I got his first name. Zachary. Looked him up. He's on the Lunastus board of directors. Clearly an asshole."

"Is that a testable fact?"

"Don't need to test anything with a name like that."

From the look on Adam's face he disagrees with Rao's assessment. "Montgomery's a potential asset."

"If he grows a pair."

"If he doesn't, do we have biographical leverage?"

"Nah. He's so boring, love. Divorcee. Amicable split. Daughter lives with her mother in Ohio. She's thirteen. No debt, no skeletons in his cupboards. His parents are dead. He doesn't have any siblings. And no form at all. Not even a parking ticket."

"Interests?"

"Christ, Adam, don't make me truth-test his hobbies."

Adam grins. "Home brewing."

"Ugh, fuck, of course."

"Anything else?"

"On Monty?"

"On the project."

Rao sighs. The golden light's dimming fast. Shapes losing resolution. Sun's dipped below the horizon. "I've been having a mare with that. I've turned myself inside out trying to find the right statements to test, but all I've got is that there's a lot more to this project and a lot more to Prophet than we know. That's it."

Adam sits up. "You can't tell?"

Rao winces. "It's weird. It's not like with you. It's a bit like those Magic Eye pictures. Autostereograms. Of dinosaurs or desert islands or something. And sometimes you almost get it, you almost see what's there, but it slips away just as you grasp it." He hates this analogy. It's terrible, but it's all he's got. "That's sort of what it's like trying to truth-test Prophet. I don't know if it's because I've got it inside me or whether Prophet and truth don't . . . coincide. It's a metaphysical headache."

"Sounds frustrating," Adam says.

"It fucking is."

"But interesting. Lack of data's still data. Don't stress it, Rao."

A little later, while Adam is out on an evening run, Rao calls Kitty Caldwell in Cambridge. He's sat on his bed with the phone Adam had given him a few times now and not bothered to dial. She's never been free before. Right now, however, he knows she's in her office and isn't teaching. He picks out the number. The wisteria, the old glass in the Gothic windows, the still fenland air in the college squares. The knowledge that those things are all still out there surprises him as he waits for her to answer: the sensation's like changing into too high a gear by mistake.

"Kitty Caldwell."

"Hello, Dr Caldwell. It's Sunil Rao. I don't know if you remember me."

"You weren't very forgettable, Rao. Kitty, please."

"Thank you. Is this a bad time?"

"No, a good time, actually. Why the call?"

"It's complicated," he says, staring at the carpet. "I think I need some help."

"I'm good with complicated. I'm not sure if I can help."

"The thing is, I'm not sure how much I can tell you. I mean, I am sure. I've signed things that make it very clear I'm not allowed to tell you anything. But—"

"You want to know if I can keep a secret?"

"Yeah. Can you?"

There's a pause so long Rao wonders if the line's dropped. It hasn't. "Yes."

Ok, he's happy with that. She can.

"So I've managed to find my way into a project working with a substance that causes nostalgia."

A beat. "Causes?"

He loves that she's nitpicking semantics. Loves it.

"Provokes. I wanted to talk to you about why this substance doesn't affect me like it does other people."

"Wouldn't you do better with a neuroscientist?"

"There are too many of those fuckers around here already."

She laughs. "Ok, how does it not affect you?"

"It doesn't make me nostalgic," Rao says. "And I think that might be because I have an unusual kind of memory."

He's been trying to truth-test it. Like so much else with Prophet, he's not been able to get clear answers, and he's starting to believe the Prophet inside him won't let him see what it's doing. It won't let him test that either.

"What kind of unusual?"

"I remember everything."

"Is it sensory memory? Emotional?"

"Everything. All of it."

"You're a savant."

"People usually call me a dickhead, Kitty, but that's a word I've heard, yeah."

She laughs. "So, apart from your demonstrating that you have an art historian's distaste for neuroscience, Rao, why did you want to call me?"

"Because your concept of nostalgia isn't based on pictures of brains. Isn't just chemicals and electrical signals. It's more than that. A cultural phenomenon. A historical one. Psychological."

"And social, don't forget."

"I didn't forget. That's just it. I want to ask you about memory. Not how it lights up the brain but how we use it. You said nostalgia can be a response to a sense of dislocation. And your book says it's an act of creation, right? It brings lost things to life, things from your past, things you remember. And the act of nostalgia forges a link between you now and a past self that's always partly imagined. It's comforting. Gives you a sense of continuity. Makes you feel you're the same person through time."

"That's not exactly what my book says, Rao."

"I know exactly what your book says. I was paraphrasing. But, Kitty, this is the thing. The way my memory works, there's no creation. Like, I don't create anything when I remember things. I don't use my imagination at all. I just retrieve the memory. It doesn't get loaded with meaning, you know? I mean, ok, I can read emotional content *off* memories. Like, I can see how the image of my bedside lamp holds associations of comfort and home. But only in retrospect. While I'm remembering it, it's just a lamp. It's that lamp, exactly. It's not an act of creation. It's pure recall."

"Hm." She sounds dubious. "What do you mean by 'pure'?"

"Pure. When I remember a lamp, it's no different from me looking at a lamp right now. It's just an object."

"That's not true," she says. "You look at a lamp right now and it'll make you feel things about lamps and life that aren't what the lamp's made of. Objects are always more than material things."

He knows she's right. He turns his eyes to the bedside lamp, the warm and reassuring light it casts on the wall, the paperbacks heaped at its base. "You can tell the difference between what's real and what's inside your head, if it's right there in front of you," he says a little testily. "Which is, well, I'm wondering if that's the difference, with me. Why I don't get nostalgic. Why I don't miss things."

"You don't miss things?"

"No. I don't have to, do I? Because they're always right there in my mind, exactly as they were. There's no loss of detail. They're perfect. Nostalgia re-creates things, right? Imperfectly. Fills the gaps in memories with feelings. But my memory doesn't have gaps. And that's why I think this substance doesn't work on me. Does that sound plausible?"

"We don't . . ." She's silent for a while. "What are memories like for you?"

Kitty thinks he's missing the point. But she's not challenging him directly, is talking around him to get him nearer to an answer. She's a good teacher.

"Like being inside a movie of my own life," he says. "Which can be pretty fucking grim. But, you know, there've been some good times."

"What about things you don't remember?"

"Pain," he says quickly. "Sleeping. Being unconscious."

"Do you dream?"

"Yeah. Vividly. But they're basically memories. I don't dream about things that haven't happened." He feels the lie. Sharply. Because he has, lately, hasn't he? He's dreamed of a lot of things.

"That's exceptionally unusual. What about emotional content?"

"In dreams?"

"In memories."

"I remember those. Feel them again when I do. Sometimes I worry I don't have emotions like other people."

"Everyone thinks that," she says. It's a throwaway line. She's quiet for a while. "Rao, I have a question for you. I think it's an important one, and I want you to think about it."

"Fire away."

"Do you miss loved ones who are gone, even though you can remember them precisely?"

He bites his lip.

"Yeah."

"Well."

CHAPTER 49

It doesn't take Hunter long to turn up after Adam lights the proverbial flare. He texted her as soon as he got confirmation her pass had been issued. The next morning he's waiting outside the facility for her to arrive. He smiles as she walks into the parking lot. Jeans, leather jacket, black tee, baseball cap. That familiar easy swagger. It's good to see her. It's always good to see Hunter. She externalizes all the things Adam keeps under his skin. Back when the military was molding them into what it estimated they could be, Hunter's externalizing was annoying. At this stage in their friendship, it's steadying. Everything could be upside down, the sky orange, birds flying backward and singing the "Ershter Vals," and Hunter would be the first to state how fucked up it was instead of doing what he would do. Adam always tries to roll with the punch, no matter where it's coming from. Hunter, on the other hand, calls a punch a punch. Their mindsets and responses are different. Complementary. Rao likes to say that Adam is some kind of operational secret weapon, and maybe he is in some scenarios, but not like Hunter is. Hunter is next-level, and she knows it.

"This is fucked up, Rubenstein," she tells him, and it's better than saying hello.

He follows her squint up to the building like he's seeing it for the first time. "Yeah."

"How much do I get to know about this?"

"I'll tell you what I can when we're inside."

"And then what?"

"Then when they release him, you and Flores can go, if you want." Adam shrugs. If she doesn't want to go in, he's pretty sure that he can ruffle different feathers than the ones he's already fucked with to get

Flores out to the front door. She doesn't look like she wants to go in. She takes out a soft box of American Spirit Yellows, taps one out. Doesn't offer one to Adam. For once, he actually wants a smoke, but he doesn't ask.

"Where are you staying?" he says.

"VQ at Buckley. Right across the street," she says, lighting up. "You looking for any help on this?"

"I don't think so."

"The fuck does that mean?"

"It means . . ." he starts, then sighs. It's hard to put it simply sometimes. Everything would be so much easier if people just did what he said when he said it, but that's not how life works. That's not how friends work. Adam doesn't have a lot of experience in that field, but he has enough. "It just means we're good, for now."

"What happens when you're not good?"

"I've got your number."

"And you don't lose that."

"No plans to lose that."

"Good to hear. But you're pulling me in all the same. I didn't haul my ass all the way over here to sit this out on the sidelines, Rubenstein." Hunter exhales an impressive amount of smoke and abandons the cigarette, grinding the unsmoked half into shreds underfoot. She jerks her head to the front doors of the facility. Wordlessly, they head inside. Hunter shows her ID, gets walked through all the paperwork she has to sign before she gets her pass, and when they're through the double doors that lead into the belly of the beast, she elbows him in the ribs. "You want to tell me why the receptionist just pissed themselves at the sight of you?"

"New receptionist. Long story."

"Is it?"

"No," Adam admits with a grin. "I just don't want to tell it. Besides, Rao makes it sound way more interesting than it was. Ask him."

"Rao, huh?"

"Yep." Adam pops his *p*.

"Lead the way, Rubenstein. God fucking help me, I'm actually looking forward to seeing the bastard."

Standing at the bottom of Flores's bed, watching him sleep, Hunter nudges Adam's foot.

"Run it by me again, Rubenstein."

He does. Goes into as much detail as he can. Tells her everything he knows about Prophet, about the project. What happened when he'd dosed himself. How Rao was the first thing he saw when he'd come out of the nightmare of reliving that day. He tells her about Flores. How Rao drew Prophet out of him just by touching him. Skin to skin. The ragged breath Flores had taken. The look on Rao's face.

"How did you get contaminated?" she asks when he's finished. He'd left that part out on purpose, but it's Hunter. She hears silences.

"I did it myself."

"Why?"

"We needed answers."

"You were getting them."

"I needed," he says, "something else."

"What?"

"Some quiet."

"You could have left the room if Rao was pissing you off."

"He wasn't the problem." Adam shakes his head. "I needed a different kind of quiet."

They're waiting for one of the medical team to talk them through the process of releasing Flores. That's all Adam needs to think about. The next task. The next task is easier than actively ignoring Hunter's sharp sideways gaze.

"Are you over this quest for quiet?" she asks.

He nods, once. It's not that simple, but it can look like it is for now. Hunter doesn't need every detail.

"You better not get out of this the stupid way, Rubenstein."

"Nah. You'd kick my ass," he sighs. "How are your folks?"

She rolls her eyes. "They're good."

"Still got our flight photo glued to the wall?"

"Yeah. Me standing next to you, you looking like a fetus dressed as a tree."

"Happy days at Lackland."

"It's all downhill after BMT."

The door opens. It's a doctor, clipboard in hand. Nervous looking and overworked, like all of Rhodes's staff. His voice is soft. Southern. He takes them through the bureaucratic hurdles that will permit Flores to be released into Hunter's care. Says he's sorry that the process will take some time. Retreats with his clipboard after promising to expedite proceedings. It's all bullshit, Adam guesses. Some way to keep Flores for a little longer or to keep Hunter on-site for as long as they need to get more intel on her—or any number of similar shitty tactics Lunastus could be running in the background. All amounts to the same thing in the end.

"Coffee?" Hunter prompts.

"There's a canteen."

"Rubenstein, you're gonna get soft living like this," Hunter observes. Moroccan lamps on every table. Woven Balochi hangings, a host of curved and gilded mirrors on the walls. In the spotlit darkness a full-size fake palm tree. He follows her gaze up to the star-shaped tracery of beams on the concave ceiling, each one set with scores of tiny, glimmering lights.

"It's supposed," he says dryly, "to represent a bedouin tent."

"The canteen? What's with Colorado and tents? Denver airport, now this. It's crazy." She lifts her cup and shakes her head. The coffee here is so good it's unholy. Adam distrusts it. It tastes like dirty corporate money and hazelnut syrup. Rao lives for it. As soon as they get back to their motel room at night, he starts complaining about having to wait all that time before there's decent coffee again. Adam's thankful they get to leave Lunastus in the evenings. Rhodes offered him and Rao accommodation on-site but they both, separately, refused her offer. The motel had been the right call, considering. Weird how quick it got to feel secure and permanent after that.

"So, it was the day your aunt died," Hunter says, breaking Adam's train of thought.

"It was the moment I should have left to go with my aunt," Adam says. Reconsiders. Clarifies. "So I guess, to me, it was the moment she died." Hunter's never heard the whole story about Sasha before. Adam hadn't told anyone before Rao.

She gets it. Doesn't linger on unnecessary questions.

"And your brain made it plop into existence because of this Prophet junk?"

"Pretty much."

"I thought you said you weren't working for the Office, Rubenstein."

"I'm not," he grins.

"Could've fooled me."

Adam's about to reply when Rao walks in. He pulls the chair next to Adam, sits, looks sidelong at Adam's coffee, then makes a series of complicated facial movements indicating his desire to take it. Sighing, Adam slides the cup in front of him.

"It's black," he warns.

"That's okay. I'm feeling *continental* today," Rao says, pleased with himself. "Cheers. What are we talking about? Alright, Hunter."

"Rao," she responds. "Good to see you."

Rao turns. "She means that, Adam."

"Congratulations, Rao."

"We're waiting for them to get the paperwork to release Flores," Hunter explains.

"Yeah," Rao agrees. "But that's not what you were talking about. That's what you're *doing*. Were you telling Hunter about my miracle-working shit?"

"You mean Raoki," Hunter says. "Like Reiki, but Rao."

"Raoflexology," Adam offers. He gets up to pour himself another coffee. Rao's glare of disgust has vanished by the time he returns. "Office Workers," he says.

"What?"

"That's what we were talking about."

Rao huffs. "Adam, I can't help but suspect that you're getting off on being obtuse right now, and I'd like it to be perfectly fucking crystal clear that I don't appreciate it."

"It's what people call the assholes who work in the Extranatural Incident Office," Hunter explains.

"Oh! Mulder and Scully."

"Yes," Adam nods.

Hunter shakes her head. "No."

"Yes," Adam repeats. "Mulder and Scully."

Rao snickers. "And by people, you mean . . ."

"Us," Hunter says.

"Service," Adam adds.

Rao hums sagely. "This would be interdivisional rivalry, then? Like the Chair Force?"

Adam lifts both eyebrows, says nothing.

"What?"

Hunter clears her throat. "He's touchy about that, Rao."

"Your dad was air force, wasn't he, love?"

Adam shrugs. "Still is, as far as I know."

"Adam?"

"Yes, Rao."

"Do you outrank your father?"

Hunter laughs into her mug, mutters something that sounds like "good coffee." Adam smiles, but it's one with teeth. Real.

"Now that you mention it, I think I might," he says slowly.

Rao beams. "You little shit."

"Mm," Adam says, as he tips his coffee and drinks.

Rhodes appears by their table. Adam's impressed he didn't see her coming; she's a natural at silent interception. She'd probably breeze through Peary. Maybe she already did. He doesn't have the intel. She's wearing thin gold bracelets. Her hair has a slight wave today. He gets why Rao's fascinated.

She smiles benevolently. "Dr. Veronica Rhodes," she says. "And you must be Hunter. You've quite a reputation." Hunter opens her mouth to reply. Rhodes doesn't let her. "Colonel Rubenstein was insistent that you be given a visitor's pass. And before it could be issued, of course, we needed to make ourselves intimately informed of your career."

"If you know so much about me, then I guess it's fair to ask about you."

"You may ask what you like, Sergeant Wood."

"I want to know what you're running here."

"I assume that Colonel Rubenstein will have—"

"I don't care what he told me. I want you to tell me."

Veronica moves to stand behind the only unoccupied chair at their table. She doesn't pull it out. Doesn't sit on it. Just rests her hands on its back as if she might.

"Lunastus-Dainsleif is in the fortunate position to have been given the chance to study, to understand, a novel substance with extraordinary properties. We've already determined that with the right application and control, this substance could be used in the field. We're taking the first steps toward completely costless warfare."

Hunter nods. "That's a hell of a spiel. You're shit out of luck, though. I'm not dumb enough to get lost in empty jargon like that."

Rhodes looks amused. "I'm unsurprised our very own Lieutenant Colonel Rubenstein keeps such stellar, straight-talking company."

"*Your* Colonel Rubenstein?"

"Ours, yes. I believe a decision on that will have already been made. What do you think of our project?"

"I think it sounds impossible."

Veronica hums, angles her head a little to one side. "Well, feel free to drop by my office or come see me in the lab if you're interested in the particularities of our impossible research. My door's always open. It's been a pleasure, Sergeant Wood."

Hunter watches her leave. Two seconds pass. Four. Ten.

"I don't like her vibe, Rubenstein," she says.

"No. Neither do I."

"She's just a psycho," Rao explains helpfully. "That's all you need to know about Veronica."

"So?" Hunter hisses, addressing Adam.

"What?"

"You're being headhunted."

"I don't think that's what she was saying, Hunter."

"Is that right?" She narrows her eyes. "Seemed pretty clear to me. What aren't you telling me?"

Adam takes a sip of coffee. "I can tell you later. It's not important right now."

She raises an accusatory finger. "Don't try to feed me that sack of shit and call it a hamburger."

Rao cuts in. "I'm . . . sorry, what seems to be the problem?"

"Rubenstein's keeping secrets," Hunter says.

"From who?"

"Hunter," Adam cautions.

She ignores him. "My guess is that he's keeping secrets from you, Rao."

"Well," Rao says. "We don't do that any longer. Do we, Adam?"

"No."

Rao folds his arms. "So what the fuck is going on?"

"Fucking—fine," Adam says. "My only angle with Rhodes is testing. I have one card to play, so I'm playing it."

"Does that make sense to you, Rao?"

"Yes, it bloody does," Rao says. "You're auctioning your, what, Adam? Your *samples*? For *what*?"

"Hunter's visitor's pass, to begin with."

Rao's eyebrows rise. "To *begin with*? And what did this pass cost?"

"She's pushing for a biopsy."

Hunter's shaking her head. Rao groans. "Fucking hell, Adam. This was phenomenally stupid of you."

"I know what I'm doing. Both of you can stand down."

"Stand down?" Rao raises his voice. "You're not my fucking CO, Adam, and now is not the time for this Captain Oates bullshit."

"Oates?" Hunter says.

"Scott of the Antarctic," Rao says, turning to her. "You know. Everyone on the expedition was starving. Oates was the guy with scurvy and frostbite who kept telling them to leave him behind, and they wouldn't.

So he hobbled out of the tent into a blizzard on purpose, sacrificed himself to save the rest of the team. Said, 'I am just going outside and I may be some time.'" Rao sits back in his seat, lets the silence hang, then turns his head to look pointedly at Adam. "And they all fucking died anyway."

"Rubenstein's not Oates," Hunter says firmly.

"Hunter, that was a spur-of-the-moment analogy, I wasn't—"

"Shut up. I get the analogy, but Rubenstein's got the best operational brains out there. He's a legend at the DIA. My advice is you put your faith in him and your trust in whatever course of action he determines is the most expedient." She looks at Adam. "Even if he is acting like a four-star idiot."

"Hunter," Adam says.

"Tell me I'm wrong."

Adam doesn't reply, just picks at the corner of his left eye. He knows it's a tell. Tiredness. Stress, maybe. Whatever. It doesn't matter.

"Rao," Hunter says. "Are they paying you for this?"

"Spending time with Adam?"

"Putting yourself inside this fucked-up project."

"They are. Lunastus values me at five hundred dollars a day."

Her eyes widen. "Jesus. Well. If you're not busy watching QVC, you're both buying me dinner later. Somewhere that isn't here. Guy on the base says there's an Indian place, it's—"

"Absolutely not," Rao interrupts.

Adam snorts. "Let's find a Vietnamese."

CHAPTER 50

His Tahoe desk is heaped with papers and meal replacement drinks. His lips are bitten raw. He's steepling his fingers. None of these signs are optimal. Veronica steels herself.

"We have to understand the biomechanics of what he does," De Witte whispers.

"That, Steven," she says, "is my goal also."

"So we can replicate it."

She nods. He shakes his head. "Your methodology has been, um, messy, Veronica. We need him in our Pensacola facility. Get him there and put him in one of your restraint units. Immobilize him. Don't give him analgesics. I don't want him sedated. Administer Prophet to him until we can model his extraction method."

Veronica knows this was inevitable. But it doesn't have to happen yet. There's so much she can learn using Rao as he is right now. While he's still willing to help. Still able to talk.

"He's useful here," she murmurs. "I'm—"

"But I don't want him there," De Witte cuts in, looking right at her down the camera. His eyes are pale, peculiarly clear. Veronica makes some rapid calculations.

"I understand," she replies in tones that sound like she doesn't. Waits to see how he responds.

"I hope issues related to his, uh, rendition aren't a concern. He already attempted suicide and was a liability to his previous employers. Elisabeth Miller is, uh, out of the frame. Except for us, nobody wants him. Not even himself."

"What about Rubenstein?"

"*A cog in the war machine,*" *De Witte says with almost no trace of his usual diffidence.* "*He barely exists as it is. Easily removed. To the wider world, neither of them matter.*"

"*I'm sure you're right,*" *she replies.* "*And of course Rubenstein's air force colleague could be sent back to Afghanistan.*"

He nods. "*She'll be deployed there anyway. She doesn't have to return. Remember the stakes, Veronica.*"

"*They're not forgotten.*"

De Witte's eyes lift beyond the screen for a moment, focus on the far wall. Then, unexpectedly, he smiles. "*Designing a repository for excess stocks of Prophet has been . . . complicated. But now we can cut that expense from our books.*"

"*You want to use him as a live disposal unit.*"

"*Absolutely,*" *he says, his smile broadening.* "*Our very own human Yucca Mountain.*"

CHAPTER 51

"**W**here's Hunter?" Rao enquires over his canteen breakfast.
"She's with Flores."

He sighs happily. "I must thank you for introducing me to Hunter, Adam. She's so incredibly emasculating. It's brilliant."

"Is she," Adam says, mouth quirked. Then his face shifts wistful. "Miller has that effect on some people too. You should see her on the range. Her groupings are insane."

Silence follows. Rao hastens to fill it. "Veronica said she'll get me to Miller," he assures Adam. "I'll fix what happened. You know I will. She'll be back on the range shrinking everyone's balls before you know it."

"Yeah," Adam says after a while, like he doesn't believe it. "You done? We should join Hunter."

When they walk in, Hunter's perched cross-legged on the bed and Flores is hunched in an armchair, a cream-coloured robe over his shoulders. His face has regained some colour, but it's still haunted. Pinched.

"Hey, Danny," Hunter says. "This is Rao, the guy who woke you up."

"Thanks," he says. "I owe you."

"You really don't. I'm glad to have helped. How are you?"

"Good. Good," Flores says. His hand trembles as he places his mug on the table by his side. "Rubenstein. Been a while. You still DIA?"

"Yeah. They looking after you?"

"Never had food like in this place."

Rao nods enthusiastically. "Have you had the tagliatelle yet?"

"It's good," Flores says, then his eyes rise slowly to the flat-screen TV on the wall, where CNN plays silently with subtitles. Footage of fighter jets. Helicopters. A sixty-billion-dollar weapons deal with Saudi Arabia.

"Fucking with Iran," Flores observes. "Keeping Saudi onside. They've been working on this one for years."

"Pretty intense for convalescence," Rao says. "Want me to switch it over?"

"No thanks. Old shows give me headaches," Flores replies. "News is ok. Hey, sit down." He nods at the button on the table. "I can get coffee, if you want?"

"No, we're all set," Adam says.

They sit watching CNN for a while.

"Flores," Adam says. "Can you tell us what happened to you?"

Flores's face twists with distaste. "I had a bad reaction to that formula. Put me in a coma. I'm just glad they found a doctor who knew what he was doing." His eyes flick towards Rao.

Rao opens his mouth but Adam speaks first. "And now?"

"Disoriented, like a concussion. It's still hard to sleep, but they're taking care of that. I got the shakes. It's sort of like the flu."

"I got dosed," Adam says. "Didn't work the same on me, but that's how I felt too."

"Rough?"

"Rough. It'll pass."

"Adam's therapeutic regimen involved bed rest and beating the shit out of a couple of goons," Rao explains.

"It helped," Adam deadpans.

Flores huffs a mirthless laugh. "June's been taking care of me. My nurse. I get a bunch of vitamins, have to drink a lot of water. But I'll pass your recommendations on."

"I spoke to her," Hunter says. "Looks like you might be able to get out of here soon."

Flores stiffens. "Will they make me go home?" He swallows. "That sounds crazy, I know. I've got to see my mom. She's not doing well. And I miss my dogs. But . . ."

"You got troubles back in Boulder?"

"No. No." He scrubs his face, embarrassed. "Feels safer here, is all. But I'm good. Really."

He doesn't look it, Rao thinks. He might be better than before, but the man's so far from right it's wrong hearing him speak. Every word is like the jolt of expecting a step on a staircase that isn't there. "Danny," he ventures. "Can you tell me what it was like, when you were out?"

His face contorts. Like Rao'd driven a splinter under a nail.

"Dr Rhodes already asked me," he says, eyes flicking towards the door.

"She's not here today," Rao says. "She's on holiday. Back tomorrow. And she doesn't know we're talking." Hunter gives him an accusatory glare. She might not, but she will. There's a security camera right above the door.

Flores bites his lip. One foot taps an anxious rhythm against the carpet. "There was this time I got sick when I was a kid," he says. "My parents put me on the couch with blankets so I could watch TV." He rubs the sore under his jaw. "*Sesame Street*. I had a fever. Bad aches. I hated every second. The blankets were too hot, but I was too weak to push them off. I couldn't even move my head. It felt like I was trapped, like I was falling through the couch, but, you know, it was comfortable, just not the usual comfortable. Comfortable because I couldn't move, and I figured there wasn't anywhere I'd feel any better than where I was. All the time there was *Sesame Street*. Big Bird. Count von Count. Painting a number five. That fucking typewriter. The pinball." He shudders all over. "Didn't matter whether my eyes were open or closed, it was *Sesame Street* inside my head, like I didn't know whether it was on the TV or inside me, and that episode went on for days. Hey Wood, can I get some water?"

Hunter gets up, fills a jug, pours him a glass. He sips at it.

"So your coma, it was like that?" Hunter says.

"Kind of," he exhales. "But . . ." His voice cracks. "I loved it. I hated how much I loved where I was. Even if it was killing me. Like an overdose." Rao's scratching his scalp, hard. White noise of fingernails against his skull. He forces himself to stop.

"The thing I remember most," Flores says, "was the feeling that I hadn't done it right."

"Done what?" Hunter asks.

He shrugs. "I was stuck in a place. It was where I wanted to be, but it was the worst place in the world, and I knew I hadn't done it right. Like when you fuck up a pass on the football field, and everyone's watching. Like that. The feeling hasn't gone away, you know? I still feel like that. Whatever happened, I didn't do it right."

"Withdrawal is a bastard," Rao observes.

An imitation of a smile spreads on Flores's face. "Looks like it."

At eight minutes past ten that evening Adam is watching motel TV. "What is the Leaning Tower of Pisa," he intones.

Jeopardy! Rao grunts, glancing up from the Jackie Collins novel he'd nicked from the lobby. He's never understood this programme. Answers that are questions. It does his fucking head in.

"What is the United States Postal Service?" Adam enquires of the screen, face as deathly serious as if he were testifying at a congressional hearing. Rao shifts his gaze to the curtains, the photographic print of mountains on the wall, then down to Adam's shoes by the door, a sock tucked neatly into each one. *How the hell does this feel so domestic?* he thinks. Decides, eventually, it's because of their daily commute. Driving to work in the morning, just like normal people. Driving back every evening. No wonder this shitty ground-floor room has come to seem like home.

"That was weird," he announces when the show's ended. Adam's on his way back from the fridge with two cans of Sprite. He hands one to Rao, cracks his own, and sits.

"What, *Jeopardy!*?"

"No, but that's weird too. I meant Flores. How he's scared to go home."

"It happens. Trauma response."

"Yeah, well," Rao muses, setting down his unopened can. "I think it might be more than that. You got dosed. How do you feel about home?"

Adam looks at him, doubt in his eyes.

"It's not a trick question, love."

"Yeah, I know." Adam stares at the TV. A Geico car insurance advert involving, for some reason, a dentist. "Home was Aunt Sasha," he says quietly after a long while, like the fact had just occurred to him. Like it was a revelation, one he's not sure what to do with. He raps sharply on the table with his knuckles, picks up Rao's cigarettes. "Smoke?"

Veronica intercepts him on his way to the restroom the next morning. "Good morning, Rao," she begins. "This afternoon—"

"Can this wait until after I've emptied my bladder?" he sighs. "I don't want to have to grab my crotch to keep it in. This is a public area."

"I'll be right here," she says, picking invisible lint from the shoulder of her lab coat.

"The early iteration Prophet test subject you requested to meet is arriving this afternoon," she informs him on his return. "I think she may surprise you."

"Doubt it. I'm losing the capacity for surprise lately."

"I simply meant she'll look quite ordinary. A civilian. Part of a test cohort drawn from a different demographic than our manifestation program. Come to the lab at two thirty, and I'll take you to her."

Veronica's eyes are shining; she's making no move to leave.

"There's more," Rao says.

"There is indeed. I want to show you something."

"Holiday snaps?" he enquires.

"I've not been on holiday."

"Monty said you were in Vermont."

"I was. There's more in Vermont than B&Bs."

"Apples," he throws out.

"Close," she says with an enigmatic smile. Tells him, as they walk to the lab, that she was following up his theory that the size of an EPGO correlates to the space surrounding a subject at the time of exposure. Tells him she'd conducted an open-air experiment on a single volunteer. When Rao asks who the poor sod was, she describes him as an old friend in the intelligence community. Someone who'd served his country admirably and was suffering from a terminal illness.

"Sorry to hear that, Veronica."

"It is terribly sad," she replies. In an improbable moment of accord, both of them smile.

"So what did you do? Stick him in a field?"

"Yes. He made a barn."

Rao makes a face. "That's not that interesting."

She ushers him through the doors. "Yes it is."

Rao sits, watches her bring up a video file on a workstation. "You left him stuck inside it?"

"No. He wasn't drawn to it."

"Why not?"

"He didn't see it. He was instructed to close his eyes during the infusion."

Rao snorts. "So where is he now? Sedated?"

"No. He's in the morgue at Northeastern Vermont Regional Hospital. It was all a little much for him. He was really rather frail."

"Your body count's getting quite impressive, Veronica."

"A blessing, really, for both him and his family. It could have happened at any time."

Rao shakes his head, looks at the screen.

It's a red Vermont barn in the middle of a grassy field on a cloudy day. Dutch roof, weather-worn wooden shingles, white window frames. Hills rise behind it. The image is so evocative Rao feels his mouth water. A vague tang of maple syrup, American apple cider.

"Pretty," he says. "Childhood memory?"

"The original was on his family farm," she says. "It's still standing about thirty miles west, though it's been converted into a home. This is, I think, exactly as the structure looked in the early 1960s."

"You could have shown me photos. Why video?"

"Because he didn't just make a barn. Keep watching."

The camera moves towards the barn at walking pace. Veronica's hand comes to rest on the door. She pushes it open. It swings inwards. Heaps of straw, feed sacks. Columns of dusty sunlight from the upper windows cast elongated pools of brightness across the wooden floor. The camera pans downwards. Lengths of discarded twine, a scrap of hessian. Detailed memories. The camera swings round and Rao starts in his seat.

"Fuck," he says.

It's a horse. Rao loves horses. He's a halfway decent rider. But seeing this one, Rao never wants to ride again. It's not a horse. It's a horror. It looks exactly like a bay Morgan—tackless, coat dappled with sunlight—but as the camera gets closer its eyes are as dead as the wooden walls behind it, and the twitch of its flanks and the shake of its neck, the repeated swish of the tail: they're on a loop.

"Fuck, it's like the radio," he breathes. "It's horrible."

"If you say so," she says. "It looks just like a horse to me."

"It's not a horse."

"Of course it isn't."

As she walks the camera around the thing that isn't a horse, Rao feels a slow wash of vertigo; bile rises in his throat. She stops, extends a hand, runs it down a flank. Presses into it with her fingers. Her hand disappears from view, the image blurs, slips and turns, and when the camera is righted, her hand is holding a penknife. She cuts, deeply. There's no flinch from the horse, but blood flows, thick, from her incision. She steps back. The looping movements continue. The bleeding continues.

The footage cuts out.

Rao sits with his head low, forearms on his thighs, breathing hard, trying to quell a swell of nausea. "Has Adam seen this?" he says, looking at the floor.

"You asked us to leave him alone."

"But you haven't. Get him down here."

Adam's head draws back a fraction as soon as he sees the horse. His jaw tightens. Then he leans towards the screen, intrigued. As the camera tracks around the horse, he says simply, "Why now?"

"Why did he make an animal?" Veronica asks.

He nods.

Rao shrugs. "He thought it should be in the barn."

"That's not what your colleague is asking, I think." Veronica tilts her head at Adam. "I suspect Prophet has undergone another change."

"Like the leap from nostalgia to making physical objects?"

"Perhaps."

When the video ends, Adam sits back, deep in thought. "Did the blood coagulate?"

"It did not."

"Is the thing still there?"

She doesn't quite answer the question. "We conducted a necropsy on-site."

"Can't be a necropsy," Rao says, "if the horse was never alive."

"You don't think it was alive?" She's amused. "Very well. Not a necropsy. We brought it into a position of left lateral recumbency on the barn floor."

"Veronica," Rao chides.

Her mouth twitches. "We laid it on one side. Cut it open. And no, I don't think the word dissection is accurate either. We . . . disassembled it."

"What did you find?" Adam asks.

"What the test subject thought was inside a horse. There's a skeletal structure, of sorts. A skull. A spine. Some ribs, mostly unattached. The lungs were well-defined but resemble human lungs more than equine ones. Rudimentary digestive system. A sac that might have been a stomach, an unconnected anal canal. Most of the horse was undifferentiated muscle tissue."

Rao nods. "Makes sense."

"Really, Mr Rao? Because the horse was nonsense. Fascinating nonsense. This is what I wanted you to see." She takes them to the other side of the lab and pulls a white plastic container printed with a diamond and the legend UN3373 from under a bench. She bends, unlatches it. Inside is a smaller box. She picks it out, lays it on the bench top. "It's the wrong size and shape, of course," she says.

"The box?"

"What's in it." She dons a pair of surgical gloves, opens the lid.

She draws out a heart.

It's a heart.

It looks like a human heart. Pale, muscular, bulbous, slick with blood, the veins and arteries running into it snipped and gaping. Rao stares. It's the worst thing he's ever seen.

It's beating.

It's still beating.

"The heart under the floorboards," Adam whispers.

"What was that?" Veronica says.

"The *Raven* guy. Rao?"

"Poe. *The Tell-Tale Heart*. Fucking hell."

CHAPTER 52

Rao is habitually late to meetings. But he's so early to this one, Adam's not here. His absence gives Rao a sudden sense of covert responsibility: he sneaks through the lab doors as quietly as he can. The lab's not busy: a few white coats sit in front of monitors and a woman with a high-spec mop is silently cleaning the floor. He overhears Veronica talking at the far side of the room.

"Yes. As we discussed. Everything you suggested. After the PET scan on Monday."

She's nodding, holding a phone to her ear. Looks across, catches Rao's eye. "I have to go, Steven."

"Talking about me, Veronica?" Rao says, grinning.

"Yes. I was."

He nods. She's telling the truth for once. Tucking her phone away she takes off her lab coat, revealing clothes of surprising homeliness: pale-grey cardigan, a floral print blouse. Hand her a pair of horn-rimmed glasses, Rao thinks idly, and Veronica would turn full municipal librarian. Behind him, the doors swing open: as Adam walks in, Veronica sends him her sweetest smile. "Glad to see you, Colonel. Shall we all head to the interview room?"

*

Soft lighting. Armchairs, lamps on side tables, a subtly patterned rug. One-way mirror on the wall. Adam sniffs. The sweet, medicinal air of this overcleaned, underused space is sharp, unpleasant.

"So I'll be setting you both in the observation area adjacent to this space," Rhodes explains.

"I want to meet her," Rao says. "I can't meet her if I'm next door picking my nose, can I?"

Rhodes rolls her eyes but not with frustration. If Adam didn't know any better, he'd think that the psychopath in the room was starting to warm up to Rao. He has that effect on people. Wouldn't be the first time he's worn someone down.

"Rao, with respect. You're not white. You're foreign. You have a beard," she lists. "She won't talk freely if you're the first person she sees."

"Did you get her in to meet me because she's a hooting racist or was that just a happy accident?"

"Happy accident."

"Stellar," Rao sighs, rubbing his eyes. "What's your plan?"

"I'll take her through some questions. I won't be mentioning Prophet, and nor will either of you. We've invited her for a qualitative interview on how she's led her town into an era of community renewal—"

"What does that mean?" Adam asks.

Rhodes wrinkles her nose, smug. "Traditional American family values. Community groups. Rallying behind their president and troops. Patriotism."

"Nationalism," he corrects.

"Same coin." Rhodes shrugs. "They're results. Ms. Crossland and the people following her in her community are success stories as far as Lunastus-Dainsleif is concerned."

Adam looks through the tinted glass of the observation room window to where the woman sits waiting. She looks patient and calm. White, graying blonde, slim build. She's wearing a knitted sweater with small appliqué pansies and ducks on the collar and sleeves and reminds him of every single teacher he had in middle school. Rao passes him the file Rhodes had handed him. He opens it and reads. Dinah Crossland. Forty-two years old but only just. Her birthday just passed. Hometown, Pahrump.

"Well," Rhodes says to Rao as she rejoins them in the observation room. "Ms. Crossland is terribly pleased to be here."

"She's from Nevada," Adam says.

Rhodes nods. "Yes, Pahrump. It's about sixty miles northwest of Las Vegas."

"I'm aware. It's an unincorporated town in Nye County. Largest census designated place in the contiguous US."

"Remarkable," she says.

"Remarkable?"

"It didn't occur to me that you'd have such an extensive knowledge of the place."

"Why not?"

Rhodes shrugs. "You're American. American dedication is a powerful weapon to wield, obviously." She gestures vaguely at the woman in the next room. "But it tends to be focused on immediate things."

"She's calling you self-centered, Adam," Rao supplies.

"Thanks, Rao."

"Just being helpful, love."

Rhodes leaves the room. They turn to the window and watch her take a seat with Ms. Crossland in the interview suite. The transition from the Dr. Rhodes they've been working with for the last few days to the charming and affable Dr. Rhodes who wants to make Ms. Dinah Crossland happy and at ease in the facility is remarkable. She laughs and smiles warmly, leans forward, seems fascinated by Crossland's replies. Right now they're discussing Pahrump's Patriot Reaffirmation Ordinance. Flying American flags, making English the town's official language: how terribly important these things are.

"She's very good," Rao breathes. He's fascinated. Adam is, too, but he has the grace to feel bad about it.

"I don't trust her."

Rao snorts. "We've covered this. I know. That's why you never use her name."

"Her name is Rhodes."

"And you're using it to maintain distance."

Adam hums. It's not like Rao's wrong.

"Is that what you do with me?" Rao asks. "Maintain distance. Only use my last name?"

"You prefer using your last name."

"Started at school. It's the path of least resistance for most people."

"Do you want me to call you by your first name, Sunil?"

Rao shudders. "I hated that," he says. Looks horrified. "Never do that again."

"Do what, Sunil?" Adam smirks. It's too easy. Somewhere, distantly, Adam knows he should be having less fun and paying more attention to what Rhodes is doing. She's talking about family. Community. Ms. Crossland lights up, speaks with her hands. They're working. He's working. He and Rao need to know more about this woman, her reaction to her contamination. Why she's like how she is. But in this second he just doesn't care.

Rao glances at him. "Prick. Come on, Veronica's given us a Look, she wants us in there."

"Dinah," Rhodes says as they enter, "I'd like to introduce you to Lieutenant Colonel Rubenstein and Mr. Rao. They'd like to know more about your success story back home."

Adam knows the kind of woman Ms. Crossland is just by how she sits up a little straighter at the sight of him. Here it comes.

"Thank you for your service," she tells him, standing awkwardly to offer an enthusiastic hand.

"Thank you, ma'am," he replies.

"It's just so welcome to meet a fine young patriot like yourself these days. Caring for Little America as well as"—she glances at Rao distrustfully—"as well as on a global scale."

Adam suspects she doubts Rao can speak English. She sits without offering him her hand.

"I've been lucky to be able to work with a range of remarkable people," he tells her mildly. "Mr. Rao here is top of the list. He'd very much like to talk to you about your work in Pahrump."

She frowns, lowers her voice to a whisper. "Arabs don't care about America in a way that keeps the country safe. Who knows what he might want to know."

"I'm from Islington, for the record," Rao says. He pulls a chair to the table, lets it scrape against the floor before he sits.

"London," Adam clarifies.

"England," Rao completes. He considers her. "Ms. Crossland—"

"Mrs."

He sighs minutely. "Mrs. Crossland," he starts again. "I'm perfectly comfortable with the two of us never getting along. Fine with that, actually. I'm not here to convince you to be decent to me. We just have to get through a few questions and then you'll never have to look at me ever again. Won't that be nice?"

"I don't appreciate what you're implying," Mrs. Crossland says icily.

Rao smiles. "I don't believe I was *implying* anything, Dinah."

Mrs. Crossland looks first to Adam, then to Rhodes, her expression shifting from cold distrust to watery discomfort. Rao sighs again, more heavily, as she pleads with Adam and Rhodes. "I didn't come here to be insulted. I can't believe how he's treating me—"

"I'm—" Rhodes starts, but Rao interrupts her.

"No, Veronica. It's fine. No hard feelings, Mrs. Crossland?" he says, getting to his feet and offering his hand. Adam sees what he's doing. He's presenting Mrs. Dinah Crossland, community racist in a hand-knitted sweater, with a choice. She can dig in her heels, or she can take Rao's hand. Be polite.

Social conditioning wins out. She takes his hand, looking furious about it.

But the fury doesn't last. The moment their hands meet, her face turns slack. At first Adam assumes her expression is revulsion, but then he sees Rao's face matches hers. Both stand there, hands clasped, open-mouthed, still as graves. Rao must be drawing Prophet from her just like before, with Flores, he thinks, though this time it looks different. But of course it's different. Dinah Crossland isn't the usual test subject: she's not immune, and she's walking around like Adam. She's special.

Rhodes moves forward. Before she can intervene, both Crossland and Rao take simultaneous, ragged breaths. Crossland stumbles but recovers and, apart from a thin trickle of blood emerging from her right nostril, seems fine. She blinks at them all. Pulls a tiny, embroidered handkerchief from the pocket of her cardigan, dabs at her nose. Her face pales when she pulls it away and sees the cotton stained red.

"I, um," she says quietly, staring at Rao. Then she closes her eyes tight, like she's making a wish. "I want to go home."

"I'd very much prefer it if you spoke to our medical staff before you leave, Mrs. Crossland," Rhodes tells her.

"No. I don't want a fuss. I want to go home."

"Let her go, Veronica," Rao says, sitting back down. He looks exhausted. Dazed. Adam kneels and checks his pupils. They're dilated, but Rao's lucid. "Let her go home."

"Let's get you comfortable first," Rhodes murmurs. Her voice is soft, but her eyes are bright and both her hands are clenched. Adam thinks on that evidence that Crossland's not heading home anytime soon.

CHAPTER 53

Bringing Adam and Hunter back to the Vietnamese restaurant for dinner was, Rao decides, a stroke of genius. After meeting Crossland, after *that*, everything—the wrinkles on his jeans, the shadow under her chair, the angle between Veronica's upraised hand and the floor, the stitching on Crossland's sleeves, the blood on her handkerchief—had shivered with sudden, terrible significance. He could barely breathe against the intuition that a revelation was at hand. That kind of apophenic bullshit is, Rao knows, pretty far down the road towards getting forcibly sectioned under the Mental Health Act—or its Coloradan equivalent. But now? Now everything's good. Everything feels normal. Deeply, wonderfully normal. And fuck he'd been so *hungry*.

He looks at the ceiling tiles, the paintings of lotus flowers, the leggy houseplants under the soft lanterns by the bar and pops a last forkful of food into his mouth. Then he pushes his empty bowl across the tablecloth, sighing with satisfaction. "That's better," he announces. "The universe is back in balance."

Hunter gives him a curious look. "You talking about dharma?"

He grins. "Not in the proper sense, no. But kind of, a bit. I've just fixed a serious injustice."

"What injustice?"

"Adam ordered this dish last time and it was delicious. Far more delicious than the one I chose. So I had to come back and right that wrong. Avenge it."

"Avenge it? You think he ordered it on purpose to annoy you?"

"Absolutely."

"Rubenstein, why did you order chicken vermicelli noodles last time?"

"To annoy Rao."

"Is he lying, Rao?"

"You tell me, Hunter."

Outside, the night air is temperate and smells of mothballs and flowers. They start their walk back to Lunastus in companionable silence.

"What's that noise up there?" Rao enquires after a while.

"Sounds like a nighthawk," Adam says.

"That's a bird."

"It is."

Rao turns to Hunter. "See? You'd never have heard that if we took the car."

"I've heard nighthawks before," she says. "And I don't mind walking. I already said."

"She told you twice," Adam says. "Hunter does a lot of walking in her day job."

"Air traffic control."

"Air traffic control," Hunter repeats, "with added peril."

Banter. Banter and dinner and the walk in soft darkness and that weird noise above them, a metallic, fizzy chime. The world is full of goodness. Rao's spirits are so lifted that he starts humming "Spice Up Your Life" as he steps along the wide sidewalk before the turn into Lunastus's car park. He's replaying the video of the Spice Girls carousing inside a dimly lit spaceship in his mind when Adam throws an arm out in front of him, stopping him in his tracks.

"Adam, what the fuck—"

"Rao," he says, voice tight.

Rao turns to Hunter. "What's he on about?"

"I don't—" she begins, then stops. Stiffens. "Shit. Over there."

She's pointing forwards, farther down the access road, and what she's pointing at is so blisteringly wrong Rao stifles a laugh. There, about thirty feet away, is a patch of blazing, shocking colour. A bright, sunlit puddle running along the edge of the sidewalk. A puddle the blue of a summer afternoon. And all around it, darkness.

"Ah," he says, rubbing the back of his neck. "Hello."

"That is fucking insane," Hunter breathes. "Wait here. I'm gonna take a look."

"She's intrepid," Rao observes as she strides towards it.

"She's fearless. She's always been like that," Adam says.

She stands over the pool of light, considers it for a while, then jerks her head to beckon them over. Adam's face is grim as he looks down at it. Uplit by the brightness at her feet, Hunter's face is set in an expression of puzzled awe.

"It's water?" she asks.

"Yeah," Rao says. "It's a puddle."

"Prophet," Adam announces.

Rao bends down. "A specific memory, this one. It's reflecting the sky on a sunny day, isn't it? And—" He crouches to change the angle. From here he can see the top of a bright-red waterslide, a reflected line of mop-headed palms. He gets down on his hands and knees, brings his head closer to the sunlit surface. More of the waterslide comes into view, and beside it a pile of artfully arranged boulders with a waterfall and beneath the waterfall, bobbing heads and waving arms. "It's a water park," he breathes.

"How did it get out here?" Adam says.

"Dunno. Maybe Lunastus's ventilation containment system doesn't work with Prophet anymore."

"Can't you tell instantly whether that's true?" Hunter says.

Rao shrugs. "Prophet's tricky shit."

"We're due east of the buildings," Adam observes. "Prevailing wind's westward. Rao's theory tracks."

"Is this thing dangerous?" Hunter asks.

"Only to the person who made it. Could be anyone. Passerby, one of the medical staff driving home, anyone."

"Not me?"

"No. You'd be facedown in it if it was yours. Also . . . what do water parks mean to you?"

She shrugs, staring down at the puddle. "Marco Polo."

"What?"

"The swimming game, Rao," Adam says. "Not the guy."

Hunter tilts her head at Adam. "What're we gonna do about this?"

"Enjoy it," Rao says. "It's ludicrously pretty. I'll tell Veronica about it in the morning. She can send someone to clear it up. I'm sure she'll be delighted to hear about another Lunastus fuckup."

Adam shakes his head. "You should call her now."

"With what phone? Besides, I'm off the clock."

"Use my cell."

"She'll never answer your number, love."

"Rao."

"Fuck. Fine. But you owe me."

CHAPTER 54

He wakes suddenly with a surge of adrenaline, heart thrumming under his ribs, eyes wide. The motel room curtains are drawn. Rao's sitting on the edge of the bed across the room, his back to Adam. He's shaking his head and laughing softly. Adam sits up. There's no visible threat, but the surge of alarm that woke him won't go away. "Morning," he calls, voice rough with sleep. Rao looks over his shoulder. His face is amused and guilty. It looks so much like his expression the last time Adam walked in on him jerking off he assumes that's what's going on here. The laughter is weird, but so is Rao. Adam stopped being surprised by what gets Rao off a long time ago.

"Morning, love," Rao says. He turns, crooks one leg up onto the bed, looks down at the covers. He's not jerking off. But he's still snickering.

"What's funny, Rao?"

"There's a lizard," Rao says.

"What?"

Rao gestures at the throw blanket, and Adam sees it. It skitters fast over the patterned cotton to the far end of the bed, where it halts, raises its head, and freezes. It's too dark in the room to make out what color it is, brown or gray, and it's kind of spiny, with a rounded head and a long, whiplike tail. Adam's familiar with lizards. They were everywhere when he was growing up. But he's never seen this kind before.

"That shouldn't be here," he says. This sparks another bout of giggling from Rao. Fuck. *Is he high?*

"No, it shouldn't."

Adam gets out of bed, walks closer, angles his head to study it. Thin toes. Claws. Lizards aren't easy, but he knows how to catch them. Sniper mindset. All you need to do is tell yourself you're part of the scenery, convince yourself you're something like a rock or a tree. Then you strike with confidence, anticipating full success. He puts himself in the right headspace, waits a few seconds, then grabs at it, pressing the wriggling reptile into the cotton, getting a firm hold before picking it up, its spine nestled against his palm, scales rough and warm against his skin, his fingers closed around its neck. Its mouth is slightly open: a line of fine, tiny teeth and a round eye, pupils wide in the darkness of the room. He drops his hand to his side, walks to the door, pushes it open, then crouches and lets the lizard run from his opened hand into the motel parking lot. It disappears over the asphalt into the shadow under a Chrysler minivan.

"You didn't kill it," Rao says as Adam shuts the door.

"Why would I kill it?"

Rao shrugs. "Because you're you?"

"Thanks, Rao. Did you want me to?"

"No. Thank you for not."

"You're welcome."

Rao's laughing again. "Shall we go in? I know it's early, love, but I'm fucking starving. Even thought about hitting reception for a serving of Cheerios in a cardboard bowl, which I tell you is a way worse gastronomic experience than anything they served me in Pentonville."

Adam looks at him and determines, again, that Rao's appreciably thinner than he had been last week. Clavicles more obvious, cheekbones sharper. Which is disturbing considering how much he's been eating every day in the corporate canteen. Rao's never been shy of food, but last night at dinner, there was desperation in how Rao stuffed vermicelli into his mouth. Twice he told Adam how delicious it was, but he was barely chewing, eating so fast Adam doubted he tasted much at all.

"Rao," he says after a second or two of deliberation. "Are you feeling okay?" It's the kind of temperature testing Rao hates, but Rao doesn't roll his eyes. He smiles.

"Never better, love. Tickety-boo."

"Tickety-boo."

"English idiom."

"Right."

"It means I'm doing fine," Rao clarifies.

"Yeah, I got that." Adam sighs inwardly. Working together before, Adam got used to seeing Rao fucked up. He'd laugh, giggle, hum through his highs. Even through his lows. Balance issues, hyperfocus, nonstop talking, eerie silences: Adam's seen them all. But Rao never seemed to lie about it. If Adam asked, he'd own up. Sometimes just to piss Adam off. Always looking for a reaction.

Now, something's off about him. Adam knows it for a fact. The kind of fact that Rao would call flat, immutable, simply the truth. Something's off, but Adam doesn't think Rao is lying when he says he's doing fine. The need to know what's going on makes Adam's skin itch, but he pushes that need away and out of his head.

"Breakfast, Adam? Surely you could eat. Even the Froot Loops there are above average."

"Yeah, Rao. Let me get dressed."

"Ticktock, love."

Adam looks at him. Watches him replay the last few seconds. Watches him wince.

"I didn't mean it like that."

"It's fine."

"Sorry, Adam."

"Rao. It's . . . tickety-boo."

He doesn't know what he was expecting from Rao, but a triumphant howl was not on the list. Grinning, shirtless, Rao starts rummaging around the room for clothes. The weight loss looks good on Rao. Under the circumstances Adam shouldn't think that, but he does. He makes an internal, passive note to get him a new belt. At the rate Rao's losing weight, his pants won't stay up for much longer. They're dipping dangerously low as it is.

"Today's going to be a good day, love. Mark my words."

"Marked, Rao."

CHAPTER 55

De Witte's in the darkened cabin of one of his Lears: in the gloom behind his shoulders Veronica can see tiger-striped wood, cream leather chairs.

"Steven. It's early. Where are you?"

"Right now I'm, uh, over Lincoln, Nebraska, en route to the event. Is Pensacola ready to receive our subject?"

"Event?"

"You don't know about the event?" De Witte closes his eyes, speaks with them shut. "I told Lane he should call you immediately, inform you of the situation."

"He didn't, Steven. He wouldn't. He sees me as a threat to your and his special relationship."

He opens his eyes. "It won't— I'll make sure it doesn't happen again."

"Tell me about the event."

"Lane got a call from security at E-MAD at, uh, three sixteen yesterday. We've had a mass manifestation of EPGOs around the buildings. He's sending in a plane to get a bird's-eye."

"How many objects?"

"Tens of thousands. Plush toys, pianos, Ford pickups, the usual kind of kind. Some are, uh, quite massive."

"How massive?"

"Boeing 747. Pan Am colours."

She takes a deep breath, holds it, exhales. "Do you have a first pass on causation?"

"Considering the quantity, I assume they were generated by our field site cohort."

"That was five months ago," she says.

"*A hundred and thirty-four days since exposure,*" *he corrects.* "*So perhaps this is another case of saltatory evolution? It would strengthen our entanglement thesis if so.*"

"*What do our theoreticians say?*"

He shakes his head. "*We lost another one. Hung himself. He, uh, left a note. It was like the last one. All about how, you know, nothing makes sense anymore.*"

She ignores that irrelevance. Something's just occurred to her.

"*Did you say the call came at three sixteen, Steven?*"

"*Three sixteen, yes.*"

She smiles then. She knows. It's Rao. Rao and Mrs Crossland. Their handshake, that skin-to-skin contact. Veronica's certain Rao somehow triggered the manifestation. Questions are presenting themselves to her now that she's very eager to answer. And right now, she decides, Steven doesn't need to complicate things.

He's looking to her for elaboration, now. "*Does that time have significance to you, Veronica?*"

"*No, Steven. Not at all.*"

CHAPTER 56

Montgomery clears his throat. This morning he grips a clipboard and his eyes are a little vague. Odds-on, Rao thinks, the vagueness is vodka, and the clipboard's partly a defensive prop. *Right*, both counts.

"Let's take you through this once more. You've agreed to extract Prophet from another test subject."

"Yes, Kent."

"And we've scheduled you for a PET scan tomorrow at eleven, to complement the MRI results so far, dig a little deeper into your metabolic processing."

"Yes. Because Prophet's not enough. You want me radioactive as well."

"Only mildly," Veronica offers.

"We'll be administering a radionuclide called fluorodeoxyglucose," Montgomery continues, stumbling a little midway through the word. "It'll leave your system in a few days. Best to keep away from pregnant women in that time."

"I'll try."

"Rao, which subject will you be working with today?"

"With? On? Or for?" Rao rapid fires. "The man with the orange blanket."

"Can you tell us why?"

"Because I'm horrified. Veronica's had his girlfriend sedated for what, a week?"

"Eight days," she says. "Her vital signs are strong."

"Fuck me, that can't be good for her. What'll you do with them both when he wakes?"

She frowns. "They signed the forms. There's no legal avenues for—"

"Lunastus isn't going to bump them off?"

"Rao," Montgomery rebukes.

"Ok, ok. Let's do this."

Rao's chosen subject is at the back of the ward, orange fleece blanket heaped in a soft pile in his arms, the ribbon stitched along one edge pressed against his lips. Tension lines around his mouth and eyes. He's already looking grey. Four nurses are clustered a few feet away. Monty takes himself off to sit on a chair against the far wall. *Fair enough*, Rao thinks. It's not like there's any point to him being here. Veronica's setting up a video recorder on a tripod by the side of the bed. Rao's tempted to step in and start the process before she's ready, but he likes that his next miracle will be on tape for posterity. He's not too proud of that.

Where's Adam? he thinks, turning his head. Standing right behind him, like Adam always is. Maybe he expects blanket man to attack Rao when he wakes. *Maybe*, Rao thinks, *he will*.

"We're ready," Veronica says. "Do you need me to—"

"No. Just make sure you get my best side," Rao says, stepping closer. Reaching out, he cradles the man's face in both hands. A wash of emotion at the sensation. Most of it unidentifiable. A lot of sadness that feels like memory. And the prickling in his palms takes longer this time, but then it catches and holds and Prophet slips through. He's waiting for the terror, but the terror doesn't come. The same intuition of measureless no-water oceans, now lit with dimmest, glimmering stars, almost familiar, and he's falling and rising inside it like breathing, as if—

Done. Like switching on a light, he's back in the room and watching the man's fingers spasm, clutch at the blanket, his eyes open wide. They're blue and bloodshot and absolutely baffled.

"Hi," Rao says.

"Doctor?"

The nurses rush towards him. Rao is pushed aside.

"Very impressive, Rao," Veronica breathes. She's standing too close. Adam's on his other side. "How are you feeling?"

He doesn't answer. Walks to the next bed. In it, a small, short-haired woman has her arms around what Rao had initially thought was a giant pumpkin, albeit one with a spout, red plastic windows, and angry blue eyebrows. Adam had informed him it was the Big Yellow Teapot, and Rao had given him shit for being overly literal. "No, Rao," he'd said. "That's its name."

"Designation."

"Name."

He smiles at the memory, pushes the woman's hospital bracelet a little farther up her arm, and grips her wrists.

This time the no-water ocean is almost a welcoming place, though it's not a place at all, and the way Prophet slips into him reminds him of something he can't quite grasp. The woman wakes with a start. The teapot rolls from her chest, hits the floor with a crack. Parts of it open, and things spill across the floor. Toys, Rao assumes, but he's already moving to the next bed, aware that the woman he's just healed is having a fit. The nurses surround her now, and peripherally he can see her kicking feet. It's not like he can help her out of it, they'll have it under control, there's more—

He studies the occupant of the next bed. Man, early forties, dark hair, gripping a G.I. Joe.

"Rao." Adam, at the foot of the bed, looking warily at him. "Do you know what you're doing?"

"First fucking time in my life, love," he says with feeling, holding Adam's eye as he presses his hands to the man's chest. Keeps looking at Adam as Prophet floods in. But his attention's torn away when he suddenly works out what this sensation reminds him of. A cold day in January in Jaipur, drinking chai from Sahu's on Chaura Rasta Road. Sweet. Hot. Fragrant. *Known*.

He moves on.

They don't all wake the same. Some don't open their eyes, their breathing turning fitful, their fingers twitching as their objects fall from their hands and arms. Others wake gasping. One with a scream. Every time Rao pulls Prophet from their bodies he feels himself sink and rise and by the eighth he's feeling so at home in the not-ocean around him it's more effort leaving it than slipping in. *Chai*, he thinks, as the last sleeper wakes. *Chai on a cold day.*

He heals everyone.

Veronica, staring at him. Hands folded together, pressed to her lips like she's praying. Like she doesn't know what to say.

"Alright, Veronica?"

"We should run some tests."

"Right. Right. But first I require a cup of tea."

*

Adam looks up to see Montgomery walking into the side room off the main ward. He really shouldn't look forward to Rao verbally punching that man as much as he does.

"Oh, *piss off*," Rao growls, setting down his mug. It's weird. Under these fluorescent lights, Monty looks like a corpse; Rao looks glowing with health. "I just healed all your casualties. Whatever the fuck you're bringing to my door, you can piss off with it, okay? Toddle back off to Veronica and tell her to bite the back of my balls. Better yet, tell her to bite yours. It'll shock everyone. You could really take charge for once, Monty. Sorry. *Kent.*"

Montgomery opens his mouth, closes it. Adam should feel sorry for him.

"Rao," he says. "I want to take a break."

"Oh! Lunch?"

Obviously. "If you want."

"I could murder a burger."

As they walk the corridors, Rao's savage mood recedes, and he starts reciting lines from his improvised ode to the Lunastus canteen. Adam's heard it on repeat since the first day, but the rhymes are getting worse, the tone more and more evangelical. There's something to be said about Rao's love of luxury and how well he's been doing at ignoring it. Apart from falling off the wagon that night with Hunter, he hasn't indulged in any kind of vice with Adam around—except the canteen.

"It's obscene," Rao says, breaking off from his recital. "I don't know how many Michelin-starred chefs they've kidnapped and got chained up in that kitchen, but eating here feels like I'm doing something highly illegal without actually going down that road."

"I was just thinking the same thing."

Rao laughs. "Go fuck yourself, love. Only I'm allowed to talk about my tendencies so lightly."

"Is that true?"

"No." Rao's smiling. "I suppose you're allowed, all things considered."

Adam shakes his head, quietly embarrassed at how much that means to him. "Very gracious, Rao," he says. He means it. Rao will never know.

Rao's smile slips. "Adam, are you cold?"

"What?"

"I feel cold," he says. He looks up, slow and unnatural. Like a wire connected to his chin is tugging his head into the right position. *Puppet*, Adam thinks. "Marionette," the word Rao would use.

"What is it?" he asks. The question has just left his mouth when he sees something trickle down from Rao's nostrils as he looks up. Blood. It's almost black.

Adam catches him as he crumples. Both of them slide to the floor. Rao's a deadweight in his arms. He's still looking up. His eyes are open, but he's not seeing a damn thing.

"What just happened?" Adam whispers into the air. There's no response from Rao. He doesn't expect one. He doesn't have to sound an alarm, either; there are cameras everywhere. Less than a minute after they hit the floor, there's a team of Rhodes's medical staff right there with a gurney. Adam doesn't fight them, and Rao doesn't react when they move him. He's taking shallow but regular breaths. His eyes are still open, unblinking. As they wheel him down the halls toward an examination room, one of the white coats drops saline onto his corneas. Adam keeps up, hand on the side of the gurney.

They get Rao settled on a bed and are hooking him to monitors when Rhodes arrives. "What happened?" she asks him. Sharp.

"Unknown," he says. "We were walking and then he wasn't."

She reaches over to close Rao's eyes. The action is sickeningly tender, and it takes everything Adam has to keep from telling her to get fucked. She's been delighting in poking and prodding Rao to get answers about what's been happening with him, and Adam's said nothing about it. Not directly. But this act of apparent kindness nearly sends him over the edge. Rhodes doesn't notice him bristling.

"He suffered from epistaxis before losing consciousness."

"You can say nosebleed, Dr. Rhodes."

She glances at Adam. "Why? You understood what I meant. You really are—"

"My ego can handle it if you focus on Rao, Dr. Rhodes, and not on how surprised you still are to learn that I can grasp the concept of synonyms."

"We'll keep him overnight," she says, leaning back enough to give the impression that she's allowing Rao space to breathe.

"No tests," he says. Acquiesces. Negotiates. It's always a negotiation with Rhodes.

"Colonel Rubenstein—"

"Rhodes, don't push me on this," he warns her. "When he wakes up, get his consent as you need it. But right now I'm telling you that the only thing you're going to do is keep him well enough to regain consciousness. Am I understood?"

Rhodes purses her lips. He hasn't used the command tone on her, until now. He doesn't do that anymore. He's not around enough soldiers these days to warrant it. But it has its uses.

"Yes, Colonel. I believe I understand your stance on the matter."

"Glad we're eye-to-eye on this, Dr. Rhodes."

"Adam?"

Rao's voice scratches Adam out of a light nap. Low medical lighting and quiet monitor beeps lulled him into a doze a few hours ago, sometime after Rhodes's people left. One of them even tried to convince him to leave. He rubs his eyes and sits up. Reaches for the glass and jug of water on the bedside table. "Rao," he says.

"What happened?"

"Good question." Adam pours and hands him a glass, watching closely for tremors or signs of weakness. Nothing. Rao looks solid. Confused but solid. "How do you feel?"

"Starving."

"We never ate. You collapsed on the way to lunch."

"What time is it now?"

Adam checks his watch. "Two a.m."

"Fuck," Rao says with feeling. He sits up, scratches his beard. Grimaces at the IV line in his arm. Sighs at his feet poking out of the bottom of the bed. "What does Veronica say?"

"The last thing Dr. Rhodes said to me was 'Tell me when he's awake.' She wants to run more tests."

"She didn't already?"

"No."

"That's not like her."

"She's not happy about it. She's had to reschedule the PET scan."

Rao snorts, settles back down. Looks up at the ceiling. Rhodes's team cleaned the blood from his nose when they brought him in and hooked him up, but Adam can still see it dripping over his lips. He blinks the memory away and tries to refocus.

"Are you defending my honor again, love?"

"Someone has to."

That makes Rao laugh. It echoes flatly. "Do you think they could get me something to eat if we tell them I'm awake?"

Adam looks at Rao seriously. The dim white light makes him look gray, but he seems okay. Maybe a little embarrassed. Distant. He doesn't look at Adam directly. Whenever he smiles or laughs, a little more tension leaves his shoulders. He could be lying about not knowing what happened. Worse, he could be telling the truth.

"Do you think you could find out what happened before they come in here?" he asks. "Do a run?"

Rao groans. "I really don't want to."

"But you could?"

"I could do a fuck ton of things, Adam. I could rip this line out and use it as a skipping rope but I'm not going to do that, am I?"

"Do the run anyway."

Rao groans again, leveling a look of pure malice in Adam's direction, but Adam doesn't care. They need to know what happened. *He* needs to know. He watches Rao give in and mutter to himself.

"Anything?" he prompts eventually.

"Alright, Adam, fuck off," Rao says, rubbing his eyes. Seconds drag past. That kitchen clock's heavy tick is somehow still in Adam's head, and he can almost hear it as he waits. He'd prefer it if Rao were looking at him, but he keeps his hand right there, blocking out the medical lighting and Adam's gaze. "It was an overdose. Run of the mill. Don't fucking talk to me."

CHAPTER 57

Hunter walks into Rao's recovery room with the specific energy of someone on a highly unwelcome mission. She tosses something onto his bed. He watches it arc and fall onto the blanket between his knees. An energy bar. Chocolate chip and peanut butter. Cartoon wrapper of a bear holding a grenade.

"Thank you? Is that beer you're carrying for me too?"

"No, it isn't." She sits at his bedside.

"Why not?"

"Because I'm not an idiot." She crosses one ankle over a knee. "How are you doing? Rubenstein said you passed out."

"Yeah, he's seen that before, nothing unusual. How am I doing? I hate these pyjamas they've given me. I know that's petty, but I am petty, and they're ghastly. Apart from that, I'm just bored. Did he make you come visit me?"

"Who?"

He snickers. "Want to sneak out for a smoke?"

She shrugs. "Sure."

"Pass me that robe on the door?"

They find a door that opens onto a flat roof at the far end of a corridor and duck out into a mild Coloradan morning. The radomes of the airbase across the road sit like unpopped soap bubbles, the sky above dotted with fist-shaped clouds. Rao lights two cigarettes, passes one to Hunter, and they look out across miles of nicotine-coloured grass to the horizon.

"Rao, how the fuck did you end up in this life?" Hunter says.

"Surprised Adam's not told you."

"He probably has," she confesses. "But I hear a lot of stories and I only remember the interesting ones."

"Hunter . . ."

She laughs. "He didn't tell me. *Jesus*, Rao. You're so *easy*."

Rao's quiet for a moment before realising he's going to tell her. Wants to tell her.

"After university," he begins, "I went a bit off the rails. Spent a few years fucking around. Spent too much of my time in the company of posh white wankers with villas and pools and good dealers. Punched out a few. Stole a car from one once."

"Highlight of your criminal career?"

"It was at the time," he says crisply. "Anyway, the last couple of years were in Berlin, and it got full-on ragged. I kind of lost the plot. I wasn't . . ." He shakes his head. He's not going to give her all the grisly details. "Then I got an ultimatum from my father. After a family birthday I try never to think about. *Sort yourself out or the money will stop.*"

Hunter blinks at him.

"Don't look like that."

"I'm not." She shakes her head. "I just don't know why you needed his money at all. You've never played poker?"

"Wouldn't be fair."

"That doesn't make sense." She frowns. Rao opens his mouth in protest; she raises a hand to stop him. "Whatever. So you got a job."

"Yeah. At Sotheby's, the auction house. Only got through the door because my mother's a specialist at Christie's. She's a very persuasive woman and she knows everyone. *Everyone.* My job was researching whether artworks were genuine."

Hunter raises an eyebrow, taps ash.

"Yeah, I know. That bit was easy for me, of course, but I still had to get physical evidence to prove it one way or the other, and that was a pain in the arse. So, I'm in my office on a foggy Tuesday afternoon in January, it's nearly dark outside, and there's a call. Someone in reception's asking for me by name. I thought it would be someone I knew from college, you know, or someone who knew someone I knew. But it wasn't."

"Let me guess," she says. "A guy with a painting he wanted you to look at?"

"It wasn't a painting. It was a beautiful red chalk by Sebastiano del Piombo. Totally real, by the way. We talked about it for a while, he got into my space, commented favourably on my cologne. I thought he'd be up for some fun. Said he worked at the British Museum, and two nights later he took me on what I assumed was a date to the Egyptian galleries." He pauses significantly. "After closing time."

"I don't know what that look means, Rao."

"Museums at night, well. You know."

"They give you a hard-on?" she guesses.

"They're *romantic*."

She laughs. "That's the worst lie I've ever heard come out of your mouth."

"Fuck off, but yeah, ok. I was thinking, why would this guy take me to a place full of funerary objects unless he had a pretty specific kink?"

She looks at him enquiringly.

"I've a very open mind," Rao says, very seriously.

She snorts. "Yeah, I know. So, what? He gave you a speech, showed you some wrapped-up mummy, got you to say it was fake, then invited you to a meeting with some people?"

"Yeah," Rao says, faintly crestfallen. Because that was exactly what had happened.

Morten Edwards had wide hazel eyes, a sweep of dark-blond hair, a pocket square that was all affectation, and a deep Welsh voice that wasn't.

"Uh, Morten," Rao had said, both of them staring down into the museum case. "Would you care to tell me what is happening here? I thought you were making a pass."

"Actually I am. In a sense. Indulge us."

"Us?"

"A government department."

"Which government department?"

"It's not Heritage and Sport," Edwards said, amused.

He's a spy, Rao thought and instantaneously *knew*. A punch of excitement under his ribcage. He'd looked back at the mummified cat. "This isn't what it says it is. But it's not a fake. More like a very ancient fraud. Depends. In this case, I don't think it matters, really. Do you?"

"I don't think it does, no. But considering what you can do, some people I know would like to have a bit of a talk with you," he murmured after a while.

"You're MI5," Rao said.

"Not them, no."

Hunter cocks her head, looks at him curiously. "So they didn't know about your lying thing?"

Rao grins. "I'm a fuckwit. I told them. Not all of it," he adds. "Only that I can tell when people aren't speaking the truth."

"When?"

"First meeting."

"You *are* a fuckwit."

He sighs. Sold himself out to the kind of authority he's spent a lifetime kicking against is what he did. That's all he's done. "I really thought I'd be helpful, you know? Save people. Make a difference."

He expects her to laugh. She doesn't. She takes a swig of her beer. "That's why we do it," she says. "I'm not as cynical as Rubenstein. No one is." Her voice is warm but serious.

"You two go back a long way, I hear?"

"Yeah, we went through basic together. This quiet Jewish kid and the asshole mixed kid showing everyone how it's done."

"What was he like back then?"

Her face grows fond. "Next-level. Like he is now." She takes another swig, reconsiders. "No, he's different these days."

"Older and wiser?"

"He's older," she says, looking right at him.

Rao's wondering if he's brave enough to ask for elaboration when the door behind them swings wide. Veronica peers out from the frame, mouth in a tight line.

"Rao. You shouldn't be out here. And you *really* shouldn't be smoking."

"Fuck off, Veronica," Rao says cheerfully.

"We need to discuss your latest blood work."

"Not now. I'm convalescing."

"If you're sufficiently well to smoke barefoot on a rooftop, you're well enough to discuss medical results."

It's phenomenally difficult to argue with that. "Bad news?"

"Inexplicable news."

"Fuck, you do know how to reel me in," he grumbles. "Hunter, where's Adam?"

She shrugs. "I'm not his keeper."

"You don't know where he is?"

"He said he was going for lunch. I don't know where and I didn't ask."

Rao bends to stub out his cigarette, flicks it into a gutter. "Ten to one he'll be eating a burger in the canteen. He hates how good they are. Or maybe . . . Veronica, you don't happen to know what today's specials are?"

"I don't," Veronica says. "But this won't take long. You're welcome to join him in the canteen when we're done."

She stands by the armchair, hands on her hips. Watches Rao get back into bed, prop himself up against the headboard. "Right, Doctor," he says, pulling his robe closer around him. "Give me the inexplicable news. I can take it."

"Your results are bizarre. Yesterday you extracted Prophet from fifteen people."

"I know I did. How are they all?"

"Good," she says. "Apart from one."

He clutches at the bed linen. He hadn't thought to check. "The woman who had the fit. The one with the teapot."

"Yes."

He's going to throw up. He is. He isn't. He might.

"What did I do? Was it broken heart syndrome?"

"You didn't *do* anything except extract Prophet from her," Veronica says tightly. "She suffered a generalised tonic-clonic seizure followed by a stroke. The neurobiology of withdrawal from Prophet will be a wonderfully fertile area for further research."

He stares at the wall miserably, thinking of the hollow crack when her teapot hit the floor. He'd been too eager to do *more*, hadn't looked back. He'd not looked at her. Hadn't even seen her face.

"What was her name?"

"Simmonds. Lab tech."

"First name?"

"Nancy."

"I was trying to help," he says dully. "Why does this always happen. It always happens."

"Rao, this has never happened before, anywhere."

He pulls his knees to his chest, hugs them. The cotton feels greasy. He's suddenly very aware of his shins. Sharp. How frail they are. How everything is.

"But that isn't the reason I wanted to talk to you. Two other things were."

He gestures at her to go on.

"Like you, Colonel Rubenstein has an anomalous response to Prophet. Both with his initial dose and then the follow-up." She purses her lips. "You know about the second dose."

"I do."

She tucks an invisible hair behind an ear. "He requested it. There was full consent."

"What have you done to him now?"

"Nothing. But his case raised the possibility that Prophet . . . refuses, shall we say, to incorporate itself into subjects who've previously been exposed, even if you've extracted all of it from their systems."

He blinks at her. She's expecting him to follow her chain of reasoning, but he's still caught up in the horror that he's killed another person. His body count is getting impressive. He—

"So I gave another dose to one of your miracles, half an hour ago."

He sits up. "For *fuck's sake*," he hisses. "Can't you just leave them alone?"

"You don't want to know what happened?"

He closes his eyes.

"Murray. Jackson Murray. Navy SEAL. Back problems invalided him out. I don't know if you remember him. His EPGO was a G.I. Joe."

He nods, eyes still closed.

"If it helps, Rao, he was barely conscious at the time. It's unlikely he felt the needle at all. But Prophet was very eager to renew its acquaintance. He created another G.I. Joe, held it in exactly the same position as before, and promptly returned to a trance state. His vitals are fine, by the way. So you might drop by the ward when you're feeling better if you're in the mood."

He doesn't engage with that.

"What was the other thing?"

"There's still no trace of Prophet in your system."

He raises his head, stares at her. That doesn't feel right. He feels full of it. Every cell in his body brimming with it. And yet—

"What did you do with it?" she asks.

"You think I'm hiding it?"

Something like a smile. "At this point, Rao, I wouldn't be surprised."

"I have no idea. I took it out of everyone. I don't know where it's gone. Maybe it vanishes into the ether. Gets absorbed. I don't care. I killed someone."

"You didn't kill them. Prophet did."

Rao has a moment of wild confusion. Indeterminacy is everywhere, he knows, but the causal structure of her statement is a fucking bewilderment. Everything true and not true and somehow *in movement*. He rubs his nape. Veronica's talking on her phone.

"Could you tell me what today's specials are? Vichyssoise, pan-fried walleye with artichoke aioli, buffalo tenderloin with prairie butter. Thank you." She cuts the call, smiles, looks expectantly at Rao.

CHAPTER 58

Adam paces around their motel room in silence. He's thinking. Rao isn't about to fuck with that before the time is right. Usually he would—and delight in doing so—but he knows he's up shit creek. He knew things would go pear-shaped if he kept on with this, but somehow thought it would go differently. Which was idiotic. He's an idiot.

The cards. *Shit.*

He'd been desperate to get out of that godawful recovery room and back to the motel but as soon as he'd walked through the door, he didn't want to be there at all. Sick of television, tired of radio, fully over the dog-eared novels the hotel lobby had supplied, he'd simply wanted something to *do*. He'd dropped the deck on the table in front of Adam, asked him to teach him how to do false cuts. Adam had nodded, glanced down, and his face had pulled taut. Shoulders too.

Puzzled, Rao looked at the deck.

The cards from the Tashkent suite. Exactly the same Russian crosshatched backs patterned red and blue, the same card stock, well-thumbed corners. He knows they'd smell the same if he lifted them to his nose and sniffed. Turpentine and bleach.

Adam had looked at them for a long while, then raised his eyes to Rao's, face way beyond demanding an explanation, and Rao, heart thumping, had known he was fucked. No way to bullshit his way out of this one.

And now Adam is pacing around the motel room, and Rao, resigned, is lying on his bed, staring up at the ceiling, waiting for what he knows he's going to get.

"What have you created?" Adam says eventually, stilling himself. "Apart from the cards, Rao. What have you made?"

"You want a list?"

"Honestly, yes. But I know you won't provide that. I'll settle for what you can remember creating and when and why."

"What do you mean, why?"

Adam exhales once, sharply. "Humour me."

"Fine." Rao sits up, positioning himself a little more solidly in the room—though it would be easier to talk to the ceiling than watch Adam's face while he speaks. "I made cigarettes. Smoked them. You had one—"

"Jesus."

"Perfectly safe. Still have three left, if you want to take a look," he offers, gesturing to the jacket hanging on the door. "They're in the front pocket. Then matches. A lighter. A chocolate bar, once, but I didn't finish eating that."

"It wasn't right?"

"No, it was perfect." Rao shakes his head. "I just misjudged how much I wanted to eat chocolate. You know how I get, sometimes, with sweets."

"Stay on target, please," Adam sighs.

"The cards."

"I know about the cards, Rao. I'm looking at them. Anything else?"

There is. There's one more thing. Two more things. They're difficult to talk about because they were the first and because that was when Rao knew he was beyond help. He knows only the worst will come of this, no matter how thrilling it is. Maybe because of how thrilling it is.

"Rao," Adam prompts.

Rao nods. "Yeah. Ok. There were lizards."

Adam freezes. Rao watches his eyes grow wide, darting around the room as he stacks this information high, clicks it into place. "The lizard in our room," he says quietly. He moves closer to Rao. Rao wishes he wouldn't. Drops into a squat so that they're eye-to-eye. "The lizard on the bed."

"Yes."

"And you laughed at it and told me to look." Yes. Rao remembers. Giddy with the sudden creation, the victory of it, the controlled chaos of it. A living thing that had never existed before, skittering on the sheets. "I put it outside."

Rao nods.

"When we were leaving, you took your time in the parking lot. I thought you were tying your laces, but—" He stops, looks at Rao closely. Stills himself to search for whatever truth he's looking for, shakes himself out of it again. The process is fascinating to watch this close. "There were lizards in the parking lot."

"There were two," Rao says. Adam lifts an eyebrow. "What? I couldn't leave the first one out there alone. Contrary to popular belief, I'm not a complete prick."

Adam's lips twitch. It's practically a smile. "I thought you were high."

Ouch. "I suppose that's reasonable enough."

"But, instead, you were creating life."

That surprises a laugh out of Rao. "Bloody hell, Adam. You make it sound so dramatic. 'Creating life,' as though it's as large as that."

"Isn't it?"

"It doesn't feel that large," Rao admits, then shakes his head at the lie. "No. It's large, just not in the way you're imagining."

"Explain it to me."

Rao frowns. "I'm not entirely sure that I can."

"Try."

That's not so easy. Rao knows how it feels, and he knows what it reminds him of. It's like heroin, but without the slowness. It doesn't put distance between him and the world, but it has the same ever-falling stillness. He's not disconnected. He doesn't get that yellow-air-in-a-library feeling, as though everything's old and dry and smells of sweet chemicals. Creating new things makes Rao feel fresh. Cold, a shock to the system. An ice bath. Breathing in morning air in the snow. Bright, sharp, as inviting as any other kind of high.

But there's no way he can say these things to Adam. The hardest thing Adam's ever done in his life is grain alcohol. He tries a different tactic, sticks as close to the truth as he can.

"It's sharp," he starts, and sees Adam focus up. "Like cutting into fabric or digging out a bullet from a wound. Only, instead of fighting to find the bullet within, the wound wants to give it up. When I do this, Adam—it's—it's as though I'm speaking a knife into the world. I make a cut. The wound gives."

Adam sighs, gets to his feet. "I thought that we had cleared up the misconception that I'm a violent psychopath, Rao." He sounds tired. He hadn't before. "You don't have to put it in terms that you think I would understand."

Rao shakes his head. "No, that's not—" He stops, seeing the scepticism on Adam's face. Lifts his hands in peace. "Fine. I might have started with that intention."

"You don't need to—"

Rao interrupts. "But what I said feels exactly right. And, rather more importantly, it's *true*."

Adam is silent again. Steps to the other end of the bed, sits. Rao feels the mattress take his weight. *A concession*, Rao thinks, though Adam's face is unreadable as ever.

"Watch," Rao says. Can hear the urgency in his voice. *Show, don't tell.*

He holds his hand open between them and inhales. Conjures in his mind the full apprehension of what it will be and then exhales, doing the thing he has no words for: opens the world to let it out. He feels the pull, just to his left, and his eyes drag towards a few square inches of bedcover. Adam's attention is drawn to the spot too; he leans towards it, intent. The air around it contracts inwardly, quivers. Like heat haze, but it's not something that can be seen. Sensed. Like an accelerating implosion, air rushing in to fill a vacuum, and—

Rao blinks—and there.

A thick glass ashtray on the coverlet, the cotton beneath it deformed under its weight. He surfs the sensation, but there's the familiar disappointment in its wake. Everything he's made so far has only ever appeared when his eyes have been closed, while he's blinked, has manifested in that fleeting moment of blindness. He's never seen it happen.

He looks over to Adam, hopefully.

"Do it again," Adam says. "I blinked."

"Adam . . ."

"Just . . . I don't know. Another ashtray. Do it again."

"Alright, but—"

"Go ahead."

He prays Adam will see it this time. He needs to know.

No dice: Adam blinks at precisely the same moment, and a second ashtray is laid on the bed.

"I don't think we're ever going to see it happen," Rao says. "Like the static on the cameras at Polheath. It won't let us see it."

"Or we're not letting ourselves see it," Adam says. "Try again."

A crowd of glass ashtrays are strewn across the carpet and piled upon the bed. One rests on the windowsill, another on a ceiling fan blade. Rao's just worked out how to make things appear exactly where he wants them; it requires a form of expectant focus that's somehow orthogonal to the process of creation, and he's thrilled with himself for getting the knack, for having managed to put one right there on the fan. He walks over, reaches to pick it from its perch, drops it next to the others on the bed; it clinks as it hits one of its siblings.

"Housekeeping's going to be a bit freaked out," he snickers, sitting back on the bed.

Adam doesn't respond. His face is no longer lit with fascination. It's turned exceedingly grave. He's picked up the nearest ashtray and is turning it in his hand, watching the light refract through it. "They're all exactly the same. Why make these?"

"I need a smoke, probably."

"No. I mean, is this an ashtray from your childhood?"

Rao shrugs. "Could be. It'll be one I've seen, somewhere, sometime, yeah." He shuts his eyes for a few seconds. "Hotel bar in Istanbul. Long vac, second year at college. Overdid the absinthe."

Adam fits the ashtray in his palm, hoists it a few times to assess its weight. Seeing it, Rao thinks of the Egyptian goddess of truth. Maat. How one of her feathers was weighed against a human heart after its owner's death. The finality of that weighing, the decision it entailed: whether the afterlife would be a fitting place for each individual human soul. He watches Adam weigh the ashtray in his hand and feels the vacancy at his core, the tiny hole that's the foreknowledge of death, and he knows it's speaking to the Prophet inside him. He doesn't know what it's saying, but he knows that Prophet is speaking back. He shivers. *This stuff*, he thinks, *it does this*. Makes him get religious. Hey ho. He's had worse.

"That lizard," Adam says thoughtfully, "wasn't like the horse. It was perfect."

Rao beams. "Yeah. It was. They were. Still are."

Adam puts the ashtray back on the bed, rocks it with a finger. "My guess is, if I'd opened it up, I wouldn't have been able to know it was a telltale."

"Are we calling them telltales now?"

"Rhodes started to use the term for the EPGOs that move. You don't like it?"

"No, it's a good name," Rao admits grudgingly, because it fucking is. For a while he contemplates the way the hotel lights refract through the piles of moulded glass, then clears his throat and assumes his best tutorial voice. "So," he says, "do you know why the lizard was perfect?"

"Because you know the truth about things."

Rao's surprised. "Yeah. Exactly."

"So when you make a telltale—"

"It isn't a telltale at all. I don't make EPGOs. I don't make telltales. What I make is properly, truly alive." He waits for that to sink in. Adam's face shows no sign it has. "You know I'm the only person in the world who can do this?" he adds.

"You made life, Rao," Adam says, low and urgent. "We're not supposed to do that."

Rao smirks. "Nah, people do it all the time. You got made, so did I."

Adam sees his bullshit for what it is, ignores it. "I don't know why I remember this," he goes on slowly, "but there's a word. It's in the first sentence of Genesis. It's *bara*. It means to create things out of nothing. Only God is supposed to create like that, Rao. It's"—he furrows his brow—"it's a serious thing. It's too serious for us to mess with."

Rao rolls his eyes. "So here's another word for you, love. *Lila*. Sanskrit. Means play. Magical creativity. Hindu gods play like that, which is how the world got made. Serious play, but play all the same." He pouts. "Also, monotheism's a drag. No offence."

Adam nods thoughtfully. He took that well, Rao thinks, surprised, before realising the response wasn't acceptance but the patient indulgence Rao's always got from Adam when he's high.

"Ok," Adam says. Glances across the room to the kitchenette. "I'm thirsty. I'm going to get some water, and then—"

"Are you fucking serious? What kind of water do you want? Come on, put your hand out flat in front of you, palm up. I'll make you a glass of water."

Adam doesn't look happy about it. But he proffers his left hand. And a few seconds later Rao watches it dip slightly as it takes the weight of a glass pulled from the air.

Adam focuses on the glass. He swallows. His hand is shaking: the surface of the water shivers. The briefest tremble crosses his features.

"It's not poison. You can drink it."

"Rao," Adam whispers. "This glass."

"Yeah, I dunno why it turned out like that. Just wanted to make you a glass of water." He leans closer. It's plastic, not glass. It's a plastic glass. It's printed with Walt Disney's signature in red at the top, and below it is a cartoon image of Cinderella in a gilded chair. Flat golden hair, an orange-and-white pinafore. She's lifting her foot to her kneeling prince. Behind her, a castle. Mice at her feet. Stars, everywhere.

"I've seen this before. One just like this. When I was a kid."

"Huh," Rao says. "Huh."

CHAPTER 59

Distant sirens outside. Rao isn't ready to open his eyes, so he truth-tests his way to the time. It's 8:12 a.m., Sunday the twenty-fourth of October. What happened on this date? He pulls a sheaf of facts from memory. Rosa Parks died. The United Nations was founded. Antonie van Leeuwenhoek's birthday. Ronnie and Reggie Kray's birthday. Release date of *The Manchurian Candidate*. The first one, not the remake. He loves that movie.

He can't smell coffee. He cracks an eye. Adam's bed is made and his running shoes are gone. So selfish. He could have made a pot before he left. Rao hauls himself out of bed, knocks the Disney glass at his feet over as he does. *Fuck*. He'd put the glass on the floor because it'd felt wrong to keep it in Adam's sight. He'd piled the ashtrays on the carpet, too, over on the other side of his bed. Is he ashamed of the things he's made? No, it's not shame. Something else. He's not sure what, but he's not been in the mood to figure it out.

By the time Rao's dressed and made coffee, Adam's returned. He vanishes into the shower, reappears in his usual government white shirt and dark tie and trousers, pours himself a mug from the pot, and stands by the window drinking it.

"See anything exciting on your run, love?"

"No."

"See anything exciting out there now?"

"No."

"That's good, I suppose. We're going in today, yes?"

"It's Sunday."

"Absolutely it is, but I want to go in."

"Ok, Rao."

On Sunday, the Lunastus facility has the hush of a business district hotel at three in the morning. There'll be a skeleton nursing team on the ward, but the upper floors are deserted. Pacing along the main corridor with Adam, Rao starts trying doors. They're all locked except two: one opens into a small meeting room and the other a walk-in cupboard full of office supplies.

"Aha. Want to nick some pens?" he asks.

Adam shakes his head. His expression is tight.

"What is it?"

"You're looking for something."

An observation, not a question. And he's right. Rao *is* looking for something. He just doesn't know what it is. Feels like the first, low ache of wanting to use. Like he's put something down somewhere and forgotten what it is, knowing the only way to remember is to find it. "Veronica's not in today," he announces, closing the cupboard door. "Monty's here, though." The second assertion doesn't feel entirely true. He mutters a few sentences beneath his breath. "He's in the anteroom to the test chamber, doing something with Prophet. Fuck knows what. Probably telling it all his problems."

Adam doesn't smile. "Something's off, Rao," he says.

Something is. Rao's known that since he walked through the doors. "It's just quiet, love," he throws out. "Sundays are always weird in offices. When I was a kid me and some mates broke into a local solicitor's one weekend for shits and grins. It was spooky as hell. *Mary Celeste* with wonky filing cabinets. We stole some biscuits."

His stupid reminiscence doesn't help at all. They both walk faster now, take the elevator to the lower floor in silence. By the time they reach the first of the double doors to the test chamber anteroom, Rao's prickling with disquiet and Adam's holding his left hand open over his sidearm. There's no real reason for this little folie à deux, Rao tells himself, this contagious paranoia. He discovers that's not true.

In the airlock space they look at each other.

"We're not imagining this, Adam," Rao says.

Adam's lips twitch. "Doesn't matter if we are. Won't make any difference if Prophet's involved."

"Ugh," Rao says. "Why does this feel like the end of *Butch Cassidy and the Sundance Kid*?"

"This isn't a movie, Rao. I'm going through."

He's back in seconds with a terse sitrep. "Montgomery's down. His dose of Prophet made a dog. He's hugging it. Unresponsive. Fridge is open, looks like the syringes have been tampered with. You ok to go in?"

"Of course I fucking am."

*

Adam's no stranger to premonition. He's experienced it a bunch of times. Service members talk about it a lot in active combat zones. Could be a sudden conviction of an impending attack, a feeling that alerts you to a hidden IED. "Spidey sense" is the term everyone uses. The Defense Department prefers "precognition involving advanced perceptual competencies." Adam knows it's nothing supernatural. It's experience. Pattern recognition. Gestalt analysis. It's unconscious knowledge is all, and that's how he's been trying to think of what keeps happening with Rao.

But Prophet must be involved. Nobody could've absorbed that much Prophet, like Rao, and not have it affect their brain. Nobody can repel Prophet the way Adam does and not have some consequence. He's pretty sure the threat he feels right now has nothing to do with anything he's seen and everything to do with what Rao is picking up.

That Disney glass last night fucked him up. But it makes sense, somehow, that that's something Rao can do. Pull memories out of Adam and make them real. It's probably his fault. He's not as guarded as he should be. He's getting too attached again, because lately it's been feeling like it felt when they worked together in Central Asia, easy as breathing. He's just obsessing. He shouldn't. But he's trying not to worry about what he's doing and whether it fucks him up. It's paying off. They're getting answers—and new questions—every single day.

Rao pushes by him, muttering that he hates it when Adam goes vacant like this, and makes his way to the fridge where Prophet is kept. Montgomery is curled on the floor in front of it, fingers flared against the fur of what looks like a rust-black-white beagle pressed to his chest, both figures illuminated by the cold light pouring from the open refrigerator door.

"Fuck's sake, Monty," Rao mutters, kneeling beside him. Montgomery's head is bowed, face obscured, forehead pressed to the dog. When Rao goes to place his palm to the bare skin of his exposed nape, the dog Montgomery is holding growls, squirms against his body to try to get to Rao. He snatches his hand back in surprise. Adam kneels, one knee on Montgomery's leg as an anchor, and holds down the dog, now snapping at Rao. It's partially inside Montgomery's chest, he realizes. Only three of its legs are visible, and under that enfolding arm he can make out flashes of teeth and a single eye. The way Montgomery has rounded his back to wrap around the animal inside him reminds Adam of how people curl their own bodies to protect an injury.

He feels an overwhelming need to get away from the beagle, from Montgomery, from this manifestation. As far away as possible from what they have both become. He presses down on the dog's neck, on Montgomery's shoulder. "Do it, Rao," he says. Silently, Rao nods. Reaches again for that exposed skin. The beagle kicks and growls into Montgomery's chest, fighting Adam's hold on them both, but Rao does what he needs to do.

Adam doesn't think he'll ever get used to seeing Rao do this. Heal people. Cure them of Prophet. It's not just that the act should be impossible. It's how Rao looks when he does it. Never the same. Sometimes his jaw goes slack, eyes open, seeing nothing in front of him. Pupils blown and far away. No way for Adam to know what he's feeling or seeing or doing, and he doesn't know how to start asking about it. Sometimes Rao's eyes are closed like he's concentrating. Brows drawn and serious. Only moving to take deep breaths, letting the inhalations move his body. This time, he's bowed over Montgomery with his eyes half closed, lashes fluttering too quickly. Adam watches and, like every other time before, he sees beads of Prophet press themselves out of Montgomery's skin before disappearing into Rao's.

As Rao takes his hand from Montgomery's neck, the arm Montgomery had wrapped around the body of the dog drops onto the tiled floor. His other arm keeps a tight grip, fingers splayed deep across fur.

"This is fucked," Rao says. He sounds far away. Voice thick like he's just woken up or as though he's emotionally overcome. "Monty? Can you let go of the dog?"

Montgomery doesn't respond verbally, just moves his mouth against the top of the dog's head. Adam frowns. Everyone that Rao's cured so far has dropped or moved away from their EPGO as soon as they were able. That's obviously impossible here.

"He can't, Rao," Adam tells him, looking at the hand on the beagle. Montgomery isn't just running his fingers through the fur. There's rust-colored fur growing through his skin. His fingernails. Rao still hasn't seen that the dog's inside Montgomery's chest. Still hasn't seen the fur through the skin. Doesn't seem to comprehend the truth of what this is. Wildly, Adam considers if he can get Rao out of the room before he does—but it's already too late. Rao's attempting to turn Montgomery onto his back, and he's seeing all of it—and more. The wild white of the dog's visible eye as it growls, whines, squirms in Montgomery's chest. The fur growing up from his neck, into his mouth, onto his tongue, as Montgomery tries to speak. "Get," he whispers haltingly. "Call—"

"I'm calling Rhodes," Adam declares, standing up. He needs to get Rao out and he needs her to take charge of this clusterfuck. Montgomery looks terrified, eyes wide, fighting for breath that isn't there. He starts coughing. Then choking.

"Adam," Rao pleads, holding Montgomery down as he convulses. Adam's already on the phone.

"Rhodes," he says as soon as she picks up. "We're in your test room lab. There's been an incident. Contamination. Dr. Montgomery is down." *He's not going to make it*, Adam thinks, looking at him as he twitches out. Lungs aren't meant to have beagles in them. He doesn't say that out loud. "Get down here."

*

Rao's seen a lot of shit. But nothing holds a candle to watching Monty's corpse jerk with the struggles of a beagle trapped half inside him. It's never getting away from him. It's trapped, and it looks terrified. He can't know if this dog is conscious or just acting as if it is. The answer is clouded by Prophet. But it can see. It can definitely see.

It's quietened itself now. Looks defeated. Its head is laid flat against Monty's cooling chest. Occasionally it licks its lips. Monty's mouth has fallen open. There's a thin trail of blood and saliva from its corner. His tongue is frosted with fur. They're waiting for Veronica to arrive. Rao's here on the floor, tightly hugging his knees, and Adam's in front of the fridge, face stark in the light streaming from its open door. *He'll be used to shit like this*, Rao thinks. Not the dog bit. Mortally wounded people he knows dying in front of him because Adam's unable to help. Maybe he does help. Maybe he puts them out of their misery, which is a crime—mercy killings are a crime—but maybe he should have asked Adam to shoot Monty. Shoot him, then the dog. Then turn the gun on Rao.

Adam turns from the fridge, puzzled. "A lot of these syringes are empty, but the seals are intact."

"Doesn't surprise me," Rao says dully. "I've lost the capacity for surprise."

"I think you should take a look."

"I don't think I can get up right now, Adam. I just murdered Monty."

"That wasn't you. Wasn't murder. Prophet killed him."

"He was alive until I took it out."

Adam picks out one of the vacuum-sealed vessels. Walks it over, holds it in front of Rao's eyes. It's perfectly intact, but there's no gleaming liquid inside. Over the surface of the glass, a tracery of frost-like lines. Delicate chasing. Rao thinks of tarakasi. Filigree silver wire. He rubs one ear, hard. Can't stop himself from touching the glass with the outstretched fingertips of his other hand. The lines fade as they sink into his skin. Just the faintest tremor inside him, now. A ticking needle on a seismograph.

"So we're working while we wait for Veronica, are we?" he grates out, when the glass is clear.

"I'm just trying to understand what happened here."

Rao hugs his knees more tightly. "Feel fucking free."

"When did he get exposed?"

Adam doesn't always get sarcasm. Rao sighs and mutters to himself. "Saturday evening," he concludes. "Yesterday. About ten o'clock."

"I think he opened the fridge when Prophet had already escaped the glassware inside. Breathed it in," Adam says.

Rao screws up his face. "He couldn't have breathed in all of it. There wasn't that much inside him, by the feel of it."

There's a faint *clink* as Adam replaces the vessel on its shelf. He walks back and drops into a crouch by Rao's side. He sits silent for a while, looking at the floor. "Rao," he begins. "You said when Prophet changes, it changes everywhere, at the same time."

"Yeah."

"I just thought of something."

"And you're going to enlighten me."

Adam nods. "If I took off my tie and draped it over that chair, the two ends would be in different places, right? If I poured water on the middle of the tie, it'd soak down through the material at the same rate. So both ends would get wet at the same time. Or they would if the tie was all the same width."

"What the fuck are you talking about?"

"It's just a way of visualizing it, Rao. I think all of Prophet's connected, like the tie. Somewhere else. We just see the ends."

Adam's face is expectant. Eager. Rao hasn't a fucking clue. He's absolutely . . . no. *Wait.* "What, you mean connected in another dimension?"

"Maybe."

Here and somewhere else.

"It's just a theory," Adam says. "Is it one you can test?"

He might be able to. He tries. Shakes his head.

"Because it's about Prophet?"

"Or because I'm full of it," he says glumly.

"About that, Rao. If Prophet is connected in another dimension, it could be how the vessels got to be empty in the fridge. Maybe it can move easily between places. And that . . ."

He looks at Rao hesitantly. Cautiously.

"What?"

"That could be why you're still walking, Rao," he says urgently. "This could be why you're ok."

"I'm not ok, you fuckwit," Rao hisses. "In case you'd forgotten, Monty's dead. I killed him. He's lying on the floor right there, and there's a dog inside his chest that's probably never going to die."

At that, Adam's face turns blank and he rises quickly to his feet, eyes fixed upon the door.

"She's here."

Veronica strides into the room in sneakers and velvet loungewear, face pale and free of lipstick, hair drawn back, a black rucksack hanging from one hand. Wordlessly, she kneels to examine Montgomery, propping the bag by her side. Hesitantly, she lowers two fingers to the dog's broad skull. It doesn't growl, just wrinkles its forehead, twitching its eye towards her. She takes her hand away, reaches into the bag, and pulls out the penknife she'd used to cut the horse. Rao winces.

"Can't the postmortem wait?" he protests.

"This isn't a postmortem," she says, running the blade through the plaid of Montgomery's shirt and tugging the fabric away. She runs a finger over the fur that spreads outwards over his chest from the dog's pelt. "Seamless," she whispers, before placing a hand on the beagle's neck, curling her fingers around it. "And a dog without a pulse. How did he die?"

"I did it," Rao says.

"Asphyxiation," Adam says. "As soon as Prophet was pulled out of him."

"Yes," she says. "That would happen." She sits back on her heels, pulls her BlackBerry from the front pocket of the bag, taps the keypad. She's calling someone on her team. Asking them to come in. Deal with the situation. After cutting the call, she gets up to inspect the inside of the fridge. "We'll manage this," she says. "No reason to cancel the test we've scheduled for you, Rao. Colonel Rubenstein, I'd be grateful if you could take him back to your hotel and call me if there's any deterioration in his health. I'll see him tomorrow at one."

PART III

CHAPTER 60

The red LEDs on the motel clock radio swim into focus: 10:36. *Ugh,* Rao grunts. *Why is it light?*

It's morning, he realises, swearing at the clock. Yesterday he'd climbed into bed as soon as they got back, pulled the covers over his head, and curled himself into a foetal position. Two seconds of that was all he could bear; felt far too akin to Monty's fatal canine hug. He'd turned onto his stomach, buried his face in the pillow. Then, like he has too many times before, he took a breath, exhaled, and let his misery and failure in. Let himself sink through it like miles of scalding water, letting it burn. Letting it burn, knowing he'd survive. Because that's the joke, isn't it. It's always other people who die.

For a few hours, that burning descent was all there was. Adam hadn't tried to make him feel better. Rao appreciated that. But he'd brought him water. Asked if he wanted food. Rao'd shaken his head against the pillow. Didn't want it, didn't deserve it.

He'd expected insomnia, a long white night coruscating with memories of Monty's last terrible moments. But he'd passed out and slept for hours. And now he can remember only brief flashes of what happened. Monty's fingernails, stiff with fur. A curved white canine below the dog's raised lip as it growled. The corner of Monty's mouth as he begged for rescue and air. And none of these memories feel like they should. They're clear but distant. Buried. Deep behind glass. Perhaps Prophet's doing this, he thinks. Protecting him from PTSD. He can't tell if that's true. Couldn't care less if it is. Or isn't. His eyes ache. Ghostly patterns branch behind his vision. And most of all he's thirsty. Dust parched. Arid. Death Valley in June. When he remembers he's nil by mouth until the PET scan at one he groans out loud. It's ridiculous Veronica's not cancelled it. Obscene.

He pushes himself up on his elbows. Doesn't feel dizzy. No nausea. He's ok. He's doing ok. And there's a toppling wash of gratitude when he sees Adam at the door of their room, signing for a delivery like a normal person.

"You've got mail," he announces.

"Give it here," Rao croaks.

His name is spelled correctly on the plastic sleeve. He tears it open. Inside is a heavy-stock cream-coloured envelope. Inside that, a letter on Lunastus-Dainsleif stationery. The familiar logo of a stylised warplane silhouetted above the concentric bands of a Wi-Fi signal. He's always been impressed by that logo. Perfectly trite, perfectly blunt.

He squints at the type. His eyes aren't behaving. He wants to ask Adam to read it to him. He doesn't.

"Fuck me," he says, faintly shocked. "They want me on staff."

"They?"

"Lunastus."

"Congratulations," Adam deadpans. A beat of silence. Then, cautiously, he adds, "What do they want you to do?"

"After this project's complete, assist with their corporate negotiations. Fuck that."

"It's a salary, Rao."

"It's a fucking massive salary. Fuck that too." Rao shakes his head. "Stuck in offices and boardrooms all day? In Sunnyvale? I'll fucking perish."

"Sure, but it's not prison."

"Fuck off with your logic, Adam."

"You hate it when I'm right."

"I loathe it." He lets out a long, theatrical sigh. "I should warn you, I'm in a very, very bad mood this morning, Adam."

"I'll survive."

Rao's just dressed when there's another knock on their door. This one is soft, almost shy. Adam moves to the window, narrows his eyes through the sheet of polyester voile.

"The goons are back. Not the same ones as before. They're carrying but they look polite," he murmurs. A twitch of his eyebrows, amused. "They just saw me and put their hands up."

"Did they? You've given us a reputation, love."

Rao pads to the door, puts his mouth to the plywood, and shouts, "Can I help you?"

"We're here for a scheduled pickup on behalf of Lunastus-Dainsleif LLC. We don't want any trouble." The voice is gruff, apologetic.

"Not on my schedule. Where are we going?"

"The airport, sir."

The helicopter is waiting for them at Centennial, rotors turning. It's a Bell 427, Rao observes. He has no interest in aviation but a few years ago he'd flicked through a Bell brochure in a GCHQ meeting room and learned all the models for a laugh.

Inside the cabin, Adam angles his head to locate the sun, checks his watch. Even before the pilot opens the throttle, he's folded his arms, leaned back in his seat, and closed both eyes. Rao envies his composure, knows the mood he's in won't permit him even the semblance of sleep. He watches the ground tilt away, golf courses and streets slipping past, turning to patterned foothills, forests, sluggish valleys.

After forty minutes, the ride gets rougher, the light sharper, brighter, hollowing out the cabin. They're over proper mountains now, snowfields, each fitful negative G plucking at the hollowness in Rao's stomach. When the Bell starts to throttle back, Adam opens his eyes, looks at his watch again, mouths: *Aspen*.

They land on a helipad near the top of a snowy ridge. The doors open into freezing air and their escorts gesture at them to leave. Ducking out onto the pavement, Rao laughs out loud, giddy with the whole Bond-movie knife-edge nonsense of all this on top of last night's horrors. But when the Bell rises through clouds of blade-lifted powder, climbs higher and straight-lines it northeast, its passage fills the valley with a collapsing, proliferating mess of echoes that remind Rao so insistently of the last few seconds before the impossible clock, he looks at Adam worriedly.

Adam's watching the helicopter rise. He doesn't look remotely concerned. In fact, he looks— *Shit*. Snow light does very good things to Adam's face. After the Bell disappears over a jagged row of peaks, he turns to Rao, jaw set tight, snow on his lashes, dusting his hair. Jerks his head towards the chalet above them, windows blank and blue with sky.

The door is unlocked. Rao follows Adam inside, boots dropping hexagons of compacted snow on the mat and across several feet of well-waxed pine. He blinks, eyes slowly adapting, and as the darkness recedes, he sees a space fitted out in full Alpine Cowboy style. A perfect log fire crackles brightly in the grate. The air is rich with cedar and cinnamon.

"Over here!"

The man on the pale-grey couch is wearing a dark-grey Pendleton cardigan and is slitting open the seal on a Cabela's sporting goods catalogue with a deer's-foot pommel knife. But somehow he's also giving the impression he's sitting back with his arms spread along the back of the seat. That's how easy he is here, in one of the many transposable spaces that wealth and power call home. Rao has seen men like him in any number of places like this, but right now it occurs to him that he's never wanted to punch one quite as much. The man's impossibly handsome. Cut glass jaw, a sweep of silvering blond hair over deep-blue eyes. Looks like a Ralph Lauren model. Paul Newman's lovechild if he'd fucked JFK.

"Hey," the man says. "Thanks for coming. I appreciate it."

"That's nice. Who the fuck are you?" Rao says.

"Lane. Just Lane. Hungry?"

Green salad and dauphinoise potatoes. Ribeye steak, very rare. They're served by a silent woman in a black cotton apron with a tight, dark ponytail and a white gold solitaire on her ring finger; she's avoiding everyone's eyes with more, Rao suspects, than purely professional courtesy. After she's finished at the table, Lane calls her over and murmurs something in her ear. She nods unhappily and returns to the kitchen.

Lane drags a bowl towards him, spoons a pile of what look like green peppercorns onto the slick of watery blood on his plate. "I grow these," he says to Rao, picking one up between finger and thumb and crunching it. "Back on the ranch. Bird chilis. You must be a spicy food aficionado. Want some?"

"No, thank you."

Afterwards there's French press coffee with single cream. Chocolate cake. Adam ignores the slice set before him. Rao shovels his down; he's not sure he's ever needed sugar more. Lane watches him eat approvingly. "Ever had cake this good?" he enquires, holding up a forkful. "We call it Death by Chocolate."

"You know, as a matter of fact, I have," Rao grates out. The cake's fucking awful and watching Lane's theatrics as he prepares himself to say whatever the fuck it is he wants to tell them is becoming an agony. Finally, Lane pulls a smear of frosting from his plate with a finger, sucks it clean, then smiles. "So, we have a time-critical situation, and a little bird told me he's a human polygraph, so I'm going to lay it all on the table for you. Literally. Ana?"

Lane pads off once the table's cleared and returns from behind a door with a bulky roll of paper. "PHOTINT," he says almost lubriciously. He flattens it out. Anchors its opposing corners with *A Celebration of Aspen Through the Ages* and a book of alpine cookery.

Rao's stomach is a knot of refusal seeing the familiar colours of it from his seat. Dry hillsides, cloud shadow; an aerial photograph of an arid landscape. He's seen broken men held over tables because of images like these. He doesn't want to give Lane the satisfaction of watching him examine it more closely, but Adam has no such qualms. He stands, bends low over the table, instantly consumed with interest. "Ten centimetre," he says. "161?"

Lane nods, his smile genuine and bright. "Friends in very high places."

Rao assumes 161's a spy satellite. *Yes.* "Where's this of?" he asks.

"Nevada. Area 25."

Adam nods. "Yeah, Jackass Flats. But what's this?" He drops a finger to the paper, taps it.

"That is the situation," Lane says.

Fine, Rao thinks, pushing back his chair.

In the centre of the sheet, milk-coloured shapes that look like the roofs of an industrial facility. Adam's index finger is laid on a darker area encircling them. Tightly packed against the buildings, the darkness lessens the farther from the site it extends, so that the pattern resembles material thrown up by an impact crater. Only the buildings appear undamaged and there is no crater. Rao leans closer. Not rocks. More like a junkyard in the desert. Where the debris is thickest it's incomprehensible, but farther out there are angles that resemble tilted roof ridges, patches of green, a fairground carousel, a stretch of golden sand bisected by what could be a marquee, and on the other side of the building, near Adam's finger, the nose of . . .

"Is that a 747?"

Adam nods. "Pan Am."

"Shit," Rao says. "Yeah, this is a situation."

"EPGOs," Lane says. "You're familiar."

"We are," Adam confirms.

"This is our main facility for the EOS PROPHET program. All this appeared around the site four days ago."

"All at once?"

"All at once."

Rao blinks. "When exactly?"

"Just after three p.m."

Rao's head itches at that. Four days ago, he was—what was he doing at just past three? Scratching his beard, he thinks back. "Fuck," he says, with a sharp inhale. So that was it. The avalanche in his head when he'd taken Dinah Crossland's hand. He'd known instantly something had happened. Something insensibly vast. A shock wave, a slamming door. Somehow, that contact had triggered the deposition of thousands of objects around ground zero. He thinks of Michelangelo's *Creation of Adam* and hates that the fresco came so quickly to mind. A spark across empty air. It's horribly self-absorbed to give himself such a pivotal role, but the problem is it's true. He's a fucking freak. *Sunil the special case.* He feels a corrosive burst of self-loathing, remembering Crossland's ashen face. The blood trickling from her nose as Veronica ushered her out of the room.

"I said, does alcohol mess with your powers, Sunil?"

Adam's giving him a warning look. It's just funny enough to pull him out of his bout of caustic introspection. "No."

Lane nods, satisfied. Produces a bottle of Johnnie Walker Blue Label, to Rao's secret amusement. Rao sets the glass down by his right elbow, surprised how little he wants what's in it. Lane takes a slow mouthful, savours it. "I let you into our Aurora facility, of course. You wouldn't have gotten in otherwise. I already knew how special you were, Sunil. Figured our project could use your ability to detect fakes. But the whole polygraph thing? Finding that out took some serious favours."

"I expect it did."

"It's ok. I was owed a bunch."

"I'm sure," Rao says. He's got Lane's measure now. He's a very particular species of charming bastard, one with an ability Rao has encountered in a few people over the years. Get too close, talk to him too long, and you'll start to feel he's on your side, no matter what bollocks he feeds you. In Rao's experience, this ability to instil entirely unwarranted confidence is the mark of a monster, but that doesn't make it any less effective, and despite his instant dislike of the man, he's having to work surprisingly hard against it. "How are Heather and Bill?"

Lane's smile turns a little frozen. "I'm sorry—?"

"Your friends, I assume? Came with us on a flight from Mildenhall. Got joined by some other friends in a broken-down van."

"Sunil, no offense was meant. We just wanted to know where you were. Keep an eye on you. Protect you," Lane says earnestly. "I thought you'd be potential assets to our project. And I was right. Speaking of which, Montgomery was very worried about what you boys did to yourselves that first day in Aurora. He's a nervous kind of guy, and things like that eat at him, you know? He thought what happened was a test. It wasn't, of course. You know that. It was what scientists call serendipity. It was highly serendipitous." Lane stumbles a little over the word the second time. He's only recently learned it, Rao determines, batting back an unwanted flash of sympathy. Lane hasn't been told about Montgomery.

"I've seen what you can do, Sunil. I watched the footage. It's truly wonderful. Extraordinary. And that's the reason I made the executive decision to pick you up and bring you here." He nods at the satellite photograph. "Let's leave this on the table. We'll get back to it in a sec. I'd like you to meet someone." He pushes back his chair. It grates on the wooden floor; with the noise, Adam rises to his feet. Watching him do so, a soft rush of apprehension climbs Rao's spine. Only lately has he learned the subtle differences between Adam's everyday demeanour and his ready-to-break-necks one. This is breaking necks, for sure. His brows are minutely raised, eyes a little darker, jaw a little tighter, and he's suffused with a sudden sense of ease, like he's just worked out the answer to a complicated question. He puts himself between Rao and Lane as the latter leads them through the lounge to the back of the lodge. Lane knocks on a pine door. A few seconds pass. He gives them both an apologetic glance and opens it.

CHAPTER 61

A large, pine-walled bedroom in near darkness. A rustic king-size bed with geometric-printed linens. An unlit elk antler chandelier. A steer skull mounted by the window, a crack of snowy daylight between the drawn curtains that catches at Rao's eyes like a blade—and a blond man on his knees on a Navajo rug between the bed and the wall. He's surrounded by sheets of paper and is scribing something on one, bent low so Rao can't see his face, just his arms and hands. Blue sweatshirt, sleeves rolled to the elbow. A Garmin watch hanging loose from a wrist that's all bone. His skin—

"Josh?" Lane ventures.

The hush is stifling. There's the deep croaking call of a raven outside and the soft scratch of pencil on paper. "The son of a family friend," Lane informs them sotto voce. "He's a weapons system officer with the 22nd Fighter Wing at Polheath. You can guess what we think happened. He . . . he isn't talking or eating. He isn't doing well." He gestures sadly at the untouched plate of steak on the desk by the window.

An en suite door opens on the far side of the room, and a person in a nurse's tabard and trousers enters. "This is Jo Seul-ki," Lane tells them. "She's taking care of Josh."

"Hi," Rao says. "I'm Rao. This is Adam. Lane told you about our visit?"

She nods. "He did, yes."

"That's good. He didn't tell us," Rao says, stepping farther into the room, soles catching on and lifting the sheets littering the floor, moving until he gets a better view of Josh's face. He's hollow cheeked, fixated on the page he's working on, staring through it to something far, far beneath. The skin of his face, neck, and arms is covered with a palimpsest of grids, some drawn in ink, others not: the darker, thinner, criss-crossing lines are beaded with dried blood.

"He did that to himself, didn't he," Rao observes.

Lane lowers his voice. "Unfortunately, yes. He stopped when we gave him paper."

Rao looks at the papers around him. Some of them are covered in letters, each one surrounded by a box. Some are carefully drawn grids. There are stars and badges and—

"Scrabble," Adam says.

"Scrabble," Rao repeats, rubbing the back of his neck and turning to Lane.

"He was on his morning run when the incident with the fire occurred at Polheath," Lane explains. "But he was fine. Never saw the EPGO we assume he made. He lost his appetite, got headaches, and was apparently a little subdued, but nothing else. He was due some leave and came back stateside to visit his girlfriend in Pismo. They were surfing when this happened. Real lucky he wasn't in the water at the time. He just sat down on the sand and started drawing in it with his fingers for hours. His girlfriend called his parents and they took him in. All the doctors thought it was some kind of psychotic break. We know better, of course. Josh's folks know I know the right people, and they asked me if I could help."

"Have you tried getting him a Scrabble set?" Adam asks. Rao is almost certain it's a joke. No. He's 50 percent certain it wasn't.

"His parents gave him one. He was excited until he picked it up, but then he lost interest and went back to this."

"It wasn't the right one," Adam says, rubbing at his mouth. He looks disgusted, like he had in Polheath after sawing through the Scrabble box that might, Rao realises, have been Josh's EPGO. No. His was the other box, the one with wooden tiles.

"When did this sudden decline happen?" Rao asks.

"A few days ago."

"How many days?"

Lane frowns. "Five?"

Adam looks at Rao.

"Just past three in the afternoon?" Rao says. He's not surprised to find it's true.

"Could be," Lane admits, then his face brightens. "You think there's a connection?"

"Yes, I do. You want me to cure him, I suppose?"

"His family and the United States Air Force would be indebted, Sunil. I'd like you to try."

"I don't try," Rao snaps, then mutters, "There is no try."

He crouches close to Josh, looks at him closely. It seems straightforward. There's no object. No Scrabble set protruding from his chest. But the emptiness that pours from the man is like chill air through an open window. And after killing Nancy the teapot lady and watching Montgomery breathe his last, after seeing the vacancy in those eyes, he's not optimistic Josh will be back in his fighter jet after this. He turns his head to Adam a little uncertainly. And Adam steps forward. Good. Adam'll be his backstop, should Josh wake in a mood of rabid revenge.

"Mr Rao?" It's Seul-ki. "Do you need assistance?"

"Not for this bit," Rao tells her. "Maybe afterwards. Thank you. Could you give us a bit of space?" He takes a breath, raises a hand, and rests it on Josh's left shoulder. Nothing. He flicks his eyes up to Adam's face.

"Ok?"

"Tickety-boo." Rao smiles, shifting his hand to the back of Josh's neck. He's not warm, he's not cold, he's not anything. There might have been a flinch. Yes. Just the merest twitch of muscles, and then Prophet ticks against his skin and he brings it in. Tides rise and ebb in that dust-wet space between and through all things. There's the familiar host of lights drifting too close, at ineffable distance, but there's more this time, a sense that Prophet's impatient, that it's leaving something deformed irreparably under its weight, and then Rao's back, waiting for the tiredness to pass, wondering not for the first time how long this healing process takes. Because he's not there when it happens, is he. Not quite.

"He's awake!" Lane exclaims. "Look, he's back with us!"

Adam's looking. Rao's looking. Seul-ki's looking. And so is Josh. He's dropped his pencil, has lifted the hand that wielded it, is staring at his fingers. Something like a sob passes through his body, and with that, Seul-ki's there, swift and certain, guiding him up into a sitting position on the rug. Josh is looking around now, as if he's taking in his surroundings, but Rao's not sure he can see them at all. There's not much change in his eyes. Still looking through, not at.

"Josh?" Lane says. "It's Zachary. We met a few years ago in Ketchum, at your folks' place."

Josh doesn't raise his eyes to Lane. "Why," he says. His voice is flat, emptiness still pouring from him.

"It was Christmas and New Year's. How are you feeling?"

"Kay," Josh says.

"Wonderful, Sunil," Lane exclaims as Rao gets up from the floor. "Is all the—"

"There's no Prophet in him anymore."

"And it doesn't . . . affect you?"

"Not dead yet."

"Amazing. Just amazing."

Josh shuffles himself up to hug his own knees, lays his tilted head against them, closing his eyes. His mouth is moving. Rao's close enough to hear him. "Kay," he's whispering. "Five points."

Lane clears his throat. "So I understand it takes time for a patient to fully recover after . . . what you do. We'll leave him in the capable hands of our nurse and you have all our gratitude." He extends a hand for Rao to shake.

"I wouldn't," Adam says.

"No. No, of course. Ha. Head back to the table, I'll join you in a short while. I need a word with Seul-ki, ok?"

"Josh is completely fucked," Rao breathes, after they leave the room.

"Yeah."

"You saw that?"

"I did. Don't know how Lane didn't."

"Wishful thinking?"

"Could be."

Rao shakes his head. "I fucking knew it was going to go tits up."

"How?"

Rao exhales heavily. "Dunno. Everything about him. Soon as I saw him."

"You got the Prophet out," Adam says. "That's all that Lane needed for his little demo."

"That was a demo?"

Adam gives him a sidelong look. "That was a demo. I doubt Lane gives a shit about Josh. Depends."

"On what?"

"On how important Josh's family is. And why we're here."

Lane returns a minute later, ushers them both back to the table, cracks his knuckles. "So," he says. "Let's get to the point."

"Josh wasn't the point?" Rao asks.

"Josh was a miracle," Lane says. "And very much to the point. The reason I brought you here," he continues, tapping the photograph, "is because we have a situation on top of a situation. Our facility has gone dark."

Adam raises his eyes from the tabletop. "Same time the EPGOs manifested?"

"No. After that."

"How long after?"

"A day after. Three days ago."

"Hostiles?"

Lane grimaces. "Yeah. We got a phone call before the lines went down. One of our engineers talking about people trying to get in. It sounded highly kinetic."

"How many personnel on-site?"

"Forty-eight."

"One person, one object. So where did all these come from?" Adam asks, like he's lost interest in the matter of hostiles.

Lane doesn't respond.

"Lane?" Rao prompts. "Do you know why there's so many objects around the site?"

"We're not clear on that," Lane says.

"Why don't we move on to things you are clear on," Rao snaps. "How about telling us exactly why we're here?"

"We need a sitrep."

"Oh, the situation's fucked," Rao announces. Adam grins at that, and Rao's just enjoying how marvellous it looks on his face when it happens. He feels the hit of absolute certainty he'll be going to this place. It begins with one of the full-body shivers like stuttering, igniting sodium, but then it hits him fully; for a few seconds it's almost overwhelming. When it recedes, the undertow continues to pull at him, hard. It's smooth and rich and cold and deep and horrifyingly beautiful. He knows instantly it won't leave him. He pulls his eyes back into focus with difficulty, past afterimages of the encircling EPGOs, the pale glow on the wings of the 747.

When he regains the room, Adam is regarding him with concern. "I'm fine," he mutters. Adam looks unconvinced.

"Everything good?" Lane asks.

"Perfect. Go on."

"You sure? You just did your . . . thing with Josh. I thought a drink would help. But if you need—"

"I'm fine," Rao says, pinching the bridge of his nose.

"Good. Good. You're both immune, and we want you in there," Lane says briskly. "I've put together a small team. Very experienced. Dr Rhodes will accompany you." He looks out of the window. "We're not sure what you'll find inside."

"A lot of corpses clutching Rubik's Cubes."

Lane looks unhappy. "Let's hope not, Sunil. We need an extraction." "Who?"

The most curious thing, then: Lane's face flushes, his eyes grow wet. His throat moves a few times. Eventually he speaks. "Steven De Witte," he says.

"Lunastus's CEO? Your billionaire? The bonkers recluse? Oh!" Rao breathes. "It's his baby, isn't it, this whole bloody project."

Lane looks defensive, folds his arms.

"Tell us," Adam instructs. "Hiding things from Rao won't work."

The struggle behind Lane's eyes flares a little brighter, then recedes. He holds up a hand in surrender. "Ok, boys. It's just, this stuff is very, very secret. Force of habit, you know? So, when site security told me these EPGOs had appeared, I called Steven."

Lane takes a breath, then: a vague flash of hurt. "He, uh, decided to take a look himself. Flew to Desert Rock early the next morning and drove in. We have him entering the facility at eleven twenty, and everything went dark just after one."

Rao shivers. Just after one. He remembers it. The sudden cold in the corridor, the sense of being stretched and pulled into threads so fine he covered everywhere, and the ice at his core so searing, so sharp, he couldn't move—and then nothing at all. Nothing until he'd woken, starving, in the small hours, with Adam by his side.

Adam's looking at him. Rao twists his mouth and nods. *Exactly, Adam. That's when it happened.*

"Of course, there may be other casualties," Lane is saying. "But De Witte is our priority. He's a brilliant mind. An important mind. We need him."

Rao raises an eyebrow. "We do, do we? Who's we?"

"America."

Rao laughs out loud. Lane is stung. "You wouldn't understand," he says. "Your partner does." He turns to Adam. "Lieutenant Colonel, you believe in America."

"Yes, sir," he says, face blank, an assent halfway between a rebuke and a snapped salute.

Lane is satisfied with this. "So you're on board?"

Adam purses his lips. "We should talk terms."

"Sure. Remuneration."

"Assurances."

"Assurances, yes, of course . . ."

"And logistics. Helo insertion?"

"Ground transport and hike in. Air's off-limits. We had an unfortunate incident."

"Adam, does he mean a plane crash?" Rao cuts in.

Lane nods sadly. "There's airborne contamination at the site. Has a pretty high ceiling."

"What did you lose?" Adam asks.

"Good men," Lane says.

There's silence for a while.

"What *aircraft* did you lose?"

"A Dash 7."

"ARL-M?"

"Yeah."

"Who's your team?"

"Six men, plus you, Sunil, and Dr Rhodes. Good guy in command. Very experienced. Captain Marcus Roberts. Ex-Delta."

"Where's your forward base?"

"Mercury."

"The secret nuclear town in the desert?" Rao interrupts. "Shit. That's brilliant. I've always wanted to go there."

Adam frowns at him. "There's not much to it these days."

"Have you been there, love?"

"Know people who have."

"Are there aliens?"

"Yes, Rao."

Rao beams at Lane's perplexed expression. Adam's taken control of the room, and Rao's having a good time watching it happen. He sees Adam's expression turn pensive, then, his eyes turn to the window. Rao follows his gaze. The light has changed out there. Bruised clouds are massed above the peaks, the shadows shifted violet from blue. Rao has a sudden apprehension of the weight of all that snow, a ghostly taste of ice in his mouth that turns to granite and quartz, salt ticking quickly on his tongue. He looks back at Adam. *He's sad*, he thinks, suddenly. *Adam is sad.*

"We're going to need more details," Adam announces. "But right now I'm taking Rao outside to confer. More coffee when we get back would be appreciated, Mr Lane. We may be some time."

It's started to snow. Outside the cabin, Rao pulls a full packet of Lucky Strikes and a silver Zippo from his jacket pocket. He frowns at the packet, then extracts two cigarettes, passes one to Adam.

"We're doing this," Rao says.

"I know."

"It'll probably end badly."

"I know that too."

Rao watches Adam drag on his cigarette and exhale, eyes closed.

"Do you believe in America?"

"Rao . . ."

"Seriously."

"I've served for a long time," Adam says, frowning. "It's complicated."

"But?"

Adam looks at Rao then. His expression is so unguarded, so openly transparent Rao's almost frightened for him. "How can anyone believe in America," he says after a while, "and keep their eyes open at the same time?"

"Fucking hell, Adam. Who are you?"

"You know who I am, Rao," he says, taking another drag and watching the smoke rise through falling snow. "I'm nobody."

"We've got a nineteen-thirty charter from Centennial to Desert Rock," Adam informs him on the flight back, voice raised against the helicopter's whine. "The team's arriving tonight. Optimally, you'd stay in Mercury and we bring De Witte to you, but Lane wants you to go in, in case we have casualties." Rao nods. He'd spent the rest of their time in Aspen lying on Lane's obscenely comfy sofa, staring at the flames of the log fire, thinking about the hollowed-out airman in the bedroom while struggling with a bout of indigestion. He looks at Adam's face, striped by sun and flickering shadow, and nods again. He's not sure how to treat this version of Colonel Rubenstein. Maybe this is how Adam always gets before action-man sorties. Rao can't know. But being near him—it's like standing at the base of the Hoover Dam, staring up at the concrete wall, millions of tonnes of water banked up behind it. Only it's not water behind Adam; it's something like grief.

"Who's on this plane?" he asks.

"You, me, Rhodes. Maybe Hunter."

"She can't go in. She's not immune."

"We need a good RTO outside."

"Big favour to ask."

"She'll do it."

"For you?"

Adam shakes his head. "No. Hunter always talks about missions like she's out there saving the world. That's how she'll see this."

He's very serious. And as Rao looks at his unsmiling face, it happens again. It's happened a few times, and it's happening more and more frequently. It doesn't go on for long—maybe a second, a second and a half—and Rao feels it like the aftermath of a punch. It's as if Adam's drawn on tracing paper and beneath it is another Adam drawn on a different sheet, and beneath that another, and beneath them a thousand more, all of them moving differently, all visible at once. Rao's been calling it double vision, but he knows it has nothing to do with his eyes at all.

Another lurch in his stomach. This one has nothing to do with Adam. The ride's far rockier than their trip out here. He looks down. Thick pine forest beneath them, verdigris glazed with ultramarine blue. Scumbled with lead white from all the snow in the air. It's cold in here. Getting colder. He thinks of Hunter and smiles. "You want her there, love. I get it. It's really ok to say so. What's Mercury like?"

"Ghost town. But they still do science at the NNSS. Our nuclear arsenal's getting geriatric, so they run experiments to make sure they still work. Conventional explosives testing. Mostly it's a training site. Special ops, counterterrorism, homeland security. How to handle dirty bombs."

"How do you handle a dirty bomb, Adam?"

"You try not to, Rao."

"Fuck's sake."

"There's supposed to be a pretty good steak house."

"That's cheering. How far away is this Prophet place?"

"Forty minutes north-northeast. It's an old building. Went derelict. Lunastus refitted it." He gives Rao a significant look. "Lane was really into telling me about the renovation."

"Christ, not another one of those boardrooms."

"Doubt it. There'll be blueprints in Mercury and an architect's model for the sand table."

"Sand table?"

"Before we go in, we'll need to familiarise ourselves with what's in the building, what's around it."

"A million Mr. Potato Heads."

Adam shakes his head firmly. "There aren't that many objects. Thirty, forty thousand."

"You're being very literal, love."

"I need to be."

CHAPTER 62

Thirty-six years since Rao took his first breath in the world. Four months and six days since he tried to take his last breath and failed. Every breath since. He could find out how many, if he wanted. He won't. He doesn't. Twenty-two days since the diner. Thirteen days since Adam's impossible clock. Since the first time he met Prophet and Prophet met him. One hour and five minutes since they took off from Centennial in a Gulfstream jet. Twelve minutes since he stared out of the window into the darkness and saw, on the horizon, flashes of light that might have been lightning, might have been behind his eyes. Eleven minutes and fifty seconds since he decided it didn't matter either way.

When he was five, Rao ran away from his mother's side when they were shopping in Selfridges on a rainy Thursday afternoon and hopped onto an escalator to the next floor. He'd long been obsessed with moving staircases. Mostly because he was frightened of them. He'd get more and more frightened the nearer to their ends he travelled. He'd turn to his parents and extend his arms, waiting for them to lift him off the ground, rescue him from being trapped and dragged under by the meshing teeth of the inexorable steps.

That long-ago day he'd known the moment he started to rise that he didn't want to be on the escalator. Knew he'd done something incredibly stupid. Gripped with terror, he'd tried to walk back down to her, but the steps were high, and he couldn't get down them fast enough. Kept being carried upwards. Tears blurring his sight, he'd watched her turn and see him. Run towards the escalator. But he knew she wouldn't get to him in time, and he'd be eaten at the end.

He wasn't. Somehow, he jumped over the last step, stood there paralysed with shock after he landed, was swept into his mother's arms a few seconds later.

Being on that escalator is exactly what this flight feels like.

No one's rescuing him from this. He's supposed to be the rescuer here, and life has taught him that's not a role that ends well for him. Not ever. He wants his mother. Her absence is terrible. Tears well up, slip down his cheeks. He brushes them away. Looks at his fingertips. They gleam with Prophet in the gloom. Only for a second before it slips back under his skin. *I'm full of it*, he thinks, self-pity shifting to darkest amusement. *Veronica is wrong, and if I survive this, I can go as a Terminator to Halloween. Scare everyone shitless at parties.*

Parties. He doubts there'll be any more of those. It doesn't matter. The flight is an escalator. They're all on it. He looks over to where Hunter and Adam sit, the walnut table between them glowing in a pool of soft white light from the curved ceiling above. Hunter has her back to Rao. She's eating an apple and nodding. Adam's frowning at her, speaking quickly. Animatedly. Rao can't hear what he's saying over the high note of the engines. His tie's vanished, the top two buttons of his shirt open. It's been like that ever since the doors shut on the plane. Makes him look half naked. Rao has no idea what it means.

Behind him, Veronica emerges from the cabin, walks down the aisle smoothing the wrinkles on her skirt, informs them they're starting their descent. The engine note has changed, and he's already feeling the lift in his chest as it falls fast through air. He buckles his seat belt and knows without knowing that he's not here to save the Lunastus billionaire.

An unsmiling guard with acne, a clipboard, and a sidearm boards the plane as soon as the steps are unfolded. He checks their IDs, issues them security passes, leaves without a word. Rao halts on the topmost step to breathe in a deep lungful of avgas and desert night and looks down to see two trucks waiting on the tarmac, hazard lights flashing. A man in a plaid shirt and a dark gilet is leaning against the bonnet of the nearest. It's Lane. "Sunil! Adam!" he shouts, waving. "Over here!"

As they draw near, Lane gives Veronica a nod. "Dr Rhodes."

"Zachary."

"Joining us for dinner? We've got a table at the steak house."

"Not tonight, thank you."

"Your loss. Food's good." He beams at Hunter. "Master Sergeant Wood? A real pleasure. Thank you for your service. Come eat with us."

"Thanks. I already ate, Mr Lane. Can I head to the dorm?"

"Sure, sure. The driver will take you." He gestures at the second truck. "Roberts is arriving with the rest of the team at midnight. Meeting at eight a.m. in the George Washington Room, classroom block. Cafeteria serves breakfast from six."

"Understood." She climbs into the truck, leans out of the window, jerks her chin at Adam and Rao. "Behave yourselves, girls."

They watch the taillights recede. Lane rubs his hands. "Let's put your cases in the back and get you dinner."

When their driver opens the rear passenger door, Adam climbs in. Rao hesitates. Looks up. The stars are bright here. Sharp. The sky feels too close. Like it could drop. Inside, the vehicle smells of expensive detailing and traces of Creed Tabarome.

After they pull away, Lane turns in his seat and starts on a history of the Nevada National Security Site. Rao ignores him and keeps his eyes on the desert road. Specks of quartz glitter on its surface; above it hangs an auratic haze of dust. After a couple of minutes, he sees the body of a small animal on the road ahead. Pale fur in the lights. Getting closer, he sees it's been crushed. Has left a trail of blood. One leg still twitches.

Their driver swerves to avoid it; the jerk draws Lane's attention back to the road.

"Roadkill. Ran under us on the way here," the driver says.

Fuck, Rao thinks. He shifts himself up against Adam's side. Leans in, whispers into his ear. "You saw that?"

"The jackrabbit?"

"Wasn't a rabbit. Come on, Adam."

Adam takes a deep breath. "You're saying it was a telltale. Out here," he says. "You sure?"

"*Adam*. It was a teddy bear."

"It bled," he exhales.

Rao nods. He doesn't know if Adam's looking at him now; something makes him not want to. He keeps his eyes ahead. Watches drifts of gravel in the headlights as they turn at intersections, rusting trailers and radiation warning signs, runs of glittering chain-link fencing, and suddenly they're in Mercury. Amber bulbs glow dimly on buildings; they pass piles of rubble under pools of light cast by sparse, heron-necked streetlights. The town is eerie as fuck, and the steak house, when they arrive, is just as unsettling. Sitting inside it feels like being trapped in an EPGO. A plastic letter board with today's offerings outside the door, red-checked tablecloths, a tired-looking server, and Lane beaming like he's entertaining at Le Gavroche.

Soon Lane's pouring zinfandel and shaking his head. "Dr Rhodes? No mistake, she's a very, very clever girl. Summa cum laude at Oxford. Before EOS PROPHET, she led Lunastus-Dainsleif's groundbreaking research into pharmacological deradicalisation."

Rao's eyes widen. "Drug-induced brainwashing?"

"Deradicalisation," Lane replies firmly. "She's a great asset to this project. But just between us, she doesn't have the connections. She can't get in the right rooms over here."

"Veronica doesn't go quail hunting with the boys?" Rao says.

"I don't think she does," Lane replies.

"But you have."

"Many times."

"And you get in the right rooms."

"I like people." Lane shrugs.

You're rich, Rao thinks.

"People like De Witte," Adam says.

Lane lays down his cutlery, leans in, crosses his arms over the tablecloth. "It's an honour to know that man. Intellects like his come along once a century. Edison. Einstein. Even when he's not speaking, you can feel him thinking. The energy, you know? His mind . . ." Lane shakes his head. "It's not like ours."

"Ours," Rao says.

Adam gives him a playful, sidelong look. It's great. Rao grins. "Steak again, Lane? It's getting to be a little tradition with us, I see."

Lane picks up his cutlery, starts sawing at his T-bone. "We're in America, Sunil. You know, I was in a place in Montana once, and one of the guys I was with ordered chicken. *Chicken.* Caused a ruckus. You can't beat American beef."

"You serve Japanese beef in the Aurora canteen," Adam points out.

"And it's excellent. Excellent. But wagyu is like foie gras. Cloying, you can't eat it all the time. Not like this." He chews with relish. "You know Steven has a ranch? Two hundred and sixty thousand acres in Wyoming. He's turning it back to prairie. Bison, the whole thing. It's incredible. Incredible."

"Seems a billionaire of many interests," Rao drawls.

"That's what makes him so extraordinary. He's the greatest visionary of our time. But everything we do, he's hands-on. Big data, analytics, defense, infosec, aerospace, energy, life sciences. His range—"

"Yeah, I can see why you want him rescued," Rao cuts in. "Lunastus would go tits up without him."

"America would. We've had this conversation, Sunil. It's not just Lunastus-Dainsleif that's relying on you tomorrow."

"America needs me. I know. So what's the plan?"

Lane chews, takes another sip from his glass. "Mission analysis in the morning, Sunil. Are you sure you don't want wine?"

*

After dinner they're escorted to a low, dimly illuminated, tan-walled dorm block with desert grass and gravel right up to its doors. Adam stands by the vehicle as Rao is ushered into a room. He's been allocated the one next door. Walking in, he sees his kit bag placed at the foot of a varnished wooden bed frame. Green woolen blankets, a single pillow, a wardrobe, a desk with an Anglepoise lamp and a single chair. Sixty-watt bulb in a metal shade suspended from the ceiling. Would have been luxury in its heyday. He peers at the faded, framed photograph of an A-bomb test on one wall. A rising cloudcap the color of rust, the shock wave bleaching the desert white beneath. A carefully inked caption: BUSTER CHARLIE, 14KT, 30 OCTOBER 1951.

He's unlacing his boots when there's a hammering at the door.

"Adam?"

"It's open," he calls.

Another knock. "Adam?" He gets up. Outside, Rao's bouncing on the balls of his feet under the light, holding out a pack of cigarettes. "Want a smoke?"

"What is it?"

Rao blinks at the cigarettes, turns them in his hand. "Look, I don't know if I should be left alone right now. What if something happens?"

"What kind of something?"

"I don't know," Rao says hotly. "Aliens. Animate teddy bears with full sets of internal organs. This is a fucking spooky place. What if I lose the plot? Fall off an emotional cliff? This is— Stop looking so unconcerned Adam. I'm freaking out. Not everyone got raised on a military base, this isn't—"

"What do you need?"

Silence.

More silence.

"Can I bring my mattress in here?"

"Yeah," Adam says lightly. "Can I have that cigarette?"

They stand outside and smoke. Rao burns through one cigarette, lights another from its tail. Halfway through the second, his attention is caught by a brown moth the size and shape of an arrowhead clinging to the wall under the light. He leans in, inspects it closely.

"What's with the moth?" Adam says. "Is it real?"

"Yes, Adam. It is. I was just remembering this time when I was small when I found a moth. An oleander hawk moth. It had just come out of its cocoon. It was beautiful. I showed it to my mother."

"You're thinking about your mom," Adam murmurs.

"Yeah."

"You should call her."

"Are you calling yours?"

"Hunter's going to take care of it," Adam says.

Rao obviously doesn't get what that means. He grimaces. "I'm not calling my mum. It's complicated, love. I can't talk to her without it being a whole thing with my dad, and that's not a good situation." He abandons the moth, turns, and leans against the wall. Sighs a lungful of smoke, watches it cloud the night air. "He's never really approved of my life choices," he says, staring into the darkness, studying it keenly.

"Your life choices," Adam repeats after a while.

"Those. He warned me once. Said if I kept sleeping with men, I'd end up ruining my life. Get addicted to drugs, go to prison."

"Huh."

"Exactly," Rao breathes. "Exactly. It's not like I can tell him it was the fucking CIA."

"I'm sorry."

"Fuck off, this isn't— That doesn't matter. You know it doesn't. And I'm not looking for sympathy. Not now I know you've Don't Ask Don't Telled your whole fucking career. I'm just explaining, right? My mother is . . ." He swallows. "She's a wonderful woman, Adam. She's the most beautiful soul. I adore her. And she's got this thing, right? It's impossible to lie to her."

Adam blinks back surprise. "You mean, she's like you?"

"She's my mother."

"No, I mean, she has an ability like yours."

"It's just impossible to lie to her, you know? She doesn't know anything about Kabul. Doesn't know I was there, what I did, the heroin, me trying to top myself, getting arrested, none of it. And I don't want her to know. She'll be disappointed and he'll be right. It's better neither of them finds out."

Adam bends and stubs out his cigarette. "I'll get the mattress."

"Why have I never heard about your mother, Adam?"

"You don't want to know about my mom, Rao."

"I do."

"You need to have another sob story about a high-functioning alcoholic in your head?" Adam shrugs. He doesn't want to talk about this. "She did her best. Her best was too much for her. I don't know what else to say."

"Ah. Is she still alive?"

"Too well-preserved to die of anything natural."

"Fucking hell, Adam."

"I told you that you didn't want to know. I'll get the mattress."

"Give me a sec. I'll come with you."

Back in the dorm, Adam drops the mattress, shoves it against the wall. Looks up to see Rao clutching his bundle of sheets, blankets, and pillow, staring wide-eyed at the framed photograph of the mushroom cloud.

"Cozy, huh?" Adam says.

"Fuck. Least it's honest about what this place is for."

"Yeah, it is," Adam agrees, his chest tight. "You have the bed. I'll take the floor."

CHAPTER 63

It's three minutes past six. Rao's been lying awake since a quarter to three, and he can't bear the press of darkness, the shape of it, any longer. It's clinging to his throat. Makes him want to cough. Shout. He throws back the blankets. Attempts to dress silently and fails. Adam's already up before Rao comprehends he's awake.

"Walk before breakfast?" Adam enquires, shrugging on a jacket.

"Yeah," Rao croaks gratefully.

The eastern sky is paling over the jagged horizon, but the just-past-full moon is bright in the west. They follow the perimeter fence. A line of Joshua trees, black against the sky. Some anonymous gardener has placed white rocks in careful circles around their trunks. Rao frowns at the absurdity of their effort in a town built for annihilation. Listens for Adam's footfalls next to his own. How does he walk so quietly? He's wearing boots. Rao's in sneakers and he can barely hear him.

"Adam," he begins. "Listen. You know they only need me in there. You don't need to do this."

"You go in, so do I."

"I'm going."

Adam nods, like it's settled.

He doesn't get it.

"I'm going, love, because it's inevitable."

Adam's lips twitch in the gloom. "Thought I was supposed to be the fatalistic one."

"It's not fatalism. It's a fact. I know I'm going to be there because it's true."

Adam doesn't stop walking, but he slows. Looks out over the desert. When he speaks, his voice is hesitant. Like someone walking out onto ice, unsure if it'll support their weight. "You can't read truth in the future, Rao. You've told me that a bunch of times."

"Well," Rao answers. "It's got a bit complicated lately."

"How?"

Rao looks down at the thin scar that runs under the silver kadas on his right wrist. An anchor, a biographical truth, a word, of a kind. He looks at it in the half light and it doesn't seem to belong to him at all. He rubs at it with a finger. "I don't know if I could even do a truth run right now. Full disclosure, the whole world's getting harder to read. Like the light's fading and I can't see what's there. But also, other things, things I really shouldn't be able to assign truth values to, I can now." He makes a face. "I think so, anyway." He takes a deep breath, lets it out very slowly, speaks when it's almost gone. "Adam, I don't think I'm very well."

"I thought—"

"Yeah, me too."

"You tell Rhodes about it?"

He shakes his head. Of course he's fucking not. The only person who's ever going to hear about this is standing next to him.

"What are your symptoms?"

"Double vision. Sometimes."

"Sometimes. Now?"

"No. Look, Adam, have you not wondered why, despite being newly possessed of an ability to make whatever I want, I've not made myself a bunch of drugs and alcohol?"

"You're clean."

"No, I'm not. I've never been less clean."

"But you're not high."

"No. But . . ." He searches for the words. "It feels like Prophet has filled all the spaces where that shit used to go. Feels like those spaces were made for it. And it's getting a little insistent."

"You want more of it."

Rao strokes his beard thoughtfully. "Not like that," he says. "It's more like I can't escape what it wants. The facility. It wants me there. Which makes it inescapable. Like it's a gravity well."

"A gravity well."

"That's a—"

"I know what a gravity well is."

"Shit, of course you do," Rao says. "Your telescope. You were a nerdy astronomy kid, weren't you? Adorable."

It's dark enough now that Adam's face is mostly in shadow, but Rao can see enough of that expression to know he's put his foot in it. Though considering their history, considering the shit Adam's had from him over the years, it'd have to be something pretty fucking bad. Something worse than calling him adorable. "What is it?"

The answer's a long time coming.

"I didn't tell you about that."

"About what?"

"The telescope."

"You did."

Adam holds his gaze, shakes his head. And watching his denial, Rao almost—almost feels it. A sensation of glassy rightness that feels like truth but impossibly distant and deeply disconcerting, like trying to pick up a grain of dust between finger and thumb.

Back at their dorm, Adam disappears for a while. Returns in fatigue pants, a towel slung over a shoulder. Rao glances up from his bed. "How're the showers?"

"Wet."

His hair's longer, now. There are tiny curls behind his ears. Rao's eyes widen in surprise.

"Fuck me, Adam," he says. "Your hair's not straight either?"

Adam snorts. "Never was."

"You're wearing dog tags."

"ID tags. I'm not a marine."

Rao recalls Adam getting beer up his nose in Racks 'n' Butts, spluttering because Hunter had just described the USMC as "lil bitches." He gets up, walks to Adam, reaches to pick the tags from his chest. *They're a big deal to him*, Rao thinks, hearing Adam take a breath and let it out shakily. He'd probably be nursing a life-threatening injury if he'd tried this anytime before. Turning the tags in his fingers he squints, moves them a little farther away. The light isn't bright in here, and the stamped-out text is so small.

"You need glasses."

"My eyes are fine."

Adam snorts again, more softly this time. "Right."

Rao holds a tag between his thumb and index finger. "What the fuck is Protestant B, Adam? I thought you were Jewish."

"I am. I served in Saudi and they don't let Jews in the country."

"Oh, it's a code phrase? That's awful. It's also fucking funny. Did you have secret services in windowless cinder block rooms?"

Adam blinks at him. "How do you know about—"

"Hooked up with a guy who'd been to one."

Adam rolls his eyes. Then, unexpectedly, he grins. "There was a rumour the rabbi smuggled in the siddur in a box of DU rounds. I don't believe it."

Rao looks at Adam's lopsided smile, feels the tension of the chain on the back of his neck, thinks of how many times he's hauled people into a kiss just like this. He lowers the tags incredibly carefully back to Adam's chest.

"You don't always wear them."

"Defeats the purpose of being undercover, Rao."

"And you're wearing them now because—"

Adam looks at him. "Because tags serve a purpose. You know what that purpose is."

Rao sniffs. "We've talked about this, love."

"No, we haven't," Adam sighs. He moves away from Rao, continues towelling his hair, and sits. He jerks his head; an invitation for Rao to join him. "We should."

"Alright, then." Rao sits. Adam doesn't say anything. "Are we not?"

"No, we are. I am."

"Could've fooled me."

"Shut up, Rao. Let me get to it." Adam lets the towel rest on his shoulders. His eyebrows draw in tight. Stressed. Adam is wearing actual human expressions now, Rao realises, but only behind closed doors. He's still full Robot Rubenstein whenever they're around Veronica or Lane. Turns dead behind his eyes. Rao'd always assumed that was just how Adam was. Steel down to the bone. Unfeeling. Because that's how he was when Rao met him. That's how he was when Miller pulled Adam out of the deck like a joker. But Adam's expressive now. Expressive like he is around Hunter, even when she's not there. Expressive like that night with the vodka and missed chances. Expressive like half light in motel rooms after mental breakdowns.

Rao's been a dickhead, hasn't he?

Adam takes a breath. A deep one. He's not looking at Rao any longer. Rao's eyes catch on the end of the scar on his collarbone, move up to the angle of his jaw. He thinks of all the times he's taken a chin in his hand to make someone look at him. He wants to make Adam look.

"This mission isn't going to be standard," Adam says in a low voice.

"No shit, Adam."

He sighs again. "Rao. Just listen to what I'm saying? It's not going to be standard. It's not going to be a case of point A, point B, hostiles, objectives. Those are the words we're using, but it's not going to be that simple with Prophet. Is it?"

Rao relaxes his own jaw to stop his teeth grinding. "It's not going to be standard, love," he agrees.

Adam nods. Reaches behind his neck. Pulls the tags over his head. "I told Hunter to contact my parents. She knows how to find them, when it's time to do that."

"Adam—"

He jerks his head again and Rao opens his hand like the command was obvious. Maybe it was. Maybe Rao knows Adam that well now. Maybe, now, Adam is just expressive enough for him to guess.

The tags and chain pool in Rao's palm. Stainless steel. He's so used to watching bright metal sink into his skin of late that it's surprising the tags just sit in his hand. They feel warm.

"You don't have to worry about contacting anyone. I just want you to have these," Adam says.

"Don't be daft."

"I don't know what that means."

"It means— Oh, fuck off, Adam. You're fucking with me right now, aren't you?"

Adam hums tunelessly. "Not all the way."

It's tempting to leave it there. Like they've cleared the air. Like the heavy shit has been talked about, looked at. And that's almost alright. But Rao can't. He can't let Adam go into this full of doom and gloom. It feels too much like violence.

Rao needs him to know that—

Adam is talking before Rao can piece his words together.

"I'm not letting you out of my sight when we go in," he says, and he's looking at Rao now. He's looking, and he's seeing, and Rao knows that there's no coming back from that promise.

CHAPTER 64

Rao halts by the briefing room door, points at the sign above it. "He totally did lie, Adam."

"George Washington? Old news."

"No, but really," Rao says. "Like, fuck your American myths."

"Yes. I know."

"You're not listening."

"He's listening," Hunter says, striding past.

Chairs, striplights, a whiteboard, projection screen, linoleum tiles. Flyblown blinds. Everything in here is tired except the soldiers sitting on schoolroom chairs. Fuck knows where Lane dragged them in from, but they look so healthy Rao's vaguely cross. He's so used to seeing Spec Ops guys in comas he's surprised by how they look when they're not. Loose-limbed, more trail runner than bodybuilder. Minus the fatigues, the one standing at the whiteboard could be a suburban dad, albeit one who shaves with a blowtorch.

"Lieutenant Colonel Adam Rubenstein," Adam says, stepping forward. "This is Master Sergeant Hunter Wood. And this is Mr Sunil Rao. Our primary asset."

"Captain Marcus Roberts," the man by the board replies. The rest of the team introduce themselves. Estrada, Baker, Garcia, Carlton, Stewart.

"We have six minutes, Colonel," Roberts says. "Mr Lane instructed me to play you the last call out of the facility before he arrives. Should we wait for Dr Rhodes?"

"No. Go ahead."

Roberts hits the key of a chunky laptop. A hiss, then a woman's voice, hushed, tight with panic.

"This is Sandra Evans, core team engineer." There's something off with the line. It's sputtering softly, pulses of silence caught up in it, though her words are perfectly clear. "I'm in the RadSafe counting room. Power's off, but it's not dark anywhere, there are—there are lights, but they're not ours. I need to report a containment failure. It's bad, it's really bad." She swallows, and the sound is louder than her voice. When she speaks again, there's a new noise—something mechanical, with movement to it, like a train going over points, but impossibly deep and slow, far too deep for a telephone line. Far too deep to be coming from the speakers on Roberts's laptop. It's like Sinatra in the diner. Right in the middle of Rao's head. He's not sure if anyone else can hear it. He's not going to ask.

"We're under attack," she's whispering. "I don't know if they'll find me here. I don't know if they can see through copper and shielding. They're everywhere. Please send help. We can't—"

The line cuts.

Dully, Rao listens to the team speculate on how the hostiles arrived, considering there'd been no recorded traffic at any height, no breach of the NNSS perimeter. They're discussing a night operation. He has to say something. But he doesn't know the right way to say it. Not to people like these. He looks to Adam. Adam knows what this is. Why doesn't he bloody say something?

In his peripheral vision, Rao sees Hunter fold her arms and give him an expectant look.

Oh. Adam wants Rao to tell them.

Fine.

"We won't need to go in in darkness," he says, a little roughly. He'd try harder to not sound a dick, but everyone here knows he is already, or will do. "It'd be pointless. Doesn't matter what time we do this."

They're all looking at Adam now.

"Listen to him," Adam says. Six pairs of eyes track back to Rao.

"What did they tell you happened in the facility?" he asks.

"Chemical spill," Roberts says. "A substance with psychotropic effects. Hallucinations, fits, comas. Sometimes fatal."

"Some people are immune," Baker adds.

Not for the first time, Rao wonders how many soldiers are psychos. This one looks remarkably fresh-faced. Just out of school. Maybe Rao's getting old. "Even people who are immune," he says, scratching his beard, "are going to see a ton of shit in there. The substance is called Prophet. It does affect the mind. But it doesn't make you hallucinate. It makes things."

"Makes things," Roberts repeats.

"Yeah. Makes objects. Makes buildings. Makes things that move, look alive but aren't. Those hostiles—they're not going to be human at all." It's true.

"I second that," Adam says. "Their official designation is EPGOs. We've been calling them telltales when they're moving like that. And considering what we heard on that call, they pose a clear threat. To incapacitate, chest and head shots will likely be ineffective. Stopping shots will be ankles and knees, or whatever structure keeps them moving."

The door swings open and Veronica enters, wreathed in floral perfume. She's wearing a light, fur-hooded jacket. *That's not coyote*, Rao thinks. *That's wolf.* There's a red flush high on her cheekbones. Looks like she wants to step on something.

"Ah, Veronica," Rao greets her. "We've just told the boys about telltales."

"Good," she says. "Lane's on his way."

He arrives forty seconds later with two henchmen carrying rolls of paper they proceed to pin upon the walls. The photographic intelligence Rao'd seen in Aspen: blueprints, terrain maps, a weather forecast with pressure lines and predicted cloud. Strange that he's not choosing to display all this digitally on full Lunastus tech, Rao muses. God help them all if it's Lane longing for better, simpler times.

As soon as Lane starts speaking, Rao stretches back in his seat. Tunes out his voice. Lets all that he hears slip into memory. He can pull it out later if he needs to. Because what's intriguing him is how obviously Veronica and Lane loathe each other. He's pointedly not looking at her as he gives his little lecture. She's staring right at him with a deathless expression. Rao smirks. He's looking forward to asking Veronica about her views on Lane.

But Rao sits up after Lane walks to a table and tugs a white sheet away from a bulky shape to reveal a detailed model of the facility. It's a far from elegant structure: a pile of steel-toned brutalist boxes like the offspring of an aircraft hangar and a cement works, a water tower held aloft on a lattice of fine wire. This scaled-down version is mesmerising. Echoes of the diner in the dark. *Scale*, he thinks. Rao's always adored miniature things. Loved how entranced humans are by the small. How we like to remake the world, magic it down to fit in our pockets and palms, turning ourselves into giants. He remembers back at Sotheby's he'd got to hold a Nicholas Hilliard portrait the size of a matchbox. It had been the kind of perfect that hurt to look at. A dark-eyed man with a pale face against depthless, midnight blue. Powdered gold, motes in darkness. It was as perfect a truth as any lie can be, which is why art has always been something Rao's drawn to.

Prophet works like that. Busy making lies that are trying to be true. *Except*, he muses, *with me. With me it makes truths.* And there's a reason for that, and he doesn't know what it is, though it feels like he did. Like it's something he's forgotten. It's a strange sensation. He takes a deep breath, lets it out, watches Lane lift away the model's roof and point inside.

"The hot bay," he says. "So called because it was designed to handle radioactive materials. The purpose of this site was to test nuclear engine assemblies. That's how this building got its name: the Engine Mainte-nance Assembly and Disassembly Facility. E-MAD."

E-MAD, Rao thinks. *Fucking hell, what a name.*

Now the screen shows a different image, a black-and-white photo of the hall in its earliest years. Men in white boiler suits, vast metal manipulator arms, barrels, platforms, everything grained and silvered like Apollo mission shots of the surface of the moon. It's phenomenally evocative but clearly irrelevant to the matter at hand. He suspects Lane's history lesson is because he sees himself as a new Oppenheimer, his fucked-up project a worthy heir to the scariest Cold War Big Science.

Rao sneaks a glance at Veronica; she's looking murderous. There's a different photograph of the hall on the screen now: pools of water on its stained concrete floor, rusting gantries, piles of rotting debris.

"This is what it looked like until our renovation," Lane intones. "And this is what it looks like now." Triumphantly, he clicks to the next image. "We kept the original green to match the historic palette."

Rao clocks the blank looks that gets from the soldier boys. Quells the urge to ask Lane if he'll be handing out special battle dress to match his heritage paint.

The renovated hot bay is spotless. Along the righthand wall, the giant manipulator arms are glossy canary yellow, and beneath them are a series of installations that resemble museum cabinets crossed with industrial machinery. Gleaming pipes, rivets, delicate traceries of glass and copper. Refracted light. Slabs of steel. Thick red lines drawn around them on the concrete floor. A whole forest of warning signs.

"Our Prophet containment system," Lane says. "State of the art. Multiple fail-safes in place. If there's been a breach, we can only assume sabotage."

As soon as Rao hears the word "sabotage," he knows it wasn't sabotage at all. He mutters some statements, finds out the containment system failed catastrophically all at once. And not just here: every single container of Prophet, including the syringes in the medical facility, had failed at exactly the same time. He doesn't have to test to know when that had happened. He knows already. He'd felt it. He'd felt it and it'd laid him out. He'd been walking down a corridor with Adam, reciting a poem, giggling at the violence of forcing entrecôte to rhyme with Truman Capote.

Here and somewhere else.

Lane is showing a series of photographs of De Witte. Most include Lane. Lane at the wheel of an ancient army jeep, De Witte hunched beside him in the passenger seat. A snowy day outside the Aspen cabin, Lane holding an axe triumphantly above a pile of firewood, De Witte swaddled in an orange parka, staring at the snow underfoot. De Witte spotlit at a podium, looking extraordinarily ill at ease in a suit and tie. He has an unprepossessing, strained face and the thin blond hair of a superannuated surfer, and the more photos Lane throws up on the screen, the more obvious it becomes that whatever Lane feels for him is far from mutual.

"We don't know his location," Lane says. "It's likely you'll find him in the hot bay or one of the labs. He was last seen wearing dark jeans, a grey shirt. When you've found him, get your medic to check him over. Then"—he gestures at Rao—"Mr Rao'll take over. Sunil, you're our special secret weapon. Tell the unit what you'll be doing."

"Not really a weapon, but yeah, I can extract this substance from people. If he's not too fucked, De Witte should be able to walk out with us. Or you can bring him out on a stretcher."

Lane opens his mouth again, but Rao's far from finished.

"So, I'm just going to address the elephant in the room," he says. "In fact, there might be an elephant in a room in there. Several. Could be Elmer, even. Or the other one. What's the other one, Adam?"

"Horton," Adam says.

"Yeah. That one. Anyway. Going in there'll be like walking into Disneyland on very, very, *very* bad acid. I'd really like to be able to tell you what you'll see isn't real and can't hurt you, but it is real, and it looks like it absolutely fucking can and will."

"We've had no cases of aggressive EPGOs," Lane protests.

"You've heard the recording," Rao says simply. "Veronica, you want to do this bit?"

Veronica nods. "To clarify, yes, this substance manifests things from people's imagination. Yes, these include animate, moving objects. And the evidence now points to these objects turning . . . being hostile."

Rao looks around the George Washington Room. Lane is standing by his giant photograph of De Witte, arms crossed truculently. Veronica seems entranced at the thought of Prophet-generated horrors. Adam looks impassive. Hunter and the soldier boys appear ready for fucking anything.

No. Someone else can talk now. He's done. "I'm going outside for a smoke," he informs everyone.

CHAPTER 65

He stands on the cracked concrete steps of the classroom block, looks out at sun-peeled trailers, piles of concrete with exposed, corroding rebars. Lighting up, dragging smoke gratefully into his lungs, he studies the desert garden across the road. Cacti, gravel, clumps of yellow grass. It looks exactly like everywhere else, only the gravel is a vaguely different shade of brown, and there's a low fence around it.

The door swings open.

"Veronica," he says as she steps through. "You had enough too?"

"There's a lot of military expertise in that room. They're talking."

"What's Lane doing?"

"Getting in the way, I expect."

He grins. "Yeah. Tell me, what is it with Lane and De Witte?"

Her lips twitch. "You noticed."

"I certainly have. It's a very embarrassing crush."

"It's not a crush. It's a father fixation. Lane lost his own early and tragically. Steven fitted his requirement for a new one."

"Steven, is it? I see."

"I can confidently guarantee that you don't."

He screws up his face. "You're right. I'm talking out of my arse." He takes another drag on his cigarette. "So, we're rescuing De Witte because Lane thinks he's his dad?"

"No," she says. "We're rescuing him because he's in possession of a brain."

He grins. "And Lane isn't?"

"Lane's a competent fixer when it comes to weapons deals. Undeclared ones are his particular speciality. He has *very* important friends."

Rao rolls his eyes. She nods. "Inexplicably, they consider him good company. Steven is a little less . . ."

"What?"

"Hail-fellow-well-met."

"Hard to get on with, is he?"

"You'll see."

"I suppose I will." He inspects the coal of his cigarette, taps ash to the concrete beneath his feet. "Veronica?"

"Yes?"

"What's the plan?"

"I'm sure Colonel Rubenstein will tell you when they're done."

"Not the Action Man plan. Your plan. Do me the courtesy, please."

She frowns. "My role on this mission? Medical assistance."

"That's not what I asked. I'm not talking about your immediate plans. I'm talking about the project. Because whatever the fuck it is, it's never been about getting ex-soldiers with broken legs to make themselves expensive guns."

She shakes her head firmly.

"Look," Rao goes on. "I'm fucked. I'm full of this stuff. Hate to break it to you, but your tests are hopeless. I cried Prophet yesterday. It came out of my tear ducts, sunk right back into my skin. I know there's no happy ending for me. Everyone that's going in is expendable except you. So, you're the one I'm asking. I'm not trying to defeat you and save the day. What am I going to do, truth-test you to death? Fuck saving the day and fuck the saving particularly. I'm over it. I'm . . . *over*, Veronica. I knew that a long time ago. I don't give two shits about De Witte. I'm only doing this because I'm a curious arsehole. That's my motivation, and I really want to know before this shit kills me."

He lets out a long breath. Some of that felt true.

"You're not expendable."

"Don't bullshit me. The next samples you're going to want are postmortem."

She looks at him carefully. He waits her out. Eventually she nods at the packet of Lucky Strikes he's holding.

"May I?"

"Didn't know you smoked."

"I don't."

He lights her cigarette. She lets the smoke slip out of her mouth, drags it back in.

"Ok," she says finally. "The EPGOs around the facility weren't made by the people who worked there."

He blinks. It's true.

"Work it out," she says.

"Can you not just tell me?"

"I don't want to tell you. I want to see you work it out."

"Fine. How much shit is piled up around those buildings?"

"Rough estimate, just under forty thousand objects."

"One person, one object."

"Correct."

He looks out at the desert, at clouds massing over the far slopes. Shivers with sudden comprehension. "It's a town," he breathes.

"It's a town. Pahrump."

"How?"

"Drinking water."

"Fucking hell, Veronica. That's wildly, wildly illegal."

She wrinkles her nose. "It's given us interesting and encouraging data."

"Has it. When was this?"

"Just over five months ago."

"So you poisoned a whole town back when Prophet just made people feel nostalgic. And now the good citizens of Pahrump have suddenly made all this? Veronica, get your story straight. You told me that once it's inside people, its effects don't change."

Her brow furrows. "Until now. In fact, I suspect you're responsible. Your handshake with Mrs Crossland was the trigger. You touched her, and Prophet made a connection. When that happened, forty thousand EPGOs were manifested around the facility."

It's true. He should feel guilty. He *is* guilty. He doesn't feel guilty.

"But why here?" he asks. As she shakes her head, he has the flash of an image that tastes of an answer. Something he saw in a magazine.

Photographs of flowers taken with UV-sensitive film. Bright patches and lines on their petals, invisible to the human eye. But not to bees. He thinks of the appliqued pansies on Dinah Crossland's sleeves. Thinks of Pahrump. Wonders what it looks like. Like Mercury, perhaps, only with fewer radiation warning signs and more American flags. Yeah, far, far more.

"Community renewal?" he says. "That's what this is for. Right. Yes. And Prophet in the water in Pahrump was, what, a dry run?"

Her eyebrows rise. "Well done."

"What kind of community renewal are we talking about, Veronica?" he says slowly.

"Well, Lane's terribly fond of slogans. He says that just like fluoride in water protects a nation's teeth, Prophet in water protects a nation's idea of itself."

"I'm surprised he's a fluoride fan. Lane's a bit precious bodily fluids, isn't he?"

"I don't know what that means."

"How have you not seen *Dr. Strangelove*, Veronica? What does 'protect a nation's idea of itself' mean?"

"Nostos," she says.

"Now you're just *trying* to be oblique. You're like my auntie Manju. She can't explain anything without—"

"Short version, Rao, is that nostalgia is an emotional weapon. And we're very keen to use it."

"We?"

"I'm not supplying names."

"Wasn't asking for them. Just, I never thought of you as a party person, Veronica."

She raises her eyebrows. "Alliances aren't the same as allegiances. People so often confuse the two. Shall we just say we're working with"—her voice shifts into a creditable Texan drawl—"important folks behind the scenes."

"Ah, yes, the no-oversight brigade. 'Nostos,' you said. Home. Your little cabal wants to dose the population to give them all a hard-on for imaginary America, right?"

"That would be one way of putting it."

"What's another way?"

"Saving America."

He snorts at that. "How is suicide by soft toy going to save America?"

"The purpose of our facility here isn't to store Prophet," she says. "It's to engineer it. We've been working on reversing these step changes in its operation. Attenuating its effects."

"Attenuating? You've been poking away at it to make it weaker? Well that's worked out beautifully for you, hasn't it?"

Veronica is unfazed. "We'll get there."

"So you're weaponizing nostalgia to engineer the conditions for a big populist government takeover."

"Oh no, Rao." She looks at him with something like pity. "No. That's not it at all. Governments are redundant entities these days. They have their uses, but they're not where power lies."

"Corporations."

She shakes her head. "People."

"People? Are we talking socialism, Veronica? Because that's a bit of a surprise, to be honest—"

She laughs. "No. Not *The People*. Persons."

"Like De Witte."

"Steven's part of the network, yes."

"Oh there's a network, is there? This isn't some Elders of Zion shit, because if it is—"

"Of course it isn't. This isn't an anti-Semitic fairy tale. It's real."

It is. Fuck.

"So what's your manifesto?"

"A brave new world, Rao."

"Come on, Veronica, you'll have to do better than that."

She rolls her eyes. "I really don't. But just for you, Rao: Think of the financial crash as the first and necessary step of a great, global reorganisation. We're freeing ourselves of the shackles of regulation to usher in a world where finite resources are managed with rare efficiency by those few, extraordinary individuals who possess the vision, courage, and commitment to see things through. And Prophet is our social engineer, the exquisite silver thread that shall shape the world to our will."

This is monologuing, Rao thinks. Vague as fuck, nonsensical, doubtless genocidal. Prophet notwithstanding, it's almost exactly like the one at the denouement of a Robert Ludlum thriller he'd toiled through a few years ago. Two weeks ago he'd have listened to this, laughed in her face, and frantically tried to work out how to save the day. Now? Fuck knows.

"So when you say 'saving America,' it's not America. It's Lunastus."

"Lunastus-Dainsleif *is* America."

Rao shakes his head, lights another cigarette. "This is some dystopian shit, Veronica."

"I'm rather surprised. I assumed you'd be over the romantic notion the world is divided into heroes and villains by now. But if you insist on that fiction, perhaps I should point out we didn't get you addicted to heroin in order to put you where we wanted you to be."

"No, you've done something worse."

She looks him directly in the eye.

"Rao, please tell me truthfully. Would you *want* to be free of Prophet right now? Would you want to be anywhere else?"

He shivers again. His answer is so perfectly true he almost retches speaking it. "No."

CHAPTER 66

Rao stabs another potato tot, chews it stoically. The cafeteria coffee is undrinkable. He doesn't care. That morning he'd made himself two copies of the finest cup he'd ever had in his life: a latte from a café by Brighton station that punished punters for the quality of their coffee by forcing them to sit on hessian-covered boxes with painfully sharp edges. He watches Adam eat a plate of mushy spaghetti and luminous marinara sauce with grudging admiration. Hunter's finished hers.

He jerks his head subtly at the soldier boys at the other tables. "Who are these guys?" he asks.

"Private security contractors," Hunter explains. "Run out of some office near Dulles, like they all are."

"Yeah, mercenaries. But they're not Blackwater or Triple Canopy."

She shakes her head. "Another outfit. Eagle Aspect. Know a couple of them by reputation. Estrada is sound. Roberts is too. Just don't ask him about God."

"That's not a challenge, Rao," Adam says. "We don't need you locking horns right now."

"I don't feel like locking anything, love. To be quite honest, I feel like a nap. What's happening now?"

"War-gaming," Adam answers.

"They're going to play Dungeons and Dragons?" Rao breathes, eyes wide. No response. *Read the room, Sunil.* "Fine. When's the mission? Tonight?"

"Nope. Lane fucked up," Hunter says. "At this rate, Estrada's going to kill him before I do."

"Estrada."

"Alejandro. Weapons sergeant," Adam explains. "Lane didn't want weapons on the plane he sent. Said he'd bring them separately. They haven't arrived. Now Lane's blaming everyone in the lower forty-eight. We won't get what we need before late this evening. H hour's pushed back to tomorrow a.m."

"Ok. Do I need to be in these war-gaming meetings?"

"You do."

Considering the madness that all this is, Rao probably doesn't need to be so covert. Habit of a lifetime. He sneaks a plastic cup into his jacket pocket as they exit the cafeteria, ducks into the empty office next to the George Washington Room, and makes himself a cup of coffee to fill it. Tucking the earthenware mug he'd magicked into existence behind a window blind, he strolls back into the meeting room, sipping as he walks. Fucking *nectar*. He nods at Veronica, perched on a desk with a bottle of Fiji Water. She beams back. It's not a proprietorial smile. It's relieved. Lane's not here. And the meeting—well. Rao's always had a bit of a thing for competence, and it turns out that watching Adam, Hunter, and six Special Forces types work out a plan of operations really does it for him. They'll be dropped off by vehicle upwind of the building, at the edge of the ring of EPGOs. They'll keep a field ambulance and EMT team from one of Lunastus's private hospitals on the far side of the ridge, leaving Hunter and Carlton with his sniper rifle on the nearside. Carlton will keep an eye on the building. So will Hunter, running the radio and relaying updates to Lane.

Taking EPGO obstacles into account, they calculate it'll take eight minutes to reach the building on foot.

The tape of the engineer's last phone call is replayed twice.

There's speculation on the motivation of the hostiles.

"It may not be hostility per se," Veronica offers. "At least, not how we familiarly use the term. Individuals exposed to Prophet are drawn to the objects they make, want to establish physical contact with them. Once that's achieved, they become unresponsive. It's possible that works both ways. Telltales may simply be searching out the people who made them. Wanting, if that word might be used for an entity of this nature, to establish physical contact with their creators."

"Contact with the people who made them by imagining them," Roberts says hesitantly. He's trying hard, Rao notes, to internalise the reality he's facing. Hasn't quite managed it.

"Yeah," Rao goes on. "Targeting them. To grab hold of them. And then—" He makes a face.

"Physical contact puts their targets down," Roberts concludes.

"Exactly."

"Are they targeting the person who made them, or anyone?"

"Insufficient data to answer that," Veronica says and smiles.

"So these telltales, they're like zombies?" Stewart asks.

"Near enough," Adam replies.

"Fast zombies." It's Estrada. He's not spoken much before.

"Likely." Heads nod.

"But unarmed."

"Who knows," Rao says. "Like, if someone in there imagined Clint Eastwood from *The Good, the Bad and the Ugly* . . ."

"That shot through the rope was bullshit," Estrada snaps immediately. "1874 Sharps at that distance?"

"It's not impossible that cinematic license," Veronica observes, "might carry into a real-world environment in this context."

"Well, that's fucked up," Estrada replies.

More nods. Graver this time.

When Estrada takes the team through their weapons list—suppressed MP5s, Beretta M9s, and a fancy sniper rifle for Carlton—Rao ascertains that everyone going in will be armed except him. Which seems remarkably unfair, considering he's supposed to be their *primary asset*.

"Why don't I get a gun?" he whispers to Adam and Hunter during a break in proceedings.

Hunter gives him a *you're fucking joking me* face.

"Because you've got me," Adam explains.

Hunter rolls her eyes and groans. "You've got more than Rubenstein. Rao, you've got a six-man team whose explicit purpose is to protect you so you can do the job we're here for. You won't need 'a gun.'"

"But—"

"Rao, have you ever fired a weapon?" she asks.

"Depends on how you define a—"

"No weapon, Rao," Adam says. "But you'll have combat uniform."

"What?"

"Battle gear," Adam says with a twitch of his lips. "You're not going in in corduroys."

"Fucking hell. That's a lot. They're not going to make me salute a flag?"

"They'll make you brush your hair." Hunter's serious voice.

"Fuck off."

When they cluster around the model to discuss their entry, sweep, and search, Rao hangs back. All he'll have to do is follow their lead, and the entirety of the model—all its rooms and floors, stairs and halls—is already in his head. So when a woman called Linda turns up with a wheeled case and says she's here with his uniform, Rao nips into the office next door with her to try it on.

It's a little maddening that the first pair of trousers she hands him fit better than the ones he's wearing. So does the shirt, the one she calls a blouse. He brushes his hands down the fractal print in little squares of grey and brown and sand. There are pockets everywhere. The boots are great. The flak vest thing is better. The ballistic helmet is . . . yeah. He hates how much he likes it.

She's looking up at him now. Small and blonde and fierce. To her, he's nothing, and he's so grateful for her lack of interest, her ignorance of whatever conjunction of the planets made him so fucking *special*, he comes perilously close to disaster. Desperately wants to walk out with her right back into ordinary life. Have a beer, a plate of tacos. Complain about the weather. She tells him to bend so she can check the helmet and chin guard. The moment passes. He waggles his eyebrows suggestively when she pulls at his waistband. Force of habit. She doesn't see him do it, thankfully. "How did you get my measurements, Linda?" he asks.

She shrugs. "I didn't. Got a case full of these. I just have to make sure one fits."

"This fits."

He thanks her. He's handed his clothes and shoes in a plastic bag. It's like he's died. Like he's dead and he's picking up the clothes he's died in. When he walks back into the room, Adam looks at him. Says nothing.

Hunter grins. "Fuck me, Rao," she says. "You've joined the marines."

"Am I a lil bitch now, Hunter?"

"Absolutely."

CHAPTER 67

They eat in near silence. There's raucous laughter from a table by the door. All men, Rao observes, none with soldierly physiques. A preponderance of glasses. One wears a Stark Industries tee. Nuclear scientists, he supposes. *Yeah.* Nursemaiding America's arsenal, making sure the end of the world will still happen if the wankers in charge want it to.

After dinner, back at the double dorm they've moved themselves into, Rao has a hot shower in an attempt to shift the blankness he's felt since he held his own clothes and shoes in a plastic bag. It helps a little. He pulls on his Union Jack tee, disconcerted by how much it's faded, a pair of grey sleep pants, then wanders back into the dorm, soles scratching on the sand he's already tracked in over the linoleum floor.

Adam's sitting at the desk examining a detailed terrain map. By his elbow, an elderly Anglepoise lamp, a steel mug, and an open box of Milk Duds. As Rao nears, he doesn't raise his eyes from the map, just murmurs, "Eleven hours fifty-two until we go in."

"Thanks, but that wasn't what I was going to ask," Rao says. Adam looks up, face jagged in the lamplight. "Wasn't going to ask you anything, actually, love. Sorry to disappoint. But now we're alone, I wanted to tell you I found out what's going on. Had a little chat with Veronica this morning. I caught her at an unguarded moment."

"Rhodes doesn't have unguarded moments."

Well, no, Rao thinks. *She doesn't.* She just assumes he's going to die. But they don't need to get into that right now. Could be a bit of a conversational derailer. "Let's just say she took me into her confidence," he says a little haughtily. "Anyway. Listen. This whole project, it's mad. It's fucking insane."

"I know, Rao."

"No. Madder than that. Much, much madder."

That gets a very tight smile. "What's the intel, Rao?"

Rao exhales. Walks to their dorm window. Looks out. The street-lights are dim. He can see high, sallow clouds lit by the moon over the desert. Must hardly ever rain here. He misses rain. Heavy rain. Cold London rain. Monsoon rain in Jaipur. Proper September rain, there, the way it feels on the skin, the way colours flood and burn in it. He doesn't think he's going to feel it again.

"Rao?"

"Sorry." He turns, leans against the frame. "They plan to use Prophet on everyone in America. To make everyone imagine a lost, perfect home and then promise they'll give it to them. They're weaponizing nostalgia to take over the world. Kitty would lose it."

"Who's they?"

"Not the military. It's a bunch of billionaire fucks and ideologues getting their cocks sucked by the military. De Witte is their little emperor. King Fuck. Veronica's his voice on Earth. The whole manifestation programme was bullshit cover. White noise. They've already done a field test, put Prophet in drinking water. That memory junkyard around the facility, it was all made by civilians."

Adam reaches to smooth the map against the desk, flattening it with one palm, brow ticking down. "At distance?"

"At distance. Prophet keeps everyone guessing, doesn't it? It's a cunt like that."

"Where's the location of the field test?"

"Pahrump."

"Mrs Crossland."

"Mrs Crossland."

A second later, Adam's wry expression vanishes. "Fucking idiots," he whispers.

"Yeah."

"No, Rao. I mean using Pahrump for field tests."

"It's convenient?"

Adam shakes his head. "You know what happened here."

"Here?"

"Nevada test site. One bomb every three weeks for twelve years. They called Vegas Atomic City back then. You could watch the mushroom clouds from your casino hotel. People came from all over to see that. The reason it's fucking stupid, Rao, is that testing stopped in 1963. There'll be folks in Pahrump who remember those tests from their childhood. You know what that means."

"Fuck," Rao breathes.

"Yep."

"Atom bomb EPGOs? It *couldn't*."

"Have you tested that?"

Rao shivers. "Holy shit. Holy fucking shit."

A long silence. Adam's stopped looking at the blueprints. He's staring into space. He's imagining it, isn't he. Out of the darkness that double flash, so bright you could put your hands in front of your eyes to block it out and see every one of your bones through muscle and skin. The silence, until the noise. The stillness, until the shock wave. The slowly climbing, terrible cloud in the desert. The searing heat of it. The dust, the death. Hard rain.

"Adam," he whispers.

"Well, that's the other way it might go," Adam says.

Rao frowns. "What might?"

"End of the world." He picks up his mug.

"Let's not be overly dramatic, love."

Adam's eyes widen perceptibly as he drinks. He sets the mug back down, stares at it. "Rao," he says very softly. "Prophet is the end of the world. You know it is. They can't contain it and it's making more of itself all the time. Nobody can destroy it. They could vaporize it, sure. But then it's just in the air. It's going to keep growing, and it's going to get everywhere."

Rao blinks at him.

"You haven't run this," Adam says curiously. And Rao shakes his head, just once. It had never occurred to him. Which is, he realises, extraordinary. And he realises something else. He knows now what Adam's sadness is. He'd felt it before. Hadn't known what it meant.

"I always thought the end of the world was going to be, you know," he says, after a deal of silence, "properly apocalyptic. Fires. Tidal waves. Floods."

"No, Rao," Adam says, the tiredness, the resignation in his voice as heavy and obvious as his conclusions. "The end of the world is just people glued to toys."

CHAPTER 68

When Rao wakes it's already light. He pulls the awful green blanket tighter around his shoulders, pushes his face into a pillow that smells of bleach. Keeps his eyes closed as long as he can, but he's so awake, and the squirming press of colourless patterns behind his eyelids is making him nauseated. He gets up, shivers, goes to the door of the dorm, and opens it.

The first thing he thinks is *salt*. Innumerable grains of it blowing in the wind across the flat expanse of gravel outside, collecting on the lee sides of rocks and clumps of grass by the door. The sky is nine tenths cloud, livid, nearly purple, the dawn light yellow, and the air is full of falling grains of salt that isn't salt, is it, of course it's not. It's—

"Snow," comes the familiar baritone. Adam's standing close behind him, already dressed.

"Is this normal?"

"No."

"Fucking hell, Prophet's changing the weather now?" Rao says. "Before anything else, I need coffee. No. Take a piss. No. Coffee first. Priorities."

"We don't have a coffee—" Adam begins, then nods. Rao conjures two mugs of Brighton's finest, one after the other, upon the desk. Hands one to Adam, who accepts it gratefully, even closing his eyes in what Rao presumes is simple pleasure after taking the first sip.

"Last cigarette, Adam?" Rao says, returning from the bathroom to stare down the combat uniform on the chair.

"Sure. You make those too?"

"Yeah, and the lighter. I'm entirely self-sustaining now, Adamski."

"You haven't called me that for a while."

"Haven't I?"

Rao pulls on his combat uniform and boots, leaving the vest and helmet on the seat, and they walk outside to smoke and watch the snow. There's so much silence, and for once in his life, Rao doesn't feel the need to fill it.

He hears the low echoing roar of their idling engines before he sees them. Rao's not seen Humvees since Afghanistan. Four of them in desert tan are parked up where the main street is widest. Snow dusts their familiar squat profiles, glows in the headlights on their toothy, bad-tempered grilles. One of them's an ambulance, red cross high on its sides. He remembers those too. From Kabul. *Shit*, he thinks. All that happened there, it's on the other side of this. But which side, he's not sure. Feels it's all still to come somehow. Garcia nods a greeting and opens the rear passenger door. Rao climbs in, swearing under his breath. Adam follows.

As the convoy pulls away, Rao stares at Garcia's gloved hands resting lightly on the wheel, then up at the wiper blades and beyond, where tunnelling flecks of snow speed towards the windscreen. Rao feels a wrench at leaving their dorm behind. It's absurd to feel so attached to a room he'd slept in for a single night. He turns his head to look out the window. An expanse of low grasses and bushes with tiny leaves silvered by snow. Dark feathery lumps that are yucca trees. About a mile out of town, he thinks he sees something running in the mid distance, ghostly suggestions of movement behind the shifting veils of snow, nothing solid. Deer maybe. Or antelopes. Yes. Those. He wonders what they're running from. Running to.

The team's talking over their radios. Their communications aren't the terse NATO alphabetised sitreps he'd expected. So far, it's mostly Estrada getting shit for that one time he vetoed Starbucks in favour of Peet's. Even Adam had weighed in on that crime. Rao listens to their banter in silence as the convoy makes its way northwest. His hands are laid on his thighs, fingers spread, just the way they were on the way to the diner, but the press on his mind is no longer a dim sense of dissimulation. It's a compass orientation. He knows exactly where they're

going. Can feel it, like his bones have been magnetised, his blood. The
submarine tow of it is so strong that every time the road veers away
from the direction of the E-MAD site, he has the distinct sensation of
being pulled onto one side. A car on two wheels. Takes uneasy, shallow
breaths that turn deep again as soon as they regain a direct heading in.

They leave the ambulance parked on the far side of the last ridge
and climb higher. The snow's falling less strongly now. More and more
of the desert around them is revealed. *Prophet wants to draw back the
curtain*, Rao thinks. *Wants to let me see.*

And he sees. They crest a rise and through the windscreen Rao
views the E-MAD buildings for the first time. They're just above Garcia's hands. They're there, outside. They're inside the toughened glass.
They're inside his head. *Scale.* He makes a low sound, tears his eyes away,
focuses on his hands. The wrinkles on his knuckles, the hangnail on
his thumb. He wants his eyes on their destination more than he wants
to breathe, but he's kicking against that need as hard as he ever has for
anything. It's a fruitless effort. As soon as he gets close, it'll all be over.
Whatever "over" is. But he's trying. He's going to hold out for as long
as he can.

They descend a few hundred yards, park up. Rao opens his door, watches
his left foot hit the ground a few inches from a Mr. Potato Head. He
ducks out and looks around, keeping his eyes low. There's a scattering
of objects around the vehicles here. One every fifteen feet or so. Nothing larger than a portable television. Strands of cotton candy snagged
in the twigs of desert bushes flapping in the cold wind. Blood singing
in his ears. The sounds of doors closing, weapons being readied. The
laughter has stopped. Voices are low. Roberts is scanning the buildings
through binoculars. Veronica stands by his side, hands on her hips. She's
dressed like a CNN reporter in a war zone. Tan ballistic helmet, dark
trousers and boots, a down jacket exactly the colour of the vehicles that
drove them in. Over it a stab vest and a black shemagh. Pale lipstick like
a 1960s snow bunny. It glitters when she smiles at Roberts. *Mad as a box
of frogs*, Rao thinks. *Madder than fucking ever.* There's another round of
check-ins on the radios. All the headsets are working fine.

After the radio check, Hunter nods to an outcrop fifty yards away. Says she's heading up there with Carlton. "Are you going to be ok?" Rao asks her automatically, feeling a flush of hot humiliation as soon as he hears himself.

"I am and will be," she says evenly. "Behind that BFR we got cover, clear lines, and our guy with the M110 tells me he was top of his class at sniper school. And if he fucks up," she whispers, "I can always call in a hellfire from Creech."

"Don't do that," he says, aghast. "It'll just spread the—"

"Rao," she says, face softening. "You're an idiot. Buy me a beer later."

"Ok," he says. She hoists her rifle and pack, and Rao's back aches sympathetically as he imagines the kind of weight she's carrying. Must hike with a pack like that all the time on ops like these, he thinks. She's so ridiculously badass. Fucking hell. He's within a whisker of asking her to marry him when she turns and looks him directly in the eye. He starts a little guiltily.

"Rubenstein comes back alive, Rao," she says. "You hear me? You have to do two things. You open your fucking eyes, and you make sure he comes back alive."

"Uh, Roger," he says.

She nods. "Then I might even buy *you* a beer."

He watches her walk away, heart strangely bruised. Adam steps in front of him, gives him a tight half smile. "Shit gets weird before this kind of thing," he advises. "Try not to take anything on. Always look to what happens after. It'll be fine."

"Is that Rubenstein fine?"

"Mission fine. Eyes forward, Rao."

The wind blows at their backs and prickles with ice. The sky all the way to the horizon is heaped with clouds. Rao stands by the vehicles, takes a lungful of bitter air. He doesn't want to look forward. Doesn't want to look back. Doesn't want to turn his eyes to the buildings he's keeping behind him. Everything out here but Adam feels unreal. And Adam is somehow almost impossible to look at. These are his real clothes Rao sees now, the reason his suits always look wrong. Helmet, tactical vest, backpack, combat pants, boots. But in battle gear he seems so absurdly slight compared to the guys around him, like a kid play-ing dress-up. When Adam drops to one knee to relace his boots, Rao knows that what he's seeing is an old premission superstition, knows that he has done this many times before. He watches Adam tying his laces tight, and his chest hurts.

"Adam—" he says as Adam rises to his feet, looks at him expectantly. But it's no good. He doesn't know what he was trying to say.

"I'm going to keep you alive," Adam says, low and urgent. "It's going to be the last goddamn thing I do."

Rao snorts. "You're a dramatic cunt, Rubenstein. Did I ever tell you that?"

Adam grins, wipes his mouth with the back of one hand. "Yeah, Rao."

CHAPTER 69

When Roberts gives the order to move out, Veronica smiles at the troops like a benevolent schoolteacher at the commencement of a class excursion. Rao's eyes linger on her smile for far longer than it lasts. She catches him looking. Purses her glimmering lips, falls into step next to him.

"How are we feeling, Rao? Excited?"

"Thrilled," he says. He's trudging behind Adam, close enough that he blocks out the sight of the buildings ahead, keeping his eyes on the ground.

"No last-minute nerves?"

"I'm *all* nerves, Veronica."

"Oh, Rao. Don't be so Cowardly Lion."

A tight laugh. "*Wizard of Oz*, is it?"

"Isn't it?"

"Not as far as I'm concerned it isn't."

"You started it, Rao. Don't you remember?" He does. He shakes his head. "You told me Rubenstein was the Tin Man. No heart."

He's sure Adam heard that.

"Fuck off."

She beams. "So who are you? Dorothy?"

"Toto," he grates.

That gets a peal of laughter. She continues to look amused for a while, then she catches sight of what's ahead and her expression shifts to fascination. The objects are strewn more thickly now and approaching on their left is the first of the larger EPGOs. It's a small section of a municipal park, tinted oddly, skewing faded Kodachrome. Thirty feet of lawn, a regimented bed of glowing red geraniums. Something that might be the back of a dog is moving fitfully among the blooms. Behind it is a houseboat, rocking slowly in the sand. He looks down the line. Credit to the soldier boys, they're still marching. Eyes forward.

A melody. Close by. Carried on the wind with the snow. It's a child's tune: plangent, unearthly. Rao instantly knows what's making those tiny, bell-like tones: it's a Fisher-Price clockwork record player, and it's playing "Jack and Jill." The crunch of feet on glittering buttons spilled over gravel, the crack of boots on a plastic Buckaroo: the music floats over and under everything. Impossible to locate, impossible to ignore.

One of the unit stops. His hands are tight fists. "I'm going to find what's making that noise," he mutters. He looks about, hooded eyes frowning under his helmet. Baker.

"No, you are not," Roberts calls to him. "Eyes forward. We have an objective."

"And I'm not going to make it there, sir, if I've lost my damn mind. I'm gonna find that thing, and I'm gonna kill it."

"It's a music box."

"It's in my fucking teeth."

"Charlie Mike," Roberts says tightly. After a moment of tense irresolution, Baker walks on.

Soon the piles of objects are so densely packed they scramble in single file. Rao slips on the icy roof of a purple Toyota Corolla; Adam grips his hand, helps him over. They have to turn sideways to squeeze their way between the walls of a small Spanish Revival house and a section of rusted chain-link fence covered in kudzu vines. And then, suddenly, they're between the trunks of tall trees, pacing across deep leaf litter, and the air is soft and warm and rich with birdsong, and the light that filters down through the greenery above is so golden, feels so impossibly safe, that Rao finds himself near tears. He hears his next footfall crunch on gravel, not leaves, and as they step out one by one back into snow, a hummingbird the colour of a wine bottle in full sun accompanies them for several feet until it halts in the air, turns back towards the warmth.

Adam stops in his tracks.

"What is it?"

"The surveillance plane," Adam whispers.

It was. Now it's something else. The wreckage is forty feet away, twisted, the plane tipped on one side, but even so Rao can see the shining aluminium wings of a smaller aircraft emerging from the sides of the fuselage near the nose.

"He manifested a Mustang," Adam says. He sounds sad.

"Pilots," Rao says. "Decidedly not immune. Romantics."

"I'm going to check it out," Adam says. He raises one hand; the group halts and waits. Rao follows him to the crash. Close up, Rao runs his fingers down the join between the plastic composite of the modern plane and the unpainted metal of the wartime one. It's seamless. Everything smells strongly of kerosene, the snow melted on the fuel-soaked ground. And though there's no sign of a fire, when Rao rubs one thumb against the shining metal, it pulls a layer of thick black ash from the surface. He wipes it away on his sleeve, looks towards the nose. There's blood inside the canopy, bright splashes of it across the complicated bisecting geometry of windows that are an amalgam of both planes. Adam hops up on one of the silver wings, peers in. "Both cut in half," he calls. "Mustang cockpit's a lot smaller than a Dash 7's. I'll check the cabin for the system ops."

He moves further along the wing, crouches to look in one of the smaller windows, then slides to the ground, walks back to Rao.

"Survivors?"

"Negative. It's a mess in there."

Veronica raises her eyebrows expectantly as they approach. Adam shakes his head. She turns and murmurs something to Roberts; they continue towards the building.

The building. It's close now. It's time. He can't hold out any longer against the need to see it. He takes a deep breath, raises his eyes, and the world clicks into a different shape.

All the photographs Rao's seen of it were taken in sunlight, sheet fasciae of corrugated steel burning white in the Nevada sun. But now the building is grey, the clouds above so low that shreds of vapour cling to gantries, shift over the upper floors. It's huge. An irregular mass of boxes like a collection of hangars, brutalist, uncompromisingly industrial, glacially cold. This close, the structure is oppressive. Feels like it's falling on him. He wants inside so badly he can taste it, feel his fingertips itch. He tries to push the need away, but it pushes back so hard he staggers on his feet.

Veronica notices. Catches at his face with one gloved hand, turns it, looks into his eyes. He looks into hers. Grey. Cold. Speculative. They're conducting a professional assessment, and it irritates the fuck out of him. He takes her wrist and pulls her hand away. "I'm fine, Veronica. Don't fuss."

"But you're so very important, Rao. I'm simply protecting our primary asset," she says. She's smiling. She's crackling with something like elation out here. It's unpleasant standing anywhere near. He's about to respond with a few well-chosen words when he sees Adam is looking at him. Their eyes meet. And with a click, a flash of intuition, of relief, Rao knows that Adam understands.

He grasps the depth of longing Rao has for what's inside those buildings. He knows it. Shares it. He's feeling it too. No. Wait.

A clench of pain deep in Rao's chest. A sudden, searing comprehension. He knows, now, what that longing in Adam is.

It's not for the building.

And now holding Adam's gaze is like trying to swim to shore in a riptide. Feels like every safety the world has ever possessed. But Rao's not strong enough. What's pulling him the other way is too powerful. The gravity well's hauling him in. He'd had no idea what Adam felt for him. How could he? Or maybe he'd known but hadn't been sure. He couldn't be sure. It's Adam. Adam's impossible. It's impossible.

It's impossible.

Adam blinks then, like he's been answered. Lifts his chin, speaks. "I got it, Rhodes."

Rao'd forgotten she was there. He feels her pat him softly, proprietorially on one cheek, sees Adam's eyes narrow as she does. Rao steps back. He's a fucking idiot. All this time. Why hadn't he—

And then what's waiting for him in the buildings ahead pulls on him hard, fanned bright like a fire in a high wind. Too bright, too hard, and he's carried towards it.

But Adam, now, is right by his side.

The objects are smaller around here, less densely packed. The last fifty yards are uneven but easy going: board games, comforters, lampshades, plush toys, sections of Scalextric track. They halt on a stretch of close-mown lawn frosted with snow in front of the personnel entrance of the concrete block annex that leads into the cold bay on the western side. Two small cushions are propped delicately against the door.

Rao knows the drill. He's supposed to wait until the soldier boys have, as they delicately described it, "cleared the room." But he makes to follow them when they file inside. Adam extends an arm across his chest, keeps him in place. He balks at it. Feels like a horse in a starting gate.

"Let them, Rao."

When the clear comes through on their headsets, Rao follows Adam inside, Veronica close behind, Baker taking rear guard cover. The space they enter is the size of a sports hall, angled forests of pipework running across green-painted walls furred with patches of white. The scurf looks old, as if minerals in the bricks had leached out over the years, but Rao doubts that's what he's seeing; the ghostly patterns resemble winter branches.

He drags his eyes to the centre of the room, where two of the soldiers are crouched over bodies on the concrete floor.

"We're not the first team in here," Rao says slowly.

"Of course not," Veronica says, close to his ear. "There've been two others."

"Always good to know we're the last-ditch fallback. Adam, did you know we were the children's fucking crusade?" He walks over, peers down at the nearest corpse. It's clutching a small tub seat upholstered in orange velvet. But the velvet isn't confined to the chair. It runs up the extended arm in a curling patch that spills over one shoulder, edges fused into the camo hazmat suit. The body next to it is curled around a dog. This one isn't a beagle like Monty's. A white feathered tail extends from under an arm, swaying gently, but the rest of its fur is patterned like camouflage. There's condensation in the visor. He's glad of it. He doesn't want to see the face.

The third body lies facedown. Things protrude from its back that look like tubes of half-melted glass.

"Alive?" Adam is asking the medics.

"Unlikely. Doesn't matter," Veronica replies. "We're not here for them."

"Hazmats aren't—"

"NBC suits are not effective, no. They wouldn't be."

The light inside the hall shifts intermittently like sunlight slipping in and out of clouds. Rao looks up. There are no skylights, no windows at all. The light has nothing to do with the weather.

"Radio's down," Roberts says shortly.

"Jammed?"

"Random noise."

"I got cocktail party," Garcia says. "Voices. Music."

"Same," Stewart says. Then, more uneasily, "It's . . . a choir?" He tilts his head, then shakes it. "No. I think I'm hearing a Pan Am commercial."

"That's fucked up."

They futz with their sets, quickly determine the radios are useless. After a brief huddle they decide to continue.

"Old school?" Rao enquires. "Hand signals and shit?"

"Yeah," Adam says. "Keep close."

MP5s readied, Roberts and Stewart slip onwards through the door into the old machine shop, refitted, Rao knows, as a conference room. Ten seconds later, Stewart reappears. "Clear. It's dark. NVGs are fucked. Flashlights."

"What—" Rao begins.

"Torches," Adam says, pulling one.

CHAPTER 70

"Why can't we at least have a go at getting the lights on now that the night vision things have decided to die?" Rao complains as they file into the room. Adam's chin strap tugs; he's not used to smiling, however grimly, when fully dressed. "We're running about in here using fucking mag lights."

"They're easy to shut off," Adam says. Smiles again at Rao's dramatic sigh.

"What's that got to do with shit?"

Roberts answers for him. "If we need to go dark, then we can without issue," he says. Stops moving. Turns around to shine his light in Rao's face. "Without too much issue."

"Fuck off," Rao mutters, squinting.

Roberts sniffs at Rao. Turns. Keeps walking.

"Prick," Rao tells Adam, under his breath.

"Mm," Adam replies. Rao's not wrong.

They continue in silence. The sweeping movements of the flashlights pick out screens, potted plants, poster presentations, the Lunastus logo in silver relief on one wall. Everyday corporate scenes, intermittently broken by EPGOs. A bright-blue bicycle, white and red streamers growing out of the handles like plastic ferns, standing in the middle of the room at an angle, like it's leaning against a wall. Adam's light catches on the face of an American Girl doll moving toward them, stopping, hobbling away. Gesturing and making sure that Rao stays close, Adam breaks rank to check it out.

The doll wears pigtails and red glasses and moves like half a human. The left half, to be precise. That half moves like it's breathing, like there are nerves under its skin, as if its glass eye can see. The left leg steps confidently, drags the right side in a limp. The eye that can see looks up at Adam. The doll stops. Backs up.

"That's weird," he says.

Rao peers over his shoulder, shrugs. "Is it? Prophet made it," he says. Bored. Explaining the obvious. Adam doesn't feel right taking his eyes off the doll, but he glances at Rao. "Prophet doesn't want anything to do with you, love," Rao adds.

"Ladies, are we boring you?" Roberts calls.

Rao shares a withering look with Adam. "Found a doll, Roberts. You know how it is."

"I do not."

"That's not true," Rao whispers.

Adam leads them back to the group. "American Girl doll. It was walking around," he reports. Watches Roberts's face tighten in confusion, maybe frustration, as he forces himself to keep up. All mission, no matter how crazy it is. No matter the struggle to maintain psychological pace.

"Hostile?"

"Complicated," Adam says. "Mobile objects seem drawn to the group but will move away from me."

"You alone, Colonel?"

"Seems to be."

Roberts's expression tightens further, making more of his scars apparent, conjuring them on his face the way Rao can think a cigarette into existence. "This team is immune," he says. Sounds out. An assumption. Adam doesn't interrupt, but he can feel Rao bounce on his heels beside him with the urge to say something. Not a great sign. "So we'll continue as planned and face any kinetic objects when and if that happens."

"Yes, sir."

They file into a wide, dark corridor, where the air is sweet like spun sugar. Reminds Adam of summer heat despite the cold. "Bazooka," Baker says. "That pink gum. You remember that? Smells like that shit."

"Less chatter," Roberts calls from the front. He takes a breath, ready to spout another ass-chewing command, but doesn't get a chance. The noise he makes is cutting. Sudden. Pain. Like he stood on something sharp.

A struggle made of light. Roberts's flashlight slashing through the dark, through the silence. Silence, except the rusty creak of what sounds like pipes to the left of the group. The team drop to their knees. Lights up, weapons switched and forward. Adam tugs on Rao's sleeve and then moves, low, up the line to find Roberts. He's not there.

Adam gestures behind him for the team to stay close, leads them on slowly. The creaking gets louder. Closer. Adam isn't just hearing it on their left any longer. It's in the air. Sharp, metallic, mixing with the sugar-sweet smell around them. His light catches movement, something shiny, polished to perfection. He moves toward it. The creaking pipes are louder, and now Adam can make out another sound underneath.

Choking. Gasping.

The light cutting through the corridor from their flashlights is selective, so it takes Adam too long to figure out what he's looking at: Roberts tangled up in the bars and spokes of the bright-blue bicycle, glittering under their lights. It's twisted around him like a snake, a living thing, but as soon as Adam reaches toward the contorted mass of Roberts's limbs and bike spokes, it starts to loosen up. Begins to move away from him.

But he's too late. He can tell from how wildly Roberts's eyes darted around, by how frantic his gasps sounded before they stopped. He's dead by the time he hits the floor, moments after the bike unfolded from around his body and let him go.

"Fucking hell," Rao breathes, eyes wide.

"Asphyxiation isn't the worst way to go," Adam murmurs. He calls back at the team. "Watch your step."

A pause. Lights tracking through the corridor to his voice, to his face.

Lights tracking down to find Roberts's body.

"Yes, sir." Estrada is the first to speak. The rest echo him.

Baker trots up. Follows orders, watching his step. Quick but careful. "Cleanup after mission success?" he asks.

Adam takes a breath. "Not my area. We continue as planned. Protect the asset, proceed to objective. Estrada, take point. Move forward."

—◆—

The team moves glacially, carefully, after the initial loss. Even Rhodes looks a little rattled when Adam checks formation. She's talking to Rao now, walking in front of him. He can hear every word.

"Roberts wasn't in a trance like the others," Rao says.

"Didn't seem to be," Rhodes agrees. "It's unfortunate that we haven't evidence to know whether he was drawn to that particular EPGO."

"He wasn't."

"Rao—"

"One day you'll trust my hunches," Rao sighs. "If you survive this."

"I'm immune."

"Roberts thought he was too."

"Yes, he did," Rhodes says mildly. "But he wasn't."

Rao exhales. A sharp hiss. "I knew it. Bloody hell, Veronica."

"Soldiers die all the time," she replies. Sounds bored. This kind of mindset isn't new to Adam. People think of soldiers that way. Cannon fodder. Human shields. Sentient robots with guns. "No one enlists thinking they're immune to bullets."

"He thought he was immune when he agreed to this mission."

Sure as shit the others think so too. Adam speaks then, low and quiet. "Volume control, Rao," he warns.

"Shit," Rao whispers. "All of them, Veronica?"

"You'll be perfectly safe, Rao. As will Colonel Rubenstein. As will I."

"D'you think? Because that murderous bike wasn't Roberts's EPGO."

"No. That *was* interesting, wasn't it? He was killed, and quickly. One might go so far as to say purposefully."

Two steps in silence. Creaks of metal behind them. Lights twinkling ahead.

"Actively hostile." Adam finally says what he assumes they're all thinking.

"Which means immunity doesn't count for shit anymore, Veronica," Rao adds. "Not when Fisher-Price fuck knows what is out there braying for blood."

Rhodes makes a thoughtful, almost melodic sound. "That EPGO was notable, yes—"

"Not the point I was making," Rao mutters.

"Since it was free roaming. Unattached from a creator. And a generalized object, wouldn't you agree? Most people had a childhood bicycle. Nostalgia manifested through shared cultural experience rather than from an individual's personal memories."

"Like the radio," Rao says, "in your ward."

"Very good catch."

"Piss off, Veronica."

"Think of what that could imply," she goes on. Adam can hear the hunger in her voice. "We already know Prophet changes periodically to suit its purpose. It could be casting a wider net."

Purpose. Rao looks back at Adam, eyes wide. Adam meets his gaze. He heard it all.

Farther down the corridor, slow, flashing lights shine from under a door, pooling on the floor. "Sweep?" Estrada inquires, calling down the line.

Adam looks back. Gives him the nod. "Go."

A quick reshuffle, with only Rao and Rhodes momentarily confused about where to stand. Adam keeps Rao close. He couldn't give a fuck about where Rhodes finds herself.

"Do you hear that?" Rao murmurs to Adam seconds before he does. Notes trilling electronically.

Adam glances at Rao. "What is that?"

Estrada cuts them off. "It's Pac-Man," he says. "Nothing else sounds like that."

Rao pulls at Adam's arm. "Look," he demands and in the same breath, "Estrada—"

It's too late. Estrada's pushing the door open enough to let the light spill out, blue and bright, getting brighter as the music gets louder.

"Rao," Adam says, stepping aside to let Rao move in. To let him lay hands. Do what he does.

"What's his first name again?" Rao asks. Adam doesn't remember but that doesn't matter. Rao knows Estrada's first name. He isn't asking for information but trying to fill the air with noise, cover the distorted beeps calling out to them. "Alejandro, mate—"

"Boards," Estrada interrupts, dropping his weapon to the floor, "is the name people used to have for levels. It's all different now."

Rao follows after and Adam behind him, but they're not quick enough to stop Estrada from moving to the source of the light. It's an arcade cabinet. Pac-Man, like Estrada said. The room smells like pizza grease and worn cotton. Instinctively, Adam looks down at his feet. He expects the carpet underfoot but not how it grows out from under the cabinet like a rash. Dark woven tendrils with haphazardly dotted russet-tinged geometric shapes designed to look amazing under ultraviolet bulbs. His feet, Rao's feet, Estrada's—their boots pull at the fabric, soaked to saturation. Too thick to be water.

Someone already died in here.

Adam is looking around for the corpse when Estrada reaches the buttons in front of him. He sighs bodily in relief. Pixelated ghosts flicker up, looping electronic notes.

"Rao," Adam says as Estrada bows over the glass in front of him. The game plays at an angle, not straight on, and Estrada's changed his stance to compensate. He bends with the cabinet, a silhouette against the flicker. He isn't suddenly unresponsive, like everyone else coming into contact with their EPGOs, but passive. His fingers are moving, one hand resting on buttons and the other driving a small joystick. Precise movements. He looks calm. In the zone. Whenever Adam hears another burst of celebratory noises, Estrada exhales like he's lining up a shot.

Rao doesn't say anything. He steps forward, puts a hand on the back of Estrada's neck, and closes his eyes. Adam expects the usual: Rao's jaw relaxing, his eyelids fluttering. He expects to see Estrada step back from the video game. He doesn't expect Rao's frown. Doesn't expect it when Rao tugs on Estrada's collar to expose more skin, place a second hand next to the first.

Adam opens his mouth to ask, but Rao is already answering. "I'm trying, Adam," he says, voice strained. Takes his hand away. Adam catches the barest hint of silver on one palm before it disappears into him like every other time. Estrada doesn't back away from the cabinet.

He turns his head. Only his head. Mouth open, eyes wild in silent fear and obvious pain. Adam steps forward to help, sees Estrada's fingers are fused to the brightly colored plastic of the buttons. Still pressing. Still playing the game. And when Adam takes that step forward, the sounds and lights judder in time with Estrada's sudden scream of pain. The cabinet's trying to get away from Adam. It can't.

Estrada doesn't stay lucid for long. As soon as Adam backs off an inch, the game continues. Even the fused hand operates like it's meant to, Estrada's eyes back on the screen.

Rao doesn't try to touch him again. Doesn't reach out to him, doesn't attempt to break the spell he's under. Just stares at the game. There's movement behind Adam. Rhodes, coming into the room to pull Rao out. Rao goes quietly. Doesn't fight her at all.

Now the flickering gets sharper, the lights brighter, the noises louder. A cascade of aural fireworks. Adam should follow Rao out of here. He doesn't. It's not about saving anyone's life in this room. They're too late for that. They were too late as soon as they heard the music in the corridor. Adam's too late. Too late to see Estrada take his other hand off the joystick and press it to the screen. Too late to see the glass get smeared with blood. Too late to realize the cabinet's hood is bowing over Estrada as he bends to get closer to the game. Adam can see the yellow wedge of Pac-Man reflected in Estrada's eyes. Knows what's happening only as it happens. Way too late to help anyone, even if he could get close enough to do something.

The hood's curve is unnatural, and the whole cabinet starts to crumple as a result. It creases like a beer can and takes Estrada's whole body with it. There's no struggle. The *wakkawakkawakka* noise of the game is deafening now. It churns in his stomach like a heavy bass through a speaker. It's the only noise he can hear.

No screams. No nothing.

When the cabinet straightens up again, Adam looks down at his boots. Even wetter now. He understands why he didn't see a body before. The screen flashes, numbers strobing in the dark.

3,333,360.

"Adam."

It's Rao. He's at the door, Rhodes's arm slung across his chest. But he's not trying to pull away. He's waving Adam back away from the puddled remains of Estrada. When Adam gets close, he sees the strain on Rao's face. "I wish I'd made a better job of it in Kabul," Rao mutters. "Because if I were dead now, then I wouldn't have had to see that."

"You don't mean that," Adam responds.

"I *nearly* mean it, Adam."

"You don't mean it."

CHAPTER 71

"Colonel, there's— Shit, what happened here?" It's Stewart, fingers tightening around his MP5. Garcia appears behind him, eyes wide under his helmet.

"We lost Estrada," Adam says. "What's the situation?"

"Baker."

"Details."

"Dead."

"How?"

"Something. I saw hands."

"You didn't investigate?"

"With respect, sir, fuck that all the way home. No, I did not."

"I saw it," Garcia says. "Someone's nonna got him."

"Nonna."

"Something like a grandma, sir."

"Whatever it was, it was fucking fast," Stewart adds. "It's gone."

And then there were five, Rao thinks.

Outside in the corridor the light is rising fast. Pearl and pink, coloured like sunrise. Tastes of distance, sea air. Rao stares at the walls as they brighten and wonders if what he's feeling is usual in lulls like these in the midst of mortal horrors. Everything's smooth and flowing fast inside; everything outside is clear, sharp edged, etched impossibly fine. And the most unaccountable thing of all—he feels entirely himself. Which is, he thinks with a shiver of surprise, an experience he's never, ever had before. Not like this. He's taken a shit ton of stuff over the years, but there's no parallel, no analogy. It's like his soul, his body, his mind have snapped into sudden, perfect alignment. He watches Adam and Garcia return from Baker's body. They've left him where he fell or was dragged;

from here he's a dim smudge of pink-washed camouflage against the wall at the far end of the corridor. Adam walks straight past Rao to Veronica.

"Couldn't close his eyes," he tells her tonelessly. "They've been torn out."

Adam isn't helping, Rao thinks. Or maybe, just maybe, he's not helping on purpose.

Then Garcia starts. Jumps. Mutters. Throws his HK to the ground. Tosses it away from him. It lands without a clatter like it's fallen on carpet, not concrete. Nothing seems wrong apart from his action, but he's frozen to the spot, staring down at his weapon.

Adam raises a hand, is at Garcia's side in moments. Cautiously, he looks him up and down. "Report," he says.

Garcia shakes his head. "I don't . . ." he starts.

"The fuck," Stewart calls. "Pick it up."

Garcia shakes his head rapidly. He's breathing hard.

"What's your situation," Adam commands.

Garcia blinks, shuts his eyes. "Don't touch it."

Rao looks at the gun. It's not right. It's not—

"It moved," Garcia says. "Swear to God. It *squirmed*."

Adam looks over to Rao, raises his eyebrows, and Rao walks over, crouches to examine the thing. It looks fine. It's wrong, wrong, wrong. He puts out a hand—

"Rao?" Adam warns.

"Yeah, you should be doing this, not me," Rao says. He runs his fingertips along the barrel, and the gun flinches like the flank of a horse.

"It's not a gun anymore," he says. "Everyone check their weapons."

Veronica already has. Her pistol has turned to glass. She holds it up in the sunrise light, entranced. Slips it back in its holster. She wants to keep it.

"Mine's ok, I think?" Stewart says. He tilts it, racks it, unclips the magazine. But as he clips the mag back in, the weapon crumbles in his hands, falls to pieces like it's made of charcoal. Soft dust sifts through the air. His gloves are black. A strangled shout from Garcia, a thud by Rao's foot, and when Rao looks down, he nearly shouts too. There's a row of tiny eyes in the slide of the Beretta, and they're blinking at him. He rises rapidly to his feet.

Adam's checking his weapons and ammo. The barrel of his HK is vaguely translucent. He shakes his head and lays it down. But it looks like his two body-carried 9 mils and clips are fine.

"You're *not* normal," Rao says, grinning. "Thank fuck."

Adam ignores that. He's looking intently at Garcia and Stewart. They're backing away from the weapons on the floor, and Rao knows without testing the truth of it what's happening.

"This is fucked," Stewart hisses. "We need to execute a tactical withdrawal."

"We're leaving," Garcia blurts.

Adam blinks, turns to Rao. "Rao?"

"What?"

"What do you want to do?"

"Oh," he says lightly. "I'm not going anywhere."

"Rhodes?"

"I want to see this through," she tells him. She doesn't sound sure, but Adam accepts her words and turns back to Garcia and Stewart.

"We have an objective," he says tightly.

"We're refusing orders, right now, sir," Stewart grits out.

A few seconds pass. Adam sighs. "I won't tell a goddamned soul. You're free to leave."

Relieved, they turn and walk away. Rao's watching their retreating backs when there's a squeal of horror. Veronica. She's got her boot on something, is pressing it to the floor. Rao can't make it out. It's green and rounded, looks like fabric, and there are flailing arms and things that could be legs—two—but somehow he's sure there are more. He watches her stamp down, hard, as if she's dealing with a cockroach, sees the thing turn as her boot descends. It's a Kermit, with bloodshot Ping-Pong eyes and a mouth full of darkness, hands reaching up towards her.

She keeps stamping until it breaks. Shatters into pieces like a bowl. She turns and vomits, moves quickly away, stands behind Adam, wiping her mouth. Garcia and Stewart had been watching, had seen it all too, and they're staring at the shards of Muppet, its limbs still writhing, when the telltale attacks.

It's fast. It's fast and earsplittingly loud. It rings like a bell. A repeated bell, a school bell. The air is chokingly thick with chalk and the scent of ketchup and sour milk. Flat shoes. A skirt. It's short but somehow elongated, a bun of mousy hair, a face that radiates infinite kindness despite lacking any features except a mouth. Rao takes in this sight in one vertiginous split second, because it's fast, it's appalling how fast it is, skittering towards them, metallic splinters pouring from it and clicking to the floor, and somehow, though heading straight for Garcia and Stewart, Rao's sure it's moving sideways, away from them.

It's not. The school bell rings, chalk dust trembling in the air. It has arms, spindly yet somehow plump, rings and fingers on the one hand that reaches as the thing slips fast across the floor. One huge hand grabs Stewart from behind, reaches over his helmet, cupping his skull, and Stewart jerks as the fingers sink into his eyes, burying themselves far past the things pretending to be knuckles, and like a shot-putter uncoiling, the other arm flashes out to grip Garcia around his jaw and throat. The fingers sink deep into Garcia's neck, sheets of blood streaming down his front, and Rao's watching the soldier boys kick out their death throes to the sounds of school. There's drumming feet in corridors, now, high, childish laughter, and there's a series of sharp retorts to his left, gunfire, and the thing's face shreds into tatters. *Automatic*, Rao thinks. *He shot automatically.* Because that headshot damage doesn't even slow it, it's coming towards Rao dragging Garcia and Stewart like they're part of it, and it's moving like a seal on a quayside, now, undulating, but Adam's in front of him now, protecting him, Rao knows, that's what he's doing, because Rubenstein makes things better, doesn't he.

Clink of shell casings. Chalk dust. Sulphur. Adam's walking right towards the thing and it's stopped its advance, is backing away from him fast, and it's going to fuck off into the bowels of the building with its dead soldiers, but it might not. It might not get away, because Adam's shooting at its knees now, and every shot connects, and it's slowing, because Adam.

Who is everything. He's focus in the midst of chaos, sanity in action, the steel-true *i* in the dot of the ocean. All the safety the world possesses, right there, and this stupid line is running through Rao's head: *Adam's brilliant at this.* Because he is, isn't he. Every round rips away more of what that thing is, and Adam is nothing like he was when he fought the goons in the motel, nothing like he was when he sparred in that backroom, it's like he's singing, now, like this is an aria and every note is perfect, pitched to shatter glass. Like the whole building resonates with every step, every shot.

Fuck, Rao thinks. *Adam.*

Adam's above it now. He's pulled a knife. The thing's not able to move away from him anymore, though it's trying to. Rao watches him sink the point of the blade into its wrist, just above Stewart's helmet. He does so speculatively, as if he's expecting to meet resistance, seeking the right path to carve through sinew and joints, but there's no resistance. The point slips right through. He pulls out the blade, changes the angle, and with a single stroke slices the limb away, freeing Stewart from the thing that killed him. He props Stewart's body against the wall, moving what's left of his head upright, then turns back and frees Garcia, whose visible skin is slack and paper white and battle dress red ruin.

Now Adam's standing, looking down at the thing on the floor, frowning. It's down but not out, dragging itself incrementally back along the corridor.

"Rao," he calls.

"Yes, love?"

"Can you make something heavy on top of it, stop it moving?"

"Like what?"

"Whatever you like. Use your imagination."

"I don't—ok."

He magics it into existence, then giggles at his creation. For no good reason he'd imagined a transparent Lucite paperweight, one of those touristic souvenirs with ferns and flowers and shells inside, but he's made it of glass and messed with the scale. It's vast. The thing's caught, trapped motionless inside it.

"Nice," Adam says.

"Shit," Rao exclaims.

"What?"

"I could have . . . before, you know? Done this before."

Adam looks at him. "Let's take five, Rao."

They sit for a while, backs against the wall like the corpses a few feet to their right. Rao doesn't look at them. Stares instead at the staples and spent casings littering the floor, the trail of smeared blood with Adam's boot prints tracked through it. And he wonders why in hell he feels fine.

"I should be more freaked out," he says suddenly. "But watching that, it was like . . ."

"Watching a movie."

"Yeah. Exactly. *The Thing*, to be specific. I saw that when I was thirteen and didn't sleep for a fortnight. The head on the table, the spider with the legs."

Adam smiles. "It was like that, yeah."

"But a teacher."

"*Substitute* teacher."

Rao snorts. "Fucking hell, love. Are you always this funny when staring death in the face?"

A sidelong look, amused. Then the faintest narrowing of eyes. "How are you feeling, Rao?"

"Less frightened than I have any right to be. Is this adrenaline? Is this why you always look so resigned? You feel like this all the time?"

"How are *you* feeling, Rao?"

"Why are you asking?"

"Your pupils are blown."

"It's dark in here."

"No, it isn't. But . . . you look steady. You solid?"

"Yeah, I'm good. Where's Rhodes?"

"No idea."

"We should look for her."

"No, we shouldn't."

"Leave no man behind?"

"She's not my concern."

"Adam—"

"Rhodes can look out for herself."

"So what now?"

"We find De Witte."

CHAPTER 72

Deeper in, the corridors are grim. The light feels singed, flutters arrhythmically. For a while the walls and ceilings are brown velvet, the floor beneath their feet buttoned like leather upholstery. For twenty feet, the stench of roses is so overpowering that Rao is forced to hold his breath; even Adam gags. A small plush purple platypus dragging itself towards them on yellow felt flippers gets pinned to the ground by one of Adam's knives and is left there, squeaking in protest.

Then follows a stretch of wood panelling punctuated with the silver of malformed sporting trophies, which turns, a few yards farther on, into a mess of beige computer casings bled into brickwork, scraps of glossy black screens winking with green DOS prompts.

The first door they try opens into a spacious storage area. Bare walls, a stack of containers and shelves. In the middle of the vinyl floor a heap of brightly coloured Tamagotchis squirm against their own chains. The noise inside the room is atrocious, an ear-splitting mess of voices, advertising jingles, laughter, snatches of *Sugar, Sugar*, the NASA Quindar tone, screams from fairground rides. It cuts out as soon as the door is closed.

The next door is faced with a sheet of polished copper.

"RadSafe counting room," Rao announces.

"Yeah. The engineer."

She's lying in the middle of the floor, a small, broken corpse in a white coat, a hazmat mask next to her, her phone still gripped tightly in one hand. Around her, equidistantly spaced, a grid, a perfect array of green plush worms with nightcaps and glowing plastic faces.

"Night-lights," Rao says. "I had one of these. Fuck. *Fuck*," he adds. There are lights beneath the engineer's skin. Inside her arms, her torso, inside her face. The grid of glowworms manifested itself right through her. He stares, swallows back something like an apology. This death is worse, somehow, than Monty's. Worse than any dealt by the horrors back there. It's so quiet. She looks so terribly alone.

The following room is dark and dense with fog. Dripping water. Smells like fall. Banks of flat-screens flicker with static CRT snow. Adam switches on his flashlight. The beam picks out a column of bark half buried in the far wall, and above and around it a tangle of branches with serrated grey leaves and shining fruit.

Rao speaks through the hiss of white noise that sounds like heavy rain.

"Fuck, it's De Witte."

He's on his knees beneath one of the branches, head bowed, hair dishevelled and damp. Both hands are high above his head, clutching an apple he'd reached for, the branch bowed with his weight. His fingers are golden, fused with the apple, spotted with pores and pits, the backs of his hands bulging horribly. Adam crouches, lifts two fingers to De Witte's throat. Rao thinks of Ed dying in the mud. Thinks of the men in cells in Kabul they kept like this, for longer than this.

"Lucky he didn't get full-body contact," Adam's saying. "His hands are gone but his pulse is strong. I'll get out of the way so you can—"

"Adam."

Adam raises his eyes.

"This isn't why I came."

"You don't want to cure him?"

"Nah. Never wanted to in the first place. Man's a cunt. War criminal. Wants to take over the world. But that's not what I mean. Helping him isn't why I'm here." Adam opens his mouth to speak, and Rao raises a hand to hush him. "Don't hold up your fingers and ask me to count them, love. It's the twenty-seventh of November, 2010, and I know who you are, and I know who the president is, and I continue to know what's true and what isn't. With the usual exception. It's just," he points at De Witte, "he is not why I'm here."

"Ok," Adam says, rising to his feet. "What's your personal objective?"

Rao reaches for an answer. He can't find one. He's pinging between the meanings of the terms "immanent" and "imminent" in his head, and he can't get past them to where the knowledge is. "There aren't words for it," he says shortly. "I know how that sounds but trust me. All I know is it was out there. I mean, it's out there." He gestures behind him. "Also, if I fix De Witte now, he's just going to be another thing for you to worry about, because from what I've heard he's a super-high-maintenance asshole, and that's before spending three days hanging from a tree."

Adam's lips twitch. "Ok. We'll come back for him when you've completed your objective. Please inform me when you know what that objective is."

"Don't nag, love. I'll let you know."

Adam smiles at that, glances up at the tree. Frowns. Looks more closely. "Huh," he says. "These apples aren't apples."

"No shit."

"They're gold. I think they're gold."

"Yeah," Rao says. "Hesperides. Doesn't surprise me in the least. You're not thinking of pocketing a few?"

Adam snorts. "Fuck off."

"Yes, let's." Rao loves it when Adam swears like that. "Things to do, places to be."

"Right. You just don't know what they are."

"You're nagging."

"No, just stating the facts, Rao." They're both grinning. The disaster this mission's become, their walking away from De Witte, shock, adrenaline, Prophet in the air: this sudden surge of elation could come from any of those things and all of them. Rao feels peculiarly porous, permeable. Wonders if Adam's caught this mood from him. The elation is a full-on champagne-bubbles birthday morning coming-up high, and it's making whatever Rao needs to do so exquisitely alluring it's hard not to bolt from the room and run to find it.

But he feels it before he hears it.

Feels it in his head, like in the diner.

Ed's gone. Ed's gone, and that stings inside him, and Nancy's gone, and Roberts is gone, and the others, too, and Polheath is done. Though somewhere, he knows, Polheath is still happening.

But it's not Sinatra he's hearing now.

Adam's already looking at the source of the music. His gun is drawn but pointed down. It's a song. A simple song, sung by someone who's not good at singing. At the end of the corridor is an archway deep enough to be a tunnel and emerging from it is a man in his midforties with greying hair. He looks untouched by any telltales. At first, Rao thinks this man walking towards them, smiling and singing, shrugging off his jacket, must be immune.

But that's not true. He knows that isn't true.

And the words of the song he's hearing are—

Rao shakes his head. He understands the words perfectly, knows what the man is singing, but the words he's using aren't English.

No, they are. They're definitely English but they're also every language he's ever spoken, ever heard, ever heard of, all at once. Each word resonates like . . . Rao thinks of how texts have described the inhuman voices of angels as the man walks easily towards him. He's singing to Rao. He's singing *for* Rao. Singing about how the weather in the neighbourhood is perfect. Asking if Rao would be his . . . if Rao could be his. The words sound like a seduction, but not the usual kind. Rao's being sung to like he's a child.

The man tilts his head. He shrugs off his jacket, lets it fall to the ground. Rao watches it drop and crumple onto the concrete, and when he looks back up, the singing man is holding a cardigan so red it hurts Rao's eyes. Technicolor.

Rao glances at Adam. He's frozen in horror. Which is impossible. Adam doesn't get horrified. Bare minutes ago, they watched a man get eaten by a training bike. *That* was horrifying. Adam's mouth is moving, silently mouthing the words to the song like he knows it by heart.

"Adam," Rao says.

Adam lowers his weapon as the singing man approaches. Silvered hair, brushed to one side. Salt and pepper eyebrows. He's the most charming person Rao has ever seen. But it isn't charm. Rao isn't charmed. The man's smile is warm in a way that speaks of absolute safety. Seeing it, Rao can relax. Like he's just walked through the door after a cold day, like his mum is in the kitchen cooking dinner and his dad is watching the telly too loudly. Safe, familiar, welcome. Warm. All in a smile.

The man is still singing. He sings of the day, how beautiful it is, how it belongs to them, how it's theirs to make the most of. He zips up his cardigan gleefully. When Adam shakes out a breath, it takes everything Rao has to look away from this serenade to check on him. Now the horror is gone from Adam's face. He looks—

Adam looks—

He looks like he does when he's sleeping. He looks like he does moments after he laughs. Glimpses of what happiness might look like on Adam's face.

The song continues. The man is still asking Rao to be his, now they are together again.

Adam's expression shifts. Rao feels it too. A pull to this man. A desperate longing for the welcoming safety his presence offers. *Prophet*, Rao thinks. Knows. No threat but Prophet.

Now the man halts. He's standing in front of Rao, eyes twinkling. That red cardigan is grafted to his skin at his neck. He's not human. But he's not a telltale. This man is different. And he's not perfect. Stupidly, wildly, Rao knows he could have done a better job. He could have made this man *perfectly*.

The smile on the man's face is softer now, as he croons another plea for Rao to be his neighbour. He offers his hand. Adam inhales sharply. All the air is gone from Rao's lungs.

The man speaks, then. A normal voice. Friendly. American. Warm, welcome, familiar. Safe.

He's glad, he tells Rao, they're together again.

Rao takes his hand.

There's Prophet in this man, and it is drawn into Rao. Bigger and badder this time. Silver behind his vision for a breath, forever, for a second. He stands, dizzy and solid, hears a soft thud.

It takes too long, this time, to blink himself back into the room.

Mercury, he reminds himself.

Adam, he remembers.

Adam's kneeling by the body of the man Prophet made. "Rao," he's saying, far away. Distant. Muffled like tinnitus. Underwater. In the past. Far in the future. *Right now*, he reminds himself. They're both right here, and it's now. "Did you just kill Mister Rogers?"

"Did you know him, love?"

Adam looks up at him, mouth open.

"Adam. He came from there. It's in there. He was *welcoming me*."

The door's green paint has curled back in hexagonal patterns to reveal the steel beneath. Very cautiously, Adam walks up, brushes its surface with the back of one hand.

"It's here," Rao says.

"This is what you want?"

"Yeah. It's where I need to be."

Adam's face contorts briefly. He lifts a hand to the side of his face, heel to ear. The tips of his fingers pale with pressure as he pushes them hard against his helmet. "I'm going in," he says. "Stay here." Sliding the door open, he slips through. But Rao can't wait. The draw of the room beyond is inexorable, and it's agony that Adam's out of his sight. He steps over the threshold into the hot bay.

CHAPTER 73

It's cavernous. Vast. An aircraft hangar. It tastes sacred. A temple. A cathedral. It's crushingly silent but singing with noise too deep to hear, a cacophony so appallingly loud Rao's chest hurts with it. Adam's a silhouette in winter light. His jaw has dropped. His eyes are wide. He's holstered his pistol. Knows there's nothing a firearm could do against this. He doesn't move, doesn't budge an inch even when Rao stands against him, shoulder to shoulder.

"Is all this—" Adam's voice is muffled like he's speaking into falling snow.

"Yes, love."

Every inch of the hall is covered with Prophet. It resembles metallic rime ice, flocked lace. Veins. Branches. The threading map of a ravenous fungus. For a moment, Rao's back in Ranthambore, walking in the groves of the banyan tree through slanting sun. His eyes slip across the buried shapes of Lunastus's storage system along the nearside wall. Prophet's slumped over them in drifts, over the far doors, obscuring the inspection windows, furring the pipework, the mezzanine, blanketing the numerous corpses spread across the floor. Rao blinks back what feels like blindness, hears Adam's voice.

"What did you say?" he asks.

"What's the plan," Adam repeats.

"The plan."

"Yes. Is there a plan?"

That's funny. It's genuinely funny, and Rao can't hold back the laugh it provokes. It feels like the struggle for breath after a storm of tears.

"I think there is a plan, love," he says. "But it isn't mine."

"Rao, we should go."

Rao looks at him, laughter gone.

"I can't."

"You can. Come on."

He's standing oddly, one foot pointed slightly inwards, hands crooked and shaking by his sides.

"I can't," he says again.

It's that point inside him. The tiny point buried deep inside. The cold. It's opened its arms and is beckoning everything in. He feels a desperate flash of refusal that's summarily dismissed, and he breathes in once and breathes out once, and knows exactly what he is. What he's for. *Funny*, he thinks. *I always knew.* An absurd memory of the moustached face of his career counsellor at school, the one who told him that his questionnaire showed he wanted to help people, and maybe he should consider medical school or joining the police, fast track. And Rao had shaken his head then, amused as all hell, and he's shaking his head now, but there's no amusement. He's recoiling from what's happening to him, but he can't stop it. The cold has opened its arms and it is beckoning everything in.

*

Adam has to blink. He blinks, and then he can't open his eyes. But he sees it all anyway. Like the afterimage of staring at the sun, the sight burns bright and close and terrible against his lids. All the Prophet in the hot bay changes state at once. It slips liquid as running glass, soft as frost on a frozen vodka bottle. Runs along the floor, slides from the ceiling, pours down the walls, flows toward Rao like it's being pulled by gravity.

It's falling into him. Adam's eyes jerk open and he can't shut them. He wants to. Both Rao's hands are held out from his sides. Sinuous ropes of Prophet are streaming up to them from the floor. His head is thrown back, mouth wide, and there's no sound but still Adam can hear him scream, and when Prophet reaches his chest and throat, it pours into his mouth and with a sickening curl like a silvered fishtail slipping underwater the last of it disappears inside.

It's all in him.

He's still standing. His head is bowed like he's at prayer, his chest is heaving, and there's no Prophet anywhere. The room is empty, and Rao is—

How can it all be in him? *How?*

Rao raises his head and looks toward Adam. Not at him. His eyes are far away. There's blood around his mouth. It's terrible to see Rao's face so still, so devoid of expression.

"Rao—" Adam begins.

"Everything's going to be fine. Wait there."

"I'm not going anywhere."

Rao shuts his eyes. His face is animated again. "I can't know, can I?" The laugh is low, delighted, conspiratorial, the laugh in the motel with the lizard. But there's something in it screwed right to the limit. "So that's why," he says. "Fuck."

A pause. "Fuck," he says again. Low, astounded. He's not talking to Adam.

"Rao?"

Rao raises a hand. "Hang on, love, just wait. Be with you in a second." His voice is precise, teetering on the edge of laughter. His punch-drunk voice. He grins. It's a brilliant smile. But his open eyes are dully shining metal, and the tears falling from them are beads of mercury, disappearing into his skin as they track down his cheeks.

Is he blind now? He's working through how this will impact his exfil in the rapidly narrowing window in which both of them survive when he sees Rao's eyes clear. They're dark now, and steady, and they're looking right at him, but the sight is almost worse. Adam thinks of the time in basic when an idiot kid jokingly put an unloaded M9 to his own head, everyone laughing. Everyone laughing but Adam because he'd seen something far too true in the kid's eyes.

He shivers. The temperature's plummeting. Sharp on his face. Every breath is fog. He looks down. Frost is crawling across the mess on the floor, furring the toes of his boots, climbing up his laces. It's mesmerizing, but his eyes won't stay where they're put.

They're pulled to the space behind Rao, where the air is crackling, rippling like a sheet on a line in the wind. Patterns are meshing through it. They're painful to look at; they tighten his temples like a migraine.

Then slowly, sickeningly, the space between Rao and the far wall begins to open inward. No. Downward. Adam steps back with a lurch of visceral panic, convinced they're both about to plummet into it. No. It's not down. It's not any direction. What's behind Rao is light. Not any color Adam's seen before. It's not bright, but it's sharp, picking at the back of his eyes like sun off a side-view mirror driving east on a winter afternoon.

The light flutters, dims, and now Adam's looking into an endless corridor thick with smoke. Dark, like burn-pit smoke, the aftermath of a high explosive charge. Inside it are flashes like miniature electrical storms that flicker, shift, and resolve themselves into points of fierce white light. The lights hang there. They're moving too. Slow constellations. Impossible to tell how many. Like the desert sky. Somehow too close, crowding in, and so distant they make his skin crawl.

Adam's useless here. Worse than useless. He's doing nothing.

No. He's doing what Rao asked. He's waiting. That makes it easier.

But the cold is a knife now, grating against bone. It's getting hard to stand. He's so tired. He wants to sleep. It's kind of funny. Never thought it'd be hypothermia. Always thought he'd be bleeding out at the end. He sways a little, knows he's seconds away from sinking to the floor and letting it happen. Doesn't seem any good reason not to.

Wait.

Rao asked him to wait.

Rao. He blinks ice away. Rao's standing right there. There's no frost on his skin, no ice in his beard, horror on his face.

"Shit, shit, I'm so sorry, love," he whispers, and Adam feels warmth envelop him, instant and entire, rivulets of water pouring down his scalp as the ice melts, coursing down his cheeks and into his mouth. It tastes, he thinks dimly, of aniseed and rainwater. The warmth brings in its wake a wave of terror. Nothing is moving except the lights behind Rao, but everything is falling toward him and everything's falling away from him, because Rao's the center of all this, and Adam doesn't know what this is. He drags in a breath, starts counting the lights behind Rao's head to keep himself sane, when everything flips. What was darkness is now the soft orange of Los Angeles sunset smog, and the pale points of light have turned into a host of black shapes, tiny flat polygons, jerking slightly, hitching and fluttering as if they're . . .

"They're kites," Adam says—suddenly, stupidly sure.

Rao nods. "They can be anything."

The kites freeze in place. Fall from what isn't the sky. They fall like shot birds, dead projectiles, onto . . . Adam can't make out what they are: things resolving from a chaos of mess and light. Containers. They're things to hold the kites, the stars, in rows. Racks of wooden trays with pale satin linings. So many. An infinity of trays. The ones right by Rao's hands are ordinary sized. The ones in the far distance are little more than dust. But they're all here. All on the same plane. It's like— Adam remembers standing between two mirrors when he was small, putting his hand up to press his fingers against the glass of the mirror he was holding, staring through it at the mirror on the wall, at his bedroom, at the posters, the folded shirts on his desk, the models of aircraft on the windowsill—and past that room into another room behind it, and another behind it, rooms receding into infinity. But flat. All in the same place.

He's standing between two mirrors. That's all.

That's what he's telling himself, though he knows it's not true, as he watches Rao reach out for the trays and start sorting through them. He's looking for something as casually as if he were searching for the right pair of sunglasses on the rack of an airport Hudson's, and he's searching with such speed and assurance Adam feels his fingers twitch, unbidden, with the memory of shuffling cards. Sees Rao halt, stop, pull at a tray. The tray is small, no bigger than a .22 round, but Rao makes it bigger, or it makes itself bigger, or Prophet does, and Rao smiles then and picks something from it. Drops it on his left palm. It's dark, and small, and round, the size of an olive. Adam's throat closes, looking at it. It's *terrifying*.

"Do you want it?" Rao says.

Adam can't speak of it. He tries. His throat won't let him.

Rao blinks, looks perplexed. "How long was that?"

"Was what?"

"Since I said something."

"About two seconds, Rao."

Wonderment. "Was it?" His voice is far shakier now. "I'm in a lot of places at once, Adam. I can't stay long." He proffers his palm again. "Do you want it?"

"Rao, I don't know what it is."

"No. Sorry. Of course you don't." He licks his lips. Swallows. "Well. I guess you could call it a second chance." He picks the thing off his palm. Holds it between his fingers. There's a star in it, Adam sees. No, not in it. It's sliding around, just below the surface.

"Asterism," Rao says. "I used to love these stones. This isn't a black sapphire, though, love, it's just what it's making one look like here. Has to be familiar things for me, for this, know what I mean?"

"Yeah," Adam lies. "So what is it?"

"It's the world where you went with your aunt."

He doesn't know the right thing to say. "Do you want me to wear this?" he tries.

"No. I want you to live it."

A low grinding noise, tectonic plates shifting against one another: Adam can feel it in his chest. Dust blows against him; it's not ice now. It's ash. He's not sure what's under his feet and he doesn't want to look.

"Rao," he says slowly. "I don't understand what you mean."

"It. You know," Rao explains, "it's not just here. Now."

"You mean Prophet?"

"Yeah. That. We brought it here, let it in, sort of. But it's not just here. You were right about that. Runs through all . . ." Rao screws his eyes tight, makes the face he does when he's searching for words when he's high. "Times. Places. Ties? Dimensions." He grimaces. He doesn't like the words he's using. "Universes. But it can't make new things. It needs us to do that." He beams. "Needs me, actually, love. Specifically."

Adam hates this. Rao is talking like he's working on finding the best ramen place in town while Prophet slides across his eyes like ink on water and his mouth is sometimes so full of it his words are unclear. When he chuckles, it sounds like his mouth is full of blood. "Vahana. I'm a vahana. I really am." He shakes his head. His voice clears suddenly. "Now changed then," he says seriously. "No, made then. Fuck. Words. Bear with me, please. Please, Adam. It's important. This is the thing. I've always been here. Right here, because the thing is, it can't create on its own. It needs a mind to do that. And there are a lot of places, universes, that don't have complicated things in them, and it likes things complicated. Complicated is life, yeah? That's what it does. Takes life to places where there's none. So . . ." Rao falls silent. No. He doesn't fall silent. He stops moving.

Everything does. Blurs, stops dead. The sensation is so exactly like looking through a defocused scope Adam wants to reach up and fix it. But he can't move. Wants to scream. Can't. Time has pressed him into glass. Then, with a low, soft crack like the slowed-down noise of ice dropped into warm scotch, everything is back in movement. More ash against his face, blown against his skin, raw citrus in his mouth.

"So I can make anything now. Make a whole world. Remake this one," Rao says, as if he hadn't stopped at all. "So this"—he holds up the sapphire—"this, and all the others, what they are, are alternate worlds. Very close to this one. Like in sci-fi."

"You don't read sci-fi, Rao."

Desperate. He's desperate for everything to be—

"It's why I can't tell. Why I've never been able to tell. Why—" His voice dies away like the words he's using have turned into something else. Adam hates how obviously he's struggling to talk. The pain of witnessing it is clean, deep, unspeakable. Then Rao relaxes, speaks quickly, mouth clear of metal, his voice soft and serious. "With you. As long as I've known you, I've been trying to read you." He frowns. "The way Prophet works, I've always known you. And I've seen all of you, all the Adam Rubensteins in all the universes closest to this one, all the choices they made, all the things they came to be, all the branching ramifications of every decision they made, everything they did and said, everything that happened to them." He pauses. "And all their truths obscure yours. Like . . . you say you grew up in Vegas? I heard that and it never felt true to me because so many of you didn't grow up there. Some didn't grow up at all. Some died later. Some . . . Let's not talk about those," he says hurriedly, face lit like it's night. His eyes are glittering. Everything else is in shadow. "You're an uncountable number of people, Adam. I can't tell what's true about any of you."

Somehow Adam summons a smile. "Figures," he says.

"What?"

"I get it."

"Do you?"

"I promise, Rao. It's not a lie."

Rao looks at the glittering black sphere. "I'm not lying either, love. This thing I'm offering. The world where you went with your aunt. Where she lived. I can show it to you."

Darkness. Instantly, Adam knows it to be persuasion. But it's not the gun-to-the-temple kind. It's like when they're on a tight schedule and Rao's nagging him to stop for lunch. Or when Rao's refusing to get out of bed, pulling the covers over his head, repeatedly insisting he's still asleep and Adam should fuck off. Rao persuasion. Soft. Soft and so familiar he almost smiles.

And there's something else.

It's staggeringly unfamiliar. No. It's not. He's felt it for a long time. He knows what it is. This is more than a place he sleeps in. And he knows, too, that it's only dark because his eyes are shut. But he doesn't need to open them, because he knows where he is. He's home. He's lying in bed, a cool breeze on the skin of his face and his chest and arms from the open window, dust and creosote bushes and desert air just before dawn. He's on leave and he isn't going anywhere soon, and there's the smell of coffee, and there's a dog curled over his feet and he can hear whistling from the kitchen, and Sasha is in Sacramento, she's visiting next weekend, and Rao is—

Rao's not there.

He sits up, opens his eyes, stares at a pair of drapes he knows he chose in a store in Summerlin and has never seen before.

Rao's not *anywhere*.

And that's enough to pull him back to the hall of horrors. The wrench is terrible. He can feel the presence of those other universes now. So close. Like someone looking over your shoulder, reading what you're reading. Exactly that same discomfort, pushed way past the limits of what he can bear. It's insanity, and it's here. He doesn't know how much longer he can stand. But Rao looks so proud of himself. So delighted to help. So expectant of good.

"That wasn't real. That was Prophet," Adam whispers.

"It wasn't *not* Prophet. It was just me showing you what's on offer. I can make that real. Right now. Sasha's alive, you're happy. You're *happy*, love. Go on."

"No, let's get out of here."

An expression chases itself across Rao's face. Bafflement or pain. Both.

"Adam," he says in his most serious voice, and it's terrible how much he manages to put into his name. He holds up the black olive again, the star slipping downward as it moves.

"I don't want it."

"Why not?"

Adam can't answer that if Rao doesn't already know. And there's no time now. He finds the butt of his sidearm, presses at it with his palm. Hands would slip right through.

"Rao, we need to get you out of here," he croaks.

Rao nods sadly, closes his palm, and the thing is gone. All of it disappears. All the trays, all the worlds, the jewels, the stars, the kites, all those possibilities slip inside themselves, pushing out a burst of searing heat that hits Adam's face like sun on an open burn. All that's left is the rippling no-color light. It's brighter now, and so is Rao, like the light is under his skin, illuminating him from within, and then it dims, stopping down incrementally, until Rao looks like himself again, just like he's standing in a bar or in their room in Aurora, though he's so much thinner, so much more fragile, so unsteady on his feet.

"We need to get you out of here," Adam repeats.

Rao looks at the floor. "I can't do what you just said," he says slowly. "I'm really sorry, love."

He raises his face again, holding Adam's eyes. There's mute appeal in his own and behind it—

Adam steps closer. The air around Rao is unreal. The thought cuts through all others, striking Adam so sharply it's almost amusing. *Unreal*, he thinks. Without reality. Like distant heat refraction, cold and close all around him. Thinking about air is a defense mechanism, he knows, because it's hard to think about Rao now. Even harder to look at him. Easier to look at anything else.

But his attention is pulled, like it always is when Rao bids it. Two days ago, Rao would have lazily said Adam's name, made a quiet noise in his throat to get his attention. Maybe he would have announced something ridiculous. That he stole Hunter's underwear and was wearing a pair right now. Anything to attract Adam's attention. As though that had ever been hard to get. But things are different now. Things have always been different.

Rao lifts his right arm. Touches Adam's chin. That's all. *Focus up*, Adam hears himself say in his head, but he stays silent. Rao sucks in a ragged breath. Torn air. What is Adam supposed to say, hearing sounds like that in unreal air?

Struggling to breathe, Rao still manages a half smile. Almost a smirk. Adam's hands hurt with how much he hates that Rao's still smiling right now. A rivulet of Prophet snakes down from Rao's hairline, slips into the corner of his left eye. He shudders. Coughs. Tries to suck in another breath.

"Rao," Adam whispers, because he has to say something over the sound of the deafening nothing around them, over white noise like he's waiting for someone on the other end of the dead comms channel. Over the sound of Rao's lungs stopping and starting. Wildly, he puts a hand on Rao's chest as though he might be able to help. He can feel it, now. The work behind the gasps.

The fingers on his chin shift. Now both hands cradle his face. Rao's movements are as jerky as his breathing, and it should be harder to be in the moment than it is. More difficult to want to cover up the sounds with words Adam doesn't have. But Rao holds Adam's face with unmistakable intent, and his near smirk turns into the kind of full-fledged smugness that's as familiar as home.

Adam tightens his hand into a fist, gripping Rao's vest to pull him down, because there's no way that he's going to end up doing all the work if they're going to kiss. *Asshole*, Adam thinks, utterly devoid of malice. He looks into Rao's eyes, his face, and he sees the smugness smooth into something gentler and far more honest. The longing in the space between them is so fierce Adam is drawn across it like he's swimming up for air, and for a second it turns exquisitely sharp, a glacial blade drawn right through his soul. His breath catches, just as Rao's evens out. The air shifts again, grows heavy and warm. The light flickers, softens, turns candle dim. Sunset light. But Rao doesn't move. Their lips don't meet. The kiss doesn't connect. It's confusing at first. Frustrating, after all this time. Then Rao sways, loses his balance. Drops his hands from Adam's face to catch himself.

He doesn't catch himself.

Adam manages to pull Rao to him before he collapses, but as soon as he feels that certain kind of weight against his own it's obvious he'll never have to worry about Rao getting hurt again. He sinks to the ground, taking Rao with him. The air around them is normal again. He knows that Prophet has gone. The lighting is bland institutional white. Debris everywhere. By their feet the tattered remnants of what once might have been a Teddy Ruxpin bear, a Howdy Doody cookie jar, a bottle promising *No More Tears!* And Adam sits in the silence, in the normal air, cradling Rao's deadweight, feeling the warmth within him, wanting to keep it there. He pulls Rao's head close to his chest, buries his face in his hair. And then what's left of Rao slips like hourglass sand through his hold, falling inward, flowing into points of tunneling absence that for a second are like spines against Adam's eyes. He feels a burst of heat against his face again, and Rao is gone. Rao is dead and Rao is gone and his arms are cradling empty air.

And Adam *wails*.

Time passes. Time passes, and there are footsteps. He raises his eyes, blinks them into focus. Across the mess on the floor of the hot bay a man with a pale, ash-streaked face is walking unsteadily toward him. For a fleeting moment, Adam thinks he's holding a pistol; his hands are linked, held out from his waist, and metal gleams there. When the figure speaks, his voice is weak and hoarse.

"You brought him? The Indian?"

Adam watches him approach. Now the man is looking down at him. His face is impatient. Expectant. Expecting what he's sure he deserves. Expecting he'll get it.

"Where is he?" De Witte demands. "I need him."

Adam pulls his M9, shoots De Witte twice in the chest.

The echoes of the retorts die in the hall. Adam watches him topple. It's done. He's done.

Hunter's voice in his ear, clear and unhurried.

—Delta 5, Delta 1, over.

He touches Transmit, speaks automatically. Sounds like a recording of himself.

—Go ahead Delta 1.
—Delta 5 sitrep, over.
—Situation's fucked. Over.
—Delta 5, do you have a medevac request?
—Won't be necessary. Over.
—I got your negative on medevac, over.
—I'm Oscar Mike. See you in ten, over.
—Roger, out.

When he steps out of the doors into the open air, the light hits him like a scald. The skies have cleared, and the sun has turned the desert gold. Everything is way too close and far too far away, like he's looking through the wrong end of a telescope. Keeping his eyes fixed on the horizon he picks his way through the rubble, the trash of hearts. It occurs to him that his face is wet. When he drags his fingertips down one cheek and pulls them away, they're painted with blood. He doesn't flinch when a jackrabbit gets up at his feet and jinks away between the objects piled around it, the pads of its feet kicking up Monopoly bills and snow. Just wonders, dully, if he'll ever regain the capacity for surprise.

Adam's used to exhaustion. He's lived inside it for months at a time. Everyone who's served has. It's nothing special. He's familiar with the feeling: ash in your blood, grit in your veins, the world turned tissue thin. He's tired, but this isn't exhaustion. He feels old, like his bones are dust, but at the same time so new and terrible it's like he's been skinned. Flayed and rolled in salt. Every step farther from where Rao died is an effort. Wading upstream through a winter flood. He has no sense of time now. The walk takes as long as the walk takes, and then it's done.

One of the hummers has gone. *Rhodes*, he assumes. He stops by the vehicles, feels himself sway, refuses to put out a hand to steady himself. Widens his stance as he watches Hunter make her way toward him.

"I got it, Rubenstein," she says, when she's close. Her face is grim. "Rhodes dropped a panicked exit, explained the situation. Just about."

"Just about."

"Took a vehicle. Said she was heading back to base. Don't know if I believe her."

"Bugged out."

"That was the look in her eyes."

"Don't care."

He hears the falling screech of a hawk above them. He angles his head to the sky, sees it wheeling against the blue. Gets lost in watching it for a while before he drags his eyes back down. Hunter's looking at him.

He looks right back at her and speaks. "He didn't make it."

Silence. "Shit, Adam."

"I need to go. We're leaving."

PART IV

It's a cutout against the sky. The sky is black. The cutout is blue.

No.

No. It's the other way around. The sky is blue, the cutout is black, and it has wings with feathers that look like spread fingers at their tips.

The bird is very familiar. He's never seen it before.

The sky it's flying through is familiar too. He knows that blue. It's high and soft and tending to lilac and—he's never seen it before. *Fuck. He's never seen the sky.*

He's on the ground, there's dust under him and the air smells of woodsmoke and the bird is a kite and there's something in his mouth that tastes of blood and regret. *What have I done this time?*

And he looks down and realises he's naked, and

Fuck.

PART V

CHAPTER 74

It's a cold morning in Mayfair and Adam is walking through Grosvenor Square. Gray skies. Bare trees and muddy grass. Gilded eagle on the American embassy roof, wings spread. He looks up at the building. *Home away from home*, he thinks, feeling nothing.

She's sitting in a soft armchair in a small, richly carpeted room on the third floor, wearing an emerald sweater, jeans, and a silver necklace. Looking solid, despite it all.

"Ma'am."

He sees the concern on her face before she smiles. "Rubenstein. Good to see you."

He takes the other armchair. She pours him coffee from the pot on the side table and asks him about the funeral. He tells her Rao would have liked it. They sit in silence for a while. Then she explains how she'd been woken by the sound of the Smith & Wesson dropping to the floor. How the nurse had put on gloves before he'd picked the revolver up and bagged it in plastic. How he'd stood there, staring at her in silence, until Miller had said eventually that she was hungry. Would appreciate some food.

"They fed me a slice of cold pork pie," Miller says wryly. "It was memorable."

"Where were you held?"

"Suburban house near Banbury. Oxfordshire." He nods. There's an NSA comms hub at Croughton.

She puts her cup down on the table. "Shall we make a start on the debrief? Informal, as requested."

He gives her an abbreviated account, but still it takes some time to relate. She accepts it all with equanimity, as he expected she would.

When he tells her Rao was overwhelmed by Prophet, her jaw tightens. She doesn't ask for details. And when she asks about De Witte, he tells her what he'd told Lane. "He was contaminated. Prophet had changed him. He was a threat."

"I understand that," she says slowly. "But the thing I don't . . . After Rao died, it was gone from *everywhere*?"

"Everywhere. There's no trace of it anymore. I guess it came, then went."

"Like a comet, huh?" There's something like awe on her face. Then she looks down, polishes her watch face with one thumb. "Clemson. My boss. I had no idea. And these people, this network, it's all still in place."

"It is what it is."

That gets him a sad smile and a long silence.

"I'm getting out," she says.

"*Out?*"

She nods. "Not corporate," she clarifies. "My brother manages a dude ranch outside Bozeman. I'll be there for a while. Teaching the worst of the bicoastal elite how to ride and shoot and fish."

"Trout?"

"Rainbow, brown, cutthroat."

"Very spiritual," he replies, smiling, and with that the pain he carries focuses. A stiletto pushing in his chest. Momentarily, he's lost. She sees him fight his way back. He hates that she does.

"Adam," she says softly.

He stares. She's never used his first name.

"You did all you could."

He's thought about that. He's thought about that a lot. Maybe it's true.

"Rao was an irreplaceable asset," he says.

"From what you've told me, he saved the world. I think that makes him more than an asset. I think that makes him a hero." She tilts her head. "You too."

He snorts. "Ma'am."

"Elisabeth," she says.

"Elisabeth."

"Not Betsy, for the love of God."

He smiles. A real one. "I've never seen a dude ranch."

"It's a pretty place. Anytime. You're back in DC now?"

He shakes his head. "I'm in Vegas for a while for cleanup."

"The things piled up around the site?"

"No. They're being moved with backhoes. I'm on disposal of animate objects."

"They escaped from the facility?"

"Some were never in it," he says. "After that's done," he adds, "I'll be moving. I got a lateral transfer."

"Where?"

"Culver City."

Her brows rise. She looks happy for him. Mostly she looks entertained.

"The EIO," she says.

"Yeah," he says. "The assholes wanted me."

CHAPTER 75

He could have put it in an envelope, sent it in the mail. He was back in England for the funeral, anyway. He still could've mailed it. He didn't.

He hesitates before the door, then raps it sharply.

"Dr. Caldwell," he says when it opens, hearing the catch in his voice. It's only a few weeks since he last stood here. Uncountable years have passed. She looks him up and down. "Thought I'd be seeing you again," she says. "Did you solve your case?"

"Yes, ma'am. Thank you for your book." He holds it out. She takes it, regards it. Raises an eyebrow. It's ruined. Rao spilled coffee on it twice and the cover's torn almost in two. "It's not in good condition," he adds.

"No. War wounds, huh?"

He smiles despite himself.

"How's Rao?"

He keeps his eyes on the book, shakes his head.

"Oh," she says. "Oh. I'm sorry."

"It happens."

That gets him a searching look that turns and tightens the corners of her mouth. "I'm very sorry," she adds more softly. "The kettle just boiled. Cup of tea?"

The tea's citrusy. An unnerving hit of childhood; lemon trees and Sunny D. It's scaldingly hot. He cradles the mug in his hands, willing the burn deeper. He can't remember how to do this. He never knew how in the first place.

"Admissions interviews start tomorrow," she says. "It's good you turned up today. Wouldn't have been free tomorrow. Thank you for the book. Was it helpful?"

Adam has no idea.

"Yes, ma'am."

"Kitty, please. And you are?"

"Adam."

She regards him seriously. So seriously he takes another sip of tea—he's surprised how much he likes it—then steels himself to hold her eye.

"So, Adam, I'm not sure if this is permitted. But do you want to tell me about it?"

"About what?"

"What happened."

Adam swallows. He knows he shouldn't want to tell her, but he does. He wants to tell her all of it. Caldwell's like Rao. Someone who inspires unwarranted confidences. He wonders, briefly, if she'd be useful. Speculates on how she'd fit an operational role. Speculates on whether she already has one. It's possible.

But hearing those thoughts—it's like listening to a ghost. He looks past her into her office. The stone windowsills, the lead frames in the glass, the wooden bookcases, the scores of nostalgic objects arranged across shelves and tables that make him feel a little sick inside. He wonders how he can tell her the truth: that without Rao, this whole calm world would have ended up gone.

When he speaks, his words surprise him.

"I miss him," he says.

"I can see that," she says.

"It got unprofessional."

CHAPTER 76

I t doesn't require concealment: he's bait. He stands in the open and
waits and they come to him. Not all the way. Thirty yards, they'll
slow. Hesitate. He'll take the shot before that.

They leave signs everywhere. Three days ago he'd found a thin
trail in the sand that wasn't a snake. A V-shaped impression that turned
abruptly every few feet, zigzagging for just under thirty yards. He
followed it to an animate Rubik's Cube tucked under a creosote bush,
rotating itself clockwise, counterclockwise, and back again. That one
he almost wanted to keep. Rao'd have loved it.

That got tossed in a bag, like all the smaller ones.

The bags get tossed in the containers in the back of the truck.

It's getting dark and he's been out since dawn. He wants a smoke.
He'll have one after he's done here.

He scans the desert ahead. He saw his target in the far distance, has
hiked toward it for a while. Couldn't identify it on first sight. Probably
got made by someone without a clear imagination. Some of them are like
that. Some are small, like the California Raisins figurine he'd trodden
into the sand. Some are too big to load into the truck. These he tags
and leaves for specialist retrieval. But apart from the truck-sized Very
Hungry Caterpillar, which required far heavier ordnance than he was
carrying, most are human-sized, like this one. Or smaller. There've been
a few dogs. Dealing with those was harder than the others. Something
to think about, when thinking is something he'll permit himself at all.

There.

He stands on the plateau, purpled slopes and peaks of Yucca Mountain ahead, and watches it approach. Snorts humorlessly when he sees
what it is. An approximation of ALF. Dead eyes. Shambling gait. He

waits until it gets closer. Exhales, takes the shot. There's a puff of white. This one is cotton wadding inside. A lot of them are. Which is a plus: ones made of ersatz flesh are heavier, filling the disposal bags with blood. But also a minus: cutting them up blunts his blade.

It takes four minutes to break it down. Twenty more minutes to walk back to the CUCV, drive it to the kill site, bag and load up. He lights a cigarette, leans against the tailgate, and looks down at today's work. There's a low, clicking *woooow* from the bag holding the first retrieval of the day. He'd heard that one before he saw it, a laughing Furby calling *bring, bring, bring* behind a pile of rocks.

A beaded Huichol jaguar. A pillowcase caught on a yucca spike he knew was a target because it was flapping on the wrong heading for the wind. And an orange cat that had walked unsteadily toward him through the desert vegetation, butting greetings at thin air. It had been out here long enough that there were more cactus spines than fur.

When he's done with the cigarette, he'll drive to the NNSS waste disposal site. There'll be the usual exchange with the guy on the gate, the only person he's spoken to for weeks. He'll ask if he's had happy hunting, and Adam will say yeah. Watch him tick them off on a clipboard, then wave to a subordinate to unload the truck and take the bags away. Sealed in shipping containers, they'll join the low-level nuclear waste and classified material in the NNSS landfill, interred under twenty-five feet of sand.

Then the drive back to Vegas. It's better than staying on-site. They've given him an apartment on East Desert Inn Road. He'd smiled grimly when he first pulled in; the place is a faded memory of 1962. Pink-washed brick, wrought iron security screens on the windows and doors, sagging palms in the central courtyard, a long-drained swimming pool. He doesn't even see it now. He'll shower. Watch TV. Find something to eat. Might, if the fates are feeling kind, even sleep.

It's Friday. Long past sundown, he sits on the couch, takes out his lighter. It's a shitty plastic one from the 7-Eleven a block away. Yellow. He holds it for a long time, flicking a flame into existence and watching it die over and over again. Darkness. Light. He already knows he won't sleep tonight.

CHAPTER 77

Adam stands by the window at the back of the apartment. Lets everything outside fall through glass into his eyes. A 737 into McCarran at two thousand feet. Palms and pines. The Wynn. The Encore. Utility poles and power lines.

It's Christmas Eve. There's a low thrum of heavy traffic and "Grandma Got Run Over by a Reindeer" playing faintly through the walls for the fifteenth time today. Strings of colored lights along the breeze-block wall of the parking lot below, where a silver Toyota Corolla is driving slowly across the cracked asphalt. He watches it turn, narrowly missing a pole holding up the sunshade roof, then disappear under the awnings. At that angle, it'll be taking up two spaces. He waits for it to back up and try again. It doesn't.

Nine seconds later he stops breathing. Looks again. Walks back through the apartment. The light is dim; the drapes are drawn. Drags a chair across the floor, drops it in the right place. Walks to the door, unlocks it, unchains it, pulls it an inch ajar. He's breathing again, but the air feels taut, full of dust. His throat hurts as he walks back to the chair, draws his pistol, and sits.

After two minutes there's the sound of whistling outside, getting closer: "Driving Home for Christmas." Hearing it brings a punch of nausea. He wills it away.

Five seconds, four.

Three, two, and the door is pushed gently.

"Adam?"

*

He's holding a gun. He's holding a gun and it's pointed right at him. He looks over the front sights and takes Adam in. His shirt collar's undone and his sleeves rolled up. He's unshaven, there's hair curling over the top of his ears, and he's far, far too thin.

"Adam . . ." The name hangs in the air. "You look like shit."

He waits for a reply. Suspects, when it isn't forthcoming, that it might not have been the right thing to say. He tries again.

"It's me."

"You're dead."

"Ah," he says, beaming. "No. It's complicated. Listen, are you going to make me a cup of tea? The drive was dreadful, and I nearly died. This truck driver pulled right out into my lane." He frowns. "No. That's not true, is it. I pulled into his. Fuck." He looks across the apartment. It's dark in here and not what he expected. There are instant ramen cups on the table, pizza boxes and empties on the floor. A small brass menorah by a heap of clothes on a cabinet top, shoes kicked everywhere. "Is that the kitchen over there? I'll put the kettle on."

"Don't move."

"You want me to put my hands up, love?"

Adam doesn't answer, but Rao raises them anyway. "Look, I'm going to explain, but this might take a while. Do I really have to keep my— Ok, fine. Right. First thing, and this is the most important thing: I'm me. I'm really me. *Really*. I remember everything that happened, all of it. I remember you giving Estrada shit for Peet's, and I remember that fucking Pac-Man that killed him, and I remember the singing man, Mister Rogers, and I remember all the rest, the . . . bigger stuff. I was there, with you, and then I wasn't. I was flat on my arse in a field in Rajasthan. Which was a bit of a surprise. As was me being naked." He makes a moue. "Ok, no, that was less surprising. That's happened before. Different circumstances, obviously. So anyway. I was in Nevada with you, and I knew I wasn't going to last much longer, and then I was in a field— You know, I can't help thinking that Prophet was a bit fucking racist putting me just outside Brahmpuri, considering I grew up in North London, but anyway. I lay there for a bit and looked at the sky and tried to work out what happened and—"

"You died."

"Adam, stop saying that. I understand this is a bit of shock, and to be honest it's quite hard trying to explain all this with a bloody gun pointed at me, but I assure you I am really me, and I know I said it's complicated, but it's not *that* complicated if you just let me explain. I got made again, right? Prophet did it. But perfectly. Down to the atom. Every memory, every part of my too-much personality, everything I've ever thought, everything I've felt, all of it. It's all here and it's all me." He makes a face. "The clothes are new, though."

There's a long silence. He speaks carefully into it. "Actually, I wasn't entirely naked. Adam, I'm going to move my arms now. I'd really appreciate it if you didn't shoot me."

He reaches into his shirt, pulls the chain over his neck and head, drops the tags into one hand, sees Adam's eyes widen a little at the sight of them, and he doesn't think he's being stupid when he tosses them across the few feet to where he sits, but afterwards there's a flash of adrenaline when he realises just how close he might have come to dying again.

Adam catches them without taking his eyes off Rao. Closes one hand over them in the air.

*

He holds his tags in one hand. Pistol in the other. Everything in him is screaming not to look away from the obvious threat standing right in front of him, talking perfectly, ceaselessly, in Rao's voice. Clicking Rao's fingers. A perfect mimic of Rao's panicked glances around the room. Everything in him is screaming not to look away. There's a threat.

There's always a threat. So what if this one is Rao-shaped? That's probably okay. If he's going to go, if he's going to lose his mind or have the last remnant of Prophet come along to finally kill him, then he's happier with Rao doing it than someone else, like Bob Ross.

He holsters the Beretta. Looks at the tags in his hand. They're his—or something like his. He'd never be able to tell without Rao around. They look perfect.

"I'm going to sit down now, Adam," it says. "I'm really very pleased you didn't shoot me. Keep that up, please."

Adam keeps his eyes on the tags as it pulls one of his armchairs, scraping loudly across the floor, to sit near him. To the left, opposite. Near the door. It's still open.

He knows that it's a bad idea to put the tags in his pocket because as soon as he does, he can't stop looking at him. It. Him. This Rao that insists he is definitely Rao.

The new Rao's eyebrows tick into a tiny frown. "Fuckload of ash rubbed into this chair, love," he mutters, flicking the fabric on the arm. He's right, the bastard. Adam knocked over an ashtray two days ago and barely bothered to clean up. "Does that mean you're indulging?"

"I don't think you get to comment on any of my habits."

"Don't I?"

Adam can't stop looking at him. Feels dangerous to blink. But he has to cover his face for a second. "You can't just come back from the dead and expect me to—"

"To what, love? Because you opened the door."

"Of course I did."

"Waiting for me. Did you see me coming?"

"Yes."

"And you haven't shot me."

"Yet."

"I understand if you're still mulling it over," Rao says, evidently amused to hell. Adam could kill him. He looks up through his fingers. Could he kill Rao, after everything? Could he have killed him before, if they'd asked? No. Adam's lines in the sand begin and end with Rao. "But, regardless, I'm still here. You're talking to me."

"I'm going insane."

"I'm flesh and blood."

"You're dead and buried."

Rao scratches his chin, looks intrigued. "Buried?"

Adam doesn't know what to say to that, so he defaults to the truth. "Your family burned something symbolic, but I didn't ask. I brought a picture—"

"Did you meet my mum?" Rao interrupts.

Adam frowns. Can't believe he missed the way Rao didn't care, had never cared about Adam getting to finish his thoughts. "Yes, Rao. I met your mother."

"That's agony," Rao says, kicking his feet. Such a childish action. Adam's chest hurts. "I was supposed to be there to smooth that whole thing over."

Adam remembers how Rao's mother had ushered him to sit with the rest of the family. How she'd taken his hand. He rubs fitfully at his wrist. "I think we managed," he mutters. Gets up. Goes to the kitchen. Finds one last beer in the fridge, pulls it out. "I'll split it with you?" he says, walking back in.

"You're day drinking too?"

"If you don't want to split it, you can just say."

*

Grief looks different on different people. Rao's seen it all: the heavy drinking, the hyperproductivity, the empty eyes, the fake smiles, the constant and unstoppable tears, the stoic silence. Kabul had shown him a lot of grief. He'd never expected to see it on Adam. Or, if he'd tried to picture it, he'd never have come up with this day-drinking, scruffy-faced, overtired, nervous-looking version of the man he once knew.

He's suddenly very close to losing it. All this time he thought he could just tell him. Just like that. Tell Adam what he'd worked out, lying in the dust.

Tell him there'd been a miracle.

That across those few closing inches between their lips had leapt a spark of creation. That all of Prophet had felt Adam's longing and known what he wanted and wanted to give it to him. Through Rao himself, it had given it. A goodbye gift, pulled into existence out of nothing.

Out of everything.

I'm made of love, he'd wanted to say. And Adam was going to look at him cynically, and Rao would tell him this wasn't Hallmark Channel shit. It was *true*.

"Are you out here alone?" Rao asks instead, hoping to hear that Hunter's been keeping an eye on him.

No such luck.

"Are you seriously asking about my love life right now?"

"I wasn't, no, but, well, since the subject's come up . . ."

Adam blinks at him. The familiar maybe-angry, maybe-disappointed blink. The slowest blink in the world. "That figures."

"What figures?"

"That this is what it looks like when I finally snap."

Rao frowns. "No, sorry. You'll have to run that past me again, Adam. You think you've lost it because I'm checking if you're single?"

"Hunter always figured I'd go postal."

"So did I, to be honest," Rao mutters. Adam thinks he's a hallucination, and who can blame him? If Rao hadn't been the one who came back from what certainly *felt* like death, he'd be questioning his sanity too.

"And I'm such a dick to myself," Adam continues. He's grimly amused now, leaning forward in his chair, beer hanging lazily from his hand, brazenly taking in Rao's features. His eyes dart around Rao's face like he'll never get another chance to see it. "I'm so inherently damaged I can't even imagine you being anything other than what you were."

"Bloody hell, Adam, that's a bit hurtful," Rao admits.

Adam snorts, waves a dismissive hand. "Shut up. You always knew exactly when to ask me about how lonely I was. We talked about this."

"Did we?"

"In that hotel, after I saw the clock."

"After you made the clock, love." Rao needs to make the distinction.

"After I made the clock and before you became a god," Adam corrects, amends, smiles sadly. Rao can't bear that smile.

"Less of a god, truthfully," Rao mutters, dropping his gaze to the carpet. Anything to get away from that defeated smile. "More like a vahana. They're the beings that carry gods, Adam. Vishnu's is a bird, Garuda. Shiva's is Nandi, the bull. Lakshmi's is an owl. They're . . . vehicles. They take gods from place to place. They help them extend their powers."

"You think Prophet's a god?"

"Why not?" He sees the expression on Adam's face and tries again. "Ok. I was more like a divine aqueduct."

"Rao."

"What?"

"A divine aqueduct?"

"Could you ever have imagined such nonsense?" Rao asks hopefully. "Surely that proves you're in possession of your reason."

Adam shrugs. "Or it's well and truly gone."

This is the worst conversation Rao's ever been part of, which is saying quite a lot. His chest hurts. His breath is gone. This talk feels like a death all by itself. "Does that mean you considered me a god at one point?"

Adam is silent for long enough that Rao has to lift his gaze from the floor to see what's going on. Sees Adam watching him, occasionally taking careful sips of beer. After far too long thinking, after two false starts when Adam takes a breath only to have the words die in his mouth—its own agony to watch—he speaks again.

"That depends on your definition, I guess."

"What was your definition, love?" Rao asks. Does he want Adam to have considered him a god? No. But he still can't help asking questions. Questions that produce answers that are never true, never false. Just Adam.

"Well," Adam says simply. Takes another one of those careful sips. He's never been much of a drinker. But judging by the empties sitting around the apartment, he's been practicing. "That doesn't matter anymore. Everything's different now."

"How so?"

"Asks the dead man."

"Fair point," Rao sighs. This is so much harder than he expected. "Aren't you happy to see me, Adam?"

That slow blink. "You really need to ask?"

"I really do."

"Rao . . ." Adam sighs, laughs, shakes his head. Looks at Rao. That sad smile again, back to strangle the air out of Rao's lungs. "I'd give *anything* to have you back for real. Whenever I go back there—"

"You *what*?"

Adam frowns at the interruption. "I still work. There's still a mess at the NNSS to deal with. I'm still one of the two people from that team that made it out alive. I'm all they have."

The work is all he has.

"You don't have to go back alone again," Rao decides, as though he has the authority. "I'm right here."

Adam laughs again, a strangled noise. Rao thinks this might be too much but he has to understand. He has to believe what's happening here. "Prove it, Rao."

If Rao didn't know better . . .

If Adam were another person . . .

But he is, now, isn't he? They both are. Rao, quite literally so.

That other Rao is gone. He's with Prophet, inside Prophet forever, always, stretched through uncountable dimensions, innumerable universes, helping it bring life to places where there is none.

But Rao is here. Adam remade him. They both, *together*, remade him. "What do you want me to do, love?" he asks, leaning forward. Adam doesn't back away but inhales quietly, sharply. Unflappable, even when flapped.

"I want you to stop calling me that," Adam says. Whispers. He closes his eyes and they're back at that hotel again, after Adam made his clock. Rao knows now what pain looks like on Adam. Or, more accurately, he recognises it. He's always seen it. It's always been right there.

"Do you?"

"No. Yes. No," Adam decides. His next sip of beer isn't quite as careful as the ones before. "I guess it would be weird if you stopped. You always used it against me before."

"What? I never did that."

"Yes, you did." Adam smiles grimly. "And it always worked."

"I was never manipulating you," Rao begins, then falters. Adam's levelling a stare at him that could strip paint. "*Fine*, dickhead, I attempted to manipulate you once or twice, but not like that. I just started calling you that to get up your arse!"

Adam blinks at him. "Rao—"

"It's a *saying*, for fuck's sake." Rao rubs his face. "I started calling you that to annoy you. You were so uptight and straight—"

"One out of two isn't bad," Adam mutters.

"Shut up. How was I supposed to know *anything* about you, Adam? Let alone your sexuality." Rao leans forward enough to snatch the half-drunk beer out of Adam's hand. He doesn't fight. They're splitting it after all. "I can't even know if you're telling the truth about what you had for breakfast—"

"Eggs."

"So the *idea* of figuring you out well enough to use a fucking term of endearment to manipulate you is insane, Adam. It's laughable. It's *mental* is what it is."

"You've never needed to do a run on me to understand what's going on and we both know it," Adam says evenly.

"We both know that, do we?" Rao says. He's supposed to be having a joyous reunion. *You are fucked, Sunil. This is all fucked, and you are the one who fucked it.*

"No one says the things you've said to me without knowing how I felt," Adam says, then takes a breath. "How I feel."

They look at each other in silence. It's too much but, perversely, Rao finds himself loving it as much as it makes him want to squirm. The electricity of it. The near disaster of it, the near triumph. The victory, not insignificant, in getting Adam to actually *say the fucking words*.

"Adam," Rao says. "Have you considered for a moment that maybe I'm just a wanker?"

"Regularly."

"Cheers."

Adam raises his eyebrows in a shrug. "You asked."

"I did," Rao sighs. Fucking Adam and his flat, unreadable, could-be facts. Fucking Adam and his spinning wheel. Adam. "But I think I'm right. Yeah? I think maybe I was just a wanker for a very long time."

No response for a breath too long. "That's a point toward you being real," Adam says eventually.

"Why's that, love?"

Rao sees it happen, this time. He's watching for it. The lightning flash of misery at the endearment. He's done real damage there, hasn't he? And he had no idea.

"As much as I hate myself, I think I would have at least fantasised you apologising properly," Adam says. "Not that I don't appreciate that one."

"Funny way of showing it," Rao huffs before finishing off Adam's now-warm beer. He regrets doing so instantly. It's rank. Flat, body temperature, slightly backwashed. "This wasn't how it was supposed to go, you know."

Adam exhales. "Enlighten me."

"You were supposed to choose happiness," Rao tells him. It's so simple. Couldn't have been simpler. "You were supposed to have a whole new go at it. Why didn't you take it? I know a thing or two about going back for what's never good for you, by the way. I don't have to tell you this, I'm sure, but maybe you're just addicted to misery."

Just like the beer. Instant regret. He shouldn't have said that.

But Adam isn't mad. He isn't anything. That blank face, beyond pain, beyond sadness, beyond grief or anger. Nothing. Smooth features. He rocks himself to standing and grabs the keys from the coffee table. "Come on, Rao."

"What? Where are we going?"

"Beer run."

*

They make it to the car, but that's about as far as Adam can manage. He should have guessed. Should have been ready for it. He wasn't. As soon as the doors close, Rao's cologne fills the car. Terre d'Hermès. Expensive and rich and cloying and somehow unique on him. Adam's seen the bottle in airports. Once, in a fit of weakness that he doesn't like to think about, he bought one. It didn't smell the same. It needed Rao. Even when he was at his best, that smell was sometimes too much for him. He's not at his best right now.

He swears under his breath, drums his fingers on the steering wheel, and ignores the interrogative look he's getting from Rao. Rao, the dead man.

"It's nothing," he lies. Waits a second to see if he gets control over himself. Another second. Another. No. His skin still aches, and he still feels like everything will end if he reaches out and touches Rao's arm. It's all he can think about. Just to reach out and—

"Could you breathe just a little?" Rao asks him carefully.

Adam shakes his head. The cologne will stay in his throat and nose for days, he knows. Linger like a wound. But he doesn't want to open the door. He can't roll down the window. He can't leave. What if this is the last time he gets to have this? His hands throb with the effort to keep from reaching out. He takes a breath.

"Thank you, love," Rao says quietly.

Adam winces. The old litany: *He doesn't mean it, he doesn't know, it's not his fault, it's all your fault, it's just a word, it's just a word you've never understood, it's nothing, it's never meant anything, you've never meant anything.* He's out of practice. He's usually so much better at handling this, at being around Rao. How was he supposed to know that he'd have to stay vigilant even after Rao died?

"It's not fair," Adam says out loud. Doesn't mean to.

"What isn't fair?"

"I'm in the middle of getting over you," he answers. He didn't expect to speak that truth. He sounds petulant to his own ears. Fuck knows what Rao heard when he said it. Nothing, probably. No truth. No lies. Nothing. That's all Adam feels like to Rao. "I'm not even doing it that well, you know? I'm fucking up daily. And you turn up at my door, and you're—"

He looks at Rao. Turns in his seat and *looks*. Sunil Rao, bane of Adam's career, world saver, royal pain in the ass, and genuinely the love of Adam's life. Healthier than he's ever looked since Adam's known him. Breathing and alive. Filling his car with his stupid cologne.

"Complicated?" Rao offers with a smile Adam knows is meant to be charming. It just looks nervous. Adam could kill him.

"You . . . Do you understand why I didn't take you up on that crazy offer?" Adam asks. The facility in Nevada, snow in the sand, lights all around them, nearly freezing to death as Rao showed him jewels. He's not imaginative enough to have made any of that up, and that's the only thought that keeps him sane most nights. It must have happened, because Adam's dull. Too dull for it not to have happened.

"I'm sorry that I said—" Rao starts, but Adam has no time for his apologies.

"Do you understand why I didn't take you up on the offer, Rao?" Adam hardens his voice in an attempt to get Rao back on task. It works. Maybe, even when out of practice, he still knows what he's doing.

"Loss makes us who we are," Rao intones. He's thought about it, and he doesn't like the answer he reached. "If you'd lived a life without the loss you had, you wouldn't be you. I understand, love, I just wish that I could—"

"I chose you," Adam interrupts him again. Rao looks at him, silent. Adam goes on. He has to now. Adam chose Rao, and Rao was supposed to survive. "I was always going to choose you. You know that. You've known that. Haven't you?"

"I know how you feel about me, yes," Rao whispers, like it's still a secret. Adam was ready for him to lie about it, but hearing him admit the truth feels a lot . . . worse, and better, than the cologne. He knows hearing Rao say it will stick to him, in one way or another, for the rest of his life. "Can I ask you a question?"

"You're going to."

"I'm going to, yes." Rao smiles, a brief quirk of lips. "Why don't you ever want to hear how I feel about you?"

That should be obvious. "I know you think that I'm devoid of emotions—"

"Adam—"

"But I genuinely think I wouldn't handle hearing the truth out loud very well," he finishes.

"The truth," Rao repeats.

"Your favorite topic."

Another brief quirk. "Yes. On that subject, in fact, I'm not sure if I've ever mentioned it, but you are aware of how I can't tell with you?"

Adam closes his eyes. *Here we go.* He's going to get some beautiful and devastating poetry about how Adam is a black hole in Rao's universe. "Yes, I'm aware."

"This extends to statements about you," Rao goes on. But Adam knows this. When Rao asked anyone anything about Adam, about his life or professional details, no truth would stick, no matter how hard Rao concentrated. He'd grill people, back when they first worked together. Adam remembers some assuming that Rao was trying to find dirt on him, that he was working an internal audit of some kind. "So I could say anything at all about you and wouldn't be able to run it."

"I knew that, Rao."

"Funniest thing is," Rao continues like he didn't hear Adam. His voice sounds almost nostalgic. "Since I woke up in that field, I've been able to take a run at two statements. I've been able to run them successfully."

The bastard pauses for effect. Adam could kill him, alright.

"I still hear you, from that time, in my head." Rao's voice dips. Not lower in register, but softer. Serious. "Hear you telling me you hated me. And I can taste it, Adam. It was a lie. You don't hate me."

"I don't hate you, Rao. I've never hated you."

Rao nods. After a while, he frowns. "Are you going to ask about the other statement?"

"Are you going to tell me if I don't ask?"

Rao looks away. Turns and looks out the window. The day is nice. Not too hot, but the sun is shining all the same. A real blue sky, no haze. Gentle breeze. Even in the parking lot, it's a nice day. Adam hadn't seen it before Rao looked away.

"Can we go back inside? I don't want more beer."

"Neither do I," Adam lies. "Let's go back in."

*

He follows Adam when they leave the car. He's not been around Adam again for more than an hour, and things between them have already shifted at least three times. Everything feels familiar. But the changes in Adam are killing Rao. New lines and bags under his eyes. The way his hands shake sometimes. Rao leans against the wall by the door while Adam jingles his keys, a quick search for the one to the apartment, and studies his hands. They're funny. Weapons. But right now, the way those weapons are fumbling with a bunch of keys puts Rao in mind of a teenager on a first date. Nerves making it difficult to get fine motor functions to work.

Oh.

He looks at Adam just as he gives up, sighing. "Rao, could you just—back off? For like a full second. Let me fucking think."

Rao speaks quickly. Takes his chance. "And if I don't?"

Adam stills. Nerves, if they were nerves, gone. Licks his lips in thought.

Rao stares at him, floored by his sudden understanding of who Adam is. How he acts. What he feels.

"If you don't back off, then I won't be able to think," Adam says clearly. It sounds like he's saying something else. Rao can almost hear the words he doesn't say. He fights a shiver. He's taller than Adam by several inches, but it doesn't feel like it. Slowly, like he's reaching to take a gun from a madman, Rao takes the keys from Adam's hands. As soon as they're free of that distraction, as though they were the very last barrier between them that Adam could deploy, one hand grips Rao's wrist.

It hurts, for an instant, like a static shock. Skin-to-skin electricity. It hurts, and then it's gone. A pinch, a spark, and then the circuit is closed. Adam sucks in a breath. That's enough. Doesn't say a damn thing and Rao still feels he can almost hear the words in the air.

**

Since the day Rao died, he's had dreams. Longing fantasies. Nightmares. Torture. All about a kiss that never landed. He's replayed the moment over and over. Thinks that if there were any Prophet left in the world, and if he pulled the same act he did back in Rhodes's lab, he'd manifest the room where Rao died.

Regret. It's an old friend of Adam's. And he knows, standing on the balcony outside of an apartment he didn't choose for himself, his fingers wrapped around Rao's wrist in a desperate attempt to keep him exactly where he is, that he won't be able to live with himself if he racks up another wasted chance in his life.

Not this time.

He pulls, telling himself that he'll feel sorry about not being gentle later, pulls until Rao bends, bows, close enough for Adam to close the distance between them. He thought that he had imagined it, a weird current through his fingers and arm when he took Rao's wrist, but then their lips meet—

**

—it's an SSTV transmission. Tones searching for an image. His brain misfiring, then chasing after the feeling. Known, that desperate hunger, but never for another human being. Not like this. Because this is love, isn't it. The *thought* of it. The pure fucking *rush* of the absurdity of that fact as it turns, solid and true, in Rao's head. He's off-balance, but he's not complaining in the slightest. For all he's got wrong about Adam, he was right about him taking charge. It's perfect. All Rao wants is to open the kiss, so he does. Adam lets him, and it's another uncontrollable rush until—

**

—he bites down on Rao's bottom lip. He's not thinking. Can't think. Just searching for the next sensation. The only thing Adam knows for sure is that he wants to know what it feels like to have Rao gasp into his mouth.

It feels like the balcony is too public. Rao is still happy to bend for the kiss, but he arches, the gasp nearing something more—

**

—which is when Adam takes his keys back and pulls out of the kiss.

"Excuse the fuck out of me?" Rao demands a touch breathlessly. "You can't stop there, love, I was just—"

"Shut up, Rao," Adam says, as solid as Rao's heard him since he turned up at his door. "Get inside. Nobody's stopping anything."

"That's a promise, yeah?"

"You're still talking."

Rao laughs and lets Adam push him into the apartment. Once the door is closed, Adam steps into Rao's space. Doesn't push. Doesn't shove. It's sudden. One step and he's sharing Rao's breath. Arresting. His eyes look up at him, knife sharp. Rao shivers. Then Adam's face softens. "Are you sure about this, Rao?" he asks quietly.

Rao's eyebrows rise. "I'm genuinely offended by this temperature check, love."

"I'm asking because—" Adam pauses. Thinks about his words. "I'm not a gentle person. That might not be what you want."

Rao can't hold in the bark of laughter that provokes. "Fuck's sake," he manages eventually. "Do you even know me?"

Adam's brow furrows. His eyes search Rao's face. Then he nods, slowly, infinitely seriously.

"I think so, yes. Yeah. I think I do."

Glossary

AFO Authorised Firearms Officer: Trained UK police officer operationally permitted to carry a firearm.

AFSOC US Air Force Special Operations Command.

ARL-M Airborne Reconnaissance Low - Multifunction: A reconnaissance and surveillance system carried on a modified De Havilland Canada DHC-7 aircraft.

ATC Air Traffic Controller.

BDU Battle Dress Uniform.

BFR Big Fucking Rock (military slang).

BMT Basic Military Training (a.k.a. boot camp).

C4 (a.k.a. Composition C-4): Malleable plastic explosive.

C-17 (a.k.a. Globemaster III): Large US Air Force transport aircraft.

CC Combat Controller.

Charlie Mike Continue Mission (radio jargon).

CIA Central Intelligence Agency (USA).

CONUS Continental United States.

Creech Creech Air Force Base, Nevada: Base for unmanned aerial vehicles/remotely piloted aircraft operations.

CRT Cathode Ray Tube.

CUCV Commercial Utility Cargo Vehicle (USA): Old-style military truck.

DARPA Defense Advanced Research Projects Agency: US Department of Defense agency for research and development into emerging technology for military use.

Dash 7 De Havilland Canada DHC-7 four-engine turboprop aircraft.

DCU Desert Camouflage Uniform.

Delta 1st Special Forces Operational Detachment-Delta (a.k.a. Delta Force): Special Operations force of the US Army.

DFAC Dining facility on US Air Force bases.

DIA Defense Intelligence Agency: Intelligence agency of the US Department of Defense.

DU rounds Depleted uranium munitions used for armor penetration.

EIO Extranatural Incident Office (fictional): Clandestine US government agency investigating unexplained phenomena.

EPGO (fictional) EOS PROPHET Generated Object.

F-15 US Air Force multirole strike fighter.

Fingerspitzengefühl German term meaning "fingertip feeling," connoting instinctive flair and intuition.

FOD walk Foreign Object Debris walk: Routine examination of flight line to remove objects that might damage aircraft on takeoff or landing.

Fort Meade Fort George G. Meade: US Army installation in Maryland, home to the National Security Agency, US Cyber Command, and over a hundred other agencies focusing on cyber operations, intelligence, and information gathering.

FVEY Five Eyes: Intelligence alliance among Australia, Canada, New Zealand, the United Kingdom, and the United States.

GCHQ Government Communications Headquarters: UK signals intelligence organization headquartered in Cheltenham.

H hour (a.k.a. zero hour): Time at which a scheduled tactical operation is set to launch. US military.

HK Heckler & Koch: German small arms manufacturer. *See also* MP5.

HVT High Value Target.

Langley Town in Fairfax County, Virginia; location of the George Bush Center for Intelligence, CIA headquarters.

M9 Beretta 92FS semiautomatic pistol: US military service weapon since 1985.

Medevac Medical evacuation.

MI5 (a.k.a. the Security Service): UK domestic counterintelligence and security agency.

MI6 (a.k.a. the Secret Intelligence Service or SIS): UK foreign intelligence agency.

Mil-spec Military specification.

MoD UK Ministry of Defence.

Moskvich 2140 Car manufactured by Soviet carmaker AZLK between 1976 and 1988.

MP5 Heckler & Koch machine pistol.

Nellis Nellis Air Force Base, Nevada.

NNSS Nevada National Security Site.

NTK Need to Know.

NVG Night Vision Goggles.

Oscar Mike On the move (radio jargon).

OSI Office of Special Investigations, US Air Force.

Peary Camp Peary: Military reservation in Virginia including the CIA training facility known as "the Farm."

Pentonville Category B Prison in Islington, UK.

PET scan Positron emission topography scan: 3D imaging method using radioactive tracers to investigate metabolic and biochemical functions of tissues and organs.

PHOTINT Photographic Intelligence.

PX Post Exchange: Retail store on US military installations.

Quindar Tones The beeping tones heard on NASA Apollo radio transmissions.

Red Zone Unsafe areas in Iraq after the 2003 invasion.

RTO Radio Telephone Operator.

SAP Special Access Program. US Department of Defense program established for special classes of highly classified information that imposes access requirements exceeding those for regular classified information.

SAS Special Air Service: Special Forces unit of the British Army.

SNCO Senior Non-Commissioned Officer.

SSTV Slow Scan TV: Method of sending and receiving static images via radio.

T1 line Historically fast digital data connection.

Telltale (fictional): Animate, moving EPGO.

UAZ Russian utility vehicle manufacturer.

UN3373 International packaging code for Biological Samples B (human or animal tissues, blood, excreta, etc.).

USMC United States Marine Corps.

VQ Visitors Quarters.

Zhen Xian Bao An ingeniously folded paper container from China, most typically used to store needlework items in Miao, Dong, and Yao traditions.

Acknowledgments

Deep thanks to Bill Clegg for his encouragement, critical brilliance, expertise and wisdom, Simon Toop for his genre-saviness and infectious enthusiasm, and everyone else at the Clegg Agency in New York. Huge gratitude to Elisabeth Schmitz, who took this book under her wing, and to Morgan Entrekin, Deb Seager, John Mark Boling, Judy Hottensen, Lilly Sandberg and all at Grove Atlantic. It's a privilege to be published by them. Thank you, Paula Cooper-Hughes and Alicia Burns, for your expert eyes.

And it's a privilege to be published by Jonathan Cape in the UK. Michal Shavit, thank you from the bottom of our hearts for your support and enthusiasm. Special thanks also to Alex Russell, Alison Davies, Suzanne Dean, and everyone on the Cape team.

This book grew from the inspiration, support and assistance of many people, many of whom read and commented on early drafts. Helen would like to thank Tom Adès, Ray Barry, Nick Blackburn, Casey Cep, Sarah Dollard, Paraic O'Donnell, Emma Gilby, James Macdonald, Debbie Patterson, Cornelius Prior, Kathryn Schultz, Anindita Sempere, Andrew Sempere, Grant Shaffer, Murray Shanahan, Denis Villeneuve and Lydia Wilson. Sin would like to thank Peter Breen, Francine Blaché-Breen, Áilbhe Hines, Eben Bernard, Adam McGhee, Ruth McCartney, Moira Purvis, Brodie Smith, Bebhinn Hare, Lauren Mehl and Frank Hicks for all the cheerleading and willingness to listen to the highs and lows. Special thanks to Rachel Purvis, who would have loved being on this journey with us.

Special thanks from both of us to Christina McLeish, Toby Mayhew, Phil Klay, Dan Franklin, Bharat Tandon, Sarah Phelps and Abigail Elek Schor. And a special thanks also to the fic writers of AO3 and the internet.

HELEN MACDONALD is a writer, poet, and naturalist. They are the author of the bestselling *H Is for Hawk* and *Vesper Flights* along with *Shaler's Fish*, a history of falconry, and two other books of poetry. They've written and presented award-winning TV documentaries for PBS and the BBC. *Prophet* is their first novel.

SIN BLACHÉ is an author and musician. They have been writing horror and sci-fi stories all their life. *Prophet* is their first novel. Born in California, they live in the Northwest of Ireland and can be found obsessing over obscure folk instruments, being an ambivalent savior to feral cats, and playing too many video games.